WHITE RIVERS

and

SEPTEMBER MORNING

D1396071

Rowena Summers is a pseudonym for author Jean Saunders. She began her career as a magazine writer, and has published over 600 short stories and some eighty novels. Ex-Chairman of the Romantic Novelists' Association, Jean lectures at writers' groups in both the UK and USA, appearing frequently on radio and TV. She lives in north Somerset and is married with three grown-up children.

WHITE RIVERS
and
SEPTEMBER MORNING

Rowena Summers

Pan Books

White Rivers/September Morning

White Rivers first published 1999 by Severn House
September Morning first published 1999 by Severn House

This edition published 2001 by Pan Books
an imprint of Macmillan Publishers Ltd
25 Eccleston Place, London SW1W 9NF
Basingstoke and Oxford
Associated companies throughout the world
www.macmillan.com

ISBN 0 330 48669 1

1 3 5 7 9 8 6 4 2

A CIP catalogue record for this book is available from
the British Library.

Printed and bound in Great Britain by
Mackays of Chatham plc, Chatham, Kent

WHITE RIVERS

One

The Pollard wedding was bound to be the society event of the St Austell calendar for 1925, Charlotte told her American cousin grandly. Skye had no doubt that Charlotte, in her important role as mother of the bride, would ensure that everything ran smoothly on the day. But from the to-do in the bedroom at the Pollard house on that fine April afternoon, it was hard to credit it.

By then, the grown-ups could hardly separate one screech from the other. The occasion was supposed to be a final fitting for the young attendants, but from the squabbles going on among the three children, anyone could be forgiven for thinking they were in a kindergarten.

Skye Norwood wrenched her daughter away from the strapping arms of Sebastian Tremayne. At eight years old, Sebby was already head and shoulders above her girls, and a champion in the old Tremayne tradition of spouting aggression whenever the situation demanded it.

Above the din, Skye yelled at him in her quick New Jersey voice, ignoring the effect that such bellowing might have on Charlotte's normally ordered household.

"Will you *behave* yourself? Just look what you've done to Celia's dress, you horrible child."

She scrubbed furiously at the grubby fingermarks on Celia's white organdie dress, but the marks wouldn't budge, and would need more attention than she could readily give. Her daughter's wailing voice was loud in her ear.

"I *hate* him, Mommy. He pulls my hair and spits at me."

"I do not spit at you!" Sebastian said, scowling.

1

"Yes you do, too," Skye's younger daughter Wenna piped up. "I saw you do it, and I hate you too."

She clutched at her sister's hand, her blue eyes large and scared, but full of bravado in their sibling closeness. Their varying expressions couldn't detract from the fact that they were beautiful girls, having inherited the glorious Tremayne looks that went back generations, black-haired and blue-eyed, with a voluptuousness that was evident, even in children. And right now they refused to be cowed by their bully-boy cousin.

Skye pursed her lips. A fine wedding this was going to be for her cousin Vera, if the three small attendants were going to be at loggerheads the entire time. With the whole town of St Austell expected to turn out for the occasion – if the bride's mother was to be believed – it would only show up the younger ones still more. Though not *her* darlings, she amended hastily. Just the abominable Sebby.

The bride-to-be came into the room at that moment, pink-faced and scowling at all the fuss. Skye smiled encouragingly at the young woman in her cream wedding gown with the hem still half pinned up, and the dressmaker scurrying around to finish it.

"The dress looks truly lovely, Vera," Skye said.

"*It* does, but I don't," her cousin raged. "I'm not made for silks and fancies. I'm too old for all this nonsense, and I can't fit comfortably into a tube of a dress when I'm not built for it."

"Vera, please control yourself," her mother Charlotte snapped. "Thirty is a perfectly proper age to be married, for heaven's sake, and there's nothing that a few extra tucks in the bodice won't disguise. Besides, every bride looks beautiful on her wedding day, and you'll be no exception."

Sebastian was stunned for no more than the briefest moment on seeing the bridal vision enter the bedroom, then couldn't resist a snigger.

"She's too fat for it, and my daddy says she'll waddle up the aisle like a duck."

"Oh, you hateful litle beast!" Vera said, reaching out to swipe him. As she did so, there was an ominous ripping sound, and the dressmaker gasped in horror at this display of temper, and the undoing of her fine underarm seams.

"Mrs Pollard, I really think—" she began nervously.

Whatever she thought was lost as Vera stormed out of the room and into another bedroom, slamming doors as she went. She might be a Pollard by name, but she was certainly a Tremayne by nature, Skye thought feelingly.

Charlotte took control of the situation in as dignified a manner as possible. "I think we'll finish for today. The children's outfits are quite satisfactory now, Skye, and Mrs Finnigan and I will deal with Vera's upsets."

They were dismissed from the proceedings, and once the children had changed back into their everyday clothes, Skye bundled them into her motor car and drove away from St Austell with a heartfelt sigh of relief. No wedding could be as traumatic as this one was turning out to be.

For a moment though, she felt a great pang, remembering how vastly different her own had been. Despite the infants still squabbling in the back of the car; despite the way everyone was getting so het up, and the number of times Vera had threatened to call the whole thing off as she failed miserably to lose the extra weight she really didn't have; despite all that, she would have loved a wedding such as Vera and Adam Pengelly were going to have in two weeks' time.

A wedding with all the trimmings, the celebrations after, and the honeymoon trip to follow. A wedding with the good wishes of friends and family, the modest gifts from the Killigrew Clay workers who had known the respected Cornish families for decades, and the newer workers at the associated White Rivers Pottery . . . Skye had had none of it.

Not that she regretted a moment of her secret marriage, even though it had been seen by her grandmother Morwen as a clandestine affair, before she and Philip Norwood went off to France in the war to end all wars, unable to bear being apart. But Granny Morwen had forgiven her in the end, knowing the headstrong romantic that she was; so like the fiery girl she had once been herself. Skye had counted on that.

*   *   *

Driving along the rough country lanes towards Truro to deposit Sebastian at Killigrew House, Skye became aware of something damp and unpleasant against her neck. She squirmed in the driving seat as she sensed the boy's hot, heavy breath on her skin.

"Please sit back properly, Sebby," she snapped. "You should know how to conduct yourself in a car by now."

"My daddy's going to buy a new one soon," he said importantly. "It'll probably be a Rover, and it'll be much bigger than this one."

"Naturally," Skye muttered, knowing it was wrong to detest a child, but finding it impossible to do much else in the case of this obnoxious boy.

Like father, like son, she found herself thinking, remembering how she and Theo Tremayne had clashed from the moment they met, when she first came from America to meet these Cornish relatives. Arriving for a year, and staying for the rest of her life . . .

So many of those relatives were gone now, she thought with a shiver. As if the war hadn't been hideous enough in killing off so many folk, the terrible influenza epidemic that followed in its wake had seen off thousands more, all over the world. Her own family had lost more than their fair share. Uncles and aunts in Cornwall and beyond, her beloved Mom in New Jersey, and her paternal grandparents in California. They were all gone now. Amazingly, Granny Morwen had defied the threat of the virus, but had gone all the same when her number had come up, as the Tommies used to say.

Skye shivered again, trying to ignore the fatalistic mood into which she was fast descending. It wouldn't do to become morose and depressed when they were all supposed to be looking forward to a happy event. She drew in her breath resolutely.

"Are you sad, Mommy?" she heard Wenna say.

She glanced around at her five-year-old, thumb in her mouth as ever, and her eyes softened. Celia, a year older, was the practical one, while Wenna had an instinctive empathy with other people. It was what her namesake Morwen would have called fey. Morwen would have *loved* her, Skye thought, for the umpteenth time.

"I'm not sad, honey," she said cheerfully. "I was just praying that Withers will be able to get the marks off that lovely dress for you."

"Withers can do anything," Celia said confidently. "Daddy says she's a maid in a million and we should think of her as a national treasure."

"Does he now?" Skye said, hiding a smile. It changed quickly as Sebby gave a hoot of derision.

"You don't call *maids* national treasures, goose-pot! They're just there to do what we tell them to do."

Skye felt her hands tighten on the steering-wheel. "You really are a nasty little boy, aren't you, Sebby?" she said as coolly as she could, considering how she was seething at such snobbery. "You should be setting an example in good manners to your cousins and your little brother."

"Why should I? Justin's a pampered pig."

Whatever she might have said to that was lost in the screams of laughter from the two girls at his daring, and with such a willing audience, Sebby elaborated wildly on the precociousness of his brother.

It took one to know one, thought Skye dryly, but at least it kept them all amused until they reached Killigrew House. And nobody could blame his mother for pampering young Justin, when she had so nearly died giving birth to him. At forty-four years old, Betsy had left it a bit late, Skye always thought, but Theo had insisted that just like royalty, you needed an heir and a spare, so Betsy had done her wifely duty and produced the second boy.

She came out from the house as soon as she saw the car arrive, Justin at her heels like the plump little butterball that he was. Betsy had grown fat and cumbersome over the years too, and there were plenty of rumours that Theo now found his earthier pleasures at Kitty's House, the bawdy abode along the coast from St Austell. Skye closed her ears to such talk. There had been enough scandal and gossip about various family members over the years for her to care about

hearing any more. And anyway, she really didn't want it to
be true about Theo and his totties. She liked Betsy, even while
she despised her a little for being so spineless. After marrying
the bombastic part-owner of Killigrew Clay, Skye had to admit
that Betsy had done litle more than produce the two irritating
sons who were destined to walk all over her. Or perhaps she
just liked it that way. Some women did, apparently, and there
was no accounting for folk, as Granny Morwen used to say.

"So how did it go at Charlotte's, me dear?" Betsy asked in
her broad Cornish voice. "Did she keep all of 'ee in order as
usual, in her prim and proper fashion?"

It was Sebby who answered. "She's a ladypig," he said,
which started Justin off, and after a startled moment of awe
at this insult to a grown-up, started Celia and Wenna off
as well.

Betsy looked at Skye in desperation. "Why Theo insisted that
Sebby should be a pageboy I'll never know. He looks a proper
fright in velvet and frills, and your two will be perfect little
angels, while this one—" She cuffed him gently about the ears,
which had no effect at all, except to send him running indoors,
still laughing, with Justin following on chubby little legs.

"It's tradition, Betsy," Skye told her. "You know what
sticklers they all are for that. Besides, I'm sure he'll be all
right on the day."

"I wish I had such confidence, then. But at least Theo will be
there to see to him if he starts his tantrums, and 'tis to be hoped
that if Lily's chief bridesmaid, she'll stand for no nonsense.
Are you coming in for a spell?"

"No, we're off home. Philip will be back soon, and he likes
me to be there."

"You've got a good man there, me dear."

"I know it," she said, trying not to notice the wistful note in
Betsy's voice. "Anyway, the children's outfits are done now,
so we'll see you on the day of the wedding."

"Oh ah. Though I dare say you'll be seeing Theo afore that.
He's fussing over summat at the clayworks now."

"Oh?" Skye was instantly alert. "Not trouble, I hope? Things
have been going so smoothly lately."

Betsy sniffed. "Well, you know what they say. When things go too smoothly, summat's bound to go wrong. And Theo's got a habit o' stirring things up, in case you hadn't noticed."

"I had, as a matter of fact . . ."

"Anyway, I don't think 'twere trouble exactly. Summat to do with exports and the like. He were more excited than upset, I'd say, but you know I don't take much heed of business dealings, not having the head for it," she said vaguely.

She wished Betsy would stop talking and let her get away. The girls were getting tired and fractious in the back of the motor now, and there was a sudden chill in the late afternoon air. She longed to be home, inside the house called New World, and to chat over the day's events with her husband.

Skye still adored Philip with a passion, and she knew that her feelings were reciprocated, but lately she had to admit that he had changed. He had always been a serious and a deep-thinking man, as befitted a college lecturer, and she had loved the discussions they had had over the years on so many different topics. It didn't matter that the discussions were sometimes more than heated. He treated her as an intellectual equal, in a way that so many husbands never did.

But lately, he had become more introverted, more tetchy and pompous, and – if she dared to put it into words – trying to run her life more than she cared for. Whether it had anything to do with the lingering legacy of the near-fatal head injuries he had suffered in France, she had no idea. They had certainly scarred him mentally as well as physically for a very long time, and she had been generous in understanding and overlooking any outbursts of anger. But in the seven years since the war ended, his manner seemed to have got worse instead of better.

Of course, it could also be put down to age. He was fifty-one now, eighteen years older than herself. It had never bothered her before, and being brought up with older parents, she had loved his maturity, but sometimes lately . . .

"Daddy's home, Mommy," Celia said, as they neared their own house. Philip's car stood outside, and Skye felt her heart sink. She shouldn't feel uneasy because he was there before her, but it was true what she had told Betsy. He liked her to be at home waiting for him, and his attitude if ever she was not seemed to reduce her standing as a woman – and women had been fighting for their rights for long enough now for Skye to resent the feeling. There was a limit as to how long you could be sweet and understanding . . .

For a moment she wondered fleetingly how her cousin Lily would react to such a situation. Lily Pollard was a declared and defiant feminist, devoted to the ideals of the Pankhursts and women's suffrage. She had been persuaded very much against her will to be chief attendant for her sister Vera's wedding. Lily had decided against marriage for herself, having seen too many women and babies living on a pittance when their menfolk hadn't returned from France, and she voiced her opinions far too loudly and publicly for her mother's peace of mind.

But Skye forgot them all as she stopped the car and opened the doors, and her two girls went running towards the front door where their father was waiting for them now. Skye went to him quickly too, putting her arms around him, and pushing aside the thought that he looked far older and more careworn today than his years warranted.

"I'm sorry, honey, we couldn't get away from Betsy. You know how she rambles," she said apologetically.

"And her brat gave you a miserable time as usual, I dare say," he said sourly.

"Sebby was no worse than any other time," she told him carefully, wondering where all his tolerance had gone. He used to have so much . . . She often thought it was a good thing he didn't have to tutor infants, or plenty of parents would be complaining at his lack of patience.

"And that says it all," Philip uttered. "But I wondered what was keeping you. Theo's been and gone, fidgeting as usual over something he wouldn't deign to explain to me, since you're his business partner, as he was sure to remind me. He'll call back this evening. I felt obliged to invite him to supper but thankfully he declined. I dare say he's got more agreeable business to attend to along the coast."

"Philip, please—" she warned, seeing how the girls were intent on his every word. She saw him frown.

"There's no use cushioning children from the facts of life, my dear."

"There's no reason to destroy their innocence too soon, either," she retorted.

Sometimes she wished she could keep them cocooned in that childhood naivety for ever, however foolish it might be. There were so many ugly and wicked things in the world, and once their Pandora's Box was opened, there was no turning back to innocence. She wished the thought had never entered her mind.

"I think you had better see to your son," Philip was saying coldly now. "He's been screaming in the nursery ever since I came home, and calling for you repeatedly. Nanny's getting flustered. It's not fair on her at her age."

"It's what we pay her for, isn't it?" Skye was stung into replying, recognising her own burst of snobbishness, and unable to avoid it.

"What *you* pay her for, my dear," Philip said, stalking off with the girls towards the drawing-room as they chattered to him about their afternoon at Aunt Charlotte's.

Skye stood with her hands clenched for a few moments, mentally counting to ten and back again. The word *Pig* came into her head at that moment, and for once she identified totally with the obnoxious Sebby Tremayne's description of whoever he hated at the moment.

Quickly, she went upstairs to the sounds of infant screaming, pushing such unworthy thoughts out of her head. Of course she didn't hate Philip. She loved him. It was just that sometimes he stretched her feelings of love to the utmost.

The baby was still exercising his lungs when she entered the nursery, his face a furious scarlet with exertion as he stood up rigidly in his cot and rocked the sides with all his might. Nanny was standing by with a bottle in her hand, its milky splashes all over her apron being the evidence of how many times young Oliver Norwood had flung it back at her.

"I can't do nothing with him today, Mrs Norwood," she

9

began in a fluster. "He's cutting his back teeth, and they're making him that fretful it troubles me to see it. I've rubbed his gums with oil of cloves, but it don't do no good at all."

"It's all right, Nanny," Skye said soothingly, as the buxom woman eyed her anxiously, clearly afraid she would be blamed for not being able to cope with a two-year-old. "Come to Mommy, honey, and we'll have a cuddle."

Oliver's arms had already reached out towards her, and Skye picked him out of the cot, feeling his hot little body still twitching from the effects of the sobs. His blue eyes were swollen with tears, and she hugged him tightly to her, uncaring how his steamy little person creased her fine beige linen frock.

"You go off and see to the girls' tea, Nanny," she said now. "I'll stay with Oliver and try to calm him."

She sat with the child in the rocking-chair by the window, crooning to him softly until the tears subsided. His dark hair was plastered to his head, but gradually the angry little face became less fraught, and his eyelids drooped.

"Poor baby," Skye whispered, seeing how one side of his jaw was redder than the other. "It pains us to get our teeth, and it pains us to lose them, doesn't it?"

She traced her finger around the curve of his cheek, thinking that even two-year-olds didn't have everything made easy, and wishing she could have the toothache for him. There must be something she could give him to ease it, but none of the doctor's remedies did any good. There ought to be some other way, some other method . . . For a second or two, her head spun, and her heart thudded, as a crazy alternative churned around in her brain. There was an old witchwoman on the moors who could concoct ancient potions that were reputed to cure all ills, the same as any quack doctor professed to do at the annual country fairs. The woman they called Helza . . .

"If you hold him that tightly, you'll crush him to death," Skye heard her husband's voice say beside her.

She had been so wrapped up in her thoughts she hadn't heard him come into the nursery, but as she lay the sleeping Oliver in his cot again, she registered that Philip looked less irritated now. As she straightened, smoothing back her fashionably bobbed hair from where it curved around her chin, he caught at her hand.

"I'm sorry, my love. I've had a stinger of a day at the college, but it wasn't fair to take my frustration out on you the minute I saw you. Can you forgive me?"

"Don't be silly," she said, twisting around until she was in his arms. "There's nothing to forgive."

And if there was, it was too sweet a moment to brood on it. She forgave him readily, the way she always did. Besides, there were always other things to think about. There was her cousin Theo, and why he wanted to see her so urgently.

One thing she was sure about was that Philip hated to be excluded from any meetings between herself and her cousin, but short of seeming to patronise him by suggesting he sat in on it and said nothing, she didn't know what else to do. He had never been overly interested in the clayworks, but the pottery was a different matter in his eyes. That was creative work and not manual labour, grubbing about in the earth.

She had never had any doings with the clayworks until coming to Cornwall, either, she thought, almost defensively. But she had known of it and loved it almost from the day she was born, simply because her mother had instilled in her the love of Cornwall and her intricate family background. And being the inquisitive person that Skye was, in the end it had been inevitable that she should see it all for herself.

"What are you sitting there smiling about?" Philip asked her over supper, when the children were in bed. "Are they private thoughts, or can anybody share them?"

"I was just thinking how lucky we were to have met on the ship coming over from New York, and how our lives would have been changed if we'd never met at all."

She hadn't really meant to say all that, and she wished she hadn't when she saw the small frown on Philip's face. Ever since coming home from the dress fittings at St Austell she had the feeling he had something to tell her, and she guessed that it was nothing to do with her cousin Theo.

"I had a letter from Ruth today," he said abruptly.

Much as she tried not to react, hearing the name was like dashing a tumblerful of cold water into Skye's face.

"Another one?" she asked, as mildly as she could.

Philip threw down his napkin with a gesture of impatience. "For God's sake, Skye, Ruth and I have known one another since childhood. You can hardly expect me to forget she ever existed."

"Nor that she expected you to marry her, and had every right to do so," she added swiftly.

She chewed her bottom lip, not wanting to be reminded in this way of the shipboard romance that had sprung up so innocently between herself and the handsome college lecturer. At least, it had been innocent on her part – but not so innocent on his, since he already had a fiancée waiting for him on the Falmouth quayside on that fateful day when Skye had set foot in Cornwall for the first time.

The sensible part of her told her not to be so petty over Ruth, and that friendships between men and women were perfectly natural. But the fiery, passionate part of her recognised her usual upsurge of tension, and the rapid, sickening heartbeats that told a different story.

It was all so long ago, and she had never truly stolen Philip from Ruth. It had been Ruth who had realised what was happening, and given him up, but Skye sometimes suspected that Philip had carried the guilt of his betrayal around with him all these years. Especially now that Ruth had begun corresponding with him again.

"What does she want this time?" she said, before she could stop herself.

"Jealousy doesn't become you, my dear," he retorted.

"I'm not jealous!" she exploded, knowing that of course she damn well was. "Why on earth would I be jealous of a—"

"Deaf woman?"

Skye felt her face flame, and she snapped back at him. "How dare you accuse me of such a thing! I was about to ask why I should be jealous of a successful teacher of deaf children? Ruth has turned the tables on her disability, and I admire her

12

for that. But don't make her out to be a saint because of it, nor me a sinner, Philip."

"I seem to have hit a nerve, though, don't I? As for what she wanted, she's visiting Cornwall with her aunt in the summer, and would like to call on us. Do you have any objections?"

"Of course not. She's never seen the children, and I'm never averse to showing them off," she said, as evenly as she could. "In fact, she and her aunt would be quite welcome to stay at New World for a few days if they wished to do so."

She was gratified to see her husband's face relax. She didn't want to be at war with him over Ruth, but no matter what he said, he was still defensive about her, Skye thought uneasily, and she doubted that that would ever change. But he reached across the dining-table to squeeze her hand now.

"That's very sweet of you, darling, but I'm sure they'll have made plans of their own by then."

Skye let out the breath she hadn't realised she had been holding, thinking fervently that she sincerely hoped so, and changed the topic of conversation quickly while they moved into the drawing-room, awaiting her cousin's visit.

Theo Tremayne had always prided himself on keeping the family business' head above water. Killigrew Clay had prospered in fits and starts since the end of the war, but now that the European markets were open to them for the spring and autumn clay dispatches again, he couldn't complain.

And with the import of expert craftsmen, the pottery had done better than he had ever believed it would. The one thorn in his side was having to have the American upstart, as he privately referred to her in his mind, as his partner. In Theo's opinion, women should be kept in their rightful places, as his wife had always respectfully accepted. One place for wives, another for dalliances . . .

He smiled with satisfaction as he drove towards New World after supper, anticipating how this evening would end at Kitty's House. The original madam had gone years ago, but the new owner was a big, blowsy woman of indeterminate years, who supplied the best for her favoured clients. Theo had been a favourite for many years, with his handsome Tremayne features and his ready purse, and his new sweetfluff was a pretty little French mam"selle called Gigi.

He felt the familiar stirrings in his loins, remembering her teasing tricks, and the softly seductive accent that aroused his senses as she whispered outrageous things against his willing flesh. Once, years ago, Betsy had been as willing, but never as inventive, he mused . . .

He didn't see the rut in the road until it made the motor lurch out of control, and he cursed loudly, knowing he had best keep his attention on the business ahead, and reserve his carnal lusting for later. First, there was the meeting with Skye, and that was enough to set him scowling again.

As if she wasn't enough, the stuffy husband kept trying to poke his nose into affairs that were none of his concern as well. Time and again Theo had cursed his grandmother for making him share his business interests with the colonial cousin. But then, Morwen had always been besotted with her daughter Primmy and her American offspring.

St Austell folk had frequently observed that the three of them were like the proverbial peas in a pod when it came to beauty and temperament, and no doubt the Norwood brats would be every bit as fiery when they grew up. They were docile enough now, compared with Theo's own roisterous boys, but that could change, he thought dourly.

And then he put them all out of his mind as he roared up the driveway towards the house known as New World, yanking on the brake as he halted his motor, and sending the gravel flying in all directions.

He was shown into the drawing-room, and gave Skye a brief kiss on the cheek, noting the fact that she always smelled as fragrant as a woodland stream. He conceded that it was preferable to Betsy's unfortunate flatulence and Gigi's cloying French perfumes, but none of it endeared her to Theo. She simply irritated him, and always would.

"So to what do we owe this honour, Theo?" Skye said with a smile, after they had made the obligatory pleasantries, and he was supplied with a glass of New World's best brandy.

Philip cleared his throat. "If you want to discuss things with Skye, I have things to do—"

"There's no need," Theo said, to his surprise. "It's good news, anyway. We've had a massive pottery order from a German firm, wanting supplies in good time for next Christmas. It's mighty early to place an order but apparently they have a huge market for such things, and while their usual supplier has been trying to push them into taking gaudy stuff, they're impressed by the way we've stuck to white embossed."

"Good Lord!" Skye exclaimed. "From what Betsy said, I imagined you were coming here with tales of imminent strikes at the clayworks or something."

Theo snorted. "Ah well, the day the clayworkers don't kick up a fuss about summat is the day pigs will fly. But you don't want to take no notice of Betsy's empty-headed prattle. Women usually get the wrong end of the stick, anyway."

"So it seems I was right about the white embossed then, doesn't it?" Skye said sweetly, ignoring the barb, and knowing that it had been all her idea to keep the image of their White Rivers goods as pure and white as the name implied, with just an indented, meandering groove around the base of every piece to reflect the image of a river, and a single embossed flower for relief. She had even invented the name for the pottery, and that had been a source of annoyance to her cousin too.

"Oh ah, I'll give 'ee that the white embossed was a brainwave," Theo was forced to admit now.

"I'd say this calls for a celebration," Philip put in. "We've a bottle of champagne in the cellar waiting to be opened, and this seems like a fair occasion for it. Will you take a glass with us, Theo?"

The cousins turned to look at him as if only just realising he was there, resentment in their identical blue eyes at his intrusion. Philip felt a small, savage shock at the look.

Even when these two were practically involved in a cat-fight, he knew that something stronger than personal dislike would always draw them together. It was something that those who married into the Tremayne clan should always be aware of, for it always put them at a disadvantage.

15

He knew it had always been the same. The closeness between all the Tremaynes had always been uncanny and unswerving, shutting out the rest of the world; even the creepy artist uncle and his seeming obsession for Skye's mother, his own sister. But when outsiders threatened, they were as immovable as a mountain, and it was a well-known fact that you couldn't move mountains.

Two

The following morning the two little Norwood girls pressed their noses against the nursery windowpane, watching for the arrival of their governess. Skye heard their squeals as they vied to be the first one to spot Miss Landon, bicycling tortuously towards the house, her sensible hat rammed and skewered onto her head at a crazy angle, due to the swirl of the onshore winds.

Cleaned, fed and belched now, young Oliver was handed over to Nanny's care, and a few minutes later Skye and the girls greeted Miss Landon in the schoolroom, where they regaled her with news about their bridesmaid dresses. And then the day was Skye's own.

Not for the first time lately, she wondered what she was going to do with it. Luxury and the indolent life was a wonderful thing to aim for when you didn't have it. But when it happened there were times, especially when your whole life had once been full and busy, when you could experience an odd sense of being in limbo, of not belonging, of life shifting sideways and not taking you with it.

She knew it was the feeling of many of the returning Tommies after the war, when suddenly there was nothing for them to do, and it was so hard to adapt to a normal pattern of life again. However terrible life had been then, whatever agonies they had suffered, or tragic sights they had seen, the purpose for their existence and the cameraderie they had shared, was gone. Each of them was Mister Ordinary again.

Skye blinked, guilt assailing her as she realised she was in danger of feeling sorry for herself, and with no good reason, for heaven's sake. Her life was still full and happy. She had a husband and three children she adored, a beautiful home and thriving business interests. At thirty-three years old, she didn't need a mirror to tell her that men still found her vitally attractive. What more could any woman want?

But the uneasy feeling wouldn't go away, and just for a moment she let it swamp her, comparing herself with those returning Tommies. It was all a long time ago now, but she too had lived with danger in France, tending the wounded, sending back true reports of conditions to the local newspaper, and writing letters home for soldiers who couldn't see, or had no hands to hold a pencil.

Dear God, it was shameful for anybody to be nostalgic for such times, she thought furiously now, as the memories came flooding back. She knew exactly what her Mom would be saying to her – and Granny Morwen too. Especially Granny Morwen.

"Get a hold on yourself, girl, and be grateful for what you have. There's many a young 'un working in a city sweatshop who'd give a sight more'n tuppence to breathe in the scents of the open moors and the sea that's on our doorstep. Go out and fill your lungs with it all."

She was right too. They were both right. She had it all. Except a purpose. And without that, she had nothing.

Ruefully, she recognised the journalist background in her that was making her think in short, staccato sentences now to prove a point. The joy of writing had been overtaken with motherhood and family life. And she was even more appalled to think, for a tiny moment, that she could resent the fact.

Once, when she had tentatively broached the subject of returning to the Truro newspaper world she had inhabited on a part-time basis, Philip had damned the idea at once.

'Your place is here now, Skye, and if you still want to dabble in your writing, do what you always said you would. Get those diaries of your grandmother out of the lawyer's chambers and start on the family history. It would be a proper pastime, and preferable to writing up local scandal stories.'

She seethed, remembering. 'Dabble' in her writing, indeed. Indulging in a 'proper pastime'! Before she met him she had worked on a highly respectable New Jersey magazine. And it had never been *her* idea to write up the family history, at least not in the way he said. He was the historian, the sometimes pompous college lecturer, and clearly wouldn't approve of his wife doing anything less gracious.

She couldn't deny that she had once thought vaguely about writing a novel based on the diaries. But ever since her grandmother had left them to her, Skye had been totally unable to read them. They were mouldering, for all she knew, in the lawyer's chambers in Bodmin. They contained Morwen Tremayne's life, all the early poverty and memories of a family beholden to the masters of Killigrew Clay, all the trials and tribulations, the loves and pleasures and heartbreaks . . . and they were private.

And yet . . . why had they been left to her, if they were not meant to be read? With infuriating logic, Philip had pointed it out more than once, and had finally given up when she had refused to even think about it, as stubborn as only a true Tremayne could be.

One day she vowed to read them, but to record her family's history in detail was something she had avoided all these years. She didn't care to think about doing it now. Unless it *was* all made into a completely fictional account, exorcising the past in a subliminal way. She didn't deny the charm and the magnitude of it, but as always she dismissed it, still certain that such intimate thoughts should be private and had never been intended for the public gaze.

She refused to think about it any more. The April sunshine beckoned her outdoors, to do what her womenfolk had always done when something troubled them, however undefined it was: take to the moors and the open spaces . . .

Once there, she parked her car near the pottery, and then set out to walk across the moors, revelling in the cleanliness of the air and the solitude; it was then she heard the voice.

"So, young madam, 'tis a goodly while since you've been upalong these parts, and wi' such a pensive look on your pretty face too. Is it old Helza you'm coming to see?"

Lost in her moorland reverie, Skye spun around, her heart thudding. If she believed in such things, she could readily fancy that the old crone had metamorphosed out of thin air, as spindly and spiky-haired as ever, her darting little witchwoman's eyes assessing every inch of the curvaceous shape of Skye Norwood.

Even as she gulped, unnerved as always by the sight of old Helza with her arms habitually full of sticks, the old crone cackled in a way that threatened to curdle the blood.

"You startled me," Skye said crossly, knowing that showing anger was the best way to hide fear. And she was no gullible child to be taken in by superstitious nonsense, for pity's sake. She was a mature wife and mother . . .

"Oh ah. And what was filling your head so much that 'ee couldn't see a body four feet ahead of 'ee, then?"

"It's none of your business."

Helza cocked her wizened little head on one side. Skye knew she should just brush past her and carry on with her walk, but for the life of her, she couldn't do it. It was as if she was transfixed by those mesmerising eyes.

"And what of *your* business then? The pots be doing well, by all accounts, and a fine living's come out of the ashes."

Skye flinched. "Is it money you want? I have a little with me."

Helza cackled again. "No, my pretty one. I want no money from you today."

"What then?" Skye said, her mouth dry.

Why couldn't she just *pass*? It was no more than coincidence that had brought her this way, much further than she had intended, to where the old Larnie Stone reared its head into the sky, and the town of St Austell could be seen through the hole in its granite middle.

She shivered as her eyes were drawn to it, knowing the old tale of her grandmother's tragic friend, the girl Skye's own daughter Celia had been named after.

"I see you ain't forgot the tale I told 'ee, my pretty," Helza said with satisfaction, as if reading her mind.

"I haven't forgotten a thing," Skye said, remembering the

hoarse way the tale had been related in the old crone's stinking hovel. Nor could she forget what she owed her – if her darkest suspicions were to be believed. Though did you really owe somebody a debt for setting fire to premises with a person still in it – however despicable that person was? It was tantamount to being a partner in the crime, and that was *certainly* something Skye had tried to forget over the years.

But she shivered again, remembering the near-rape in the old linhay at Clay Two, when the oafish Desmond Lock had overpowered her before Helza had appeared, to terrify him. And then the horror of discovering that the linhay had mysteriously burned down, with only the boot from Desmond's clubbed foot to be found. Skye's eyes glazed, hearing Helza's cackling laugh, and she closed her eyes tightly for a few moments, willing the memories away. When she opened them again, the witchwoman had gone.

"You're becoming as moonstruck as that one," she said furiously, talking to the air, then twisting her lips as she realised how the action matched the words.

She struck out purposefully towards the splendid edifice some distance ahead of her now, and tried to force back into her veins the familiar warm glow of pride in its conception.

White Rivers Pottery had grown, truly like a phoenix from the ashes, from the humble linhay of Clay Two, to the splendid workshop and showroom it was today. The whole site of the old Clay Two pit had been landscaped and sculptured into an attraction in its own right.

The old dirt tracks had been transformed into proper roads, where visiting folk could drive their motor cars and watch the potters at work if they were so inclined, and then browse to their hearts' content in the showroom. Some astute advertising in *The Informer* newspaper had ensured that the opening day had been well attended, and in the six years since the pottery had become a reality, it had never looked back.

Gradually, Skye felt herself relax, calling herself all kinds of foolish names for heeding an old moorswoman's taunts. Sensible folk scoffed at Helza anyway – at least, they did so once they were well away from her, Skye admitted. But in these more enlightened days, the general feeling among younger folk was that Helza had inherited few of the reputed powers of her so-called sister-witch, Zillah.

Skye swallowed. She hadn't felt so confident some years ago when she and a distant relative by the name of Lieutenant Lewis Pascoe of the American army, had visited Helza's hovel, and been almost knocked back by the stench of it. They had learned of events in their mutual past that were too horrific to accept, and yet too appallingly believable to be anything but true. Things that linked them together, and drove them apart. Things concerning her grandmother Morwen, and Celia Penry, her own daughter's namesake . . .

She pushed the memories away as she saw the young lad approaching her now.

"Are you took bad, Missus – Ma'am? You've been standing so still it made me fret for you. Are you needing a doctor, or a quiet sit down, maybe?"

At that moment the concerned boyish voice was like balm to her ears, especially after the raucous sounds that Helza had made. She smiled swiftly at the young apprentice, clearly on his way back to the pottery from an errand, and blush-red now at speaking so personally to the vision that was Skye Norwood.

Skye forced a smile to her cold lips. "You're a honey, Ethan, but I'm perfectly well, thank you, and I'm just daydreaming, that's all. So tell me, how is everything at White Rivers? Have you become an expert potter yet?"

As they fell into step, she made herself sound interested in the work – which she was, of course, she reminded herself hastily. And so was this likeable lad, the spit of his brother Adam who was going to marry her cousin Vera in two weeks' time. He was a generation younger than Adam, and Vera referred to him as his parents' little afterthought, although there had been a brother between Ethan and Adam who had been killed in France. The oldest Pengelly brother, Nicholas, lived in Plymouth; he had clearly broken away from the family circle, if only moving over the border separating Cornwall from Devon. But to Skye, it was odd, and endearing – and sometimes a little alarming – how so many Cornish families seemed to rotate and intermingle; even the American branch of her own. It was almost incestuous – but not quite – and she quickly veered her thoughts away from the ugly word as she listened to Ethan's stumbling reply to her question.

"'Tis all going right well, Missus – Ma'am – and I'm starting to throw a fair pot, so me brother says."

"I'm sure you are. It's not as easy as it looks, is it?"

"Have you ever done it, then?" Ethan asked in some astonishment that such a vision should ever dirty her hands with the clay.

Skye laughed. "That I have, and a silly mess I made of it, though at the time Mr Lock was kind enough to say it wasn't a bad first effort."

"Would that be old Tom Lock that died t'other week? They say he had a weird son who worked up here long afore the pottery got properly built."

Skye kept her voice calm. "They both spent some time here in the old linhay a long time ago, and it was the son who died when the place burned down." She resisted a huge shudder, remembering again how the weird Desmo Lock had forced himself on her, and was only stopped by the very witchwoman she seemed so fatally attracted to contacting. After the linhay had burned down, with Desmo Lock in it, old Tom Lock's brain had been turned because of it all.

Two tragedies, and all on account of her – if her own beauty could be blamed for such a thing. Her thoughts became self-mocking for being so high and mighty as to think she was some twentieth-century Helen of Troy . . .

"Did you know 'em very well?" Ethan went on curiously, unwilling to leave the old tale alone.

"No, I didn't," she said crisply, "it was all a long time ago, and it's best forgotten. And since we're going to be related in a couple of weeks' time, hadn't you better start calling me Skye?"

His fair-skinned blush deepened to scarlet. "I dunno," he said uneasily. "What will folk think?"

She laughed, squeezing his arm at the innocent question. "When you're all dressed up and slicked down, they'll think

what a well-mannered young man you are, and a credit
to the family. And who gives a red cent what any other
folk think!"

His eyes were filled with admiration at this daring way of
talking. But everyone knew that Mrs Norwood – Skye – was
more progressive than most around here. It was because she
was American, thought Ethan – and wished that he was too,
if he could have a ha'porth of her self-confidence.

"Me brother Nick's comin' back for it, Miss – ma'am – Skye
– missus," he said, more confused than ever now. "He's too
busy to come back to see us too often."

"Well, I'm sure your mom will be glad to see him then," she
said, thinking Nicholas Pengelly sounded a bit of a cold fish.
"And it's just Skye, remember?"

By the time Skye reached her car for the return journey to New
World, she had recovered her composure. It was too golden a
day to be in the doldrums for long, and things that were past
and done with were best left in that secret place. After all, there
was a wedding to look forward to, and her girls were going to
look like angels.

Her spirits began to lift at once, and she could laugh at
herself for being briefly discontented with her lot. She might
not be the mother of the bride, with the self-styled importance
of Charlotte, but she was certainly the mother of the two
smaller bridesmaids, and her own outfit had reached the final
dressmaking stages.

It was a dream of an ensemble, she thought, as she drove
her car back down the hillside. A long, slim jacket in shades
of green, over a straight-skirted frock of matching shot silk
that was all the rage in Paris, the local dressmaker had told her
earnestly; although, fairly predictably, Charlotte had exclaimed
in horror on seeing the swatches of fabric. She remembered that
brief, heated exchange now.

"You can't wear *green*, Skye. It's unlucky, and it's bad
enough that Vera's changing her name and not her letter
without adding more chances of misfortune!"

Skye had looked at her in exasperation. "I haven't the

24

faintest idea what you're talking about, but I'm not changing my mind about the outfit because of any old superstitious nonsense, Charlotte. Anyway, I don't know what you mean about changing her name and not her letter."

"Oh well, I suppose we can't expect you Americans to know everything," Charlotte said, clearly stung. "Our surname begins with P, and so does does Adam's, and everybody knows it's a bad omen for two similars to wed."

Charlotte's red face told her she believed everything she said, but Skye was too riled to spare her any sympathy.

"And you honestly think that because a Pollard marries a Pengelly, this will spell disaster, do you? What about my own parents? That was more than a coincidence of letters. It was a Tremayne marrying a Tremayne, and there was no happier marriage in all the world!"

But wasn't she also aware that there was some dark secret about her parents' beginning? Some reason why they had fled to America before a great scandal broke . . . and her Uncle Albie was undoubtedly involved somewhere along the line.

But whatever the trouble was, they had survived it all, and it certainly hadn't involved a premature birth, which would have been the worst disgrace of all. Skye's brother Sinclair hadn't arrived for some years after the marriage, and she was even later. As much of an afterthought as young Ethan Pengelly, perhaps, but a much-wanted one for all that. But she wished her cousin Charlotte hadn't even put the memory of those thoughts into her mind.

Driving back to New World from the moors, and passing the glittering, sunlit tips of Killigrew Clay on the way, she knew the answer could very well be in those old diaries of Morwen Tremayne. And that was another thought that wouldn't seem to go away.

The answer could also come from Uncle Albert, she realised, but there were questions she never wanted to ask him. The last time her mother had been in Cornwall, when her own sweet Celia had been born, Skye had virtually seen the truth of it without the need for words.

25

The brother and sister, Albert and Primrose – Primmy – Tremayne, had had a relationship that was once as close as sharing the same heart. No matter that it had been physically unfulfilled – and Skye was *sure* of that – just as she was sure that Albie had loved her mother with an agonising love.

It could only have ended in one of two ways. Either lust would have won, or love would have superseded it. And thank God, love had came along in the shape of Cresswell Tremayne, Skye's father.

She jerked the car to a halt outside the house, realising her hands were damp. She knew so little of those past, shadowy days that were none of her business . . . and yet, sometimes it seemed that the memories that didn't belong to her jostled to to be known. As if someone was pushing them into her subconscious . . .

"Dear Lord, I'm truly going crazy," she muttered. "I'll end up being as mad as a country loon if I'm not careful."

Skye removed her hat and gloves, and went into the elegant bathroom alongside her bedroom to splash cold water onto her heated cheeks and hands, gazing at the face in the mirror. Morwen's face. Angrily, she turned away, wanting to be herself and nobody else. For two pins she'd burn the damn diaries and be done with them; then she could never know the truth, and nor could anyone else. The hell of it was, she didn't understand why it should be so important to her, anyway. No one else in the family gave a damn that Morwen had left them to her, or wanted to delve into the past.

Deliberately, she made herself think of other things. Of the coming wedding, and the beastly little Sebby who could even overawe the inoffensive Ethan Pengelly at times. She fervently hoped the marriage between Vera and Adam would be a happy one. Vera deserved it.

They had become friends during the war, and Skye didn't forget how Vera had been such a brick when Skye had been terror-stricken at having to go on the wards in a French hospital and deal with sights that no young lady was ever meant to see. This was a humdinger of a thing to think about, she told herself now. But she only began to relax by imagining how cousin Lily would cope with being chief attendant, considering her lack of interest in all things romantic.

Lily had apparently met the oldest Pengelly brother while attending a rough-and-ready women's rights rally in Plymouth a few months back, and Vera and Adam had insisted she should call on him for politeness' sake. Lily's report was that he was very agreeable, but that she still wasn't interested in men, thank you very much, and that if Vera's idea had been a matchmaking scheme, it had failed dismally.

Skye smiled, thinking of Lily's indignant face at the time, and Vera's innocent one. But it proved her own theory. There was something inherently not quite right in the way these people wanted to cling to each other and to intermarry. Her smile faded slightly, remembering that her own folks had done the very same thing.

Plymouth had been home to Nicholas Pengelly for some years now. He was a practical man, and there was no yearning in his soul to return to the heart of Cornwall and his roots. Plymouth was near enough for his allegiance. He sent money home to his folks from time to time, but he always said it would take something very special to make him go back for good, and he hadn't discovered it yet. But he had never believed in the word never, and a lawyer always had to see every side of things.

The arrival of the strident Lily Pollard at his town house certainly hadn't been the catalyst to make him think any differently. He wasn't looking for a wife, and if he had been, she definitely wasn't for him. He hoped the sister was a mite softer in temperament, for his brother Adam's sake.

He liked women as much as the next man. But at thirty-seven years old, he hadn't seen one yet who made him want to give up his bachelor status. He freely admitted that, in part, the war years had seen to that, as they had done to so many others, instilling a sense of restlessness in their souls that had never existed before.

Some of the men who had never ventured far from home prior to the war had become adventurers, looking for more than was under their noses. Nicholas had seen plenty of marriages broken up because of it. He had listened to enough of their heartaches, and tried to help them come to terms with what was left of broken dreams.

His latest clients had been such a pair, and he was still fraught with their problems and bemoaning the fact to his partner who shared his chambers in the elegant riverside town house.

"Will you just listen to me!" he said now. "I'm starting to sound like a lonely hearts' adviser, instead of a hard-headed lawyer."

"You need to get away," William Pierce said. "This family wedding you're going to is just what you need. Take a week or two off, Nick, and unwind properly."

"You think that's what I need? To see my brother tie himself up to the sister of that impossible woman who came calling on us?" he scowled. "I'll give it two years, and then he'll be getting in touch with us to disentangle himself."

"My God, when did you become so disillusioned? This isn't like you, Nick."

"I know, so what do you say we get out of here and go down to one of the seamen's pubs this evening, drink ourselves silly and pick up a couple of floosies on the way back?"

William began to laugh, because this wasn't like him either, and he only ever spoke like it in a fit of melancholy. But he went along with it as he always did, knowing nothing would come of it.

"Why not?" he said breezily. "And you can tell me some more about this family your brother's marrying into."

"There's nothing to tell," Nicholas said abruptly. "And there's too many to worry my head about them anyway."

"What about that semi-famous artist bloke among the relatives? He sounds interesting enough."

"Albert Tremayne," Nicholas nodded. "I might call in at his studio in Truro while I'm there to take a look around."

"If there's anything half decent, you might pick it up for me, Nick. He may not be a Rembrandt, but you never know, his work might appreciate when he's dead."

"He's half dead now, by all accounts," Nicholas retorted. "Most of them are, if what Adam's told me about them is anything to go by."

Apart from seeing his brothers and his parents again, he admitted he wasn't particularly looking forward to going back to Cornwall. And yet there was still a corner of his mind that wanted desperately to see it all again, if only to note how small and insular it had all become in retrospect. And the tiny tug that he couldn't deny made him all the more resentful of the fact that Cornwall could still have a hold on his heart. Lawyers didn't go in for all that romantic nonsense. As for the restlessness that had pervaded his soul as much as any other man's when the war to end all wars had ended, well . . . He smiled ruefully; being stuck in a lawyer's chambers was as far removed from travelling as from deep-sea diving.

Sometimes he still felt an urge to get out and see more of the world. But that was where he and his partner differed. William often spoke about one day buying an antique shop and surrounding himself with the antiques that he loved. If they sold up their successful practice, they could each follow their dreams, Nicholas mused . . . and that was probably all romantic nonsense too.

Romance was furthest from Philip Norwood's mind at that moment. He glared at his wife's cousin across the desk in the plush St Austell offices of Killigrew Clay. Theo was being as obstinate as ever, but Philip had always reckoned he could match him in that respect. Besides which, he had all the richness of an academic's language at his disposal, while Theo Tremayne, for all his brashness, came from common stock, and frequently betrayed it.

But today, he knew damn well that Theo was getting the better of him, and he could feel the old wound in his head throbbing as his blood pressure rose.

"'Tis no use you showing me that black face, Norwood," Theo bellowed. "Much as I dislike the thought of partnering a woman in business, 'tis laid down legal and proper that the clayworks and the pottery be divided between your wife and myself, more's the pity, and I ain't persuading her to do nothing different."

"I'm perfectly aware of that fact—"

"And the only way you can be a part of it," Theo went on relentlessly, "is if Skye herself hands her share over to you now, or makes a legal thing of it in her will. And I doubt that she'll do any of it. We Tremaynes be a stubborn bunch o' folk, as you've discovered over the years. We keep what's ours. And anyway, I can't see your wife passing over yet. She's too bloody healthy for that, barring accidents. You ain't seeing fit to poison her to get your hands on the business, I suppose?"

"Don't be insulting. Such a thing never entered my head, and I'll thank you not to countenance such evil thoughts."

"And when she and I go underground," Theo went on crudely, "there's your young Oliver all set up to go into partnership with my Sebby and Justin. She'll not want an outsider to take a share, especially a poncey schoolteacher." His face hardened still more as he stood up, leaning on the desk, and almost spitting out his final words at Philip. "So, Norwood, I'd suggest you keep your hands out o' my clay if you know what's good for you."

"Is that a threat?"

"No. It's a promise."

Philip left the St Austell offices more shaken than when he'd arrived. The man was vicious and uncouth, and he would never like him as long as he lived. In that respect, he agreed with his wife. But he couldn't deny that in another respect, he and Theo were in agreement. Neither of them thought a woman should be in business to the extent that Skye was. She held the family purse strings as well as the house that had been bequeathed to her, and the whole bloody watertight facts were galling to a man of importance, such as a college professor.

As he strode along unseeingly, freely accepting the snobbery of his thoughts as his manly right, they switched to an unwanted direction. If he had married Ruth Dobson as he had always intended, he would have had a subservient and mild-mannered wife instead of the sparky and beautiful daughter of the Tremayne dynasty. . . . His thoughts changed just as quickly, wondering what the hell he was thinking of, to be so dismissive of the love he and Skye had known over the years.

Ruth was his past, however guilty he could still feel over the way he felt he had abandoned her. She had ended the engagement herself, but he had always known it was because she could see he was so passionately in love with the woman he had met on the ship bringing them both to Cornwall. Such a twist of fate that had changed all their lives . . .

"My goodness, Philip, you're deep in thought today," he heard an amused voice say, and he forced a smile to his face as he met the bright eyes of Vera Pollard. "What are you doing in St Austell?"

"I might ask the same of you," he countered, with the ease of tutorial rhetoric. Vera laughed.

"Oh, I'm visiting Betsy, just to check that Sebby's got over his latest tantrum. If he plays up at my wedding, I'll throttle him. But it's a bribery visit, I'm afraid. What do you think of this?"

She opened the brown paper bag she carried, and brought out a toy soldier with a key in its back. When she wound it up, the soldier saluted continuously until the mechanism creaked to a halt.

"Very nice," Philip said, oozing sarcasm. "Just the thing to remind children about the existence of war."

"Oh, Philip, don't be so stuffy," she said crossly, never one to mince her words. "Sebby's too young to know anything about war, and it's only a toy."

She flounced off, realising she still didn't know why Skye's husband was wandering about St Austell like a lost soul, instead of tutoring at his college in Truro. He was a secretive man at times, thought Vera, and no doubt his own war experiences had a lot to do with his frequent scratchiness, but she wasn't sure that she really liked him. It had never occurred to her before, but it occurred to her now.

31

Three

Two days before his brother's wedding, Nicholas Pengelly came back to Cornwall. With Adam's nervousness and young Ethan's exuberance, he managed to hide his shock at the way his mother had aged in the last few years. His father too seemed to spend far too much of his time staring out of the window, and was clearly still of the opinion that his dead son was coming home from the war.

It made Nicholas more than uneasy. He was also filled with guilt to realise the few times he had returned to the St Austell family home. And how small it all seemed to him now. . . . He knew such observations were commonplace when folk moved on, but it didn't lessen his uncomfortable feelings to know it. Nor the fact that once he had been inside the house for a while, he felt a real urge to get out.

"I'm going to take a drive over to Truro to look up a few people," he said casually the next morning. "Why don't you come for the ride, Mother? It will do you good."

She shook her head. "There'll be enough excitement for me with having to meet all these Pollard folk and t'others at the wedding, but you go off, Nick. You don't want to stop in wi' an old couple when you've got folks to see."

He gave her a swift hug, feeling how frail she was now, compared with the robust woman he remembered. But he had to go. The thought of sharing their empty, endless days began to stifle him as much as the house.

It wasn't good for Ethan, either, he thought suddenly, to face the prospect of caring for two aged parents. Not that he guessed the boy had even considered it. Neither had Nicholas, until now, but when Adam was married and had set up home with his new bride, it was going to be inevitable. Ethan would be the only brother left in the house. His guilt began to magnify as he realised that sending money home for their little comforts didn't compare with companionship, and the way his mother's eyes had lit up on his arrival told him as much.

But for now, he put it all behind him as he drove towards Truro. As yet he hadn't met any of Adam's future relatives, although he had been to see the White Rivers Pottery, where Adam was such a proud and experienced potter, and where Ethan was fast learning the craft.

He had duly admired the gleaming, virginally white products, with the initials WR entwined with KC on each base, depicting White Rivers and Killigrew Clay. There was clearly no intention of separating one from the other, and rightly so, he supposed. He had known the whole area since childhood, though his family had never been involved with the china clay business or it owners. But everyone knew the importance of Killigrew Clay around here, and the way the pottery had come into being after the end of the war. Adam had told him that Mrs Norwood herself, the part-owner who had once been Skye Tremayne, had thought up the name of White Rivers.

To Nick, she sounded a pretty formidable woman, and probably in the mould of Lily Pollard who had come calling on him unannounced. It wasn't an appealing picture.

But he instantly forgot about her. Because today, after he had visited several old acquaintances, he intended calling at the artist's studio, with the firm intention of buying a future masterpiece as a gift for his partner.

Albert Tremayne didn't relish the prospect of attending a family wedding. He accepted that he had become more reclusive as the years had gone on, in complete contrast to the heady greenstick days he had shared with his sister, Primmy.

Before his wife Rose had become so dependent on him, she had constantly complained at how garrulous he was with clients and Truro folk, and he had insisted that he owed it to be civil to the folk who considered him a local celebrity. But after Rose had died, and there was no more need to go out of the studio for relief from her grumbling, he had turned inward on himself.

He took few commissions now. He probably should, because until he got them working, his fingers were becoming stiff with arthritis, and he had lost much of his enthusiasm for his work. He took longer to begin his day each morning, but since he was now seventy-two years old, he hardly cared what folk thought about him any more. He knew that some thought him a queer fish, but amazingly, this aura of mystery and aloofness seemed to enhance his stature as an artist.

Albert scowled at the insistent knocking on his studio door on that sunny April morning. It was barely ten o'clock; he had just finished a late breakfast, and still wore the Chinese silk kimono one of his more grateful travelling clients had given him. His hair was lank and long, and he peered at the smartly turned out young man at his door with an air of irritation.

"I'm not open for business yet, and I don't do sittings without a prior appointment."

"Mr Albert Tremayne?" the man enquired. "My name is Nicholas Pengelly, and I believe we're shortly to become related, at least in a roundabout manner."

Nicholas forced a smile, though personally he found the sight of the artist a disgrace to humanity. Bits of food clung to the sides of his mouth, and he looked and smelled none too clean. No wonder he needed prior appointments for his clients' sittings, if only to tidy himself up. The clients would need fair notice too. But he wasn't here to criticise.

Albie's eyes narrowed. "Related, you say? How the devil do you make that out?"

From his dishevelled appearance and the tremor in his voice, Nick guessed that the man had probably been drinking the night before and his brain was befuddled, or he would surely have recognised the name Pengelly. Nick spoke slowly, the way one did to the very drunk, or the very stupid.

"I apologise for coming here unannounced, sir. And it's my brother who is about to be married to your niece. I refer to the marriage of Adam Pengelly and Miss Vera Pollard."

"Charlotte's girl," Albie growled. "And not before time,

34

neither. Not that I suspect any funny business between 'em, you understand, but she's getting a bit long in the tooth."

The man was an oaf, thought Nicholas, but he had met enough celebrities who thought they could get away with any insult they chose to use. They always attracted enough adoring sycophants, no matter what they said, so their party trick was to become as obnoxious as they could, to see just how far they could go before their audience fled in disgust.

In his profession, he was used to summing up people very quickly, and he would be surprised if Albert Tremayne wasn't just such a person. But he'd come here for a purpose, and he wasn't going to be put off, nor rise to the bait as Albie stood with folded arms, awaiting his response.

"Then I hope my brother knows how to handle her," he said coolly. "But that's their business, and not mine. Now then, Mr Tremayne, I want to purchase a special gift for my business partner, and as he's very keen on supporting modern artists, this is my purpose in coming here."

"Oh, your *business* partner, is it?" Albie sneered, his voice heavy with innuendo. "Well, I've heard bedmates called some fancy names, so I dare say that's as good as any. And what makes 'ee think I need supporting in my old age?"

Nick looked at him steadily. "From the look of you, man, I'd say you need a pot of strong black coffee to support you. And perhaps I could give you my card. It might also serve to remind you not to make insinuations about people unless you want to be accused of slander."

He handed over the gilt-edged card with the words 'Pengelly and Pierce, Solicitors at Law' embossed on it, and the address of their Plymouth chambers beneath.

Albie took it, staring at it fixedly for a few seconds while his brain took in the information. It had been said so smoothly that he wondered if he had even been censured at all.

"So if you're quite satisfied that I'm not here to ravish you, sir, perhaps I could step over the threshold before you startle the local virgins and horses alike by your unkempt appearance," Nicholas went on pleasantly.

It was the shock approach, and it usually worked. For a

moment, Albie said nothing, then he roared with laughter and stood back to give Nicholas admittance.

"By God, you're a rum fellow, but I like you, sir," he said, when he could draw breath.

Which was more than Nicholas could say about Albert. But personalities didn't come into business dealings, and he knew that well enough.

"Well, in the circumstances I dare say I can trust 'ee not to run away wi' any of my work," Albert added, unable to resist the barb. "So you can wait in the studio and take a look-see while I get some clobber on, then we'll get down to business. Would 'ee care to take some coffee with me – or something stronger, maybe?"

"Thank you, nothing," Nicholas said, not wanting to risk having a drink laced with anything unidentifiable. "I'm happy to wait until you're ready."

"Come through, then," Albie grunted, and led the way to the studio before he stumped upstairs to his living quarters. He had plenty of paintings for sale from his more feverish days, and he was sure he could palm off this lawyer fellow with a suitable scene and make a handsome profit.

Nicholas tried not to notice the fine layer of dust on the studio furnishings. He was not fastidious to the extent of prissiness, but he disliked squalor. This place didn't qualify for the term yet, but it was clear that Albert Tremayne's business acumen must be going downhill fast. He felt a brief pity, because once, he knew, the artist had really been a somebody in this town. A glamour figure, in his way, almost as much as the new movie stars were becoming now.

He turned his attention to the work on display. There were plenty of paintings for sale, on easels and hanging on the walls. Some were quite small and delicately painted, while others were bold and masterly. The man was a fine artist, Nick acknowledged, and no one could take that away from him. He moved towards the group of unframed paintings stacked against one wall, and idly riffled through them. Some were pastoral scenes, but others were portraits. Then, without warning, his breath caught in his throat, and he pulled one of the paintings out from all the rest and stared at it.

The woman portrayed on the canvas was more beautiful than any woman he had seen in his life before. And it was obvious to anyone with any sensibility at all, that there was a world of passion in her extraordinary blue eyes, and that the artist had painted her with a matching passion in his soul.

For a hard-headed lawyer like himself to have such an instant reaction was unusual enough. To be aware that his heart was racing and that he could feel more than a stirring in his loins just by studying the voluptuous red mouth and the curvacious figure dressed in the extraordinarily flamboyant garments, was something he was totally unable to explain.

And that beautiful hair . . . that long, gleaming black hair, dressed in a style that was not a style at all, but was decked with beads, and flowed freely and uninhibitedly over her slender shoulders. She was no more than a canvas portrait, but to Nicholas she was uncannily alive. . . . She was Aphrodite and Cleopatra, and every temptress that ever lived in life or in legend. . . .

"That painting's not for sale," he heard Albert Tremayne say harshly.

He hadn't heard the artist come downstairs again, but now, dressed more soberly than in his garish Chinese garb, Albert strode across the studio floor and almost wrenched the portrait out of Nicholas's hands.

"I'm sorry. I was merely looking around as you suggested. But she's such a beautiful woman. You must have known her very well. Who is she, or who *was* she? Your wife, maybe?"

Nick felt as gauche as a young boy asking the questions, clumsy in his need to know the identity of the woman.

"She's nobody who exists. She's a dream, a fantasy, and she's not for sale. So if you would tell me your business partner's tastes, perhaps we can strike a deal, sir. I have clients to see today, and don't have much time to spare for idle chitchat."

Nicholas was damn sure there were no clients in the offing, but as Albert tucked the portrait away at the back of the stack on the floor, he knew he would get no more information out of the man. And he had best keep to the business in hand, instead of being totally bowled over by a beauty that apparently didn't exist. Or so the man said.

Long after Nicholas Pengelly had gone away with an overpriced painting of Truro overlooking the Lemon River, Albert sat clutching the portrait of Primmy in his hands. He had forgotten it was even there. It wasn't meant for public viewing, and he cursed the fact that he had allowed the stranger free rein in his studio.

Once, he had wanted to display Primmy's likeness everywhere, and God knew he'd done enough paintings of her in his time. But now, with an almost possessive greed, he wanted to keep them all to himself, and he took the portrait upstairs to his bedroom and put it in the cupboard with all the others.

It was ironic, and inexplicable, even to himself, that he couldn't bear to look at them. He simply wanted to possess them to the exclusion of all others. It was the only thing now that made her totally his.

He still cared about Primmy with a undimmed passion, but more than being a comfort, he knew it had become a curse he was obliged to live with until the day he died. And if that wasn't enough to feed a body's sense of fate being against him, he didn't know what was.

He cared little what became of the paintings he sold, and had lost interest in himself as a celebrity, except when it suited him. Even then, he was more self-mocking than laudatory, with the effect that even the strongest admirers of his work thought him unduly sarcastic and arrogant. It was certain the Pengelly fellow had thought as much, but he dismissed all thought of him as easily as swatting a fly.

Nicholas drove around the countryside for quite a while before he thought of going back to St Austell. It was ludicrous how impossible it was to get the face of the woman in the portrait out of his mind.

He had no idea who she was, and he realised that the artist

had been totally unforthcoming in identifying her. Perhaps it was true what he said – that she didn't exist and never had, and was no more than a dream, a fantasy . . .

He wasn't a superstitious man; he left all that twaddle for more gullible folk, but he was a Cornishman for all that, and a feeling deep in his gut told him that the man was lying. The woman did exist, and no artist, however sensitive, could have portrayed that amount of sensuality in a woman without having known her. And loved her.

By the time Nicholas got back to St Austell he was calling himself all kinds of a fool, and had determined to put the image out of his mind. He had more important things to attend to than chasing someone else's dream. He was to be best man at his brother's wedding.

He smiled ruefully. Having met two members of the clan so far, he wasn't impressed. The strident Lily and the uncouth Albert Tremayne were hardly candidates for most popular folk of the year. He only hoped Adam wasn't heading for disaster.

They had arranged to go out to a local hostelry that evening. They both knew their father wouldn't join them, and no matter how much Ethan begged to do so, he was told firmly that he was too young to frequent such places.

"I'm near to being fifteen," he defended himself. "I can hold me jug of ale, same as the next 'un."

"I hope you haven't tried it, sprog," Nick said sharply. "It won't do the family reputation much good to have you thrown into the local jailhouse for drinking."

"*Your* reputation, you mean," Ethan sulked. "Bigshot lawyer."

"No I don't. I mean your brother's important new family, and the ones who provide your weekly bread and butter. How would it look if Adam had to explain to his new bride and her family that you can't be at the wedding because you're sleeping it off in a cell?"

Ethan scowled, half of him sensing the pride in being able to boast of such a thing to his contemporaries, and the other half fearful of the cuffing he'd get from his brothers.

"You'll let me have a taste at the feast, though, won't you? I know Mrs Norwood won't be so all-fired fussy. She's my friend, and she said I have to call her Skye now we're near-related," he added importantly.

Nick began to laugh at such cheek, and Adam gave Ethan a cursory clip about the ears.

"Don't be disrespectful," he snapped. "I never heard such nonsense, and you mind and keep a civil tongue in your head. I'm sure Mrs Norwood never said anything of the sort."

"She did too," Ethan howled. "I seen her up at the pottery t'other day, and 'twas her idea, not mine, so there."

"What's this Mrs Norwood got to do with the wedding, anyway?" Nick said with a smile, trying to play down the growing tension between them.

Now that Adam was joining the clan, so to speak, he probably should have kept in touch with the goings-on down here, but he'd lost track of the large Cornish intermixing families a long while ago. His mother spoke up.

"She's the daughter of the Tremayne girl who went to America and married her cousin. There was some fuss over it at the time, but 'tis all water under the bridge now. This here Mrs Norwood is old Morwen Tremayne's granddaughter."

Nick's heart jolted. Of course there were going to be Tremaynes and Killigrew descendants at the wedding, but the names had never been as prominent in his thoughts as now, after leaving Albert Tremayne's studio.

"And her name is Skye?" he said casually.

His mother sniffed loudly.

"American. I told you," she said, as if that explained everything. "And she be as uppity as all on 'em, from what I hear. Owns half the pottery, so that should tell you."

Nick found himself laughing at her indignant voice, and Adam joined in.

"Ma thinks women should stay home and bake bread or take in washing for richer folk. She forgets that plenty of 'em used to be bal maidens for Killigrew Clay in the old days, and that plenty more went to do war work."

"We want no talk of war here," his mother said sharply, with a glance at her husband in his creaking rocking chair by the window. "Anyway, she don't *make* the pots, o' course, just rakes in a share o' the proceeds."

"She *can*, though," Ethan said. "She told me she once threw a pot afore the old linhay was burned down years ago. She can do anything," he added with adoration in his eyes.

"Hell's teeth, she sounds like a real tartar," Nick said in an aside to his brother. "Are you sure you want to marry into this family?"

Adam's eyes were suddenly mischievous. "Oh, brother, have you got a surprise coming to you! But I ain't saying no more, and we're wasting valuable drinking time."

"You be sure and keep him sober, our Nick," his mother called out as a passing shot. "We don't want no faltering at the church tomorrow wi' all they posh folks watching."

It was late in the evening by the time they reached the Dog and Duck Inn on the St Austell waterfront, and the taproom was thick with smoke when they entered.

Adam had assured Nick that he knew what he was doing; that he adored Vera, and that she was the only woman in the world for him, and in any case he was marrying her, not her entire family.

Still with the thoughts of the two he had met so far, and the imagery of the progressive American, Mrs Norwood, firmly fixed in his mind now, Nick could only hope that Adam was man enough to cope with them all.

The door of the taproom opened and shut, bringing with it a blast of evening air, and Adam groaned.

"Christ, I hadn't expected him to be here tonight," he muttered. "It's Vera's uncle Theo, Nick. One of the Tremaynes. You'd have met him tomorrow as he'll be giving her away, so you may as well be introduced to him now."

Nick watched the large man moving forcefully towards them. There was a faint likeness to Albert Tremayne, if only in the eyes. This one was much younger, though – in his late forties, Nick assessed.

"Well, Adam, taking your last taste of freedom, I see," Theo greeted him. "And this must be the brother who escaped."

"Escaped?" Nick said, not sure how to take this.

"Theo thinks everyone who moved away from Cornwall did so because they had something to hide," Adam said shortly. "Take no notice of him."

"Now then, you young bugger, we're not fam'ly yet, so you mind your manners," Theo said, giving him a dig in the ribs, but chortling and expansive all the same.

From the look of his fiery cheeks and unsteady gait, Nick guessed he'd already had a bellyful to drink before coming here. There was a whiff of something else on him too. Perfume. And cheap French perfume at that.

Adam snapped a response. "Well, as you rightly suppose, this is my brother Nicholas, who's a respected lawyer in Plymouth, if you call that escaping."

"A self-imposed grockle, then. Well, if we need another lawyer, we'll know not to get in touch with 'ee, won't we?"

He roared at his own joke and Nick looked at him steadily. So this was another choice sample of Adam's family-in-laws . . . but even as he thought it, his mind cleared. They were Adam's, not his. Once the wedding was over, and he had spent a few more days at home, he could go back to Plymouth any time he wished. He didn't have to stay for the couple of weeks William Pierce had insisted he needed.

"You'm a sober one, by the looks of 'ee, boy," Theo said thickly now, glowering back at Nick. "Don't 'ee have a store of lawyer's jokes to tell at the feasting tomorrow?"

"I do not," said Nick. "And in my business, we take marriage seriously. Too many of them come unstuck for me to enjoy listening to the kind of jokes you're referring to."

"For God's sake, Nick, don't bait him, or we'll be here all night."

"You pompous *prig*," Theo spluttered, his mind too muddled to really be any threat. "I'll have to see if I can dredge up some jokes about lawyers then, to keep the crowd amused."

"You do, and I'll break your neck," Nick said, so pleasantly that the others wondered if he had said the words

42

at all. He drained his ale, and told Adam it was time to go.

"That's right," Theo bellowed after them. "Take the boy home to get his beauty sleep, for he'll get none tomorrow night, unless he don't come up to expectations."

"*Leave* it, Nick," Adam said, clutching his brother's arm as he made to turn back, his fists clenched. "He won't remember a word of it tomorrow, and it don't mean a thing, anyway. Everything's all right in the lower department."

Nick grinned at him as they went out into the fresh air and headed back to his car. "So you and Vera have—"

"Once or twice," Adam said ambiguously, and then exploded into laughter. "Oh ah, broth, we've made contact all right, if you know what I mean. And they bedsprings in that little hotel in Newquay are going to sing out a joyous song of welcome tomorrow night when me and my Vera get thrashing. Shocked you, have I?"

"Good God, no," Nick said, laughing. "I've heard far worse than that."

He wasn't shocked, nor even surprised, except by his own sudden feeling of envy. Whatever Vera Pollard was like, she had obviously captivated his brother, and they were clearly head over heels in love. He wished her and Adam all the love and luck in the world, and for the first time in a long while, he knew what he was missing.

Into his mind at that moment came the image of the woman's face that had been haunting him all day. A sensual and beautiful face, that probably had no more substance than a will-o'-the-wisp. And it was a foolish man indeed, who fell in love with a dream.

Trying to make conversation at the dinner table at New World that evening, Skye found herself wishing the wedding was over and done with. Philip was not in the mood to celebrate other folks' nuptials, and the thought of being on parade tomorrow, as he put it, was making him more argumentative than usual. Finally, Skye could stand it no longer.

"Honey, just for once, will you accept that this is a family occasion, and therefore important to me, and try to look as if you're enjoying it?"

"I don't know why they're so damn important to you, when they probably don't give a fig for you."

She felt herself flush deeply. "How dare you be so insulting, Philip. Truly, I don't know what's got into you lately."

"Well, face it, *honey*," he sneered, exaggerating her tone. "You were always your grandmother's favourite, and it didn't help matters when you were left this house and half the pottery, did it? You were the American upstart, remember?"

"Is that how you saw me? How you see me now?" Skye said, becoming more upset than angry now.

Philip shrugged. "I married you, didn't I? It would have made no difference to me if you were black or yellow or spoke Chinese."

"It might have made a difference to me, though," she retorted. "If I'd been any of those things, I may not have been able to tolerate your British snobbishness." She listened to her own voice with something like horror, hardly knowing how this argument had begun, or where it was leading. She heard him push back his chair as he threw down his table napkin.

"It may seem like snobbishness to you, but it's normal behaviour to me, to want my children brought up in a civilised atmosphere, and not among—"

"Go on. Say it, why don't you? Among savages, maybe?"

"You're putting words in my mouth now," he said coldly.

"Oh, I don't think so. They've been in your head for long enough. You despise my family just because of who they are, don't you, Philip? You've always despised them, because they don't match up to your intellectual standards."

She saw his hands grip the back of his chair, and noticed the way the hard veins stood out on his forehead. She knew that these signs heralded a bad night. His head would throb and the nerve-ends would stab, and he would end up sleeping in the adjoining room, instead of sharing their bed with her. And she didn't care. She didn't damn well care . . .

"I'm sorry if it offends you, *honey*," he drawled now. "But if you want to know the truth, then yes, some of them are less than civilised. There's the Irish pair, who are rarely seen here, thank God. And the farming yokels, who I suppose we have to be hospitable to for a night or two. Then there's the drunken artist uncle, to say nothing of choice cousin Theo—"

"Stop it, Philip," Skye snapped. "You've said enough, and if you shame them by your taunts, you shame me too, and I'll listen to no more of it. Granny Morwen left me this house in all good faith, and she and my mother would be horrified to know you thought so little of it all."

"Oh yes, the famous Tremaynes who weren't so bloody wonderful that there weren't a few secrets in their past."

Skye flinched, wishing she had never been so reckless as to confide in him about secrets that weren't even her own.

"Every family has secrets," she said sharply.

"Mine didn't."

"Oh, I know you were Mister Perfect," she said, close to tears now, and hardly knowing what she was saying. "I dare say you didn't even feel a flicker of lust for your precious Ruth. If you'd married her, any future children would have involved an immaculate conception—" She gave a cry as he came around the side of the dining-table and hauled her cruelly to her feet.

"I won't deign to ask what your parsimonious Uncle Luke would have made of that remark. But if it's lust you want—"

Before she knew what he intended, he had thrust one hand behind her neck and brought her face close to his, fastening his mouth over hers in a savage kiss. She tried to twist away from him, but he overpowered her, and she lost her balance and fell to the floor, with him on top of her.

It reminded her all too graphically of that other time, but this wasn't Desmond Lock, and she was no longer a young girl. This was her husband, Philip, whom she loved . . . she realised she was sobbing now, as his hands fumbled for her skirts, and she tried to plead with him.

"Philip – darling – not here, please. Think about where we are. Let's go upstairs – please—"

Suddenly she felt him leave her. He stood up, looking down

at her coldly. She drew in her breath, anticipating what was to come. They had been down this road before.

"Tidy yourself before the servants come in. You look like a whore with your skirts all rucked up. As for going upstairs, you'll be undisturbed tonight. My head is too full to bursting to play any more of your harlot's games."

She watched him leave the dining-room, tears streaming down her face and her heart near to breaking at his crudity. He professed himself a gentleman, but he frequently treated her as far less than a lady. The doctor had told her these vicious mood changes were due to the pressure inside his head, and one day . . . one day, it might all be too much for human tissues to withstand.

She understood, and she forgave, knowing she could do nothing else, when these raging personality conflicts were none of his doing. It had nothing to do with drink or drugs, just a terrible injury inflicted on him in a war. But it was gradually tearing him apart, turning him into two separate beings in one body, and it was tearing her apart too.

She still loved him, even though that love was often sorely tested, and she desperately wanted him the way he used to be. But the more time passed, the further apart they seemed to be, and she knew in her soul there could be no going back.

Four

By the following morning, the day of the Pollard wedding, no one would have known of Philip Norwood's savage mood change, and he appeared to have forgotten it. That was the way it always was, and Skye was grateful enough that he was his old self, at least for now. When Em and Will arrived from Padstow to the squeals of delight from the children, he was charm itself towards them. That was a bonus too, as he often implied that the farming pair were a cut beneath the others.

"So what be 'ee wearing for the event, Skye?" Em wheezed, large and ungainly as ever in an unfashionable frock and jacket. Skye's thoughts soared with pleasure as she described the elegant green shot silk ensemble. She saw Emma's doubtful look and gave a sigh.

"Oh, don't tell me you're going to be an old fusspot like Charlotte, just because I'm wearing *green*! It's just a colour, Em, and nobody can be so dumb as to think it can influence anybody's future!"

Emma snorted. "And you a Cornishwoman! Even if you'm an imported one, you can't deny the senses that were given you at birth, and you'd do well not to scoff at superstition, my girl, nor sneer at them that believe in 'em."

"I don't sneer," Skye said quickly, realising that for all Emma's affability, she was really put out now. "But I have my own opinion on style, and knowing what suits me."

She bit her lips, wondering if Emma would see this as a further slight. Whatever Em wore to the wedding, she was going to appear lumpy and red-faced and breathless – and perfectly content with her lot. To Skye's relief, she saw that her aunt was laughing now.

"Don't you worry none about style as far as me and Will are concerned, Skye. We go our own way and always have done, and they who starch themselves up to the nines for the wedding must take us as we are."

Skye gave her a hug. "And love you for it," she commented, suddenly husky.

Of all the long Tremayne dynasty, by whatever name they now were, these two were the most contented of all. It may not be a fiery, passionate relationship – and only Em and Will knew the truth of that – but there was a lot to be said for the easy, loving companionship they shared.

But Skye admitted that for herself, in the glorious, fulfilling prime of her life, such thoughts were more depressing than encouraging. She wasn't ready to settle for easy, loving companionship . . . any more than Morwen Tremayne would have been, at whatever age.

Skye's eyes gleamed, remembering her grandmother's sometimes more than vague hints on just how passionate a girl and woman she had been. Reminding Skye that passion didn't have to end as the years advanced – providing the two people concerned felt the same way. Providing that passion didn't become ugly and turn into abuse . . .

"Are you cold?" Emma said as she shivered. "'Tis a lovely day for a splicing, but if that silk affair you'm planning to wear be too thin, you'd best think of summat else."

"Stop it, Em," Skye said, laughing at her blatant guile. "I'm wearing green, and that's that."

The New World family and their relatives arrived at the church shortly before the due time. Baby Oliver had been left behind with his nanny until later in the day, and knowing of the girls' restlessness and excitement, to have brought them any earlier would have been disastrous.

As it was, Sebby was already challenging the hapless verger and a furious Lily in the church porch, saying he was too hot in his rubbishy outfit, and he might decide not to march up the aisle behind the bride and the little idiots after all.

"Oh yes, you will, you little brat," snapped Philip, wrenching Sebby's arm and taking charge. "You spoil this day for your cousins and I'll throttle you."

"Philip, go on inside the church with Em and Will," Skye said, knowing she had to stop this before it came to blows. "I'll stay outside with Lily and the children, and join you in our seats later as arranged."

She didn't miss the verger's thankful glance, and guessed he'd been sorely tested before they arrived. But they had been almost the last, until the horse-drawn carriage arrived with Theo acting as proxy father of the bride, and Vera looking as unlike Vera as Skye had ever seen her. Love – and wedding nerves – made all the difference, she conceded.

"Will I do?" she whispered to Skye through the filmy veil covering her face.

"You look perfectly beautiful," Skye assured her, "and Adam will love you for ever."

But it felt a little strange to Skye to follow the bridal procession up the aisle, feeling that she really had no place to be there at all. It hadn't been her choice to do so, but Lily had insisted that she couldn't control Sebby as well as the Norwood girls if trouble erupted between them.

It was hardly the way to regard a wedding day, but Skye couldn't deny the possibility. So as the strains of the traditional bridal march began, she followed at a reasonable distance behind Theo and Vera, Sebby and her daughters, and finally Lily.

There was a lump in her throat as she saw how people turned to gaze at Vera and smile at her. So many family members and friends, all wanting to wish her well on her special day. And at the far end of the church, where the preacher awaited them all, Adam and his brother Nick, his supporter, stepped forward and turned to see the vision who was approaching them now.

Nick Pengelly was curious to see this woman who had captured his brother's heart. He knew she was no young flapper, he thought irreverently, but she and Adam obviously suited one another. He couldn't see Vera's face clearly behind her veil, and he felt momentarily guilty that he hadn't made the effort to call on her when he arrived back in Cornwall.

But there had been so little time, and anyway, it was too late now for such thoughts. He always said that if you couldn't change things, then you simply got on with life, and didn't let past regrets get the better of you. It was something he frequently tried to impress on his clients.

He glanced beyond the bride and her uncle, to the scowling young boy and the fragile-looking little girls in their white organdie frocks, to the strong-faced older attendant, whom he now knew was Vera's sister, Lily. And then his heart stopped.

Paintings didn't come to life. He knew that. Someone whom he had been told didn't exist couldn't suddenly appear in the flesh – and such delectable flesh that it curled his toes and tightened his loins. A woman who had been described as no more than an illusion, a dream, couldn't possibly be here, as if she had emerged as fully formed and beautiful as Aphrodite rising out of the waves . . .

Dear God, thought Nick, *poetry was never my strong point* . . . and it had no place in a hard-headed lawyer's thinking. But seeing this startlingly beautiful woman garbed in the silken sheen of a sea-goddess or a shimmering mermaid was turning his mind . . .

He swung away abruptly, concentrating on the fact that Adam was moving towards his bride, and that he was supposed to stand beside him, ready to perform his supporter's duties. But not before he had caught someone else's glare, directed straight at him from several rows back.

He knew at once that Albert Tremayne had interpreted his reaction. Albert Tremayne knew just what his feelings were, because he had once shared them. In that instant, Nick knew himself to be just as capable of the so-called Cornish intuition as any of them. You could move away, but you could never escape your roots.

Skye was aware of her heart beating erratically as she slid into the seat beside Philip, as close to her girls as possible. She was perfectly confident at meeting strangers and always had been. It was part of the American psyche to be confident and outgoing, and so she was. She had held down a job for many years, against all the odds of a male-dominated world, gone through a war and seen sights in a foreign hospital that no sensitive young woman was ever meant to see, and she was a mature wife and mother.

And yet one look into a stranger's eyes had suddenly filled her with feelings she hadn't known for years, if ever.

She had never denied the instant attraction she had felt for Philip all those years ago, but love had developed gradually. It had been held in check by the knowledge that he already had a fiancée, and she had had no intention of breaking up another woman's relationship. To his credit, neither had he. She should remember that now, since she was hardly a free woman.

The incongruity of such fleeting, irrational thoughts didn't escape her mind. But nor could she deny the heat that seemed to sear through her veins as her glance locked with Adam Pengelly's brother. It was frightening and overwhelming, and more shiveringly exciting than a feeling had any right to be on a solemn occasion like her cousin's wedding.

The realisation of where she was brought her back to her senses, and she forced herself to concentrate on the procedure of the wedding service, aware that she had missed half of it already. The sweet litany of the vows stirred her, as always, to remember her own.

'Do you, Adam, take Vera to be your wedded wife? Will you love her and cherish her . . . Forsaking all other . . .' Skye had done that. '. . . In sickness and in health . . .' She had done that too. '. . . Until death do us part . . .' Well, wasn't that what every couple intended at the onset of their lives together?

As the service proceeded, Adam's brother placed the gold ring on the vicar's prayer book, and for one more breath-stopping moment he glanced at Skye again, then looked away.

"What's the matter with you?" Philip hissed. "You're fidgeting worse than the girls."

She felt as if she could hardly speak, as if she was sick with a fever she couldn't explain. It was madness . . . but as Wenna began to droop and reach for her mother's hand, she clutched at it as if it was a lifeline, pulling the child into the seat beside her until the central figures moved towards the vestry to sign the register.

This was her life, she reminded herself, just as if anyone was daring to question it – her husband beside her, her daughters behaving like little angels, and baby Oliver asleep at home until he was made sweet and fresh and brought to the reception to be displayed and crowed over. There was no room for anyone else.

Charlotte was firmly in control of her daughter's wedding, and at the reception in the big marquee in the garden of the Pollard house, the guests were all shown to their appointed tables. Family by family, group by group, the closest ones were placed nearest to the bridal table. With Celia and Wenna being an official part of the bridal party, the Norwoods had been given due prominence.

But by the time the speeches began, the girls had joined their parents, and only Sebby and Lily sat alongside Vera, Adam, Charlotte and Theo – and Nicholas Pengelly.

As he stood up to make his speech, Skye heard his voice for the first time. It was a rich Cornish voice, but more modulated and educated that Adam's or young Ethan's. Families were a mishmash, she thought, and most of hers were distinctly unalike. Emma and Charlotte might be sisters, but in every respect they were different. It was a wonder any of them got on together, so perhaps there was more than a thread of truth in the old saying of blood being thicker than water.

Oliver began to get fretful then, reaching out for her, and noisily rejecting the arms of his nanny, and Skye concentrated on being a mother and not a philosopher.

Once the formalities were over and the cake had been ceremoniously cut, the whole tempo became more relaxed as the adults began to mix and talk over old times. The children, however, quickly became bored. Inevitably, she saw with a sigh, Sebby became the ringleader of some noisy arguments. He was ready to fight with everyone, and his young brother Justin soon left him for the safety of his mother's wing. Celia stood up to his taunting as long as she could, then she kicked out at Sebby in frustration, ducking out of his way as he went to swipe her. His arm landed heavily on the side of Wenna's head, making her squeal with pain.

Before anyone else could move, Sebby was quickly hauled out of the way and told in no uncertain manner that he was a bully and a pig, and he should learn to respect girls.

Wenna stared in awed astonishment at the way Sebby scowled for a few silent moments at this verbal attack, and then stalked away to find some other prey. She was only five years old, but she knew a red-faced champion when she saw one. And as she was asked awkwardly if she was all right, and if she would like some lemonade, she nodded, letting Ethan Pengelly take her hand, and following him adoringly to the buffet table.

"Will you just look at that?" said an amused voice beside Skye. "Is that a future romance in the making, do you think?"

Skye felt as if she turned her head very slowly, hardly knowing if she intended to savour this moment – or to put it off as long as possible. The stranger spoke again.

"I'm sorry if I startled you. I should have introduced myself formally. I'm Nicholas Pengelly, Adam's brother."

Skye looked at him properly then, seeing the slightly incredulous look in his dark eyes, and not understanding it. Her own eyes imperceptibly widened, and Nick caught his breath at their incredible colour. She swallowed, not too happy at being caught off guard like this, and reacting so naively.

"Skye Norwood," she murmured, and then, as if to defend her position, "mother of the smaller bridesmaids and the infant Oliver, who's now been taken away to be tidied."

She knew the words were inane, but it seemed somehow important to establish herself as this staid figure, even though her appearance totally belied such a label. She saw Nicholas Pengelly offer her his hand, and had no option but to place her own in his for a moment. His fingers tightened around hers, and she tried not to snatch them away.

"I'm delighted to meet you, Mrs Norwood, but I must confess that I can hardly think of you so formally, for we have already met before."

"Oh, I think not!" Or she would certainly have remembered it . . . .

Nick gave a short laugh. "Well, perhaps that was a stupid remark to make. But I've seen your portrait – dozens of them, in fact, but I was given to understand that the portrait was of someone who didn't exist. Of course I knew that couldn't be true, but the artist seemed oddly reluctant to tell me the lady's identity, so you remained a mystery until today."

He began to feel fraught with embarrassment. For if this Skye Norwood was the woman in the portraits, and if Albert Tremayne had been in love with the sitter as Nick believed, then there was something very ugly in an old man's obsession with her. And what were her feelings towards him? He would almost rather not have known that she existed at all . . .

"You are truly mistaken, Mr Pengelly," he heard Skye say lightly. "I presume you are referring to my Uncle Albert as the artist, but I assure you that any portraits you may have seen in his studio are not of me."

"Then who?"

"My mother. Primrose Tremayne."

"*Ah.*"

He couldn't deny the huge relief he felt that there was no incestuous relationship between this lovely young woman and that disgusting old man. At least, not a physical one, nor even one that she was aware of, he guessed. But the likeness between the mother and daughter was so intense that he could easily believe the artist still lusted over them both, unable to separate one from the other in his twisted mind. Nick had seen too many deviants in his line of work to disbelieve anything, or be shocked by it.

"Ah, indeed," said Skye, with no idea of his thoughts. "Now, I must see to my children, Mr Pengelly."

"Of course. But please call me Nick – or Nicholas, if you prefer. We are related by marriage now, and how enchanting it would be if these two children continued the trend."

She followed his amused gaze to where Ethan had put a protective arm around Wenna's shoulders. And her little daughter's adoring look towards her fourteen-year-old hero was nothing short of flirtatious now. Even at Wenna's young age, a female knew the value of a look from glorious blue eyes and a tremulous smile. The Tremayne look . . .

"Don't be ridiculous," Skye said shortly. "And please excuse me, Mr Pengelly."

Skye had to get away from him. She had never quite believed in the power of an aura; that invisible shield that surrounded and protected a person. But she had felt Nick Pengelly's aura, drawing her into him as if they were soul mates whose destiny linked them inescapably together. It was a powerful and frightening sensation that she wanted to run from while she still could.

She looked around in desperation for Philip, and saw him entertaining some of Charlotte's more erudite acquaintances with intellectual conversation. He was having a good time on his own level now. Philip hadn't missed her. None of the children had missed her, and were playing happily.

She started, because of course no one had missed her. She hadn't been anywhere. Her brief chat with Nick Pengelly had taken no more than moments, and yet she felt eerily as if she had leapt a great distance in time. Nothing was as clear-cut in her mind as before, and whatever lethal concoction had been in the so-called fruit cup that Theo had generously provided for the reception was definitely swirling her brain.

It was at that moment, against all her better judgement and without warning, that the craziest thought entered her head. Maybe she should consult old Helza, and demand to know what the future held for her. She had to know if Nick Pengelly was destined to play any part in that future – but not with any intention of anticipating any clandestine romance! If Helza were to confirm such absurd thoughts, she could then do all in her power to go against destiny. She was in control of her own life, and always had been, and she was oddly uplifted by the thought, dismissing any notion that you couldn't go against fate, however much you tried. If she *did* consult Helza – and it was no more than a fleeting thought – then she would disprove such nonsense for good and all.

"How are you, Skye?" she heard Albert's slurred voice ask a few minutes later. "The babes played their parts well, but you don't look up to par now, if I might say so. I didn't know you'd taken to drinking more than is good for you."

He grinned at his own forced joke, and she shrank away from him as his drink-sodden breath filled her face. How could her mother ever have loved him? But in their halcyon days, he hadn't been this odious, creepy old man whom Skye didn't even like touching her. He had been dashing and flamboyant, and she could still feel pity for him – if she tried hard enough.

"Weddings always make me a bit sad. Silly, isn't it, when they should make one feel just the opposite."

"It depends on the wedding," Albie said darkly. "Though I can't say I care for throwing everybody together for the occasion as if they're the most sociable of folk. Half of 'em would probably prefer to cut each other's throats, given half the chance."

Skye began to laugh. "Oh, come on, how can you say that?"

"Easily. Look at Charlotte now, playing up to the monied folk for all she's worth, and dying to get her corsets off if the strained look on her face is any indication. And there's Em, wishing she were back wi' her pigs. Theo can't stand any of 'em, nor your pompous husband, and as for you, my pet—"

"Yes? What about me?" she said quickly, ignoring his snide reference to Philip. "I only said weddings made me a bit sad, but I've got no arguments with anyone here."

"I could see that by the way the Pengelly brother's taken a shine to you, and the way you responded, even though you tried not to show it. He's got a shrewd eye that sorts out the gold from the dross."

"I don't like to hear this kind of talk, Uncle Albert, and Philip wouldn't like to hear it either."

"Well, I'll not be the one to tell un," Albie slurred. "You mark my words, though, that one's got his eye on you."

She was glad to get away from him as the bride and groom approached on their informal chat with their guests. Adam's eyes were full of mischief now that he was a married man with the dreaded formalities behind him, and he was more confident than usual towards his elegant new relative.

"Went well, didn't it, cuz? I told our Nick he'd get the surprise of his life when he saw you."

"Did you? Why was that?" she said, fixing the smile on her face, but wondering if it was a weird conspiracy for folk to link them together. First Albie, now Adam . . .

"Well, knowing of your reputation as part-owner of the pottery, and then our Ethan's comments about you, he began to think you were a real harridan," he chuckled. "And we had no intention of putting him right."

"I told him he was mean, Skye," Vera put in, "but that's what brothers are like, and I'm sure Nick has formed his own opinion of you by now. You look marvellous, by the way."

"Thank you."

"So what do you think of my clever brother?" Adam asked.

"Clever? In what way is he clever?" She realised she knew nothing about him or his life, except that he had moved away from Cornwall. She didn't care, either . . .

"Well, being a lawyer and all that learning stuff. Poor Vera got lumbered with less than the cream of the family, I'm thinking," he said with a laugh, but as Vera told him off in teasing terms, Skye had no doubt that they had both got exactly what they wanted. Lucky them.

So Nick Pengelly was a lawyer. That explained the educated voice, and the slick way he had delivered the wedding speech, in such contrast to Adam's awkward, but none the less sincere words.

"When do you plan to leave for the honeymoon?" she enquired, moving the conversation away from the focus of attention that Nick seemed to have become.

"As soon as it's decent," Adam said meaningfully. "I've had more than enough socialising and I want my wife to myself."

Vera laughed, her face blush-red. "I don't mind you saying that in front of Skye, but you just stop short of saying it in front of my mother or anybody else, you hear?"

"Yes, Ma'am," he replied. "You see how she's got me hogtied already, cuz?" But the way he said it confirmed again that it was the only place he wanted to be.

*   *   *

For once, Skye was thankful when Oliver started playing up and she could use him as the excuse to get her children home. They were all tired, and she had a lot of thinking to do. But why did she? She couldn't explain the strange feelings that had come over her, and she was glad that presumably Nick Pengelly would soon be leaving to resume his legal career, wherever it was, and she was unlikely to see him again.

Even as she thought it, her mind cleared, and the nonsense of going to consult old Helza vanished. Why was there any need, when their paths would never cross again?

When they retired to bed that night, she turned to Philip with a rush of affection, holding him close to her and pressing her warm lips into the hollow of his throat, to which he immediately responded.

"What's all this?" he said, humouring her. "Have I suddenly become God's gift to womanhood?"

"No, just God's gift to me, and to blazes with the rest of them," she murmured, unable to resist smiling at the irreverent thought. But she held her breath all the same, because Philip could so easily revert to being his most pompous self again, if he thought she was being too daring.

She had long ago realised that he always had to take the initiative, and it was something that constantly frustrated her. Love-making should be a mutual enjoyment, but in Philip's eyes, that meant the man was always in control. An American author had written a book with progressively modern ideas on the subject, and Skye had secretly read and devoured its concept, but so far she had never dared to put any of the ideas into practice. Philip would be shocked to think she even knew about them. And for now, she was more than content to have his loving arms around her, to feel his hands reaching for her, palming her breasts, and for his mouth to be seeking hers and kissing her with an urgency that stimulated all her senses. He was her husband, her lover and her best friend, the way he had always been, and there was no room for any other in her life.

The honeymooners had gone off to their blissful heaven, and

Emma and Will had returned to their pigs and sheep, and for everyone else, life quickly returned to normal.

Philip left the house early on Monday morning, while the girls clamoured to be taken out for the day. Their tutor had arrived that morning with a bad cold, and rather than have the whole household sniffling and snuffling, Skye sent her home. However long ago it was now, the lingering memories of the flu epidemic were still too real in people's minds to take any chances. But now she had the girls pestering her to take them out for the day. God bless Oliver, thought Skye, who was still content to spend half the day sleeping or playing with his toys in the care of his nanny.

"All right," she gave in to her daughters with a smile. "You can choose where you want to go, as long as you both agree. I want no squabbling, mind. So what will it be? The seaside to collect shells, or the moors to collect wild flowers for pressing? Or we could go into Truro and look around the town like tourists, or go visit Aunt Charlotte or Aunt Betsy . . ."

Celia pulled a face at the thought, and Wenna squealed impatiently. "I don't want to see that horrible Sebby again," she wailed. "And Justin's a baby, always doing what Sebby says."

Skye hid a smile. Justin was all of a year younger than Wenna, but in her eyes that made him a baby.

"Where then?" she said impatiently. "I'm not going to drive around aimlessly, so if you can't make up your minds, we'll stay home and make some candy."

"Cook won't like that," Celia said loftily. "Anyway, I know where Wenna wants to go."

"Do you? And where's that?" Skye saw her younger daughter's face go bright red as Celia began to chant.

"Wenna wants to go to the pottery to see soppy Ethan Pengelly! She's gone all soft over him, just because he treated her like his little pet at the wedding."

"I'm not soft over him!" Wenna screamed. "And he's not soppy. He's nice, and you're just in a huff because he didn't take any notice of you."

"For pity's sake you two, stop acting up this way. The pottery's not a bad idea, anyway, because I promised to look in on things while Adam's away. So stop glowering at your sister, Celia, and go fetch your coats."

She was sure it was quite unnecessary to check on anything at the pottery, but Adam was so conscientious that he had almost begged her to do so. And it was her domain. If she had never felt quite at home at the clayworks, and didn't understand half of its intricacies, at least she knew what the pottery was all about.

So later that morning she was driving away from New World and up to the moors above St Austell town; the air was so clean and fresh on that April morning that Skye opened her car window and breathed in the mingled moorland scents with an almost sensual pleasure.

There were already half a dozen motors parked outside White Rivers, and she was gratified to think that the tourists were discovering their whereabouts so early in the season. Much of that was due to David Kingsley's generous advertising in *The Informer* newspaper, she acknowledged.

"Can I try to make a pot, Mommy?" Wenna asked tentatively, at which Celia hooted.

"You couldn't make anything with those fat little fingers, could she, Mommy?"

"Yes, I could," Wenna said, almost in tears. "Ethan would show me how."

"*Ethan* won't have time for messing with little girls, you ninny. He's supposed to be working. Isn't that right, Mom?"

Before Skye could think of a suitable reply, she registered that Celia was in danger of turning into as pompous a little prig as her father if she wasn't curbed, and then two familiar figures emerged from the pottery. Her heart leapt as she saw them.

"Well, this is a pleasant surprise," Nick Pengelly said, coming towards the trio with his arm outstretched to shake Skye's gloved hand. "Ethan promised to show me around, so I thought today was as good a day as any. It seems as though we both had the same idea."

"But Mrs Norwood – Skye – won't be here as a visitor, Nick," Ethan put in quickly, visibly nervous at the assumption. "And I should be getting back to my work."

"I'm sure the rest of them can spare you for a while, Ethan,"

Skye said gently, reassuring him. "It's not every day your brother visits with you, and I'm sure he'll want to know what you're doing before he returns to—?"

"Plymouth," Nick supplied. "I share a practice with my partner there, at least for the time being."

"Oh? Isn't it permanent then?" She held her breath. It was no business of hers, and it didn't matter to her whether he practised his lawyer's trade in Plymouth or Timbuctoo.

"Our Nick's thinking of coming back to Cornwall," Ethan said eagerly. "Me Mam's ailing and me Dad's away with the pixies half the time, so Nick thinks it might be best now that our Adam's wed and moved out."

"Now, don't you go jumping the gun, Ethan. I only mentioned the possibility, and it'll take some thinking about," Nick chided him.

As the two older ones seemed suddenly tongue-tied, Ethan smiled down at the two little girls. "Do you want to learn how to throw a pot, then?"

"*Yes*!" screamed Wenna excitedly.

"No thank you, and *she*'ll never be able to do it, but it'll be fun watching her try," said Celia.

"Is it all right, Mrs Norwood – Skye?" Ethan asked, suddenly remembering their owner – apprentice relationship.

"Of course it is," she said, laughing. "Go on, all of you, and I'll join you in a minute."

She watched them go, aware that now only the two of them remained, herself and Nick Pengelly, and the sensuous scents and whispering bracken of the moors all around them.

"Well, I suppose we shouldn't stand out here forever," she said, after what seemed like an endless moment.

"Shouldn't we? I can't think of anything more desirable than being with you forever."

Skye felt her heart begin to drum more loudly. She spoke in a low, troubled voice. "Please don't say those things to me, Mr Pengelly."

"It's Nick, remember? And since I have so little time to be here, there seems no point in dressing up all my feelings with fancy words."

She ignored the last part of his sentence. "You didn't mean it then – about coming back to Cornwall permanently?"

"Would you want me to?"

She was getting progressively more agitated at the tone of this conversation. His voice was rich and possessive, and for the life of her she couldn't stop imagining how it would sound and feel as the timbre of it deepened against a woman's skin in more intimate surroundings. She gave a small shiver.

"What you do has nothing to do with me, does it? We only met a few days ago, and I hardly know you."

"You've always known me, just as I've always known you. I knew you the moment I saw your mother's portrait in your uncle's studio. I knew then that this was the image of the woman I wanted to share my life with—"

"For God's sake, will you stop this! I'm going to join my daughters, and I'd be glad if you would leave me alone."

Skye went to push past him, and his hand reached out and held her. She felt the small caress of his thumb against her arm, and she shivered again.

"For the moment. But anyone with an ounce of Cornish blood in them knows that you can't deny what fate has in store for you. You're not so colonial that you don't know that."

She tried to sound withering, even though her voice seemed no more than a husk of sound to her right then.

"And everyone knows that a clever lawyer has the where-withal to twist any kind of fate to his own advantage, so don't try to blind me with such nonsense."

She walked away from him then, and he made no attempt to stop her, but she felt decidedly wobbly as she entered the familiar confines of the pottery saleroom, and was greeted deferentially by the staff.

She tried to smile and respond naturally, and then went through to the working area where her daughter Wenna was enveloped in a huge overall now. Ethan Pengelly stood close behind her, guiding her small hands over the misshapen pot she was creating, while she laughed delightedly and adoringly into his face. And giving Skye the most unwelcome sense of *déjà vu*.

Five

Nick drove away from the pottery at high speed, asking himself furiously what the hell was the matter with him. Skye Norwood was a married woman for God's sake, and in his work he'd dealt with enough pain and misery in marriage break-ups to indulge in that kind of caper himself.

He must be having a brainstorm, and the only way out of it was to get as far away from her as possible until the fever in his blood cooled down. For there was no denying, at least to himself, that he wanted her with a raging passion. Ever since he had seen her he hadn't been able to sleep properly for thinking of her, and imagining her in his arms.

He wanted her like hell – but ruining a woman's reputation went against everything he believed in. Or so he had always thought, when dealing with other people's marital problems. It was one of life's ironies that the tables had finally turned on him, and the one woman he wanted in all the world was the one he couldn't have.

Anyway, whatever madness had possessed him speak to her as he had outside the White Rivers Pottery had probably been enough to frighten her off for good and all. And a bloody good thing too, he thought savagely.

He drove back to his parents' house, full of self-condemnation, and resolving never to see Skye Norwood again. The thought of coming back here to live was fast receding. There must be some other way of ensuring that his parents were cared for, and that all the burden didn't land on young Ethan.

His lawyer's brain got to work. Providing the house was to be left exclusively to Ethan when his parents died, then a living-in relative was the obvious answer, and Nick could easily afford to pay all the expenses. There was a cousin down Penzance way who had lost her son during the war and her husband to the flu epidemic, and had found it hard to make ends meet ever since in her miserable rented cottage. She had always been fond of his mother, and might well fit the bill.

Knowing how sensitive older folk could be, Nick knew he would need to sound things out with all concerned before he made any move, but already things were clearing in his mind. And since there was no time like the present for seeing what his cousin Dorcas might think, he told his mother he was taking a drive down to Penzance the following day.

"Do you want to come? You always got on well with her, didn't you?" he said, sowing the first seed.

"Aye, so I did, and 'twould be good to see her again, but the old un wouldn't like me to leave him for a whole day, Nick," she said wistfully. "If he weren't up to attending his own son's wedding, then he won't want me gallivanting off down south."

Nick hid a smile as she made it sound like the other end of the country instead of thirty miles or so away.

"Then I'll just give her your best, and tell her all about Adam's big day."

So the next morning saw him driving down to Penzance alone, and finding his way to the little cottage on the windy hill where his cousin Dorcas lived. The buxom and homely woman gaped in astonishment when she saw who was standing there.

"Well, the saints preserve us, if it ain't our Nick. There's nought wrong wi' your Ma or Pa, is there?" she said anxiously, giving him just the lead he needed. He shook his head, smiling as he asked if she was going to let him in, or if he had to stand on the doorstep all day, courting gossip between a mysterious stranger and a well-set-up widow-woman. Dorcas chuckled at once.

"None of your nonsense, now! There's none around here who'd look twice at me, and nor would I want them to. Since my Jed died, I've no use for anything in trousers. But come in and have a brew of tea, and tell me how the family in St Austell fares. I heard about your Adam's wedding, o' course, but I'm

not one for attending such things nowadays. They didn't take
no offence, I hope?"

"Of course not, Dorcas. My father wouldn't go, so Mother
felt she should stay home with him. But I know she'd like to
have seen you on the day, and it all went well for Adam and
his bride. I tried to persuade Mother to come with me today,
but she doesn't get out much now. They're both getting old."

As his cousin bustled about preparing the tea, she gave him
a shrewd look. She might be a countrywoman, but she didn't
lack anything upstairs, Nick thought.

"And you think mebbe a visit from me might give 'em a bit
of interest in life, is that it?"

"It's not a bad idea," he said carefully.

She laughed again, pushing a plate of home-made biscuits
towards him, then speaking more sharply. "Now why don't you
tell me what's really going on in that devious lawyer's mind o'
yourn? You ain't come all this way just to take a cup of tea wi'
me, have you?"

He grinned, taking a long drink before he spoke again. "And
I thought I was being clever," he said, boosting her sense of
intuition. "So let me tell you what I've been thinking about
these past few days, and then you can tell me if I'm taking too
much for granted, and kick me out if you feel like it. It's only
an idea, mind, and you're the only one to hear of it so far."

She listened patiently, and she didn't say anything for what
seemed like an endless few minutes.

"So you ain't even asked your Ma and Pa what they think
about all this?" she ventured at last.

"No. I told you. You needed to think about it first."

"Well, you just go back and ask 'em, and if they agree,
I'd be more'n willing to give up this draughty old place and
come and care for them in their old age," she said, her eyes
suddenly filling up. "It holds no special memories for me, after
all this time. But you'd best be sure that young Ethan won't
take umbrage at having a bossy widow-woman moving into
his house."

Nick gave her a hug that had her tut-tutting at such soppy
behaviour. But he was jubilant. All he had to do now was

to sort out the rest of them. And not for one minute did he consider himself a manipulator, while relieving himself of any obligations other than monetary. It just seemed like the best solution all round. Any vague thoughts he'd had of returning to Cornwall himself, except for occasional visits, could simply be forgotten. Better still, all thoughts of Skye Norwood could be relegated where they belonged.

Once Wenna had had her fill of making her pot on the previous day, Skye took the girls for a walk across the moors, partly to give them some exercise, and partly to try and rid her mind of the outrageous things Nick Pengelly had said to her. Even Philip had never been so outspoken on such short acquaintance, but she reminded herself that Philip had already been engaged when they met, while Nick, presumably, was totally unattached.

But was he? She knew very little about him, except that he was Adam and Ethan's brother, and he was a lawyer in Plymouth. And as Celia shouted at her to 'come on before the old woman reached them', she realised with annoyance that far from getting him out of her thoughts, he was very definitely taking up a large part of them.

"What old woman?" she asked, but of course, she should have known. The bent figure stumbling towards them at a rate that surely defied her age, could only be one person. Helza.

"Let's go back to the car," Skye said quickly. "We've gathered enough flowers for pressing now, so we'll take a drive down to the sea and look for shells and fossils."

"Who is she, Mommy?" Wenna whispered, drawing nearer to Skye and half hiding her face in her skirt.

"*I* know who she is," Celia declared importantly. "Sebby told me about her. She's a witchwoman, and when I grow up I'm going to ask her to tell me my fortune."

"No, you are not," Skye snapped. "And if I hear you talking such nonsense again, I shall slap you hard."

Both girls looked at her in astonishment. She didn't believe in slapping, and if she ever scolded them physically, it was only in the mildest way. But as Helza reached them as if the distance

66

between them didn't exist, Skye cursed Sebby Tremayne for putting such ideas into Celia's receptive head.

"So you've brought your pretty maids to see me today, have 'ee, lady?" Helza wheezed.

"Not at all. We're just out walking, and now we're going to the seaside, so good day to you," Skye said swiftly.

Even here, with no more than a soft breeze blowing, the stench of the old woman's herbs and her insanitary hovel was strong and pungent about her. Celia pinched her nose, while Wenna was too dumbstruck to do anything but widen her vivid Tremayne eyes at the apparition. Helza cackled.

"You've a fine pair of sprogs there, missus. I'll wager that just like t'other two, one will be lucky in love, while t'other – well, who knows what will happen to t'other un? And I ain't in the mood for telling!"

She turned and hobbled away, still cackling, while Skye felt her nerves tingle with an unreasoning fear.

"Who was she talking about?" Celia demanded, still full of bravado now that Helza had gone. "What other two did she mean, Mommy?"

"Nobody. Nobody at all. She tries to frighten people, but sensible ones take no notice."

"Do you *know* her, Mommy?" whispered Wenna.

"No, of course not. She's out and about on the moors for much of the time, but it's best to keep away from such folk. Now then, who can race me back to the car?"

It took their minds off the disreputable figure for the time being, but Skye might have known that the outspoken Celia couldn't resist telling Philip of the encounter when he returned home from college later that day.

"You surely didn't take the girls to see her, or let them speak with her?" he said explosively.

"Of course I didn't! But the moors are free to anyone, and I could hardly stop her approaching us."

"Then I forbid you to go anywhere near that part of the moors again," he snapped.

"You *forbid* me?" Skye said sarcastically. "I've never had anyone forbid me do anything in my life before—" She gasped

67

as he gripped her arm, trying to keep cool as she saw how scared Wenna suddenly looked, and even Celia was silenced at this verbal attack which was in danger of turning into a physical one.

"I seem to recall you promising to love, honour and obey me – or do your marriage vows mean nothing to you any more?"

"You know they do," she whispered, her eyes smarting at the way his fingernails were digging into her flesh. "Mean something."

"Only something? I thought they were supposed to be more important than that."

"Don't twist what I say, Philip. I know that cleverness with words is your stock-in-trade, but you can't deny that I've always been a loving wife to you, even when—"

Skye bit her lip. There had never been any recriminations on her part for the times when he had been less than a man to her. She had understood the ravages that wartime experiences could have on a man, the frustration, the fears, the impotency . . . but in time all those things had been overcome.

She knew the extent of his head injuries and how it affected him: the violent moods, the burning pains, and the risk to his long-term health. But the last thing she wanted to do was to make a martyr of herself because of it.

Philip suddenly let her go, and Wenna gasped at the ugly red weals on her mother's arm. She glared at her father.

"You hurt Mommy," the child said shrilly. "I *hate* you!"

He looked at her contemptuously, seeing the telltale trickle of urine run down her small legs, as it sometimes did when she was frightened and upset.

"See to your disgusting daughter," Philip said coldly. "The other one can come with me, since I've something to show her in the study."

Celia followed him with barely a glance at her mother and sister, and Skye felt cold inside. They were becoming a divided family, she thought in some hysteria, and through nobody's fault. But in times of crisis, large or small, it seemed as though each girl sided with one parent, and always made the same choice. Only Oliver, at two years old, threw his allegiance towards whoever was available at the time and was offering comfort. A little like a neutral country throwing in their lot with whichever invader was the most profitable at the time . . . To Skye, it wasn't the most comforting of allegories.

"Mommy, I'm wet," she heard a thin, plaintive voice say. "But I'm not 'gusting, am I?"

Skye swept Wenna up into her arms, ignoring her tackiness against her fine linen skirt. A soiled bit of linen was a small price to pay for the love and security of a child, she thought indignantly. Philip never seemed to realise that.

"Of course not, honey," she said swiftly. "Five minutes from now we'll have you sweet and dry again, so don't take any notice of what Daddy said."

"But he's always cross with me," Wenna persisted, her blue eyes huge and drowned with tears. "Does he love Celia better'n me?"

"What a thing to say! Parents love all their children the same, though they don't always show it. Why, when I was small, my Mommy spent more time with me than my brother, because we liked doing the same things. But she loved us both the same!"

She spoke briskly as she took Wenna upstairs to wash her and put her into fresh clothes. But she didn't altogether believe her own words. Primmy had lavished all her love on her daughter, while the moodier Sinclair was always out in the cold, even if it was by his own choice most of the time.

Right there and then she resolved to write to her brother, realising guiltily how she had been neglecting such a duty lately. And she the writer too . . .

For a moment she felt a real sense of nostalgia for the heady days of journalism. Words had always been *her* stock-in-trade too . . . even those she had written at the wartime hospital in France, when she had insisted on reporting the true facts from a woman's point of view for *The Informer* to print. But as Wenna asked in a small voice if they could play a game, she pushed away all thoughts of being nostalgic for wartime days. It was wicked to even think such things.

Theo stormed into New World a week later, abrupt as ever.

"The honeymooners are back, and I've ordered Adam Pengelly back to work on Monday morning. I've also hired another experienced potter to start getting this German order into production. I trust this meets with your approval, cuz?"

"And good afternoon to you as well, Theo," Skye said shortly. The man was an oaf, and it was hardly surprising that young Sebby followed in his ungainly footsteps. She was thankful that Philip wasn't around to add his sneering comments to her own thoughts. There weren't many of her family that Philip tolerated, let alone liked, she reflected. He had adored her grandmother, but apart from her . . .

"*Well*?" Theo said disagreeably. His dislike of having to have business dealings with a woman was patently obvious, as always, and Skye stared him out blandly, knowing how this irritated him. But she couldn't stay bland forever, not while she seethed at his high-handed remarks.

"I hope you didn't *order* Adam to return to work. For pity's sake, Theo, the man's a craftsman, and he's one of the family now."

"No outsider's one of the family as far as I'm concerned," he snapped. "Just because he married Charlotte's daughter don't make him one of us."

"You're a pig, Theo. I've always thought so, and how Betsy's put up with you all these years, what with your ill manners and your—"

"My what?" he said, his eyes narrowed.

Skye shrugged. The children were with their governess, Oliver was alseep, and there was no one else around to hear. It was high time someone told Theo what they thought of him. Morwen would have done so.

"Your dalliances, for want of a better word," Skye replied. "Do you think folk don't know of them? They either snigger behind your back, or are scandalised by it all. And what does that do for the proud name of Tremayne?"

"Whatever I do is no bloody business of yours," he shouted, his face scarlet with rage. "You should look to your own folk before you go criticising others. Your mother and dear old Albie for a start."

Skye gasped, and before she could stop herself, her arm had lashed out, catching Theo a stinging blow on his cheek. He grasped her hand viciously, making her cry out.

"You bitch," he snarled. "You can deny it all you like, but you should be thankful there were no little bastards coming out of that liaison."

"Get out!" she screamed at him. "You disgust me."

"Oh ah? You think yourself so high-and-mighty pure, don't you? I saw the way you and that Pengelly lawyer looked at each other at the wedding. There's plenty of hot Tremayne blood in you, my girl, and your man should be thankful the lawyer fellow's gone back where he belongs."

"Has he?" Skye said in a choked voice. "And why should I care about that? He's nothing to me."

Theo gave an ugly laugh. "So you say, but everything about you gives you away, cuz. Your eyes and your mouth, your voice, and all the other luscious parts of your anatomy."

Insultingly, his gaze wandered over her taut figure, to where her breasts had peaked in anger. It infuriated her to know it, and to see that Theo was well aware of it. The straightness of the current fashion did nothing to hide the womanly shape inside it, and Skye felt a violent urge to press her hands across her chest to flatten the telltale nipples. But even as she drew breath to scream at him again, Theo turned on his heel and left her with a crude comment.

"You'd best calm down your heated cheeks and your fiery blood, unless you aim to give your man the benefit of it all."

She just managed to resist the childish urge to hurl something at the door after him; but one glance at her face in a mirror told her he was right about one thing. She had the look of a wanton, and it wouldn't do for Philip to come home and see her in this state. She drew a shuddering sigh at the thought, and all the fire in her was subdued. Because there had been a time when all her feelings would have been for Philip, and he would have recognised the longing in her eyes, and swept her up in his arms with a matching desire. Now, it seemed as though she trod on egg shells as she waited to see what mood he was in. And that was no way to conduct a marriage.

As she splashed cold water on her face, Theo's words suddenly filled her head. Nick Pengelly had gone back to Plymouth. He hadn't tried to contact her again – and why would he? She knew that he definitely *shouldn't* . . . but she felt an unreasoning sense of resentment that he hadn't. So much for an instant attraction that was mutual – and dangerous.

Skye called on Vera on Monday, with no ulterior motive other than to see the modest new house she and Adam now occupied, and to welcome her home after the honeymoon.

"Well, there's no need to ask if you had an enjoyable week," she told Vera archly, as she saw her cousin's glowing eyes and pink cheeks. "Marriage obviously suits you, honey."

Vera laughed. "I should hope it does, after just one week! You're our second caller, as a matter of fact, but Theo was in a blazing hurry as always, so I can give you the leisurely guided tour of the house, and then we'll have tea."

"I can guess you weren't too pleased to see Theo," Skye remarked, when she had duly admired everything, and was treated to Vera's attempt at aptly-named rock cakes.

Vera pulled a face. "Oh well, if he thought he could upset Adam and me, he had another thought coming. We're too happy to let anything bother us, and Adam told him he'd report for work when he was due, and not a minute before. I was proud of him. Oh – and did you know he's hired another potter?"

"Yes," Skye said, when her cousin paused for breath.

"Adam's glad. He couldn't possibly cope with all the extra orders on his own, and Ethan's not up to scratch for the finishing work yet. Adam said Nick used to be good with his hands, so it's a pity he wasn't interested in following the same trade, instead of lawyering, or whatever you call it. It would have been a *real* family concern then, but Adam knows the new man, and says he's a first-class craftsman."

Vera seemed too wound up and excited to stop talking, mentioning the name of her beloved at every opportunity. Skye drank her tea to try to soften the rock cake, as the unbidden imagery of what Nick Pengelly could do with his hands threatened to overwhelm her. She suddenly heard Vera giggle.

"Oh go on, throw the blessed thing away. I'm no cook, but I'll learn, and Adam seems prepared to eat anything."

From the newly-wed aura surrounding her, Skye would have been surprised if he'd noticed anything he ate.

"You know Nick's already gone back to Plymouth, I suppose? It's a pity. Adam wished he could have stayed longer, but everything happened in an all-fired hurry, I gather."

"What do you mean? What happened?"

"We called on Adam's folks as soon as we got back, and Nick was just preparing to leave. He's moved in some female cousin from down Penzance way to look after his parents, and Nick is paying all the expenses. It's relieved Adam quite a bit, I can tell you, and Ethan's happy, since this Dorcas is a wonderful cook and he's getting proper meals now. I'm thinking of asking her for some lessons," she added with a grin.

"Well, Nick Pengelly certainly moves fast when he wants things done," was all Skye could think of to say.

Vera looked at her thoughtfully. "Are you all right? You look a bit peaky."

"I'm fine, but I'd better go. Philip's arranged for us to go to a concert this evening with some of his college people, and then supper, and I'm not looking forward to it."

As she heard her own words, she began to ask herself in alarm what had happened to the self-assured young woman she had always been, when meeting new people and going to concerts had been an exciting part of her life. But that was before Philip's mood changes and condescension had begun to crush her spirit. . . . She was shocked as the thought entered her head.

She kissed Vera swiftly, and told her airily to rely on good old Cornish recipes rather than try out anything new. Adam wouldn't notice them, anyway. But she went home feeling unaccountably gloomy. However foolish it was to dwell on it, the comparison between her own marriage and Vera's couldn't be more marked. Skye's had begun in wartime with a ceremony that they had kept secret from most of the family for several years. It had been dramatic and exciting in its way, and if Celia hadn't been conceived, who knew how long the secrecy would have gone on? And if Philip hadn't been wounded with such long-term and unanticipated results, who knew how different their lives would have been? Or how much happier they might have been. . . .

Life was full of what ifs and if onlys, Skye reflected. She didn't want to think like that, but the thoughts wouldn't leave her alone. But she knew she had to make a conscious effort to resist them or they would bring her down even more. It was no way to feel before an evening out with her husband, when she was to be virtually on display to his college colleagues. And she had better stop thinking that way too.

Skye dressed with care, wearing a sophisticated bronze-coloured dress that was long and slim, but the supple silkiness of it accentuated her shape every time she moved. Nothing could disguise the fact that she was a sensual woman. She added a long string of bronze beads, and wore silver-edged tortoiseshell combs in her hair. Her gloves were long and made of cream silk, and a soft stole and shoes finished the ensemble.

When they were ready to leave, she and Philip presented themselves to the children for their approval, since they always clamoured to see their parents 'poshed-up', as they called it.

"You look beautiful, Mommy," Celia said admiringly, while Wenna breathed that she looked like an angel. Oliver simply looked at her sleepily and held out his arms to be hugged.

"Don't let him mess you up," Philip said sharply. "These are important people we're seeing tonight, Skye."

"These are important people too," she murmured, but not loud enough for him to hear. It was best to let the moment pass, anyway, and when they were driving towards Truro, she covered her brief attack of nerves regarding the evening by making ordinary conversation, and telling him she had called on Vera that afternoon.

"I trust the holiday was satisfactory," he commented.

Good Lord, she raged silently, *you were always pompous, but when did you become so damn hateful too*? And yet, what had he really said that was so awful! But it was just the *way* he said things lately . . .

"Of course!" she said coolly. "But then, Adam's a very physical man, so I doubt that they'd have any kind of problems. After all, it was their *honeymoon*, Philip."

"Please don't make those sort of innuendoes in front of the college staff," he said, to her utter amazement.

"Innuendoes? I did no such thing, and I'm hardly likely to talk about intimate family matters in front of strangers!"

"That's just the sort of talk I mean," he said.

"My God, you're insufferable sometimes," Skye burst out. "I wonder why you bothered to marry into my family at all, if you think they're all so far beneath you."

"You know the answer to that. I loved you then, and I love you now, and the rest of them don't matter."

His tone was about as romantic as telling her he loved steamed fish for Friday night's supper, and sent her temporarily speechless.

"By the way, I've had another letter from Ruth," he went on, oblivious to her reaction. "She and her aunt would like to visit us for a few days in mid-June, if that's all right with you. She's keen to see the college, and she'd like to bring a friend with her as well. Can we accommodate them?"

"Why not? Let them bring the whole of south Wales with them if they feel like it!"

"Don't be ridiculous. I'd like you to add your piece to my letter welcoming them. We'll do it tomorrow."

Skye felt numb. She wasn't jealous of Ruth Dobson in the slightest, but nor did she have any great desire to see her again. She could invite Vera and Adam for supper one evening while they were here, she thought suddenly. Both Vera and Lily had had an amazing rapport with the deaf girl when they first met, and the more people there were around, the more it would help to ease any sense of embarrassment.

"If they're coming in mid-June perhaps we could have a small family party for my birthday while they're here," she said, with a flash of inspiration. "I'm sure Ruth would like to see Vera and Lily again."

"Are you?" Philip shrugged. "I'll be taking the visitors off your hands most of the time, anyway."

"Sometimes, Philip," she said deliberately. "You make me feel less of a wife, and more of a background accessory."

"Now you really are being ridiculous," he said, clearly not having a clue to what she was taking about.

The concert was a great success, according to everyone in their party who liked chamber music. Skye didn't. It was far too dreary, and she didn't enjoy the earnest, after-concert discussions into how the orchestra had interpreted the composer's thoughts. And supper, at the currently fashionable Truro restaurant where everyone liked to be seen, turned into a loud, pseudo-arty affair of the worst kind, in her opinion.

She spent far longer than was necessary in the ladies' powder room, applying a touch of rouge to her cheeks and mouth in defiance of the crêpe-skinned female professors listening adoringly to Philip and the other men.

"You look bored to kingdom come with all that stuffy talk," she heard a broad cockney accent say alongside her. "How d'you put up with it, gel, or d'you just turn a deaf ear? I know I would!"

The thought was so incongruous, considering the deaf woman who was coming to stay at New World, that Skye turned stiffly to the would-be confidante, ready to snub her. And then her mouth dropped open.

"Good Lord, it's – it's—"

"Oh, I don't expect you to remember me, ducks," the woman said with a chuckle. "After all, we were only in the same hospital in France for a few weeks before I was moved to another place, but I often wondered about you and that man you were so mad about. The name's Fanny Webb."

"I *do* remember you!" Skye said in some delight. "You could always make the poor boys laugh by making fun of the sisters. And the man I was so mad about is with me in the restaurant – the one I married."

"Gawd almighty, pardon my French! I expected him to be a real Valentino instead of a stuffed shirt – and now I've done it again, haven't I? Put me bleedin' foot in it, I mean."

Skye burst out laughing. The blowsy Fanny Webb had been a

breath of fresh air to the soldiers dying by degrees, and she was a breath of fresh air now. If she dared, she would love to ask her to join her at their supper table. She dismissed the thought, knowing that Philip would disown her.

"But what are you doing here? Away from London, I mean."

Fanny spoke carelessly. "I got restless after the war, and when my old mum died, I travelled round the country a bit. Cornwall's a real graveyard, ain't it? I shan't stay long, but I got no ties now, 'cept my gentleman friend, and he's only temp'ry-like, so I please me bleedin' self what I do."

"Oh Fanny, you've got to come and see me while you're here. My children would love you."

"I ain't so sure about that. What would your old man think? He looks a real toff – and so do you, come to think of it. My gentleman's paying my way tonight, or I wouldn't be in this 'ere establishment at all."

It didn't take much deduction to know what kind of gentleman was paying for her supper, but that didn't bother Skye. Fanny Webb was still the breath of fresh air she needed so badly, and hadn't even known she did until right now.

"Come to tea tomorrow," she said impulsively. "Ask anyone the direction to New World, Fanny. Take a taxicab and tell them the fare will be paid on arrival. I mean it."

"Cor blimey, you've come up in the world. Or maybe you were up there all the time. No, I ain't sure about this."

"Tea. Tomorrow afternoon. Four o'clock. I'll be expecting you," Skye said, blowing her a little kiss as she returned to the restaurant, smiling sweetly at Philip's disapproving look at her rouged cheeks and lips. She didn't know why she wanted to annoy and shock him, but she did – not least because she sensed the more than glancing approval of his male colleagues at her heightened colour and high spirits.

Her thoughts ran on. Naturally, Philip would violently disapprove of Fanny, but if he could have his friends coming for a visit, then so could she. Not that she was inviting the woman for anything more than afternoon tea and a sharing of old memories. They hadn't been close friends, except for the quick and easy friendships that occurred in wartime.

But compared with Fanny Webb and her colourful vocabulary, Skye realised she was becoming as pale and chaste in spirit as the purest china clay that formed the White Rivers pottery.

Far from pleasing her, it was an irritating thought. She was in a rut, however comfortable it was. And the only way out of a rut was to jolt yourself onto a different pathway. She could almost hear old Morwen Tremayne telling her so.

Six

"Mommy, who is that funny lady?" Wenna whispered, as they saw the taxicab depositing Fanny Webb at New World the following afternoon.

"She can't be a proper lady," Celia put in before Skye could answer. "Daddy says ladies don't wear bright colours in the daytime because it's common, and you should leave all that to the birds."

Skye felt herself bristle at the child's imperious tone; her father to the life. As Fanny stood arguing with the taxicab driver, she saw the housekeeper hurry outside to pay the man, as she had been instructed to do. Skye turned to her daughter and spoke firmly.

"Now you just listen to me, Celia. I met that lady in France during wartime, and she did a great deal to help keep up the poor soldiers' spirits when they were very ill, so you just mind your manners. I've invited her to take afternoon tea with us, and we must all make her feel welcome."

Even as she spoke, she knew what Philip's interpretation of the extra services Fanny did in France would be. And she wasn't at all sure in her heart that he wasn't right. There was more than one way to boost a soldier's spirits. But that was Fanny's business, not theirs.

The housekeeper showed her into the drawing-room with a slightly incredulous note in her voice, and Skye had to hide a smile at the garish costume Fanny wore, together with the fake ocelot fur stole slung over her shoulders.

"Thank you, Mrs Arden," Skye said. "You may serve tea now, and would you ask Nanny to bring Oliver downstairs when he wakes up, please?"

As the housekeeper went out of the room with an ill-disguised sniff, Fanny spoke in some awe.

"My Gawd, Skye gel, you fell on your feet and no mistake. Did you marry a bleedin' millionaire or what?"

The girls gaped at this free and easy talk, while Skye answered as coolly as she could. "As a matter of fact, this is my house, Fanny. My grandmother left it to me."

Fanny stared, settling herself down on the silk-covered sofa, smoothing its luxurious surface with red-tipped fingers, and exuding a strong whiff of cheap perfume.

"Bleedin' 'ell," she said at last, recovering herself. "Well, it's like I always said. When it's wartime, and everybody's wearing the same uniforms, you never know who you're rubbin' shoulders with, do you? Nor nothin' else, if you gets my meanin'!"

She gave a snigger, and Skye remembered at once just how coarse she could be. She had forgotten after all this time, and although she prided herself on not being a snob, the last thing she wanted was for the girls to pick up any of Fanny's favourite expletives or snide remarks.

"How long are you planning to stay in Cornwall, Fanny?"

"Oh, don't fret yourself," she said, laughing. "I ain't thinkin' of movin' in. My gentleman's taking me back to London tomorrow, and we're going to see some shows."

Tea and cakes were brought in then, but the vision in their drawing-room was of far more interest to the girls, and to Celia in particular. Skye could see that she was absorbing everything about Fanny to report to her father. Last night it had been a mixture of defiance and a whim on Skye's part to invite Fanny here, but now she wasn't sure it had been so clever after all.

"So how old are these little charmers?" Fanny said, when she had slurped her tea to the fascination of both girls, with her little finger held at an impressively high angle.

"I'm six and a half and Wenna's five," Celia told her importantly. "Our brother's only two, and he's a crybaby."

"Well, when you're only two you've got a right to be, I dare say," Fanny said with a grin. "And where's your pa today?"

"At the college," Celia continued in her best voice. "He's a professor, and he's very, *very* clever."

"Bleedin' 'ell!" uttered Fanny, her scarlet mouth dropping open in surprise.

The arrival of Nanny with Oliver stopped any more discussion about Philip, and the infant and the visitor eyed each other with mutual unease. Fanny didn't care for babies, and Oliver didn't care for strangers. As she leaned towards him, clucking inanely, he let out a howl of alarm, and she leapt to her feet.

"Gawd almighty, I didn't mean to scare the kid, but I'm no good with babbies. Anyway, I should be going. This place was farther away than I thought, and my gentleman will be wond'ring what's become of me."

"You won't stay and meet my husband then?" Skye asked, praying that she wouldn't, and yet half hoping that she would. Philip would absolutely *hate* her, and why that should make Skye feel so mischievous, she didn't even know.

"I ain't no good with professors, either," Fanny said, edging away. "Just point me in the right direction for St Austell, and I'll start walking back to the hotel."

"You can't walk all that way in those shoes," Skye remarked. "I'll drive you there in my car."

"Bleedin' 'ell," said Fanny.

She didn't take the children, and when she had deposited Fanny at her hotel, Skye breathed a deep sigh of relief. She opened the car windows to let out the strong scent of Fanny's perfume, and decided to call on Betsy while she was in the area. She was in no mood to go back home just yet.

"What on earth's that smell?" Betsy said at once, wrinkling up her nose. "Have you been in one of those places where Theo gets some of his orders, Skye?"

Skye laughed as she passed off the innocent question with a light reply, but she felt decidedly uncomfortable at guessing the kind of places Theo frequented, if he came home wreathed in cheap scent. And Betsy didn't deserve it.

"I thought I'd just call in to say hello and see if Justin's recovered from his cold," she invented. "Theo said he was a little under the weather."

"Oh, 'twere only a little sniffle. Theo's taken the boys for a drive, so you've missed 'em. He'll be sorry about that."

No he wouldn't be, and neither was she, Skye thought silently, and she wondered again how this nice, ordinary woman could be seemingly so content with her boorish husband, who played away from home more often than not, if the rumours were to be believed.

"Do you want some tea?" Betsy asked now. "I've got fresh-made scones and jam in the parlour."

"You're a love, Betsy, but I've just had a visitor at the house and had tea already. No, this was just a brief call, and I didn't realise how the time had run on. I won't stay, or Philip will be home before me."

Even as she spoke, she felt a small surge of alarm. Before Philip arrived home, she needed time to brief the girls on their language. They might have been reluctant to say very much while Fanny was there, but they would have taken it all in. In particular, Celia was a fine little mimic, and Skye could just imagine Philip's reaction if . . .

The moment she reached home and heard the shouting, she knew the worst had happened. Celia was Philip's pet, but as with any close relationship, when they clashed, it was as fiery a ding-dong battle of wills as that of any two folk in the Tremayne dynasty.

"I only said what *she* said," Celia was yelling. "Bleedin' 'ell, you'd think it was something terrible!"

"Bleedin' 'ell," Wenna said, clearly just as charmed by the colourful phrase as was her sister.

"I want you both to listen very carefully to me, and to take very good notice of what I'm about to say," Philip bellowed on, his voice near to exploding. "What you have just used is gutter language, and the only people who use it are either wicked or common, because they don't have the gumption or the capacity to use a better vocabulary. If the language of this woman didn't make her lack of class clear enough, then you can tell the type of person she was by the stink she left behind."

"Mommy said the lady did a lot of good work for the soldiers' spirits in the war," Celia yelled back at him.

"And we all know what kind of good work *that* was," Philip almost spat out the words.

"What kind was it then?" Celia persisted, still aggressive, and eager for knowledge as ever.

Skye couldn't bear to hear Philip expound any further. Nor could she risk him deciding to educate her daughters and take away their innocence with his stiffly worded explanations of the particular comforts that soldiers could get from a woman of loose morals. She could practically hear his words in her head now, as clearly as if he spoke them out loud. He was so utterly predictable . . . which came from his years of college tutoring. The spiel was the same, and only the students changed.

His anger was directed at Skye the moment she walked into the room, his face an ugly puce, and all puffed up with self-importance and fury.

"What on earth were you thinking about, bringing a woman of ill-repute into my house and infecting my children with her gutter filth?"

Skye felt the room spin for a moment. *His* house, and *his* children?

"Aren't you forgetting something?" she snapped at last.

"I don't think so," he threw back, astute as ever, and not pretending to misunderstand her. "If you're about to remind me whose house this is, let me remind you that you promised to obey me, and while I live and breathe, I'll not tolerate my children being subjected to the kind of language such people use."

"I also promised to love and honour you, but sometimes you make it damned difficult, Philip," she stormed.

She hardly saw Nanny enter the room and take the girls silently away from the two ranting adults. The two of them stared at each other. They were barely a foot apart in reality, but the distance in spirit between them was enormous.

"What exactly do you mean by that remark?" he roared. "Haven't I given you everything you wanted over the years? My love and protection, and the children. I've never strayed from my marital duties, nor wanted to, which is more than can be said about your wretched cousin."

"Marital *duties*?" Skye almost screamed. "Is that how you see it, Philip? Am I no more than a duty to you now?"

Dear God, whatever happened to the passion between them that had made them unable to contemplate being apart? The passion that had made her risk her family's wrath in following him to France after a secret marriage? Risking her very life, in being so near to the front line in all those terrible years. . . . But it had been unthinkable to be apart from him, and while duty for their country had been part of it, duty between the two of them had never entered into their decision. Only love.

The antagonism still smouldered between them, and to Skye's horror and dismay, Philip slept in another bedroom that night, saying coldly that his head troubled him appallingly and he didn't want to disturb Skye with his thrashings, but they both knew it was more than that.

The separation continued until Skye's birthday was imminent, and their guests were due to arrive from Wales. By then, she had never felt more remote from her husband, nor more bereft at the way neither of them seemed able or inclined to reach the other. But once Ruth Dobson and her aunt and friend arrived, she thought hopefully that he would surely move back into their marital bed, and they could become loving partners once more. . . .

"I'll use my dressing-room while the visitors are here," he told her. "I've discovered that I sleep marginally better when I'm alone."

"Do you?" she said woodenly. "I seem to remember a time when you couldn't bear to be apart from me, Philip."

"My dear girl, we've got three children, and we're too old for all that nonsense now."

"For pity's sake, I find that a depressing statement. I hardly think I'm entitled to be put on the back shelf when I'll be only thirty-four years old in June!"

"And I'm fifty-one, and ready to take life at a more mature and steady pace than you and your frivolous friends."

Skye felt her face go hot. Fanny Webb hadn't called on them again, but her brief influence was still evident in Celia's occasional 'bleedin' 'ell', whenever she thought no one in authority was listening. Skye was well aware that some of the kitchen maids thought it hilarious, which made Celia say it all the more. And Philip wasn't going to let Skye forget it.

"Oh, sleep where you like, then, for as long as you like," she snapped in frustration.

This wasn't what marriage was ordained for, she thought, except in certain royal circles, by all accounts. But any attempt to suggest such a thing to Philip now would be to see his pompous face again. And she'd had enough of that. Let him please himself. It dawned on her that he always did, anyway. Maybe Ruth's presence would lighten his sour looks. . . .

Any thought of that disappeared the moment the visitors arrived. Ruth had hardly changed from the pale girl Skye remembered, except to look more confident now. Her aunt had aged, and then there was the stranger . . .

She and Philip had simply assumed it would be another teacher from the school where Ruth taught now. Another woman. Instead of which, it was a man of about her own age who clearly wasn't deaf, but was adept in sign language and patently adored Ruth.

Once they had all greeted one another and the ladies had removed their gloves for afternoon tea, it didn't escape Philip's notice that Ruth wore an engagement ring.

"What's all this?" he said, pointing to her left hand.

It was the stranger – Jeffrey – who supplied the answer. "Ruth wanted to keep it a surprise, and in fact, it's only just happened, Philip – if I may call you Philip?" He didn't wait for a reply and went on speaking, facing Ruth so that she could understand all that he said. "I teach at a similar school to Ruth, but I've been offered a post in Canada, and I can take my wife with me. As I don't have a wife, I decided it was time to make an honest woman of her."

Ruth's laugh denied the unintentional innuendo that Skye thought charming, and Philip obviously didn't.

"And what do you say to all this, Miss Dobson?" he said at last, turning to Ruth's aunt.

In amazement, Skye realised he was playing for time, and also needed an ally in his discomfiture. He was *jealous*, damn him, she thought, and even if he didn't want Ruth for himself, he clearly didn't want anyone else to have her. What a hypocrite!

Miss Dobson replied warmly. "I'm included in the package, thanks to dear Jeffrey," she said. "A house goes with the teaching post, and there's room for us all. Ruth and I couldn't be happier that we'll still be together."

"So when is the wedding going to take place?" Skye asked.

"In a month's time. We sail to Canada at the end of July. It will be a very small affair with my family in London, or we would have invited you all. This flying trip around the country is by way of saying goodbye to England."

Ruth spoke then, in the slow, flat drawl of the deaf, her eyes unblinking at the man she had once expected to marry.

"Be happy for me, Philip."

"My dear girl, I'm delighted for you. How could I be anything else?" he said, moving swiftly towards her. He lifted her hand and kissed the back of it in a continental gesture.

They all looked slightly relieved, and Skye knew that the atmosphere had been evident to them all. But only she guessed at how Philip still seethed beneath his bland good manners. His scarred mentality had made him increasingly selfish over the years, and while he no longer wanted Ruth for himself, it didn't please him to see her glowing eyes every time she looked at her fiancé.

It had been a shock to him, and the effect of it resulted in him coming to their room that night, and forcing himself on his wife with no attempt at finesse. It was marital rape, thought Skye, when at last he slid away from her without uttering one word of love, and only his animal gruntings told her that he was enjoying the act in any way at all.

She did not. He was rough and she was sore. She felt the slow tears trickle down her face as he went out of the room as silently as he had entered it. She was no more than a thing to him, and she had never felt it more. She was used, and abused, as if he had needed to prove his manhood just because his old love was in the house.

Thankfully, he seemed to have recovered his equilibrium by morning, and was charming and friendly to Ruth and Jeffrey, insisting that he showed them around his college and took lunch with him in Truro. He effectively shut out Miss Dobson from the offer, but since she was more anxious to meet the children than to be involved in academic activities, such rudeness went unnoticed. Or so Skye thought.

"You've a strong personality in your husband, my dear," she observed, when the others had left the house in Philip's car.

"He's always been used to saying what he thinks, and it was quite a shock for him to see that Ruth was engaged when she hadn't told him anything about Jeffrey."

"But he couldn't have expected her to remain unwed all her days, after – well, forgive me, Mrs Norwood, but after what happened between you all."

"I'm sure he didn't. But Philip had a difficult war, and the repercussions of his injuries are far from over, I'm afraid. We don't talk about it, but we're always aware of it."

And she had no intention of discussing details of it with Ruth Dobson's aunt, pleasant though she was. To her credit, she didn't ask any more questions, and happily turned to the children when they were brought down from the nursery.

"Would you like to visit the pottery this afternoon?" Skye enquired, when the playtime was exhausted. "We could all take a drive up there, if you wish. Perhaps you could help me choose something for Ruth and Jeffrey. It would seem a more personal wedding gift coming from White Rivers."

"That's a charming idea. Yes, let's do that."

They chose a set of tableware and tureens that would be shipped to Canada with the rest of their belongings. There was no point in swearing the children to secrecy, because the gift would be presented to the couple before they left Cornwall. But Skye insisted that they keep quiet about it until Philip had seen it and approved. She was sure he would. It would please him to think that Ruth would be using something of the business in which he was involved, however slightly.

She realised she could almost be accused of being jealous too, but she wasn't, not any more. It alarmed her to know how indifferent she really felt as to whether or not Philip was attracted to anyone else, past or present. And that the real sense of envy in her soul was that these visitors were shortly to be crossing the Atlantic. A great sense of nostalgia for her parents and her old home swept through her at the thought. Canada wasn't New Jersey, but it was nearer than Cornwall . . .

"It was a very nice idea," Philip said, when she showed him the pottery that evening. By now, he was expansive and genial, and she guessed he had had a good day, well in control of himself again. "We had best give it to them this evening, before the girls spill the beans."

"Why, Mr Norwood, that sounded almost human," Skye said, too softly for him to hear, and she didn't repeat it.

Knowing that it was Skye's birthday soon, there was a small gift for her too, a pretty tortoiseshell brooch that was almost Victorian in its design. Skye loved it at once, and hugged Ruth as she thanked her.

"It's a birthday and farewell gift in one," she heard Jeffrey say. "While we were all out, your housekeeper took a message for me to call my people urgently. My teaching post has been advanced by two weeks, otherwise there will be a lengthy delay. Ruth and I have discussed it seriously, since it obviously means rearranging the wedding details and an earlier passage to Canada. In the circumstances we have decided to leave for London tomorrow."

Skye couldn't deny her huge relief to hear it. They were nice people, but they were strangers all the same. And Ruth and Philip would always share a past that excluded her.

And if June had been an oddly traumatic time for Skye, July passed smoothly. She immersed herself in domestic matters, and with the added pleasure of knowing that White Rivers was doing exceptionally well this year with the influx of seasonal visitors. She could forget all the mad nonsense of Nick Pengelly's intimate remarks, since he was no longer in Cornwall to remind her, and the days of summer were warm and fragrant and uneventful.

Just like the calm before the storm, Skye's grandmother always used to say, and just as untrustworthy. . . . And Skye had always laughingly pooh-poohed such remarks.

She took little notice, therefore, when she saw the telegraph boy toiling up the hill on his bicycle towards New World. The wartime days when such visits brought terror to people's hearts were long gone. And the boy was probably taking a roundabout route to his destination, just to savour the early August sunshine and the long summer days.

When he turned into the driveway leading to the house, crouched low over his machine to give him more impetus, Skye felt her heartbeats quicken. She was sitting in the conservatory, enjoying a lazy afternoon, with the house quiet. She had been idly reading but, without being aware of it, the book fell to the floor and she was suddenly standing, very still, hands clenched by her sides. Her sense of premonition was strong and painful, and her palms were sweaty. It was bad news about her father. It had to be. She was sure of it.

The boy caught sight of her and came straight to the conservatory. He handed her the telegram, turning away at once, ready to free-wheel back down the hill, and not waiting for a reply. The neglect of his duty was ominous to Skye, but she had no breath to call him back. In any case, her mouth was too dry for her to speak. She ripped open the envelope quickly, and stared at the words in total shock and disbelief:

'SINCLAIR KILLED WASHINGTON DC 8 AUGUST DURING KU KLUX KLAN RALLY. COME HOME AS SOON AS POSSIBLE. DADDY.'

The terse words danced in front of her eyes like darting tadpoles in a stream. Her thoughts were just as distracted. She was totally off-balance, and had never felt so alone. Philip had taken the girls for a walk, but would surely be back soon. Oliver was asleep. And there was no one to share the weight of a tragedy she didn't even understand . . .

The next moment she felt someone's arms go around her. She seemed to have difficulty in focusing her eyes. All the same, she knew the arms holding her weren't her husband's. She blinked hard, forcing herself to react.

"David," she said in a high voice that didn't sound like her own. "What on earth are you doing here?" And then she slid to the ground as David Kingsley tried vainly to stop her hitting her head on a jardinière.

"I think she's coming round," she heard a man's voice say. Philip? No, not him. Not one of her relatives either. Her father? Impossible. Sinclair . . . ?

The pain of remembering rushed at her so fast she was in danger of throwing up all over the sitting-room sofa where she realised she was lying now. She struggled to keep the nausea under control, and looked into the face of David Kingsley, editor of *The Informer* newspaper, and then at the frightened eyes of Mrs Arden.

"Steady, Skye," David said gently. "Take it slowly . . ."

"I wish Mr Norwood would come back," Mrs Arden whispered in agitation, as if Skye wasn't there at all. "She'll be needing his strength, poor soul. And perhaps I should send for the doctor too . . ."

"I don't need a doctor," Skye croaked. "I'm not ill."

And *Philip*? What good would he be, with his platitudes and his lack of understanding of the remorse and guilt that ran through her like a knife-edge now, remembering all the times she had despised and ridiculed her brother Sinclair, for his fringe attachments to politics.

And look where it had got him, she thought in anguish. She was appalled at the clarity of her thinking regarding her brother, and also her husband. That was guilt, if you like. She *should* be needing him, but right now, the solid good sense of the newspaperman, from whom she was sure she could get some sensible answers, was like a lifeline.

"Mrs Arden, can you get Mrs Norwood some hot sweet tea, please?" she heard David say briskly now. "And perhaps a drop of brandy to revive her. She was only out for a few moments, but she's had a severe shock."

"Thank you," Skye said briefly, when they were alone. "I can't bear to have someone wringing their hands over me. Now tell me what you know, and how you come to be here." She was recovering quickly from the initial shock, and her keen mind needed to know all the facts.

"The general information came through for the newspaper. Then I saw the name of the victim, and from what you had told me of his involvement in politics," he said delicately, "I realised at once that it had to be your brother. I hoped to get up here to tell you gently before the telegraph boy, and I almost made it."

"I didn't even hear your car," she muttered, as if such an inane remark mattered.

"That's understandable. You were hearing nothing but the words your father sent you."

"Oh God, my *father*," Skye moaned. "He'll be distraught by this. He had such faith in Sinclair." She bit her lip, knowing she hadn't shared that faith.

"Listen to me, Skye. From what I can gather, none of it was your brother's fault, nor the government's. Sinclair just happened to be in the wrong place at the wrong time." David said brusquely, "Are you ready to hear the details?"

"Of course." She took a deep breath, her journalist training overcoming her horror at hearing the details that affected her own flesh and blood.

And in like fashion, David told it concisely and without expression. The Ku Klux Klan parade in Washington DC had been properly organised and approved, and no violence had been anticipated. Perhaps 40,000 members, wearing their white robes and conical caps, had taken part, and huge numbers of spectators had watched the march towards the Washington Monument. By the time it was nearing the conclusion it was raining and the sky was dark. The rain prevented the planned finale of the ceremony and the burning of an 80-foot cross, and by then tempers were at fever pitch on both sides.

"Then there was an incident," David said carefully. "There had been many small fights among the crowd, apparently, and it seems there was also a crowd of anarchists out to make trouble, and they soon swelled into a mob. A dozen people were injured, some of them seriously. And there was one fatality."

"My brother," Skye said. He expected her to cry, she thought woodenly. To fall apart. To be a hysterical female. She had fainted, but that was as much out of concern for her father as anything else, she realised, consumed with a new guilt. She and Sinclair had never truly got on, nor understood one another.

To most men, hearing such news should result in predictable female reactions. David was no exception. She could tell that by the way he seemed intent on holding her, squeezing her arms so hard now that she was sure she would have bruises on them.

But she couldn't cry. Not yet. She was still numb with shock, and brandy was only going to make her light-headed, dulling the pain. Her journalist training was forcing her to be analytical about it all, keeping emotions at bay until a suitable time. A suitable time for weeping . . . She swallowed the sudden lump in her throat, wondering if these really were the thoughts of the emotional and passionate Skye Tremayne . . . But of course they weren't; these were the thoughts of the mature and dignified Skye Norwood, wife and mother, but still the journalist, with the monstrous ability to see the drama in a situation, however close to her heart . . .

She felt the thrust of a glass against her cold lips, and swallowed a minute amount of the bitter spirit. She hated its taste, grimaced, and said she would prefer the hot sweet tea, if nobody minded.

"She's such a brave lady," she heard Mrs Arden whisper again. "And 'tis such a terrible thing to happen, on account o' they terrible people dressed up in their comic hats."

Comic hats indeed . . . such an innocent phrase for men with such evil intent to hide behind. It was the one thing, the only thing, that had the power to scatter all Skye's senses, and the tea went flying as her nerve broke, and she seemed to lose control of her limbs.

"That's right, my love. Let go and cry as much as you want," David's muffled voice said, as she fell against him in a torrent of weeping. "You'll be all the better for it."

* * *

92

How long she stayed there, she couldn't have said. She was hearing nothing but the sound of her own keening and her ragged heartbeats. And then she heard Philip's outraged voice.

"What the devil's going on here?"

Before anyone could answer, Skye caught sight of Mrs Arden rushing into the room behind him, and of her daughters' frightened and disbelieving eyes at the spectacle of their mother in the arms of a stranger.

"Mr Norwood, sir," the housekeeper said. "Please bring the children outside for a moment while Mrs Norwood composes herself."

Skye expected a bombastic remark from her husband, but something in the urgency of the housekeeper's voice, and her own obvious distress, apparently alerted him that this was no clandestine meeting, but something far graver. She saw Philip shoo the girls out of the room, and struggled away from David Kingsley at once, highly embarrassed now at losing control of herself so badly.

"I'm so sorry," she whispered.

"For what?" he said gently. "For being a woman, with all a woman's tenderness and compassion? I would never have expected anything less of you, Skye."

She caught her breath, wishing he would go now. Needing to think. Needing to know what to do next.

He stood up. "Look, you'll want to be alone with your husband, so I'll get back to town and see if any more news has come through. I'll telephone you tonight, if I may, to see if there is anything I can do for you. I have some influence with the shipping company, and if you need an immediate passage—"

She looked at him, not understanding for a moment. And then she did, and it all became clear what she must do.

"Thank you, David. And there is something you can do right away. Would you send a telegram to my father, saying I'll come as soon as possible?"

"Of course."

She went to the little bureau in the corner of the room, wrote down the address and handed it to him. Her hands shook, but she was oddly calmer inside, knowing what she had to do.

She had to go home. Her father needed her, and there was no one else. Out of all that huge, generations-old, widespread Tremayne family, she was the only one who could comfort him. The only one left of his own.

Seven

No matter how hard Skye resolved to put all thoughts of the children out of her mind, the memory of their tearful faces and clinging arms as she said goodbye to them kept haunting her. She would be an unnatural mother if it were any different, and it had been hard not to let them come and wave her off at Falmouth, but that would have truly finished her. As it was, they stayed at home with their father, and it had been the ever-supportive David Kingsley who had taken her to the quay on that sunny August morning.

True to his word, David had got her an amazingly early passage on a ship bound for New York, and it was David Kingsley who had hugged her and wished her well, just as though they were a normal, loving couple. His last words reminded her that once, long ago, he had had every hope that they would be. . . .

"Take care of yourself, Skye. You're very precious to a lot of people," he said softly.

"Good Lord, that sounds most unlike your usual pragmatic self," she said, her eyes bright.

"I know. But at times like these, a little poetic licence is permissible, isn't it? Even in a hard-headed newspaperman."

"Of course," she said, hugging him back, and uncaring that they were in a public place. In any case, it was the kind of place for hugs and kisses and emotional farewells. "You've been a good friend, David, and I won't forget it."

"Just come back safely, and you know we'll all be thinking of you."

She nodded. The trip itself was traumatic enough – travelling back to where she had once belonged – without such a sad time ahead of her. The funeral would be delayed until her arrival, and her father's last telegram had been effusive and lengthy, and almost pathetic in his thanks for her presence. As if there had been any doubt that she would be there. . . . Her next thought had been her firm intention to bring him back to Cornwall with her.

Cresswell Tremayne would be a lonely man now, she reflected sadly. His wife was gone, and so were his parents. His beloved daughter had continued his link with his Cornish heritage, but there had always been Sinclair, staunchly American, the son of whom he was inordinately proud, despite his priggish ways. Skye knew that. A man's son was always a man's son . . . and now he too was gone.

She leaned on the ship's rail, shivering in the coolness of the sea air, and watched the receding Cornish shoreline until she could see it no more. Her eyes were blurred, torn between the need to be with her father, and her anguish at leaving her own small family behind. There had been no question of any of them coming with her, of course. The children were too young to come on such a sad mission and Philip's place was with them.

"Can I get you anything, ma'am?" a deferential American voice said, close beside her, and she turned to see one of the ship's young stewards.

"Nothing, thank you," she told him, shaking her head.

"Don't catch cold, then, ma'am. It can turn chilly very quickly once we get out to sea."

"I know it. And thank you again."

She was cheered by his familiar accent, the first American one she had heard in a long while. In fact, one of the last ones had been that of Lieutenant Lewis Pascoe, the soldier who had turned up at New World near the end of the war, and had turned her grandmother's life upside down, reviving such evil memories of the man who had raped Morwen Tremayne's best friend, so many years ago. . . .

Skye shivered again, and went down to her cabin to unpack properly. Memories were strange things. They came back to haunt you at the most unexpected times. Even now, even here, on this return voyage to her homeland, she kept remembering another voyage, the one where she had met her husband, and started a chain reaction that had sent them into one another's arms.

She closed her eyes, picturing the moments. Philip had been so dashing then. So educated and forceful, and so *everything*, when she was feeling so young and gauche to be crossing the Atlantic alone on the great adventure to the country of her mother's birth. But from the moment they met, she had known she was no longer alone.

Skye gave a small sigh, peering through her porthole at the last sight of land for days. The ocean was very calm, the dying rays of sunlight gleaming on its mirrored surface and the shadowy silhouette of the Cornish coast. An artist's paradise. . . . As the phrase entered her head, her thoughts turned at once to Albert Tremayne.

She had naturally informed all the family of her brother's death, but since none of them had ever known him, she was met with no more than the usual platitudes. Except from Albie, when she called on him to say goodbye.

"Your mother would have been grief-stricken," he said unnecessarily. "Primmy was always an emotional woman. This news would have devastated her."

"And my father," Skye reminded him.

She still wasn't comfortable in thinking of Albert and her mother in the same breath. Her moments of compassion for him were fewer now, though she was alarmed to see that he had gone downhill fast in the last few months. He was a rheumy-eyed old man now, and none too clean.

"Oh ah, your father." The sneering note was in his voice again, and any sympathy for him vanished. He was never going to forgive Cress for taking his beautiful Primmy away from him, she thought, but it was all so long ago, and time now for forgetting and forgiving on all sides.

"I'm hoping to bring him back with me, for a long visit, at the very least," she said coolly. "He's got no one else now. I hope the family will make him welcome – *all* of them."

"I dare say they will," Albie remarked, non-committally. As she turned to go, he caught at her hand. "What? No kiss goodbye, when you ain't even been to visit me for weeks, and it took a knife in your brother's guts to bring you to my studio? I'll not be seeing you for God knows how long—" his voice became whining, with the petulance of the self-centred elderly.

"Goodbye, Uncle Albie," she gasped, claustrophobic at the very nearness of him, and needing to get out of his presence while she could still feel untainted by it. It was terrible to feel that way, about the man, the *brother*, whom her mother had loved so dearly.

But perhaps Primmy had been more innocent than Skye had ever been. Primmy hadn't seen the horrors of war the way Skye had, nor heard the tortured tales of lust and downright evil inhumanity that some of the dying soldiers had whispered to her, in order to appease their consciences.

Compared with what Skye had experienced, Primmy was an angel in heaven . . . and she undoubtedly *was* now, she thought, her breath catching on a sob. And Primmy's ever-ambitious son was probably organising his portion of heaven already, came the more irreverent thought.

But she sobered at once, remembering where she was, and why she was leaving Cornwall. She lay on her bunk for a while before the bell was due to call the passengers for dinner, and closed her eyes. She didn't sleep, although she was exhausted by the speed and trauma of the past few days. But lulled by the rhythmic motion of the ship, she seemed to see a succession of people and places passing through her waking dreams.

So many people . . . her own sweet children, and Philip, holding them close to him. Albie . . . her thoughts slid away from him. Theo and his unexpected concern for her, followed by a more predictable swift return to last-minute discussions about the pottery and the clayworks, which were far more important. . . . Her own last visit to the pottery, surrounded by the purity of the products she loved, to oversee and check with Adam Pengelly that all was well with the new man Theo had so arrogantly installed. . . . Nice young Ethan pressing a bunch of flowers into her hand and wishing her well . . . And Nick . . .

Her heart jolted. She hadn't seen Nick Pengelly since the

day he had made the outrageous comments to her outside the pottery, but his face was suddenly there in her mind, as if it was the only one that mattered. His rich, deep voice was filling her senses, as caressing as a lover's touch. Her nerve-ends tingled, and she felt herself curling up on the narrow bunk, hugging her arms to her chest, her breasts, as if it was someone else's arms hugging her, holding her. Nick's arms . . . Nick's hands . . .

Her eyes were open, but dilated now, not seeing anything but the knowledge she had seen in his eyes and his face, and knowing that the feelings were reciprocated in her, or could be, given the chance . . . and thank God, there was no such chance. But even as she thought it, she was aware that the spectacular rhythmic sensations she was experiencing had nothing to do with the throbbing of the ship's engines. They were deep and exquisite within her, reminding her that she was a passionate and sensual woman, with a woman's longings and needs, and a yearning that she hadn't felt in a very long while – a fierce and primitive desire to be loved by a man who wasn't her husband . . .

Nick Pengelly didn't believe in telepathy. Nor did he logically expect Skye Norwood to be giving him a second thought. He was a dealer in logic, in facts, but he also had a fair acceptance of fate putting in a hand from time to time. Because of all those things, he also accepted that he could never forget the woman with so much beauty and grace who had made such an impression on him, and that he thought about her far too often.

They had met so few times, and yet she was already imprinted in his heart and soul. He had breathed in the scent of her, and seen the answering knowledge in her eyes at the frisson of magnetism between them. She may resist it, but she couldn't deny it. Even if she refused to do anything about it. . . . And assuredly wouldn't, Nick thought savagely. She was too sweet and upright, too bloody marvellous a woman to do anything but honour her marriage vows. And he was a lawyer who couldn't afford such sentiments or even admit to such a raging desire to make her his own, whatever the cost.

Almost wildly, he thanked God that he could keep far away
from her in Plymouth. And when his brother Adam telephoned
to tell him his mother was ill and calling for him, he learned
at the same time that Skye Norwood's brother had been killed
in street fighting, and she had gone to America to be with her
father. The tragedy aside, Nick decided that this was clearly
meant to be providential.

Whatever God was up to, He was keeping them apart. He
didn't intend them to meet and be lovers. The word slid into his
mind before he could stop it, conjuring up unbidden images of
Skye lying naked in his arms, and being everything in the world
he'd ever dreamed about.

"Christ, what's happening to me?" he muttered. "I've never
hungered for another man's wife in my life before."

"Are you all right, old boy?" he heard his partner say mildly.
"You've been staring at those papers for God knows how long.
Is it that difficult a case?"

"No," Nick snapped. "Just that I seem to have lost heart in it
for the moment. Thinking of my mother, I suppose, and trying
to fit in my schedule as best I can before I have to go down to
Cornwall. I'm sorry to leave you at such a time, William."

He heard William clear his throat. "Actually, there's something I've been meaning to speak to you about, Nick, and
I've hardly known how to begin. But now seems as good
a time as any, to give you time to digest it while you're
away."

Skye couldn't have said who she met on board ship, or who she
dined with, and she was so obviously a woman in mourning
who preferred to be left alone that the other passengers mutely
respected her wishes. It suited her. She didn't want transient
company; she missed her children, and she longed for the
voyage to end, where once she had longed for another voyage
to go on forever. How far she and Philip had travelled, in so
many respects, she thought sadly, when at last the ship was
within sight of the New York skyline.

But as always, the sight of that vibrant city revived her spirits,
despite the sadness that had brought her here. The ship's purser

had sent a telegraph ahead, and her father would be there to meet her.

It was the reverse of her one-time departure from America, but the moment she caught sight of Cresswell amid the crowded quayside, the usual streamers and bunting heralding a ship's safe arrival, and the crazy jazz music the bands were playing, she felt a deep, profound shock.

She hadn't seen him since Celia was born – nearly seven years – and in that time he had changed dramatically. Losing his beloved Primmy had done that . . . but Skye had not expected him to look so *old*, so desperately old. He was no longer the glamorous young man her mother had so adored. Not even the father she too had adored, and who had been at such pains to let her lead her own life, even though it took her far away from home. Nor the man who had encouraged his only son to go to Washington DC and follow his dream, even though it was obvious to all of them that Sinclair never really had what it took to be a politician.

Cresswell Tremayne looked exactly what he was: a broken man, lost and bereft, and desperately seeking the one person in all the world he longed to see. The only one he had left. He had always been so strong, so large, and now he seemed to have shrunk in every way.

Skye pushed away the sense of shock and waved madly, until at last he saw her. And the look on his face was so joyous, so wonderfully joyous, that her heart broke for him.

"Daddy," she said chokingly, when at last she was clasped in his frail arms. "Oh Daddy—"

She couldn't say any more, and he couldn't speak at all. They simply stood and held one another, jostled on all sides by the disembarking passengers, and not noticing it. But at last they became more composed, and he led her to a waiting car that was taking them home to New Jersey.

"An official car, no less," Cresswell said huskily, with the ghost of a smile. "We've been accorded that honour, Skye, and a few minor government people will come from Washington for the funeral tomorrow. I refused to let it be held anywhere else. It's what Sinclair would have wanted.

Your mother too. They'll be buried side by side in the family plot."

His voice broke, and she squeezed his hand, grateful for the glass screen that separated themselves and the driver. Sinclair would have loved all this, she thought ironically. To be fêted with an official driver, and to have some of the semi-bigwigs attending his funeral. Oh God . . . even now, she couldn't put his pomposity out of her mind. She was a monster, she thought. A real, honest-to-God monster. . . .

"How long can you stay?" she heard her father say next.

"Until you agree to come back with me, if only for a visit," she said, plunging right in. "I'd ask you to come for good, but I have a feeling you won't agree to that."

He shook his head. "Not while your mother's here, and she's not moving anywhere." It was the nearest he got to anything like humour – if humour it was.

But after the ordeal of the funeral was over, Skye realised that in death her brother had become something of a local hero, if nothing else. It did much to bolster up her father's waning spirits, which Skye could see were alarmingly low. She spoke to him more urgently about coming back to Cornwall with her. Here, in her old home, sitting out on the porch, surrounded by the fragrance of the roses and shrubs her mother had grown, and with the strong sense of Primmy and Sinclair surrounding them, they sat together on the old swing, and spoke about the people they loved. And since they were talking more candidly than usual in their mutual grief, Skye felt the loss of Primmy more sharply than ever before.

"She's still here, you know," Cress said gently, as if reading her thoughts with uncanny accuracy. "I feel her presence every single day. When I pass her piano and I ripple my fingers along the keys, I see her smiling, playing for me, and telling me that she didn't regret a single thing about our lives together. I smell her perfume, and sometimes I hear her voice in my head. When you've known such a love as we did, you know that death isn't the final parting."

Skye was mute at such an impassioned, yet quietly dignified speech, and she shifted uncomfortably, knowing that his words were going beyond the things she wanted to hear. *Shouldn't* be hearing, since they were too private and intimate for anyone else to share.

"I'm sorry. I'm embarrassing you, my love," Cress said with a wry smile.

"A little. But only a little," she lied.

"And you seriously want me to leave my Primmy behind and come to Cornwall with you, do you?"

"Only for a while, Daddy," she said, certain now that it was hopeless to expect anything more. If he was destined to live out the rest of his life as a lonely widower with only his memories for company, then so be it. What right did she, or anyone have, to try and change his wishes?

"I want you to come because you have grandchildren who need to know you," she continued, and then played her trump card. "I'm sure Mom would want you to do this, Daddy. You know how she always set such store on the family background, and how she used to tell me and Sinclair so much about them. I felt I knew them all even before I set foot in Cornwall. It was comforting and gave me a great sense of continuity."

"I know. The charm of it all meant a lot to her too." He gave a deep sigh. "And as the years pass, there are fewer of them left. So how is that old reprobate, Albie?"

Her heart leapt at hearing his name. He could have mentioned any one of them. But it had to be that name, among all the others in this big, tangled family. The one name that had meant the most to her mother, before she and Cress had fallen in love so madly that they couldn't bear to be apart.

"He's well enough for a man of his age," she said cautiously.

For the first time since she had arrived, she heard her father laugh. "Careful, honey. We're much the same age, in case you forget."

"But you haven't lived the kind of life he has," she replied swiftly. "He's a self-indulger, Daddy, a hedonist, if you like, and it all shows in his face, and in the way he's become so debased and sarcastic, and mean."

And, dear God, if she wasn't careful, she'd be delving into forbidden territory. What in hell's name had made her mention that word *hedonist*? A pleasure seeker of the worst kind . . .

"You don't need to tell me, Skye. But those days are long past, and best forgotten."

Unfortunately, the past had a habit of bearing quite strongly on the present, and Skye shivered, remembering the possessive way Albie had looked at her, his eyes burning, seeing not the daughter, but the mother . . . *his* Primmy . . .

"So will you come home with me?" she persisted. "To make your acquaintance with Celia and Wenna and Oliver?"

He didn't speak for a long moment, gazing into the garden as if seeking affirmation, and then: "All right, I'll come back with you for a visit, since your mother would wish it. So do I, of course, though it's a long while since I had anything to do with children. But this is my home, Skye, and it's here that I'll be returning."

She had to be content with that, knowing she couldn't press him further, nor suggest a possible date for the voyage. Not yet. Not while he still grieved for Sinclair, and messages of sympathy were still coming to the house daily. Yet she knew in her heart that this homecoming to New Jersey had meant more to her on her mother's behalf than her brother's, and her guilt was paramount again.

"I'll want to show you the pottery too," she went on, turning the conversation to less emotive matters. "You've no idea how it's flourished in the past few years, and now we've got this large new Christmas order from Germany that Theo's forever crowing about."

"Is he still as loud-mouthed as ever?"

Skye laughed. "I see you don't forget much, do you, Daddy? Yes he is, and he and I frequently clash. But for all that, I think we make reasonable business partners."

She said it in some surprise, but she supposed that it was true. Business partners who didn't always see eye to eye, and could thrash out ideas until they reached a sensible conclusion, were preferable to those who were each afraid to upset the other one, agreeing mouse-like on every topic and heading for possible disaster.

"And how does Philip see your business partnership?" Cress said idly, but with his blue eyes as astute as ever.

Skye shrugged. "Philip was never wholly happy about it, and I don't suppose that will ever change."

"And you? Are *you* happy?"

"With the business? Of course."

"No. Not with the business."

The words seemed to hang in the air, and it was the first time anyone had questioned her on the state of her marriage, or her relationship with her husband. Or was it? She dismissed the uneasy thought that Nick Pengelly had done just that, whether in words or looks or feelings . . . and she waited too long before she answered.

"Well, of course I'm happy. I've got three darling children, haven't I?"

"So you have, but that's not what I asked."

She stood up, feeling a chill in the air as a small breeze rustled the branches on the trees and wafted the scent of roses towards them. As if it was Primmy admonishing her to tell the truth now, the way she had said it when Skye was a child. But she was a child no longer, and such confidences were not invited or wanted.

"I think it's time we went inside, don't you? I'll make us some coffee and then I think I'll have an early night. We have some of Sinclair's old buddies calling on us tomorrow, and we'll both need a steady head to deal with them."

And she couldn't bear to sit here on the old swing on the porch one minute longer, pretending to her father that she still loved her husband with the passion that had made their union inevitable. The shock of finally realising the truth was almost as great as learning of her brother's death, and that was the most terrible thought of all.

"When is Mommy coming home?" Wenna said plaintively to her father, her small chin sticking out mutinously. "I want Mommy. Mommy plays with me and tells me proper stories."

Philip counted to ten, wondering how it was that he could be so voluble and erudite to a group of earnest students, debating intellectual topics for hours, when he couldn't seem to string two sentences together that would satisfy his five-year-old daughter.

"I've told you proper stories," he almost snapped. "I've told you *Goldilocks and the Three Bears*, and *Cinderella*, and *Little Red Riding Hood*."

"I *know* all those," Wenna howled, not ready to give an inch. "Miss Landon tells me those. I want to hear the stories Mommy tells me, about the uncles and cousins and Granny Morwen. And 'sides, I don't like witch stories."

Celia sniggered, looking up from her painting book. "She wouldn't mind hearing a story about the old witchwoman on the moors, though, *would* you, ninny?"

Wenna howled again, and Philip turned on Celia. "No one is to mention that old crone in this house, do you hear me? Your sister will have nightmares, and besides, she's not a witch. Witches don't exist."

"They do too," Celia dared to yell back as always. "Mommy says so, and so does Ethan."

"Who the devil is Ethan?" he said, forgetting.

"He's the nice boy who works at White Rivers," Wenna said, her lips quivering. "Ethan says—"

Philip spun around, uncaring what Ethan said, and shouted for Oliver's nanny to come and get these two ready for bed. Then he went down to the drawing-room and poured himself a large whisky. And then another. It was against doctor's orders, and unless he drank enough it did the burgeoning pains in his head no good at all, but it was the only panacea he knew.

And the more he drank, the more resentful he became about his wife's absence, wishing to God that she would come home and see to her children, because they were beyond his capabilities to handle. By the time he had drunk himself into a near stupor, he staggered up the stairs and threw himself across his bed, snoring like a bullfrog.

"Are you quite sure about this?" Nick said slowly to his partner. "You've really thought it all through carefully, and weighed up all the pros and cons, have you?"

William Pierce nodded, his face and voice determined. "God knows I've dithered for long enough, Nick. If I don't make the break now, I'll always look back and think what a fool I was to miss the opportunity. I've got the chance to buy the place I want, lock, stock and chattels, and it's a going concern. I'd be obliged if you would go through all the details with me, though, and give me your expert opinion."

Nick laughed. "Soft-soaping me isn't in your character, Will, and you don't need me to tell you if the thing is viable. You're a better lawyer than that, and I know damn well you'll have gone into it thoroughly before you mentioned it to me. If your heart is really set on going into the antique business, then who am I to try and stop you?"

"It's been my dream for years. You know that. I'd ask you to come up to Bristol with me this weekend to look the place over, but I know you want to get down to Cornwall as soon as possible. And yes, it's viable. What concerns me more is dissolving the practice. I couldn't give you much time to find a new partner, Nick, and that truly worries me."

"Then don't let it," Nick said briskly. "Good God, man, do you think I'd stand in your way, when I can see how much all this means to you? As for finding a new partner – maybe this is a good time for us both to think about the future."

His thoughts were moving fast, in a new direction. He didn't yet know how bad his mother's illness was, but Adam had sounded serious on the telephone. And he and William both knew that to sell the practice as a thriving concern to new people without the strings of one surviving partner, would be to ensure a far more handsome price.

The worst scenario he envisaged, depending on his parents' health, would mean he was needed in St Austell for a long while. He was far from being a pauper, and in any case, he would be affluent enough with the half profits from Pengelly and Pierce, to bide his time before looking for anything else. He might then seek out new premises to begin again on his own, or to see what partnership openings there were in a reasonably close area to his family.

Not in St Austell itself, he thought, without examining his

reasons why. But near enough to be of help when the time came. He faced facts. There were bonds that couldn't and shouldn't be broken. They went far beyond monetary help, and he knew it had been a mistake to put all the responsibility for his own aged parents on to young Ethan and his cousin, Dorcas. And Adam had his own commitments now he was married. It was time for him to go back.

"Go and see your antique shop, Will, and then decide what we both intend to do. For what it's worth, you have my wholehearted blessing, but if you go, then so do I. The firm of Pengelly and Pierce will simply be at an end."

"Christ, Nick, that makes me feel so guilty—"

"Then don't let it. If it's fate taking a hand, blame it on my Cornish blood for finally calling me back, even if it's only for a time. My gut feeling always told me it would happen one day, anyway."

He didn't necessarily believe it, but he tried to be flippant, knowing it would relieve William's conscience if he thought it was the answer for both of them.

Just as long as he didn't have to see *her* every day. . . . He didn't even allow her name to enter his thoughts. He didn't need to.

Adam had taken the telephone call at the pottery with some relief, and reported it to his wife that evening after their evening meal, at which Vera was now improving.

"Our Nick's coming home for a spell. It's only right that he should see how bad Mother and Dad have got lately, and 'tis not fair to leave it all to Dorcas to care for two invalids, nor Ethan," he said, echoing Nick's words.

He avoided her eyes. They could have Ethan to live with them after the inevitable happened, but they were still newly-weds, and too selfishly in love to want to share their home with anyone. Vera and he were both in accord with that, and her arms went around him, nuzzling her lips against his neck for a moment.

"It's Nick's responsibility too, my love, and he obviously sees it that way, so there's no need to fret over it."

"I know. But our Nick's such an important man, and he's talking about giving it all up. 'Tain't right, Vera love," he said, still troubled.

She loved him for his loyalty and his honourable nature, but she couldn't let that pass.

"You're an important man too, Adam Pengelly, and don't you ever forget it," she said fiercely. "You're a marvel with your hands, and not only on those old pots of yours . . ."

She heard herself giggle in a ridiculously girlish fashion, but she knew she could say anything to Adam and he'd quickly pick up her mood, however daring. Which was more than Skye's pompous old Philip would, she thought fleetingly, seconds before Adam had twisted around to grab her in his arms and let his hands slide down over her rounded buttocks.

"So I'm a marvel with my hands, am I, wench?" he chuckled. "Now just what do you mean by that, I wonder?"

"I can't rightly remember," she said airily. "You'll have to remind me all over again."

And her teasing laughter was still ringing in his ears as he chased her up the winding staircase to their bedroom and fell across her on their bed, pinning her arms behind her head and kissing her soundly, their eyes glowing and their bodies ready for love. And all else forgotten.

Eight

It was more than a month before Skye and Cresswell returned to Cornwall. By then, the initial shock of Sinclair's death had receded for her, but not for her father. For her sake, she guessed that he was trying to conceal the extent of his grief, but it was obvious to Skye that it went very deep. She prayed that meeting his grandchildren would give him the boost to his morale that he badly needed.

As for herself, she ached to see her children. New Jersey hadn't been home to her for a number of years, and many of the people she used to know had left. Even a brief visit to the magazine offices where she had once so enjoyed working, had a different editor, and new staff who didn't remember her.

"I felt like a stranger," she said in bewilderment to her father that evening. "All the people I knew have gone. Everyone was busy and didn't have the time to spare for someone who had once been a part of it all. It was strange."

"People change and move on, honey," Cress told her. "There's no stopping it. But they would all know about Sinclair, and your reason for being here, so I dare say there was a certain amount of embarrassment too."

Of course. Why hadn't she thought of that? But he was right. People did change and move on. However sad it might seem, she admitted that it was healthy and inevitable.

And the nearer the homecoming to Cornwall, the more eager Skye was to be in familiar surroundings again, and to hear her children's eager chatter. She had missed them so much, and she couldn't wait to hold them in her arms again. Philip had promised to check on the time of the ship's arrival, and would bring the children to Falmouth to meet it.

At first, disembarking in the crush of passengers, Skye couldn't see him at all, and she was sick with disappointment. Surely he would know how important this was to her . . . and then she glimpsed his car at the far end of the quay, the doors opening, and her little daughters spilling out of it.

"They're here," she breathed to her father, and seconds later she was running along the uneven quay, picking up the fashionable hobble skirt that was hampering her progress, and gathering them both up into her arms, hugging them as if she would never let them go.

"Oh, I *missed* you both, my darlings!" she gasped. "You can't imagine how much!"

"We missed you too, Mommy!" Wenna wailed, and immediately burst into tears in the sheer release of tension after the long wait for the ship to dock.

"Well, she's back now, so don't be such a crybaby," Celia snapped, resisting her own chin-wobble with a great effort. "Have you brought us anything, Mom?"

Before Skye could catch her breath at this, Wenna dug her sister in the ribs.

"You know you're not supposed to ask right away. Daddy said so. Celia's cross because he smacked her for saying *those words*, Mommy. You know the ones," she said, unable to hide a nervous giggle.

"Welcome home, darling," Philip said, coming into her focus, and kissing Skye on both cheeks. *Très* continental, she thought. And totally without the emotion she felt inside.

He was obviously ignoring Wenna's indiscretion, unless he hadn't heard it properly in the general quayside confusion and excited babble. His words were warm – just – considering he was glaring at both his daughters now, but Skye felt desperately let down. As a learned professor he made it a rule to keep his dignity in public at all times, but she was his wife and had been away from him for more than a month . . .

"You didn't bring Oliver then," she said, simply because she couldn't think of anything else to say to this stranger who was her husband.

"I did not," he said, his eyes becoming steely despite himself, and she guessed at once what this month of child caring had been like for him.

Poor Philip, she thought, sympathy overcoming everything else for the moment.

And then at last her father had caught up with them, having supervised the baggage unloading with one of the quayside porters while the little reunion was going on.

"Daddy," she quickly drew him into their family circle. "Come meet your granddaughters, Celia and Wenna."

She pushed Celia forward, still sulking, still black-faced at being shown up in public. But Wenna went straight into his arms, and his heart was lost to her for ever.

Wenna sat close beside him as they drove back to New World, with Celia on his other side, and as the girls chattered, Skye could sense how he was trying to relax. This journey had been an ordeal for him, she thought suddenly, and wondered why she had never realised it before. She had only thought of doing good by him, but she should have known that his memories here were very mixed.

His engagement and subsequent marriage to his cousin Primmy had been far too hasty and suspicious for the rest of the family, even though it had assailed the darker suspicion about Primmy and Albie. Primmy had often laughed about their varying attitudes when relating the old tales to her daughter, and there had been no embarrassment, no hint of scandal to keep hidden away.

Skye was fully aware of the family history that linked brother and sister together, however wrongly. But seeing her father's haunted and dark-shadowed eyes, she was full of self-doubt at bringing him home with her at this vulnerable time for him, knowing that the therapy of it was as much for her peace of mind as for his. She prayed it hadn't been a mistake.

"Has Theo been a problem while I've been away?" she asked Philip, immediately thinking it was a foolish question to ask, and worded in such an infantile manner. As if Theo was another child, instead of a grown man.

Philip snorted. "No more than usual."

But she was in tune with the wariness in his voice even before Celia cut in, important with knowledge as ever.

"Uncle Theo came to the house and he and Daddy had an awful fight. A *big* fight, with lots of shouting," Celia had announced, before Philip told her to be quiet and to stop telling tales before her mother had even reached home.

Skye turned to him at once, her heart sinking. She could imagine how Theo would react if Philip had started interfering in clay business. Theo *hated* interference of any kind.

"What happened?" she said quietly but insistently.

"The man's a fool, and has completely taken leave of his senses," he exploded, clearly unable to hold himself in check any longer, until he glanced at the older man sitting silently in the back seat of the car. "I apologise for this, Cresswell, you didn't want to be thrust right into the middle of it – and I haven't yet said how sorry I am about your son."

Dear God, was there ever an afterthought so tactless? Skye fumed, aghast at his words.

"Get it off your chest, man, whatever it is," Cress said roughly. "We all know that life has to go on."

Philip nodded. "Well then, that bast – that *imbecile*, and I can't think of him in any other way, has taken Anglo-German relations too far, and the clayworkers are already at loggerheads about it. There'll be a strike before long, you mark my words, or something worse."

"Perhaps this discussion is best left until we get home after all, Philip. Little ears are quivering," Skye said swiftly, seeing how Celia was leaning forward in the car now, sensing something dramatic going on between the grown-ups, and agog for the bits of information that she didn't yet know. But she had to put in her piece.

"I already know some of it, anyway, and Sebby told me his father said you weren't going to like it one bit when you heard. But it was more his clayworks than yours anyway, and so was the pottery, so he went ahead and did it."

"Be quiet, Celia," Philip snapped at her, seeing that her garbled words made little sense to Skye except to alarm her more. "This is a fine welcome home for your mother, and your grandfather will think he's come into a crazy house."

"Not at all," said Cress, the coolest of them all. "I'm a Tremayne, remember?"

Which was more than Philip was . . .

"I'll hear no more of it until we get home," Skye said fiercely. "Not – one – more – word, Celia."

She couldn't be sure, but as her elder daughter turned her imperious little face to the car window, she fancied she heard her mutter 'Bleedin' 'ell', and she had a hard job not to let her mouth twitch. Or it might have done if she didn't sense already that something dire was in the air. Something that affected Killigrew Clay and White Rivers, and therefore *her*, and all of them.

As if belatedly realising he should make a greater effort to be sociable after the unfortunate incident, Philip spoke directly to his father-in-law.

"You'll be seeing some changes since your last visit, Cresswell. There are fewer of the old family members left now, of course, but the Pengelly fellow joined the ranks when he married Vera."

Considering that Cress's own son was one of the depleted family members, it was a doubly tactless remark that Philip apparently didn't see, and which Cress chose to ignore.

"Oh yes, the wedding. Skye told me all about it and how beautiful these little honeys looked on the day."

"Am I a honey, Grandad?" Wenna asked, charmed by the word as always.

"You surely are, babe," Cress went on, exaggerating his accent. "As sweet as the honey from a hiveful of bees."

"We seem to have been invaded by a hiveful of Pengellys now," Philip said, his voice edgy and clearly not enjoying this transatlantic jargon. "What with the boy apprenticed at the pottery, and now the older one coming back to Cornwall—"

"The older one? You mean Nicholas?" Skye spoke as evenly as she could, giving Nick his full name as if to distance herself from any intimate knowledge of him.

"The very one," Philip nodded. "The parents are practically

at death's door, I gather, so he and his partner have dissolved their practice in Plymouth and he's taken up a partnership with Slater in Bodmin. The Pengellys will be privy to all our family business soon."

"So is he living in Bodmin now?" Skye tried not to sound too interested, and didn't rise to the bait that Slater was *her* family's solicitor, not his, and always had been.

"No. He's taken a house in Truro."

"Oh well, I'm sure his family will be glad to have him fairly near."

She glanced round at Wenna as she spoke, as if for reassurance that she had her own family, and that whatever Nick Pengelly did had nothing to do with her. As she did so, she caught her father looking at her.

He knew, she thought. With the uncanny intuition of the Tremaynes, he knew that this information meant more to her than the disquieting news that there was about to be trouble brewing between herself and Theo and the clayworkers. But how could anyone *not* know, when she was so aware of her pounding heart, and the heat in her cheeks, just by hearing his name? Dear God, what was happening to her?

"Daddy, you must think we're being terribly selfish, going on about things you know nothing about," she said quickly.

"Of course I don't. It's strangely refreshing to be caught in the middle of family ups and downs again, no matter what they are. I hadn't realised how I'd missed it."

But if she thought this meant he was likely to stay forever, the slightest shake of his head at her hopeful look, told her differently.

Philip spoke again. "You'll be wanting to meet all your folks again, I dare say. We could arrange a small get-together for them all while you're here. Not exactly a party, of course. You wouldn't want that, I'm sure," he added, accentuating the gaffe.

"Thank you, but in the circumstances I'd prefer to see them all separately in my own time. I don't want any fuss."

"No. Of course not."

There was dignity and dignity, Skye mused, as they all fell

silent for a few embarrassed moments. Philip had it when it suited him, especially in the company of adoring students or academic contemporaries, but her father had it all the time. And to his credit, she could see he was just as determined not to put a damper on his daughter's homecoming, and he spoke cheerfully about making the acquaintance of young Oliver Norwood.

"He won't talk to you for days, Grandad," Celia said at once with a superior giggle. "He'll just stick his thumb in his mouth and bury his head in his nanny's bosom."

"*Celia!*" thundered her father. "I won't have you using such words."

"Oh, for pity's sake, Philip," Skye said, starting to laugh. "Don't go on at her so. She could have said far worse!"

"And we all know where she got that from, don't we?"

Once they had arrived at New World, and the infant Oliver was brought down to study the grandfather he didn't know, he did exactly as Celia had said, sucked his thumb and buried his head into his nanny's bosom without a single word.

Cress gave a small smile as he felt Celia's hand creep into his and squeeze it in triumph, and he gave her a surreptitious wink that made her giggle. It took time to get to know people, but already he felt he was beginning to understand this precocious little one quite well.

Skye could hardly wait to tackle Philip about the trouble with Theo. Once the girls had insisted on taking Cress to his bedroom and then showing him their garden and the plants they were growing in their special little plot, she put all other matters out of her head and demanded to know what had been happening while she had been away.

The comment about Anglo-German relations had more than alarmed her. The war had been over a long time now, and people had to get along with one another, no matter how many compromises had to be made.

"As I told you, your lunatic cousin's gone right over the top this time," he said, blind to the irony of the tragic phrase. "Of all the wild schemes he ever had, this has got to be the worst. He's so hand in glove with these foreigners now, he's invited half a dozen young German workers to study the clayworking methods from beginning to end, to see how the clay is transformed into the pottery for export to their factory."

"Well? That doesn't seem so unreasonable to me," Skye began uneasily. "Time's getting short, I'd have thought, and the export order must surely be well under way by now."

"I'm not talking about all that." He brushed the importance of it aside as if it was nothing. "Anyway, from the mutterings among the clayworkers when he first suggested it, you might have second thoughts about the wisdom of inviting foreigners. But it hasn't stopped there."

"Go on, then. What happened next?" she said, biting her lip as he seemed too short of breath to go on. Maybe she shouldn't be pressing him, but she knew only too well she wouldn't stop him, despite the way the veins on his forehead stood out like purple ropes. It was a pity he couldn't stay calm in the telling the way he apparently did with his students. How was it he could explain the most intricate things to them, in infinite and patient detail, and yet anything to do with Killigrew Clay or White Rivers had him near to apoplexy? But she knew the answer to that, of course. Teaching was his domain, while the rest was hers.

"The next thing, my dear sweet wife," he said insultingly, "is that he's offered them temporary jobs while they're here, putting them on the clayworks payroll without even consulting you, and sending a kiss-my-ass 'so what?' to everybody else." As she gasped at this rare vulgarity from Philip, he stormed on. "And you don't need me to tell you how the clayers have reacted to that. You know the list of names on the memorial cross in St Austell as well as I do. Do I need to remind you of how many were wiped out in one day in France? Or have you forgotten the Killigrew Pals' Battalion so soon?"

Skye flinched. No, she hadn't forgotten. How could she, when she had been the one to write home to every one of the families when the news had come through to their army hospital in France? When she had written of the tragedy so emotionally for the readers of *The Informer* newspaper?

All those young boys . . . All of them Killigrew Clay boys,

whose families had worked for Killigrew Clay for generations past. *Their* boys . . . Her tolerance to the foreigners was fast disappearing.

"How *dare* you accuse me of forgetting!" she said.

"Nor do the clayers," he retorted. "I warn you, there'll be strikes at the very least, and bloodshed at worst."

"Bloodshed? What do you mean by that?"

But a cold shock was running through her, knowing of the temperament of the clayers. They didn't have the hardships of their predecessors now that things were more mechanised, but the heart and soul of them was the same. They were hard, tough men, as hard as the granite memorial cross in St Austell, and they wouldn't have forgotten, either. They were a tight-knit community, and they had all lost sons and brothers and fathers.

"I need to speak to Theo," she said, through cold lips. "We must do something about this before it's too late."

"I doubt that you'll get him to change his mind. It'll mean losing face to send them back now."

"Then I must speak to the clayworkers myself."

"*You*! You're a woman!"

"Oh, for pity's sake, Philip. Haven't you been listening to anything except what's in your own head these past years? Women do have a voice now, you know. Ask Lily!"

"Your cousin Lily's a feminist of the worst kind," he sneered. "Marching and banner waving and screeching like a banshee hardly becomes her."

"And neither does sitting on the sidelines and letting things happen when you can do something about them. Morwen Tremayne wouldn't have stood aside and let a man make a perfect fool of himself. Even if that's all it is."

But she knew in her heart that Philip was right about one thing. There could be strikes – or bloodshed . . .

"You set a mighty great store on what Morwen Tremayne would have done, don't you?"

She heard the resentment in his voice now, and gaped at him in astonishment and sorrow. Philip had loved and respected her grandmother, but his twisted thought processes meant that his

118

feelings for people could change with chameleon-like swiftness these days. Her throat was thick as she put her hand on his arm, knowing it wasn't his fault. It was a relic of the evil, bloody war – and she understood too, his own personal reason for resenting Theo's action. He couldn't help the way he felt, and she had to keep reminding herself of that fact or it would destroy her. She spoke more softly.

"You always set a great store by Morwen's opinions too, Philip, and I know that in your heart you still do. But let's leave it for now. I won't do anything until I see Theo, and I don't want any of this business to spoil my father's visit. He's suffered enough without having to hear us bickering like magpies."

It was more like two dinosaurs head to head, she thought, but to her relief he nodded, and she was glad to turn away from him as they heard the children bringing their grandfather back to join them.

Cresswell settled in remarkably quickly, and he was offered the use of a family car whenever he wanted it to visit his relatives. Thankfully, there was no more talk of a family reunion for him. It was the last thing he would have wanted right now. He had varying memories of Cornwall, and the happiest were those when he and Primmy had fallen in love. But it had never been his home, the way it was with all these others. He had been born in America, the son of Morwen's brother Matt, but his Cornish links were strong, through his father, and his darling Primmy, who had become his wife.

But he had already resolved that this visit shouldn't be prolonged. He knew how much Skye wanted him to stay, and he loved her for it, but in his heart he knew that a couple of weeks would be enough, and at night he already found himself longing for the familiarity of being back home.

Within the first few days, he had called on the ageing Luke, and was glad to get away from the wheezing and ponderously speaking old man. He visited Charlotte and heard her cloying sympathy about Sinclair, and he drove out to the farm to call on Emma and Will, and was clasped to Em's ample chest. He was invited to supper with Vera and her new husband, whom he liked enormously for his fresh honesty and obvious devotion to Vera.

His visit to Theo and his family was brief, and neither man mentioned the trouble Cress now knew was imminent, though he felt disinclined to advise Skye on what to do or say about it. Having been uninvolved in the war himself, and knowing the attitude of some British folk towards America's late entry, it hardly seemed his place to do so.

He also knew he was putting off the visit to Albert Tremayne's studio in Truro for as long as he could. It wasn't that he felt any resentment towards Albert any more. All that was past, and besides, he knew the absolute truth of the rumours. Whatever incestuous thoughts there had been, they were all in Albie's mind and never Primmy's. And it had never come to fulfilment, thank God.

No, the reason he didn't want to go to the artist's studio – could hardly bear to contemplate it, if the truth were told – was because he knew it would still be so full of Primmy. She had had such a happy, heady, bohemian life there – and he simply didn't want to think of her belonging in any other place but their home in New Jersey.

"You're a bloody foolish old man," he told himself savagely. "The life she and Albie shared was nothing compared to the life she shared with you. It may have been wild and unconventional at the time, and caused folk to raise their eyebrows, but it was no more than an episode long past."

But the fact that he could still feel jealousy was a torment in his soul, and he finally knew it wouldn't be assuaged until he faced the lion in his den. And when he did, he stared in disbelief at this bedraggled old man – no more a lion than a shuffling insect, and clearly the worse for drink – who opened the studio door to him and peered short-sightedly at the visitor.

"Yes? Who is it?" Albie growled.

"Don't you know me, Albert Tremayne?" Cress said quietly.

It never promised to be a good meeting. For Cress it was simply something he had to do, as if Primmy was compelling him to at least make contact with her brother. But they could never be friends; never more than two men bound by ties that went beyond the tangled relationships of the Tremayne family. Two men who had loved the same woman.

"Heard you were here. Didn't expect to see you. Don't get many visitors, 'specially fam'ly ones," Albie said, his voice slurred and his head disorientated. He tried hard to remember something important. "Bad news about your son. A shock."

"Yes. But Skye's presence helped."

"Ah – Skye. How is she?" Albie enquired.

"She's well. She's young, and gets over things. And she has her own busy life, of course."

"Of course."

"The children will be of help to her. Children take away the hurt," Cress went on, almost desperately.

They each listened to themselves, talking in stark, staccato sentences, each knowing that the gulf between them was too wide to ever cross. It was the strangest thing, thought Cress. They had the most fundamental thing in the world in common, and yet it was the very thing that kept them apart, and always would.

It had been a mistake to come here, despite Primmy. He felt a violent need to get back to New World, to the healthy, boisterous antics of his grandchildren, and as far away as possible from this gloomy old man who seemed to live half in the shadows in the almost fetid atmosphere of the studio.

"Well, it's been – good – to see you," he said finally, realising he hadn't even been offered a chair, and thankful now that he hadn't had to pretend a relationship he didn't want.

"No, not *good*," Albie said, a shade more lucid and taking him by surprise. "I'll always be a – a *question* in your mind. Won't I?"

Cress felt his heart begin to thud. If this evil old devil was about to pretend to him now, that he and Primmy . . . *he and Primmy* . . . He saw Albie give a twisted smile, but although his words were less muddled, they were slower and more deliberate, as if he climbed a mountain in trying to get them out, but was determined to do so.

121

"Let me say it. Primmy. Everything – in the world to me. We loved each other. You – knew that. Our life here was – total harmony. I'd have given my life – to make her mine. You know damn well. But I was just her brother. Her best-loved brother, but *only* her brother. Nothing more. Ever. Question answered?"

"What question?" Cress said steadily, but he felt increasing alarm as the other man's eyes burned as if with a fever, and he began to sway. Albie coughed, exhausted after such a long speech, and there was blood on his lips.

Cress caught at his arm. "You're ill, man. Can I do anything for you? Can I get you a doctor?"

"Not ill," Albie croaked. "Just tired of living."

He slumped to the floor then, and as Cresswell felt his pulse and saw his sickly grey pallor, he knew this was more than a drunken stupor. His heart plummeted, unable to cope with another fatality so soon after Sinclair . . . but then common humanity took over, and he knew he couldn't just leave the man here like this.

He telephoned New World and spoke to Skye. She gave him the name of a Truro doctor and said she would come to the studio immediately. Since it was a considerable distance, the doctor was there long before her, and by the time Skye arrived, Albert had been taken to hospital in an ambulance, and the doctor had remained behind to have a long talk with Cresswell. He reported it gently to his daughter.

"Albert has had a stroke, Skye, but although the doctor doesn't seem to think it's serious, there are other, more serious problems."

"What other problems?"

She didn't want to get involved. Didn't want to have to think about Albert Tremayne at all, and she was quite sure her father didn't want to, either. But here they were, the only two of the family on the scene when they were needed. She hated the thought, and yet she had the strongest intuitive feeling that it was what her mother would have wanted. Primmy wouldn't want Albie to be deserted. She drew a deep breath, concentrating on what her father was saying now.

He spoke as unemotionally as possible, not wanting to distress her by repeating the doctor's scathing words that when the artist drank to excess and his senses got out of control, he resembled a raging bull.

"The doctor has been treating him for some time, for alcoholism and senility, darling. He's been insisting for months that Albert shouldn't continue living alone, or he'll end up doing himself real harm."

At the implication of what he was saying, Skye felt horror creep over her, and her voice was shrill with panic.

"He can't come to us! Philip would never agree to it. And the children – no, I won't subject them to it—"

Cress clutched her shaking arms, but she knew that her outburst had nothing to do with Philip or the children.

It did in part – but her prime feeling was one of terror at just having Albert Tremayne in her house, ogling her, wanting her . . . She caught herself up short, reminding herself that he was a pathetic, shambling old man, and her mother had loved him, but for the life of her she couldn't produce any sympathy at that moment. All she could do was shudder.

"There's no suggestion of that," she heard her father say. "What the doctor's strongly suggesting is that he's placed in a home where he can be properly cared for."

"Oh God no, not an asylum," Skye whispered. "Mom would never agree to that!"

She clapped her hands over her mouth, her eyes wide and brimming above her fingers. But here in Albie's studio, where he and Primmy had shared all those reckless bohemian years, she seemed to hear her mother protesting violently that they couldn't do this to her beloved Albie. Primmy's voice was so strong in her head, and she prayed desperately that her father couldn't hear it too.

"No, darling, and neither would the family," Cress said steadily. "The doctor says there are excellent rest and care homes where he'll be looked after properly until the end of his days. We'll insist that he's found the best."

"No matter how much it costs," Skye said.

"No matter how much," he agreed.

*　　*　　*

"You're not planning on paying for the old boy's keep forever more, I hope?" Philip asked her, when at last she and Cress returned to New World, totally exhausted.

She looked at him speechlessly. The visit to the hospital had been harrowing. Albie's health had declined so fast it was almost unbelievable. The stroke had been a minor one, but it had been the trigger to destroying him. It was easy to see there was no going back to the studio for him, nor living alone, and the trembling hands that had produced such delicate paintings would never hold a brush again.

"I certainly am," she answered Philip, furious. "You seem to forget he's my uncle, and he was my mother's dearest friend as well as her brother. What else would you expect me to do?"

Philip shrugged. "I think you take on too much, my love," he said, the coolly uttered endearment such a contradiction. "There are others in the family who should help."

"But none who were ever as dear to Uncle Albie as Mom and me," she dared to say, knowing her father was listening.

"And if the expenses bother you that much," Cress put in, "I'll be more than willing to share them with Skye."

She looked at him, and had never loved him more. But perverse as ever, Philip shook his head.

"That won't be necessary. I'm just concerned for Skye, that's all." He put on a more practical voice. "So, assuming that he'll never return to his studio, who's going to clear it out and put the place up for sale? It won't be the most savoury task, I suspect."

"It's far too soon to think of that. Besides, no one can do that without his agreement," Skye said swiftly, the thought of it appalling her.

"They can, if he's so deranged that a doctor and lawyer decree it. Consult your Pengelly man and ask his advice."

Nine

Theo, Charlotte and Emma were called in to the family council. Luke Tremayne had declined to attend; probably thinking that he'd be the next to go, Theo had said sourly. Luke was not yet sixty years old, but since his long-ago conversion to religion, he had turned into a latter-day Methuselah, according to Theo. And no doubt Luke's pious presence always made Theo feel uncomfortable, considering his own extra-marital activities, thought Skye shrewdly. But this was no time to dwell on personalities. Albert Tremayne's future was an important matter, and the only other direct older members of the family were too far away to be consulted.

Cresswell had intended going home to New Jersey as soon as he decently could, but from Skye's present state of mind he knew he must stay until these proceedings were finished. As for Philip, once he realised the family was closing ranks on any decision, he ignored the entire feudal business and let them get on with it.

The family council was quickly arranged to take place in Truro, at Theo's home. Killigrew House seemed the obvious place to hold it, and those present included Dr Rainley and the family solicitor, and Skye felt her heart jump when she saw Nick Pengelly walk into the drawing-room.

"Good afternoon, everyone," he said quietly. "I apologise for Mr Slater's absence, but he has to be in session in Bodmin for the next couple of weeks. I'm fully conversant with all the details of this case, and I trust no one has any objection to my presence? If so, the whole matter will have to be postponed until a later date."

"Just get on with it, man," growled Theo. "We all know why

we're here, and there's more important clay business to sort out than the future of a senile old man."

The doctor cleared his throat, while the others stared stonily ahead. They were all used to the insufferable Theo, but he could be guaranteed to mortify them by his crudeness in front of outsiders. Dr Rainley spoke unemotionally.

"I've had a consultation with other senior doctors, and we are all of the same opinion regarding the health of Mr Albert Tremayne. I have obtained signed statements to that effect, which I will show to you all, and then pass on to Mr Pengelly. They all affirm that Mr Albert Tremayne is no longer competent to live alone, and would be a danger to himself and possibly to other people. Because of his unpredictable nature, we do not advise any of you to offer him a home."

"Thank God for that," Theo said feelingly.

"Shut up, Theo, for goodness' sake," Emma said, red-faced at such a lack of charity. "Albie's our family, after all."

"Oh ah. Were you thinkin' of movin' him in wi' you and your farmer then? Got a suitable hen house for him, have 'ee, Em?" he sneered.

"What *do* you advise, Dr Rainley? We want the best for him. Our mother would wish it." Charlotte asked, ignoring him, and clearly wishing herself anywhere but here.

Dr Rainley was her family physician, and she tried to hold on to her dignity. She could see how upset Emma was now, and probably liable to lapse into coarse farming talk at any minute if she and Theo began wrangling. And she had no wish for Theo to let the side down any more than he had to. Neither did Skye. Charlotte knew that by the way she was staring into the distance.

In fact, Skye was finding it very difficult to concentrate in the stuffy atmosphere of the drawing-room that Betsy always kept at near to hot-house temperature. But she knew Morwen would have wanted the best of care for her adopted son, Albie. So would Primmy, and so did she.

She caught Nick Pengelly's glance, was held by it for a timeless moment, and swiftly looked away. But just for that one brief moment while the others squabbled, she had the strangest

126

feeling that no one else existed for either of them. His unspoken sympathy for her, on account of all these impossible people, was obvious. But she knew there was far more than that in the magnetic exchange of glances, and she didn't want to admit that it meant anything at all, not for one second.

She forced herself to listen to what he was saying in his lawyer's voice now, as the doctor passed the signed statements over to him. He scanned them quickly.

"These documents are legally and unquestionably sound," Nick said. "You may all examine them, and I will provide copies for you all in due course. And if it is the family's wish that Mr Tremayne be committed to a place of care, then I will deal with all further legalities."

"As long as it's a *decent* place of care where he can be looked after with every kindness," Skye said emphatically. "I refuse to sanction one of those awful asylum places."

"No, indeed!" Charlotte added. "We could never hold up our heads in public if poor Albert was sent to such a place."

Skye looked at her coldly. "That was the least of my concerns, Charlotte."

"Well, of course, Americans see things differently, don't they?" Charlotte said, unable to resist the small barb.

"I think what Skye means," Cresswell put in, "is that we want every comfort for our brother, until the end of his days."

Skye had never loved him more. Albert wasn't *his* brother, and if anyone here had cause to resent their concern for him, it was her father.

"Can we get on with it?" Theo bellowed. "Em will want to get back to her farmyard, and Skye and I have urgent business of our own to deal with, in case you've forgotten, cuz."

"I haven't," she snapped. "But it can wait until later. Please go on, Nicholas – Mr Pengelly. What do we do next?"

"Dr Rainley has advised me of several suitable rest and care homes of the type your uncle needs," he said, addressing her as if they were the only two in the room. "Unfortunately none of them is in Cornwall, and the actual location is a decision the council will have to make. There's no question of an asylum since the family is well able to support Mr

Tremayne in his last years. I presume that *is* agreeable to you all?"

"Oh my goodness, yes," Charlotte said. "Whatever it costs, I'm sure the family will rally round."

"It won't matter where the bugger is, if he don't even know what day it is," Theo scowled.

"I'm very much afraid Mr Tremayne is right in that respect." The doctor ignored the outraged gasps from the others. "His condition has deteriorated swiftly, and it's doubtful already whether he would know any of you for more than moments at a time. I understand from Mr Slater that your lawyers can be given power of attorney if the client is incapable of making personal decisions, so whatever happens to his property will eventually be your joint decision."

"He'll certainly get no visits from me, wherever he is," Theo retorted. "Just find him a suitable place and let us know the fees. We're none of us paupers, though I'd have thought he had assets enough, considering all his paint daubings. Unless he's drunk it all away, of course."

At that moment Skye hated the lot of them. Theo for just being Theo, which said it all; Charlotte for her snobbishness; even darling Em, fidgeting uncomfortably in her dowdy clothes and sensible shoes, and clearly wanting to get away. She was totally out of her element here, and it showed.

"Please listen a moment." Skye said, knowing she had to take the initiative or they would get nowhere. "Theo is right again, however tastelessly he puts it. It's reasonable to assume that all Uncle Albie's costs will be met out of his estate, since he has no direct descendants to leave it to. But when that is exhausted, then his every comfort will be continued to be paid for by funds from the Killigrew Clay estate. It's what Granny Morwen would have wanted, and I'm sure Mr Pengelly and Mr Slater can arrange things, once we have found the right accommodation."

She shivered. She hadn't intended to make such a lengthy speech, and she knew she was being far too bold in some folks' opinion. Despite having lived in Cornwall for thirteen years, where her roots were, she would always be the interloper

. . . the American cousin, as her father had been before her. But since no one else seemed to be making any sensible decisions . . .

"You can rely on us," Nick said, his eyes telling her that she was the only sane one among them, as far as he was concerned. Except for her father, of course.

"Then I think this initial meeting is at an end," said Dr Rainley briskly. "You are all at liberty to visit Mr Tremayne in Truro hospital to see him for yourselves, of course, though he probably won't know you. I know Mrs Norwood has already done so, and will confirm my words."

Skye nodded, preferring to forget that traumatic and horrendous visit when Albie had thrashed about in the bed like a madman, threatening to harm everyone near him before he was sedated. And wishing she could also forget the way his face changed as the drug relaxed all his muscles, and seeing in him the flamboyant and youthful brother her mother had loved.

"And I'll be in touch about further arrangements as soon as possible, Mrs Norwood."

Nick ignored Theo now, making Skye the central figure in the procedure. Before the rest of them made thankful exits, he had one last comment to make.

"There's no need to do anything about the studio yet, providing it's securely locked up. Once everything is proceeding, I'll put the legal wheels in motion, then the studio can be cleared out, and put on the market."

Skye shuddered. Poking and prying through Albie's studio was something she didn't want to think about, nor to take any part in. But yet again she seemed to hear her mother begging her not to let it be left to strangers to touch Albie's personal, intimate belongings . . . some of which would surely still belong to her, since Skye knew full well that he had never truly been able to let Primmy go . . .

As Betsy bustled in with a tray of tea and home-made scones for those who weren't making hasty excuses to get away, Skye suddenly found Nick at her side. He handed her his business card, which included details of the Bodmin chambers, and his home telephone number and address in

Truro. She barely glanced at it, and just stuffed it inside her glove.

"Please let me help you when the time comes," he said quietly. "Adam tells me your father will be leaving for America soon, and you shouldn't deal with this alone. Since you have shown more consideration towards your uncle than the rest of them, there may be items at the studio that will upset you. From the look of things, none of these charmers will want to be involved in any of it."

She looked at him mutely. She didn't want to be involved, either, but she was. And so was he.

"Thank you," she whispered.

"Now then, cuz, what the hell are you making such a song and dance about these German fellows for?" Theo yelled at her, when the rest of them had finally gone, and they were alone in his study. "We need to get on with this export order for Kauffmann's at a fair rate now. They're bloody good workers, and keen to learn, and I see nothing wrong in it—"

"You wouldn't, you stupid oaf," she screamed at him, her temper exploding, and wondering how he could be so bloody, *bloody* insensitive as to go on at her so, right after the distressing family council about Albie. She needed time to recover herself, even though she knew this confrontation was long overdue. But she was too vulnerable right now, and he knew it, damn him.

"So tell me," he snarled, arms folded as he glared across his desk at her. She didn't sit down. She stood there, taut and furious, knowing she was at a disadvantage, but uncaring.

"They're *Germans*," she screamed again, aghast at the blatant prejudice she hadn't even known still simmered inside her, but unable to stop it.

"So? Their orders put bread and butter in your mouth, same as mine. They ain't going to taint your precious pots."

"Tell that to the clayworkers! I've been up to Clay One, Theo, and I've spoken to a number of them. Oh, I grant you that the German boys are good-looking and agreeable enough, but the clayers only tolerate them because they're doing the menial

130

jobs. But some of the Germans are boasting that they could do the work far quicker and with better equipment."

"Mabye we should see this better equipment then. I'm always open to a bit o' streamlinin'"

"You suggest that, and I doubt that you'll have any Cornishmen left to work at Killigrew Clay."

Theo suddenly stood up, knocking over his chair as he did so, and leaning right across the desk, an inch away from her face. She flinched, but she didn't move away.

"You know your bloody trouble, don't you, woman? You can't forget that the war's a long time over. We've got to make progress and forget that we were ever enemies. Anyway, these young buggers were only infants when the war began."

"And there would be plenty of Cornish boys of their own age working in the pit now, if their fathers hadn't been part of the Killigrew Pals' Battalion that was wiped out in a single day," she whipped out, close to tears. "If you can't see how these boys are a constant reminder of that, then you're an even bigger fool than I took you for."

Theo said nothing for a moment, and then sat down again, hands clenched, and his face a furious colour. "Well, it's too late. We have to get these orders out fast now, if they're to get from the German factory to the shops in good time before Christmas. 'Taint no good having a pile of goods arriving on Christmas Eve, when all the shopping's been done. In fact, to speed things up, I'm thinking of sending a couple of the boys to work in the packing shed at White Rivers. Will that please you?"

"It will not!" she said, incensed. "How dare you be so high-handed? White Rivers is as much my concern as yours, and you had no right to do any of this without consulting me."

"Well, since you were out of the country at the time," he sneered, not even seeing how his words wounded her, "I had no intention of sending a message by carrier pigeon over the water to ask your permission. The day I ask any woman for permission to do any damn thing is the day I pack it in."

Skye turned on her heel. As if her brother's cruel death hadn't been enough, the last few days had been terrible, answering folks' enquiries, fielding off rumours about Albie, and then culminating in this ghastly afternoon. There had been no time, until now, to confront Theo about the Germans, and now she didn't know if she felt shame or outrage, or both.

She just had to get away from him. Her father had gone back to New World, and she had said she'd go to the college and wait for Philip to take her back. Now, she didn't even know if she could bear to do that. He'd assume she had gone home with her father, anyway. And he'd want to know everything that had happened, and in the end he'd wash his hands of Albie, the way he always did.

Or perhaps not. In Philip's perverse moods it was just as possible that he would act as though he didn't know or care where she had been that day, and not even refer to it. Either way, Skye didn't want him. She definitely didn't want him.

At that moment, something seemed to die within her. All the years they had shared together; all the dangerous months in France, never knowing if they were going to get out of that evil war alive; all the closeness, all the love . . . all of it was slowly dying within her, and she couldn't hold on to it. She couldn't get it back . . .

Skye left Killigrew House, hurrying through the Truro streets, seeing no one, hearing nothing, as if her mind was a total vacuum. She walked and walked, hardly realising she had reached the river, and for once its meandering beauty didn't touch her. On the far side of the bank was Albie's studio, but her senses simply refused to acknowledge it. It didn't exist, any more than she did herself in those disorientated moments.

"For God's sake, Skye, be careful," she heard a voice say close beside her. She felt a hand on her arm, pulling her back from the glittering, beautiful water's edge, and for a moment she couldn't focus at all.

She couldn't see the face of the man with sunlight behind him, until he moved out of its aura, and Nick Pengelly appeared before her for the second time that day. A nervous laugh that turned into a sob tore at her throat, because he surely couldn't think she had been going to throw herself in . . .

"Don't worry, I'm not about to do anything stupid," she said painfully. "I just had to get away from them all, and Lord knows what you must have thought of them."

She was babbling, aware that he kept hold of her arm, as if he still wasn't sure of her intention. She felt her mouth tremble. She didn't know either. She had always thought herself so strong. She had come through a war, for pity's sake, and seen and coped with unmentionable horrors from the trenches in the field hospital . . . and now she felt as though she was slowly disintegrating. Without knowing that she did so, she leaned against the tall, hard body of the Pengelly man, as Philip called him.

"I'm sorry," she muttered. "You must think me terribly feeble . . ."

"Don't be ridiculous," he said, his voice rough. "You should know by now that I think you're the most marvellous person who ever lived. As for the rest of your wretched family – I've seen and dealt with far worse in my profession."

Her heart was doing its rapid jungle beat again, and she gave him a crooked smile, needing to take any hint of intimacy out of his words.

"Is this the usual bedside manner you employ for foolish clients, Mr Pengelly? Maybe you should have been a doctor instead of a lawyer."

"There's a certain similarity," Nick agreed, unwilling to admit how those simple words *bedside manner* had fired his blood and stirred his loins.

He told himself again that she was a married woman, and he couldn't risk any scandal – then reminded himself in the same instant how fate had thrown them together. His partner had wanted to dissolve their Plymouth practice; his parents had needed him, but now that he was near at hand, they seemed to have had a second lease of life, however temporary; and he had been called in to deal with the tangled fortunes of the Tremayne dynasty, by whatever name. If that wasn't fate playing with him, he didn't know what was.

And now he held this beautiful, sensual woman in his arms, and he wished he could hold her there for ever.

Skye became aware that they were in a very public place, and that people were glancing their way. It simply wasn't done for strangers to be standing so close, even if she knew in her heart that they were never strangers. She shivered, not wanting to believe in a force larger than herself that was racing her towards a place she knew she shouldn't go. Fate should *help* people, she thought angrily, not test them to their limits. The anger helped her to speak more curtly.

"I'm sorry. I'm acting so unlike myself. I must go."

"You can't go anywhere yet. You're far too agitated. Come and take tea with me. Doctor's orders," he added.

She didn't even smile. "I can't. My husband – my children will be waiting for me. I shouldn't stay here any longer—"

"But you will. Won't you?"

She didn't speak for a moment, and then, "Just tea then," she said, weakening.

"Of course."

There were several tearooms in the twisting streets of the town nearby, and she kept her eyes downcast as he tucked her hand in his arm and walked her briskly away from the river and the sight of Albert Tremayne's studio. She walked as if she was in a dream, still caught up in the drama of past days, not wanting conversation and not offering it.

She hadn't even realised they had turned into a tree-lined residential street, until she looked up, startled, at the tall house where he was unlocking the front door.

"Where are we?" she said.

But she knew. Of course she knew, and instinctively she shrank back. But Nick kept her arm squeezed to his more firmly so that she couldn't pull away.

"My house. It's more private than any noisy tearooms, and I promise you I'm a dab hand at making tea. It's one of the advantages of living a respectable bachelor life."

She didn't know if that was meant to reassure her. She only knew, with an instinct that Granny Morwen would have applauded, that if she once stepped across this threshold, her life was going to be changed for ever.

"This isn't a good idea," she said.

"Do you think I'm never alone with a female client in my

chambers?" he answered coolly. "*I* have a reputation at stake, as well as your own, my dear Mrs Norwood. Do you think my intentions are anything but honourable towards you?"

For a frisson of time she wanted to shriek at him: *Yes, yes, yes, I think your intentions are anything but honourable towards me . . . and it's what I want, what I need and what I crave . . .* She flinched as if frightened that the words were written clear across her face.

"I would never do anything to harm you, Skye. All I'm offering is tea," she heard him say quietly, and she was lost.

He was indeed a dab hand at making tea, as he put it, and she stayed far longer than she had intended. But he was charm itself, putting her at her ease, and showing her all around the small house he had bought, with all the eager pleasure of a child showing off a new toy.

She was bemused and enchanted by this side of him that she suspected few other people ever saw. He could probably be a hard and ruthless lawyer in court, but here, on his own territory, he was a man any woman could love.

"I really must go soon," she murmured, as she finished her second cup of tea. "I said that if my father didn't take me home from Theo's, I'd meet my husband at the college."

They both heard a church clock strike the hour, and she looked at him in dismay at realising how late it had become.

"Then I've kept you here far too long, and I'm sure he will have left the college by now," Nick said. "You must let *me* drive you home instead."

"Oh, that's not necessary. I can take a taxicab. I seem to be putting you to so much trouble."

"My dear Mrs Norwood," he said, using her full name like a caress once more, in a way that made her nerve-ends tingle, "don't you know that nothing I do for you would ever be too much trouble?"

"Nick, you promised—"

"That I would never harm you, yes. And nor I will. But that doesn't stop me wanting you."

She drew in her breath, knowing that marriage and children – and recent bereavement too – didn't stop her wanting him, either. There was a matching fire in her veins, and she had to turn away from the desire in his eyes, fumbling for her hat and gloves, then feeling his arms go around her as he arranged her stole around her shoulders.

Without realising that she did so, she leaned back a fraction towards him and she felt his hands tighten, then slide down her arms and turn her slowly round to face him, until she was held in the circle of his embrace.

"I would never harm you, Skye," he said, for the third time that day. Like Judas, she thought faintly, or was that analogy better applied to herself, knowing she had already betrayed Philip, in thought if not in deed?

But the notion was only half-formed in her mind before she felt the touch of Nick Pengelly's mouth on hers, and then she was kissing him back with as much wild abandon as if there were only moments left in the world.

"Please take me home," she murmured against his mouth when the kiss finally ended, yet keeping in the closest physical contact; once the contact was broken, so would be the spell. "I shouldn't even be here – and I daren't stay any longer."

And they both knew why . . . Shaken, Skye suddenly wrenched herself out of his arms, her face white where seconds before it had been hot with passion.

"Of course I'll take you home, and I'll explain to your husband that you felt ill and needed to rest before returning. It's a perfectly feasible explanation, considering recent events," Nick said, shaken himself. "And we need never refer to what happened here ever again – if that's what you want."

She couldn't lie to him. "It's not what I want. It's what has to be," she said simply.

Philip wasn't concerned about her absence, except in the way her lateness might have disrupted his own plans. He had been invited to a gentlemen's club with several colleagues in St Austell that evening. As the name implied, it was a meeting-place for men only, he informed Skye grandly, so there was no need for her to tart herself up.

It was said so arrogantly that Skye felt herself siding vigorously with her daughter Celia's currently expressed views that all males were 'pigs' . . . whether they were a chief hog, like Theo, or a piglet in the making, like his offspring, Sebby. The thought, more attributable to her daughter than herself, didn't even amuse her.

But it had been such an exhausting day for her that she was mightily relieved that Philip was going out; that she could have an hour with her children before she put them to bed; and then unwind after supper by taking a glass – or two – of wine with her father. She didn't need Philip's company.

"So what was the council's final decision?" Philip asked, when he emerged from their bedroom, spruce and elegant in his dark evening attire.

It was said as such an afterthought that Skye had to jolt her mind back to what he referred to, and then it came back to her with a rush. How *could* she have forgotten, even for a moment!

"Dr Rainley's looking out a suitable residence for Uncle Albie," she said delicately. "There's no question of him ever returning to live alone. Once it's all arranged, the studio will have to be disposed of, and actually, I've had an idea about that—"

"Tell me another time. I'm late, but I'm sure your father will be interested."

He went off without kissing her goodbye or showing the slightest interest in what her idea might be. He just didn't care any more, she thought sadly. And what was more, neither did she.

But far from comforting her that at least they seemed to be growing away from one another at the same drifting tempo, it alarmed and upset her. Theirs had been such a wonderful, ecstatic marriage, and she could see it all crumbling away like sand through her fingers.

Much later, when all three children were sleeping, and she and Cresswell had eaten supper and were sitting comfortably in the drawing-room with their glasses of wine, she broached her idea to him.

"It's only a thought as yet, but the kind of home best suited to Uncle Albie seems likely to be out of Cornwall. People will forget him – if they haven't done so already," she added, "and he was too important a local artist to let that happen. As a family, we owe him more than that."

"Go on," Cress said. "What do you have in mind?"

"I'd like to make enquiries about holding an exhibition of some of his paintings in Truro. There are dozens of them at the studio, portraits and landscapes and so on, and he deserves that recognition, don't you think?"

"Including portraits of your mother?" Cress asked.

"Well, some, of course," she said carefully. "Would that bother you, Dad?"

"It might, if I was going to be here to see them," he ventured. "So this seems a good time to tell you *my* idea. I'll be going home soon, darling. There's a ship leaving for New York in two weeks' time, and I intend to be on it."

She wanted to weep at his words, but she held herself together with an effort. It was his life, and he had always given her free rein with hers. It was her turn to let him go.

"I won't try to stop you Daddy," she said slowly. "It just seems as if I'm losing everybody at once. Sinclair, and Albie – and you." *And Philip*, she added silently.

"We never really lose the people we love, honey," he reassured her, and she knew he was thinking of Primmy right then. Primmy, the love of his life – and she was in New Jersey, where his heart would always be.

With true Cornish logic, Skye didn't think it in the least odd that she could think that way. She hesitated, but there was something else she knew she must say to him.

"Daddy, there are lots of portraits of Mom at the studio. You should choose whatever you want to take back with you."

To her huge relief, he shook his head. It was far too soon for her to think of going there, but she would have done, for her father's sake.

"I don't need any more reminders than the ones I've already got, and most of those are in my heart," he answered.

Then, before they got too maudlin and sentimental, he

said something surprising. Though, thinking about it later, it shouldn't have surprised her at all.

"Why don't you go and telephone Nicholas Pengelly and tell him what you've got in mind?"

"Why on earth should I do that?"

"Because I suspect that as your lawyer, he may want to be consulted over any exhibition plans, and he's the one person outside all of this who I'd trust to make sensible decisions with my daughter. I was very impressed with him."

Despite herself, she found her mouth curving into a slow smile, and it felt as though it was the first time it had happened in days.

"So was I," she said softly. "But I shouldn't call him at home at nine o'clock at night, should I?"

Without warning, her pulses throbbed as she said the words, and she averted her eyes from her father. She must be in the grip of some Indian summer madness, she thought in a panic, and it musn't happen. It *musn't*.

Her inner senses argued with her. What was so wrong with calling your own lawyer at night, to discuss with him an important idea? But she knew very well she wouldn't be calling Mr Slater in Bodmin at this hour, no matter what the reason.

"Go call him, Skye," she heard Cresswell say. "After what I've seen today, he seems to be the only one you have a rapport with right now."

"Except you," she said swiftly.

"But that's not the same."

She didn't question what he meant. She knew, just as he did. They had always had a special empathy with one another. All three of them, she thought: Cresswell, and Primmy, and Skye. Only Sinclair had seemed oddly out of touch with the thoughts and feelings that the other three shared. She swallowed, wishing she had learned to understand her brother more.

As she passed her father's chair she leaned over and kissed him, and for him the moment was filled with the summer-fresh scent that was essentially Skye and Primmy. His throat was thick as he watched her go to the hallway to the telephone, knowing he was pushing her towards her destiny.

*   *   *

"Nick, I'm sorry to call you at home," she told him, seconds after she had heard his professional answering manner. It changed at once when he recognised her voice.

"It's true then," he said enigmatically, his voice deeper and warmer than before, and making her heartbeats race.

"What is?" she asked inanely.

"That miracles do happen if you wish for them hard enough. And ever since we parted I've been wishing I could have held on to you a little longer."

She gave that small, nervous laugh again. "You shouldn't be talking to me like this . . ."

"Why not?" he spoke teasingly, humouring her. "You're in no danger from physical assault when you're at the end of a telephone."

No, it wasn't *physical*, thought Skye. But it was surely unethical, and far too intimate, and seductive . . . She realised she was leaning against the wall, standing on one leg, with her other foot wrapped around her ankle, the way she used to do as a child when something especially excited her. And when she looked in the mirror above the telephone table, her eyes were wide and lustrous and dreamy.

She turned away from her own image, knowing exactly what it was telling her. She unwound her foot from her other leg and spoke more severely.

"I should hope not, indeed. I'm actually calling you on a professional matter, but this was obviously a bad time—"

"No it wasn't. In fact, I probably willed you to call," he went on. "Being Cornish, I presume you believe in all that telepathy stuff?"

"I'm not Cornish."

"You are, where it counts."

She took a deep breath. This wasn't how this conversation was meant to be going at all, and she had to think very hard as to why she was calling him in the first place.

"I've had an idea, and I wanted your professional advice on the feasibility of it."

"Fire away."

"It's to do with my uncle's paintings. There are masses of

140

them at the studio, and something will have to be done with them. But oh Lord, I feel dreadful discussing this as if he's already dead."

"Any lawyer would tell you it's sensible and practical. So go on," prompted Nick.

"Well, I suppose the family should have their choice of the paintings eventually, but before all that happens I was wondering about staging an exhibition in Truro where he's well known. What do you think?"

"I think it's an excellent idea. Once all this residential business is concluded, we'll catalogue and price them all and then approach suitable premises."

"Oh, I was only asking for your opinion, Nick; you're far too busy to spend time doing all that."

She hadn't given a thought to the practical details of it all. Cataloguing and pricing, and premises . . . it had been just an idea, as ephemeral as the wind. Pricing them – and selling them? She hadn't thought that far ahead, but what else would they do with them? But she was suddenly nervous, realising what she was taking on.

"It will be my pleasure," he assured her, and she knew he wasn't merely talking about the work.

"Then we'll talk about it again at a more suitable time. Goodnight, and thank you," she said quickly.

"Goodnight, my love," he answered, and she slammed the receiver down, her hands shaking. She wasn't his love, and he had no right to use those words to her.

But after Philip came home very late, and went stumbling into another bedroom so that he wouldn't disturb her, it was Nick Pengelly who filled her dreams. And while she could resist her acknowledgement of feelings and emotions, she couldn't control the sweet eroticism of her dreams.

Ten

Theo faced an angry barrage of clayworkers the moment he stepped out of his motor car at Clay One. He felt his skin bristle, knowing they would have seen him coming up the hill towards Killigrew Clay, and had quickly gathered into a formidable mob.

He also knew what it was all about, of course. It was the influx of the small group of German workers. But he was the boss, damn their no-good eyes, and it was his decision who he had working for him, and it had seemed a good idea at the time when Hans Kauffmann had proposed it. He had dismissed querying Skye about the decision with as much indifference as brushing away a cobweb.

"What's all this, then?" he bellowed now, as he saw the mob of clayworkers moving towards him like a surging tide. "If you buggers ain't got enough work to do, and can stand about idling, I'll have to be docking your wage packets."

"We ain't idling, Tremayne, and no fat-assed clay boss ever accused we of doing so," came a mutinous yell from the back of the crowd, echoed by the rest.

He couldn't see who had begun the uproar, and the others wouldn't be telling. He scowled, feeling his blood boil. They were bloody sheep, the lot of them. They were paid to do a day's work for a day's pay, and there was an end to it in his opinion. He couldn't be doing with strikes and minor complaints, and that should all be left to the pit captain to sort out. Where *was* the bugger?

He saw the hard-hatted man come out of his little hut, hurriedly stubbing out a cigarette and waving the smoke away, and his face darkened even more. When his father, Walter, had been in charge here, no pit captain would have been tardy in coming to meet the boss. He'd have bet it never happened in old Hal Tremayne's day, either. Things had got sloppy, and it was high time that changed.

"What's going on here, Yardley? Can't you control these buggers no more? It's what I pay you for."

"What's going *on*, Mr Tremayne, sir, is summat you should've seen coming a while back," the older man said insolently, standing his ground. "In case you'm too blind to see what's under your nose, and want it explaining, they'm objecting to the new workers you've put among 'em, and insisting they'm sent back where they belong. Mr Walter would never have stood for the insult, and he'd have listened to his clayers. He'd not have spent his time in other pursuits. He'd have seen what was happening here and put a quick stop to it afore it all got out of hand."

Tom wasn't normally given to making long speeches, but he'd be damned if he'd be spoken to like this in front of the men by any blustering womaniser, boss or no boss. The inference didn't go unnoticed by any of them, and Theo's eyes narrowed as the men muttered noisily among themselves now, and one or two of them sniggered and made crude gestures. Tom Yardley was old enough to be slung on the scrap heap, Theo thought furiously, and he'd be there fast enough if he didn't mind his words. Especially in front of the clayers.

He saw his pit captain fold his arms and stare him out, too old and dour to fear this young whippet, and Theo cursed the day he'd kept him on out of loyalty after Walter died.

"Leave my father out of it," he snapped. "You'll get back to work, the lot of you, and stop all this bloody nonsense. And I can promise you there'll be no bonuses at the end of the year unless you do."

"There's more at stake than your pittances, Tremayne," bawled one of the clayers. "My boy was killed by one o' these German bastards, and so was my sister's boy, *and* his brother too. And I ain't working alongside no child killers."

Trying to make himself heard amid the roars of assent, Theo yelled back. "These here boys weren't responsible for what happened to your family, any more than you were, you snivelling toerags. The war took sons and brothers on both sides, and I dare say some of these would have similar tales to tell 'ee, given half a chance."

But he had to grit his teeth as he spoke, since he wasn't normally so magnanimous. Truth to tell, it mattered little to him who did the work, as long as it was done. But the clayers clearly saw his words as more than an insult to their families' memories. It was an incitement to riot, and the next minute he felt a stinging blow to the side of his face as a stone was flung at him from the back of the mob, and then another.

He felt the hot trickle of blood run down his cheek, and with it came the red rage of a maddened bull. "You bloody lunatics," he screamed, losing all sense of dignity now. "I'll sack the lot of you, and then where will you be? Go and ask your womenfolk how they'll enjoy being turned out of their cottages and left to scratch for food to put in your babbies' bellies."

He dabbed a white handkerchief to his cheek to stem the blood, and after his tirade he saw Tom Yardley pushing his way forward, his face shocked and his arms outstretched to the crowd now as if to ward off any further attack on the boss. Strikes were one thing, but physical assault was ugly, and he was of the old school that didn't permit such acts towards your superiors, however much you disagreed with them.

"Think about what Mr Tremayne says, men," he shouted. "You'll lose your homes as well as your livelihood if you threaten him wi' strike action. We all know you've got grievances, but this ain't the way to deal with 'em."

Bloody turncoat, Theo thought savagely. Even though Yardley was starting to placate them by his common sense, he knew the reason for it was because Tom knew which side his bread was buttered. It didn't make Theo warm to the bugger.

"You'd best keep the foreign muckers away from us, then," came the final united roar from the clayers. "The minute they get any plum jobs, we're out, and see how your bloody export orders get along then, wi' no clay for your friggin' pots."

Theo strode through them, hustling them aside like Moses parting the Red Sea. He walked stiffly over to the edge of the clay pool, where the sullen group of German boys had been listening and brooding on all that was going on.

"We have done nothing to provoke them, sir," one of them burst out at once, his grammatical English excruciatingly and infuriatingly correct to Theo's ears. "It is not right for us to be blamed for the sins of our fathers. It is not honourable, nor charitable, nor civilised."

Christ, give me patience, thought Theo. The way they spoke made him feel as though he was dealing with a bunch of saints, and he'd wished more than once that he'd never agreed with Kauffmann's bright idea of inviting them to Cornwall. But he was buggered if he was welshing on it now. Especially with the tales of anarchy these turds would have to tell.

"Just keep out of their reach as much as possible," he snarled. "Their memories are long, and that's something that ain't going to change, no matter what we do. But to calm things down a mite, I'm sending a pair of you to work in the packing shed at the pottery. We need to get the orders off to Kauffmann's pretty damn soon now. Who's volunteering?"

All six of them stepped forward at once, and he gave a grim nod. It told him more than words what the atmosphere had been like these last few weeks. The sooner this export order was finished, the better, and in future he'd have no more infiltration of the enemy.

God damn it, he raged, as the word slid into his head, *Even I'm thinking in those terms now . . .*

"You, and you," he pointed to the nearest two. "Report to Adam Pengelly tomorrow morning. And the rest of you, for God's sake try to merge into the background as much as possible."

"But why should such a thing be necessary?" The spokesman was clearly the leader of the pack and ready to argue, his eyes flashing with self-righteous anger. "We are not here to do penance, and we do our work well, do we not?"

"Look – Gunter, isn't it?" Theo said. "If you know what's best for you, you'll just keep out of trouble. Make friends with the younger ones. They have no axe to grind."

"What is this axe that you speak of?" the boy said, his brows drawn together with deep suspicion.

Theo gave a raucous laugh. "It's nothing. Just an English expression, that's all. I've got no more time to stand about exchanging pleasantries, and neither have you. Time means money, so I suggest you get back to earning it."

He strode back to his car, thankful to be away from the clayworks and to get back to Truro. *Bastards*, the lot of them, he thought, his cheek stinging more than ever now. He needed somebody to soothe his jangling nerves, and he couldn't stand the thought of Betsy fussing and farting around him. At the last minute he swung his car away from the direction of home, and went to find comfort elsewhere.

Skye's second hospital visit to Albie was as futile as the first. He either didn't know her, or didn't want to. In any case, he simply lay on the bed and stared at the ceiling for the entire time she was there. His eyes were as blank as if someone had turned out the lights.

She knew it would be due to the sedative drugs they were giving him, but it was so awful to see him like this. So lacking in spirit, when that had never been attributable to him! In the end, she found it impossible to sit beside this silent shell of a man any longer, and she went in search of Dr Rainley to ask what progress had been made.

"None, as far as his health is concerned, Mrs Norwood," he said candidly. "The situation is still the same, and is unlikely to alter. But I do have some news for you. There are two places available to Mr Tremayne. One is in north Wales, and the other is in Bristol. I would recommend the Bristol one, since the facilities there are far superior to the other. It's vastly more expensive, of course—"

"That is of no importance. As long as it's the best."

"The very best. I'll give you a brochure to take away, if you wish to consult your family about it," he added.

"Has anyone else been to see him?"

His eyes were guarded as he replied in the negative. But he needn't have worried. It was just as she had expected. Albert

Tremayne was a forgotten man already, and Skye was sickened by the family's lack of concern. There used to be such a strong feeling of kinship among the Tremaynes, but over the years it had simply disappeared.

Morwen had been the pivot of them all, with the ability to hold them all together during her long lifetime, Skye thought, but after her death, nothing was ever the same again. And *she* certainly didn't have that same strength. As she thought it, her self-confidence began badly slipping. How could she ever have believed she was the epitome of her grandmother?

"Was there anything else, Mrs Norwood?" she heard the doctor say. "I do have other patients to see."

"I'm sorry, I'm taking up too much of your time," she said quickly, pushing aside the momentary misery that had swept over her. "Thank you for the brochure, and I'll let you have my opinion soon. I presume it will be in order that we inspect the place before the final decision is made?"

"Oh, naturally. I would heartily recommend that you do. It will be Mr Tremayne's home for the rest of his days, after all," he said delicately.

Skye left the hospital gladly. The unavoidable smell of the overpowering disinfectant that was meant to disguise the far more degrading mixture of human smells, was almost as nauseating. It added to her already jittery feeling, reminding her as it always did of the French hospital where she had been stationed during the war. When she had followed Philip with all the urgency and passion of a woman following her man, no matter where . . .

As she went out into the clean fresh air of the hospital grounds, she forced herself to remember other memories of those years too. Good times, not just the bad.

Times when she and Philip had managed to spend secret hours together, when no one knew they were husband and wife, and where such meetings were so few and far between, and so intensely precious, because they never knew whether each one would be the last.

She caught her breath in a painful sigh, and told herself not to waste time dwelling on the past, when there was a man's future to be arranged.

She went straight to see Charlotte before going to Killigrew House to consult Theo. She knew that Em would go along with whatever was decided. But she could have anticipated the outcome of her visits after they had scrutinised the brochure the doctor had given her.

"It looks perfectly fine," Charlotte said. "You have my blessing to go ahead with it, Skye."

Not, *Yes, let's go see it together before we decide.*

And Theo too. "Do what you like. He was always more partial to you and your mother than the rest of us, so I don't know why you want to bother me with it. Let's get down to more important matters. Two of the German boys will be reporting to White Rivers tomorrow morning, so I trust there'll be no trouble on that score."

He couldn't keep his mind on Albie for more than an instant, Skye raged to her father later that evening.

"You're wasting energy thinking you'll ever change him, honey," Cress said mildly. "Go see this place in Bristol, and if you're happy with it, then there's an end of it."

"Come with me," she pleaded. "I know Philip won't. He hates travelling anywhere farther than Truro these days."

Her husband was becoming an old man long before his time, Skye thought sadly. Spending his time with old men, and not wanting to play with his children more than he had to. As for her . . . she realised that her father was answering her seriously.

"By the time the arrangements are made, I'll be on my way home, darling. I think you should ask one of your lawyers to accompany you. They'll have a stake in it too, remember."

"Why should they?"

"They'll be dealing with Albie's estate, and will need to ensure that it's financially viable. A lawyer can assess things more independently than someone as highly involved as yourself. What's wrong with asking Pengelly to go with you?"

"I think you know," she said slowly.

"And I think I can trust my daughter to know what's right," Cress replied.

Oh, really? Sometimes she wondered if he knew her at all. Or if anyone in the world really knew anyone else. Because the thoughts that were spinning around in her head at the prospect of going to Bristol in Nick Pengelly's company were anything but *right*, in the way he meant it . . .

"Mr Slater might agree to come with me," she pretended to muse, while knowing that wild horses wouldn't get her to travel anywhere with that boringly pedantic elderly gent.

Cresswell laughed, reading her mind. "And I'm damn sure there's no way you'll consider asking him!"

"Well, I'm not asking anyone for the moment," she said crossly. "There's no great rush, and I just want to enjoy our last days together, Daddy. If they *have* to be our last days."

"I'm afraid they do," he said, and she knew, as she had always known, that he would never change his mind.

But once his visit had finally come to an end, it was time to bid him an emotional farewell on the quay at Falmouth, and she tried hard to hold back her own tears and comfort her daughters, who were bereft now at losing their grandfather.

Oliver had been left at home, too young to understand the implications of the parting. And Philip had had obligations at college for which Skye had been guiltily thankful. This day belonged to themselves, to Cresswell and his daughter, and her daughters, and Skye found a simplistic beauty in the threads of family continuity.

"Will Grandad ever come back again?" Celia wept, more open with her emotions now than when he had arrived.

"I don't know, honey," Skye said, unable to fob her off with half-truths. "But when you grow up you might go to America to see him, and to see my old home."

"That's what I'll do then," she announced, always quick to see other possibilities coming out of adversity.

"So will I," Wenna sobbed in a small voice.

They sniffed and snuffled all the way back to New World. Skye toyed with the idea of taking them somewhere, maybe to see their cousins, but she quickly resisted that idea. Sebby and Justin would make such fun of the girls' puffy red eyes, and she couldn't bear to sit and make small talk with Betsy. No, home was the only place to be, to try to regain some sort of normality.

Once the girls were settled with biscuits and milk and telling Oliver and his nanny all about the ship that was taking their grandfather to America, and of their own plans to go there one day, she knew they were quickly recovering.

They were the lucky ones, thought Skye, wishing that she too was six years old, with all the resilience of childhood . . . She went into her father's bedroom and stood quite still for a moment. The room had already been efficiently cleaned before their return home from Falmouth, but Skye could still sense his presence.

She opened the lid of the little writing bureau where he had often sat in the evening recording everything that had happened that day, and her heart leapt as she saw the envelope addressed to herself. She opened it quickly, sitting on the bed, and hearing his voice in her head as she read the words he had written to her.

'Darling Skye,
    These weeks with you have been wonderful, but we both know this may well be the last time we ever see each other. Don't be sad about that. You made your choice to live in Cornwall many years ago, and you went with our blessing.
    I'll miss you and your beautiful daughters and sweet baby Oliver, but now it's my choice to be back with my Primmy. If you'll take a bit of fatherly advice, then live your life to the full, the way we did. And if there's a telephone call this evening, smile when you answer.
    Always your loving Daddy.'

Her eyes were damp when she finished reading. It was so like him to know that she'd be wandering through his bedroom, breathing in the lingering traces of him. So like him to leave this little reminder – and a telephone call this evening as well? Were there such facilities from ship to shore? With the magic of modern machinery these days, she supposed there was, though she had never thought about it before. But it would be his way of still keeping contact, of not losing her too completely, too soon . . .

The children were safely in bed by the time the telephone rang much later that evening, and she rushed to answer it, elated that he had kept his word.

"I've been going crazy, waiting for your call," she said joyfully, smiling into the receiver as he had instructed. "And this is just *darling* of you!"

"Well, that's the most spectacular reaction I've ever had to a telephone call," said Nick Pengelly's warm voice. "Your father gave you my message then?"

Skye stared at the wall stupidly, unable to get her thoughts together for a moment. And then it all became clear. The letter had said nothing about *Cresswell* phoning her. It had just told her to expect a call, and to smile when she answered it. And she had done that, and more, smiling like a Cheshire cat and saying it was just *darling* of him to call . . .

"Skye? Are you still there? You do know who this is, don't you? It's Nick."

"I know who you are, *now*," she said in a brittle voice. "I thought it was going to be my father, calling from the ship. I don't normally answer the phone in that ridiculous way."

And now she felt more like crying. Nick Pengelly's charisma was as exciting as chalk for all that it hit her at that moment. She didn't want him. She wanted to hear her father's voice one more time, as she had expected. But she swallowed her disappointment, her quicksilver thoughts rushing ahead. Nick must be calling for a reason. And what's more, her father must have known of it. Or planned it. Suspicion was suddenly high in her mind.

"Are you all right?" he said, almost more gentle now than she could bear. "This day will have been an ordeal for you."

"Yes. But life goes on, doesn't it? And I cut the apron strings years ago." She groaned, listening to herself talking in cliches, in banalities that had nothing at all to do with the misery in her heart. Making her sound as shallow as any flapper who ever danced the night away without a care for tomorrow . . .

"I'd like you to meet me at my chambers in Bodmin tomorrow afternoon, Skye. There are things I need to discuss with you regarding your uncle's future. I can give you an appointment at three o'clock if that suits you."

For a second, she marvelled that this businesslike voice she heard now could belong to the same man who had clasped her in his arms and kissed her so passionately.

But of course it could. She knew full well how people put on different faces and voices for different occasions. She did it herself. Everyone did. It was a useful defence mechanism, and after a momentary silence she replied in the same business-like way.

"That will be quite convenient," she confirmed.

"Then I'll see you tomorrow. Goodnight," he said, his voice perceptibly softening.

Skye replaced the receiver carefully without answering. The acute disappointment that it hadn't been her father on the phone was receding now, and she was becoming curious about why Nick should want to see her officially at his chambers.

"Who was it?" Philip enquired, barely looking up from his book as she returned to the drawing-room.

"The lawyer. Wanting to see me in Bodmin tomorrow," she said. "Something else to do with Uncle Albie, I expect."

She didn't elaborate that it wasn't Slater who called, and he didn't ask.

Nick's secretary brought them both a cup of tea as she sat opposite him in the wood-panelled chambers she remembered of old. Her heart was thudding, finding as always any command to be here as unwelcome as a visit to a doctor's surgery to hear bad news. It was ridiculous, but it never failed. And why were all lawyers' premises so predictably identical? she found herself wondering. The dusty, book-lined rooms were always the same: the desks were always solid, suggesting honesty and efficiency; the pictures on the walls were of ancient, previous partners who

152

had gone to that happy lawyers' hunting ground in the sky . . .
it was only the present incumbents who ever changed, and some
of those were as dry and dusty as their predecessors.

Skye looked into Nick Pengelly's eyes, and knew that such
a comparison could never be applied to him.

"So why have you brought me here?" she asked, taking a
nervous sip of tea.

"You make it sound more like a royal command than a
request," he said with a smile.

"Wasn't it?"

He opened a drawer and drew out an identical brochure to
the one Dr Rainley had given her. The words 'The Laurels,
Exclusive Residential Rest and Care', shrieked out at her,
and she had to admit that it looked a truly lovely place. It
was beautifully situated on the hills they called the Downs –
which seemed such a contradiction in terms – and it overlooked
Bristol's River Avon and the splendid structure of Brunel's
Clifton Suspension Bridge.

"What did you think of it?" Nick said, pushing it towards her
across the desk. "I presume you've had time to study it, and to
discuss it with your father before he left."

"And my husband," she said deliberately.

But she avoided his eyes, remembering that Philip hadn't
shown the slightest interest in the brochure. Just as long as
Albert Tremayne didn't become *his* responsibility . . .

"You'll want to see the place, to assure yourself that your
uncle will have every care," Nick went on. "Will your husband
accompany you? Or any of your relatives?"

For a moment she wanted to shout angrily "Why me?" Why
shouldn't one of the older relatives, who had known Albie far
longer than she had, inspect the place where he would live out
his life? But she knew the answer. None of them really gave a
damn for his welfare, and as long as she was willing to do it
. . . But the thought made her feel unutterably sad, because it
was so terrible for a man to have no one left in the world who
really cared about him. . . .

"Of course I intend to view the place, with or without anyone
else," she said, as if there had been any doubt. "I'll ask Dr

Rainley to make the necessary arrangements, and to find out details about the train journey."

"Would you allow me to do that, and to accompany you? I want to see my ex-partner in Bristol on a business matter, and as your lawyer I have an interest in seeing that The Laurels is suitable. Mr Slater has approved the idea."

Skye kept her eyes fixed on the brochure. So they had already discussed it, had they? What a nerve lawyers had! Anyway, she was perfectly sure that Nick Pengelly had no need whatsoever to view The Laurels. It was just a contrivance for them to spend time together. She had checked on the distance between here and Bristol. They would need to stay in the city for at least one night. It was a dangerous thought. And Philip would never agree to it.

She remembered his indignant reaction at having to look after the children for the time she was in America. Yet, what difference had her absence really made to his life? It had continued in exactly the same way without her. As for more personal needs – they rarely made love any more, but she dismissed the thought from her mind. It wasn't the issue here.

And the children themselves – the girls had had their governess to keep them in order, and Oliver's nanny had been at hand at all times. The staff at New World had undoubtedly fussed over them, and seen that they didn't miss her too much . . . and here she was, worrying over Philip's reaction to being away for two days on a very good cause. She felt herself weakening by the minute. Thoughts whirled around in her head, knowing Nick wasn't giving her too much time to think.

"Dr Rainley advises that your uncle needs to be settled as soon as possible, Skye, so I suggest we go to Bristol at the end of next week. We can leave on Thursday morning and be back by Saturday night. You can leave all the arrangements to me."

She was angered by the way everyone seemed to be manipulating her movements. "You take too much on yourself, Nick! I haven't agreed to any of this yet. I'd certainly want to talk it over with my husband before I made any such decision. And as for staying two nights, I'm quite sure he wouldn't approve of that."

"My dear girl, I'm not suggesting an elopement, and we'll stay in a respectable hotel. Separate rooms, naturally," he drawled, making her feel as if she was acting like a frightened virgin in protesting so much. But she wasn't, and she knew how it felt to be so carried away by passion that nothing else in the world mattered. . . . And she knew how much he wanted her.

"As I said, I'll talk to Philip about it and let you know," she repeated, standing up and preparing to leave. "In any case, I'm not sure I should be away from home at this time. My cousin is stirring up trouble among the clayworkers at Killigrew Clay and it's spilling over into White Rivers."

Nick came around the front of the desk and caught at her hand. "Well, providing you're not actually thinking of digging the clay yourself, and turning a few pots with these fair hands, I suggest you leave it to the men to deal with. Theo Tremayne may be a hothead, but he's a businessman, and I'm sure Adam won't let him get away with anything."

"Men aren't necessarily the best people to deal with anything involving hot-tempered clashes," Skye retorted. He was standing far too close to her, and her senses were in danger of being overwhelmed all over again.

She could hear his secretary noisily tapping away on her typewriter in the little outer office. It was all too excitingly reminiscent of the hours she had spent in Philip's college rooms before they were married . . . dangerous, clandestine hours, with the risk of being discovered adding to the seductive thrill of it all . . .

"I must go," she gasped, wrenching her hand away from his, and knowing he was about to kiss her again. And he mustn't. He had his reputation to think of. And she had hers.

"If you think it's necessary, I suppose I have no objection," Philip said, when she had outlined Nick's suggestion in as offhand a manner as possible.

She felt unreasonably mad with him. He *should* object, loud and strong. He should offer to take her to Bristol himself, like any caring husband would.

"Don't you have any worries at all about my travelling all

that way and staying in hotel with another man?" she demanded, hoping to provoke him. Damn it, she *wanted* him to forbid it, to take the decision away from her.

He gave a short laugh. "Skye, the man's a lawyer. Lawyers and doctors are sacrosanct, aren't they? Not to say sexless, if you want a more common word for it. Delving into the dregs of humanity in their various ways as they do, I doubt that they have the time or inclination for dallying. I'm sure you'll be perfectly safe with the Pengelly man."

And you're the most short-sighted fool in the world, if you believe all that, thought Skye.

"So you think I should agree then."

"Of course. Anyway, I'd trust you to do nothing untoward, even if I didn't trust him. You're a wife and mother, and a sensible matron now, my dear."

She was incensed by his condescending words. She might be a wife and mother, but that didn't turn her into a drab. Her mirror told her exactly the opposite. She had inherited the Tremayne beauty and colouring, and her shape was still voluptuous enough to attract admiring glances wherever she went. It was only Philip who couldn't seem to see it any more.

She went straight to the telephone before she could change her mind, and called Nick at home.

"Please go ahead and make all the arrangements, and let me know the details." She didn't elaborate, knowing there was no need to do so.

"Right," he said briskly, allowing no emotion to colour his voice. "I'll contact Dr Rainley and The Laurels first thing tomorrow morning, and I'll be in touch as soon as everything's confirmed."

"Thank you."

Skye replaced the receiver, not wanting to prolong the conversation, and knowing that for good or ill, she was going to spend three days and two nights with the man she was growing far more attracted to than she had any right to be.

Eleven

For someone who was so content with her lot now, Vera was openly envious when she heard about Skye's forthcoming trip.

"What are you planning to take with you?"

"What do you mean? What should I be taking?" Skye said, not quite following her cousin's line of questioning.

"Well, clothes, of course. I've never been to Bristol, but it's a fashionable city, by all accounts."

"*Vera*, you know very well I'm going to view a rest and care home for Uncle Albie, not going there to fritter my time away. This isn't a pleasure trip."

Her cousin pulled a face. "Oh, I know all that, of course, and I'm sorry if I sounded uncaring. But neither Lily nor I had much time for creepy old Uncle Albie, if you must know. And you're not going to spend *all* your time looking around a musty old house, are you?" She gave a mischievous grin. "I envy you Nick's company too. Not that I'd exchange him with Adam, but Nick's going to be quite a catch for somebody. You'll both turn folks' heads."

"I doubt that such a thing has occurred to him, and it certainly hasn't to me!" Skye said dismissively, ignoring the quickening of her pulse at Vera's words.

"Oh Skye, sometimes I could shake you! You were always so spirited and daring, and the envy of us all. I don't know what's happened to you lately. You've become – well, I certainly wouldn't say matronly in appearance, but in outlook, just a *little*, darling. Truly."

Skye was startled as Vera echoed Philip's exact word, even if it wasn't in the same context. Or maybe it was. *Had* she

157

become matronly in her outlook? She certainly wasn't ready for that label yet, and if it were so, then she must rectify it immediately.

"So in order to redeem myself in your so worldly eyes, what clothes would you suggest I take for this pleasure trip that isn't a pleasure trip?" she demanded of Vera. She saw the other girl's eyes become dreamy.

"Well, I know it isn't a honeymoon . . ."

"For glory's sake, it's anything but *that*!"

Vera's face went a violent pink. "Oh Lord, you know I didn't mean that at all. But I dare say you'll be staying in a swanky hotel, where folk dress up for dinner and suchlike," she said, the words tumbling out in an embarrassed rush. "You and Nick are both so elegant, and you'll make quite a dash in the dining-room, so you *must* take a couple of special outfits, like the one you wore to my wedding."

As Vera paused for breath, a swift memory of Nick Pengelly's eyes widening as they met hers in the church, soared into Skye's mind. That scintillating instant when she knew that for good or ill, here was someone special. . . . She abandoned the thought angrily.

"That outfit would be far too grand."

"No it wouldn't," Vera insisted. "You looked so beautiful in that colour, Skye, no matter what my mother said."

"You mean about green being unlucky?" Skye said, starting to smile. "I don't believe any of that nonsense, anyway."

"Then take it with you. Have you worn it since?"

She hadn't. There hadn't been a suitable occasion – and this certainly wasn't it. She wasn't going to Bristol to make a poppy-show of herself, nor to impress Nick Pengelly, she thought defiantly.

But when the appointed day arrived, both the shimmering shot silk outfit, and her favourite bronze silk evening frock, were placed carefully inside folds of tissue paper in Skye's small suitcase. It was only for the reason Vera had implied, she told herself. She wouldn't want to let Nick down in any fashionable establishment by appearing the country bumpkin.

She couldn't deny, though, that she was nervous, and the

further the train took them on the long journey away from Cornwall, the more she asked herself just how wise she had been to agree to this. To her relief, Nick's attitude during those long hours of travelling was businesslike and professional, and it was only as they neared their destination that he smiled with any real warmth.

"Do you know you've hardly said a word for the last half an hour or so?" he remarked.

"I'm sorry. I've been admiring the changing countryside, and also feeling a little sad at how far away from home Uncle Albie will be. I didn't mean to be rude."

"You weren't. Anyway, I doubt that Albert will be too bothered where he is, so don't look so edgy. I'm not going to eat you, Skye, so please try to relax."

She felt her face go hot. "Do I seem so much of a country hick to you? If you understand what I mean?"

He laughed. "Of course I do, and I'm fascinated by your transatlantic vocabulary. Don't ever lose it. And no one could ever take you for anything but a beautiful and sophisticated woman. William will love you."

She stared at him suspiciously, knowing he referred to his ex-partner. "I'm hardly likely to meet him, am I? I assumed that while you had your meeting with him, I would take a look around the city by myself."

"Oh, did I forget to mention that he's arranged a small dinner party on Friday evening, and that we're invited?"

"You certainly did forget to mention it! How long has this been planned?"

It was ludicrous to feel angry and upset, though it wasn't simply on account of being invited to a dinner party. She wasn't exactly a recluse, and would normally look forward to it immensely. It was the fact that she was being manoeuvred again, and that he was doing the manoeuvring.

"Why don't you trust me, Skye?" Nick said at last, ignoring her question, and reaching out his hand to cover hers for a moment.

She looked at him helplessly. He must know the answer to that. He must know she was dangerously close to falling in love with him, or could be, if she once let herself forget that she was a married woman with three children. A wife and a mother and a *matron*, for God's sake. . . . As the word filled her head she tilted her chin up high. Did she have a mind of her own, or not! It was up to her whether or not she let this man come within one breath of her senses . . .

"Of course I trust you," she said. "You're my lawyer, aren't you? With a reputation to protect."

"Touché," he said softly, and then the train was steaming into Bristol's Temple Meads station, and there was no more time for talking in the general mêlée of alighting and hailing a taxicab outside the grand edifice of one of Brunel's engineering masterpieces.

"The Georgian Hotel," Nick told the taxi driver who was already putting their suitcases inside the boot of the car. And within minutes they had left the railway station and were merging into the hustle and bustle of the city's trams and motor cars and drays, and there was no turning back.

Skye couldn't have said why that particular phrase entered her head, but once it had, in an odd way she found it easier to relax than at any time during the day. There was little point in doing otherwise now.

So she was here with Nick. They were staying for two nights, and they would oversee the home where Uncle Albie would live out his days. And tomorrow evening there would be a dinner party, and in her suitcase was the glittering shot silk ensemble that Nick had so admired at Vera and Adam's wedding.

Even then, all her womanly instincts had told her it was far more than mere admiration. His eyes had told her how beautiful and desirable she was to him, just as his words had told her since then. And despite all her misgivings, the tingling excitement filling her veins now was something she hadn't felt in a very long time.

Her own fatalistic thoughts filled her head once more. There was indeed no turning back now. Primmy and Morwen would have echoed the sentiments. Tremayne women believed in fate.

Skye looked away from Nick before he could read what was

in her heart. She tried to concentrate on what she could see of the city, knowing the children would want to hear all about it when she returned home. She was enchanted by it already, so vibrant and alive, from its bustling heart around the river, where tall ships still vied for position with busy little river tugs, to the soaring green Downs above.

She knew this had always been an important seafaring port, from the days of the infamous slave trade to the commercial exports of the day. But what made her draw in her breath was the sight of the beautiful, slender span of the Clifton Suspension Bridge, the second of Brunel's great Bristol marvels.

"I never imagined it would be like this! It's so exciting a city, and yet in a way so terribly sad."

"Sad?" Nick said, not understanding.

"For Uncle Albie," she replied, more soberly. "He would have loved to paint all this, and now he'll appreciate none of it."

"But if it wasn't for his state of health he wouldn't be here at all. You can't have it all, darling. None of us can."

She wouldn't comment at his endearment. Nor the unbidden thought that entered her head that they couldn't have it all either. They could only have these few precious days that would be as fragile in the great scheme of their lives as a loose leaf torn out of a book.

"The Georgian Hotel's just ahead of us now, sir." The broadly spoken driver swivelled his head back towards them, his gaze fully approving of the goddess-like vision in his taxicab. "If you and your lady wife will go along inside, I'll bring in the bags for 'ee both."

Nick's hand on her arm prevented Skye from making the light observation that she wasn't his lady wife. What did it matter what he thought? They would never see him again.

She looked instead at the impressive hotel where the cab was drawing up. It was grand all right, and Vera had been quite right to advise her to take suitable attire. And at last she accepted how lovely it would be to dress up in her finery and enjoy herself for a few days, with no cares on her mind of the clayworks or the pottery; no worries about the children or of Philip's black moods. She could just be herself.

When Nick had registered for them both, a young lad in the hotel uniform of plain trousers, green striped waistcoat and matching striped pillbox hat, jumped to attention and carried their luggage up the curving staircase to the adjoining rooms on the second floor. A few minutes later, Nick tapped at Skye's door, and she flew to let him in.

"Is everything all right, my lady?" he enquired with a smile.

"It's very much all right! I even have my own bathroom – and have you seen the wonderful view from the window, Nick?"

He followed her across the room. The hotel was perched above the dizzying heights of the Avon Gorge, and far below them they could see the winding, sluggish waters of the river as the tide receded into the Bristol Channel.

"It's spectacular," he agreed. "And so are you."

"Please don't say such things," she replied quickly. "You promised."

"And when was paying a compliment to a lovely woman so very wrong?" As she felt his hands on her shoulders, she tensed slightly, but he didn't move away. "Your husband should be proud of a wife who can cope with whatever life throws at her, Skye. That's just one of the reasons why I think you're a very special woman."

She shouldn't ask. She *knew* she shouldn't ask. . . .

"One of the reasons? You mean there are others?"

He laughed, dropping his hands from her shoulders and turning away from her. "Plenty, but you're not going to tempt me into saying them now, or it will take for ever. I'll send down for some tea to be sent to both our rooms while we unpack, and then I intend to take a bath. I have my own bathroom too. It's one of the luxuries we pay for in this hotel. Later, we could take a short stroll around the Downs before we change for dinner this evening. How does that sound to you?"

"It sounds perfect," she said, half relieved that she was going to have some time alone, half annoyed that he hadn't continued the provocative conversation she had begun. "And when are you going to see your ex-partner?"

"Tomorrow morning. If you wish, I'll order a taxicab to take you shopping or sightseeing. In the afternoon we'll visit The

Laurels, which is very near here, and once we've satisfied ourselves that it's the right place for your uncle, our business will be officially over. We can enjoy William's dinner party with a clear conscience."

She avoided his eyes, knowing that the feelings inside her involved anything but a clear conscience. They were alone together in a hotel – disregarding all the other guests – and once their business tomorrow was over, they were free to enjoy themselves. And before that, there was tonight . . .

Skye shivered as he left her. She had never intended to let these few days become a liaison, and nor had she ever betrayed Philip – except in her thoughts and dreams, her guilty conscience reminded her. But the thought that occurred to her more and more often was, *would Philip even care*? He was so wrapped up in himself and his students lately that she seemed no more than an appendage in his life. But she had a life too, and it had become singularly empty without the fulfilment of her husband's love. She was restless, frustrated, and probably a ready target for an unscrupulous man who intended to seduce her.

She flinched visibly, knowing she would never accuse Nick Pengelly of being such a man. Any seduction that occurred would be one of mutual desire and longing. . . . All her nerves were on edge again, and her hands were damp as she answered the door and let the maid inside with her tray of tea and biscuits.

"The gennulman in room 204 said he'd see 'ee in half an hour, ma'am, so would you like me to run 'ee a bath while you drink your tea?" the girl asked, her accent as broad as the taxi driver's.

"Yes please," Skye said quickly, glad to be diverted from her own wayward thoughts. A bath would be wonderful, to wash away the grime of travelling, and to get her thoughts properly organised again, and away from the dangerous direction they were leading her.

Later, to her relief, she discovered that Nick was decorum itself. She needn't have worried. As they strolled around the heady greenness of the Downs, high above the city, he tucked her hand inside the crook of his arm in a friendly, but not too familiar way. They might have been brother and sister . . . as Albert and Primmy had been . . .

They walked for a long time, while she admired the steep sides of the Avon Gorge, and the glimpse of the ships docked further along the river, so miniaturised from this height. On the opposite side of the Gorge from the Downs was a vast stretch of dense woodland, in stark contrast to the elegant buildings on the Bristol side.

As they turned away from the stomach-churning height and began to walk along one of the winding roads that circumvented the Downs, Nick pointed some distance ahead.

"You see that large building set well back from the road?" he said. "That's The Laurels."

"What!" Skye exclaimed. "I imagined we'd have to travel some distance."

"Not at all. It seemed a good idea to stay in a hotel within walking distance, and my ex-partner recommended the Georgian as being very comfortable. This part of the city is an acknowledged healthy area, well away from the industrial heart and the stench of the river – which I'm told can get pretty strong in the summer."

She wondered if he was saying all this to calm her. They were so close to Uncle Albie's new home. They could go there now and be done with it all . . . they could go home tomorrow. . . . As if sensing her thoughts, his arm squeezed hers.

"It's too late to visit The Laurels today, Skye. The staff don't welcome visitors without appointments, and the place where a man will end his days deserves proper consideration, don't you think?"

"Of course I do." She wasn't sure if he meant to censure her, but she was mildly irritated by the words. *Of course* she would want to see that all was well. "Can we go back to the hotel now, please? I'm feeling chilled."

"I'm sorry. I'm not having much consideration now, am I?"

But she sensed that he was. He must know how jittery she was feeling, and not only about Uncle Albie. But she had also given him the impression that she was some feeble little female who couldn't walk ten steps without complaining . . . and for a woman who had once been in the thick of wartime hostilities in France, the idea was ludicrous.

"Thank God I've said something to make you smile – though I'm not sure what it was," she heard him say. "You've been very un-Skye-like for the past hour."

"Really?" She looked up at him defiantly. "I doubt that you have any idea what the real Skye is like!"

"But I'd like to, very much," he said softly, which made her instantly mute again, pursing her lips and turning away from his gaze. *Like a frightened virgin*; the phrase slid into her mind again.

For dinner that evening, she wore the bronze silk dress with her long bronze beads, and then fastened a beaded headband around her forehead. Philip had always disapproved of the fashion, saying it should be left to the Red Indians to adorn themselves in such a way, but she had always adored it. And Philip wasn't here . . .

"You look sensational," Nick told her, when they descended to the dining-room together. Apart from that one compliment, he was extremely civilised for the whole evening, and she couldn't fault him. But if it was the only verbal compliment, what she saw in his eyes and gestures said far more than words. She knew he wanted her, and she was fraught with nerves once more when they retired to their separate rooms, wondering how she would react, if . . .

"Goodnight, Skye. Sleep well," he said gravely, raising her hand to his lips as he left her at her door.

She went inside, almost slamming the door behind her, trembling, her knees shaking. And calling herself all kinds of a fool for the raging passion inside her. He was her lawyer, for God's sake. He would never compromise himself, certainly not in a public hotel. He respected her . . . and she almost wept with frustrated longing, knowing that she wanted him with all her heart. She felt utterly rejected – and disgusted with herself for her own stupidity.

She undressed quickly and climbed into the unfamiliar bed, burying her face in the pillow and trying to make her mind a complete blank. Anything, rather than imagine Nick Pengelly in the room next door . . . sleeping in a bed similar to hers, with only a wall separating them. For all that, it might as well have been an ocean.

Despite spending a restless night, by the following morning Skye felt more composed. They were going to visit The Laurels later, and that was the sole purpose of the afternoon. Meanwhile, while Nick went off to see his ex-partner, he had already arranged for a taxicab to take her around the city for a little sightseeing.

It was a pleasant way to spend a morning, she conceded, though eventually she dispensed with the driver's services and wandered through the little backstreets with their quaint, old-fashioned shop fronts that seemed as if they were of another age. She bought a few trinkets for the children from a Friday market stall, and found the taxi driver again at the appointed time and place to take her back to the hotel for a light lunch. By then she was more than thankful to sit down.

"Did you have an enjoyable morning?" Nick asked her.

"Very, thank you. And you?"

"Oh yes. William seems highly pleased with his new life here, and he's looking forward to meeting you."

They were behaving like strangers. And if it was because she was symbolically holding him at arm's length, it was because it had to be. They both knew that. By the time they set out for The Laurels that afternoon, she knew it was safer to keep things on a very cool footing between them.

"So what do you think?" he asked her at last, when the matron had tactfully left them alone after showing them over every inch of the place, including the sunny room that was available for Albert Tremayne, its windows looking out onto a wide expanse of the Downs. It was quite luxurious, but that very fact saddened Skye even more.

"I was going to say I think he'll be very happy here – but he won't, will he? He won't even know where he is."

"The important thing is that this is a specialist home, caring for people in your uncle's condition. And you'll always know that you did your very best for him."

She nodded slowly. She could almost hear her mother's unspoken approval in her head. Primmy would be glad her daughter had done her best for her beloved Albie.

"Then I think we should confirm it," she said unsteadily.

Nick reached out and squeezed her hand. "Good girl. We'll go and see about the paperwork and then it will be done."

He was as efficient as ever, while Skye felt as exhausted as if she had climbed a mountain. She was oddly disorientated, and for a few breathless moments she felt the strangest sensation, as if her mind was skimming backwards over the years in a life that wasn't entirely her own. Watching all those others in past times, as if she was seeing them through a moving camera . . . especially the womenfolk.

Skye had never known her great-grandmother Bess Tremayne, but she knew all about her. And Bess's stoical image was suddenly real, moving with her family from the poor cottage on the moors to the pit manager's house. Going up in the world.

Morwen was even more real. That wild and beautiful young girl, marrying the son of the boss, Ben Killigrew, and raising three children who weren't her own, including Primmy and Albert, then their own two. Then came Morwen's second marriage to Ran Wainwright, and the three chidren of that union. All of them strong, in their different ways. Primmy, Skye's mother, had been as wild and wilful as any of them in marrying her cousin Cresswell against all advice.

And Skye was just as strong as any or all of them, or so she had always believed herself to be . . .

"Drink this, my dear."

She heard the female voice close to her ear, and blinked hard. She never fainted . . . but she presumed that she must have fainted now. She did as she was told without thinking, and grimaced at the bitter taste of brandy. The arms holding her tightly belonged to Nick Pengelly, openly concerned as the matron of The Laurels took the glass from her lips.

"Are you feeling better?" he asked. "You had a momentary lapse of concentration."

If he was being kind in calling it thus, the matron was more adamant in suggesting that their resident doctor should take a look at the young lady.

"That won't be necessary," Skye said, struggling to regain her composure. "I'm perfectly all right, and it was simply a case of trying to cope with the fact that my uncle must come here. Not that I can fault it, Matron, and I know you will do your best for him," she added hastily.

"Naturally," the woman said.

Nick insisted that she sat still while he dealt with the paperwork that didn't need her signature, and by the time they left The Laurels, Skye had recovered. It was a *fait accompli* now, and Albert Tremayne would shortly begin to live out the rest of his life in this place.

"Thank goodness for this evening's little dinner party," Nick said as they made their way back across the Downs. "You need a bit of cheering up after that little ordeal."

She looked at him with active dislike, wondering how he could be so insensitive. He never even asked if she felt well enough to go out, nor had he questioned the reason for her strange mood at The Laurels. But when she looked into his eyes, she knew that he cared, and that this was his way of showing it right now. If he had acted any differently, she would probably have simply fallen apart.

But it had been more of a traumatic afternoon than Skye had anticipated. She felt as if she had literally signed Albert's life away. She had never wanted to feel responsible for him, but that choice had somehow been taken away from her. She was the only one – apart from Nick – who had cared enough to do this, but far from making her feel noble, or even resentful, it simply set her nerves on edge.

She was thankful to return to the hotel and take afternoon tea in the sunny lounge overlooking the Avon Gorge, and to start to feel like a normal person again.

"Better now?" Nick asked.

"Did I make an awful fool of myself in front of Matron?" she asked, feeling as gauche as a schoolgirl at asking the question.

Nick laughed gently. "Of course not. This has been an ordeal for you, Skye, but I hope that this evening will restore your usual spirits."

She dearly longed to say she had no wish at all to go to a dinner party in the company of strangers. That all she wanted was to go to her room and stay there until they could take the train back to Cornwall in the morning. But that would be churlish in the extreme after all Nick's kindness.

Later, wearing the beautiful ensemble she had worn at Vera's wedding, her own reflection did a great deal to revive those flagging spirits. Nick came to collect her for the evening, and she couldn't miss the admiration in his eyes as he stepped inside her room.

"I'm glad you wore this tonight," he said simply. "It reinforces the feelings I had, the first time I saw you."

"I'm sure I shouldn't ask what you mean by that," she murmured. "So I won't."

"Then I won't tell you," he said maddeningly. "But no Cornishwoman would deny the truth of love at first sight."

"But I'm not a born and bred Cornishwoman. I'm an American, and an ex-journalist," Skye said brutally. "And we don't pay so much attention to all that mushy stuff."

"No? Anyway, I didn't fall in love with you on my brother's wedding day."

"Didn't you?"

Whether he did or did not, why should she care, or believe his nonsense? He was only saying these things to keep her light-hearted after the tension of the day.

"I fell in love with an image of a woman more beautiful than anyone I had ever seen before. A portrait of a goddess that stayed in my mind and wouldn't give me any peace until I found her. And when I did, she was more beautiful than ever in a shimmering green outfit."

"Stop it, please Nick," Skye said quickly, aware that the teasing had stopped and that he was becoming far too serious for comfort.

He caught at her hands. "Can you deny that we've come full circle in a way, my darling girl? I saw your image first of all in your uncle's studio, and then I found you. Your uncle had more than a hand in our fate, whatever you might think. And now we've come here together to settle his future."

"But not *ours*," she said jerkily. "And it wasn't my portrait that you saw. It was my mother's. Everything you're saying is a sham. You can't love me – you musn't. I have a husband and children. I have a life that doesn't include you."

She knew she was pushing them oceans apart again. But that was the way it had to be, even if it broke her heart.

Nick turned abruptly, as if unable to bear seeing the truth of it in her eyes. It was time they left, anyway, and the cab he had ordered would be waiting for them. He was once more the cool-headed lawyer, so adept in switching off his emotions, while Skye's were still churning inside.

She tried to keep her emotions under control as the vehicle took them down to the centre of the city, and into a small side street where William Pierce had his double-fronted antique shop and living quarters above.

It was time to put on a social face; prepare to meet and talk with strangers, and to be what she was – Skye Norwood, wife and mother and matron, and nothing else. And then they were ushered inside a cosy living room, where a man and a slender, dark-haired girl rose to greet them.

"Come in, both of you," William said warmly. "So this is the beautiful lady I've heard so much about. I began to think you were a myth, from the way Nick has kept you hidden away all this time, Mrs Norwood, but now I see why!"

"Please call me Skye," she said, a little taken aback at such blatant flirting, and already wondering if there were to be any other guests besides themselves.

"Skye it is, then. This is my fiancée, Queenie, and tonight the four of us are going to celebrate our engagement. Quite a turn-up, wouldn't you say, Nick?"

"I certainly would, you old devil!" Nick exclaimed, clearly stunned by the announcement. "Why didn't you tell me this morning? I knew there was something you were keeping from me, but I never guessed it was this! And my apologies for seeming ungallant, Queenie, but this old rogue has been a confirmed bachelor for so long, I never thought any young lady would snare him."

"I think you should quit right there, Nick. You're putting your feet further and further into your mouth," Skye said, laughing with the other girl, who didn't seem to take any offence as she linked her arm in William's.

"Oh, it's perfectly all right," Queenie said. "Will and I expected raised eyebrows at our whirlwind engagement."

"And when is the wedding to be?" Nick said, clearly unable to think of anything else to say. It was the first time Skye had seen him nonplussed, and it pleased her to know he was human after all.

"Next summer. And you'll both be invited," Queenie said.

There was a small silence. How could they both be invited, in the way Queenie said it? They weren't a normal couple, even though this dinner party now seemed more like a romantic quartet than anything else. Skye accepted that Nick couldn't have known of it though. And once the intital awkwardness was past, she admitted too that the other two were nice people, and the evening was highly enjoyable.

She found herself wishing that she and Philip had such friends with whom to spend an evening, and realised, almost with a shock, that they did not. They had relatives, and he had his college chums, but apart from that, they hardly socialised at all.

For the first time in years, she also realised what she was missing from her busy working days at home in New Jersey. Those days were so long ago, and yet they suddenly surfaced in her mind, vividly and nostalgically, and she was shocked to think she had become so insular as to be almost anonymous. . . .

She pushed such ridiculous feelings aside, determined not to cloud the other couple's happiness. But for all her pleasure in sharing the social evening, she was glad to return to the hotel. When you were on the outside looking in, such obvious happiness was almost too much to bear. . . .

"Why so pensive, Skye?" Nick asked, as the taxicab took them back to The Georgian Hotel. "I hope you enjoyed the

evening as much as I did, though I must admit the engagement
was a big surprise to me."

"I enjoyed it very much. I liked William, and I thought
Queenie was charming. They'll make a good marriage."

"But?" he asked. He leaned towards her in the darkened
cab, and she could feel his breath on her cheek, warm and
wine-sweet.

"But nothing," she said steadily.

"Maybe you think the engagement happened too quickly?"

"It's no business of mine."

"You have a right to your opinion. After all, William's hardly
been in Bristol for five minutes, and here he is, his future
already settled while I'm still searching for mine."

"Are you?" She turned her head too quickly, and without
warning she felt his lips brush hers. She moved away at once,
remembering who she was, and where she was, and that there
was a third party in the vehicle with them.

She heard Nick give a soft laugh. "No. But it's my misfortune
that the lady doesn't feel the way I do."

She refused to rise to the bait, and was relieved when they
reached the hotel, and she didn't have to sit beside him in such
close proximity.

It was very late by now. Most of the other guests had retired
for the night long ago, and there was only a sleepy-eyed porter
on duty as they entered the foyer. He bade them goodnight, and
as they quietly climbed the stairs, Skye found herself imagining
that they were truant schoolchildren, sneaking in after hours . . .
but children they were not.

"We could be the only two people in the whole world," Nick
whispered, as if reading her mind as they reached the second
floor. "And I wish to God that we were, then I would never have
to let you go."

Skye caught her breath, aware that her heart was thudding,
and that her fingers on her door handle had been covered by
his.

"But we're not the only two people in the world, are we?" she
whispered back.

"We could be, just for tonight," Nick said, his arm reaching for her, and drawing her into him. "Just for this one night, my sweet darling Skye, we could be all that fate intended us to be to one another."

Her pulses were pounding so hard now that she could hardly breathe. He was so close, and so dear, and she wanted him so much . . . and had done so for so long. . . .

"Just for this one night." She repeated the words in a huskiness of sound, as if it was a litany. As if she was giving her consent, as she had always known she would. As if it had always been inevitable that they would become lovers. . . .

And then Nick was opening her door, and they moved inside the room as if they were one person, still holding one another, still clinging together as if they would never let each other go and this night was never going to end.

173

Twelve

Skye awoke slowly, her limbs relaxed and filled with a delicious feeling of lethargy. Dreamily, she wished she could lie here for ever. The day ahead was not wanted. She wasn't ready to face it yet, nor to fully come to her senses. She was in a sort of blissful never-never land, her eyes still closed, the bed a soft cocoon of warmth. . . . Then she felt the touch of someone's mouth covering hers, his body as close to hers as if it was a second skin. Her arms automatically wound around his neck . . . and her eyes inched open.

Memories flooded her mind in an instant. Wanton memories of a night that held the wonder of love and lust combined, of exquisitely intimate kisses and caresses that went far beyond those of tentative young lovers. . . . Of herself and her beloved passionately exploring one another, glorying in one another, hungering for each other, and of her need for him soaring to meet his for her in every respect. Without shame. Without guilt. With only love.

Were they truly memories, or part of a wild and erotic imagination? But she knew. Of course she knew. But she still needed to ask, to be reassured that this was love. . . .

"Nick." His name was no more than a breath of sound in her throat. "Tell me it really happened. Tell me it wasn't all a dream."

His answer was to gently pull the sheet from her naked body and kiss her breasts. She felt the sweet tug on her nipples, and there was an instant, answering flame of desire in the core of her. How could she ever doubt that this was what she wanted with all her heart for all of her life?

"If it was a dream, then we're still dreaming and I want to

go on loving you for ever and never have to wake up," he murmured against her willing flesh.

"Neither do I – but we know that we must," she whispered again as reality took over her consciousness. "We have to go back to being what we are. We can't escape our obligations."

But she couldn't yet allow her husband's name to enter her mind, nor her children's. She couldn't bring their vicarious presence into this room, or this bed, where she had experienced all the sweet seduction a man could give a woman. And where she had responded to all the love she had craved for all these months since first setting eyes on him.

Her mouth was dry, her eyes frightened, knowing at last the all-consuming power of love. And knowing too, that it couldn't be for ever, no matter how strong their desire for one another.

"The dream can continue a little longer, my love," Nick said softly. "It's still early, and we have a couple of hours yet before we have to put on our proper faces again."

Our proper faces . . . and what were they? The lawyer, and the part-owner of a pottery and clayworks. The so-respectable couple, whom no one, not even a husband, would suspect of having a clandestine affair . . .

Deliberately, knowing exactly what she was doing, Skye shut them all out. There was only here and now, and these last few hours of belonging that had to last a lifetime.

"I love you," she said with a catch in her voice, for she had only said those words to one man before him. "You know that, don't you? I will never be able to say it again after today, so I want you to be sure of it, and to always know it."

"I do know it. Just as you've always known of my love for you. Haven't you?"

"Yes," she whispered.

He folded her into him and she felt him hardening against her, and the blood flowed faster in her veins with an urgent need to be a part of him just once more. It was easy then, to simply stop thinking of anything beyond the pleasure his seeking hands and his mouth and his body were giving her.

It was as strange and nerve-racking a journey back to Cornwall as it had been in the opposite direction, but for very different reasons. With every mile the train covered, Skye knew that something precious and wonderful was ending. And thankfully for her peace of mind, Nick knew it too. She had been fearful for a while that this would turn into some hole-and-corner affair, and she didn't want that. Couldn't bear that. And, it seemed, neither could he. There was no question of their continuing what had so magically begun. It was not a rejection, simply an acceptance of what had to be.

He only spoke of it once, when their carriage was empty but for themselves, and they were nearing their destination.

"I won't try to contact you unless our business affairs demand it, Skye. But if you ever need me, you only have to call and I'll be there."

"Yes. It's best," she murmured, and even if her heart was breaking, she was deeply aware of the heritage of the Tremayne women. They loved passionately, but they never let their family down. They were strong when they had to be, and if ever Skye needed that inner strength, she needed it now.

Before the train drew into the station, Nick raised her hand to his lips as he had done so many times before. But now he turned her hand over to kiss the inside of her palm and symbolically closed the kiss inside. It was a sweetly intimate gesture, and her eyes filled with tears, her throat thick.

"So this is goodbye, my love," he said quietly. "We'll be obliged to see one another from time to time, but this is our real goodbye."

"I know." She wanted to say so much more, but the train was already scorching and grinding to a halt, and it was time to take down their luggage from the rack and return to their ordinary, everyday lives. It was suddenly an appalling prospect.

But even as she thought it, she glimpsed two small, excited faces through the train window, and her heart jolted.

Philip had brought Celia and Wenna to meet her, and her world was being turned the right way up once more. The girls looked so vital and alive, so excited to see her again . . . and Philip looked so stooped, so professorial, so *old*, compared with her virile young lover . . .

176

Swallowing hard, she turned to say something inane to Nick, but he was already holding out his hand to help her down, his eyes steady and understanding. Letting her go . . .

Within seconds, her children were rushing into her arms, and she was holding them and hugging them, and exclaiming how big they had grown, even in three days . . . and knowing that she had to forget that those three precious days had been as meaningful as an entire lifetime.

"It's good to have you back, my dear," Philip said formally, never one to show emotion or to embrace on public railway stations. "Did your mission go well?"

For a second she couldn't think what he meant, and then his words shocked her into remembering. How *could* she have forgotten, even for an instant, the reason for going to Bristol! If anything was calculated to fill her with guilt, that fact hit her very hard at that moment.

"Yes, it did," she said quickly. "I'll fill in all the details when we get home, Philip, but I can tell you I was pleased with all that I saw at The Laurels. It had everything Uncle Albie will need for his comfort."

"Good. Then we can leave the formalities to you and Dr Rainley now, I presume, Pengelly?" he said, bringing Nick into the conversation as an afterthought, and ready to dismiss the so-called mission from his mind once he was assured that he need not be involved in it.

"Of course. Though if you and Mrs Norwood wish to escort Mr Tremayne there when the time comes, I'm sure that could be arranged with the hospital," Nick replied coolly.

"Oh, I think not," Skye cut in at once. "I've done the preliminary investigations, and I think it's up to someone else in the family to do anything more."

If Philip thought she was showing some indignation for her family's unconcern at last, she was sure he wouldn't argue with that. But how could she bear to go to Bristol for a second time, especially with *Philip*, retracing her steps and letting her imagination take her into that hedonistic world of pleasure that belonged to her and Nick, and no one else. . . .

As the imagery of herself and her lover together swept into

her mind, she avoided both men's eyes, thinking herself a shameless woman to be having such thoughts. But Nick would understand her reasons for not wanting to go back to Bristol.

"Well, it's a damn good thing you're back," Philip said, after they had parted company from the lawyer. "There's been such a furore at the clayworks, and your hot-headed cousin's upset every apple cart as usual. He doesn't have your tact."

Skye wasn't aware that her forthright manner had ever involved much tact, but compared with Theo, she supposed anyone's would.

"What's happened now?" she asked sharply. "I dare say it's to do with the young German workers?"

Philip glanced back at his daughters, who were silent and clinging onto every word now. His voice was short.

"You've a knack of sensing things, my dear, that I don't, nor ever professed to have. It's all down to your Cornish blood, I suppose. Or so they say."

"Please tell me what's happened, Philip," she said again, annoyed at his patronising tone. But for once, she thanked God that he didn't have any kind of intuition, or he would surely sense her misery and loss at parting from Nick.

"Not yet. When we get home will be soon enough," he said, with insufferable patience. "We don't want little ears picking up gossip and passing it all around the county."

"Considering the children rarely leave the house and grounds except in our company, they would hardly do that. But first, tell me how Oliver is. Is he quite well?" she uttered in exasperation, knowing she would get no more out of him yet. She hated his habit of dangling a hint in front of her, and then refusing to tell her more until he was ready. She was also alarmed and distressed that they were already bickering, when they hadn't even reached home yet. Where had all the tenderness between them gone? she wondered again.

"Oliver's perfectly well. My dear girl, you've only been away for three days, not an eternity."

Skye stared stonily ahead, her mind in a turmoil, and refused to let her thoughts dwell on the irony of his words. It would be fatal to let everything he said twist a knife in her heart. She was glad when it became impossible for the little girls to keep quiet any longer, and they began clamouring to know all about Bristol. She forced herself to be informative.

"Well, it has a wonderful river flowing into the heart of it from the sea, and a high bridge spanning it. Lots of ships bring their goods for sale from faraway countries. There are splendid houses and hotels, and – and little markets where people can buy all kinds of things," she went on hurriedly as she felt her throat tighten.

"Did you buy us anything, Mommy? *Did* you?" Wenna squealed, and she laughed.

"Of course I did, honey, and you'll see what as soon as we get home and I unpack my things."

Giving them their gifts and assuring herself that Oliver truly wasn't sickening for anything was her first priority. Then she joined Philip in the drawing-room and demanded to know what had been happening that had caused Theo to upset the clayworkers again.

"You were right," Philip said curtly. "It's all to do with the German workers. Your cousin was a damn fool if he thought it was all going to go smoothly. But we all know he's got no more sense than a baboon, don't we?"

"Will you please *tell* me?" Skye said, ignoring his sneer.

"It's the usual story. It seems one of the German boys took a shine to the daughter of one of your clayworkers and has been seeing her on the quiet. Couldn't keep his hands off her, by all accounts."

"You mean he was courting her, I suppose?"

She tried to dignify his words, while her stomach churned uneasily at the implications. She knew the clayworkers. They wouldn't tolerate one of their own being violated, especially by those they still considered the enemy. It would be like setting a match to a tinderbox. But how long could this go on? she wondered despairingly.

Philip gave a coarse laugh. "I'd hardly call it courting. Most likely the wench threw herself at him. Common country girls always set their caps at any chap who's a bit different from the ordinary. And no lusty young fellow is going to refuse what's offered to him so willingly."

Skye was furious at his assumptions. His pompous, college lecturer's assumptions that took no account of two people falling in love, no matter how different their backgrounds or how impossible the match.

Like Morwen Tremayne and Ben Killigrew – the clayworker's daughter and the heir to Killigrew Clay. . . . Like her own mother, Primmy, and her adored cousin Cresswell . . . like herself, a married woman, and her family lawyer . . .

"Sometimes, Philip, you can be so short-sighted," she snapped, her nerves as taut as violin strings.

He looked at her, clearly affronted. "I don't know what's got into you this evening to be acting so vinegary. I fancy the trip to the big city has addled your brains if you can't see that we have a serious situation on our hands."

"Oh, *we* do, do *we*? And since when was it any of *your* business what goes on at Killigrew Clay?"

The moment she had said the words, she clapped her hands to her mouth in horror. No matter what went on outside, she had always thought of New World as a haven of calmness and peace. But she hadn't been back in the house an hour yet, and already they were spitting angry words at one another, and she was doing the very thing she had always vowed never to do: remind him that this was her house, and that Killigrew Clay was her business.

"You bitch!"

He was ugly and purple-faced now, the veins standing out like ropes on his forehead. "So we have the truth at last, do we? You've always resented every word I've ever said about your bloody clayworks, however much you tried to hide it, but now it's out. And from now on, you can stew in your own juice as far as I'm concerned. Your cousin's coming here tonight, and you can deal with him on your own."

"Where are you going? Philip, please don't do anything reckless," she almost screamed at him as he stormed towards the door.

"Why should you care?" He shouted back. "You obviously

don't want me here, so I shall go somewhere more congenial. And you can rest assured that I won't be disturbing you in your bed tonight, or any other night."

Skye shuddered at his words. After Nick, the last thing she wanted was to share a bed with her husband, but she knew her wifely duty, and she would have done anything to preserve the harmony of their marriage. Or rather, to regain it, since it was more often disharmony than anything else. But she hadn't wanted any of this to happen, and moments later she was aghast as she heard his car engine roar into life as he drove crazily away from New World. He missed Theo Tremayne's car by inches, and never even noticed.

"Your madman of a husband nearly ran me down," Theo yelled, the moment he entered the room, slamming the door behind him. "What the hell have you been saying to him?"

"Nothing. He's in one of his black moods as usual, and it's none of your business anyway," she shouted back, wondering if the whole world had gone berserk. The raised voices must have been heard all over the house, and she prayed that the servants had gone to their quarters for supper by now.

"It would have been somebody's goddamned business if he'd killed me," Theo roared. "But since he didn't, let's get on with what I came for. You've heard the news, I suppose?"

"Philip said something about a German boy and a clayer's daughter," she said delicately, annoying him even more.

"Oh ah, and I dare say he dressed it up wi' fancy college talk," Theo sneered. "To put it bluntly, cuz, that bloody young fool Gunter couldn't keep his breeding tackle inside his trousers where it belonged!"

Skye gasped, and not just at Theo's coarseness. "I'm sure you're mistaken. He wouldn't be so stupid, and none of the moors girls would go that far."

"Oh no? They were seen, my sweet innocent, cavorting on the moors late at night, the wench half dressed, and he with his weapon stuck up her, forging away like a piston engine—"

"*Theo*! For God's sake, keep your voice down," she said, outraged by his graphic description.

"'Tis too late for covering up, cuz. The whole area knows

of it. The boy's had one beating already, but the uppity wench is saying she ain't going to part from him, so the clayers are baying for more blood if he don't leave her alone."

"Then we must send the group home at once."

"What? And lose some of the best workers we've seen for months, and all on account of some little tart who's willing to drop her knickers for a few coppers?"

Skye slapped him hard across the face, and ignored his hollering and his earthy language in reply. He pulled her towards him, shaking her hard, but she wrenched away from him, her teeth chattering with rage and shock.

"You disgust me! You're not worthy of our family name. You'd risk having a strike, or even worse, just for the sake of a bit more clay?"

And so would his father, Walter. So would Ben Killigrew, and Morwen's brothers, and all the rest of them with clay in their souls, instead of flesh and blood. . . .

"For the sake of your precious pots as well, my fine noble cuz! Just remember that your flourishing White Rivers may not be doing so well wi'out these packers. We're almost there with the Christmas orders, and I ain't jeopardising things at this late stage to pander to no snivelling clayworker's daughter. Are you willing for that – *cuz*?"

Skye stood quite still, breathing heavily, hands clenched by her sides, her breasts heaving and her eyes sparkling with explosive fury. This – this – *oaf* knew exactly how dear the pottery was to her heart.

No matter what the joint names on the deeds said, the pottery was *hers*, she thought passionately, and in that instant, she knew exactly how the Tremaynes had always felt about the clay. It was a primeval, possessive feeling that was inexplicable to any outsider.

She heard Theo give a savage oath, and the next second she felt his arms go around her. His hand was behind her head and she couldn't move away as he pressed a violent kiss on her mouth. It was hard and insulting, his tongue pushing through her unsuspecting lips and digging against her inner softness in a simulated act of sex. She almost vomited as she thrust him away from her, scraping furiously at her mouth until she removed the tender skin and tasted blood.

"What do you think you're doing, you bastard?" she screamed, wondering if she was about to be raped by her own cousin in her own house. He was bullishly strong. There was no one to protect her and she was suddenly very afraid.

Then she heard him give a harsh laugh; he turned away from her and insolently poured himself a glass of brandy from the decanter on the side table. Her legs threatened to give way beneath her, and she sat down quickly on the edge of a chair, rather than have the indignity of collapsing in front of him.

"You needn't worry, my plum, I've no intention of ravishing you, however delightful a prospect that might be to some. I just wanted to show 'ee how easy it is for a young woman to be aroused and ready for a coupling. And your own sweet buds prove that even an uninvited kiss can do the trick."

Skye didn't need to glance down to be aware of how her nipples had hardened during his assault. But it was through shock and anger, not lust. She would never lust after her cousin. Even so, she was honest enough to admit that there had been a frisson of response in her. But as for a *coupling* as he called it . . . she would never betray Nick. . . .

She lowered her eyes at once, shocked anew to know that any betrayal in her mind had been on her lover's account, and not on her husband's. And that was surely the ultimate betrayal of all!

"So, cuz. We must think seriously how best to deal with this situation," Theo went on, as calmly as if he was able to simply put aside the fact that he had just crudely insulted her, or that her lips were swollen and bruised from his attack and her need to be rid of his touch and taste.

But then, lust was second nature to him, if his dalliances were to be believed. It meant nothing beyond the moment, and she realised for the first time that if Betsy knew or suspected his weakness, his wife had nothing to fear from his mistresses. He always went home to her and his sons.

Skye tried to think sensibly, and answered in the same icy manner. "So what do you suggest we do about it that's any better

than sending the whole group back to where they came from?"
It was really the last thing Skye wanted to do, as Anglo-German
relations could be so well cemented by this visit and had proved
amicable enough until this present situation. But human nature
between a boy and a girl was something no one could deny
or avoid.

"There's another way round it. You don't know these clayers
as well as I do. They'd sell their souls for a few extra coppers
jingling in their pockets."

Skye clamped her lips together before she exploded with
rage. His father, Walter, had loved the clay with a passion,
and he'd also loved and respected the men who worked it.
The clayworkers were stalwart, loyal men, who had served
Killigrew Clay well for decades. Theo had little or no understanding of people's feelings and certainly no compassion,
confirmed in his next statement.

"So we pay the wench to go away, and put a bit of money her
father's way to persuade him to calm the rest of the hotheads
down until the orders are completed, and then we send the
Jerries back. Nobody loses face then. The wench could turn
out to be carrying a by-blow, of course, but that needn't be a
problem. I know a quack who'd deal with that."

Skye felt murderous towards him then. To carelessly scheme
to rid a young girl of the possible child she was carrying, was
evil as well as severely against the law. Only someone with the
black heart of a devil could concoct such a plan.

At the same moment, she felt a stab of fear as Theo's words
brought home to her something she hadn't even considered
before. She too could be carrying a child, a child that wasn't
– couldn't be – her husband's. The shock of it almost numbed
her brain.

"I see that you ain't averse to the idea," Theo went on more
smoothly when she said nothing. "I'll set things in motion, then,
shall I?"

Skye let out her breath, feeling as if she had been holding
it forever. Her voice shook with rage. "I'd never agree to it.
It's wicked. Tell me the name of the girl and I'll go and
talk to her."

"And what the hell good is that going to do? I tell you, if this ain't nipped in the bud, we're in for big trouble."

"I insist that you let me see what I can do, Theo. I'll go and see the family tomorrow. Where do they live?"

He glowered at her, his face dark with fury. "In one of the cottages overlooking Clay One."

"You mean where our parents and grandparents once lived?"

She knew this would infuriate him. Theo never liked to be reminded that his family had such humble beginnings, but it seemed eerily ironic to Skye that many of the problems the Tremaynes and Killigrews had faced over the years began and ended in the same place, in a never-ending circle.

"The same," he snapped. "And it's Roland Dewy's daughter who's the troublemaker, name of Alice. But you'll do no good, unless you take a pay-off with you. It's the only thing these yokels understand."

"Get out, Theo. I'll let you know the result of my meeting with Mr Dewy and his family when I'm ready to do so," Skye said deliberately, giving the clayworkers all the dignity they deserved.

"Well, don't leave it too long with your bloody do-gooding," was Theo's parting shot. "I won't be responsible for any trouble brewing, and don't say I didn't warn you."

Skye wilted after he had gone. It was terrifying how quickly life changed. This morning she had lain blissfully in her lover's arms, and already it seemed like a lifetime ago. Since then she had met with her husband's accusations and her cousin's vile, bruising insults. And now she had undertaken to do what she could with the Dewy family, while wrestling with the fact that Alice Dewy's problem could be her own . . .

She suppressed her panic with great difficulty. There was no use worrying over something that may not happen. The more urgent thing was to see if she could placate the Dewy family, and persuade Alice not to see the young German again.

She felt a swift sympathy for her. If the girl was as taken up with the boy as Theo so unpleasantly described, and as

185

passionate a clayer's daughter as most of them were, then she knew she had a pretty hopeless task ahead of her.

By now, she felt completely wrung out. It had been an exhausting day, from the long train journey home and saying goodbye to the love of her life, to Philip's bad temper, and then Theo's boorishness. She had borne the brunt of it all, and she wished desperately that she could bury her head in the sand like an ostrich and not have to contend with any of it.

To make matters worse, Philip didn't come home all evening, and she spent frustrated hours wondering whether or not to sit up for him. To risk his wrath and get more tongue-pie as her mother used to call it, or to be ready with sympathy and understanding if he was in one of his rare contrite moods . . .

In the end she went to bed, remembering he had said he wouldn't disturb her and hoping he meant it. She tried to make her mind a total blank. She wouldn't think about tomorrow, and she couldn't bear to think of yesterday. . . .

Skye was woken abruptly by the sound of rapid hammering on her bedroom door, and by the housekeeper's voice calling her name urgently. It was still very dark outside, with only a pale moon and a sprinkling of silvery stars to lighten the night sky. It was still a long way from morning.

In an effort to gather her senses, she realised she thought she had been hearing other voices in her head, but she had simply thought she was dreaming. Now she knew that she was not, and she grabbed her dressing-gown and wrapped it tightly around her, filled with dread as she opened her bedroom door.

"What is it, Mrs Arden?" she said thickly.

"Oh, Mrs Norwood, ma'am," the housekeeper gasped, avoiding her eyes as much as possible. "There's two constables downstairs, and they've come wi' such terrible news. I don't rightly know how to tell 'ee . . ."

Skye pushed past her, and hurried down the stairs to where the two young constables were standing awkwardly. She felt almost sorry for them, knowing they could never be the bearers of good news in the middle of the night. And knowing exactly what they had come to tell her. It was more than a sixth sense. It was an inevitability.

"It's my husband, isn't it?" she said quietly.

"I'm afraid it is, ma'am," the first one said. "There's been a terrible accident, and the poor man stood no chance, no chance at all."

"Would 'ee care to sit down, ma'am? And maybe the house-keeper could fetch 'ee some brandy," suggested the other.

"I'll do it right away," Mrs Arden said, standing close behind her and clearly glad of some direction now. "The poor soul will be needin' her comfort, after hearing such a shock."

"I don't need it," Skye snapped. Were they all fools? She didn't need anything, except to be told that it wasn't true.

"Please take the drink, ma'am," the first constable urged uneasily. "'Tis quite often that the shock don't properly register at once, see?"

"I see," she answered, obliging him and leading the way to the drawing-room. What happened now? she wondered. Did she have to go and identify the – the – she suddenly flinched, as the word refused to come into her head.

"Please tell me exactly what happened," she said instead, her voice a mite shriller than before.

One of the young constables cleared his throat. "It seems that Mr Norwood was taking a drive up on the moors and lost control of the car. Do you know if he'd been drinking, ma'am?" he asked. "You understand that we have to ask these questions, and I don't mean to upset you unduly."

How much more upset could she be, than hearing that her husband was dead? But she tried to answer the question. "He may have been drinking. I'm not sure. I had only just returned home from a visit to Bristol when he left the house. I don't know where he went from here."

She saw them glance at one another and pushed down the rising hysteria. Maybe she should say he'd probably gone off like her cousin Theo did, to visit some floosie or other. . . . But that wasn't Philip's style, any more than killing himself was. She couldn't bear the thought of that. Skye smothered a sob and drank down the brandy Mrs Arden handed her, at a single stinging gulp.

"Please go on," she managed, after a moment or two.

"Well, ma'am, Mr Norwood's car crashed into the old standing stone up on the moors near the clayworks. The one they call the Larnie Stone. It has a strange hole in the middle where you can get a glimpse of the sea, and 'tis meant to have magical powers, some say, but you may not have heard of it, not being from these parts . . ." His voice trailed away uncertainly as the woman in front of him began to laugh hysterically now.

Oh, she'd heard of it all right. Wasn't that where the old witchwoman once told her that Morwen Tremayne and Celia Penry had taken a potion to see the faces of their true loves? The place where Celia had been raped by Ben Killigrew's cousin, and then the two of them had committed the ultimate sin in getting rid of the child before Celia drowned herself with the shame of it all. Oh yes, Skye knew of the Larnie Stone all right. . . .

It was said that shock affected folk in different ways, but the constables had never seen anything like this before, and they didn't care to see it now. 'Twasn't right . . .

"You two be on your way now, and I'll see to her," Skye heard Mrs Arden say, as calmly as if she was bidding her sons goodbye. "Come back tomorrow and we'll sort things out then when she's got some of her family around her."

And then Skye heard no more as the motherly arms of the housekeeper went around her as she lost control of her senses and fainted for the second time in two days.

Thirteen

The doctor gave orders for Skye to be sedated and allowed to recover from the shock of her husband's death in her own time. For three days the house was hushed, as if everyone needed to walk around on tiptoes for fear of disturbing Mrs Norwood. But her nerves were so on edge that no amount of sedation made her completely unaware of what was happening.

As if any of it made it any better. As if the muted voices took away one iota of the sheer horror of knowing that after a blistering argument, her husband had driven off in a wild rage and killed himself. As if there was any way of blotting out the fact that history had yet another hideous way of repeating itself.

Reminding her that the Larnie Stone had played an important part in her family's past, and reviving a long-forgotten garbled memory that Charlotte had once gossiped to her. How much of it was true, or how much had been embroidered over time, Skye never knew. But part of Morwen's turbulent and romantic past had included a bittersweet affair that had begun when she had travelled to London with Ran Wainwright on a business matter, and shortly afterwards Ben Killigrew had tragically died.

Admittedly, Ben Killigrew had already been ill and had died from a heart attack, Charlotte had said . . . but the circumstantial similarities constantly tormented Skye. She too had been away from home on a business matter that had developed into a romantic liaison and then her husband had died. And even the doctor's assurance that it hadn't happened from any act of self-destruction, but that the final bursting of the horror inside Philip's head had caused the car to skid and crash . . . even that couldn't quench the overpowering sense of guilt in her mind.

It was a similarity too poignant to face, yet too terrible to ignore. For three days she simply closed herself off from everything, her senses dulled with the prescribed drugs, which did no more than put off the grieving time.

It was her children who finally drew her out of her abject misery, as Wenna clung to her and begged to know when their father was coming home.

"He's dead," Celia said, brash with her own anger and pain. "You know Mrs Arden told us so and that we shouldn't talk about it because it will upset our mother."

"Why shouldn't we talk about it?" Wenna wept. "I want my Daddy, and Oliver cries every night because he can't see him."

"He's just a crybaby and so are you," Celia declared rudely.

"I'm not," Wenna said fearfully. "Mommy went away and she came home, so why can't Daddy?"

Listening to them, Skye dragged herself from the depths of her own guilt, recognising the fear in Wenna's young voice and following her reasoning. She had been lying on her bed, resisting the need to return to reality, but now she opened her arms to the little girls. Wenna rushed into them, while Celia stood sullenly by, finding it too difficult to show the emotion she held tight inside, and burning up with the sense of betrayal that her father had left her.

Her father's daughter to the limit, thought Skye.

"Listen to me, my darlings," she said huskily. "It's true that your daddy is dead, but we can talk about him whenever you want to. We may not be able to see him any more, but as long as we still talk about him and think about him, he'll always be alive in our hearts."

As she went on in the same controlled manner, Wenna continued to snuffle against her mother's shoulder, but she was soft and pliant and ready to take in everything Skye told her. Celia stood stiffly, unable to accept anything but the inescapable fact that Philip was dead.

When her pet rabbit died, it was Philip himself who had told her in his clinical way that once something was dead, it was dead, and those that were left had to go on as best they could. And she was having none of this nonsense about her father still being in their hearts.

After a few minutes she flounced out of the room, and left the other two together.

"You won't go away and leave us again, will you, Mommy?" Wenna whispered fearfully.

"Of course not. We're all going to look after each other, the way Daddy would want us to."

She shivered as she spoke, sensing that she might have more of a problem with Celia than the other two. Wenna was so trusting, and Oliver was too young to really understand what was happening; but Celia had an old head on her shoulders, questioning everything, and totally resentful of the fact that Philip had died.

There was a hardness in Celia that Skye hadn't even realised before now. It would stand her in good stead on many occasions, but right now she seemed determined not to shed a single tear for her father. And that wasn't healthy.

"When are you coming downstairs, Mommy?" Wenna said with a new tremor in her voice as Skye leaned back against the pillows for a moment with her eyes closed.

"Right now, darling," Skye answered at once.

She discovered how wobbly her legs were as soon as she put her feet to the ground, but she knew this had to be done. It was the first step back to normality, and she couldn't let others do the things that were her responsibility. She knew that Charlotte had been here, and that she and Theo and Betsy had already organised the burial, which was only four days away now. How could the widow hide herself away as if none of this had anything to do with her?

Skye flinched as the word came into her mind. Widows were very old ladies wearing black who were only a step away from death themselves . . . and the minute she thought it, she knew it was far from the truth. Since the Great War, there were many young widows in the parish, and many children who would never know their fathers. And here was she, hiding behind her own guilt and grief, when they had dealt with it all so stoically and bravely.

She walked unsteadily downstairs, holding her daughter's hand, and when Mrs Arden saw her, there was more than a hint of relief in her eyes.

"'Tis good to see you, ma'am. For a while we feared . . ." Her voice trailed away with embarrassment, and Skye finished the sentence for her.

"For my sanity, I suspect, Mrs Arden."

"Ah well, when a lovely young woman such as yourself loses her man, 'tis a tragedy that would turn anyone's mind. But you'm strong, the way your family's always been strong."

And besides, now that I'm no longer tied in marriage, I can always turn to my lover to cheer me up. . . .

Skye caught her breath as the wicked thought surged into her mind. It was a thought she didn't want, and wouldn't entertain. In fact, the last person she wanted to see right now was Nick Pengelly. It would only compound her feelings of guilt, and nor could she bear to hear the platitudes that everyone made at such a time, especially from him. It would simply twist the knife in her heart.

"Ever so many folk have sent their condolences, ma'am," Mrs Arden said, following her and Wenna into the drawing-room. "There's flowers and letters and cards come for you too."

"I see them," Skye murmured, her eyes filling at the kindness of people. The floral scent in the room was almost cloying. She wished the housekeeper would take them all away, but it would be too churlish and ungrateful to say so, and she couldn't bear to read all the cards and letters until later.

"That Mr Pengelly has telephoned half a dozen times," the housekeeper went on. "He wanted to see you, but I put him off. I hope I did the right thing. The doctor said you were to stay in bed until you felt the need to get up yourself and not to see any visitors you didn't want."

"You did quite right," Skye mumbled, ignoring the way her heart had jumped at the mention of his name. And hating herself for the feeling.

"Besides, 'twouldn't have been right to show him into your

bedroom, even if 'twere on business," Mrs Arden went on innocently.

But he had been there before. In her bedroom, in her bed and in her heart. He knew every part of her more intimately than any man had ever done . . . was more inventive a lover than Philip had ever been . . .

"Mr Theo said you'll have to see un sometime, o' course," Mrs Arden went on uneasily, seeing how Skye's gaze had become fixed. "There's legal things and all to see to, but there's plenty of time for that after – well, after."

"After the funeral. Yes, I do know the word, Mrs Arden. And I must do something about it."

"I told you 'tis all taken care of, ma'am. And Mrs Vera Pengelly has already arranged to take care of all the children on the day – yours and Mr Theo's."

It was like listening to the funeral arrangements of a stranger. Others had done everything necessary, and she was being gently put aside as if it had nothing to do with her, like an anonymous extra character in a drama. It wasn't right. It wasn't fair to Philip to back away from giving him his final send-off in the way the generous-hearted Cornish folk referred to it.

The realisation of it finally roused Skye from her shock and lethargy. Everyone was kind, friends and family . . . and she recalled how she and Vera and Lily had leaned on one another and supported one another during the dark days of the war in France, and she drew a shuddering breath.

"I want to talk to Vera. Please send a message for me, Mrs Arden, and ask her to come as soon possible."

The housekeeper's relief was obvious. It was the first positive thing Skye had said since hearing the dreadful news. Her thoughts were still muddled, her brain still dulled, but she knew there were other things to be considered. Things that were far removed from the very personal tragedy of her husband's death, and the forbidden memory of Nick Pengelly. She had read the brief note accompanying his roses, and then torn it to shreds, unable to cope with its hidden meaning.

The note simply said: *"I'm here if you need me. Nick."*

But she knew there were other things that needed her attention, if only she had the strength to face them. There was a problem with a German boy and a clayer's daughter, and something to do with Uncle Albie. Not the removal to The Laurels where he would be cared for – that was clear in her head – but something else that had to be organised. She couldn't think what it was, and by the time Vera arrived, the frustration of it all was making her angry.

"Sweetheart, you've had such a dreadful homecoming," Vera said, taking her straight into her arms. "We're all so very sorry about Philip."

"Tell me what was planned for Uncle Albie," Skye said, pushing her away. "For the life of me I can't remember and it's driving me crazy."

Vera stared at her, alarmed at this reception, so different from what she had expected. She knew Skye was strong, but this was a different Skye. She was hard, her eyes tortured and dry, when Vera had been prepared to hold her in her arms and let her pour her heart out.

"Uncle Albie? He went to Bristol yesterday, so that you wouldn't have any more distress. Nick arranged it."

"Did he now? How *thoughtful* of him." She couldn't stop the sarcasm in her voice, without knowing why it was there. She just had to hit out at someone – anyone – and hearing his name merely produced more feelings of guilt.

After a moment's silence, Vera spoke gingerly. "Skye, did something happen between you and Nick? He's been so strange these past few days, hardly speaking to anyone except to snap, and Adam thinks you must have had a terrible row or something—" She stopped, appalled at her cousin's sudden hysterical laughter and the tears that finally streamed down her face. And this time, when she put her arms around her, Skye didn't push her away. "My poor love. What a terrible time it is for you."

"It's not that," Skye said chokingly against Vera's ample bosom. "It's something too awful to talk about, so don't ask me. Please don't ask me—"

"Of course I won't," said Vera, thinking that Skye should see a head doctor, and quickly. She was so clearly deranged and not thinking sensibly.

Skye sobbed, wondering what on earth was wrong with her to feel so perverse, knowing that she *wanted* Vera to wring the truth out of her, so that she didn't have to keep the awful guilty secret to herself. In the end she knew it was no good. She had to speak out.

"I have to tell you something, Vera, but swear not to breathe a word to a soul, not even Adam. Especially not Adam."

The moment she said his name, she knew she should keep it all to herself. Adam was Nick's brother, and all their lives were so intertwined, the way the Tremaynes and Killigrews had always been. It never ended, she thought fearfully . . .

"I won't tell a soul, not even Adam," Vera promised, sure that nothing could be dire enough to bring this wild look into Skye's eyes. She had always been so open, so honest.

"It's Nick. Me and Nick. Nick and I, or however you people put it. I can't remember, and what does it matter, anyway? It doesn't change things."

"What things?" Vera said in a hushed voice, but already anticipating what was to come, and trying to hide her sense of shock. And yet seeing things she should have seen a long time ago. The look in Nick's eyes when he spoke of her. His need to bring her name into the conversation whenever possible, and the way he spoke her name, lingeringly, like a caress. The tight, lost look on his face now that shrieked of his own guilt to Vera far more eloquently than mere words.

Skye spoke brutally, before she could change her mind. "We had an affair. A very brief affair, and now it's over."

"Is it?" Vera said into the silence.

"Well, of course it is! Do you think I'd carry on now, with my husband not yet buried?" *But she had carried on while he was alive, and that was a greater sin* . . . She went on deliberately, not sparing herself. "I'm not sure if you know exactly what I mean, Vera. When we were in Bristol, we spent a night together. We were *lovers*, and my penance is the guilt of my husband's death."

"Don't be daft. Philip's death has nothing to do with you, or

Nick," Vera said harshly, still taking in the enormity of it all. "We all knew his time was coming, and if you want to put the blame anywhere, then blame the war that caused his head injuries. It's not your guilt, Skye."

"No? And what about the timing? Don't you think that's significant? You, with your Cornish omens and superstitions! Why did it have to happen at this particular time, if I wasn't meant to feel guilt? Tell me that if you can."

"You'll be telling the whole house if you don't keep your voice down," Vera said sharply. "Just listen to me, darling. You've got the ordeal of the funeral to get through, and then you have to get on with your life. You have three beautiful children, and the last thing they need is to see their mother constantly berating herself for reasons they couldn't possibly understand. Guilt is a huge waste of emotion. Philip would have said as much. He was always a great one for spelling out such things. You don't need me to tell you that!"

Skye stared at her through tortured eyes. She heard all that Vera was saying as if she was hearing it through a fog, and it all meant nothing until her final words. Vera was exactly right. Philip was – had been – a great one for logical and pacifying explanations. More than anyone else she knew, Philip had never believed in wasting emotions on things that couldn't be changed. And the two things in her life that couldn't be changed now were the inescapable fact of his death, and the fact that she and Nick Pengelly had been lovers. She nodded slowly.

"Thank you, Vera," she whispered. "You were the only one I could have faced with this."

"Then face it, accept it, and let it go," Vera said briskly. "Now then, are we having some tea or not? I'm parched after all this soul-searching."

Skye gave her a wan smile. "I'll order it. And Vera—"

"You don't need to ask. I know nothing. And maybe what you were wondering about Uncle Albie was about that exhibition of his paintings that was talked about."

"That's it! How could I have forgotten?"

"It's hardly surprising," Vera said dryly. "Rather a lot has been happening in the past week, after all. But I know David

Kingsley has taken an interest in the idea, and is willing to make a big splash about it in the newspaper when you feel like doing something about it."

"Or when someone else in the family deigns to get involved, you mean," Skye said with a flash of her old spirit.

Vera was more than thankful to see it. Unknown to Skye as yet, ever since the news of Philip Norwood's death had become common knowledge, everything in the vicinity seemed to be holding its breath, according to Vera's husband. The clayers had become eerily silent, and the German boys had made themselves scarce at every opportunity. Roland Dewy had packed his daughter off to some relatives, but nothing had been resolved. There had to be a reckoning. But not yet.

It wouldn't last, Adam had declared ominously. It was all due to shock at the accident, and out of respect for Skye and her family. But it wouldn't last. It was the calm before the storm, and the storm was just waiting to happen.

After Vera left, Skye forced herself to receive visitors, rather than face them all for the first time on the day of the funeral. There were plenty of callers, family and friends, clayworkers and pit captains, all offering their awkward condolences. Only one caller was missing. The one she yearned to see the most, and yet couldn't bear to face.

'*I'm here if you need me*', he had written. And she knew he wouldn't come unless she sent for him. Not until they met formally at the graveside of her dead husband, for as the family solicitor, he would naturally be there. It would look very odd if he wasn't.

"We don't have to go to the funeral, do we, Mommy?" Wenna said for the tenth time, by now having heard all kinds of gruesome tales of the dead and dying from the housemaids.

"*I* want to go," Celia said.

"Well, neither of you is going and nor is Oliver," Skye told them. "You're all to spend the day at Aunt Vera's with your cousins."

"I don't want to see that awful Sebby, and Justin's an idiot," Celia howled.

"Will Ethan be there as well, or is he too old to play with cousins?" Wenna said.

"I don't know," Skye shrugged, having forgotten that Ethan Pengelly was a relative too, and that the clayworks and the pottery would both be closed for the day.

Celia hooted. "Wenna still thinks Ethan Pengelly likes her in a soppy way. As if he'd look at a baby like *her*."

"I'm not a baby," shrieked Wenna. "And you like him too, I know you do."

"I do not," Celia was red-faced with rage now. "He talks like a clayer, anyway."

Skye had a hard job not to strike her daughter then, but slapping the child when the whole house was tense with nerves and mixed emotions would do none of them any good. So she held on to her temper with difficulty.

"That's a very snobbish remark, Celia, and you should never forget that your grandmother's family were all clayers. If it wasn't for their hard work, none of us would live in this fine house and have all the privileges that we do."

After a few mutterings which may or may not have been an apology, Celia stalked out of the room, and Skye felt a surge of alarm. Her daughters were just children, but they were close in age, and already she could sense the undercurrents of jealousy between them. If ever they fell in love with the same man . . . but she was being absurd again, and the Cornish legacy of a wild imagination was running away with her.

But for a few moments it had taken her mind off the coming ordeal of the funeral and being the centre of attention of all the people attending. Watching and assessing and noting every scrap of emotion on her face, and naturally expecting her to be the distraught widow.

Which she was, of course. Except that deep in her heart she was also aware of a huge feeling of release because Philip had been so difficult to live with these past few years. But it was a thought that only added to her guilt.

When the day finally came, the family gathered at New World where the cars were to follow the hearse to the church. Luke had been persuaded to conduct the service, even though he'd virtually retired now, but somehow it seemed right, as it always had, for the family to close together in as tight a circle as possible.

But not only family, Skye realised, as the enormity of the occasion dawned on her. Clayworkers had turned out in force, even though they had had little time for Philip Norwood. But he was part of the tapestry that made up Killigrew Clay and White Rivers, and was therefore to be honoured in death, if not in life.

And there were so many strangers, few of whom Skye recognised. But from their demeanour, so different from the awkward country folk, she knew they were college colleagues and students, and was made acutely aware of the different lives she and Philip had led.

Until she stood at the graveside and watched the coffin being lowered, hearing the sombre tones of Luke Tremayne committing Philip's body to the earth, she hadn't fully realised that there was no one here who was truly her own. There was no one left. Not her mother and brother, who were both dead. Not her father, too far away to attend, but who had sent messages every day. Not her children, too young to be there. All these others standing sentinel until the ceremony was over, these Tremaynes and other relatives and friends . . . none of them truly belonged to *her*.

Her eyes were drawn momentarily to a figure standing silently on the far side of the grave as she threw the handful of earth onto Philip's coffin. The sound was a dull thud, echoing the thud of her heartbeats as she saw Nick's briefest nod, supporting her with his mind and his love, even if he couldn't do so openly.

As she lowered her eyes quickly, it was the womenfolk who drew her away. Charlotte and Lily and Betsy, and Em. Dear Em, who was robust and brisk and unable to express her feelings in words, but had brought her plants and produce from her garden as a gesture of love. And a whole side of pork for later.

The house was oveflowing with people for the bunfight, as

Theo disrespectfully persisted in calling it. Only a few of Philip's colleagues attended, and none of the students. But the family was there, and a handful of clayworkers, curious to see the inside of this splendid house. And the Pengelly brothers.

"Thank you for coming," Skye said formally to Adam.

"Why would I not? We're all family now, my dear, and Ethan here wanted to pay his respects as well. Though I fancy your young uns might have preferred it if he'd stayed with Vera and the rest of the cousins."

Skye saw Ethan's colour rise. It was a shame to bait him, and a boy of fourteen was so vulnerable to teasing.

"Our Nick said it would be all right," he muttered. "And if our Nick says so then 'tis all right by me."

"Whatever *our Nick* says is all right with him," Adam grinned. "He's the boy's hero."

"Everybody needs one at that age," Skye murmured, wishing they'd stop talking about Nick, as if they thought she would be remotely interested.

"Needs what?" He was suddenly at her side, a plate of roast pork sandwiches in his hand. "I've been asked to hand these round, since few folk seem inclined to help themselves."

She took one automatically, and Adam warmed to his words.

"Everybody needs a hero, that's what. And I was just telling Skye that I reckon you're our Ethan's."

"Excuse me," Skye said quickly as he glanced at her, needing to get away before Ethan asked artlessly if she had a hero too. It would be too awful on this day, in this gathering. But he was just a boy, and really out of his depth. He should have gone to Vera's after all, she thought. She paused, and then put her hand on his arm, taking the initiative since no one else seemed to want to do so.

"Ethan, why don't you go back to Vera's now and have proper tea with the others? I'm grateful that you came, but all this chatter is very boring for you now, I'm sure."

Even as she spoke, she knew it was her family doing the talking and reminiscing over times past, the way most families did at any such gathering. Half listening to them now, she realised that they spoke about missing family members, the fluctuating price of clay, of good deals and bad ones.

Hardly anyone spoke about Philip, or had any particular memories of him that were worth sharing. He had been part of her life for so long, but he had never been one of them. Even in death, they were unwittingly shutting him out. And she accepted it because there was nothing else she could do.

"I'll need to see you about the will," she heard Nick say quietly a few minutes later. "It's quite straightforward, and there's no hurry, so I suggest we leave it until next week. I could come here, or you could come to my chambers in Bodmin. Whichever you prefer."

"Bodmin would be best," she said, discussing these arrangements as if with a stranger. Somewhere impersonal would definitely be best, while she and her lover discussed the personal bequests of her husband. The irony of it didn't escape her, and she moved slightly away from him.

"Until next Friday then. About three in the afternoon," he went on, as coolly as if they had never lain together, or loved so wildly, or needed one another to the exclusion of all others in the world.

He held out his hand to shake hers in farewell, and only by the slightest pressure of his fingers on hers did she feel anything between them. She was cold, lost and alone, and yet she welcomed the feeling, because she couldn't bear to interpret any sweet, unspoken sense of intimacy between them at this time.

She was thankful when everyone left at last, save for her cousin Lily, and Emma the homebody, busily helping the maids to clear the remnants of the feast away. As they sat amiably together, Lily looked at her shrewdly.

"There's a good man going to waste there," she said.

"What? Who do you mean?" Skye said, taken off-balance by the odd remark.

"Nick Pengelly, of course. He should be married with children. Don't you think so? He'd be a natural."

"Are you applying for the job then?" Skye asked, refusing to allow the rush of jealousy at her cousin's words.

Lily laughed. "Not me, love. I'm not interested, and in any case I wouldn't stand an earthly. The man's only got eyes for one woman, and you know it."

Skye felt her face burn. Surely Vera hadn't said anything . . . but she was instantly certain that she hadn't. It was merely conjecture, but she didn't pretend to misunderstand.

"This isn't the time to be saying such things," she said.

Her cousin reached forward and squeezed her hand.

"Darling girl, I don't mean to be intrusive. I know that when you and Philip were in the first flush, you were like two halves of the same coin – and I'm hardly the world's most poetic creature to be saying such things, so it must have been obvious at the time. But that time's gone now, Skye, and you must look to the future."

"Well, I just wish people would stop telling me so!" Skye said angrily. "For pity's sake, Philip's only been – been gone a week and we only buried him today. It's still painful and unbelievable to me, so don't start pairing me off with anyone else just yet, if ever! Especially not—" she stopped abruptly.

"Nick Pengelly? Oh well, we'll see. But you can't mourn for ever. And I know I'm an insensitive pig for saying so."

"And now you sound more like the abominable Sebby, oink oink," Skye said without thinking.

After a moment's startled silence, they both began to laugh. Emma walked into the room, gaping in astonishment at the unlikely scene, having just ushered out the last of the family and preparing to stay at New World for a few days to give Skye some comfort and support.

"Well, this is more like it. What's the joke?" she asked, her voice showing relief that she needn't tiptoe around any longer. "I allus say there should be more jollity at a funeral wake. The dear departed wouldn't object, I'm certain sure."

At which ludicrous comments the two younger women laughed harder than ever, while Skye was just as certain sure that Philip at his most pompous would most definitely object.

"Em, you do me more good than everyone else put together," she gasped, her eyes watering.

"Do I? So why don't we have a slice or two of that nice belly of pork I brought you over from the farm? Funeralising allus makes me hungry."

"Oink oink," said Lily, remembering Sebastian Tremayne, at which they convulsed again.

Fourteen

S kye refused all offers to take her to Bodmin, preferring to drive herself. She wasn't an invalid, and she also defiantly refused to continue wearing the required black garb of the widow. If it raised eyebrows, no matter.

According to some, she was still the eccentric American cousin and always would be, so she might as well live up to it. Besides, wearing black only made her feel more depressed. So she chose a sombre grey hat and coat, which she considered suitable enough to remind folk that she was in mourning.

What was of more concern to her was the ordeal of seeing Nick again, and hearing him read out the contents of Philip's will. There was an irony about his part in the whole procedure that she disliked intensely. It wasn't wicked or obscene, but it wasn't far off. It would have been far better if old Mr Slater had dealt with the matter instead, but he was ailing now and Nick was left in sole charge of the lawyers' firm more and more often.

It wouldn't be long before he took over completely, thought Skye, knowing him to be an ambitious man. Knowing him. And wondering just how long Cornwall would really hold him.

She shivered. No matter how much she tried, she couldn't forget what had happened between them. But instead of being a prop to sustain her, it was a barrier between them that she couldn't cross, nor even know if she wanted to. Too much had happened. Too much, too soon.

Nick greeted her formally, as much for the benefit of the young female secretary in the outer cubbyhole office, as through wariness at the tight, pinched look on Skye's face. Her beloved face. He pushed the thought aside, knowing that she wanted none of their previous relationship to intrude at this time. And nor it should. Nick was not an insensitive man, and he could guess at the range of her tormented feelings and emotions. He was not unaware of the same feelings in himself.

"Please sit down, Skye," he told her. "My secretary will bring us some tea – or would you prefer coffee?"

"Like the colonial cousin that I am, you mean?" she murmured, with a feeble attempt at a joke. She didn't know why she said it, but she kept her eyes lowered as she sat down on the proffered chair and slowly peeled off her kid gloves.

"No," said Nick evenly, trying not to notice the way she unconsciously caressed the soft black leather with those delicate fingers; remembering how she had caressed his skin, slowly and erotically, and the way he had caressed hers. "I just happen to know you prefer coffee to tea."

"Thank you, but tea will be fine," she said perversely, refusing to be reminded for a moment how they had shared intimate breakfasts in a Bristol hotel, and even breathing in the seductive aroma of steaming, freshly-ground coffee had seemed a hedonistic and sensual affair. Like theirs.

Once the secretary had brought in the tea and left them alone, Nick opened the file containing Philip Norwood's will. He hadn't wanted to deal with this either. He wished himself anywhere but here, and so did she, he thought. They were suddenly oceans apart, where they had once been closer than if they shared the same heart.

He forced himself to be professional. "I shall read the entire contents of the will to you, Skye, and then we may discuss any points you wish to go over before I give you a copy of it. It's a very short document."

He paused. He enjoyed his chosen profession, but he sometimes wondered how it felt for clients to realise that their lawyer knew more about the deceased's wishes than they did themselves. In most cases, they were just grateful to have everything cut and dried and taken care of by a third party.

In this case he had the unsavoury task of opening a Pandora's box of raw emotions. He had no idea how she was going to take it. It may not be as bad as he suspected, of course. And he couldn't put it off any longer.

He read out the formal phrases unemotionally. For someone as wordy as Philip Norwood had been in life, it was indeed a short will. It left everything of substance to his wife, and on her death, to his children. They were normal, everyday bequests, and Skye still kept her eyes lowered, saying nothing as he paused again, sensing that there was more to come.

"Please go on."

"There are only two other bequests aside from the bulk of Philip's estate that I have already outlined," Nick said.

She looked up sharply. She knew every nuance of his voice so well, and there was definitely something odd in it now. But he continued without further comment.

"'To my college, I leave the sum of £200, to erect a bench in the grounds in my name for the pleasure of future students, and perhaps to provide some other small memorial.'"

Skye felt her face scorch with embarrassment. It was so very egocentric of Philip to have thought of something like this. It was the very essence of his pomposity and self-importance. . . . She heard Nick clear his throat.

"And to Miss Ruth Dobson," he went on, "I leave my set of leather-bound encyclopaedias, with my best affection."

"*What*?"

The mixture of Skye's emotions at that moment was indescribable. Her hands were clenched tightly together with her fingernails biting into her palms, and her eyes burned with fury, rage, and a sick, unreasoning jealousy that she hadn't felt in a very long time.

How *dare* he do this? In physical terms, the encyclopaedias were the most valuable thing Philip possessed, and she knew he had prized them above everything. She had always expected them to be passed on to their children. Instead of which, his one-time fiancée, Miss Ruth Dobson, was the beneficiary. Leaving her his beloved books, and his *best affection*! Not for his wife, or his children, but for the woman who had once meant so much in his life. Even if Skye had never wanted the wretched books for herself, she knew how much they had meant to Philip, and this act was a betrayal from beyond the grave, she thought hysterically.

And maybe more than that. Maybe it was a punishment for the way she and Nick Pengelly had betrayed him. . . .

She felt Nick's arms go around her, and she pushed them away with a sense of horror. Her voice was shrill.

"No, don't touch me! I'm perfectly all right, and I'm simply overreacting, I'm sure."

"And I'm sure that you're not," he said angrily. "You've had a shock, and I should have prepared you for it."

"How? By betraying your client's confidence? I think not. We betrayed him, so this is no doubt well deserved. After all our life together, I have to believe now that Ruth still meant a great deal to Philip. And if you think that fact excuses *our* situation, I promise you it does not."

She couldn't explain her impenetrable anger. She was finding it hard to breathe properly, and although Nick tried to make her sit calmly for a while, they both knew it was impossible. She had to get out of these claustrophobic rooms. But even though her senses were spinning, there was one last thing she had to settle.

"I've no idea where Miss Dobson is now."

"It's not your problem, Skye. It's our business to find her and acquaint her with the news. If it's your wish, we can also arrange for the volumes to be packaged and delivered here until that time."

"Please do so. And when you find her, impress on her that there is to be no contact between us. I want no condolences or expressions of remorse. Any explanations can be made through you. She was not my friend, nor ever could be. Will you do this for me?"

"I will do anything for you. You know that."

"Please Nick—" she put out her hand to ward off any physical contact. "No more. Just advise me when it's done."

She couldn't get away from there quickly enough, her nerves ragged, her feelings bruised and humiliated. It was even worse that he had known of Philip's wishes, and must have known for some time. That really seared her heart. She felt completely disorientated and lost.

Then, like the women in her family before her who needed solace, she drove towards the open moorland and halted the car with her hands still shaking. She sat there for a long while in the quiet solitude, trying to understand and to compose herself. She had once loved Philip so much, and in those early, wonderful days she knew how desperately he had been in love with her . . . but in a single moment he had thrown all that love back in her face.

Unless this was his way of assuaging his own guilt for the way he had reneged on his promise to Ruth. For such an articulate and intellectual man, he was also very proud, and he would have found it difficult to put those inner feelings into words. But maybe, by giving Ruth all that he could of himself, even at this late stage, maybe he still hoped for some salvation in heaven . . .

"*Bull*," Skye said aloud, her voice echoing in the keen air. "He never believed in all that hereafter stuff, and he was just appeasing his conscience over Ruth, that's all."

The scathing sound of her own voice was startling in the silence of the moors. And the incongruity of what she was saying startled her even more. Not that there was anyone to hear. There was only the whispering of the bracken and the soft breeze soughing through the clumps of wild yarrow.

Was she going mad? If so, at any minute now, she could expect to see old Helza hobbling towards her over the rough terrain, with her own brand of head-nodding knowledge, and her wizened cackles that she'd been certain sure all along that Philip Norwood had never been the true love of her life.

"Stop it," Skye snapped to herself. "You're going to end up as loopy as the old girl herself if you don't watch out."

Anyway, there was no sign of Helza nor anyone else up here. This wasn't *their* moors. Killigrew Clay and White Rivers were some distance away, with life going on as usual. Yesterday was over.

And now that she had had some time to recover, she was coming to terms with the things Nick had told her. It was no use fighting it and she would never be so base as to ignore the terms of anyone's will. In any case, the children were too young to even be aware of the precious encyclopaedias. They were always kept locked in Philip's study, and once they were out of the house no one need ever know of their existence.

The sheer logic of her thoughts was worthy of Philip himself, she thought, with a grimace. But it was helping her to calm down. Looking at it sensibly, it really didn't matter a jot to her who had the books. Just as long as she didn't have to hand them over herself.

And providing Ruth Dobson didn't come calling, or write, or want to further their acquaintance . . . if this was being selfish, then so be it.

In any case, Ruth was engaged now, she remembered, and she couldn't imagine that the bequest would drive a wedge between her and her new man, so there was no reason why it should affect Skye either. She made herself believe it, and in the end, she did believe it.

By the time she drove more slowly towards the moors above St Austell her nerves were slowly calming down. The sight of the distant clay tips, glinting in the thin October sunlight, soothed her as always. She had received a shock, but it could have been far worse. She couldn't think exactly how, she just knew it could. And at least Philip wasn't an important enough person – despite what he might think himself – for his will to be made public. She was saved that humiliation.

And who was full of saving face now!

She carefully avoided the area where the Larnie Stone stood, knowing that she couldn't bear to see the place where Philip had died. But when she found herself alongside the row of cottages at the top of the moors, she half wished she could stare beyond the outer stone walls, to feel enveloped by the warmth of all those Tremaynes who had started the dynasty, trying to imagine those times when Morwen Tremayne was a young girl, as wild and unpredictable as the moors themselves.

A woman came out of one of the cottages, and stood for a few moments, staring at her as she leaned on the steering-wheel of the motionless car as if transfixed. After a second's hesitation, the woman walked across to the car, her voice deferential and uncertain, and as thick as Cornish cream.

"Excuse me, ma'am, but be 'ee quite well? If you'm ill,

perhaps you'd care to step inside the cottage for a spell and take a brew, if you'll forgive the liberty of asking."

"Oh, that's very kind of you," Skye said, feeling the weak tears spring to her eyes. "Would you mind very much if I did? I'd dearly love to see inside the cottage."

Dear Lord, how patronising that sounded! Skye groaned inwardly as soon as the words had left her lips, but the woman seemed to take no offence. Instead, she looked quite pleased to have a lady wanting to see her humble dwelling.

"It will be my pleasure, ma'am. Come you in and sit you down by the fire and get warm. You look fair perished with the cold."

Skye stepped inside the cottage, and was immediately struck by how small it was, yet so cosy and compact. It was truly *darling*, she thought, just the way Americans imagined the quaint old English homesteads to be, but she was careful not to say as much. It was obvious by the way the woman was glancing at her fine clothes that she knew Skye was a lady, and she had been unwittingly patronising enough. Even so . . .

"My relatives once lived in one of these cottages," she couldn't resist saying, as she was offered a drink of cordial.

"Is that so?" the woman said, clearly disbelieving that such a vision could come from the likes of such humble stock as clayworkers. But by now she had begun to have her suspicions about who the lady could be.

"My name's Flo Dewy, ma'am," she said abruptly. "My man's a clayer for Killigrew Clay. You've mebbe heard on 'em?"

Skye gasped. "Then your husband must be Roland Dewy—"

"The same. Troublemakers allus get known afore the rest, I dare say." She nodded at Skye now. "And you must be the poor lady who's just buried her man, God rest his soul."

"That's right. I'm Skye Norwood."

"Then I'm right sorry I asked 'ee in, ma'am. You'll not want to be gossiping with the likes o' we folk at such a time," she said, poker-faced.

"Please don't worry," Skye said quickly. "I'm grateful for your kindness, and my people are still walking around on tiptoe for fear of upsetting me."

Neither woman said anything for an embarrassing few

moments, and then Skye had to speak up. "Actually, I had intended calling on you and your husband, Mrs Dewy, on account of some bother with your daughter. Alice, isn't it?"

"Oh, you needn't fret none about her now, ma'am. She's been sent off to her auntie down Zennor way. There won't be no more trouble until these here foreigners are sent back where they belong," she said, averting eyes that suddenly flashed.

"There won't *be* any trouble, will there, Mrs Dewy?" Skye said deliberately. "The young men have a perfect right to work here and to return home unscathed."

"You may be right," Flo Dewy said, but more defensively now. "And 'tis true my Alice came to no harm. You'll get my meaning, you being a woman of the world. But that don't mean she ain't been interfered with and spoiled, and my Roland ain't the only clayer to take a very black view o' that. A very black view indeed, ma'am."

As the atmosphere inside the cottage subtly changed, Skye was glad to leave. From the woman's warning words she had an uneasy feeling that the matter was far from settled, and she knew she must speak to Theo about it at the first opportunity.

But at least the nubile Alice was out of harm's way, and her own uncertain condition had righted itself that very morning. There would be no *issue* to remind her of the weekend she had spent with Nick Pengelly, she thought, using the legal jargon as if to distance herself from the intimacy of it all.

It had been an unsettling few moments all the same, and she didn't feel like returning home yet. The children would be taken care of by their nanny, and the fresh air was healing her wounded pride far better than a houseful of well-meaning folk. She drove around aimlessly, edging along the coastline and wondering what her father was doing now, all those ocean miles away. Still missing her mother and her brother, and grieving on his daughter's account, she had no doubt.

She realised she had driven right into St Austell and was near to Killigrew House. She stopped the car and walked to the front door, anticipating the shocked look on Betsy's plump face when she saw her visitor.

"Yes, it's me and not an apparition, Betsy," she said abruptly.

"Is Theo at home? I need to discuss a business matter with him quite urgently."

"Well, yes, I believe he's here," she said, flustered. "But are you sure you're ready for business? I mean, well, it's so soon, and I'm sure there's no need for you to bother with such things until you feel more like yourself."

"For pity's sake Betsy, don't baby me! I never felt more like myself, and if anyone expects me to shut myself away for months on end like some latterday Queen Victoria, then they don't know me as well as they think they do."

She heard a slow handclap coming from the open sitting-room, and the next moment Theo sauntered through it.

"Well said, cuz. I always knew you had more fire in your belly than the rest of the clan put together. So what's this business matter that won't wait?"

Betsy melted into some retreat of her own without even being noticed. Skye followed Theo into the sitting-room and shook her head at his offer of a snifter of brandy.

"I've been to see Roland Dewy's wife," she said.

He paused in mid-pouring. "Good God. Was that wise? I wish you'd leave such things to me, girl."

"Why should I? Anyway, it was quite accidental. I had stopped my car for a breather and she thought I was unwell and invited me into her cottage. I had no idea who she was, and she didn't know me until we introduced ourselves."

"And I'll bet she was almighty pleased to see you," he said sarcastically.

"She was fine, and Alice is fine too." She wasn't going to elaborate on *that* little matter. He could work it out for himself. "But I'm sure Roland hasn't finished with it yet. I reckon he'll want revenge for his girl being spoiled—"

Theo hooted. "*Spoiled*? You think that was the first time she'd lifted her skirts? You don't know these slappers like I do, cuz, and it would have been just another mark on her bedpost to have been shafted by a German boy."

"You disgust me, Theo," she said coldly. "But never mind that. What do you propose to do about the boys? I say we let them go now before something happens that we'll regret."

212

"Like starting another war, you mean?" he sneered. "No, my sweet one, they've been hired to do a job of work, and they'll stay until it's finished. Otherwise, we'll just be seen as giving in to these scumbag clayers, and no Tremayne has ever been accused of doing that!" He swallowed his brandy and poured himself another. "Anyway, what did your fancy lawyer friend have to tell you? If you're as rich as Croesus now with some wild idea of paying Dewy off, then you're even madder than I thought."

Skye stared at him, not comprehending for a moment, but of course he had known where she was going today. And not for all the tea in Asia was she going to tell him what Philip's will contained. She lifted her chin up high.

"If I am, it's no business of yours," she retorted.

"No nasty little surprises in the will then?" he said, his eyes narrowed.

"None that I can't handle."

It was true, she thought, driving away from the house and back to her own domain. The first shock of Philip's bequest to Ruth Dobson was fading a little. She would handle this crisis as she had handled all the others in her life. And it was hardly a life-threatening crisis! Dear Lord, she had come through a war and faced her mother's death, then her brother's, and her darling Morwen's. She had dealt with Uncle Albie and risen above any thought of scandal surrounding him and Primmy. She had had a love affair and put it to one side where it belonged. For now. She was strong. She was a survivor. She used the words as a mantra, repeating them to herself all the way back to New World. And for once it wasn't Morwen Tremayne's voice inside her head, approving her thoughts. It was her own.

And she didn't even realise she hadn't once put Philip's death into her reckoning.

Theo took her words at face value after all, Skye discovered. He had already taken the German youths away from the clayworks and put them onto the packing at White Rivers, where the Christmas orders were in the last stages of completion now.

He also insisted that they kept to a strict curfew. So, with luck, nothing was going to happen on the Dewys' account after all, and Skye breathed a little easier.

Two weeks later Nick telephoned to say he'd be calling at the house with an assistant to collect the encyclopaedias, and whether or not that meant he'd located Ruth Dobson, Skye didn't ask. She arranged to be out of the house on the day he was due, knowing she was being cowardly, but unable to see this last act of spite on Philip's part being carried through.

By now, that was how she chose to see it and she gave instructions to Mrs Arden to give Mr Pengelly access to her husband's study, and to obtain a receipt for whatever he required. Everything businesslike and impersonal.

David Kingsley had also telephoned one afternoon.

"I know it's too soon to discuss other matters, my dear, but it may take your mind off things," he said awkwardly.

Like my husband dying, you mean?

"Go on, David."

"It's this proposed exhibition of your uncle's work. I mentioned it to Mr Theo Tremayne, and we both thought that after Christmas might be a better time. I'm thinking about *The Informer* doing a big spread about it when the time comes, of course, with perhaps some background information on the artist that you might like to write yourself."

And how much background information were you thinking of? A suspected relationship with my mother, the artist's sister? Or the way he had transferred that unhealthy lust to me?

David was still talking as she gripped the telephone receiver in her hand.

"I understand you have a rather large business project on right now, and also, after Christmas would coincide with the proposed selling of the studio and effects."

Her heart jolted at his words. "Who told you the studio was to be sold?"

"Oh Lord, I'm sorry if I'm treading on someone's toes, but Mr Tremayne intimated—"

Her quick temper subsided. After all, wasn't it the only sensible thing to do? Albie would never return to Cornwall.

The doctor who had helped her through Philip's death said he was slowly going into a complete decline, but that he was well and happy in his new home. As far as it was possible to be, for a man in his twilight condition, he had added significantly.

"We'll leave everything until after Christmas then, David." And meanwhile, she would ensure that others in the family took on some of the responsibility. It wasn't just hers. It wasn't fair to expect it of her, especially now. . . .

"Mommy, are you crying?" she heard Wenna's fearful voice say as she put down the telephone.

"Of course not, honey," she said, blinking back the tears. "I was just thinking we should do something while the weather is still fine, and a walk by the sea might be the very thing. What do you think?"

Wenna clapped her hands and then eyed her mother cautiously. "But Celia's doing lessons, and Oliver's asleep."

Skye recognised the hope in her wistful voice. Wenna not only wanted her mother to herself, she *needed* her exclusive attention. She wanted to feel that sense of belonging between the two of them. In an instant Skye remembered the times when her brother Sinclair had insisted on being with her and Primmy, when she too had wanted her mother all to herself.

"Then it will be just the two of us," she promised, rewarded by the glow of pleasure in the small, beautiful face.

It was something she needed too, Skye realised, as they walked briskly towards the shore and the small sandy cove beneath the cliffs. To feel the bonds that existed between mother and daughter, and to remember that Philip's legacy to her was more precious and important than all the encyclopaedias in the world. How could she have been so foolish as to let it cloud her common sense? Whatever Ruth Dobson had, Skye had her children, but she refused to wallow in sentimentality, and she and Wenna spent a joyful hour tossing stones into the oncoming waves, and screaming with laughter as they scrambled back from the creamy swell.

"Is it all right to laugh, Mommy?" Wenna said once.

"Of course it is. Daddy wouldn't want us to be gloomy for the rest of our lives, honey."

"But Miss Landon said we shouldn't be too noisy and upset you. She said we should have respect for the – the dead . . ."

Skye caught her up in her arms and looked into the troubled blue eyes. "We'll always have respect for your daddy, darling. But we can't live in the past. We have to go on living in the here and now."

"Does that mean we can still have a tree at Christmas – and presents?"

Skye laughed. "Of course it does! Why on earth wouldn't we?"

"Miss Landon says it might not be right—"

"Miss Landon isn't your mommy, and if I say it's right then it's right," Skye said, resolving to have words with the children's nanny about one or two matters. She was a treasure, but there were certain house rules that she had to understand, and one of them was to let the children recover from their father's death in their own way. Shunning all thoughts of childhood fun certainly wasn't the right way.

By the time they returned to the house, Skye was feeling more refreshed than when she left it. The road ahead was one without her husband, but life went on. You couldn't stop it, and nor should you want to.

The children needed their childhood, and Albie needed his exhibition, whether he would be aware of it or not. He deserved recognition for his talent, and despite her earlier resolve, Skye knew she was destined to be the one most closely involved in seeing that he got it. The mourning time for Philip wasn't over, but she was starting to see things more clearly now and to look ahead to the future.

A few days later she went up to White Rivers to see for herself how the Christmas orders were progressing. The staff were somewhat embarrassed to see her, but when they realised she was here to discuss business, they visibly relaxed.

Adam Pengelly was openly pleased to see her. In his married state as a relative now, he had lost his one-time awkwardness with the elegant lady boss.

"Our Nick came and had a meal with us t'other evening," he told her. "He were saying he hadn't seen anything of you lately, and I told Vera we should have asked you too, to get you out of yourself."

"I'm fine," she replied, smiling at the quaint phrase, "but thank you for the thought."

"Ah well, Vera said you prob'ly wouldn't want to do too much mixing wi' folk just yet."

And Vera would know the reason why she wouldn't want to do too much mixing where Nick Pengelly was concerned . . .

"So tell me, how are things going here?" she went on determinedly. "No problems with the helpers?"

Adam's face darkened a little. "We had Mr Theo up here t'other day, and he gave us all a good talking-to about not making trouble, as if 'twas one of us who was sporting wi' the moors girls. Anyway, young Gunter gave him back a right mouthful, and said he'd please himself what he did, and who he did it with."

Skye felt her nerves tighten. "I was told that the Dewy girl's been sent away—"

"But she ain't the only one, is she? There's talk, see, and the damn fool can't stop his boasting, nor keep his tackle where it belongs, begging your pardon for being so frank."

"I told Theo they should be sent home," she snapped.

"And he's a stubborn mule," retorted Adam. "You'll not be rid of 'em until the job's done. But most of the shipments have already been sent off, so we're well on course."

"Then thank goodness it's nearly over and done with, Adam. But I don't like to get such news second-hand, and you'll be seeing far more of me from now on."

As she left the pottery, she realised that for all her unease her spirits were strangely uplifted, knowing it was far better to be involved in something than to languish in misery. Even if it was something that could still have an unpredictable outcome. The clayers were volatile at the best of times, and the simmering resentment against their one-time enemies could as soon erupt into a cauldron of hate, with unforeseen consequences.

Fifteen

The reckoning came one dark Friday night in early November. The clayworkers had been biding their time out of respect for Skye's bereavement, but after the Dewy girl's departure it was discovered that Gunter and several more of the brawny German youths had been sporting with other girls in the warm linhays at Killigrew Clay, and boasting about their conquests.

It was more than the clayers could take. They lay in wait for the youths, setting about them and beating them about their heads with sticks, knowing that these easy come easy go workers didn't have to report for work until the following Monday morning.

Although they fought back, the young men were heavily outnumbered. And as if to emphasise that the Cornishmen meant business, the little white rivers of claywater began to run red with German blood as their gory heads were plunged under the milky water time and again until they came up gulping for air, pleading and fearing for their lives.

"That'll teach you forrin buggers to mess wi' our maids," screamed one, and echoed by the other clayers, not sparing any one of them.

"You fools," the boys screamed back. "They only get what they want. What they *ask* for, instead of how we were told your bastard English Tommies defiled our German girls—"

The merest reference to the war incensed the clayworkers more. Every one of them had lost someone dear to them and their vengeance was raw and violent. The beatings went on until the boys lay groaning and near-insensible, their heads and bodies a bloody mass of pulp. Only then did the clayers walk away, satisfied that in their eyes, honour had been done.

*　　*　　*

There were no German packers at the pottery on Monday morning. By then, still nursing their wounds, they had sullenly refused to leave their temporary lodgings, barracading themselves into their rooms and frightening their landlady with their foul-mouthed oaths. And long before then they had broken into the White Rivers packing room, leaving the remainder of the Christmas orders smashed to smithereens.

Adam Pengelly discovered the carnage with his workmates when he went to unlock the main door to the pottery early on Monday morning and found it broken open, the door creaking on its hinges.

"Christ Almighty," he said hoarsely, as he took in the magnitude of the sight in front of him. In the packing room he strode over the smashed plates and pots, feeling as if he walked on the remnants of his very heart as he did so. But suppressing his unmanly distress as much as possible, he reached for the telephone and called Theo Tremayne.

"The bloody buggering swine!" roared Theo predictably. "Whoever did this, I'll have 'em strung up by the bollocks!"

"Ain't it obvious?" Adam said bitterly. "The forriners ain't reported for work, and if 'twas them that did it, they'm keeping well out of sight. Young Ethan said he saw a gang of clayers with bloodied faces over the weekend as well."

"So it came to a fight, did it?" Theo snarled. "Well, what's the extent of the damage? Do we have enough stock in the showroom to replace the last of the orders?"

"Maybe, with a bit of luck."

"Then the bastards will just have to come back and do the work they're being paid for! I'll fetch 'em myself and frogmarch 'em back to work if I have to."

"I'm not sure that's wise, Theo."

"You're not paid to be wise," he snapped. "Get on with the clearing up and I'll be there as soon as I can."

The line went dead, and Adam stared at the phone in resentful silence. He was a skilled craftsman, not a cleaner, but with one sentence Theo Tremayne had reduced him to a menial worker. Without moving another muscle, he quickly spoke to Skye on the telephone, relating all that happened, and his certainty as to who had done the damage.

"Dear God, I knew something like this would happen," she raged. "I've feared it all along – and Theo will only make matters worse. He must see now that we must send the Germans home right away. If the clayers get wind of them returning to work we'll have a strike on our hands – or worse."

"'Tain't only the clayers neither," Adam snapped, beyond trying to keep his temper now. "We all lost family at the hands of these buggers, and there's plenty here who'll refuse to work with them after this."

"Not you, Adam? You wouldn't strike, would you?" Her voice rose shrilly as everything seemed to be falling apart.

"You ain't seen the damage," he shouted. "All our finest work's been ruined, and no craftsman can be expected to put up with that outrage."

Skye knew he was seriously understating the searing blow to his pride. "I'll come at once," she said, and put down the telephone with trembling hands.

If the potters, the undisputed linchpins of the business, went on strike, then everyone else at the pottery would follow suit. The showrooms always did well at Christmas time, since David Kingsley was generous in advertising their local products as being the pride of Cornwall for Christmas gifts. But with no staff to price and sell the goods . . .

Skye's thoughts sped ahead like quicksilver. She wasn't so bloody grand that she wouldn't do it all herself, but it would take more than one person. . . .

She drew a deep breath. This time, she knew that if Adam refused to work, she couldn't expect any help from Vera. You couldn't, and shouldn't, split the loyalties of husband and wife. But there was Lily, who certainly wouldn't have patience with any strike nonsense, and would stand shoulder to shoulder with Skye as stridently as if she was one of Mrs Pankhurst's suffragettes.

Before she even left the house to see what was happening at White Rivers, Skye telephoned her cousin in Plymouth and explained the situation as briefly and succinctly as possible, considering the way her stomach was churning. But it was better to be forearmed, than to wait and see what further damage Theo would do in his bull-headedness.

"I'll be there as soon as I can," Lily said in answer to her garbled words. "Don't worry about a thing. You and I will be shopkeepers and to blazes with the rest of them."

Skye felt her eyes fill with tears. Lily was so loyal, but by now she was already wondering if shopkeepers would even be needed. *The Informer*'s advertising had worked wonders for the pottery in the past, but the clayworkers could turn their hands to propaganda as well as anyone else. If the whole county turned against them for employing Germans, there would be no customers for Christmas, if ever. And if the boycott continued, White Rivers could be ruined because of this folly. But they had no option. They had to try.

Skye stared in horror at the ruined packing room. Theo was shouting loudly at the regular workers, standing around awkwardly and not knowing what to do. Skye walked carefully over the broken pieces of pottery to confront him.

"For pity's sake, control yourself! This isn't doing any good. We have to see how we can repair the damage."

"Oh, do we, my fine feathered cuz? And how do you propose we do that? By setting the potters to work day and night and paying them an extortionate rate to get the orders finished?"

"Yes. Exactly that," she said calmly. She turned to Adam and his fellow craftsmen, standing silently by.

"How long would it take, Adam?"

Unbelievably, she saw him fold his arms, his face mutinous. All the others followed suit. Like sheep. Like bloody aggrieved sheep, she thought hysterically.

"We've had a meeting, Mrs Norwood."

She stared at him, startled, as he used her formal name, but he stared her out and went on grimly.

"We ain't prepared to continue with this order. If Mr Tremayne gets the toerags back to work, then we go on strike. And if you expect us to work all hours of the day and night to provide plates and pots for the forriners' tables, then you can think again."

"Adam! For God's sake think what you're saying. You'll all benefit from extra wages, and what does it matter where the goods end up? We need to expand and export—"

"It matters to we, ma'am," one of the others put in. "My missus is still grieving over our boy who was killed in the war, and I ain't ready to think of some forrin fam'ly enjoying our hard labour."

Theo snarled. "Hard labour, is it? You're not gouging out the clay from the earth and getting your feet and your brains soaked in all weathers – if you've got any brains, that is."

"I did once, and so did my father before me, and so would my son now, if he weren't lying dead somewhere in France."

There was total silence for a few moments, and then Theo's voice was practically spitting fire. "But you can't seriously mean to strike, you stupid buggers. Your womenfolk will give you plenty of tongue-pie if you don't bring in your Christmas wages."

"We'll put up with that," Adam retorted. "Meanwhile, this is the deal—"

"*Deal*?" Theo yelled. "I don't make deals with minions!"

Before she could stop herself, Skye slapped him hard across the face. He had humiliated these good men, and he had humiliated her too. He made to lunge at her, but before he could retaliate, several of the men had pulled him away.

"Listen to what Adam says, Theo, and stop making a bigger fool of yourself than you already are," she said in a choked voice, touched that these men should champion her so visibly.

"The deal is this," Adam went on forcibly, "we'll work for Mrs Norwood and get some goods ready for the showroom, but we'll have no Germans here, and we'll have nothing more to do with the German order. It was a mistake in the first place."

"No, it was never a mistake, Adam," Skye put in swiftly before Theo could draw breath. "And what you're suggesting is just perpetuating what was over a long time ago. I know individual feelings have run very high lately, but the overall business scheme was always a good one. Bringing the boys here was the big mistake."

"And I ain't sending 'em back until I'm good and ready," Theo continued to roar, his face purple with rage. "I ain't being dictated to by workmen and women as to what I do."

"Then we strike as from now until they're gone," Adam said. "Every man here is at liberty to follow his own conscience, so those who are with me will be leaving now."

He turned on his heel, and the others followed him silently. At the broken door, one of the men turned and glared back at Theo with pure hatred in his eyes.

"You've had this coming a long time, Tremayne, and I'm warnin' 'ee that it ain't finished yet. My two brothers work at Killigrew Clay and if we strike, they strike."

Skye gasped and made to protest, but Theo stopped her.

"Let 'em go. They'll soon come crawling back when they've got no money to pay for food for their children's bellies."

"How can you be so *stupid*? You risk putting the whole of Killigrew Clay out of production as well as White Rivers, and whatever else you think, these people are vandals and should be sacked immediately."

"Oh ah, my clever little cousin. And I thought you were all for forwarding Anglo-German relations, as you called it?"

"So I was, and I still am. We must look forward and not back, but you handled everything badly, Theo, the way you always do. And while we're on the subject of *your* men and *your* goods, this is a good time to remind you that White Rivers belongs to me, and not to you."

He glowered at her. "Then you can do what you like with it from now on, for I've done with it. But I ain't sending those boys back home until I see fit to do so."

He stalked out, his feet crunching on broken pottery and leaving her alone in the mess that was once her pride and joy. There was no one else here now. Even the women who normally appeared for work had clearly got wind of the situation and decided to stay away. Or more likely had been forbidden by their menfolk to work for a boss who consorted with the enemy.

Skye felt an almost hysterical laugh bubbling up inside her. Didn't they realise – couldn't they understand – that she had as much to condemn the Germans for as they did? Her husband had suffered a terrible injury because of them, and he had finally died from its legacy. But they all had to go on, to rise above it all, before bitterness became a cancer that in time would destroy them all. If she could forgive and forget, why couldn't they?

Yet here she was, little more than a month after her husband's death, plunged into a war of her own, and having to face it entirely alone.

Into the silence of the once-thriving pottery, she heard a small sound. She spun around, her heart pounding, wondering if she was about to be molested, or worse, and faced the scared young face of Ethan Pengelly.

"What are you doing here?" she choked out.

"I work here," he said uncertainly. "I just passed a gang of angry folk on their way to Killigrew Clay, and Adam told me what had happened. He said I mustn't speak to you, but that ain't right, is it, Mrs – Skye? We'm fam'ly, and fam'lies stick together. That's what Our Nick allus says, anyway."

And if Our Nick says so, then it must be right.

"Come here," Skye said, holding out her arms to him, her heart full. He was such a darling boy, and *Our Nick could always put things right* . . . and she had never yearned for him more than she did at that moment.

But she realised that in his loyalty to her this young boy was about to split his own family in two, and she couldn't allow that. Although hadn't that already been done? Vera would stick by her husband, no matter what, and Lily was on her way here right now. Two sisters were already on opposite sides.

Ethan moved towards her uneasily, wondering if he was going to be clasped in Skye's arms and full of adolescent embarrassment at the thought. Sensing his feelings, at the last moment she reached for a broom.

"Then if you're going to stay, you can help me clear up all this mess for a start," she said as calmly as she could. "We'll put it all into the packing boxes and then I'll arrange for someone to take it all away. We're going to have the showroom open for business as soon as possible, no matter what anyone else thinks."

Ethan's eyes sparkled with hope for a moment. "Then do 'ee

think maybe I could throw a few extra pots, Mrs – Skye? I'm a dab hand at it now, so Adam says."

"Why not?" she said. "We'll show them all."

She wasn't sure herself just what she meant, but already she had a glimmering of an idea. She was good with words. Journalism had been her job, and she had written extensively in the past, sending back authentic articles for *The Informer* newspaper from the front line, and revealing the truth and the heartbreak of wartime from a woman's viewpoint. Why not make use of that expertise again, turning a bad situation into a positive one? And there was one person who could help her.

"Well, this is a turn-up," Lily whistled, when her boneshaker of a car finally rattled up to White Rivers that afternoon. She tried to hide her shock at the state of the place, although by now, Skye and Ethan had done a fair job of clearing up. There was still dust everywhere, choking and cloying, and turning the pair of them into ghostly white figures worthy of the clayworkers themselves.

"You should have seen it this morning," Skye said hoarsely, her throat dry. "But we've been working like Trojans, and it's beginning to look quite respectable now."

But as Lily gazed around, unable to disguise her horror, Skye's eyes filled with tears. It still seemed a thankless, insurmountable task, but she was going to see it through if it killed her in the process. Old Morwen Tremayne would have expected nothing less of her. But it was hard not to feel defeated. She was limp with exhaustion and the tension of the morning, and she was also very hungry, she realised.

As if anticipating her thoughts, Lily dumped the hamper she was carrying, seeing that Skye looked all in.

"Food and drink before anything else, my girl," she announced. "No army ever won a war on an empty stomach, and we three will have a jolly picnic before you tell me your plans."

Skye gave a short laugh. "What plans?" she shrugged.

"Oh, I'm sure you must have some by now," Lily said. "You were never short of ideas, however far-fetched they seemed."

"Well, I have thought of something," Skye murmured. "But it will depend on how far David Kingsley will go to help me."

"The newspaper chappie? Oh well, that'll be no problem, will it?" Lily said with a grin. "You'll get no opposition from him. He was always your willing slave, ready to do anything you asked."

"Not always," Skye said, aware that Ethan Pengelly was becoming more interested by the minute at this female talk. "But at least he's a more impartial newspaperman than most, and I think he may agree to champion our cause."

Lily looked at her thoughtfully, seeing her white face and her luminous blue eyes, as beautiful as ever, but seemingly almost too large for her face now.

"Are you really ready to do battle, Skye? So soon after Philip, I mean?" she asked, more gently.

Skye gave a brief smile. "I'm more than ready, and you know as well as I do that Philip was always one to champion a cause too."

Not that he'd enjoy the spectacle of his wife becoming a shopkeeper, or wrangling with common folk, or writing impassioned articles for a provincial newspaper. But since it was her choice and not his, she didn't feel the least bit of guilt in recognising that his opinions no longer mattered.

"So where do we begin?" Lily said, when they had finished the bread and cheese and bottles of lemonade that she had so thoughtfully brought.

"Ethan has already begun," Skye told her, giving him a warm smile. "I've telephoned for a locksmith to come and fix a new lock on the door and make it safe, and I shall speak to David Kingsley this evening. Meanwhile, we'll finish clearing this mess up, and put up a 'Temporarily Closed' sign."

"What do you think Theo will have to say about that?"

"I don't give a tinker's cuss for what Theo thinks. This is my property, not his. Granny Morwen left it to me, and I've no intention of letting her down by throwing in the towel after one little setback."

"That's my girl," Lily said softly. "She'd have been so proud of you. But then, she always was."

It was a sentiment that left Skye glowing for the rest of the day until she finally said they had done enough. By now the door was fixed, and Ethan had gone home.

Since they both had their motor cars at the pottery, Lily followed Skye down the undulating slopes of the moors until they reached New World, where Lily would stay.

"Mother will probably wash her hands of me, anyway, when she hears the stand we're about to make," she had told Skye cheerfully. "*Lady Charlotte* always had to hold her head up high in the community, no matter what anyone else did. She missed her vocation in not being born a Killigrew."

Skye laughed. "You do me so much good, Lily, and the children will love having you here. This house has been so gloomy lately, and I really can't bear it."

"Poor love. Do you miss him so very much?" Lily said sympathetically.

Skye lowered her eyes. For a horrible moment she had been tempted to tell the truth and shock her cousin rigid. To say that no, she really didn't miss Philip at all, and the house was a much more relaxed place without him . . . it was just gloomy with the aftermath of a death in the family and its required sense of hushed reverence. If the whole truth be told then this resolve to do something positive about the pottery had given her just the boost she needed.

"I'll survive, Lily. And thankfully, the children seem to be taking things in their stride now."

"Children are very resilient," said Lily, not realising how neatly Skye had turned her thoughts away from the widow's own feelings.

"So let's decide what to do next. I suggest that when I call David I'll ask him to come here for a meeting. I don't want to say anything over the telephone. What do you think?" Skye said, bringing her into the plans.

"I think you're bloody marvellous," her cousin replied.

"But apart from that?" Skye said solemnly, before a smile broke over both their faces.

Before they thought of doing anything else, though, they spent an hour with the children in the nursery to help settle

them down. Lily was totally undomesticated and had no maternal instincts on her own account, but she was always ready
to play rough-and-tumble with the three of them. Oliver in
particular, adored her.

"I could be jealous," Skye said mildly, when he screamed that
he would let no one else put him to bed but Lily.

But she wasn't. Lily was like a sweet breath of moorland
air inside New World, and she resolved that from now on, no
one should treat this house of mourning as somewhere akin
to the grave itself. Victorian protocol was of another age, and
tomorrow Skye would order that the curtains should be drawn
right back from all the windows, instead of still half shading
the daylight. Others could think what they chose. This was her
house, and she made the decisions.

Glory be, she thought. *I'm in danger of becoming as strident
as Lily!*

Not that that was any bad thing. But all that was for tomorrow,
and there was still tonight. . . .

"David, it's Skye Norwood here."

"Skye, my dear, how are you?" his voice said cautiously. It was
odd how you could detect every nuance in a person's voice over
the telephone, she mused, sometimes more acutely than when
you were facing them. And he was clearly wary of how she was
reacting to her husband's death. He had sent the usual card of
condolence, but nothing more.

"I'm well enough, thank you, but my state of health is not why
I'm calling. There was some trouble at Killigrew Clay a few days
ago, and I fear that it's overlapping into White Rivers. Maybe
you've heard something about it already?"

"I'm afraid I have. Such news travels fast, Skye. I presume
you'd like me to print your side of it?"

Of course the news would have travelled. Clayworkers were
never slow to air their grievances, but his words gave her the
perfect opening. "I'd rather not say anything more over the
telephone, but I wondered if you could come here this evening
to discuss a plan of action with my cousin Lily Pollard and
myself? And I'll give you the correct version, David."

It had suddenly struck her that he might have already heard a very different and damning version.

He spoke again. "This evening, you say?"

"Yes. Why don't you come to dinner?" she added hastily.

"Are you sure about this?" he asked. "I mean, do you feel up to having an extra dinner guest?"

"I never felt more up to it," she repeated quaintly. "And I need your support, David. About seven o'clock?"

"I'll be there."

Skye replaced the receiver slowly and drew a deep breath. She had begun the process that she hoped was going to stop the total annihilation of everything she had worked for all these years. Everything Morwen had approved for her.

Lily said, "You handled that very well. Just as long as he doesn't think you're harbouring fond thoughts about him."

"I shouldn't think so. We dealt with all that a long time ago. And besides—"

"Yes, I'm sorry, love. I just didn't think. No one would dream of your having such thoughts about anyone else so soon after your husband's death."

They certainly wouldn't dream of her having yearnings for Nick Pengelly, but that thought had been uppermost in her mind at that moment. It wouldn't go away, no matter how much Skye tried to make it. And it was David himself who brought up his name once dinner was over and the three of them sat companionably in the sitting-room of New World.

By then Skye had told him everything about the attack on the German boys and the outcome of it. And of her plans for Lily and herself to become shopkeepers, aided at present only by young Ethan Pengelly.

"I admire you both greatly," David said. "But I presume you've alerted your insurance company to assess the damage and make a sensible claim? And you must certainly be advised by your lawyer to see where you can press charges."

"I don't intend to press any charges," Skye said, but she was quickly realising she hadn't been nearly as efficient as she should have been. Or rather, she had been *too* efficient. She had cleared away all the visible evidence . . . and she hadn't yet given a thought to any insurance claim. "My cousin Theo refuses to send these youths home, and I've no intention of allowing them back to work to stir up more trouble. But the mere fact that they remain in Cornwall will have just as explosive an effect on the clayworkers as if they were working, so we're at stalemate."

"Then what is it you want of me?"

"I want you to write a brief and unemotional article for the newspaper detailing everything that happened here the other night, and what's happened since. I'll give you all the details, names and everything. And then I want you to print my personal article alongside it, written in the way I wrote those I sent home from the front. This time I shall try to appeal to people's reason, to try to make them see that this hostility has got to end, or we shall never attain a real peace. I also want you to do some extensive advertising for the pottery showrooms, and I will already have stated frankly the reason why Lily and I are there. What do you say?"

Her voice had become impassioned, but she felt her heart leap as he looked at her uneasily without speaking. Surely he wasn't going to refuse? It had all seemed so cut and dried when she and Lily had discussed it.

"Don't you think it's a good idea?" Lily demanded. "Isn't she marvellous to want to put things right?"

"I've always thought she was marvellous," David said dryly. "But I have to tell you something. When I said I had heard something about the attack on the Germans, I didn't tell you the whole truth. One of my reporters has a relative working at Killigrew Clay, who was quick to pass on the story of the beatings. He's already interviewed some of the clayworkers and got their side of the story, and I'm afraid it will appear in the next issue of *The Informer*, with plenty of self-righteous quotes from those concerned. And there are still plenty of folk who agree with their sentiments."

"Then include your impartial viewpoint article alongside it to counter the damage that's been done!" Skye said swiftly. "I'll get my own copy out as quickly as possible – not that I've even begun to work on it yet. Everything's been happening so fast. . . ."

Her voice died away as he shook his head. "It can't be done, my dear. The next issue has already gone to press, and whatever we have to say won't appear until a week later, and I fear that public opinion will already be swayed by then."

The two women stared at him with sick hearts. The plan had seemed so perfect, so courageous, and now it seemed that the clayers had successfully undermined even that. At that moment Skye hated them all.

"But you'll still do it?" Lily snapped. "You won't let us down, will you? And we need the advertising too. We don't intend to let these devils win, David."

He saw the fiery resolution in her eyes. Those goddamned, treacherously beautiful Tremayne eyes, no matter what name any of them married into. One of these women alone was strong enough. The two of them together were formidable.

"Of course I won't let you down," he said.

After he left, each of the two women tried not to show how depressed they were. But they knew the timing was all wrong.

If only Skye had got her words into the newspaper first. They both knew that if public opinion hadn't actually been swayed by her article, then at least the voice of reason would have been heard. She was well respected as the granddaughter of old Morwen Tremayne, even if she was an American. As it was, if feelings ran high enough for the townsfolk to join forces with the clayworkers while the German youths were still here, it could so easily turn into a witch hunt. And God only knew how it would end.

"It's all Theo's fault," Lily burst out. "If he wasn't so bloody pig-headed—"

"It's no use blaming him. Lily. We should all have seen this coming."

"And who arranged for them to come here in the first place? It was Theo, wasn't it?" Lily demanded.

"All right, but don't let's talk about it any more," Skye said wearily. "I've had just about enough for one day."

She turned almost thankfully when Mrs Arden announced that there was another visitor, and handed Skye a business card. She read Nicholas Pengelly's name on it, and it was more than she could do to turn him away.

"Please ask Mr Pengelly to come in," she told her house-keeper.

"*Adam?*" Lily said, clearly preparing to stand her ground and argue the toss with her sister's husband.

"No, it's Nick."

"Then I'll make myself scarce. He obviously wants to talk to you about business matters, and I could do with an early night. Goodnight, darling."

As she left the room, Skye felt a moment's panic, wanting to say that there was no need for her to go. And that anything she and Nick had to discuss could be said freely in front of Lily, since the two of them were temporary business partners now. But the words stuck in her throat as Nick came into the room, his face stormy.

"I've been talking to my brothers, and wondering if the whole world's gone mad, and you in particular," he said. "What the hell do you think you're doing, Skye?"

Sixteen

S kye stared at him, open-mouthed. This certainly wasn't what she expected, or deserved. It had been one hell of a day, and her temper erupted.

"What do you mean, what do I think *I'm* doing? Have you the faintest idea of what's been happening here while you've been sitting on your backside in Bodmin?" She saw slight amusement twitch his mouth as the unlikely word slid from her lips. It only infuriated her more. "And I suppose you think it's funny that I'm probably about to be ruined, and that most of my family relationships are in tatters!" *To say nothing of ours* . . .

"I don't think it's funny at all," he said sharply. "What I think is that you've been an idiot for allowing yourself to be drawn into this situation because of the rank stupidity of your cousin."

"You think I don't *know* that!"

Her mouth suddenly trembled violently, and without either of them knowing quite how it happened, he had crossed the room and she was being held tightly in his arms.

"Sweetheart, this last month must have been sheer hell for you, and I have never felt more impotent at being unable to help you," he muttered against her burning cheek.

Impotent? the mischievous little devil inside her echoed the word; he was never that . . . But she sobered at once, because this was no time for such thoughts. She clung to him for a moment longer and then pushed him away. "Nick, we can't – not yet, not now . . ."

"I know," he said, more gravely. "We have serious business to discuss."

"Do we?" she asked, not yet knowing why he was here, nor why he had railed at her so furiously. She moved away from him and sat down abruptly on an armchair, her hands crossed primly in her lap.

He had to force out of his mind the image of her in a far less formal pose, when she had lain so erotically in his arms, each pleasuring the other, with nothing between them but their own glistening flesh. And love. So much love.

"I've done something wrong, haven't I?" she said, half defensively, half apologetically.

"You could say that," Nick sighed, seating himself on another chair and careful to keep his distance. He had already forgotten himself once, when faced with her haunting beauty, but this was still a house of mourning, and some servant or other might appear at any moment to offer him refreshment that he didn't want. He only wanted *her*. . . . He cleared his throat.

"What have I done?" she asked. "You know what's happened, and by now the whole community is probably taking sides."

"That's not what I'm here about. Ethan tells me you and he spent hours this morning clearing up the mess in the pottery, and that you and Vera's sister intend to manage it yourselves until things get back to some kind of normality."

"Is there anything wrong with that?"

"Just this, my sweet, headstrong little idiot. You should have touched nothing until the police and the insurance assessors arrived. You should have telephoned me at once for advice, not rushed into things with all the rashness of Theo Tremayne."

"Well, thank you for that!" Skye said, blazing now. "If you wanted to heap insult onto insult you couldn't have done a better job. But for your information I don't intend to press any charges and stir up even more trouble."

"You'll stir up trouble if you don't! Can't you see that folk will simply think you're letting these vandals get away with it?"

"And what of *them*? Do you think they'll be pressing charges against the clayers who half killed them? There's been no sign of them since that night, and I should imagine they're too scared to show themselves. I prefer to let sleeping dogs lie, and Lily and I will do exactly what we've decided to do."

He saw her challenging eyes and shrugged. "Then I can't make

up my mind whether you're a courageous woman or a blind fool.
I know one thing though."

"What's that?" Skye snapped, resentful to her fingertips at his
high-handed attitude.

"Those German boys have got to leave Cornwall."

"Try telling that to Theo. He won't listen to me. They're still
owed some wages, and I doubt that they'll go peaceably without
that, either."

"Let's leave Theo out of this. If you've got the details and the
funds here, we'll do the job ourselves."

Skye stared at him, not understanding. This was the upright
lawyer who never put a foot wrong, and right now he sounded for
all the world like a villain planning a robbery. Or something else.
. . . Surely he wasn't suggesting that they smuggle the German
boys out of the country?

"What job?" she queried.

In the early hours of the following morning, Skye and Nick
returned to New World, exhausted, but having achieved their
goal. After thrashing through their plans, they had gone straight
to the lodging house, surprising the German youths. And dealing with them hadn't been nearly as traumatic as Skye had
anticipated.

By now they were more like frightened children, cut off
from society and virtual prisoners in their lodgings. The once-
sympathetic landlady was glad to be rid of them, and the boys
were almost pathetic in their anxiety to return to Germany
on the night packet from the St Austell port at Charleston.
Nick's authoritative voice was enough to make them agree to
anything.

They were still bloodied and bruised, but the wages for the
work they had done pacified them, even though they were denied
the bonuses in order to pay for the damages. It would never
cover it all, but Skye was prepared to go halfway. Nick had
been openly disapproving, and was more for sending the boys
home in disgrace with no favours at all.

"What good would that do?" Skye argued. "I need to continue
good relations with our export clients, and Hans Kauffmann will

get a detailed letter from me explaining the situation. He's a fair man, and I know he'll understand."

"Then you have more faith in human nature than I do," Nick said dryly.

But they had finally got the youths onto the packet ship and breathed a sigh of relief as they returned to New World. They had taken two cars in order to transport them to the port. There was no need for Nick to return with her, she told him, but the night was dark and she would be a woman alone, so chivalry won. But for the first time Skye felt awkward as they stood outside the house together.

"Don't come in," she murmured. "It would look odd, you being here at this hour, but I do want to thank you, Nick."

"I don't want your thanks," he said roughly. "I just want you to turn to me whenever you need me. And I want you to need me, and to miss me, damn it!"

"You know that I do," she whispered with quiet dignity. "But I can't think about anything but the pottery right now, and how to salvage things. Theo will be furious when he discovers what we've done."

He could see that she was too exhausted to think of more personal matters, and no matter how he longed to take her in his arms and kiss away all the hurt and fears, he knew that he must not. Her spirit was strong, but there was a fragility about her now that touched his soul.

"Then let me put one worry at rest. I'll contact the insurance people and assure them that I've seen the damage and can vouch for what happened. And that you needed to get reorganised as quickly as possible for the Christmas business. It won't please them, but they'll take my word for it."

"Thank you."

He hesitated, but it had to be said sometime, and now was as good a time as any. "And one last thing, Skye. Through a business colleague I've contacted Ruth Dobson, and the encyclopaedias are on their way to her. She fully understands your wishes not to make any further contact."

He didn't elaborate, but he saw the tightening of Skye's mouth as she nodded, turned, and went inside the house. And he got back into his car and drove away like the wind, savage with frustration that he couldn't do more for her, and be with her, and love her. He hated himself for having brought up Ruth Dobson's name at this time, but he was ever mindful of fulfilling his legal obligations.

Which was about as hypocritical as he could get, he thought angrily, considering what he had persuaded Skye to do tonight. Hustling those boys out of the country and giving them their freedom, when by rights they should be brought to justice for their vandalism.

But so should the clayers for their brutality, his inner voice argued. And he gave up the intrusion of his bloody legal training that made him see two sides to every question and went home to bed for a couple of hours of much-needed sleep. The next issue of *The Informer* was due out that morning, and both he and Skye knew they could expect to see the garbled and one-sided reports from the clayworkers about their rights, and the indignant backlash against hiring the German boys.

Skye had no doubt that every clayworker who had a voice would have said they'd been against the import of the youths from the start, and they had only got what they deserved. By the time the article ended, the clayers would be whiter than white, and their actions against the boys would be seen as no more than rightful retaliation.

And didn't she know only too well how an astute choice of words could always sway folk to whatever conclusion was intended? She shivered as she crawled into bed, knowing she must get her own article started as soon as possible. As soon as she could get her thoughts together. But first thing tomorrow morning there was something else she had to do.

"You've done *what*!" Theo exploded when she telephoned him from the showroom, having decided to be as far away from him as possible when she did so.

"The German boys went back on the night packet from Charleston, so there'll be no more trouble from them. I've already telephoned David Kingsley to make sure he includes the information when there's a fuller report on events in next week's newspaper," she said in a clipped, decisive voice.

"You had no right to do this without consulting me!"

"Theo, I've consulted you until I'm blue in the face and got nowhere. Can't you see that now we've removed the obstacle, there's nothing to stop the clayers and the potters from returning to work?"

There was silence for a moment, and then Theo snapped into the phone, "I doubt that very much! You bloody Tremayne women have always taken too much on yourselves."

"Thank you cuz, I take that as a compliment," Skye said sweetly, but her heart was pounding all the same.

"It wasn't bloody well meant to be," he snarled. "And don't be so sure that'll be an end to it, either. The clayers will feel you've betrayed 'em again."

"Why will they? You said they'd strike if the boys returned to work, so how long did you expect to keep them here doing nothing?" she said, but her stomach was clenching with anxiety. "They paid the price for being normal healthy young men, and you were never slow to blame the girls for enticing them on."

"And you think that excuses the shitheads for smashing up White Rivers, do you? Christ Almighty, woman, you're more bloody forgiving than a barrelful of nuns!"

Skye slammed down the phone while he was still ranting on. She shook all over, but she still believed she and Nick had done the only thing possible. And she was still determined not to press charges. Foolish or not, it was her decision, and she intended to stand by it.

"Are you all right, Skye?" she heard Lily's voice as if it came from a long distance away. "Don't let the swine upset you. He's not worth it."

"You're right. He's not," Skye said, drawing a deep breath. "So let's get on with what we intend to do."

But Theo's words had shaken her more than she wanted to admit. Surely, with the German boys gone, there was no reason why work couldn't resume as normal. Theo had always been in the wrong to bring them here in the first place, and to insist on keeping them here now. But she knew she was reckoning without the perversity of the clayworkers, and the way her cousin could twist folk around to his way of thinking.

He had been in the clay business far longer than she had, and he knew the men. They had wanted blood and they had got it, but maybe now they would see Skye's attempt to pacify things as a shifty way of getting the boys out of harm's way, and to her own advantage for selling her pottery goods.

If it were so, then despite all the damage that had been done to her property, she would be seen as being still more on the foreigners' side than her own countryfolks'.

Not that these *were* her countryfolk, her being from over the water and not a true Cornishwoman . . . in some folks' eyes, she was still as much a foreigner as the Germans. . . .

As clearly as if she could hear Theo putting his inciting arguments to the clayers and adding his snide remarks to demean her, she knew exactly what was going to happen. He would be prepared to rest on his laurels and let her be the scapegoat for all that had happened. Somehow, Skye Tremayne Norwood would be getting all the blame.

"Sit down," she heard a voice say sharply, and then Lily was pushing her head between her knees as the world seem to swim in front of her eyes. She felt a cup of cold water pushed against her lips and she swallowed automatically. But she was made of stronger stuff, and as she recovered almost at once, she looked into the scared eyes of Ethan Pengelly.

"It's all right," she said huskily. "I just felt faint for a moment, but it's nothing to worry about."

Lily spoke swiftly, seeing her pinched white face. "You don't have to be here at all today if you don't feel up to it, Skye. Ethan and I will get on with things."

"Of course I have to be here. No one's going to say I'm hiding away, and I'm going to start on the window posters to say that we're open for business as usual."

But she avoided Lily's eyes then, knowing that each of them were wondering if there was going to be any business to speak of, and not wanting to put their doubts into words.

She forced herself to be optimistc. The Christmas advertising would be going into *The Informer* newspaper very soon, and when Ethan had shown Skye his efforts at pottery making, she was surprised to find how adept he already was at it. He was definitely an asset, and they would survive. They *must*.

By the middle of the afternoon the posters were in all the windows, and the clearing up of the damaged showroom was complete. The final Christmas orders for export were ready for dispatch, and had just made their quota by depleting the showroom shelves. Ethan was in his element in the workroom, with a tray of pots already waiting to be fired in the kiln – and as many others discarded. His efforts weren't always up to standard by any means, but he was keeping busy at doing what he liked best. And there was always a ready market for less than perfect items at a cheaper price, Skye had discovered. It wasn't only the rich who needed pottery goods for their tables and displays.

Ethan at least was happy . . . while the two women waited for customers that never came, and filled in time by rearranging shelves, and washing and dusting the goods that had got covered in a grey film during the German boys' rampage. It was necessary work, but it didn't compensate for having no interested townsfolk admiring the potters' work, nor a clutch of determined shoppers wanting something specifically Cornish to give to their friends and families on Christmas morning.

"It's only November, Skye. Folk don't start their buying for weeks yet. Most of them leave it until the last minute," Lily tried to reassure her as the hours dragged on.

"It didn't happen that way last year, nor the year before," Skye said. "We might as well face it, no one's going to come here. But there's no point in worrying, and I'm sure that next week it will all come right, after David prints my piece in *The Informer*."

But before that she had to write it, and she was almost afraid to admit that right now she was experiencing a block in her mind such as she had never known before. Words had always come easily to her, but they had never been so important as these words. And even as she thought it, she felt ashamed. However important this business was to her, it was still a shallow thing compared to the comfort and hope she had given to Cornishwomen when she had written so honestly and sincerely from the front. No words had ever been so important as the words she had sent home during those dark days, nor ever could be. She could only hope that the compassion she had shown then would stand her in good stead, and that the readers would recognise her for her honesty and sincerity, now, as they did then.

"I think we may as well go home," she conceded eventually to her fellow workers. By now the daylight had begun to fade a little, and the chill of the November day was beginning to depress them all. There was no point in staying here any longer, and after her feeling of lethargy, Skye was suddenly itching to get home and find paper and pencil to formulate the words that were going to restore the pride of the clayworkers as well as saving her business. She hoped.

"Hold on a moment. We've got a customer," Lily exclaimed.

Skye's heart leapt, but not with anticipation. "Oh no, not her. That's all we need."

"Who is it?"

Ethan spoke up, his voice half fearful, half full of bravado. "They say she be a witchwoman that can work magic spells," he uttered, eyeing the hobbling gait of old Helza as she approached the pottery.

"Oh yes," Lily said, starting to laugh. "Well, if you believe that, maybe you'd best ask her to weave a magic spell to put things right here."

"I ain't asking her nothing!" Ethan told her, and backed away into the workroom, leaving Skye and Lily alone as the doorbell tinkled and the old crone came inside, wafting her own air of rankness before her.

Lily, fresh from Plymouth and with a more sophisticated Truro background than that of moorsfolk, stared the woman out.

Skye spoke huskily. "Yes? Can we help you?"

Helza cackled. "'Tis more likely that I be able to help you, lady, if all that I hear be right."

"What have you heard?" Lily said sharply. "Don't waste our time with nonsense, old woman."

Skye didn't need to ask such a question. She may not be Cornish born and bred, like Lily, for all her upcountry manners now, but she was canny enough to know that Helza wouldn't have needed to be told anything. Helza would just *know* all that had been happening.

She saw the old crone put her head on one side, her little black eyes as darting as a bird's, her mouth a thin slash in her grizzled face as she studied Lily.

"You'd be a mite improved wi' a good man to rest your feet on of a night," she said sourly. "'Twould make 'ee less of a shrew." Before Lily could catch her indignant breath, Helza turned to Skye. "And you'll still be missing yourn, I dare say, lady, but there'll be another un for you, never fear. And not so far off neither."

Lily's face was puce now. "How dare you come here, upsetting my cousin like this, you old witch," she stormed. "Don't you know she's in mourning?"

"'Course I know it, and I came to see how the pretty one fares after the recent trouble, not to bandy words wi' the likes of you, madam."

"I'm well enough, Helza," Skye said quietly, oddly touched at the old woman's concern, if that's what it was.

Helza nodded. "And the corner will soon be turned for 'ee, my pretty. I seen it in the stars."

Skye heard Lily snort, but by then Helza had turned full circle towards the door, almost as though she was on a pivot. At the last minute she turned back and glared at Lily.

"I pity the man who falls for 'ee, lady."

"What damn cheek!" Lily raged as the door slammed behind the old woman. "As if I was interested in men, anyway. I haven't seen one yet who I'd give a tuppenny toss for."

"No?" Skye said with a grin, thankful to steer the talk away from their present problems for the moment. "And I thought there was a certain look passing between you and David Kingsley last night." *Was that really only last night? Already it seemed like years ago*, thought Skye in shock. And then she caught sight of Lily's face. "My Lord, I was right," she squealed.

"Rubbish. I merely thought he was more interesting than most, if you must know," Lily said airily. "At least he can talk about something other than clay blocks or throwing pots. You found someone intellectual in Philip, and I'd aim for nothing less, no matter how charming. And oh God, I didn't mean to upset you by mentioning Philip."

"You didn't. I don't want to forget his existence and nor do the children. And now let's go home. I've had enough of White Rivers for one day." She called out to Ethan. "You can come out now. Helza's gone, so if you want a ride, we'll take you home."

Ethan's scared little face peered round the workroom door before he came out, wiping his hands on a rag.

"Me mammie says that t'other old un that used to live on the moors never died at all, and the one called Helza's really the same. If she touches you, she'll put her spell on you."

"Good Lord, will you listen to the child?" Lily said. "The tales some folk will tell!"

"Come on, Ethan, there's nothing to harm you here," Skye said gently. "Even if it were true, everyone knows there are good spells as well as bad ones."

It may have mollified him, but from the look Lily gave her, it was clear she was thinking her American cousin was as batty as the boy.

The next day they were feeling slightly more settled. Skye still hadn't found the right words to write, and in any case the children had been enchanted to find that Lily was staying at the house, and they had both romped with them until bedtime. There were no unexpected visitors or telephone calls, and as things had surely got as bad as they could get, the women began to feel a sliver of optimism for the future. It was shattered in a moment when they reached the pottery.

"Oh God, who could have done this?" Skye croaked.

"It's bloody obvious who's done it," Lily snapped. "It's Theo's precious clayworkers, that's who!"

Every window in the place that had been proudly proclaiming that the showroom was open for business, had been daubed with red paint saying TRAITORS in large letters. Except that in places the word had been misspelled. It hardly mattered. The effect

243

was just as heart-stopping and sickening, however illiterate the writers.

"I've been trying to get some of it off, missus," Ethan's shrill voice came from around the corner. "But 'tis all dried on and 'twill need paint-stripping stuff and we ain't gone none." He sniffed, wiping his nose and eyes on his sleeve, and near to tears at his inability to work miracles before they arrived.

"You did well, Ethan, and you're right," Skye told him, thinking rapidly. "I'll go down to St Austell to get some paint-stripping stuff to clean it up properly. Meanwhile, you and Lily make some more posters and paste them on the outside of the windows to cover up the red paint. We'll go on doing it until they stop. They're not going to win."

She couldn't think of the proper name for the paint-stripping stuff any more than he could, but that didn't matter. What mattered to all of them was that they were doing something to put things right. She left them planning the new posters and drove down to the nearest hardware store in St Austell, her hands shaking.

After trying every shop in town she began to realise that whether they had the stuff or not, she wasn't going to get any. She was met by either hostile silence or by clipped negatives. Folk in the streets stepped out of her way and didn't look at her. Where she had once been so popular, she now felt like an outcast.

And it had nothing to do with the fact that she was the grieving widow respectfully left alone. It was more to do with the fact that she had been on the German youths' side. She had expected folk to be pleased she had rid the town of them. Instead of which, she was becoming more and more suspicious that in doing so, she hadn't let them have their full pound of flesh. She had helped the enemy to escape. In Skye's mind it was a ludicrous statement, and those young boys were no more the enemy than she was. They would have been mere striplings during the war. And even though she knew what long memories some folk had, couldn't these people see that she had averted a far worse catastrophe?

Skye hurried back through the town, suddenly nervous at the unspoken aggression she felt all around her, and as she passed the war memorial she saw that there were fresh flowers surrounding the base, as if to rebuke her for consorting with the enemy, even though those who had perished during and after the war had eventually included her own husband. . . . But he had never been one of them, any more than she was, she thought bitterly, and certainly not now. In all her life, she had never felt so alienated. She was in the right . . . but nobody else seemed to believe it, or understand her motives.

It was midday by the time she rushed back into the sanctuary of White Rivers, ashen-faced. She hardly noticed the other car outside as Lily stared at her aghast.

"Skye, what's happened? You look terrible. David's here, and we were just having a bite to eat."

"David, thank God," Skye gasped. "You've got to do something. You've got to help us—" She swayed alarmingly, and sat down heavily on one of the chairs they provided where customers could sit and browse. Those mythical customers who were shunning them totally now – and from what she had seen today, looked set to do so for the foreseeable future, unless they did something drastic.

"That's just what I'm here to suggest," David Kingsley said calmly. "Otherwise there could be a very *un*civil war among the inhabitants of Cornwall."

"Don't I know it," Skye muttered. "For the last couple of hours I felt that at any minute I'd be stoned at best, and deported to America at worst."

She didn't stop to consider what order she had put the choices in. She *belonged* here now, damn it, and she wanted to hold her head up high, the way her predecessors had done. Those proud Tremaynes and Killigrews, who had forged the dynasty that commanded respect and love from the community. Until Skye Norwood had introduced her own radical ideas and ruined everything. And it was so unfair. Theo had been the one to insist on keeping the boys here, and he was no doubt lording it about Truro, having washed his hands of her.

"Listen to what David has to say," Lily urged her now.

Skye looked up dully, but unable to miss the sudden vibrant look that passed between the other two. She wondered briefly if she was unwittingly providing some lonely hearts service . . . ironically so, since she was the one with the loneliest heart of all. . . .

"I'm afraid Theo Tremayne's been quick to put his side of things wherever folk will listen, and if we waste time it will only get worse. So I suggest you get your article written today. I want it to be mainly your voice that's heard, then I'll print a special newsletter to be delivered to every house in the neighbourhood free of charge before the next regular issue of *The Informer* is due out. It's the only way to stop him at his own game."

Her mouth dropped open. David was a shrewd businessman but she knew he believed in a cause. Even so, he couldn't do this free of charge. As if he read her mind, he grasped her cold hand and squeezed it hard.

"Call it my Christmas good deed, Skye, and take advantage of it – and it's also good public relations," he added, in case she thought he was going soft.

"I think it's darling of you, but you must let me pay for it," she choked. "I insist."

He shrugged. "You can meet the costs halfway if you must, but don't deprive me of my entire moment of glory!"

"David really wants to do this for us, Skye," Lily said. "Isn't he wonderful?"

It was pretty obvious now that Lily was smitten. How curious, thought Skye, when she had never shown the slightest interest in men before, except for a passing fancy for Nick that had quickly fizzled out. What was even more amazing was that David, never short of female company, seemed so struck by Lily's heightened colour and rapturous expression.

"We'd better get on with it then," Skye said, reverting to business before she let her imagination run away with her. "I need to be at my desk, and I've no stomach for sitting here twiddling my thumbs today, anyway. Let's shut up shop."

"No, we mustn't do that," Lily shook her head, taking charge. "You go home and do your writing, and we'll keep the place open. Ethan's keen to practise his pottery, and I'm quite capable of dealing with any intruders."

She was too, Skye thought. Lily was no weakling, and David

Kingsley clearly admired the handsome woman that she was, far more than the simpering females who fancied their chances with him.

"Well, if you're sure."

"I'm sure. Besides, we had another visitor while you were away and I shan't be alone."

At that moment Vera came through from the workroom, smiling sheepishly at Skye. Her voice was defensive, but as determined as her sister's.

"Adam's still on strike, and I told him I'm quite ready to go on strike in the kitchen as well unless I'm free to help you both. We have to make a stand sometime and follow Mrs Pankhurst's lead, don't we? Otherwise it was all for nothing."

As if unconsciously imitating the lady's doctrine, the two sisters moved closer together, standing resolutely shoulder to shoulder, and Skye had never loved them more.

Seventeen

The news that the German youths had gone spread with the speed of a moorland fire, but instead of solving everything, it resulted in the clayworkers at Killigrew Clay becoming totally divided. Some were furious, believing they had been done out of their rightful scourging since Skye had helped the foreigners to flee under cover of darkness. Many of them bitterly blamed her for her female interference.

Others were in a state of complete uncertainty, wanting to get back to work and nagged by their womenfolk for not doing so. Christmas was coming, and there were few enough treats for large families when the menfolk were idle and not bringing home their wage packets. But the pit captains were adamant that nothing was to move until they had thrashed things out to everyone's satisfaction.

Vera was able to throw more light on what was happening, and reported it to the other women. "Not that Adam was being disloyal to the rest of them in speaking up, you understand," she told them. "But when a man gets between the sheets with his wife, she can always turn pillow talk to her advantage."

"Why, Vera Pengelly, are you saying what I think you're saying?" Skye gave her the ghost of a smile, thinking there was precious little else to laugh about in these tense days.

Vera's face went pink. "I dare say I am. There's more ways than one of making a man do what a woman wants, and depriving him of his needs is one of the oldest."

"So you didn't only go on strike in the kitchen then?" Lily grinned as her sister's colour deepened still more.

Before she could think of a suitable answer, Skye exclaimed,

"Vera, you're a marvel! I'm still struggling with my article for David's newsletter, but you've given me the best idea."

Two nights of poring over paper and discarding most of what she had written had finally produced a telling and perfectly competent article on the short-sightedness of perpetuating a conflict that was long since over, and with it the need to move on and look to the future. But she still wasn't completely satisfied with it. Now, with Vera's artless words, she realised there was a different angle she could use, and she suggested that she might take the rest of the day off.

"Why not? We're not exactly rushed off our feet," Lily said. "We've had one sale of a pot in two days, and even that was to Vera."

"It had dividends though," her sister told her triumphantly. "It was one of Ethan's, and Adam was so impressed by his brother's work that I could see he was dying to be back here himself. Who said women aren't clever enough to be the driving force behind their men!"

"Can I quote you on that?" Skye said.

The words that were going to change everything – she hoped – were already in her mind, and she tingled with the need to get them down on paper, and the style of the article became clearer by the minute as she drove back to New World.

David needed the finished copy by tonight, and now she was sure she could have it ready. All the muddled words she had somehow been unable to express were unravelling in her head, and once she had assured the children that she was here to work and not to play, she spent the rest of the morning and half the afternoon writing and rewriting until she felt she could refine the article no more.

Although it wasn't so much an article as a letter, written intimately as if from one woman to another. Those were the people who counted. Vera had given her that thought, and she was ever grateful to her. Women were the backbone of every marriage and every family. She made their role abundantly clear, detailing it in brutal, often painful truth, in words that men usually turned away from.

The women bore the pain of childbirth and nurtured their

children; fed them and clothed them and cared for them with a gentleness that hid the very steel of their fabric. They were the ones who had held homes together during the dreadful years of war, and who deserved every man's respect because of their suffering, which in its way, was as deep as any man's.

It was to the women that Skye's words were written, knowing that every one of them would take note and relay her sentiments to their husbands and brothers. She wouldn't be so indelicate as to urge them to deprive their husbands of their conjugal rights in so many words, but the inference was as smooth as silk.

Her final paragraphs were straight to the point, and would either endear her to the county or damn her prestige for good and all, she thought grimly. She read them aloud, trying to imagine how others would see the words she had written.

'Dear friends, despite the variations in our accents, you and I speak the same language and you will understand what I'm trying to say. We share the same hopes and feelings and emotions. We have husbands, fathers and children that we love.

'Some of us lost those husbands, fathers and children during the war, or from the effects of it, and we still grieve for what might have been. But we should never forget that the main aim of the struggle was to make a better life for us all, through peace, the natural end result of war.

'The women of other countries speak a different language from ours, but the wives and sweethearts and mothers of our old enemy grieve for their menfolk too. They share our pain, and in that we are all sisters under the skin.

'I freely acknowledge that I was responsible for sending the young German workers back to their families. I deeply regret that it was necessary, since to me it represents failure in that common humanity and decency we all profess to have. But I did it in the hope that the incident that provoked such bad feeling, dividing friends and families could be forgotten once and for all. There has to come a point where we say that enough is enough, to get on with our lives and welcome strangers as friends.

'Don't let us become so insular and small-minded that we

cannot see beyond yesterday towards a brighter tomorrow. That was the hope that our loved ones died for.'

Two days later every household in a wide area around Truro and St Austell was waking up to a newsletter pushed through their letter boxes. It had taken a team of David Kingsley's staff and any casual lads they could round up to deliver them, and he was paying handsomely for the privilege. But by now he was as caught up in the project as Skye, and he wished he could have been a fly on every wall to gauge the reaction to her uninhibited and impassioned words.

"What the hell is this?" Theo Tremayne spluttered, as his son pushed the pamphlet towards him over the breakfast table.

"Aunt Skye's telling everybody that she and Aunt Lily are shopkeepers now," Sebby chortled, proud of his reading skills after scanning the first, businesslike part of Skye's message. "They say if the men are too soft to work, then the womenfolk must do what they can to earn a crust."

"Earn a crust! More likely crumbs," Theo snarled. "What do they know about men's work?"

"A good deal, if I remember rightly," Betsy said, reading over his shoulder and quickly skipping the first part to read Skye's more intimate writing.

"Your womenfolk all worked as bal maidens at Killigrew Clay, which was how your grandmother met and married Ben Killigrew, so don't scoff at the power of women," she added, charmed by Skye's particular way of phrasing things.

"Oh ah. And I suppose you're thinkin' of going up to White Rivers and manning the showroom too, are you? Not that there'd be any buyers . . ."

"Why not? Do you think I'm incapable of doing anything but cook your meals and make your bed?"

"You don't even do that. The servants do it," he sneered.

Betsy's eyes flashed. It was a long time since she had challenged Theo, but she knew what an oaf he was, and she was also well aware that he took his bodily pleasures elsewhere. She knew it by the sickly whiff of cheap scent on his clothes whenever he stayed out late. But he still expected her to do her wifely duty whenever he chose to lift her nightdress. He treated her so casually and carelessly, as if she was no more than a chattel – and that wasn't what women had been fighting for all these years. And she wasn't so dumb that she couldn't recognise Skye's guarded hints that a woman could exercise her power over a man in more ways than by shifting clay blocks.

"Then maybe the servants can see to the rest of your home needs as well," she snapped. "For I'll be locking my bedroom door to you until you come to your senses and get the clayworkers back to work."

She heard Sebby gasp, not quite understanding the gist of it, but never having heard his mother speak like this before. He looked at her with new respect.

"Can I come to the pottery and be a shopkeeper with you and the aunts, Ma?" he said, his eyes sparkling with glee at her getting one over on his father at last.

"You bloody well will not. You'll go nowhere without my say-so," Theo roared, turning on him.

"Yes he will. We'll both go. Get your coat, Sebby."

Theo's face was a picture of shock and rage, and for one pleasurable second of triumph Betsy wished she could have borrowed old Albert Tremayne's skills to capture it on canvas.

"Good Lord, will you look at this?" Lily said in astonishment. "That surely can't be Betsy and Sebby getting out of that posh car! And who are those other women with them?"

"It's working, Lily," Skye said softly with a catch in her throat. "I knew it would. Women will always show their strength when it matters."

She crossed the showroom to greet Betsy with a kiss at the door. Two well-dressed townsladies got out of the front seats of the car after her and shook Skye's hand as Betsy introduced her.

"It's a privilege to meet you, Mrs Norwood, and we wish to say how completely we agree with your sentiments in the newsletter. We're here to do what we can to show our support in your efforts to stop this male foolishness."

"Mrs Anderson lost a son at Passchendaele, Skye," Betsy

said soberly. "But she thinks, as we all do, that the time for recriminations is past. Sebby and I were on our way here when she and her sister gave us a ride in their car."

"Then I thank you sincerely, Mrs Anderson," Skye said to the lady, choked at this unexpected support from Betsy, and amazed at her proving to be such a spokeswoman. "I thank you all! This is wonderful, though I'm not sure that there's very much for you to do." *She could hardly ask such obvious ladies to soil their white hands on menial tasks!* "As you see, we don't have too many customers . . ."

"But you do now, my dear," the second lady put in grandly. "You have us."

As the day progressed more and more women appeared at White Rivers until Skye began to wonder if there was anyone left at home at all. They came to applaud her, to admire the goods at the pottery, and to buy. Those who couldn't afford to buy anything, like many of the clayworkers' wives and daughters, merely stayed outside in the pottery yard and took up their stance like immovable statues.

"'Tis a real turn-up, ain't it?" Ethan Pengelly said, his eyes glowing, his hands dripping with sodden clay, when Skye went into the workroom to take him a bun to eat. "And even this young un is discovering how good it feels to get his hands in the wet clay and fashion a pot or two."

Sebby glanced up from his determined attempt to throw a pot. Skye looked at him in surprise. The little horror of old was actually getting his hands dirty and enjoying it. What was even more odd, he and Ethan seemed to have found a new regard for each other. In Sebby's eyes, Ethan was already a man.

"Well, I can see we'll have to find you a job here eventually," she said at last.

"Will you, Aunt Skye? You can make it right with my father, can't you?" he said hopefully.

"Now hold on a minute, honey! I was only joking. Besides, you have to go to school for years yet, and I dare say you'll have changed your mind about becoming a potter long before that," she laughed.

"I won't. I know I won't."

He turned back to his dollop of clay and threw it with gusto onto his wheel, already forgetting her. And knowing what a strongly opinionated boy he was, just like his father, Skye had the strangest feeling that he wouldn't change his mind either. And wouldn't Theo just love that! It would be like hammering another nail in his proverbial coffin.

For an entire week the support for the pottery never wavered. The women turned up loyally every day. Those with money bought everything in sight, and those without money just came up to the moors anyway, wanting to be part of what was becoming known as Skye's Crusaders. Who named it thus, Skye never knew, but the newspaper reporters were out in plenty, obtaining quotes and praise for Mrs Norwood, and interviewing anyone who would say anything at all.

The next regular issue of *The Informer* was full of it all, and the name of Skye's Crusaders was blazoned all over the front page, together with letters the newspaper had received, all giving their support to the venture and condemnation for the men's continuing strike action now that the situation had been resolved.

"I'm sure the letters must have been suitably chosen for publication," Skye said. "But all credit to David for that."

"And it must be a constant thorn in every man's side to see a White Rivers pot or plate on every mantelpiece and table," Vera chuckled. "Adam examines every piece I bring home, and from the way his hands move so lovingly over the glaze, I just know he's itching to be back at work."

"And are they moving just as lovingly over you?" Lily dared to tease her as they pored over the newspaper together.

"They are not! And I don't care to talk about it," Vera said primly. "It's private."

"I won't tell you my news then."

Vera perked up at once. "What news? Have you been keeping secrets from me, Lily?"

Lily glared at her sister. "Hardly. It's just that when everything calms down here I've decided not to go back to Plymouth. I'm moving back home with Mother."

"What? But you've never got on, and you'll be at each other's throats in a minute."

"She's getting old, Vera, and I have a duty. Besides, David's offered me a job at the newspaper. Not reporting, of course. I'd be no good at any of that, but I'll be working as a sort of secretary-cum-dogsbody. It's only temporary until I decide what I want to do."

But she said it all so casually, far too casually . . .

"Aha!" declared Vera in triumph.

"Aha nothing," Lily said, and then her face broke into a smile. "Well, *maybe* aha. It's too early to tell yet. But we do seem to get on extraordinarily well. And I suppose you're never too old . . ."

"Good Lord, you ninny, you're in your prime – and so is David, I'd say," Vera added with a grin. And for no good reason at all, the two sisters hugged one another, more in accord than they had been in a long time.

Theo arrived at White Rivers the following Monday morning. The clayers' wives stood outside defiantly and silently as he strode through their midst and into the showroom where he was virtually ignored in the bustle of activity inside.

Through the open doors to the workroom he couldn't fail to see that by now young Ethan Pengelly was a star attraction as he demonstrated how to throw a pot to the many interested folk eager to try their hands at the craft, and these demonstrations were a facet of the business that Skye was noting for the future.

He was also infuriated to see that his own son was fetching and carrying for the Pengelly boy and following his instructions to the letter. It was the ultimate blow to Theo's pride, and he was having no more of it. He walked straight up to Skye and put his hands on the counter.

"All right, madam. You've had your fun, and it's time to put an end to it. I have already been to the clayworks, and as from tomorrow morning Killigrew Clay will be fully operational again. So I suggest that you get these females and children off the premises as quickly as possible and let the craftsmen get back to work."

Once the cheers had died down, Skye spoke sweetly. "Are you telling me how to run my own business now, sir?"

Theo scowled, aware of the giggling around him. She had completely scored over him and was still doing so in reminding him that White Rivers belonged to her and not to him. And they both knew she could run it very well indeed without his help.

"Heaven preserve me from interfering in anything you see fit to do," he rapped, "but since one business is reliant on the other, it would seem like a sensible idea to get your own people back at work."

"Then I thank you for the suggestion, cuz," Skye said with quiet dignity.

She turned away from him to speak with another customer, but before he was even out of the showroom, the women had pushed him away, crowding towards her, and applauding her loudly. Theo felt like less than nothing, while Skye, for the first time in years, felt as if she had the whole of Cornwall at her feet and in her heart.

It was inevitable that after the hiatus and the traumatic days, and then the triumph of it all, there would be a feeling of let-down. There was no need for Skye's Crusaders to make a stand any longer, and both Killigrew Clay and White Rivers quickly resumed their normal working days.

The return to work of all their own men and the several women who normally worked in the showroom, meant that Skye and Lily and Vera were no longer needed. They were redundant, when for those few heady days it had been a case of everyone pulling together, the way women had done during the war.

But now Vera was openly thankful to resume her life as a new wife again. Lily had already left New World to settle everything in Plymouth and to move back home with Charlotte in Truro. All was as it was before, except for Skye's emotions.

Everyone said she had achieved a miracle. A very ugly situation could so easily have turned into a disaster, and David Kingsley had warmly congratulated her on the way her sensitive article had turned the corner for them all.

"Aren't you proud of what you accomplished?" he asked. She seemed more listless than overjoyed when he called on her some days later with the many letters of congratulation that had since poured into the newspaper offices.

"Of course, but it wasn't only me," she said. "It was everyone. It was common sense prevailing over stupidity."

"And now that Skye's Crusaders have retreated back into obscurity, their leader has nothing to do," he concluded softly. "Am I right?"

She shrugged. "I suppose so. It's silly, isn't it? But suddenly I feel so useless. I have no goal any more. Nothing to keep my mind occupied and alert. I have no – no—"

Without warning her eyes filled, and his arms went around her, providing a much-needed shoulder to cry on, without a shred of sexuality involved. If there had been, it would have been rejected at once, and they both knew it.

"You have no husband," he said gently. "And now that your cause is over, you have too much time on your hands to remind you that it's almost Christmas, and that families should be together at this time. But you have your children, Skye, and Philip will always live on in them."

She snuffled against his shoulder. He was being very kind, saying what every woman would want to hear at such a time. Except her. She hadn't given Philip a single thought during the strike, and all her longings now were directed towards Nick Pengelly – and her resentment too. She needed his praise above all things, but according to Ethan, Nick was out of town. *On a case*, as he called it importantly . . .

Consumed with guilt at her own restless and wanton feelings for a man other than her own husband, Skye broke away from David and gave him a thin smile.

"You're perfectly right, and I know I've been neglecting the children lately. They love decorating the house for Christmas, and are probaby wondering if we're even going to have any celebrations this year. But we must, of course. Philip would have wanted it," she added deliberately, still making him a part of it all.

Even though it all seemed more sad than joyful to her,

she knew how the children needed her involvement, and she resolved from that moment to make their first Christmas without their father as happy as possible. She echoed her own brave newsletter words; they all had to move on.

She felt David Kingsley kiss her forehead lightly. "We're all proud of you, my dear, and Philip would have been proud of you too," he told her. "Together you were a formidable partnership, but you'll survive whatever comes your way. The Tremaynes always do."

It was the sweetest compliment he could have given her, and after he had gone, she washed her face and straightened her shoulders. Then she went to the nursery, where the governess was giving Celia and Wenna their afternoon lesson of letters and numbers. Oliver was curled up asleep on a cushion in a corner, oblivious to it all.

"You can finish for today, Miss Landon," Skye told her. "The children and I are going to the beach to collect some driftwood to decorate the house. We must look for fir cones and berries to paint too, and make some new paper chains to remind us that it's nearly Christmas. What do you say to that, my honeybees?"

After an astonished moment, their answer was to fling their arms around her neck and whoop with delight. Above their clinging arms, Skye met the approving eyes of the governess, and nodded mutely. The worst of the dark days were over.

There was nothing compared with children's innocent acceptance of things to obliterate your own worries, Skye thought later. The four of them spent the rest of the afternoon at the beach and she promised that tomorrow they would start to gather the berries and greenery and make the homely decorations that would bring New World back to life again.

By now the children had accepted Philip's death far more easily than she had expected. She still missed him. You couldn't spend so many years of your life with a person and not feel his absence deeply. But she was honest enough to admit that what she missed most was the Philip she had first loved so passionately. The Philip he had become was nothing like that man, and if anyone could blame the effects of war on a change of circumstances, it was herself. But there was no use wishing for things that could never be. It was something her mother had always impressed on her, and Skye knew the value of it.

Her grandmother too, had been full of so many wise sayings, and her lyrical Cornish voice was in Skye's head at that moment. *If you can't change something, my love, then don't waste your time in fretting for the moon. You only have one life, and 'tis meant to be lived to the full, not wasted on regrets.*

Oh, Granny Morwen, thought Skye, watching her children at play on the beach, scrambling back and shrieking with excitement every time the waves threatened to surge over their feet . . . do you know how many emotive ways those words can be interpreted?

But of course she did. Morwen Tremayne hadn't wasted a moment of her life. And Granny Morwen had always known exactly what she meant whenever she gave out some of her wise advice.

At that moment, Skye resolved not to make this Christmas a gloomy one, and it seemed that other members of the family had had the same idea. Betsy called on her the next day and spoke all in a rush.

"I know you're still officially in mourning, Skye, and even though our children don't always get on together, we'm all family, so me and Theo would like it if you'd all join us for Christmas dinner."

"*Theo* would like it?" Skye queried, her eyebrows raised at this unlikely prospect. But there was a new assertiveness in Betsy nowadays.

"Me and Theo have had a talk, and he knows I ain't prepared to be a doormat no more. That's all thanks to you, Skye, so please say you'll share Christmas Day with us."

"Well, just part of it then," she said, knowing she couldn't be so churlish as to refuse this bridge-building gesture. "We'll want to be home by evening."

Vera had also mentioned them all getting together, but Skye had rejected the idea, saying that she and Adam should spend their first Christmas dinner as a married couple on their own.

Her own words had stirred up bittersweet memories, remembering that she and Philip had spent their first Christmas together, somewhere in France . . .

As though Vera's thoughts were in tune with Betsy's, she telephoned Skye that same evening. She suspected there had been some collusion between the two of them.

"Nick and Ethan are coming here for a late supper on Christmas Day, so when you've put the children to bed, you're to come and join us. Lily's coming too, with a guest – and you might guess who that will be. *Please* say you will, Skye. The house will be bursting at the seams, but we really want to do this. Oh, and Nick will come and collect you because the moors are sure to be misty by the time you leave here."

And they wouldn't want any more accidents . . .

"Aren't you taking him for granted? Nick, I mean," Skye said, as Vera paused for breath. It sounded all too cosy – too wonderfully, *ecstatically* cosy.

"Not at all. He suggested it. Did you know he's back from Bristol now?"

Skye's heart jolted. "I didn't know he'd been there."

"Well, apparently his ex-partner recommended him for some difficult legal case. I'm sure he'll tell you about it."

And maybe he wouldn't. She was angry that she hadn't known . . . but then, why would she? She never invited Nick to call or visit. She held him at arm's length, because she was too afraid of letting him into her heart. It was too soon. Too impossibly soon . . .

Her feelings were so mixed, but she knew it was safer to keep the anger simmering, rather than let any other emotion in. But *Bristol* of all places . . . and she knew very well why he wouldn't have told her. He'd know she would be imagining the time they had been there together. . . .

When the phone rang again she almost snapped into the receiver. She had been left discreetly alone after Philip's death, and now it seemed as if no one would leave her in peace, when all she wanted was to be alone with her children.

"Em, I'm sorry," she stammered, hearing the Cornish-cream voice. "I thought it was going to be someone else."

"Well, whoever it was, I reckon he was about to get a taste of your tongue," Em chuckled, having no idea of the sweet, erotic irony of her words. Skye pushed the thought right out of her mind as she listened.

"Me and Will thought you might like to bring the babbies to the farm for Christmas. Now just say if you don't want to, and there'll be no offence taken, but the offer's there."

"Oh Em, it's darling of you, but everybody seems to have had the same idea." She hesitated. "Maybe we could come for the New Year instead. Would that be all right?"

"'Course it would, my lamb. Just come when you'm ready, and we'll fatten you all up with some good country cooking."

Skye felt a touch of hysteria threatening, but she knew Emma meant it in all sincerity, and resisted the feeling with a great effort.

"I do love you, Em," she said huskily instead, and put the phone down quickly, knowing that Emma didn't go in for all that mushy nonsense, but needing to say it all the same.

When the telephone rang for a third time that evening, she simply mouthed into it, wondering who felt it their Christian duty to invite the poor widow-woman this time, and unable to stop the cynical thought.

"*Yes?*"

"Well, I've had better responses," Nick said calmly. "I have something I need to discuss with you, Skye. Is it convenient for me to call on you this evening?"

She stared into the phone, her heart thudding at hearing his voice, rich and deep and intimately near, and yet so businesslike too. "If you're going to tell me you've been to Bristol, I know," she said, almost rudely.

"That's only part of it," he replied, completely unperturbed by her reaction.

But that was part of his training, never to be shocked at anything a client told him. But she was not his client. Well, yes, she was, but she was his lover too . . .

"I'll be there in half an hour," he said, when she didn't answer, and then the line went dead.

When he arrived she greeted him coolly, and pointedly sat some distance away from him in the drawing-room. Her emotions were in turmoil, and she couldn't think what they had to discuss that couldn't wait until daylight. She stared at him unblinkingly, and Nick found himself cursing the effect those beautiful Tremayne eyes were having on him. But there was business to be done, and there was no shirking it.

"First of all, I must congratulate you on your achievement over the recent strike. Adam sent me the newsletter while I was away, so I was well aware of it all."

"Thank you."

"Skye, for heaven's sake—" His professional manner slipped for a brief moment, but she lifted her hand as if to ward off any more personal reactions. He shrugged. Such reactions were imminent, anyway. "You know I had to go to Bristol for an important legal case."

"So I believe. I trust you were successful."

"Thank you, yes," he said, angry at her politeness, and preferring her to rant and rave the way he knew she could. Being his volatile and passionate Skye, and not this cold, unemotional statue he couldn't yet reach. But he would. For good or ill, he would. When the time was right.

"While I was there I visited The Laurels. You've been receiving weekly reports, I understand, and you'll know that your uncle has settled in remarkably well."

She had hardly looked at the reports, she thought guiltily, and she hadn't expected this. It was kind and dear of him to visit Albie, and her mouth trembled as she nodded.

"They say he has brief times of near-normality, but that it makes no difference to the eventual outcome."

"He was quite lucid while I was there, although very slow-speaking. But he fully understood when I told him we intended to show an exhibition of his paintings in the new year. He seemed quite pleased."

"I had forgotten," Skye said in some distress, keeping her eyes lowered now. How *awful* to have forgotten. Even her father, so many miles away, never failed to ask after Albie in his letters, while she had simply forgotten him and the exhibition.

There was some excuse for it, considering the happenings of the last few months, but even so . . .

"He was so lucid, in fact, that he asked me to draft a document for him. It's legally binding, and was witnessed by several members of the nursing home staff and the regular visiting clergyman."

"What kind of document?" Skye said suspiciously.

Nick drew it out of an envelope. "You had better read it for yourself. It's very short, but I assure you it's perfectly in order, and dictated of his own free will."

She was almost afraid to take the document from Nick's hands, but she knew that she must. She read it aloud, her heart swelling as she did so, imagining Albie's stumbling words as he dictated it.

"'This is not my Last Will and Testament. I am not bequeathing my goods and chattels after my death. It is a gift of love and enduring affection to my niece, Skye Tremayne.'"

She glanced at Nick, her eyes tormented now.

"The ommission of your married name is of no consequence. In any case, you are his only niece," he said.

She read on, her voice becoming increasingly wobbly. "'I wish to make a gift of my studio and everything in it, including all my paintings, to the daughter of my beloved sister, Primrose Tremayne, in perpetual memory of other days. The gift is to take effect immediately.'"

That was all. It was dated and signed by Albie's wavering, scrawling hand, and witnessed by half a dozen other signatures before the name of Nicholas Pengelly was written across his legal seal.

"How can he do this?" Skye wept. "I don't want it. I won't have it."

"You must. It's the last thing you can do for him, and for your mother's memory," he urged relentlessly. "Would she have wanted you to throw his gift back in his face?"

"I hate you," she raged.

"I know," Nick said. "It's a blinder, isn't it? But when you've had time to calm down, you'll know that Albie meant what he says. This is a gift of love, and I'm sure he wasn't expecting you to live at the studio. Once it's been cleared out, you can sell it or rent it out, or do anything you like with it."

"I can't even face going inside there! You know that."

"We'll leave it until the new year," Nick said more gently. "But you know we have to sort things through then, in order to set up the exhibition. But don't be too hasty in your wish to be rid of it, Skye. It's a valuable property right on the riverfront, and it could also be the base for a very useful business venture."

"And just what did you have in mind, masterbrain?" she said with a touch of sarcasm, still unable to take it all in, or to see where his words were leading. And not really wanting to. Couldn't he see how upset she was by all this? Where was the empathy that had been so beautiful between them?

"That's up to you. But if you want my professional advice – well, your showroom at White Rivers is pretty much out of the way, and unless there's constant advertising, few people get to know of it. You don't need me to tell you that. But a riverfront property in the heart of Truro could really open things up for you."

Skye stared at him, her thoughts finally coinciding with his. "A White Rivers Pottery shop, you mean?" she said slowly.

"Why not?" Nick said, thankful that there was some spark of interest in her eyes at last. "You would need someone trustworthy and enthusiastic to manage it, of course."

They looked at one another, and after a moment they both spoke at once.

"Lily!"

Eighteen

The family was openly supportive when Skye revealed the contents of Albie's document to them. Especially when she insisted that from now on, she would also be solely responsible for his upkeep at The Laurels.

"That's generous of you, Skye, and I doubt that there will be any arguments from the rest of them," Lily said, the sharpest of them all. "All the same, darling, you deserve to have the property if anyone does. You're the closest to him, after all. But what on earth will you do with it?"

"As a matter of fact, I wanted to talk to you about that," Skye said carefully. "You rather enjoyed being a shopkeeper, didn't you, Lily?"

Her cousin started to laugh, never slow to catch on, but getting it slightly wrong this time. "You want me to be the warden of a picture gallery? Oh, I don't think so. I always thought Uncle Albie was more than a little creepy, and having all those spooky painted eyes following me about the place wouldn't suit me at all."

"Would the idea of displaying and selling pottery as manageress of the White Rivers Pottery shop sound unsuitable or demeaning to you?"

Lily's eyes widened, and she didn't say anything for a moment, and then, "You mean it, don't you?"

"When did you know me to say anything I didn't mean? I have to do something with the studio, Lily, and this would still keep it as a family concern. That would please Albie, whether he was aware of my plans or not. And I know it would have pleased Mom that I wasn't going to sell the place where she and her brother spent so many happy years."

Skye realised it no longer pained her to say it. She was sure that whatever had happened between Primmy and Albie had been mostly in Albie's mind, and it was all so long ago that it was of no consequence to anyone any more.

"Then I accept," Lily said with alacrity. "But how did you come to think of it?"

"I didn't. It was Nick."

By Christmas Day, New World was heavily bedecked with holly and paper decorations. The tree in the corner of the drawing-room was adorned with tinsel and fir cones made beautiful with glitter and glue, and the silver-painted driftwood was transformed into strange and wonderful art forms, according to each child's imagination.

After the children had opened their presents with much excitement and given Skye their own modest offerings, they all ate hot mince pies as they opened their Christmas stockings, each containing an apple and an orange and a bag of nuts, and various small treats. In every way, it was as comfortably relaxed a Christmas morning as Skye could have hoped for, she thought with some relief.

The day was crisp and sunny, with none of the bad weather experienced upcountry, or habitually in Skye's native New Jersey at this time of year. And later, snuggled into their winter coats, Skye drove them all into Truro and arrived at Theo and Betsy's house in time for the midday Christmas meal.

As expected, the decorations here were far more lavish, but the children's exclamations of delight took away the initial awkwardness on the part of the adults.

"Thank you for inviting us," Skye said simply. She hadn't seen Theo since the day he came to White Rivers, but now he held her shoulders lightly and kissed her on both cheeks.

"Might as well get used to doing it the Contintental way," he said airily, which covered all explanations and apologies in an instant. It was the best way.

And naturally, the turkey was larger than anyone could ever need, the plum puddings were overrich and laced with far too much brandy for young tastebuds, but the atmosphere was so jolly and homely that Skye readily forgave Theo everything.

Not least, was the remarkable change in Betsy. From having been the downtrodden wife, she now appeared to be an equal marriage partner in every way. She had *blossomed*, thought Skye in amazement. There was no other word for it. Few women would have envied her in the past, but they might well do so now. It was not her business to know how Betsy had accomplished it, but she was delighted to see it.

The boys too were far more amenable than of old. Sebby was still in charge, with Justin faithfully following his lead, but they were quite happy to play games with their cousins, from hide-and-seek, to hunt the thimble, to guessing games. By the time the Norwoods left for home, Oliver was fast asleep in the car, and the girls weren't far off.

"It was a lovely day, Mommy," Celia said sleepily. "Daddy would have loved it all, wouldn't he?"

It was such a rare and lovely comment from her reserved little daughter that Skye could only nod.

"He'd have been watching us from heaven, anyway," Wenna said confidently.

Skye glanced round at Celia, her eyes daring her to scoff, and for once her elder daughter did as she was mutely told. She was growing up, thought Skye, her throat tight. She was no longer a baby, and it made her both proud and sad to realise it.

But they were all ready for bed quite early, thanks in part to Betsy's brandy-soaked plum puddings. And then Skye had to get ready for the evening celebrations. She could easily have asked Lily and David Kingsley to pick her up, rather than have Nick go out of his way to fetch Ethan and then herself en route to their brother's house. She hadn't, but she was glad Ethan was included. It made it less of a conventional social gathering of three couples. Much of the talk was of Albie's unexpected gift to Skye, and the new venture they were all involved in, and the evening progressed from being a normal Christmas evening, to one of excitement and tentative plans for the future.

"We're so lucky to have David as a good friend," Vera observed. "Newspaper advertising for the new Truro shop will ensure its success. Not that there will be any chance of failure, considering Skye's popularity now."

"We should all drink to Skye," Adam Pengelly said, in the solid, methodical tones of the very drunk.

"And you should be in bed by the sound of you!" said Vera.

"Not unless you come with me, wench," he said wickedly, and while everyone laughed at such daring in company, Skye carefully avoided looking at Nick.

How sweet it would be if they could do like these two, and retire to bed after such an evening. Not that Adam would be much use for any physical pleasures, she thought in amusement. But any man could be forgiven for taking a drop too much when he was so clearly relishing the fact of having a loving wife and a good job, and being host to a houseful of friends at Christmas.

It was very late when Lily and David decided they had better leave. By then, the finer points of the new shop had been discussed many times, and Skye was sure that most of them would be forgotten by morning. But the planning had been fun, and while they were all exhausted and had talked themselves out, inside she felt more exhilarated and alive than she had been in a long while. And a little while later as she saw Vera stifle a yawn, she murmured that it was high time she went home too, if Nick and Ethan were ready.

"I think Ethan had better stay where he is for tonight," Vera said. "There'll be no rousing him, anyway."

Skye saw then that he was sprawled out on the sofa, oblivious to the world. So that meant that she and Nick would be leaving together. And as predicted by Vera, the mist had risen over the moors in a filmy white layer. Nick drove slowly and carefully, inching his way along the lanes, and they might have been in a strange and alien world where no one else existed but themselves. They seemed to be floating on a sea of ghostly white mist. Far above them was the clear dark sky, studded with stars above the earth's gossamer atmosphere, and the only things visible against the darkness were the soaring white tips of Killigrew Clay.

"My mother used to call them sky-tips," Skye said suddenly, breaking the silence between them. "I first heard the name when she told me stories about her childhood in some wonderful far-off place called Cornwall."

"And has it lived up to your expectations?" Nick asked softly.

She hardly realised that the slowly inching motor had stopped now, and they seemed to be suspended in time and space. She could see the sky but not the earth. It was eerie and spectacular, and they could be in danger of plunging over a precipice into a claypool for all she knew. She should be afraid, but she wasn't, not with Nick . . .

"It's everything I thought it would be," she said slowly.

The next instant she felt his lips on hers, his arms crushing her to him, and the aching longing she had felt for him all this time flared between them. She felt him caress her breasts, his tongue seeking the inner softness of her mouth. His hands and his fingers sought for her body, and hers responded in the same seeking, feverish manner. She wanted all of him, here and now and for ever, as much as it was blatantly obvious that he wanted her. . . . But to her shocked surprise, he put her gently away from him after a few passionate moments.

"Not here, and not now," he whispered hoarsely. "This is not what I want for us, Skye."

"It's what you wanted once," she almost wept.

"I want you more than anything in the world. I think of you every minute of the day and night. But not like this. Not in some clandestine affair. You mean more to me than that, and we both know it's far too soon to think of anything more."

"Because my husband died, you mean?" she said savagely. "You didn't worry about it when he was still alive."

"But I worry about it now. I don't want your name to be involved in a scandal, my darling girl."

"Are you sure it's not your good name you're thinking about? It would never do for a lawyer to be involved in a scandal, would it?"

He didn't answer, and she was conscious of the sound of their breathing; his deep and heavy, hers ragged and painful. She couldn't believe that it was so wrong for a woman to feel the same deep emotional and physical needs as a man, so why was it so wrong for her to express it?

"I will always love you, Skye, and our time will come, but there are conventions that we shouldn't ignore, my beautiful, headstrong love. One of us has to be sensible, and deep down, you know I'm right. Meanwhile, we both have work to do that will keep us together."

"Thank you for those crumbs," she choked, but knew that he was right. So infuriatingly right.

He gathered her to him once more, kissing every inch of her face. When he spoke, his voice was tight, and she knew how he was restraining himself. It didn't help. She was her mother's daughter, and when she loved, she loved with all her heart, and she wanted him *now*.

"Darling girl, don't ever doubt my love for you, and when our time is right I promise you we'll be together for ever."

"And when will that be? A month from now? A year? How will we know? And do you think I care a fig for conventions, any more than—"

Appalled, she stopped abruptly, her heart thudding wildly. Knowing exactly what she had been about to say.

. . . any more than Albie and Primmy did . . .

And as swiftly as a bolt of lightning striking her, her feelings did a complete reversal. How *could* she be so insensitive as to forget the past few months, as if Philip had never lived? Nick was right and she was wrong.

"I think you understand now," Nick said gently. "A close-knit community has long memories. I care too much for you to want to risk raking up old hurts."

Skye moved carefully away from him, but unable to bear this unfulfilled closeness with him a moment longer than necessary.

"Take me home, Nick," she said in a strangled voice.

He started the engine again, and they continued the journey back to New World in silence, while her heart felt as if it was breaking all over again.

"Will you be all right?" he ventured at last.

"Of course. Tremayne women are survivors. Didn't you

270

know?" She drew a deep breath. "Do – do you still intend to help me sort out Albie's paintings for the exhibition? Lily's too superstitious to go inside the place until it's all cleared out and repainted." And fumigated . . .

"Of course I'm going to help you," he said roughly. "Do you think I'd let anyone else do it? And now that we've got the shop to think about, I suggest we put all other considerations out of our minds, and plan the exhibition for the middle of February. Then with luck, we can get the shop ready for spring, when the townies start arriving. You know what they say about spring, don't you?"

"No, but I'm sure you're going to tell me."

"It's a time for new beginnings, and you and I will have a wedding to think about."

"Oh, so you really think I'm going to marry you," she said, her voice brittle. God, who was being insensitive now!

"I wasn't asking you," he retorted, just as brutally. "I'm talking about my ex-partner's wedding. It's arranged for June now, and you promised to come, remember?"

So she did, in what seemed like a lifetime ago. She nodded, and got out of the car before the wanton part of her suggested anything rash, like inviting him in for a last drink, and enticing him to her bedroom . . .

"Goodnight, Nick," she said determinedly. "And thank you for everything."

Even to her own ears it was a goodnight that sounded ominously like a goodbye. But, in a newly puritan mood now, she was just as determined to curb her own feelings as he was. She might be a headstrong Tremayne, but she still had her pride, that damnable quirk of human nature that spelled doom to so many relationships. She could only pray that theirs wasn't going to be one of them.

"Well, you do look peaky, my lamb," Emma exclaimed to Skye on New Year's Eve, when Will had taken the children off to see the new chicks at the farm. "Lily phoned me the other night, and from the way she was bubbling over about this new idea of yours at Albie's studio, I thought you'd be bubbling too."

"I'm all right, really, Em. It's just Christmas. You know. Keeping up the jollity for the children's sake," she lied, knowing it was the only way. She had discovered that it effectively shut off any further probing, even from Em, who wasn't known for her tact over personal matters.

"A good meal of pork and taters will perk you up," she declared, with her own brand of therapy. "So when will you start converting the studio to a shop?"

"Oh, not yet. We want to set up Albie's exhibition first. Nick Pengelly's going to help me with all that, and David Kingsley's going to organise the advertising."

"You're moving in high circles, Skye, like I always expected," Em said admiringly. "But then, nobody could doubt that you'd have men falling at your feet from one look from those lovely eyes. You make the most of it, my love," she finished with a chuckle, failing to see the shine of tears in those particular eyes as Skye turned away.

She didn't want to manipulate men into doing what she wanted. She was obliged to accept help to get the exhibition ready, and to get the studio cleared out. Then there would be a team of professional builders and painters called in to turn the studio into a shop.

And since Nick was her lawyer, he would insist on seeing that everything was done properly, and that she wasn't being exploited because she was a woman doing business in a man's world. Even Theo had shown an interest in the new venture, since the sale of the White Rivers Pottery pieces would be to the advantage of Killigrew Clay as well.

She couldn't avoid the men's influence, but instead of pleasing her, it alarmed Skye to know how much she was starting to resent it. She surely wasn't turning *frigid*? – that almost forbidden word that only cropped up in learned medical books as an unfortunate condition among women. Or in brown paper packaged beneath-the-sheets manuals advising on sexual matters . . . Skye smiled ruefully, knowing that no one as uninhibited and sensually aroused as she had been with Nick Pengelly in a certain hotel in Bristol, could ever be called *frigid*. . . .

*   *   *

After five days of relaxation at the farm, during which the children had a wonderful time and Will Roseveare realised his potential as a pseudo-father figure, Skye knew she wasn't relaxed at all. She felt as if she was living on a knife-edge. Finally, as they drank cocoa together in the farmhouse kitchen on the last morning, Em asked her outright what the devil was wrong with her.

"And don't tell me 'tis all to do with losing Philip, my love, tragic though it was. 'Tis summat more than that. And I've a ready pair of ears and a buttoned-up mouth if you want to unburden yourself."

Skye couldn't even raise a smile at her quaint words. "You're right, Em. And I lost Philip a long time before he died, or rather, we lost each other, and now I'm so full of guilt and regrets it's eating me up."

"You'm a fool to let it," Em said crisply. "What's past is past, and no good ever came of wasting time on regrets."

"You sound just like Granny Morwen."

"Why shouldn't I? She was my mother, and I learned every wise thing I know from her. So since you and Philip lost your way a long time ago, what else do you have to feel guilty about? Or perhaps I should say *who* else?"

Oh God, tact was certainly *not* Em's strong point, thought Skye, feeling her face flood with heat. If she wanted to know a thing, she came right out and asked it . . . and there would be such sweet relief in the telling. . . .

"Nick. Nick Pengelly," she said in a small, raw voice, feeling like the child she had once been, and far removed from the mature woman that she was, and the mother of three chidren. Feeling young and gauche and lost. . . .

"And you love him. Does he love you in return?" Em asked.

She was unshockable, thought Skye. How odd. She was such a typical countrywoman, so isolated from worldly affairs, and yet she understood and didn't stand in judgement. There was nothing she wouldn't understand.

Within minutes Skye found herself pouring out her heart to her aunt, sparing nothing of her feelings for Nick, or his for her. Revealing the shame and the ecstacy of the night they had spent

in one another's arms in Bristol, and of their vow to keep that
love forever sacred in their hearts, because at that time Skye
still had a husband . . .

"Poppycock," Emma said, startling her. "I'm sorry, love, but
living on a farm makes you see life for what it is. You're a
sweet, lovely girl, and I admire you for your loyalty, but you
could be dead tomorrow. You know that after what happened
to Philip. He's gone, and you're still young, so don't keep your
man waiting too long."

"I can hardly think of courting so soon after Philip's death,
can I? I do have some sense of morality."

"Well, just don't be too set on making a martyr of yourself,
that's all. Now go and wash your face and hands and make
yourself presentable before your children come back."

But her soft eyes belied the harshness of her words, and Skye
went to do exactly as she said. It was direction she wanted.
Someone to tell her what she must do and how she must behave.
But she and Nick had already worked that out for themselves,
and she wasn't so spineless that she couldn't wait a few months
until it was accepted in society that a widow-woman could start
courting again.

Besides, she had her children to consider. How would they
feel if she was open about a new relationship when they were
still acutely aware of losing their father? She should consider
them above herself.

And she was being so damn self-righteous now, it was
sickening, she thought, with a spark of humour. But the
common sense that had threatened to desert her, began to
return. It was right to have this breathing space, because it
meant she didn't have to make any decisions at all.

By the time they all finished their goodbye hugs, she
felt as though she was starting to get onto an even keel
once more, and she whispered her thanks to Em, just for
listening.

"Don't thank me," Em said simply. "If you've sorted out your
feelings by now, then thank yourself."

Whenever they met now, Skye couldn't deny the tension

between herself and Nick. There was a barrier between them that they were both unwilling to cross. They kept to business matters with excrutiating correctness, as if determined not to allow personal feelings to spill over.

But when they arranged to go to the studio on a Sunday morning to choose the paintings for the exhibition, it could never be anything but emotional for Skye.

"So much of my mother's past is here," she murmured. "So much of *her*. Almost more than Albie. Isn't that strange?"

"Not really. She was a very beautiful woman, and he was so intent on painting her in all her moods, that her presence almost eclipsed his."

"That's very perceptive of you, Nick," she said, touched by his words. "It's almost poetic!"

"Do you think a lawyer only has at his disposal the dry and dusty words on legal documents?"

"No. I don't think that."

How could she, when she so often imagined his voice in the night, whispering against her flesh the words that had once come so fluently from the lips of a lover?

She blotted out the memory with a huge effort. "I thought I would offer everyone in the family one of Albie's paintings after the exhibition," she said quickly. "I'll keep some for myself, of course, and send the best ones of Mom to my father. But some of the exhibition paintings must have a 'No Sale' label on them."

"You intend to sell them, then?" he said in surprise.

"There are just so many, it seems the only thing to do. But I'd like your opinion on that, Nick."

"It's your decision. You must do what you think best."

She glared at him. "I'm asking for your opinion, damn it. Stop wearing your lawyer's hat and tell me what *you* think."

"I think there's time enough for further discussion when we know what's going into the exhibition."

She clamped her lips together. She knew she was taking up his precious weekend time, and after they had worked solidly for more than two hours, she needed to get out and into the fresh air. The studio was stifling her, and by now they had selected the major paintings to show.

There were many likenesses of Primmy, landscapes of the moors and 'sky-tips', and exquisite watercolours of Truro itself. The exhibition couldn't fail to charm people, thought Skye. Albie had had such talent, and people should know it. There was just one thing, though . . .

"Time to go? Or are you still seeing ghosts?" Nick enquired.

She realised she had been standing motionless in the middle of the studio. She smiled shakily.

"I guess I was. I'm just wondering how Mom would feel about having her portraits on show for all to see."

"Well, you could either remove the portraits, which would be a great pity – or put your 'No Sale' labels on them, then they'll still belong to you. You have the choice."

She wondered if there was a hidden meaning in his words, but apparently not. There was no need for double meanings, anyway. They were both perfectly clear on the choice they had chosen for themselves. And right now, love seemed a very long distance away from friendship.

"Then let's get it all set up, and arrange with David to do the advertising," she said quickly. "I'll take the ones I want home with me now."

As she spoke, Primmy's face smiled out at her from the canvases, beautiful, self-confident, her glossy black hair and lustrous blue eyes the trademark of all the Tremayne women. It was a face that had been painted with expertise and love, and her daughter carefully placed the tissue-wrapped paintings in a soft blanket before she broke down and wept.

The Albert Tremayne Exhibition was reported in *The Informer* newspaper as a tremendous success. David had done extensive advertising of the event, together with an additional feature about the connection between the artist and Skye Tremayne Norwood, and the proposed change of the studio to the White Rivers Pottery shop.

Lily had adamantly refused the offer of occupying the living quarters above the shop, so it was decided that it would be used solely for storage for now. There was no doubt that it would be well patronised, and after the exhibition ended with plenty of sales, Theo organised a celebration for the family and all concerned, at Killigrew House.

"I have to hand it to you, cuz," Theo said. "You've a good business head on those pretty shoulders, and turning old Albie's studio into a pottery shop was inspirational."

"It was Nick's initial idea, not mine," she protested. "He should take most of the credit."

"Ah well, the two of you make good bedfellows – nothing salacious intended, o' course," he added hastily, seeing his wife's frown.

Skye avoided looking at Nick. The exhibition had lasted longer than anyone could have forecast, as people continued to come and view the local artist's work. Family members who wanted one of Albie's paintings had been given their choice, and Skye had sent her father the two that she was sure he would love the most. Theo, commercial as ever, commented that once the old boy was gone, the paintings would probably escalate in value, so it was a good investment.

By the beginning of March the builders and painters were busily at work at the studio, ripping out old fittings and putting in new ones, and transforming the place into gleaming new business premises. Soon, the shop would be in its pristine state, ready for spring, and new beginnings.

And Nick Pengelly wondered how long it was reasonable to wait before he followed his heart and asked Skye to marry him. How long before the community thought it no longer scandalous for a man to propose to a women who had lost her husband? Was six months too short a time? To Nick, it seemed as if he had already waited a lifetime to hold her in his arms again.

But she was so remote now, so unapproachable compared with the loving woman he had known, that it sometimes seemed to Nick that they had never been such passionate lovers at all. Never shared their hearts and bodies . . . as if he had dreamed it all, or else her heart had simply frozen, and if it had, then he had no idea how to melt it.

But the situation couldn't go on indefinitely. He was a red-blooded man, and he wanted her so badly that in the end he had to speak out. They were reviewing the end of progress on the shop, admiring the newly furbished interior and breathing in the smell of new paint that replaced the dank atmosphere of the old studio, and made it live again.

"They've done a wonderful job," Skye said at last. "I couldn't have asked for better, and Uncle Albie understands a little of what's happening. I wrote to the matron, asking her to explain it, and she said he seemed pleased."

"That's good. When the pottery displays are in the window, we'll take some photographs to show him when we go to Bristol for William's wedding. Or even before then." He saw her flinch, and he took her hand. "Skye, don't shut me out. We can't go on pretending for ever that there's nothing between us. It's our time *now*."

"Is it? I don't think so – unless some guardian angel came to you in the night and told you so."

She bit her lip, wishing she hadn't said those particular words. It was too much like superstitious mumbo-jumbo, and she was done with all that.

"You know I want you, don't you?" Nick persisted, refusing to be put off by her angry eyes. He sought to find something to persuade her. "Is this how your mother, or your grandmother would have reacted? They were strong enough to know what they wanted out of life. I didn't think you were a lesser woman than they were."

"I'm not!" she declared, once more his volatile darling. "Or maybe I am after all. Maybe I need to know what Granny Morwen would have said. She married the two men who loved her, so she must have had to decide when the time was right too."

Skye looked at him as a glimmer of memory filled her mind. Her grandmother had died shortly after Celia was born, so she could no longer ask her for advice. There had been many times when she hadn't needed to do so, for Morwen's ethereal voice was so often in her head when she needed it.

But there was another way. There had always been another

way, and it was only now that she intuitively knew the reason for something Morwen had done so long ago.

"Nick, could we go to your chambers?" she said, her voice wavering. "I want to see Granny Morwen's diaries."

Skye didn't really know what she was looking for, and when Nick had finally brought the bulky box of journals to her, she looked at them in bewilderment, not knowing where to begin, and aware that she still couldn't bear to read them all. It would be impossible, anyway, for they represented a woman's lifetime. She tentatively opened one or two of the books, still feeling as if she was prying into someone's innermost thoughts and feelings, and then realised that the yellowing entries were often sketchy, haphazard accounts, recorded whenever anything significant occurred in Morwen Tremayne's life. But however brief, always written with the passion that was in her soul.

"You'll want to be left alone," Nick stated, making her jump. "I have papers to deal with in the outer office, so just call me when you've found what it is you're looking for."

He left her then, and she flipped through the pages of the early diaries quickly, pausing to read of Morwen's anguish when her brother Matt, Skye's own grandfather, fled to America with the infamous Jude Pascoe. And then how her beloved brother Sam died in Ben Killigrew's railtrack accident, and how she and Ben had later adopted the three orphaned children, Walter, Albert and Primrose.

Other pages were filled with joy, such as when she and Ben had their own children, Justin and Charlotte. Skye turned the pages quickly, covering the years, her emotions at fever-pitch, almost frantic for what she was trying to find, without really knowing what it was she sought. But she was driven to it, and an instinct stronger than reason told her that here, somehow, she would find the answer.

And then at last she found it. She caught her breath. Morwen had been no scholar in her early years, but simple words were often more eloquent than the most lyrical ones, especially when they were written in capital letters.

'TODAY, RAN WAINWRIGHT CAME INTO OUR LIVES.'

To anyone else, it might have been an odd, disjointed statement. To Skye, looking for answers, it was significant. *He* was significant. It needed no elaboration. At that time, Morwen was still married to Ben. And as she read on, skimming the dates, Skye could sense the torment in Morwen's heart because of her growing attraction towards another man. It mirrored her own life, except for one thing.

Morwen had still loved Ben, and was tormented by her own conscience, while Skye had fallen out of love with Philip long before Nick came to mean so much to her. Did that make a difference? She smothered the thought.

There were many gaps in the diaries, and many disjointed references, especially after Ben Killigrew's death, while Morwen struggled to do what was right by their large family of children. Then Skye's eyes widened and her nerves prickled.

'I'm going to copy out the letter I sent to Ran', Morwen wrote, 'to remind me that if everything goes wrong, I have only myself to blame. He wants to marry me, but 'tis too soon after Ben, and so I sent him away. I wonder now if I shall regret it all my life.'

Skye couldn't bear to read more than small sections of the letter, feeling as if she was looking into another woman's soul. Yet she was very sure she could feel Morwen's loving presence as she read her letter to Ran.

". . . I know that nothing matters but the feelings of a man and a woman, and to have your love again I would gladly give away Killigrew Clay and everything I own. It was never really mine, anyway. It was always Ben's, and part of a man's world. . . . I'm no good at being noble, so don't expect me to dance at your wedding to one of the Pendewy girls, because I shan't! I love you."

That last part was so – so *Morwen*, thought Skye, defensive to the end. And of course she knew that Ran Wainwright had never married a Pendewy girl, but Morwen herself. The entry ended there, and dated some while later there was a single line that needed no capitals to make it the most important entry of all.

"Today, Ran and I were married, and I am whole again."

Skye slammed the ledger closed, her eyes stinging. That was it. That was the feeling. She had been in some kind of No Man's Land for months now, feeling only half alive, and torn by guilt at wanting to be whole again. To be part of someone again. Someone that she loved with all her heart.

She heard him enter the room, and she turned her head very slowly, then heard him catch his breath as he saw her brimming eyes. In seconds he had crossed the room to her and held her close to his chest. He spoke roughly, unable to hide his own emotion.

"Leave the diaries for another day, my love. There's far too much to take in all at once, and it's upsetting you."

She shook her head, her voice soft, but full of a new determination now. "I shan't look at any more of them, ever. I know all that Granny Morwen wanted me to know, and now I shall burn them all, and no one else will ever see them."

"Do you think that's what she would have wanted?"

Skye wound her arms about his neck, and kissed Nick's mouth with an uninhibited passion, and as she felt his instant response, her spirit soared.

"I know it," she said simply. "The way we Tremayne women always know these things."

SEPTEMBER MORNING

One

Almost crushed by the crowds in the swelteringly hot stands, amid the noise and rapturous applause, Celia turned to her companion and hugged his arm. She knew that solemnity should be coupled with the excitement of the event she was witnessing but, outspoken as ever, she couldn't resist whispering in his ear.

"What a funny little man he is," she said with a giggle.

Franz Vogl glanced round, shushing her at once. Besotted as he was with Celia, he couldn't let the slight to his hero pass. Handsome, fair-haired and typical of his race, Franz's nature was as passionate as that of the Cornish girl he adored, but his national pride in the Fatherland and its leader was paramount.

"You must be careful what you say, Celia. Would your English folk be so pleased to hear your King Edward described as a funny little man – especially as–·"

Celia pulled a face as he paused abruptly, but she knew what he was thinking. European and American newspapers were rife with the stories and rumours that Fleet Street had had strict orders to suppress – that of the scandalous affair between the British king and an American divorcee.

But even if it had nothing to do with ordinary people, Celia was prepared to defend her king and his right to love. It was so very romantic – and any hot-blooded seventeen-year-old girl could hardly think otherwise. All the same . . .

"*Verzeihen Sie* – I'm sorry. But I would never describe King Edward as funny, because he's not. He's very dashing and very royal. But your Mr Hitler. Well—"

She giggled again at the memory of the German Chancellor pronouncing the Games open with his rasping voice and sporting his weird little moustache. Try as she might, Celia was unable to distinguish him in her mind from Charlie Chaplin. She straightened her face at once as her mother nudged her, and whispered

1

disapprovingly, "Behave yourself, Celia, and remember that we're guests of Franz's parents while we're here."

Celia nodded. It was pure luck that she was here at all. She had only been allowed to take her stepfather's place at the Berlin Olympics because he was involved in an important legal case and had been obliged to stay behind in Cornwall while she and her mother travelled to Germany. Her sister had begged to be allowed to come as well, but they had only been offered two tickets, and Wenna had never been interested in sports anyway. Celia airily brushed aside the fact that it wasn't so much the sports that excited her, as the thought of all those healthy, virile young men who would be panting around the tracks or leaping over the hurdles.

She felt a momentary pity for her young brother Oliver. He would have loved all this – but two seats meant two seats, and the moment of regret for him passed quickly.

Her mother was now deep in conversation with their German host, whose company imported White Rivers pottery, the business she owned and managed so successfully. Celia greatly admired her mother for her business skills, and also for having learned the German language so fluently and easily. She and Wenna had struggled with its vowels and complicated sentence structure at their Swiss finishing school.

Both girls adored their American mother, Skye, and the smile Celia gave her now was almost dazzling.

Skye caught her breath at the sight of that smile, marvelling as always how alike all the generations of women in their family were.

Skye's uncle, the artist Albert Tremayne, had done a remarkable job of transferring their likenesses onto canvas. His paintings were now fetching handsome prices in Cornwall and beyond. Skye thought it a charming way for the heritage of the Tremayne beauty to be perpetuated. Especially in the case of her own mother's portrait. The empathy between Albert Tremayne and his sister Primmy had been particularly strong.

But this was no time for reminiscing, Skye reminded herself. Today was a wonderful day, the first of August with Adolf Hitler opening the Olympic Games. If the great American athlete, Jesse Owens, lived up to expectations, then she could take an extra pride in one of her own countrymen winning a gold medal. She felt a thrill at the thought. It was many years since she had left America for Cornwall to try to find her roots, and stayed for a lifetime. But deep inside her there was still that tug of home and always would be.

Since she had read some of the American newspapers, she knew very well what the more lurid ones were saying about the new king and Mrs Simpson. Rumours all, according to her husband, which she shouldn't pay any heed to.

"Don't believe any of it until or unless you hear it from reliable sources," Nick had advised her. "These scandal-rags will say anything to further their circulation."

"They can't say just anything, Nick," she had replied uneasily. "You, of all people, should know the legalities of printing libellous material."

"And you, my love, know very well how a clever journalist can get around that little problem with carefully chosen words." Her luminous blue eyes seemed darker in contrast to her pale face, and her classically beautiful features were drawn and anxious. He had already guessed the reason why. "Darling, you really can't take all this personally," he'd said quietly, "it has nothing to do with us."

"I know it," she had answered, forcing a laugh.

And of course it didn't. They lived in the far west of Cornwall and events in London and the rest of the country had always seemed very removed from their own small world. So it was impossible for Skye to try to explain her feelings to Nick, her clever lawyer husband with the so-logical brain that didn't allow for hunches and sixth senses. Nor could she really explain them to herself. It was crazy for a long-exiled American woman to feel this unnecessary defensiveness, almost bordering on guilt, for pity's sake, on behalf of a slicker, more sophisticated and worldly American divorcee.

Except, of course, that her countrywoman was no ordinary woman. She moved in high places – the very highest. And if all these foreign newspapers were shrieking out the truth, she could be the catalyst for the unthinkable to happen: for causing the King of England to abdicate, and possibly even to bring down the monarchy. Such a shameful eventuality would touch every one of them.

At that moment Skye had felt the American newspaper taken

out of her numb hands. She had smiled briefly at Nick, knowing she was seeing what wasn't there – might never be there. That was the Cornish part of her, her legacy, and she told herself severely that such problems were for others to solve.

"Don't they look simply marvellous?" Skye heard her elder daughter say, and she forced her thoughts back to the present and the parade of athletes through the vast Berlin Olympic stadium.

At seventeen Celia was boy-mad, Skye thought, and it was a relief to her that Franz was such a steady and upright young man. He had strong opinions of his own too, which wasn't such a bad thing and might curb her headstrong daughter.

While they were in Berlin, she and Celia were guests of his parents. The very middle-class Vogl family lived in a mansion situated in a cool shady avenue of old buildings that exemplified the very best of European architecture. Skye counted herself fortunate to have such good European connections, both in business and socially.

Skye saw her daughter lean towards Franz and his blue eyes lit up at the sight of her. His blondness was in sharp contrast to Celia's glossy black hair. She felt a momentary frisson of unease at the way the girl smiled so teasingly into his eyes. At times, Celia's nature was too tempestuous and passionate for her own good. Everything had to happen at once for her.

Skye smiled faintly. Celia was certainly her mother's daughter in that respect. It could take no longer than a locked glance between two people for them to fall in love. She didn't want that to happen to Celia yet. She had her whole life in front of her, and the opportunities for women were so much wider now. But tempting though it was, Skye knew she must not indulge her own dreams through her daughters.

Instead, she too concentrated on the fine parade of athletes and the seemingly endless preliminaries before the Games could officially begin. This was the spectacle they had come here for, as well as making a tour of the factories using Killigrew Clay and the shops selling White Rivers pottery. She felt a glow of pleasure at her own success – as important to her as anything these athletes would accomplish.

In just over two weeks all the ballyhoo was over. Tears had been shed for the losers and plaudits given to the winners. Jesse Owens was the undoubted hero of the Games with a clutch of gold medals, but to Skye's disgust – and the fury of the American press – Adolf Hitler had refused to shake hands with him because he was black. It said much about Hitler, in Skye's opinion, but because of her obligations to her German hosts, she wisely kept those opinions to herself.

By the time they were well on their way home, Celia was declaring dramatically that she had fallen madly in love with Franz. She was trying to persuade her mother to invite him to Cornwall during early December, when she would be back from Switzerland to share in her belated November birthday celebrations.

It had already been arranged that Celia would return to finishing school next month for the winter term, even though her course was officially over. She had obtained a post as the school's art class assistant, to keep Wenna company for her last year, and to keep an eye on her – or so she said. According to Wenna, it was more likely to enable Celia to keep her eyes on the young French and German buckos who flocked to the area for the skiing every winter. It was so unlike Wenna to criticise anything Celia did that Skye was perfectly sure it was true. Celia was the one who needed watching, if anyone did.

"You will ask Franz to visit us, won't you, Mom?" Celia begged, as they finally reached the end of their voyage back to Cornwall.

Ahead of them they could see the twin castles on the headlands of Pendennis and Mawes, as the welcome outline of Falmouth harbour came into view from the prow of their ship.

"We'll see, honey."

"Oh, you always say that! Why can't you just say yes? It would return Herr Vogl's hospitality to invite Franz. We could invite his parents too," Celia added as an afterthought. "I'm sure they would like to see the pottery, and the Killigrew Clay works."

Skye laughed. "You're so transparent, Celia. I'm quite sure that's not the only reason you want to invite the entire Vogl family."

"Of course it's not. I've already said so," Celia replied candidly. "Oh, please, Mom. Say, yes, so I can write straight back to Franz and invite them."

"You've only just said goodbye to him, Celia."

"I know," she said, suddenly miserable. "But it already seems like years ago. The minute he'd gone I missed him. You wouldn't understand . . ."

Celia felt Skye's arm round her shoulders, and her mother gave her a squeeze.

"Believe me, I do understand, my love," she said softly.

Skye gazed at the familiar shape of the harbour and the many ships that jostled in its deep waters, but in her mind's eye she was seeing herself on another ship in another time approaching this very harbour. A time when she too had fallen recklessly in love with a man she had only known for the duration of the ship's voyage. A man who had been engaged to someone else at the time, but whose love for Skye Tremayne had been too strong to deny. A man called Philip Norwood who had swept Skye off her feet and had eventually married her and fathered her children.

Now the eldest of those children was declaring herself in love with a virtual stranger too. Skye gave a small shiver in the cool evening air. History had a habit of repeating itself, and the endless cycle seemed more pronounced in the long history of the Tremayne family than in any other. Or so it had always seemed to Skye, although she had no doubt that other families would say the same thing of themselves.

"Mom, are you all right?" she heard Celia say.

"Of course I am, and if it will keep you happy, then, of course, we'll invite the Vogls—"

Her reward was a cry of sheer delight. The next minute she was hugged tightly by her effusive and beautiful daughter.

Anyway, the German family might not come, Skye thought privately. Why would they want to leave their home at Christmastime to stay with virtual strangers? By then, four months from now, Celia's butterfly passion for Franz would probably have waned. At seventeen it happened, and absence didn't always make the heart grow fonder.

"Do you see them?" Celia was saying excitedly, craning her neck to catch the first glimpse of the rest of her family. It was barely dusk and the dockside was filled with motor cars and larger vehicles awaiting the disembarkation of the passengers.

"Not yet—" Skye began, and then her heart jolted as she saw the tall figure of Nick Pengelly on the quayside, with two excited young people jumping up and down beside him. Wenna, at sixteen, was not yet too grown up to smother all her excitement, and the finishing shool had done nothing to change that. Skye hoped it never would. While Oliver, at thirteen, would be blatantly expecting presents.

"There's Daddy," Celia screeched.

"Yes," Skye said softly. "I see him."

There was no way her daughter could guess how her heart raced at the sight of Nick, or that Celia could comprehend that love became more constant when you were nearing your middle years. The young believed that love was invented solely for them, but the feelings in Skye Pengelly's heart for the man who had become her second husband, were as achingly longing as when Nick had been her clandestine lover for a few brief hours of stolen bliss.

He and the children caught sight of her and Celia then. They began waving madly, and Skye's wanton feelings momentarily vanished, but she knew they would return, and a shudder of warm anticipation ran through her veins. Once the family reunion was complete, all the talking was done and the excitement had died down a little, she and Nick would be alone at last, with the whole night ahead of them to spend in each others' arms.

"The Games apart, the visit was a success?" Nick asked her a long while later, when they lay, replete and fulfilled, their bodies as intertwined as if they shared the same skin.

"It was wonderful," Skye told him. "But I wish you could have been there, Nick. The showrooms are so elegant, and our goods are displayed with such importance."

"Why wouldn't they be? White Rivers is really on the map now, darling, and the shops here are flourishing."

Skye loved the way he was so pleased for her success. Many men wouldn't be, she thought fleetingly. Many men would resent having a businesswoman for a wife. But there weren't many men like Nick. There was no one like Nick . . .

She held him more tightly for a moment, knowing how lucky she was to have found such love twice in a lifetime. But at his words, the second most important thing in her life took prominence, and her enthusiasm bubbled over in the soft warm darkness.

"But it's nothing like the huge department stores and showrooms they have there in Germany. I can't wait to see Lily and show her some of the brochures I've brought back. They're so keen on advertising. They send out brochures to their regular clients – and they also have them available for indulgent papas to send out to prospective wedding guests. Isn't that a marvellous idea? Imagine all those new brides receiving a complete set of White Rivers pottery to begin their married life with."

Nick laughed. Her enthusiasm was having a different effect on him.

"I don't know about new brides. I would rather concentrate on the one I've got in my arms."

"Hardly a new bride," she murmured, feeling his mouth seeking hers, and thrilling to the fact that he could be so readily aroused again, even after ten years of marriage.

"But every bit as desirable," Nick told her, and as he matched the deed to the words, she gave up thinking at all.

The following day while Celia was busily regaling her brother and sister about the delights of her stay in Germany, and no doubt giving away a few secrets to Wenna about the attentions of the lovely Franz Vogl, Skye made a telephone call to her cousin Lily in Truro.

"You're back!" Lily squealed unnecessarily. "How was it, Skye? Was it marvellous, or were you a bit scared? Right in the heart of the enemy and all that."

"Lily, stop it," Skye said, laughing. "All that was a long time ago. They're not our enemies any more. They're our best customers, don't forget."

"Oh, I know. There are still plenty of folk who can't forget, though, and David's not so tolerant with all the rumours he gets to hear. Still, as you say, we need them."

"How is David?" Skye said swiftly. "And I'm longing to see my nephews. I thought of coming to visit this afternoon."

"Good. David's fine apart from his arthritis, and the twins are driving me mad as usual, so it'll be lovely to have some adult conversation," Lily added cheerfully.

Skye hung up, the smile still on her face at hearing Lily's no-nonsense voice. The twins had come late in her life, but she was coping with everything, the way she always had. It was good to know that some things stayed the same, no matter what . . . and why Skye should think such a thing at that precise moment she couldn't have said.

She was looking forward to seeing Lily, with whom she had such a good rapport, but part of her was also keen to learn any snippets of information Lily's husband may have given her on the Mrs Simpson situation. David Kingsley was the owner of the *Informer* newspaper, and as such, was privy to much of the information withheld from the general public. Personally, Skye thought it ludicrous that the British public were cushioned from important and dramatic events that might shape their nation. It was their right to know. This suppression of news would never happen in America.

Before his death, Skye's brother Sinclair's brief love affair with politics had revealed how many aspects of public life could be inspected under a miscroscope. It wasn't always desirable, but at least it was honest.

She put such thoughts out of her mind. The children were sitting in the garden now with Celia holding court as she discussed the finer points of the Berlin Games with Oliver, and still boasting about meeting the handsome Franz Vogl – for Wenna's envious benefit.

Skye left them to it, and drove her car into Truro, revelling in the warm sunshine, with the fragrant summer scents wafting down from the moors on her left, and the sparkling blue sea on her right. As always, this route gave her a lift of the heart just to be where her ancestors had always been, from the start of their association with Killigrew Clay, when her grandmother, Morwen Tremayne, had married Ben Killigrew, the owner's son. The same great clayworks that Skye now part owned. No matter how often she travelled this road, the memories never failed to stir her heart. And if ever there was any doubt that she had inherited her family's Cornish sense of romance, this was the place she knew it most.

" 'Tis called fey, my love."

She could almost hear Granny Morwen telling her now, as she had done so often years ago. She almost turned her head to answer her with a smile, and knew how foolish that was.

But it was a fact that a person didn't have to be physically near for someone to feel their presence. Even now, Skye was sometimes aware of and charmed by it. It wasn't spooky at all – to use one of Olly's favourite words of the moment – and that was part of the Cornish legacy too, she thought with satisfaction.

When she reached Truro, she paused for a moment after leaving her car to gaze with unabashed pride at the frontage of what had once been Albert Tremayne's artist's studio. This was where Albert and his sister, Primmy, had spent so many happy years in bohemian bliss before Primmy had married Skye's father and gone to America.

The place was completely transformed now. Skye hadn't known what to do with it after Albert had bequeathed it to her. She certainly hadn't wanted to keep it as a dusty museum or art gallery as some kind of ghostly memorial, but the answer had come so joyfully and realistically when her inspired White Rivers Pottery had begun to prosper. The old studio was now an impressive shop and showroom, frequented by all the best people in Truro and the surrounding district. But always mindful that poorer people needed plates and dishes, too, Skye had insisted that they kept a special section of the shop for misshapen and less than perfectly thrown pieces.

Together with David's advertising strategies in the newspaper, it had proved to be a winner. The gleaming window displayed the pure white pieces, which were produced from the finest clay from their own clayworks, with their distinctive winding river decorated on the base of each piece. At Skye's suggestion the backdrop for each wide shop window was a deep blue, showing the china off to its best advantage.

The door of the old studio burst open, and Lily's well-rounded figure rushed through. Lily managed the shop and she and her family lived in the rooms above it. She used to be quite gaunt, but a happy marriage and two enormous twin sons had put paid to that, and she looked all the better for it. The five-year-old boys were at her heels now, like two fat little butterballs.

"It's so good to see you, Skye," Lily exclaimed. "And you look so well! Different, somehow. You were always elegant, but I reckon the continental style has rubbed off on you."

"What rot. I can't have changed that much," she said with a laugh. "It's barely a month since I saw you."

"It seems longer," Lily assured her. "I missed you. We all did, didn't we, boys?"

She always referred to them collectively as boys, even though she knew perfectly well which was Frederick and which was Robert. Skye sometimes wondered if it was going to give them a complex, but then the rest of the family never knew which was which. At their mother's question they hurtled towards Skye, and she was nearly knocked over as they clamoured to be held in her arms.

"Good Lord, they're going to grow up to be boxers at this rate, they're so strong," she gasped.

"That's what David says," Lily said happily. "I can't think where they get it from. Anyway, now that they've seen you, they can go into the garden and play, while we have some tea and you can tell me everything about Berlin."

That was Lily: tell me everything, in one fell swoop. But Skye relished her cousin's sharp mind, for it matched her own.

"Did Celia behave herself?" Lily asked over tea and toast, but before waiting for an answer, she rushed on, "Which reminds me, I saw Betsy the other day, and she thinks you were very modern in taking Celia to Germany by yourself. I think she was admiring your courage, but you can never be sure with Betsy, can you?"

Skye screwed up her nose. "Betsy's getting old and crusty just like Theo," she said, knowing she would have to meet their mutual male cousin quite soon, since she and Theo were co-owners of their various enterprises. "Anyway, why on earth shouldn't two women travel alone? You and I and plenty of others did far more during the war."

"True, but it was acceptable then, because they needed us. Now that we've all become *respectable* again, for want of a better word, we're supposed to take a back seat and sit at home knitting socks for our menfolk."

Skye grinned at the thought, knowing it was quite alien to Lily's nature. Lily had been a foremost feminist, and she and her sister Vera and Skye had served together in France in the war. Travelling unescorted had been seen as a serving woman's right at that time. Now, it seemed that the male population was only too anxious to keep its women chained to the kitchen sink once more, as one progressive cartoonist had portrayed it.

"I hardly think we come into that category," Skye said. "And they can like it or lump it."

"Sometimes, Skye, you're still so deliciously *American*," Lily said with a chuckle.

"*Still?* I always will be, nothing's ever going to change that! Anyway, you wanted to know about Celia, didn't you? She found a beau, of course."

"Well, was there any doubt? She's a Tremayne, no matter what label she goes under now. They were never short of beaux, even though it took some of us longer than others to discover what we wanted. And did you see that horrible little man?"

"If you mean Mr Hitler, yes we did. And yes, he is—"

"David doesn't like the situation at all," Lily said, apparently going off at a tangent. "He calls Hitler a rogue character and quite unpredictable. David sees dark times ahead if we're not careful."

"You don't mean another war? There's no likelihood of that, surely. All the German people we met were exceptionally correct and genteel."

"But ordinary folk don't rule the roost, do they? Oh, forget I said anything. It's probably nothing."

The trouble was, Skye couldn't quite forget it. David Kingsley had access to too many sources denied to other people. And this nasty little Adolf Hitler had already stirred up more than one hornet's nest by entering the Rhineland in March, throwing the French into confusion over whether to keep their dignity and refrain from comment, with the more belligerent of them shouting for instant military action.

Warmongering had been evident then, and when one newspaper claimed that Hitler was merely re-occupying what was rightfully his, it was pointed out that it was also a hundred miles nearer to French territory. Skye felt a shiver of real unease, and tried to shrug it off as she drove home to New World, deciding to call in on Theo and Betsy on the way.

"Betsy's out visiting, so you'll have to put up wi' me. So how were the bastards?" Theo asked her, with his usual charm.

Nearing sixty now, he was more portly than ever, and wheezing with the extra weight he carried, which did not improve his looks or his habitual lack of finesse.

"If you mean the Germans, they were delightful people," Skye snapped. "Why must you always despise everyone, Theo?"

"My God, but you've got a short memory, girl. Have you forgotten how those young German workers wrecked the pottery and half killed one of the clayworkers into the bargain?"

"For pity's sake, all that was more than ten years ago!" she said, exasperated. "You can't keep dredging up the past for ever."

"Why not? If it weren't for the healthy accounts we get from our exports, I'd say good riddance to the lot of 'em. They were our enemies in the war, and as far as I'm concerned, they're our enemies now and always will be."

His son Sebastian arrived home from the pottery in time to hear his father's usual blistering onslaught.

"Pay no attention to him, Skye," he told her with a grin. "He's always worse when the gout plays him up. I only wish I'd had the chance to go to Germany with you and Celia. How did it go, by the way?"

"It was wonderful, Sebby," she said, thinking it a marvel that he had turned out so agreeable. As a child he had been as obnoxious as any youngster she had ever come across. But now, working at the pottery with the clay he loved, alongside her own young brother-in-law, Ethan Pengelly, Sebby had turned into a fine young man, albeit with a roving eye for the girls.

"And she got a glimpse of the chief bastard, so don't bother asking her," Theo snarled.

"What was he like?" Sebby asked, ignoring his father.

"Charlie Chaplin," Skye said solemnly, as irreverent as Celia, and within seconds the two of them were laughing hysterically at the image.

After an hour, when she had repeated yet again everything she had told Lily, she finally headed for home. By then she knew that all was well at the pottery, though she sensed a small hesitation from Sebby as he had said so. Skye guessed it was due to a little bit of healthy friction between him and Ethan, which was understandable in two such creative young men, and nothing to worry about.

At least there were no current complaints from Killigrew Clay. That was a small triumph in itself, she thought, knowing the volatile nature of the clayworkers.

The memory of the German Chancellor still wouldn't leave her mind. It was one thing to scoff at a person's appearance, but the power that the man held was indisputable. And he was greedy. Surely the impossible couldn't happen again, when the younger members of her own scattered family were of an age to be involved? She shivered, thankful that Celia and Wenna were girls, and Olly still only thirteen.

But Sebastian was nineteen now, and his brother Justin a hefty fifteen. Even Ethan at twenty-five, would be more than ready to go if the call came, avenging the brother he had lost in the Great War.

Skye tried to shake off the unreasonable sense of disaster. It was madness to let passing remarks dwell in her mind and fester. It was even crazier to start imagining events that would probably never happen. Hitler's desire for power would be just as likely to fizzle out and disappear when some new ambitious politician challenged his right to lead the German hierarchy.

She comforted herself with that thought, and spent the evening with her husband and children gathered around her, as if to assure herself that together they were a stronghold that no one could violate.

Two

C elia knew she was taking out her ill temper on her sister. She also knew it wasn't fair but she couldn't seem to stop it, as a natural deflation after the visit to Germany replaced her exhilaration.

Wenna was by far the gentler of the two sisters and, though she was by no means spineless, she had always been a useful scapegoat for Celia's sharper tongue. But this time she was goaded beyond measure.

"If you're so mad about the stupid boy, why don't you just go and live in Germany?" Wenna finally burst out.

"I wasn't even talking about Franz," Celia snapped, ignoring the little leap of her heart at just saying his name.

"You don't have to talk about him. You've been mooning over him ever since you and Mom got home from Berlin. Where's the sense in wasting your time dreaming over some boy who's so far away? He won't come here so near to Christmas, anyway, and we don't want him. We have enough family of our own without having strangers in the house."

Celia curbed her rage with difficulty. "Well, we all know *you* dream about someone much closer, of course, and a fat lot of good it will do you. Ethan's not going to bother his head over a little ninny like you. He still sees you as a schoolgirl – which you are!"

It was the final moment of triumph, and she saw Wenna's face flush a deep red at the insult. It wasn't Wenna's fault that Celia was more than a year her senior, but her sister never let her forget it. Nor did Celia ever forget that Ethan Pengelly had always championed Wenna, and teased Celia in a mocking way that constantly affronted her, and made her feel more like a good pal than the desirable young lady she purported to be.

But Ethan was a man now, and Wenna must know he didn't

look at her in any way but as Celia described it. If anyone was wasting her life dreaming about the impossible, it was Wenna for ever thinking that a man of twenty-five would waste his time on a schoolgirl who had just turned sixteen. There was a limit to how long she could fool herself that Ethan was just waiting for her to become an adult.

At Wenna's suddenly downcast look, Celia's demeanour softened without warning. Her frown vanished, her blue eyes sparkled and her mobile mouth curved upwards in a laugh.

"Just listen to us, will you? Mom would have a fit if she knew how the family coffers were being wasted on a good education by the way we're always bickering. We're supposed to be turning into young ladies, aren't we?"

Wenna laughed back, her sunnier nature never allowing her to stay cross with Celia for long.

"I wonder why a Swiss finishing school is supposed to be any better at that than anywhere else? At any rate, I always thought it was healthy for sisters to be competitive."

"Oh, is that what we are? I'll have to watch out when Franz comes to visit then." Celia grinned, complacent about her own sensuality and confident that such rivalry was never likely to happen. She hugged Wenna's arm. "Anyway, we're supposed to be looking round Mom's old pottery today, so that should please you, seeing dear Ethan up to his bare elbows in wet clay!"

She felt an odd tingle in her veins as she said the words. She had no particular feelings for Ethan Pengelly, her stepfather's brother, but she had to admit that if Wenna fancied someone like mad, she felt it was her bounden duty, as the elder sister, to prove that she could attract him too. It never meant anything as far as Celia was concerned. She treated her male cousins in the same way. It was just harmless flirtation, and it had the safety valve of being within the family. It was nothing at all compared with the way she felt about Franz Vogl.

Ethan Pengelly and Sebastian Tremayne were inspecting a particularly fine set of tableware they had just completed for Skye's approval. It was an experimental design, and Sebby knew he would have to win his aunt round to agree to it. She preferred to stick with tried and trusted methods, but you had to move on or you became stagnant.

His aunt was in his mid-forties now, and in his opinion a little staid in some respects, though hardly in the way his mother was. Skye was still considered a beauty, while his mother had always been old, even as a young wife, and when he was a child Seb had been perfectly aware of his father's little peccadilloes. He doubted that they still continued, what with Theo's gout and his preference to stay at home at night, or to frequent the local hostelries rather than going further afield. But Seb had been blessed, or cursed, with his father's roving eyes for the female sex, and was well aware of the way his beautiful girl cousins were growing up.

Cousins or not, it was a good thing, as far as he was concerned, that they spent so much of their time in Switzerland, he bragged to himself, or . . .

"What's put that stupid grin on your face?" Ethan asked him. "If you're planning how to win Skye round with your nonsense, you'd better think again. If this new design is not going to be a viable proposition, she won't agree to it, and we'll be accused of wasting time and materials."

Seb scowled at once. Ethan had a knack of putting things in a sensible perspective and, although they rubbed along remarkably well, he was the more headstrong of the pair. Since Ethan's brother Adam had retired from the business, Ethan was in charge of White Rivers now. He had been persuaded against his will to produce the set of tableware that now bore an entwined W and R at intervals around the edge of the plates and the base of the cups. It was elegant, but it wasn't Skye's design. It was Seb's.

"My father agreed with it," he reminded Ethan.

"Of course he did, since he was sure Skye would oppose it," Ethan said, knowing Theo's contrariness only too well. "When did you ever know him to be happy to think a woman had the upper hand in his business dealings – and especially an *American* woman?" he added.

"She does though, doesn't she?" Sebby said thoughtfully. "She always has, the way they said her grandmother did."

Ethan, paused, sluicing his hands under cold water to rid himself of the wet clay remains that clung to them.

"You never knew her, did you, Seb? Old Morwen Tremayne, I mean. That's how folk always referred to her, even though she'd had two husbands."

17

"Well, since I was only a baby when she died, no, I never knew her. Why – did you?"

Ethan shook his head. "Not really. My family weren't involved with them then. I saw her once, though, when she was a very old woman. She had these amazingly blue eyes that seemed to look right through you, even though she must have been about eighty years old at the time. I was about seven, and it scared me, I can tell you. It was just as if she knew every damn thing I was thinking. Of course, they always said she was more fey than most."

Seb stared at him. It wasn't exactly the way his father had described Morwen Tremayne to him. Theo was Morwen's grandson, and he had loved and feared her in equal measure, but his aggression was mostly because he could never accept the idea of a woman being in charge of business. And what a woman. Seb was well aware that no one who had known Morwen Tremayne had ever been in doubt of her strength of character. She was practically a legend around St Austell and the Killigrew clayworks.

This was why he knew damn well he must never under estimate Skye's reaction to his new pottery design. She walked only too well in Morwen Tremayne's footsteps. So Seb knew he must tread cautiously, even though he and Ethan had worked bloody hard to bring the new design to a perfect finish before displaying it to her. But even so, he couldn't forget his father's sarcastic aside that if Skye hated it, then Sebby would just have to give the set to his mother for an early Christmas gift.

"Bloody cheapskate," Seb muttered beneath his breath.

"Thank you for that!" Ethan said indignantly.

"I didn't mean you. Anyway, you'd better perk up. Aunt Skye has just arrived with the girl cousins."

They both looked through the workroom window to where Skye was getting out of her car with Celia and Wenna. Contrary to most of the large and scattered Tremayne family and their descendents, neither the sisters nor their brother Oliver had the remotest interest in clay. After finishing his education, Oliver was determined to follow in his stepfather's footsteps and become a lawyer.

"My God, but Celia improves every time I see her," Seb commented. "It's at this time of year you appreciate that women are wearing shorter skirts. She's also growing outwards as well as upwards, if you see what I mean. What a luscious pair – and I don't just mean her and her sister."

His coarseness hid the sudden nervousness he was feeling. He had hardly realised himself how vital the acceptance of this new pottery design was to him until he saw Skye. He had been in his father's shadow all his life and, although working under the Pengelly brothers had been perfectly acceptable to him while he served his apprenticeship, he never forgot that he was a Tremayne. He was now as skilled a potter as any man, and he needed to assert himself in the family business.

He ignored Ethan's snappy rejoinder to mind his manners. Pengelly had better mind his, Seb thought, and to remember who he was – and more importantly, who he wasn't. He strode through into the pottery showroom to greet his relatives.

"It's good to see you again, Aunt Skye, and I hardly need to ask how the world is treating my lovely cousins. You both look blooming, girls."

"Now then, Seb, enough of the flattery," Skye said with a laugh, aware he was sizing up her daughters. "Your father tells me you've got something to show me."

"Did he? It was meant to be a surprise."

"Well, since I have no idea what it is, it's going to stay a surprise for ever unless you show me, honey," she said coolly. "And how are you today, Ethan?" she added as he entered the showroom, hastily pulling down his shirt sleeves to cover his bare arms.

"I'm well enough, thanks," he said, still wiping the remnants of clay from his hands. He wondered how it was that Seb could always look so spick and span moments after finishing work, while he always felt as though he looked as dishevelled as a dishrag, especially in front of finely turned out folk like these three.

"Have you heard about our visit?" Celia asked him, cutting across the formalities. "If not, I'm sure Wenna's dying to tell you everything at second-hand."

"Seb's passed on most of it," Ethan said, "but I'm always glad to hear anything Wenna has to tell me."

"All right, you two, stop this bantering and let Sebby show me the surprise," Skye said briskly, seeing how Wenna's face began

19

to colour. The poor girl had always looked up to Ethan, and her adoration had never wavered since she was a child.

I wish it would, Skye thought suddenly. There was far too much intermarriage in the family already, and she didn't relish any more. She immediately thought how foolish she was being, to interpret a childhood fantasy in such a way.

"Before I do, I'd be glad if you would say nothing until you've counted to ten," Seb said.

"My goodness, what have you done, Seb – set fire to the workroom?" Celia giggled.

"Be quiet, Celia," her mother said sharply.

There had been a time, long ago, when these very premises had been reduced to ashes in a blistering and maliciously started fire. But they and the business had risen, triumphant and phoenix-like to begin again, and she wanted no reminders of that time.

The three women followed the young men into the workroom. They were *all* women now, Ethan realised, even little Wenna was the epitome of the fabulous Tremayne beauty. She was no longer a child. He felt a throb of desire in his loins which he thrust away. The girl was no more than sixteen, for God's sake. No matter how much rapport had always existed between them, it wasn't right to think of her in that way.

He caught the glimmer of mockery in Celia's eyes right then, and knew she had been perfectly aware of the way his thoughts were going. Bloody knowing wench, he thought savagely, reverting to the earthier speech of the clayfolk, as if to relieve the feelings in his surging lower regions.

Seb had arranged the set of tableware on a dark blue cloth, the way the sale pieces were displayed here and in the Truro shop and showroom. Their own Killigrew clay produced the finest and whitest of Cornish china clay, and their pottery was acclaimed country-wide and beyond. He had no doubt of the quality of his work, just Skye's reaction to it.

Once they were all assembled in the workroom, he pulled off the covering cloth with all the aplomb of a magician pulling a rabbit out of a hat. He looked anxiously at his aunt, his heart thumping. He truly didn't want to displease her, but he couldn't miss the frown on her wide forehead as she looked at his new design.

"My father says that if you absolutely hate it, I must give it to my mother for an early Christmas gift, and forget all about creating any new designs. It was no more than an experiment, you see," he heard himself say quickly, despising himself for doing so.

He was normally a brash and self-confident young man, but these three women, with their glorious blue eyes gazing on his work – his creation – were practically dissolving his innards.

"It's beautiful, Seb," Celia declared, breaking the silence. "Isn't it, Mom? And if no one else wants it, I'd be glad to have the set for my hope chest."

She challenged her mother to deny it. Seb laughed, more nervously than usual.

"Hope chest? You're hardly out of the nursery, cuz. It's far too early to be thinking about such things."

"It's never too early, providing it's no more than a distant dream," Skye murmured without thinking, while taking in the fact that the two men had been mighty busy while she had been away. But she had to be fair. "I like the result. But I'm not sure I want to go into production with it. People know what to look for with our goods."

"But that's just it. We've become too predictable, and perhaps the time has come to move forward, Aunt Skye," Seb persisted, becoming bolder now. "It's called progress—"

"I know what it's called, thank you. Anyway, I suggest you do as your father says and give this set to your mother, and I'll think about progress."

He had to be content with that for now, but there was something else he wanted to ask his aunt about.

"Would you object to my inviting Celia to a tea dance next Saturday afternoon at the Regal Hotel in Truro? If she'd care to come with me, that is."

Celia burst out laughing. "Dancing? You?"

"I do have some social graces, cuz, even if my father sneers at them. And I have been known to trip the light fantastic, as they say." He was cucumber-cool, but his eyes glinted dangerously, and her heart skipped a beat.

She composed her face, even though the image of her large cousin waltzing serenely round a ballroom was so unlikely. But she realised Wenna had drawn in her breath. Not that she had

21

been invited, Celia thought at once. Everyone knew that an afternoon tea dance was at once respectable and slightly decadent, so why not? Even with Seb Tremayne.

There was always the chance there would be other handsome young men there. Dancing was so deliciously innocent a pastime, yet so intimate as well. The next moment she heard Wenna's explosive gasp.

"If Celia goes, can I go too, Mom?"

"I haven't said she can go yet," Skye said.

"She can't go without a partner, anyway," Celia put in at once. "It would look silly for one man to escort two girls. She'd have to sit at the side like a wallflower all afternoon."

"I wouldn't allow that," Seb said, though it hadn't been part of his plan to include Wenna in the invitation. It hadn't been his plan to go dancing at all, except that his mother was always urging him to do these things in her attempt to make him as different from his uncouth father as possible. He was already wishing he hadn't been so impetuous as to virtually kowtow to his aunt. It wasn't his style.

"You'd divide yourself between them, would you?" Skye said, her eyes beginning to twinkle at the way these three were revealing their feelings. Celia, aching to be grown-up and escorted to a dance . . . Sebby wanting a girl to himself, despite the way his father would probably mock him when he heard of the invitation . . . and Wenna, so envious that she wasn't old enough yet to be thought of as a suitable dancing partner, and knowing she would be only there on sufferance.

"If Wenna didn't think me too old a partner, I'd be glad to offer myself as a fourth person – or a chaperon, if you prefer it," Ethan said.

"I accept," Wenna said, suddenly overwhelmed at the thought of swaying in his arms to the strains of the waltz. "And I don't think you're too old to be my partner at all."

"Now, just a moment, young lady," Skye said sharply, and then saw the pleading expression in her daughter's eyes, and recognised her longing to be considered grown-up enough to do this. She looked at Ethan. "Can you dance?"

He coloured up at once. "No. Never tried. But maybe Wenna would teach me."

Celia hooted. "She couldn't teach anyone."

22

"Of course she could. Her music teacher says she has a marvellous sense of rhythm and timing—"

"That's piano playing, Mom! Teaching someone to dance in public would be just too embarrassing. You can't let her do it – I'll be mortified," Celia wailed.

"Then Ethan must come to the house every evening and we'll give him some private lessons," Skye said firmly.

It wasn't what Celia had had in mind at all, but seeing her mother's steely eyes, she knew she had to accept it.

As for Wenna, she had the dizzy promise that Ethan Pengelly was to be her dancing partner on Saturday and all the evenings in between, since she was quite sure that Celia would be set on flirting with Sebby Tremayne.

While they were at the pottery their brother Oliver was grumbling to Justin Tremayne from their moorland vantage point by the clay pool at Killigrew Clay.

"We've got to have this big eighteenth birthday party for Celia in December. You'll all be invited, of course, and now she wants to include this German fellow she met in Berlin," Olly complained. "I can't see what all the fuss is about. She'll be putting on even more airs and graces than usual once she's a so-called teacher at that finishing school of hers."

"At least you can bet Wenna won't get so stuffy," Justin said, skimming a pebble across the clay pool and watching it dance over the milky green surface.

"No. Celia was always the uppity one, even before she left Cornwall. From the moment she could talk, I dare say."

Justin laughed sympathetically. His older brother Seb had been the same with him once, until he discovered Justin had his own way of dealing with insults and had then simply ignored him. Justin had more than come into his own since then. He was two years older than his cousin Olly, but they had become as thick as thieves recently. Both were dark-haired, strapping youths, and more tolerant of each other than of their own siblings.

"You worry too much," Justin said. "You should be more like your mother or blood will out, and you'll end up as pompous as your father was."

"I hardly remember him. Was he really so awful?"

"Not awful. Just a picky minded professor. You have to forgive them for that, because that's the way they're made," Justin said easily. "Anyway, you get on all right with your stepfather, don't you?"

Olly's face cleared. "Oh, yes, Nick's spiffing!"

"Does he mind you calling him Nick?"

"Why should he? It's his name. The girls call him Daddy, but he's not my father and I believe in keeping things right – even though we all agreed to take his surname when my mother suggested it. But I'm still my father's son," he declared.

"My God, Olly, you're definitely a lawyer in the making, you pompous little twerp," Justin said with a grin.

Olly gave him a swipe across the arm, and the next minute they were tussling good-naturedly on the turf. They rolled over and over, and Justin finally declared himself the winner, sitting astride Olly and urging him to surrender.

"All right, you bastard," Olly squealed, and as Justin relaxed, he reversed their positions and sat heavily on his cousin, bumping up and down in triumph.

Justin felt a familiar and pleasurable surge in his groin. One of the more erotic discussions between his school contemporaries lately was of this discovery which could be so amazingly potent and produce such spectacularly joyous results under cover of the bedsheets. Sometimes it literally just happened . . . as if your mind had no control over your body, no matter whether you were a scholarly swot – which he certainly was not – or the son of a clay boss, which he was.

He tried to ignore the feeling as he rolled well away from Olly, and squirmed at the tacky dampness in his drawers, praying that Olly wouldn't notice it. Sometimes, close as they were, the two years between them could seem as wide as a chasm.

"Here, you two young uns, what are you about? Don't 'ee know this is private property?"

At the sound of the angry voice, the boys scrambled to their feet and brushed off the clay dust clinging to their clothes. They turned to face the burly man bearing down on them and, at the sight of his hard hat and shiny boots, they recognised the garb and suspicious face of the pit captain.

"We're very well aware of it, as a matter of fact," Justin said in his best school voice. He saw the man's expression change at once.

"Oh, I'm sorry, young sirs, I didn't see it was the two of you. We get some queer folk around here at times, see, and not always up to any good. Beggin' your pardons, I'm sure. But you should mind these clay pools all the same. They'm quite deep in places, and there's been more than one accident in 'em over the years."

"That's all right, Mr Vickery," Olly said. "You did quite right to question us, and thank you for the warning."

"Good day to 'ee both then."

As soon as the man had stumped off, Justin turned to his cousin. He frowned, his eyes squinting in the sunlight that dazzled on the mountains of clay waste – the pale sky tips glinting with the deposits of mica and other minerals that were a vivid reminder to upcountry folk from England that they had reached the far west of Cornwall.

"Why do you defer to these people so easily?" Justin complained. "You should remember who you are, Olly."

"I do remember, but I haven't had such a fancy education as you to put plums in my mouth. Anyway, things have changed since the clay bosses were kings around here. Even Killigrew Clay is down to one pit now, instead of four. I know your father still lords it over the clayfolk whenever he comes up here, but you're not the son of God, Justin."

"I'm not the son of a piddling pottery owner, either!"

"Well, at least we have something to show for the work that goes on there, instead of just piddling lumps of clay!" Olly said rudely. "You're a prize snob too, and if you want to know what I think, I reckon you and Celia are two of a kind."

His young voice, cracking with tortuous adolescence, rose higher. He was red with anger and always defensive of his mother, whom he adored. They had grown even closer over the years, especially since he had declared his intention to follow his stepfather's profession. To his secret shame he sometimes wished that his sisters would stay in their marvellous Switzerland, and never come home at all. Every time they did, things changed, and he had to share his mother with them.

Justin saw the sudden misery in his cousin's eyes and bit back the retort he had intended to make. Instead, he gave Olly a playful punch on the shoulder.

25

"Well, I haven't seen her since she came back from her visit to Germany yet. But I doubt that your high-and-mighty Celia will even deign to talk to her country cousins any more – especially Seb. She was always superior to him."

He grinned, remembering the spats they had all had as children, and since such occasions had usually ended in rough and tumbles, and then the inevitable pacifying parties from the grown-ups, he felt a passing regret that such a childhood couldn't continue for ever. And that was a bloody pathetic way for a healthy, red-blooded fifteen-year-old to be feeling.

It was a feeling that didn't last long though, not now that he was learning the new delights of approaching manhood, and knew there were so many girls in the world just waiting to be loved, and so many exciting experiences still to be tried. Not that he had done any of it yet. But he would, he thought confidently. In that respect he was certainly his lusty father's son, and so was his older brother.

"You've done *what*?" Theo asked Sebastian when the Tremayne family were sitting down to their evening meal.

Seb looked at him resentfully.

"I'm taking Celia Pengelly to a tea dance on Saturday, and Ethan Pengelly's bringing Wenna as well just to make it a family occasion and keep the numbers even."

"That's very nice of you boys, Sebby," his mother began.

"It's bloody poncey!" Theo exploded. "Working wi' the Pengelly fellow's one thing, but hobnobbing with him socially won't do your standing in the town any good at all."

Seb laughed carelessly. "Since when did you ever care what folk thought? And there's no need to cut Ethan down to size, not when his brother's married to Aunt Skye. Nick Pengelly's an important man in his own right in these parts."

Theo glowered at him. His foot was playing him up like billy-oh, and he could do without his son scoring points over him. T'other one could stop that stupid grinning too, he thought, and he snapped at Justin at once.

"What's funning you, then, boy?"

"Nothing. Well, just something Olly said."

"Oh, ah. And what was that?"

Theo heard his own voice coarsening, and knew it was

because, God dammit, he had sent the boy away to a posh school, and now he found his tidied-up accent as irritating as a cactus burr.

"Just that the pottery has something to show for the work they do, instead of just piddling lumps of clay. Maybe you should never have sold the pottery to her—"

Theo's eyes narrowed. So the little runt had been talking out of turn, had he? To Theo's amazement Seb suddenly turned on him, his eyes blazing.

"Olly's right. You should *never* have done that, Father!"

"Why the hell not?" Theo roared. "I'll do what I like and it'll take more'n the likes of you to stop me!"

"But can't you see what it means to me now?"

Theo leaned back in his dining chair, arms folded. He looked scathingly at his son.

"Why don't you tell me, if what I do with my business is so all-fired important to you?"

"You know damn well what the reason is," Seb flashed at him, ignoring his mother's tut-tutting. "When you sold out your half of the business to Aunt Skye it meant it would never come to me. All the work I've put into it all these years will be for nothing."

Theo crashed his chair forward again.

"And whose fault is it that you went straight into the potting nonsense instead of getting a proper education like your brother? You had the chance, but no, you had to do what *you* wanted," he yelled, not caring that he was totally backtracking on his opinion of what London schoolmasters were doing to Justin's speech.

"It was what *you* wanted, wasn't it? To have at least one of your sons knee-deep in clay."

"Knee-deep in it is one thing. Moulding fancy pieces of china for namby-pamby rich folk to enjoy is summat else. Especially bloody foreigners. And there's nowt wrong wi' clayworking, you young bugger. My father and grandfather all held their heads up high working in an honest Cornish occupation, not prissying about—"

Whatever else he was about to say was lost as Seb threw back his chair.

"If that's your opinion of me, then the less we see of each other, the better," he shouted back. "And I'm still taking my cousin dancing on Saturday, however prissy an occupation you consider *that*!" With that, he strode out of the room.

27

There was silence for a few minutes, as Theo strove to contain his anger and Betsy calmly continued to serve up three dishes of bread-and-butter pudding.

One of these days, she thought, eyeing her husband's puce-coloured facial contortions, his temper will get the better of him, and we'll all be happier when he's six feet under – and may God forgive me for thinking so.

As she anticipated, Theo's silence didn't last, though the words he muttered savagely beneath his breath were mostly unintelligible. This newly contrived habit was supposed to relieve Betsy from having to listen to his obscenities, but she didn't need to hear them to know how verbally inventive he could be in cursing anyone who angered him.

When they had all finished eating, she heard Justin clear his throat in the annoying way he had developed lately when he was about to make some clever pronouncement. Betsy gave a sigh, having looked forward to a quiet evening, and prayed that he wasn't about to enrage Theo even more.

"Father, I wonder if this would be a good time to discuss my future with you?"

Three

W enna looked forward to Saturday afternoon with tremulous anticipation. It would be the first proper dance she had ever attended. At St Augustine's Academy for Young Ladies near Gstaad, rudiments of the dance was on the curriculum as a desirable accomplishment for every well-bred young lady. But dancing there had been confined to holding another girl semi-close while meticulously following the instructions of an eagle-eyed dance mistress who considered too much proximity with another person to be unhealthy, which was why she had been given the secret nickname of the female eunuch.

Now, true to Skye's promise, each night after supper, Wenna's parents put a suitable record on the gramophone, and she swayed to a waltz or a slow foxtrot in the arms of Ethan Pengelly, which was like a dream come true. Or it would be, if only he didn't have such clumsy feet and trod on hers more often than not. Even more so, if her sister didn't hoot with laughter every time they stumbled into one another.

"Does Celia have to stay here, Mom?" Wenna finally burst out. "She's just being beastly, and she's putting me off."

"I agree. Go and do something else, Celia," Skye said firmly, seeing Wenna's heated face, and her elder daughter flounced out of the room.

"Now then, honey, you come and wind up the gramophone, and Nick and I will demonstrate to Ethan how it's done. It will probably be easier for him to watch the man's steps, and then copy them."

Skye saw Ethan breathe more easily. Poor lad, she thought, plunged into the middle of something he probably didn't have the remotest interest in. But once her daughters had decided on something, no man was safe. She smiled up into her husband's eyes, remembering how he had once said the very same thing about all the females in the family.

According to Nick, they weren't wily, just irresistible. It was a long while since they had danced together and she had forgotten how very enjoyable it was. Maybe they should accompany the girls to the tea dance, but immediately she had thought it, she knew such a suggestion wouldn't be welcome. Young girls wouldn't want their parents around when they were doing their best to be alluring to two personable young men. The thought was only a fleeting one, but it startled Skye for a moment, relegating herself and Nick, as it did, to an older generation.

They *were* the older generation, for pity's sake, but you didn't always want to be reminded that time moved on more swiftly than you ever noticed. Here she was, with an almost eighteen-year-old daughter, when there were still times when she felt just as young and foolish as when she had been that age.

She was the one to stumble over Nick's feet then, and she forced herself to laugh.

"You see? We can all make mistakes, Ethan. But you'll be fine by Saturday, I promise you. A few more lessons and you'll be a proper gigolo."

"Good God, I hope not," laughed Nick.

"What's a gigolo?" Wenna said, frowning.

"Officially it's a male professional dancing partner," Ethan said, poker-faced. "But they sometimes do other activities as well."

"Do they? Well, I don't think there's much chance of you ever turning into one of them without more practice. I hope you never do, anyway," Wenna added. "You're much too nice to do something that sounds rather horrid."

She wasn't quite sure what those other activities might involve, but she blushed more deeply as she said it, and prayed that her heart wasn't actually throbbing on her sleeve as all the penny dreadfuls had it. If any of her family had the faintest idea of how passionately she had loved Ethan Pengelly all her life, they would probably be highly alarmed and forbid her to go dancing with him at all. At sixteen, they considered her still a child. Ethan was nine years older and already a man. But her feelings for him were far removed from anything childlike although she was mature enough to hide them – most of the time.

* * *

Seb Tremayne and his father were at loggerheads again. Seb's own aggressive streak which always simmered just below the surface, was very much his father's legacy to him. When the two of them clashed their anger could sometimes blow up into volcanic proportions. He had a pretty shrewd idea that Theo was losing much of his interest in Killigrew Clay, which was a major shock to Seb, indoctrinated in it as he was.

He knew his family's sometimes violent history. He knew that Morwen Tremayne had been a young bal maiden working at Killigrew Clay when she had caught the eye of the owner's son, Ben Killigrew, and had eventually married him. He knew of her feyness and her reputed sixth sense, and although he would have ridiculed any such nonsense in himself, Seb knew what the future held for him if his father sold out his half-share of the clayworks, either to Skye, or to some other ambitious buyer. There were no supernatural fantasies about what such a pro-spect would mean to Seb: There would be no inheritance for him if the clayworks went outside the family. Even if it remained, prestigious though it was, it was long past its heyday, and Theo was cantankerous enough to sell out just to spite his son. He had already sold out his shares in the pottery to Skye, and although Seb loved getting his hands in the wet clay and producing something beautiful out of nothing, he was Tre-mayne enough to want the clayworks to continue within the family. It was their backbone, their strength.

Seb also guessed that in due course Ethan would be granted full control of the pottery by way of seniority, and he would be no more than a dogsbody employee. He seethed at the affront to his pride, but he'd put up with it, providing the Tremaynes were still the owners of Killigrew Clay as well.

He hadn't fully realised just how much he wanted the family continuity to remain. It occurred to him that he was the only one with the proud name of Tremayne who felt that way. Justin wasn't interested. But it was important to Seb that the name shouldn't die out and lose its meaning or its position in the community.

"I don't know you why you waste your time worrying about any of it," Justin said, when Seb sought him out later that evening. "Although, I admit that the clayworks are far bigger than any tin-pot business – sorry for the pun, bruth – and china clay sells everywhere for a multitude of purposes."

"You don't understand, do you? You never had any interest in any of it, unless you were thinking of trying to throw a pot or two as a pastime," Seb said, nettled.

Justin shook his head. "Of course not. But I've just had an interesting conversation with Father about my future."

"Oh, *your* future is it? I didn't think he was in the mood to talk sensibly with anyone, not even his blue-eyed boy. So what's going on? Don't tell me you're planning on becoming a clay-worker after all, and risk getting those nice white hands dirty."

"I'm going into medicine. I've been recommended by my tutors and I've just informed Father of the fact."

"Christ, Justin, why can't you talk in plain English for five minutes? *Informed* Father, for God's sake? What kind of talk is that?"

"It's something you wouldn't understand," Justin said, refusing to be riled. Then he grinned. "Actually, I thought Father would throw a fit about my wanting to study in London, but he was remarkably calm about it."

Seb snorted. "Why would you want to go to London? What's wrong with learning doctoring in Cornwall, if you *must* consider such an unsavoury occupation. Don't Cornish folk need their coughs and colds sorted out?"

Justin flushed. "I'm not being a snob, Seb, although you all seem to think I am. But Father's willing for me to go to university and then to medical school and who knows where I may end?"

Seb stared at him, seeing the determination in his face and a new authority that he'd never noticed before.

"My God, sometimes I wonder if I know you at all, bruth. Does your new best pal know about all this ambition?"

"If you mean Oliver, no, I haven't told him yet."

"Oh well, I suppose the future doctor and lawyer will make fine bedfellows – and don't take me literally."

Justin grinned. "You needn't have any fear of that," he said, thankful they were on sociable terms again and that the great trauma of revealing his budding hopes to his family was out in the open. He had to move forward, and Cornwall didn't hold him in spirit as it did the rest of them.

Unknowingly, he had a similar thought to that of his cousin

Oliver right then. Everything changed. Nothing stayed the same. But in Justin's case, it was a welcome thought.

It was the final weekend before Celia and Wenna were to return to Gstaad for the new term. Saturday was to be a highlight they hadn't expected, and they were both in a tizzy as they got ready for Ethan to call for them and drive them into Truro to collect Seb on the way.

"I wish I had jubblies like yours," Wenna wailed, as she tried in vain to push her bosom up higher into the white afternoon frock. "Mine are pathetic."

Celia preened in front of the mirror, admiring her own curvaceous figure in her best blue organdie afternoon frock. Then the pose softened as she giggled, standing with her hands on her hips for a moment.

"Now then, girrrls," she said, in a fair imitation of their Scottish female eunuch dancing tutor. "Young ladies should never refer to brrreasts in any shape or form. Indeed, we must try to forget we even have them. It's unhealthy to dwell too much on our bodies, and especially on our brrreasts."

Wenna giggled. "Well, you can't forget *you've* got them," she said. "I just wish mine would grow."

"Never mind, Ethan will love you just the same," Celia said lightly, meaning nothing, and not realising just how her sister's heart beat faster at the words.

At the sound of the motor-car hooter, they turned and raced each other downstairs, calling out goodbye to their parents and running out into the sunlight in a scrabble for the front passenger seat.

"And there go our so-called young ladies," Skye said with a laugh to her husband as they waved them off. "Have we wasted all our money on an expensive Swiss education, do you think?"

She felt his arm go around her and he nuzzled his chin into her neck beneath her glossy hair as she leaned back against him.

"If they turn out as beautiful and desirable as their mother, then we haven't wasted a penny of it," he told her.

She twisted round in his arms. "Why, Nicholas Pengelly, for a stuffy old lawyer, that was almost poetic."

"Oh, I have my moments," he said, following the words with a very satisfactory kiss.

Skye sobered a little. "I hope they enjoy themselves. I hope it's everything they expect it to be."

"Why on earth shouldn't it be?"

"With our family? You know better than to believe that everything will go smoothly, honey."

Celia smiled provocatively up into Ethan Pengelly's face. Seb had gone to fetch four glasses of lemonade and Wenna was nursing a sore toe from Ethan's enthusiastic dancing.

"So are you going to ask me to dance? There's no rule that says we can't change partners now and then, is there?"

Ethan laughed. "I don't think you'd want to risk it."

"Why not? I'm game, if you are," she said challengingly.

Truth to tell, she felt a small thrill as she said it. She had seen the admiration in his eyes as he had watched the way she and Sebby had whirled so expertly around the floor. She had been astounded at the way Sebby could dance, and privately congratulated her Aunt Betsy for pushing him into it. He was a very good partner, but he was just Seb, and she suddenly saw Ethan Pengelly in a new light.

"Ethan won't want to dance with *you*," she heard Wenna say. "You'll only make fun of him."

"No I won't," Celia said softly. "Well, Ethan?"

Imperceptibly, she held out her arms to him a fraction, and the next moment Wenna saw them moving slowly around the room together, and experienced the searing pangs of jealousy.

She felt a glass of lemonade being pushed into her hand as Seb returned, and saw his mocking glance towards the other couple.

"I pity the poor fellow. Celia will make mincemeat of him if he attempts anything other than a regular one-two-three."

"Don't you mind?" Wenna said, choked.

He looked at her properly then, and saw everything there was to see in her face.

"No, and neither should you, sweetie," he said roughly. "Pengelly's not our sort, however skilled he is at making pots, and Celia's going to run through beaux faster than blinking. It doesn't mean a thing to her, so get that jealous frown off your pretty face, and let's show them who can dance and who can't."

"You mean me and you?" she said, forgetting every aspect of correct grammar in her astonishment.

Seb laughed out loud. "Good God, is it so distasteful to you to be seen dancing with me? I'm not my father, cuz."

Wenna felt her face burn. "I'm sorry. I didn't mean to imply anything—"

"Then stop talking before your tongue gets into a tangle. Stick your nose in the air, and let's dance."

Wenna did as she was told. It was an extraordinary feeling to be championed so thoroughly by the cousin she had always thought had little time for either of then, but not disliking the feeling at all, especially when she she caught sight of Celia's piqued face as she and Sebby executed an expert twirl around the dance floor.

Dance classes in Gstaad were never the same after that. Not that Celia was involved with them any more, now that she was a part-time assistant in the art classes. But Wenna's contemporaries were eager to hear how she had been to an afternoon tea dance and danced with not one, but two eligible young men.

"Of course, one of them was my cousin, and the other was my stepfather's brother," she said, honest as always, even though she had never thought of Ethan as simply that.

"But you must have enjoyed it," her close friend Helene Dubois said. "Did you dance close – you know – the way Miss Macnab says we mustn't? Did they press against your jubblies?"

Wenna laughed, suddenly finding their way of referring to their bosoms as silly and childish.

"If you mean, did they press against my brrreasts," she said darkly, "well, there were so many couples dancing, they couldn't help it."

As Helene and the other girls gasped at this daring declaration, Wenna knew that she had suddenly gone up in their estimation. At the memory of the one time when Ethan had stumbled against her and held on to her tightly, she felt her nipples prickle against the regulation winter dress she wore.

"Is Ethan the one you always had a fancy for?" Julia Fletcher, the daughter of a church minister asked.

"He might be," Wenna said mysteriously, "and then again, it might be the other one."

"Well, you can't marry your cousin," Julia said.

"Yes I could – if I wanted to! But I don't – and you should ask your father about getting your facts right, Julia."

She was put out by the very suggestion that she might want to marry Seb Tremayne, and even more so by the suggestion that cousins couldn't marry at all. Of course they could. It had happened in her own family, and she wasn't having any self-righteous minister's daughter telling her otherwise.

Not that she could ever think of Sebby in that way. He was just, well, Sebby. She had always been a bit scared of him, but she had to admit that he was much nicer than he used to be. He didn't tease her about Ethan like Celia did.

Then the little group got into a more interesting discussion about the young men they had met during the holidays, and she forgot all about him.

Celia had forgotten the whole incident long ago. In her own room, away from the four-girl dormitory she had inhabited as a student, she was busily penning a letter to Franz Vogl. She implored him to come to Cornwall in December when the current term ended, and added her mother's invitation for his parents to accompany him for a week or so.

> My birthday will have come and gone by the time the term ends, but my mother is planning a big party for me, and I do so want you to be there, Franz. Mom is sure your father would like to see the pottery and the clayworks. The end of the year is never cold in Cornwall and I know you would enjoy the balmy weather and meeting the rest of my family.

She paused, wondering if it was quite true. The Vogls were so elegant and well bred, and some of her family were – well, she tried to be loyal, but for a start, her Uncle Theo could be guaranteed to let them down if he felt so inclined, or if he and Seb got into an argument. She ignored the thought and carried on with the letter.

"Anyway, please write back, Franz. It would be so nice to get a letter from you here."

Celia didn't dare to end it with love and kisses. It wasn't done, and she was sure his straight-laced mother wouldn't approve. She simply signed it with her name. Two weeks later she got a reply.

I would very much like to see your home, Celia, but my mother would prefer it if the invitation to include us all came directly from your parents. It would be more correct, would it not? So we will anticipate that event, and meanwhile I send you my best wishes and hope that we will see one another quite soon.

It was far more formal than Celia might have wished. There were no hidden messages that she could detect, nothing between the lines or any sign of the dashing young German she remembered. She felt oddly let down, but she had no intention of showing her disappointment. Instead, she wrote to her mother immediately, imploring her to write quickly to Frau Vogl, and issue the invitation to the family.

Once it was all a *fait accompli*, she could crow to Wenna and anyone else who would listen, about her handsome German beau who was coming to visit.

The weeks passed quickly for Celia in her new role at St Augustine's, and it seemed no time at all before she and Wenna were on their way back to Cornwall at the end of November. Franz and his parents would be arriving a few days later, and her party was fixed for the following Saturday.

Skye had seen to everything. It was to be a wonderful party, with all the relatives they could muster coming from far and wide.

"Not that there are that many now," Skye said sadly to Nick as they surveyed the final invitation list.

"There's enough of them," he said, scanning the names. "The house will be filled to overflowing if they all turn up."

"Oh, they will. When did you ever know a Tremayne or a Pengelly turn down an invitation?"

"And then there are these German folk," he said thoughtfully.

"It doesn't bother you, does it? You stood by me all those years ago when we had to hustle the German youths out of the country so hurriedly."

"I remember. I also remember the antagonism of so many local people when one of the German lads started messing about with a clayworker's daughter – and the ugliness that followed. There were always suspicions about just why she was hurried away into the country, so don't be fooled into thinking folk will have forgotten," he added.

"It's nothing to do with them," Skye said. "This is a social occasion, and anyway, the Vogls had no connections with us then. We all have to forgive and forget those bad times. I said it then, and I'm saying it now, and heaven help anyone who tries to interfere with my family."

The stupidity and short-sightedness of local folk had almost brought her business to its knees once, and she wasn't prepared to let it happen ever again. The bigots had objected to the young German lads coming here to work, and blood had been spilt because of it. But if they were foreigners, then so was she, and they would stand together if need be.

She began to wonder just what wildness was making her think this way right now. Her husband laughed gently at her vehemence.

"I doubt that any of them will forget the impact of Skye's Crusaders either, darling," he said softly. "You and David Kingsley together could conquer the world if you tried. It's a pity other folk don't have your kind of rhetoric instead of using their fists – or worse."

Skye smiled faintly. "David always said that more battles could be won with words if only people would listen to them – or read them – and he was right."

"But it was your words that won the day then. He had the wherewithal to publish the newspaper, but it was your skill and compassionate writing that made people see sense."

"Why, thank you, kind sir," she said, touched at this tribute. "So now, can we finish deciding on who to invite to Celia's party, and who we can legitimately leave out?"

As the evening of the party approached on the fifth of December, Skye realised she was looking forward to it as much as her daughters were. Such get-togethers had a sense of family solidarity about them. No matter what else failed, the family was always strong, and they were always there for one another.

There had been a party to celebrate her own arrival from America all those years ago, when she had met all these unknown relatives who were to become so much a part of her life. Her parents had urged her to come, to get to know Cornwall and to sense the joy each of them had known in finding one another in the place of their family roots.

The memory of that time was always an emotional one for Skye. She still remembered how she had had an almost hallowed feeling when she stepped onto Cornish ground for the first time in her twenty-three years. And then seeing all the places that her mother, Primmy, had told her about, and the mystical feeling she had experienced at one and the same time, at the strangeness and the familarity of them.

And now the house where she had discovered such an empathy with her grandmother, Morwen Tremayne, was to be host to another large gathering, and she was the hostess, the matriarch. She shivered suddenly, as the charm of it was replaced by a far less comfortable feeling.

The years passed, and with them the next generation took over the limelight, and the older ones began to fade . . . it was rightly so, and sometimes scarily so . . .

"Are you laying ghosts again?" she heard Nick say.

She realised she had been staring into the firelight in the drawing room for a very long time.

She spoke softly. "Just a few. But they're nice ghosts for the most part, Nick."

"Then let them be, and let's get ready to greet our guests," he told her, just as softly.

He took her hand and they went upstairs together to change into their finery for Celia's party. It was the last time they would be alone for hours and Skye savoured the moments. The girls were excitedly dressing and Olly was grumbling at having to look like a tailor's dummy, and the house guests were separately preparing to do justice to Skye's beautiful daughter.

She drew in her breath as she and Nick entered their bedroom, and she put her arms around him for a moment.

"We've always done right by Celia, haven't we, Nick? She's turned out just as Mom and Granny Morwen would have wanted her to be, hasn't she?"

"She's a credit to all of you, darling. She's a Tremayne woman to her fingertips, and I can't give higher praise than that. They would be proud of her, and I'm proud of you."

"I haven't done anything—"

"Then stop angling for me to tell you you're the most ravishing woman on God's earth, or I may just have to halt the party proceedings in order to prove it to you," he said, with a meaningful smile.

She laughed and moved away from him, the introspective mood broken and her spirits rising. Everyone would love both her beautiful daughters tonight, wearing the gorgeous evening dresses Nick had so generously bought for them. Celia's was the most luxurious, in a sensuous shade of deep blue velvet, and Wenna's was a stunning bronze shantung silk.

Skye's own gown was her favourite forest green, the shade that had so alarmed her cousin Charlotte when she had chosen to wear it as mother to the little bridesmaids when Vera had married Adam Pengelly. Skye had always refused to believe the superstitious nonsense that it was an unlucky colour. If anything was to prove to her that green was far from unlucky for her, that had also been the day that she and Nick had first set eyes on one another. The day they had both fallen instantly, and irrevocably, in love.

The German guests were ultra correct, and Theo's whispered aside that they resembled waddling penguins went thankfully unnoticed by all but his wife, who shushed him at once.

"Behave yourself, Theo," she said severely. "This is Celia's night, so try to be gracious for once in your life."

"Bloody women," he muttered, before trying to persuade David Kingsley to tell him what juicy bits of news were being kept from the general public.

The newspaperman looked at him coldly. Whatever there was, Theo Tremayne wouldn't be the one he confided it to. There was certainly something, and he intended to find a quiet corner to discuss it with Skye some time during the evening. But not now, when the Pengelly family was putting up such a happy and united front as their guests continued to arrive.

He felt an unexpected pang, watching them. The girls had the delicate yet sensuous beauty of all the legendary Tremayne women, but in his eyes nothing could match Skye. She was radiant tonight, and he could never quite forget how he had once wanted her for himself. He pushed the feeling aside as his little boys claimed him, overawed in such splendid surroundings and with so many people. He smiled at Lily, and his wife smiled back, and his world righted itself again.

"I wonder what's keeping Mother and Vera and Adam," Lily said. "I hope everything's all right. Vera said Mother was having trouble with her breathing the last time she saw her."

"None of us is getting any younger, my love," he commented, and for a man who avoided cliches as much as possible in his writing, he visibly cringed at the inanity. But he couldn't ignore the worried look on his wife's face, and he prayed inelegantly that her mother, Charlotte, wouldn't choose this particular evening to pop it.

He saw Skye smiling slightly at him, and knew she was guessing how he would sum up this party occasion for a brief mention in the *Informer*. Anything to do with Tremaynes and Pengellys merited a mention, and he considered himself very much small fry in the Cornish hierarchy of name dropping and heritage in this particular part of the county.

But he was doing his best to expand the dwindling family, he thought, as Frederick and Robert clamoured to know when they could have a drink of lemonade. If he had his way, he and Lily would have more children, but Lily was perfectly content with the two she called her late ewe-lambs.

"What are you grinning at?" she hissed at him.

"Just thinking how glad I am that I never married a pompous woman," he said. "And even more glad that you got all this feminist nonsense out of your system and married me."

Seeing the way her eyes sparkled, he knew it didn't mean that she didn't have a mind of her own. She was never afraid to use it either, and he was glad of that too.

He moved away with his boys and sought out the lemonade table, happy to be a part of this big, sprawling family in a way he had never expected to be. To his relief, his sister-in-law Vera and her husband arrived shortly afterwards, with Charlotte as well as ever.

As he gave Vera a dutiful peck on the cheek, David realised how enormously fat she had grown through compulsive eating, which Lily said was a compensation for not having the children she had wanted. Adam always said loyally that there was more of her to love, and all credit to him for that, but in his earthier moments David sometimes wondered how the hell they managed it with all those rolls of fat to contend with. Did they tuck them up and flatten them out, or . . .

* * *

"Ladies and gentlemen – and children," he heard Nick say some while later when they had all gorged their way through a mountain of party food. "This is not going to be a formal speech and we all want you to enjoy yourselves. But before we continue, Skye and I ask you to raise your glasses in an eighteenth-birthday toast to our lovely daughter, Celia."

As they did as they were told, Celia blushed and received kisses from everyone in the family until only the Vogls were left. She looked expectantly at Franz.

"May I be permitted to join in this expression of affection?" he asked.

"Of course!" Celia giggled, her heart beating wildly.

To her absolute mortification he took her hand in his and raised it to his lips in the continental way, clicking his heels together as he did so. She wasn't sure whether to be charmed by such old-world courtesy or enraged at the non-appearance of an acceptable kiss in company, when she heard Seb and Justin snigger. Even Olly managed a weak smile, knowing that he shouldn't, but unable to resist it as the three youths crowded together in a corner.

"Your young men seem to find our customs amusing," Herr Vogl commented to Nick.

"I assure you they mean no offence by it. The young are sometimes thoughtless, aren't they?"

"It rather depends on their upbringing, and perhaps we are stricter with our young men that in other cultures. *I* do not mean to offend either, sir. I merely make an observation."

"Of course," Nick said, privately thinking the man a bumptious ass, and praying that Celia wasn't serious about his son. If Franz Vogl turned out as prissy as his parents, his spirited girl would have a far less easy life than of old. He was glad when someone else claimed his attention.

Wenna had already joined her brother and cousins and was chuckling in a corner. They leaned together, their dark heads almost touching, in a solid family unit.

"Did you see it?" Olly said. "What a twerp."

"Shush, Olly, they'll hear you," Wenna hissed, happy to be included in their circle which excluded her sister. They had all had several glasses of fruit cup by now, and Wenna no longer minded quite so much that Ethan had asked to bring along a friend to the party, although initially she had been devastated to discover that the friend was female.

Seeing them together had made her cling to her cousins even more, as if to prove to Ethan that it didn't mean a thing to her that he was so attentive to the daughter of Tom Vickery, the pit captain at Killigrew Clay.

"Just look at that toe-rag now," Seb said, as if following her thoughts. Since lacing his innocuous drinks with a smidgin of brandy his voice was becoming slightly slurred, and it was making him bolder. He nodded in Ethan's direction as he spoke. "He's gooey-eyed about the Vickery tart, and we all know she'll drop 'em for a tanner. Mebbe that's the attraction."

It took a couple of seconds for what he meant to sink into Wenna's brain. When it did, she gasped, her face burning with embarrassment, and with it a sharp sense of loss for the feelings she had always attributed to her hero.

"How dare you say such things, Seb. You're disgusting, and you're spoiling everything, just like you always did. I thought you had *some* manners now, but you don't. You're just the same as you always were – a – a prize *pig*!"

The childhood name she had always given him came readily to her lips, which trembled visibly as Seb and the boys shook with laughter at her indignant face.

"Oh, come on, Wenna, he didn't mean anything," Justin said roughly, taking her arm. She shook him off.

"He shouldn't have said it then. And Ethan's not like he said. Nor is – is Jessie," she said, fighting to remember the Vickery girl's name.

"Oh, well, believe what you like," Seb said carelessly. "But you should grow up and open your eyes to the real world, Wenna. That posh school's obviously teaching you nothing."

The foursome broke up as Wenna flounced off, and Olly slunk away, not wanting to get into a family fight, especially when Sebby was in one of his belligerent moods.

Skye watched the little incident from a distance. She had heard nothing of what had been said in the general mêlée and excitement of the party, but she could read Wenna's body language. She knew full well the reason for her younger daughter's changeable moods that evening. The pangs of first love were never easy, but Wenna must always have known that Ethan wasn't for her, and that someone nearer his own age was far more suitable. Jessie Vickery was a pretty girl, and probably not as black as some people painted her, Skye thought generously.

"Can we snatch a moment to talk?" David Kingsley said, at her elbow and, as she saw his troubled eyes, her heart leapt with unease.

Four

Skye always thought how strange, and how useful it was, that two people could manage to hold a private conversation in the midst of a crowd. From the back of the room, watching the dancing from a distance, she looked at David Kingsley, seeing from his face that his news had to be something momentous.

"What is it?" she murmured.

"My sources in London say the abdication is imminent," he said abruptly. "An announcement is expected very soon."

Skye gasped. "Are you sure?"

But she knew he must be. He had the nose for a story, and the integrity not to print it before it was proven. He also knew that he could trust her above all people not to divulge what he told her.

"I expect the wire to come through at any time. I'm holding the front page of the *Informer* each day until the very last minute. The nationals have reported that the Duke and Duchess of York have arrived in London from Scotland, which is a clear indication that something's afoot. It can't be long before the whole thing is out in the open now and Beaverbrook will be unable to stop it however much he tries. Why the devil shouldn't the British public know what's common knowledge all over Europe and America, anyway?"

"So once it happens, there will be a new king, and the two young princesses will have their lives changed for ever." Skye spoke slowly, ignoring David's sense of outrage at not being able to do his job and report everything he knew.

She tried to take it all in, imagining for a brief, fantasising moment, how it would be if her own daughters were to be suddenly plunged into a situation none of them had ever dreamed about.

"What are you two plotting now?" she heard her cousin Vera's voice close to her a moment later. "Sometimes I swear that you

45

must both have printer's ink in your blood. Doesn't it make our Lily jealous?"

David laughed, making an obvious effort to sound normal. "It does not! She knows me well enough, and you wouldn't expect the glorious Skye to look at anyone else but her husband, would you, sister-in-law dear?"

Vera laughed too. Skye noted with a small stab of alarm how she wheezed as she did so. She resolved to speak to her cousin about her excess weight, and to try to convince her to eat a healthier diet. Though, remembering Vera's wonderful suet dumplings and her addiction to the bread-and-butter pudding that she and Adam loved, she doubted that her advice would have any effect. Her own mouth watered at the memory of Vera's steamy and aromatic kitchen.

As the other two drifted away into the party crowd, Skye became aware of someone else hovering close by. She smiled dutifully into Jessie Vickery's pretty face.

"I jest wanted to thank 'ee, Mrs Pengelly, for allowing me to come to the party. 'Tis real neighbourly of 'ee to let me come along of Ethan."

"Well, that's perfectly all right, Jessie," Skye said warmly, trying not to notice the clumsy speech of the clayworker's daughter, and trying even more not to feel snobbish about it, when her own family history was the very same as this girl's. Even Granny Morwen had lapsed into the soft, sing-song lilt of her clayworking background at times, which Skye had found endearing.

"Well, I jest wanted to tell you I 'preciate it an' all," Jessie persisted, as if determined to pin Skye into a corner with her voluptuous figure.

Her face was bold and vivacious. If you ignored the knowing eyes you could think she was just a simple country girl with no more ambitions than to wed a simple country boy, thought Skye. Why such a idea entered her head at that moment, she couldn't quite imagine. Jessie's next words clarified it all too well.

"Me pa says I'm not to get above me station, though, but there's nuthin' wrong in wantin' to better yerself, is there? And if me and Ethan want to go courtin', I reckon there's nuthin' he can do about it," she said, with a reckless giggle that spoke of having imbibed rather too well.

Ethan hustled his way through the crush of people and caught at Jessie's hand impatiently. Skye listened to his words with a sense of inexplicable unease.

"Come on, sweetness, let's show Seb Tremayne that me and my girl can do a turn or two on the dance floor. Anything he can do, we can do better!"

Jessie followed him with a laugh that was a mixture of excitement and triumph. Skye felt her heart skip a beat and a small frown creased her brows.

"What's wrong, darling?" Nick said as he came to join her. She composed her face at once and hugged his arm.

"Nothing at all. What could be wrong on a night such as this, when everyone's enjoying themselves so much?"

He knew her too well to be fooled, but she had no intention of spoiling the party by revealing her thoughts. Not for the world would she put into words the idiotic ideas that had swept through her mind at that moment. Ideas that were more like a presentiment, which was one of the Cornish traits her grandmother had bestowed on her.

Nor would she tell anyone, not even Nick, that just for one crazy moment she had visualised the likes of Jessie Vickery marrying her young brother-in-law Ethan. That between them and the influence of the clayworking community they would reduce *her* pottery and *her* clayworks to the humble beginnings of a century ago. If Theo were to insist on selling out, the clayworkers would rule the sophisticated empire that she still thought of as hers, by right, by her own efforts, and by the loving legacy of her grandmother, Morwen Tremayne.

"Sit down, Skye," she heard Nick say as if from a long way away. "What did David say just now, or can I guess? I warned you not to take this Mrs Simpson business too much to heart. Is that it?"

She clung to the lifeline he had thrown her. "I suppose so, and I promise to forget it, and mingle with our guests before Theo throws an almighty spanner in the works and outrages Frau Vogl with his coarseness."

She bit her lip, knowing she was doing it again. She was unwittingly separating herself from the very heartbeat of her family by thinking herself better than the rest of them. It had never occurred to her before, but it occurred to her very strongly now, and she didn't like what she saw. No wonder Theo had been so scathing about sending Celia and Wenna to a Swiss finishing school. If he sneered at his own son Justin for being a bit of a snob, then she was a worse one by far.

She and Nick made their way towards their house guests, currently being entertained by Theo and Betsy. The Vogls were clearly not at their most comfortable in their company, and Skye sympathised with both sides. Herr Vogl was stiff and starchy and although Betsy was a darling, she was a countrywoman to her bootstraps and unable to make the kind of conversation they would expect. And Theo was . . . she could hear him now, loud and bombastic as ever, and she groaned.

"Our china clay is the finest in the world, and 'tis a pity it never took on the Tremayne name when the Killigrews passed on. A real thorn in my side, that one, and if I had my time over again I'd probably insist on it. But female ownership had other things to say to it as usual."

"Theo, I'm sure Herr Vogl doesn't want to hear our family business," Skye cut in quickly as Theo's face darkened.

Jessie Vickery wasn't the only one who had had a drop too much to drink. In the girl's case it had merely emboldened her to speak to Skye, and she was now whirling on the dance floor with Ethan, while Theo was ready to do verbal battle with whoever encouraged him. Herr Vogl couldn't know that.

"I find it most interesting, as a matter of fact," the German said, his voice carrying. "In my country, we do not encourage women to enter into business in the same manner."

Every sentence was a speech with him, Skye thought. He had been a pleasant host in his own country and was a good business connection, but she didn't really like him at all. He continued speech-making, holding his small audience captive.

"I, too, believe that a man's name is most important. It's his personal attribute that no one can take away from him, and should therefore be preserved at all costs."

"Like Mr Hitler," came a smothered whisper from somewhere in the room behind him. "Preserved in aspic, perhaps, with his Charlie Chaplin face and his funny walk!"

Skye felt her face flame, and prayed that Herr Vogl didn't have such acute hearing as she did. Maybe he didn't, but Theo did. She heard him roar with laughter as he turned and clasped Celia around the waist, to her utter disgust as he breathed whisky fumes in her face.

"You've a witty tongue on you, girlie, but I doubt that our German friends will appreciate the insult to their leader. Charlie Chaplin indeed! But now that you mention it—"

He burst into more raucous laughter that started him coughing and retching, and had Betsy slapping him on the back. She led him off to the drinks table, her face puce with embarrassment, still apologising for him as they went out of sight. Skye also felt obliged to apologise for her loathsome relative. If Herr Vogl hadn't got the gist of Celia's words before, he certainly knew them now.

"Please forgive my cousin, Herr Vogl," Skye said, mortified to be doing this, and thankful that Frau Vogl was sitting with Charlotte and unaware of what had passed. Of Franz there was no sign. "Theo is a litle wild at times, and I'm afraid he always speaks first and thinks later."

"It would seem to be a national trait, I believe," he said, his voice stiff. Skye felt doubly mortified at this slight, said so icily and with so much meaning.

As for Celia, Skye seethed with anger at her daughter's indiscretion. Birthday girl or not, such an insult to their foreign visitors was unforgivable. Now was not the time to chastise her, but it later would be, Skye vowed. Of that Celia need have no doubt.

It was the early hours of the morning by the time the last of the revellers went home and most of the household had gone to bed. Only Skye, Nick and Celia were left downstairs, and Skye rounded on her daughter at once.

"What on earth did you think you were saying, Celia? Have you no consideration at all? The Vogls were your personal guests, and you went out of your way to insult them. I don't know what Franz must have thought of such rudeness."

"In case you hadn't noticed, I hardly saw Franz all evening," Celia exploded, her eyes sapphire-bright with tears she tried to hide. "Didn't you see the way he ogled that cheap Vickery girl? He even danced with her while Ethan was fetching her a drink. She's nothing but a miserable, common moors girl and she didn't belong here at my party."

Before Skye could stop herself, she had struck Celia's cheek. They both gasped, and Nick strode forward to intervene as Celia's hand automatically rose to defend herself.

"That's enough," he snapped. "The girl was a guest like everyone else, and you'll apologise to your mother at once."

"*Me*, apologise to *her*? She was the one who hit me!" Celia screamed. "I won't apologise for what I said about Jessie Vickery. I hate her, and so does Wenna."

She was ramrod stiff with fury, but Skye didn't miss the stark misery in her eyes. Nothing had ever thwarted Celia in her life before, and she felt it doubly hard. Dear God, it was not only Celia, but both her girls, Skye thought with a small shock, both of them were smarting and insulted by the Vickery girl, because both their young men had danced with her, and Ethan was apparently courting her.

First love could be traumatic as well as beautiful, and she felt her daughters' pain as if it was a physical thing, but before she could find any tactful words to try to make amends, Celia had twisted away from both her parents.

"I'm going to bed," she shrieked. "And thank you both for ruining my party."

There was silence for a moment after she had gone and then Nick folded his wife in his arms. Until that moment she hadn't realised how much she was shaking.

"Let it go, darling. A good night's sleep is what you both need, or what's left of the night. Things always looks brighter in the morning."

"You can guarantee that, can you?" she asked bitterly. She took a deep breath, suddenly very calm. "What I need more than sleep is to talk to you, Nick. I want you to call a meeting between Theo and the two of us, and to draw up a legal document to ensure the continuity of the family business that's absolutely watertight."

"It already is watertight. You know that."

She shook her head. "What I want is to add a codicil to the wills that Theo and I made, to the effect that if none of our children want to take over the clayworks or the pottery then they are to close down. Under no circumstances must anyone but our direct descendants inherit or make any offer to buy us out. When Theo and I die, our children will take over, or Killigrew Clay and

50

White Rivers will be no more. We have five children between us. We must persuade Theo to agree that one or several of them must inherit, without marital considerations, or we close down. Theo has no shares in the pottery now, but I'd have no objection to his sons being included in the arrangement if they wished."

Her thoughts came thick and fast and wild and without proper order, and she had to pause to catch her breath, but at her impassioned words Nick became white with anger.

"My God, is this all you've had on your mind at your daughter's party? Do you think Theo will agree to this ridiculous ultimatum?"

"It's not an ultimatum and I haven't thought it out at all. I'm just sure in my bones that it's the right thing to do. I'm protecting what has always been ours, and what must remain ours, or be no more."

"Oh, no, my dear, I think you mean what has always been *yours*," he retorted. "You and your womenfolk have always tried to undermine what's rightfully a man's prerogative, but no man is willing to be emasculated—"

"Don't try to blind me with long words, Nick. I know them all," she snapped. "And we do not try to emasculate you—"

"Really? I seem to recall that when you went on your crusade to keep the pottery open some years ago, Vera withheld her favours from Adam, even though they were newly-weds. If that's not emasculating, I don't know what is. You may think you're strong, Skye, but—"

"How did you know about that? Did Adam tell you? Do you discuss what does or doesn't happen in the bedroom in some public bar for everyone to hear?"

"Calm down, and think what the result of your proposal would be. Do you really want to throw all the clayworkers out of work because of a selfish female whim?"

She started at him, realising she certainly hadn't thought the idea through. And, as she looked at his angry face, she wondered how on earth this wonderful night had ended so painfully. She could hardly bear to look at him, knowing how little he must think of her. Her erratic plan to draw up a legal document that was watertight for the succession of the joint businesses had been for one reason only, but as he went to the door, she realised Nick had seen it entirely differently.

"You might also reflect over the insult you're doing to Ethan, Skye. And to me, since no marital considerations, as you call them, come into it. Not that I ever had any aspirations to be a clay boss, in case you were wondering."

She could easily dismiss his last ridiculous statement, but not the first one.

"What has any of this to do with Ethan?"

But she knew instantly. It had been at the back of her mind all along, even if she hadn't thought it through properly. All she wanted was to ensure that whatever little trollop married into the family couldn't get her hands on what her family had worked so hard to achieve. And that included Jessie Vickery. It was *all* on account of Jessie Vickery, who was courting Ethan Pengelly and hurting her younger daughter so.

"If you don't know, then you're more stupid than I give you credit for," Nick said coldly. "Ethan has given his life to White Rivers, and if you were to sell out, if anyone deserves to buy into it, he does."

"You're not listening to me, are you? I'm not talking about selling out. I'm talking about closing down, flattening the whole area, not letting anyone else take what's mine—"

"Exactly," he said, when she stopped abruptly.

Her heartbeats began to race. Suddenly it seemed as though she was staring at her own mortality, planning for a future when she no longer existed, and it frightened her.

"Nick, please let's sleep on it," she said. "I've obviously made a mess of trying to explain the way I feel, and anyway, we're talking about something that's hopefully years ahead. I'm not planning to quit this life just yet."

She tried to make him smile, but putting such thoughts into words always seemed like tempting fate, and she couldn't resist crossing her fingers as she said them.

"I sincerely hope not," Nick said curtly. "How the hell would I survive the humdrum of it all without these regular spats between us?"

She was too tense to see any humour in his reply. When they went to bed she curled up into a ball between the cold sheets, as far away from him as possible, wishing she had never said anything at all. She knew in her heart that she would never insist on her wild plan if Nick strongly disapproved. He always saw things so much more logically than she did, and of course she wouldn't want to put the clayworkers out of work. Whole families had given their lives to Killigrew Clay, including her own in years past.

She lay in the darkness, dismissing the whole crazy idea, but her last waking thought was the hope that Ethan would be as sensible as his brother, and marry someone far more suitable than the Vickery girl.

Celia was quick to apologise the following morning. She came into Skye's room and stood diffidently beside the bed.

"I'm sorry for everything I said, Mom, and I can't bear it if we're not friends. Please forgive me, and I'll grovel to Herr Vogl too – if I must," she added, with a watery smile.

It didn't really solve anything, but one look at her daughter's pleading face after a sleepless few hours, and Skye opened up the bedclothes and Celia snuggled inside them.

"You really were abominably rude," Skye told her. "You wouldn't like it if Franz said something horrid about the king, would you?"

"Everyone's saying horrid things about him and Mrs Simpson," Celia muttered. "Why can't they leave him alone and let him marry her if he wants to? What difference will it make to us, anyway?"

Skye gave her a hug. Celia was many things, but she wasn't intolerant of other peoples' relationships, except where it affected herself. In that she was certainly possessive and selfishly independent – just as a good Tremayne woman should be, Skye thought, wickedly cheered.

"Where's Daddy?" her daughter said suddenly.

"He was up early to attend to some business," Skye said vaguely. "We should get up too. What will our guests think?"

"They're already up. I saw Franz and Herr Vogl out walking earlier on."

"My goodness, they're energetic, aren't they?"

Celia shrugged. "It's the German way. A healthy mind in a healthy body, or some such tosh."

"Do I take it that the great romance is not as great as it was once expected to be?" Skye said carefully.

Celia turned to her. "Oh Mom, he's so *stuffy*! They all are. I didn't realise it until I saw him here among all our own folk. Even Sebby's like a breath of fresh air compared with Franz."

So obviously the little matter of him dancing with Jessie Vickery hadn't meant so much to her daughter after all. That was one relief, anyway. The last thing she wanted was for Celia's heart to be broken, but she had always thought that Franz Vogl wasn't the one for Celia. It was something her girl had had to find out for herself though, the way everyone did.

"Well, they'll be gone soon. Two more days and we'll have the house to ourselves again, and we can look forward to a peaceful family Christmas."

Providing she and Nick weren't at each others' throats, she thought. Life was too short to waste it on petty quarrels, and when she saw him later, Skye told him stiffly that he should forget the things she had said the previous night.

Was sacrificing the family businesses in all their glory really preferable to seeing them fall into the greedy little hands of the likes of Jessie Vickery? To her shame Skye knew that was the main reason for acting the way she had. She had simply been seeing things that weren't there.

She was thankful that she and Nick had patched up their differences and the house was harmonious again. The German family had gone home, making them all sigh with relief. The announcement they had all been anticipating was broadcast on the night of 11 December.

"At long last, I am able to say a few words of my own . . ." came the king's solemn voice, at which Nick muttered audibly beneath his breath.

"More like a dozen advisers putting the right words into his mouth," he commented, shushed at once by his womenfolk as they crowded near the wireless set.

Wenna, soft-hearted as ever, was openly crying as the tragic announcement unfolded, while Celia's voice was brittle as it came to an end.

"Well, I still think it's all wrong that he has to give up the throne for the woman he loves." As her sister wailed even louder, she turned on her. "Oh, do shut up, Wenna, you little sissy."

"Oh, you're hateful! Didn't you hear what he said? He

couldn't remain king without the help and support of the woman he loves. It's so tragic!"

"It's mad. Why should he listen to what the church and the government tell him? He should be strong and defy them all. What's the point of being king otherwise?"

"Well, he's not the king any more, is he?" her father pointed out, trying not to smile at her outraged face. "And even kings have to obey the rules, just like everyone else."

The girls were still in the middle of a heated discussion and solving nothing, when the telephone rang. Skye left the room thankfully to answer it. When Celia was in this mood, there was no changing her mind, and by now Olly was having his say as well, scoffing at them both.

She recognised David Kingsley's voice at once.

"I take it you heard the broadcast?" he asked, barely unable to contain his excitement. "Quite a turn-up, isn't it?"

"Is it? I thought it was what you were expecting."

"Yes, but not in quite such a way. The royals have never been known for expressing their feelings or emotions in public. He sounded almost human. It's quite a scoop to be able to print it word for word in the *Informer* – along with every other damn paper in the country, of course. Nobody gets an exclusive on this one."

But she could feel his enthusiasm as if it was tangible, and she could also feel a matching adrenalin in her own veins. Reporting a sensational story was every newsman's dream, and in this case it didn't matter that every other paper had the story too. They would all interpret the facts in their own way.

"Actually, I'm quite sorry for her," she said. "Whatever her aspirations, and however much of it was truly the king's own decision, she'll never be able to forget that she cost him his throne. That's a heck of a noose around anybody's neck."

She could almost hear the thoughts ticking over in David's brain before he spoke rapidly again.

"You wouldn't care to write it up for me from that angle, I suppose? As a favour, Skye. As a woman, and as an American. What do you say? It could be a stunner."

"Oh, I don't think so."

"Why not? You, of all people, know what it's like to be up against the rest of the community. Remember the German

workers' fiasco when the pottery was boycotted, and you organised Skye's Crusaders to keep it open with just yourself and Lily
and Vera to help until the other women joined in? Remember the
articles you sent home from the Front during the war that touched
the heart of every woman who ever agonised over what was
happening to her man? You're the best and most compassionate
woman reporter I know, Skye, and if Mrs Simpson has had a bad
press before, she's certainly going to get more of it now. You could
do a little bit to redress the balance, if you wanted to."

She warmed to his praise of her. It wasn't all flannel, of course,
he was too hard-hearted a newspaperman for that. She knew she
had it in her to do as he asked, too. Redressing the balance a little
– why not?

It took two people to fall in love and to commit themselves to
marriage and so far Mrs Simpson had had the worst of the
rumours, as the wicked witch who had schemed and manipulated
her man. By implication it had diminished the self-esteem of their
king – ex-king she reminded herself.

"I'll do it," she said quickly.

"Good girl, I knew you would. Get the copy to me first thing
in the morning, if not sooner."

"But that means I'l have to work on it all night!"

"Well, that's the way every good reporter is prepared to work.
Isn't it?"

"Yes," she said, laughing. "I'll see you in the morning."

Nick didn't approve of her involvement. She'd known he
wouldn't, even though the girls were intrigued by the idea of
their mother championing a romantic cause.

"You could be putting yourself in a bad light," Nick warned.
"The country has been divided against this liaison from the start,
however much it's been kept under cover."

"But you can't prevent people falling in love, and I don't see
how any sensible woman would think differently. I'm just going
to put my side of things as an ordinary woman, the way I've
always reported things."

"My love, an ordinary woman you're not, and never will be,
thank God," he said. "I just want you to think what you're
taking on, and to think carefully, that's all."

"Are you going to try and stop me?"

He gave a crooked smile. "I wouldn't even try," he said.

So she spent the next few hours in his study, among the familiar smells of leather and old books that always reminded her of the heady days when she herself had worked in the offices of a magazine in New Jersey. By the time she went wearily to bed, the article was ready to deliver to David the following morning.

"I'll drive in to Truro myself," she told Nick. "It will be interesting to be in the office at this time, and David wants the copy as soon as possible."

She just managed to avoid saying she couldn't resist being at the hub of it all, to be in on any news that was breaking over the wires.

David was delighted with her article, as she had known he would be.

"It's brilliant, as always. You have the common touch, Skye, with all the rhetoric of the skilled reporter. It's a formidable combination, and you're wasted out there in the sticks."

She had to laugh at that, but as always, his praise stimulated her.

"My husband wouldn't thank you for describing our life as being out in the sticks, thank you very much!"

"But you miss all this, don't you?" he said slyly, noting how she was avidly reading the newspaper columns and the incoming wires, and breathing in the pungency of the printer's ink.

"Of course I do, but if you think I could be lured back to work for you, think again," she retorted. "I've a business and a home to run, and three children to care for."

"Three adolescents who can perfectly well take care of themselves, you mean. The girls are young women now and don't need nursing any longer, and I gather that Olly already has ideas about his future, and good for him."

"Has Lily put you up to this?" Skye said suspiciously. "Does she think I should get out more or something?"

"No. I merely see the way those gorgeous eyes sparkle when you're involved in something other than domesticity, and I think what a waste of a good brain it all is."

And just for a moment he let his guard slip, and she knew instinctively he wasn't simply thinking about her domestic life. There was still a strong link between them, even if most of it was on David's side as it always had been.

"Anyway, I'm not here to discuss my future. It's the future of the country that should concern all of us," she said, more briskly. "What will happen now?"

"It's already happened. Our ex-king left Britain in the early hours of the morning to join his lady friend in France. We now have a new king, George the sixth, God help him. We know little about him and his family as yet, but that will soon change. The scandal-rags that have had their knives in Edward will soon want to show George as whiter than white."

"My God, how cynical you are!"

"And how right," he said drily.

With the release of the publishing restrictions ordered by Lord Beaverbrook, every newspaper in the country was full of the news, and Skye's article in the local Cornish newspaper brought mixed reactions. There were telephone calls, some praising and supporting her views, while others openly abused her for her disloyalty to the crown and siding with the woman they called the royal enemy. Some people turned their backs on her when they saw her in the street, but the final straw came when Ethan telephoned from White Rivers to say the walls of the pottery had been daubed with paint during the night with the words 'American Witch Lover' scrawled large.

"It's just like what happened when we had the young German workers here," she raged to Nick that night. "How short-sighted these people are. How *stupid* and insular—"

"Careful, my love, you're in danger of setting yourself above them," Nick said. "I warned you this might happen, didn't I? I'm afraid you've added fuel to the flame by reminding them that you're American and supporting your countrywoman."

"I don't see that she's done anything wrong, since the king chose her above his throne. And why shouldn't I remind them that I'm American and proud of it?"

"Because they're not, and some of them will always think of you as the colonial upstart. Remember how your grandmother used to talk affectionately in that way? Not against you, of course, but outsiders have always made Cornish folk close ranks. Feelings are running high, even so far from London, against what some see as the usurper stealing their king from under their noses."

"What absolute nonsense! They won't stop me saying what I think," Skye said. "No one has ever done so before."

She hadn't felt so mutinous for years, and was completely at one with her daughters in supporting the cause of true love. So it came as such a shock when Celia came home from Truro a few days before Christmas, her dress torn and her hair dishevilled.

"My God, what's happened, honey? Has someone hurt you?"

"You could say that," Celia said in a choked voice. "I took a walk over the moors on the way home to collect some greenery for the Christmas tree, and a couple of young clayworkers began taunting me about my mother being being a Yankee lover. I couldn't let them get away with it, Mom, so I yelled back at them, and they rushed at me and began pulling at my dress and hair—"

She stopped on a sob, and Skye hugged her tense body close. Celia was so unused to anyone opposing her in anything that this was doubly shocking.

"The sooner I get away from here, the better," Skye heard her say in a savage, muffled voice. "Don't you see what you've done? I can't wait for Christmas to be over so I can get back to Gstaad. This whole vacation has been a disaster. I hate Cornwall and all those dreadful people."

Blaming her sent a further shock through Skye. Dear Lord, but she had never meant this to happen. She had wanted to help, to put things into a sensible perspective, but it seemed as if her carefully worded article had backfired on her in a way she had never expected.

Those bloody, *bloody* clayworkers, she thought in a sudden rage, thinking they ruled the earth and taunting her daughter. They were to blame for this latest upset, turning Celia against everything Cornish, at least for the present. For all her brash ways Celia was as vulnerable as the next person when it came to wanting to be loved. She couldn't bear to be so hated, and blamed the taunting on her mother's interference. Oh yes, it was the clayworkers that were at the heart of it all.

But there was something far more urgent to think about right now.

"They didn't actually hurt you, did they, darling?" she asked carefully. "I think you know what I mean."

Celia gave a brittle laugh, more chilling than Skye thought possible from a girl of little more than eighteen summers.

"If you mean did they try to shove their hands down my dress or up my skirt, no they didn't. But there are more ways of being hurt than by sexual rape, Mother."

By addressing her in that scathing, adult way, Skye knew they had lost something precious between them for ever. It would be something to mourn in the long weeks ahead after the girls had gone back to Gstaad.

Five

Vera's illness progressed so violently that by early January everything else was forgotten. Interest in both state and business matters faded in view of the very real family crisis.

Skye made daily visits to her cousin's house to carry out the doctor's instructions, even though the cloying smells of coal tar medication and herbal chest rubs made her want to heave. But the chronic bronchitis didn't improve as the weeks passed, no matter what remedies were tried. By then Lily and Skye were taking turns in caring for Vera, since Charlotte couldn't face the journey up to the moorland house to make regular visits to her elder daughter. Skye and Lily even discussed the idea of resorting to the quack methods of the moors healing woman, but just as quickly discarded it.

In any case, Skye wanted no truck with any weird potions that could stun the brain to the point of hallucinating. In ages past these old crones would have been burned at the stake, and she wasn't so sure that the ancient woman who lived in the hovel on the moors now, wasn't in the same category.

Even if her evil-smelling concoctions might help Vera . . . but she shuddered, her conscience clear in that respect, knowing that neither Vera nor Adam would agree to it.

"Adam's mother swore by a bread poultice and red flannel to bring out any impurities, and mine always gave us a good dose of expectorant. But none of it's any good if your time's up. It's between me and God when that day comes."

Vera constantly wheezed out such words in between her agonising bouts of coughing and the disgusting bloody mucus she had to spit into a container for the doctor's inspection.

Skye shuddered squeamishly at the covered receptacle, wondering how she and Vera and Lily had ever coped with the sights and sounds and smells in the French field hospitals during the war. But that was then, when it had been a necessity and their sense of duty towards the poor soldiers and an endless procession of new cases numbed their senses. This was now, when she did it out of love and anxiety for her cousin, but with every day Vera got progressively weaker.

"It doesn't look good, Adam," Skye said, once they had left Vera tortuously sleeping. "If only she didn't have all this weight it would ease her breathing. As it is . . ."

"As 'tis, it looks as if I'll be losing my Vera quite soon, don't it?" he said, with the stark simplicity that couldn't disguise his agony at being without her.

Theirs had been such a love match, such an unexpected and spectacular love match, and one that had brought his clever lawyer brother Nicholas, back to Cornwall and into Skye's life. She could never forget that, and she always felt a special closeness to Vera and Adam because of it.

"It looks like it," she said quietly, not taking away his dignity by pretending otherwise.

She saw his shoulders begin to shake, and without warning he started to sob, great heaving sobs that tore at her heart and made her put her arms around his great bear-like body and hold him to her as if he was the child he and Vera never had. It took a long while for the paroxysm to cease and, when it did, he wiped his eyes and squared his shoulders, and made no apology for such an unmanly show, which only made the sense of heartbreak more poignant to Skye, knowing he loved Vera so much. Only a strong man would weep publicly for his wife and never mind who knew it.

"Would you like me to stay here tonight?" she murmured.

"Aye," he said. "In case I should have cause to go for the doctor. I wouldn't want her to be here alone."

But he faltered for a moment as he spoke, avoiding Skye's eyes. They both knew what he meant. This night was likely to be the last one on earth for Vera Pengelly.

In the early hours of a cold February morning she slipped from this world to the next, with her husband holding one hand and her best friend holding the other. It was over.

There was no possibility of Celia and Wenna coming home for the funeral, and Olly preferred to stay away since Adam said roughly that it made no difference who was there and who wasn't. The only person in the world who mattered to him wouldn't care one way or the other. He was living in a twilight world of his own now, Skye told Nick worriedly, and seemed to want Vera buried with almost indecent haste.

"Everyone has their own method of coping, darling," Nick said, their own disputes a thing of the past in view of this far more fundamental tragedy. "Adam must deal with it in his own way. You know that."

Skye knew it was an obscure reference to the way she herself had coped with the deaths that had touched her life. Her brother Sinclair, hit by a crazed fanatic's bullet . . . her beloved parents . . . Granny Morwen . . . her first husband, Philip . . . All of them gone, reminding her of the relentless march and insecurity of a life span.

Lily was as stoical as ever at Vera's passing, but their mother, Charlotte, who had always resented Vera marrying a common man, as she put it, was vociferous in her show of weeping over the open coffin.

" 'Tis never right for the child to go before the mother, is it, Skye? 'Tis the wrong order of things."

"I know it," Skye said, not wanting to be the comforter for this elderly woman, but having no choice since Charlotte had begged to be told every detail of her daughter's passing. "So many parents had to face the same thing during the war, Charlotte. It's never right, but we just have to go on as best we can."

"Well, you never had to face such a thing, did you?" Charlotte said, suddenly aggressive. "You don't know what it is to lose a child."

Her innate selfishness overflowed as she glared balefully at Skye. Vera had been forty-two years old and hardly a child, but Skye couldn't find it in her heart to be angry.

"No," she said quietly. "Just a husband."

Charlotte crumpled then, and Skye let her sob against her, trying not to dislike her so much.

The small crowd of black-clad family mourners and friends was enlarged by the respectful clayworkers and their families who stood at a distance as Vera Pengelly was laid to rest in the moorland churchyard on a chilly afternoon.

"Turning out so ill-dressed for a funeral," Charlotte whispered to Skye, glancing at the clayworkers' everyday garb and dismissing them.

"They come to pay their respects, not to be a poppy-show," Skye said sharply, "and I shall make a point of asking one or two of them back to the house if they care to come."

New World was the venue for the beanfeast, as Theo always called a wake. He had ordered Killigrew Clay to close for the day, and Skye had closed the pottery and the Truro shop. She ignored Charlotte's outraged face as she walked across to the pit captain and other clayworkers and made the request.

"Thank 'ee kindly, Mrs Pengelly, but we'll get back among our own if 'ee don't mind," Tom Vickery said awkwardly. "My girl might want to go with 'ee though, if that's all right."

"Oh, yes, of course," Skye said, wondering how she could have missed Jessie's bright hair among the crowd.

Ethan's interest in her seemed to have waned partly due to the ragging he was getting about the flighty girl, Skye suspected, and a good thing too. But if she wanted to come to the house for a bite, she could hardly refuse her now.

Thankfully, it seemed that she didn't, and she saw father and daughter wrangling at the back of the crowd.

Jessie probably had other fish to fry by now, Skye thought fleetingly, while Tom wasn't ready to let the better-heeled Pengelly fish off the hook completely. She let the words slide in and out of her head, pushing aside the sadness of the occasion for the moment, and sought out her husband. It was time to return to the house and some kind of normality.

She saw Nick and Ethan supporting their brother Adam, taking him away from the open grave towards Nick's car before he totally collapsed with grief. There were other cars available, and she could return to the house with Lily and David. When she found them she spoke quietly about something that had been puzzling her.

"Do you know who that girl is? The one at the back of the crowd."

They followed her glance to where a slim young woman dressed all in black was standing motionless, as if intent on imprinting the scene on her memory. She wasn't a clayworker, and Skye had never seen her before, but from the top of her beret-clad head and long dark hair, to the erect way she held herself, there was something dramatically familiar to her.

"Never seen her before," David said. "Do you want me to go and speak to her?"

"No, don't," Lily put in quickly. "We don't want strangers intruding today. This is a family affair, and it's getting very cold. Let's just get away from here, please."

Skye glanced at her. It wasn't like Lily to sound so agitated. Lily was always the calmest one of them all, the solid, no-nonsense one, who had kept Skye's swooning spirits in check when she had been near to collapse and horror in the French hospital wards all those years ago. Lily was as pale as death now . . . reminding Skye that she had just buried her sister.

"You're right. The sooner we get away from this place now and get something hot inside us, the better. Mrs Yardley will have hot soup and tea waiting for us."

The crowds were dispersing, and when Skye glanced back the girl had gone, as mysteriously as she had appeared. Or was she going crazy, seeing things that weren't there? A ghost, or an apparition, a phantom brought about by the rising mist that had already begun to shroud the moors so insidiously?

She shivered, colder than the February day itself, but if it had been an apparition, then David and Lily had certainly seen it too, and that was not the way of things.

She put it out of her mind and concentrated on being the hostess for Vera's wake, trying to be as cheerful as possible, and in particular, caring for Adam's welfare. He refused to stay at New World, and returned with his memories to the moorland house he and Vera had shared for more than ten years.

"He'll need watching," Nick said much later, when they were finally alone and in their own bed. "Vera was his life and I'm not sure how he'll cope without her."

"I know," Skye said, "somehow it always seems so much more tragic for a man to cope alone."

"Well, it's not going to happen to me, darling, since you're as fit as a flea."

"I'm not sure I like the comparison, but thank you anyway," she said, knowing he was trying to lighten the gloom that had descended on all of them on this sad day.

But it couldn't last for ever. Mustn't last for ever. Life had to go on, however trite it seemed, and she held him closer, wanting his warmth and comfort and to know that they were still alive, still in love, and still needed each other.

She remembered the girl the following day.

"Did you see her? I had the strangest feeling about her, Nick, and it was almost as though Lily recognised her."

"I doubt that. You know how that weird yellow daylight distorts things, especially when the fog is about to cover the moors, and we were all in a highly sensitive mood by then."

"Maybe," she said slowly. "But something tells me it was more than that."

"Or something Granny Morwen's telling you?" he said with a grin. "You can't blame everything on her, Skye!"

"Well, *I* didn't say it, *you* did," she retorted.

He moved away from the breakfast table. "I'm going to see that Adam's all right," he told her. "I'll fetch him back for supper tonight if he'll agree, and Ethan too. None of us should be alone at such a time."

She watched him go, loving his concern for his brothers. Loving him, and thinking how lucky she was to have found such love for the second time in her life. Not everyone was so fortunate. Only herself and Granny Morwen out of this whole, tangled family network, she reflected.

Halfway through the morning the housekeeper came to the sitting room where she was trying to compose letters to her daughters to tell them everything that had been happening recently. Mrs Yardley's creased face was anxious.

"There's a person to see you, ma'am," she said. "I told her 'tis a house o' mourning, in a manner of speakin', but she says 'tis of some importance. I think she's an Irish person."

Mrs Yardley's tone implied that this was comparable with being a tinker, and Skye hid a smile, as her own family had an Irish connection. Not that Morwen's brother Freddie had been Irish, nor her much younger son Bradley, but they had both lived in Ireland for many years until their deaths.

She gave a small sigh. "Show the lady in, please, Mrs Yardley. If she says it's of some importance then I'll hear what she has to say."

"You jest mind that she's not come here beggin'," the house-keeper muttered with a sniff.

The girl entered the room. She wore the same black clothes as before, and stood just as still and composed, apart from a slight tremor of her gloved hands. At a quick assessment, Skye guessed that she was about twenty-three or four. She was exquisitely beautiful, her hair long and dark in a completely unfashionable style, and there were dark shadows beneath her large blue eyes.

Skye rose slowly, a strange feeling inside her.

"Who are you?" she said, her voice unaccountably rough.

"My name is Karina, ma'am," the girl said, her accent soft and melodic. "Karina Tremayne."

There was silence in the room for a moment, and then Skye gestured to a chair, her heart thudding.

"I think you had better sit down and tell me what it is you want," she said at last.

As she did so, the girl's cool manner suddenly crumpled a little. She pressed a linen handkerchief to her eyes without any fuss or show, and quickly replaced it in the neat black bag she carried. The words tumbled out.

"I'm sorry, Mrs Pengelly, especially now I know of the circumstances here. When I made enquiries, the folk in Truro told me about your loss. I didn't mean to intrude, and I know I shouldn't have gone to the burying, but it seemed a way of observing without being observed, which sounds even more terrible to me now. But Mother of God, I didn't mean to upset anybody, and I don't think anybody really noticed me."

"They did. *I* did."

"Ah well, so be it then," the girl said softly. "But sure and I meant no harm by it."

"What do you want here?" Skye repeated.

The girl looked down at her hands. "My mother has recently died, God rest her soul. She left me some letters and documents. The lawyer gave them to me, but I didn't know what to do about any of it. He said I should come here and consult an English lawyer, but I don't know one."

"Don't you?" Skye said, her compassion over the girl's be-reavement tempered by suspicion. It was a bad time to come here with some sob story, but then, what better time, when they were all feeling vulnerable?

The one thing she couldn't overlook, though, was what she should have seen all along. The thing that Lily had evidently seen, and that was the trademark of the Tremayne beauty. This girl had it all. Skye overcame her suspicion with an effort and asked gently if she would like some tea.

"Oh, that I would, ma'am. 'Tis a cold day and I've walked from Truro, so I have."

"My heavens, have you?" Skye said, startled.

That was something Morwen Tremayne would have done in her youth and thought nothing of it, in the days before people became soft and relied on motor cars to take them from place to place. Granny Morwen would have easily walked from the cottage at the top of the moors to the bustling streets of Truro for the thrill of the annual fair.

But she was more than thankful when Nick arrived home and took the questioning out of her hands. She was out of her depth for once, and didn't know how to handle this situation. As yet, she didn't even know what the situation was, since they had simply made awkward small talk after the girl's brief revelations. She seemed awed by the size of the house, and was reluctant to show her precious letters and documents to anyone but a lawyer.

"As I told you, my husband is a lawyer, Miss Tremayne," Skye told the girl formally. "Whatever you have to say I suggest you say it now, and we can sort out the mystery of why you're here."

It wasn't like her to remain patient for so long, but she was almost afraid to ask any more, and Nick had his own methods of dealing with clients, so she took a back seat while he dealt with their uninvited guest.

He scanned the letters and documents and opened the Dublin lawyer's letter which was addressed to whomever it may concern. Finally, he looked up.

"It all seems to be in order, and Mr Flynn affirms everything here. You are the daughter of the late Aileen Hagerty and Bradley Tremayne—"

He heard Skye gasp, and held up his hand.

"I am, sir," Karina said in a low voice. "But I had no knowledge of who my father was until my mother's death. It came as a great shock to me, but as you will see from some of his personal letters to her, he loved her and, unknown to me, he arranged for regular amounts to be paid to her for my upkeep.

You will see that he also wanted me to contact my Cornish family one day, especially if I was ever in need."

"And are you in need?" Skye said sharply, hardly able to take all this in.

"That I am not, ma'am," she said with quiet dignity. "I am well provided for. It's not why I'm here. 'Twas my parents' wishes that I contacted you and made my existence known, and now that I've done so there's no more reason for me to stay."

She stood up, holding out her hand for the return of her documents. Skye didn't miss the way her hands shook, and realised what an ordeal this must have been for her to carry out her parents' wishes.

"Of course you must stay. You're part of our family, after all," Skye heard herself say.

Karina gave a slight smile. "You're very kind, but I'm sure this must have been just as great a shock to you as it was to me. I have taken a hotel room in Truro for several nights, and then I must go back to Dublin."

"Do you have money?" Nick said, always the practical one.

"I have enough, but eventually I will seek employment, since idle hands do not suit me. I like to be busy, so I do."

Skye made up her mind. "My husband will drive you back to Truro to collect your things. I confess I know little about Bradley Tremayne and the Irish connection, but you can't simply pop into our lives and out again. I won't allow it."

"My mammie always said the Tremaynes were bossy folk," Karina said with an apologetic smile. "She took on my father's name in later years, although they never married."

"Was there any reason for that?" Skye asked.

The girl lifted her chin high. "My mother was already married. He was a wastrel who eventually drank himself to death and they had already parted when my father met my mother and I was conceived. I'm sorry it's such a sordid tale. According to the letters she left me, my father died when I was very young, so they had no chance of marrying. But I believe they truly loved each other, and of course, the priest always had to believe that I was her husband's child or Mammie would have been disgraced and ostracised by everyone."

"You'll be a Catholic then," Nick said.

"Lapsed, but none the less honest for all that."

Skye took control as she saw the strained look on the girl's face. She was exhausted. It must have been a shock to find herself in the midst of another bereavement so soon after her own. Fate sometimes had a strange way of dealing with folk and making them face up to things.

"I'd like you to stay here for a few days at least, Karina," Skye said gently. "My children are away from home, and it would be good to have a young person about the place for a while. Besides, the rest of the family would never forgive me if we didn't introduce you to everyone."

Although just how Theo was going to react to the fact of his Uncle Bradley having fathered a child, she couldn't think. She had met Bradley once when he had been on a visit to Cornwall years ago, and all she knew of him was that as a precocious and wayward child he had gone to Ireland to live with his Uncle Freddie and Aunt Venetia, where they had raised horses until the stud farm was sold after their deaths.

She would find out more later. First though, once Karina had returned from the Truro hotel, she would show her to a guest room and assure her that she was welcome, which, to Skye's surprise, she was. Karina was still grieving for her mother, but she brought a breath of fresh air into this rambling empty house.

You can't keep her, said a voice in her head.

Whether it was her own, or the echo of her grandmother's, she wasn't too sure at that moment. And of course it would be disastrous to try to replace her beloved daughters with this girl. Disastrous, and dangerous.

Nick's discreet telephone conversation with the Dublin lawyer confirmed everything Karina had said. He took her into Truro and collected all her clothes and cancelled the hotel booking, and that was enough for one day.

But later that evening, with the other two Pengelly brothers joining them at the dinner table, and the talk becoming more general than morbid, Skye was even more thankful for Karina's presence.

"I'd be glad to show you around the area, Miss Tremayne," Ethan offered. "You certainly can't walk everywhere, and I have a small car, even if Nick does call it a bone-shaker."

"Then I'd be glad to accept," she said shyly. "And my name is Karina."

"Karina it is then," said Ethan, the word as soft as a caress on his lips.

Theo was predictably coarse when he heard the news.

"Christ Almighty, I never thought old Bradley had it in him," he chortled. "Some even thought he was one of the limp-wristed brigade, what with he and old Freddie closeted up like two old women in that farm of theirs after Venetia died. Must have wanted to get his oats somewhere though."

"All right, Theo," snapped Skye. "You've had your fun, and you're not to say any of this to Karina. She's a lovely girl. Lily and David have met her and like her, so don't you dare put your evil spoke in, you hear?"

"Christ, but you're the spit of your grandmother when your eyes snap fire," he snarled. "All right. I'll be good – which is more than old Brad was," he couldn't resist adding. "So what's this meeting all about?" he asked, changing the subject.

They had concocted something to take his mind away from Karina's presence, though by now, Skye had seen the sense of not putting her previous plan into operation. Whoever Ethan or any of their children married they had to trust that they would have sense enough to keep the business in the family names, and that had to be ensured by proper documentation. Killigrew Clay would remain Killigrew Clay in perpetuity, and White Rivers, the name she herself had chosen for the pottery, would never be changed. If it was a compromise, it was a reasonable step to take. By arranging the meeting at Theo's house, they could kill the two proverbial birds, by also telling him about their new relative. Betsy, of course, had predictably been charmed at the thought of another girl in the family to fuss over.

Theo was surprisingly willing to listen to Skye's proposal, which made her increasingly wary. Theo being docile always meant trouble, and she didn't trust this mild-mannered attention for a moment.

"You do understand what Skye's proposing, don't you, man?" Nick said sharply, as if her own mistrust was fast transferring itself to him.

"Well now, I ain't too sure," he said, leaning back in his study with his arms folded behind his head, exuding a far from pleasant odour in the confined space.

71

"All I want is to ensure that the businesses continue with the family or chosen names, or not at all," Skye said before she could stop herself, and immediately bit her lips as he pounced on her words.

" 'Tis a mite selfish of 'ee, ain't it, cuz?" he said lazily, but his eyes were starting to flash now. "Seems to me like you'd happily put all the clayfolk out of work just because of a bloody female whim. Has this new Irish tart put more daft ideas into your head?"

Skye felt her face flush. "Karina doesn't come into it. There's no need to be insulting. I hadn't considered putting anybody out of work. Nick will vouch for that. Of course I don't want to sell out. I just want to keep the names intact. Is that too much for your pea-brain to take in?"

She should have held her tongue, she thought furiously. Instead she had implied that they might sell out if things didn't go her way, and she might have known what interpretation Theo would put on that: bloody female interference again.

Nick had warned her to let him deal with this instead of confronting Theo herself, and she hadn't listened to him. But why should she, when it was between herself and her cousin, she thought angrily? But now she was faced with Theo's smugly malicious face.

His hands suddenly left the back of his head and his fists smashed down on his fine oak desk.

"Well, I'll tell 'ee just what I think, cuz. I think you've gone too far above your station with your fine schools for your children, and your grand ideas, and 'tis the clayworkers who bring in the pennies for you to make your pretty pots, and don't you forget it."

"Why must you always twist my words?" she stormed. "I'm just trying to save everything we've always stood for, you damn idiot, by making sure that the registered names are a condition for the future. I know how hard Granny Morwen fought to stop another woman clay boss buying us out all those years ago and turning it into Pendragon Holdings or some such nonsense," she invented wildly. "All I want is to preserve Granny Morwen's values."

But God help her, she knew that wasn't the sole reason. It was seeing the covetous, greedy eyes of Jessie Vickery that had brought on all this frantic assessment of the future and prompted her to think so irrationally.

"Aye, and if Morwen and Ran Wainwright had sold out to Harriet Pendragon at that time, we'd all be sitting pretty by now, instead of having had to deal with depressions and strikes over the years, and having bloody po-faced Germans as our main markets," Theo said, turncoat in his thinking as always.

He just about managed not to hawk and spit as he said these last words. Others might be Jerry-lovers, but he was not one of them and never would be.

"He has a point, Skye."

Unbelievably, she heard Nick's comment, and felt her blood surge with rage.

"Are you siding with his bigoted views now?"

"All I'm saying is that you can't deny that china clay has always had its ups and downs, and in recent years the downs have taken precedence. I know you're shipping large quantities of raw clay to the German factories, and your own pottery exports continue to be good, which is to your credit. The new markets to America that you're so proud of are cautiously profitable, but in general, production is not at its best. The expensive electric machinery we installed seriously depleted profits for a long time, and they have never fully recovered. We're only just holding our heads above water."

Skye stared at him. She was no accountant, and neither was he, but he made regular visits to their Bodmin accountants, and knew their affairs better than anyone.

"Why haven't you said any of this before?"

He shrugged. "There was no need. I wanted to get Theo's reaction to your proposal first, and then put one of my own."

"What is it?" Theo growled.

In one respect he was in agreement with his cousin, and one respect only. He didn't want outsiders involved in their affairs. As far as he was concerned Skye would always be on the fringes as the American upstart, and even more so, her husband.

"Sell now," Nick said calmly.

"Are you out of your mind?" Skye gasped, and then she screamed as Theo shot around the desk like a streak of greased lightning and grasped Nick by the throat.

"What kind of backhander have you got your sights on, you

inferfering bugger? This is *my* business, not yours, and I'll see hell freeze before I let any snot-nosed lawyer tell me what to do with my business."

He was strong, but Nick was stronger and younger, and he had soon wrenched Theo's fingers from his throat.

"Sit down, you old fool, and listen to some sense," he snapped, pushing Tho away from him.

The thick-set man stumbled and fell, and for a moment Skye felt real fear in her heart when he didn't move for a moment. Then he scrambled to his feet and sat down heavily on his chair, no more than winded, his features puce with humiliation at this insult in his own home. His voice was harsh with derision.

"Whatever it is, it had best be good. Killigrew Clay has been in our family for nigh on a hundred years, and we ain't selling it on no lawyer's say-so. I thought your wife had some family feeling, but she don't need the money now, o' course, with her profits from old Uncle Albie's paintings."

His jeers stung Skye almost to tears. Albert Tremayne's paintings had become valuable assets after his death, and she had received a staggering amount of money for the ones she had sold. It was so like Theo to demean the things that other people held dear. He was a hateful, hateful man . . .

Nick spoke calmly and deliberately, ignoring the tension between them. "I'm no prophet, and far be it from me to foresee any trouble in Europe, but the fact that Hitler is building aircraft carriers doesn't make easy reading for those who remember the last conflict all too well. If the worst happened, all those overseas markets would be closed, just as they were in the last war."

"Good God, man, I don't have any truck with the heathen buggers, but you're away with the fairies if you're seeing another war coming up on the strength of a few goose-stepping idiots and the screechings of a madman," Theo sneered.

Nick ignored the jibe and went stolidly on.

"As you know, many of the smaller china-clay works that have struggled to keep afloat have decided to join the big conglomerates, and it may be time for Killigrew Clay to do the same. Selling now, and continuing to receive dividends through a central control would mean we wouldn't throw anyone out of work. Then, if anything untoward *did* happen, we would have the buffer of a shared business interest."

"And if that went down, we'd all go down," Skye said. "Granny Morwen never wanted us to be part of a large concern. It was her pride that Killigrew Clay always stood alone."

"Aye, it was the family's pride an' all." Theo added mutinously. "You're off on the wrong track here, Pengelly. We ain't merging with no big concern, and that's that. In fact, we ain't selling out at all, and as far as I'm concerned this here discussion is at an end."

He stood up. Skye glared at her husband and turned to Theo, swallowing her pride.

"We seem to have lost track of my original suggestion, Theo. Nick has turned this meeting into something quite different from what I intended. Perhaps you and I could talk about it together sometime? It seems a very simple matter to me, to make it a legality that the names of the two businesses never change."

So damn simple . . . no more than a few lines on a legal document . . . yet between them these two had turned it into an argument. She deliberately excluded Nick in her comment to Theo. She was seething with anger that he could have done this without warning her beforehand.

She sided with her cousin at that instant. They were family, and Nick was not. He was the outsider. She might bear his name, but at heart she was still a Tremayne and always would be, with a fine tradition behind her. Whatever happened, it would be a Tremayne decision.

"Come back tomorrow afternoon, cuz," Theo said after a moment, clearly finding a sly amusement in the conflict between them. "Bring the Bradley sprog with you if you like and let Betsy have a chinwag with her."

He went out, crashing the study door behind him, leaving them to make their own way out of the house. Once in the car, Skye looked at her husband, white-faced with anger.

"How dare you? Your role is to advise, not to issue me and my family with ultimatums."

"Thank you for putting it so succinctly, my dear. I thought my *role* as you put it, was to look after your interests and keep you happy, but it's obvious that I fall far short in both my marital and my professional roles."

"Don't twist my words, Nick. I feel very let down, and when

Theo and I decide what to do about the business – if anything – we'll be sure to inform you as our family lawyer."

"I never doubted it. And incidentally, I agree with the oaf in one respect. Are you quite sure old Morwen Tremayne expired nearly twenty years ago? If ever she had an influence on you she's exerting it now – or else she's doing a damn good job of reincarnation."

He drove off in a rage, while she stared dumbly ahead in the seat beside him. Far from enchanting her as it once would have done, his words chilled her. She didn't believe it was Morwen's influence telling her what to do. She was capable of using her own instincts. She was a level-headed American, not a fey-minded airhead like some of the spookier Cornish folk pretended to be for the benefit of upcountry strangers.

She didn't want to be anybody's reincarnation either, she thought fearfully, not even her beloved grandmother's, and she hated Nick even more for putting such disloyal thoughts into her head.

Things were still strained between them when she met Theo the following afternoon. By now Ethan was escorting Karina around, and she couldn't miss the attraction between the two of them. Skye simply refused to think how Wenna might react to it. There had never really been a future for her and Ethan but Wenna was too young and too romantic to be convinced of it. And in any case, Karina was so much more suitable for Ethan than the flashy Jessie Vickery.

Skye tried to push all of them out of her mind as she again faced Theo. The cousins were in agreement for once in total opposition to selling out on the grounds Nick had suggested, and Theo was adamantly pooh-poohing any idea of another war. Everybody knew the Great War had been the war to end all wars, and nobody would want to risk another, not even the power-hungry Nazi leader.

Theo had obviously had time to mull over the things Skye had said, and he agreed that they should make things watertight for their successors. The one and only thing she could admire in him was his loyalty to his family, and he had a strong second in Sebastian. Skye was sure his son would want to carry on the business, even if Olly didn't. She had more or less discounted her girls along with Sebby's brother Justin. And then Theo made her heart jump.

"Seb's the only fly in the ointment," he said, scowling.

"What? Surely he'd want to keep it in the family. He's passionate about his craft, and only Ethan's a better potter than he is."

"He's got restless lately. Wanting to travel and see a bit of the world some day, he says."

"He could go to Germany and see the other factories."

"Over my dead body, woman! You know what I think about them buggers. The only way I'd see him over there is in fighting gear, and that ain't going to happen."

"For pity's sake, don't say such things," Skye said quickly. "It's tempting fate, Theo."

"Anyway, I daresay 'tis all a long way off, but I'm just warning you that when the time comes to take over, it may be down to your sprog and not one of mine."

"Olly wants to be a lawyer, like Nick."

Theo became more thoughtful. "That don't stop him, or Seb, for that matter, being absentee owners, does it? What say we make a joint codicil to the effect that when we pop our clogs, the two of 'em are to be joint owners? That'll ensure that the names go on, and we'll insist on it legally if we must."

"Cut my girls out, you mean? Oh, I don't think so. It has to be the five of them or none at all."

"Done," Theo said, and she wasn't at all sure that she hadn't been. Or that they weren't back at square one.

Celia found it surprisingly easy to forget Franz Vogl. She would have hotly denied the suggestion that she was shallow, but her philosophy was that if someone didn't care for her, then she wouldn't care for them. It had the effect of sometimes making her seem harder than she was, but it also prevented too much heartache. And she hadn't really fallen for him . . .

Her new post at Gstaad was taking up all her energy and, besides, there were always new young men to talk to from a nearby college, who were only too eager to teach the beautiful young English sisters and their friends to ski on the winter slopes at the weekends. Even though she made a nominal protest at chaperoning her younger sister, Celia was secretly glad to have

Wenna with her, since she was far less sure of herself than her outward appearance revealed.

As the year rolled on, and winter gave way to a fragrant early spring, the experience at the hands of the jeering clayworkers faded, but she couldn't quite forget how vulnerable she had felt that day. Springtime in Gstaad and the surrounding area was exhilarating, with a plethora of brilliant wild flowers on the meadows and slopes, although by evening the temperature had usually begun to drop.

She and Wenna had got used now to the fact that there was a new female relative installed at home in New World, and Wenna in particular, had got over her jealousy when she had heard that Karina had taken on the job of nursemaiding Lily's little boys.

"Well, since Lily's boys are such a double handful, the new nursemaid cousin probably needs to be a dragon," Wenna had surmised. "Good luck to her, I say."

"She can't be that old," Celia said. "Mom says Olly's taken to her as an older sister, but then, anyone over twenty is ancient to him."

While the vagueness of Karina Tremayne's background was so intriguing to Wenna, Celia wasn't going to let on that Skye had also intimated in her letter that Ethan Pengelly was becoming ever more interested in her. For all their competitiveness, Celia didn't want to be the one to break her sister's heart.

"You have a letter from Berlin, Miss Pengelly."

She started when Madame Doubois, her immediate superior, handed her an envelope late one afternoon when lessons were over and the tutors were relaxing in the lounge in front of a unseasonably necessary log fire. All her life, Celia would remember the particular and piquant scent of those pine logs.

"Do you have a beau in Germany, Celia?" Monique, who taught deportment and elegance, asked teasingly.

"Not than I'm aware of," she said slowly, with a small leap of her heart.

She no longer had any contact with Franz, and was sure he wouldn't have written to her after so many months, but when she turned the envelope over, it was to see the seal and stamp of Herr Vogl's Fine Porcelain Distribution Company. She took out the letter at once, hoping there was nothing wrong. But if there was, she couldn't see why it would have anything to do with her.

My dear Miss Pengelly,

This letter will no doubt come as a surprise to you, but in recent correspondence with your mother through our mutual business concerns, I understand that you will be leaving St Augustine's Academy for Young Ladies in September of this year, and I have a proposal to put to you. I know how proficient you are in languages and your mother tells me of your interest in expanding your knowledge of Europe.

There will be a vacant post as personal assistant to one of my business managers in November in the company's central office here in Berlin. If you would be interested in the post a small apartment would also be available in the company hostel, which is securely supervised.

I have your mother's approval and knowledge that I am writing to you. Naturally, there is no need for a hasty decision, but please consider the matter and send me your thoughts.

With many felicitations, I remain etc., etc.

"Good Lord," Celia said out loud. "I've been offered a job in Berlin from next November, if I want it."

"What kind of job?" Monique said curiously. "You should be be careful in Berlin, *chérie*. I'm told it's a very bohemian and decadent city these days."

"Really?" Celia said, interested. "I can't say I saw anything like that when I was there with my mother last year. Anyway, I hardly think being a personal assistant in a long-established company is going to corrupt me in any way."

"Don't be too sure. There's personal and personal," Monique said meaningfully. "And of course, you were there with your mother at that time, weren't you? And well chaperoned!"

"Oh, well, I don't have to decide right away. I've got ages to think about it."

But she already knew she would accept. Living at home in a Cornish backwater, idyllic though it was, was already a long way behind her. This was a heady chance of adventure and independence she couldn't refuse.

Six

O liver Pengelly's hand shot up that May morning as his current affairs tutor related the news story of the previous day. Irritated at being interrupted in his dramatic description of the *Hindenburg* disaster, the tutor told him to be quick about it.

"I don't want to be excused, sir," Olly said, red-faced as his classmates sniggered. "It's just that my mother was born in New Jersey."

"Well now," the tutor said. "Perhaps she will be able to rouse your interest in your lessons, young man. But for now, please concentrate. As I was saying, the giant airship *Hindenburg* exploded in mid-air in the state of New Jersey, in the United States, killing thirty-three of its passengers and crew. She began her flight across the Atlantic from Frankfurt. Who can tell me the location of Frankfurt?"

As the voice droned on and more hands shot up, Olly lost interest. He already knew about the disaster, anyway. David Kingsley had telephoned his mother when the news had broken the previous night. It had happened nowhere near the town where she was born, and she had no relatives there now, but she had been white-faced and shocked.

"I can't believe it! All those poor people," she had said. "I always had a horror of those great airships. Travelling in them always sounded horribly risky and claustrophobic. Just think about all that terrible gas just waiting to ignite."

"I imagine that Herr Hitler will have to ban fuelling the things with hydrogen, at least," Nick agreed. "Be thankful that we're going to London by train," he added prosaically.

They were leaving for the capital on Monday, and Olly was going with them for the royal occasion of the year. The drama of the abdication was well behind them now, and the splendour and pageantry of a coronation was just what was needed to raise the nation's spirits. Wenna had begged to be allowed to join them, and had been granted a special time away from the academy. She was wild with excitement at being included in a trip without her sister for once.

Olly's pal Justin hadn't been at all impressed at the idea of hob-nobbing with royalty, as he called it.

"Not that you'll get within miles of 'em," he said, as the two youths strode over the moors on the bright Sunday afternoon before the Pengellys left for London. "We'll see more of the procession through the London streets on my father's new television set, and you won't be allowed inside Westminster Abbey anyway," he added for good measure. "You'll just be squashed like insects by the crowds."

"You're just jealous," Olly retorted, refusing to let his pleasure be dimmed. The horror-filled accounts of the recent *Hindenburg* disaster were already receding in his mind as the excitement of London beckoned.

"What, of seeing all the fuss made of the new king and queen? It's for sissies."

"So you won't be watching it on your new television set with the rest of 'em then?" Olly said slyly.

"I might," Justin said. Then he grinned. "Oh, well, all right. In fact, my mother wants to invite all the relatives to come and watch it so she can show it off. Pity you won't be there. The new cousin's sure to bring Ethan as well."

Olly scowled. Since Karina Tremayne had effectively cut her ties with Ireland and looked like staying at New World with his family permanently he had been torn over whether to write to Wenna and mention Ethan Pengelly's attachment to her, but had decided against it. What brother wrote to a sister, anyway? That was for sissies if you like.

It would all have been for nothing, in any case. Now that Wenna was home, she seemed to have no particular feelings for or against their new Irish cousin, and she never mentioned Ethan Pengelly at all. Oliver simply didn't understand girls.

He forgot the lot of them as he and Justin raced across the moors, flattening the bracken beneath their feet. The stench of the old moorswoman's hovel reached them even before they saw the smoke curling from its chimney.

"Let's go and ask the old crone if Ethan Pengelly's going to marry Wenna or Karina," Justin said mischievously.

"I'm not going anywhere near her," Olly said at once. "My mother forbids it."

"And since when did you do everything your mother says?" Justin taunted him. "Are you scared of the witch woman?"

They heard a screeching noise behind them, and they whirled around to find the bent old woman leaning on a stick, her wisps of grey hair almost non-existent on her balding pate, her mouth full of blackened teeth.

"If you ain't scared, then mebbe you should be, my fine pretty boys," she said and cackled.

Justin spoke boldly. "We mean you no harm."

The cackle became louder. "*You* harm *me*? Now there's a dandy thought. So what do 'ee want old Helza to do for 'ee both on this fine May day? 'Tis never mere chance that brings 'ee this way."

"Yes it is, you old witch," Olly snapped, gaining courage from his cousin. "We're just taking the air."

"Oh, 'takin' the air,' is it?" she mimicked. "Well, mebbe you should mind and watch your feet instead of keepin' your snotty young noses in the air. There be plenty of ruts to catch 'ee unawares and stop your funnin'."

She went off still cackling, and the boys strode away as fast as they could so as not to lose face, before breaking into a run. They were on the downhill stretch, a stitch creasing their sides, when Olly gave a sudden yelp at a wrench in his ankle as he went headlong into the bracken.

"The old witch has cursed me with her talk of ruts," he moaned, trying not to cry out still more at the stinging pain and the sight of his twisted ankle rapidly swelling and bruising.

"Don't be stupid. There's not even a rut there. You just didn't look where you were going," Justin snapped, unnerved at the sight of him. "Get up and let's get home."

Olly tried, but the pain was excruciating.

"I can't," he whimpered. "I think my ankle's broken, and a fat lot of good you're going to be as a doctor if you can only stand there wringing your hands. Help me to Adam's place, Justin. He'll telephone my father to come and get me."

With Justin acting as a ungainly crutch, they somehow managed to cover the short distance to Adam Pengelly's house. Justin was practically hauling his cousin along, and Olly was near to swooning with the pain. He was trying to be manly and not to give in to tears but he knew his chance of going to London was gone. Even if it was only a sprain or a bad twist, he wouldn't be able to stand for hours among the crowds and cheer on the newly crowned king and queen.

Once Nick had collected him from Adam's house and the doctor had been called out, it was confirmed that it was a severe sprain, which had to be kept strapped up and rested for at least a week. Much later, his sister tiptoed into his room and sat on his bed, anxious and sad for him.

"I'm really sorry you'll miss our trip to London, Olly. But you should have taken more care on the moors."

"Oh, thank you very much for that advice, brainbox! But there's not much you can do against a witch's curse, no matter how much care you take," he muttered beneath his breath.

"What did you say?" She had caught the gist of the words but she wanted to hear them again.

"Nothing. I didn't want to see all the pomp anyway."

"Didn't you? You won't want to know what Daddy's been arranging for you then."

"What?" Olly asked, too sorry for himself to care.

"Uncle Theo has telephoned, and Daddy's arranging to take you to his house on our way to the train station. You're to stay there for the few days we're away so that Aunt Betsy can fuss over you, and you'll be able to see the procession on their television set!"

"I suppose that's the next best thing," Olly said grudgingly. "In fact, Justin says we'll see more that way. He was crowing over it."

"Well, it's not so bad after all then, is it?"

Wenna spoke cheerfully, as sunny-tempered as ever, feeling a mite selfish in thinking how good it would be to have her parents all to herself in London. She would never have wished Olly any harm, but it was odd how fate took a hand sometimes. And she scoffed at the thought that old Helza's words might have had any substance towards that end at all.

London was *en fête* on the day of 12th May, despite the threat of rain in the air. Nothing could stop the excitement and, with everyone surging forward to get a glimpse of the golden coach and the royal procession, the Pengellys were squashed by the crowds. They had left their hotel early in the morning to be as near as possible to Buckingham Palace and get a reasonable vantage point.

Their feet were sore and aching by the time the unseen ceremony inside Westminster Abbey and the street pageantry was all over. But at last, their patience was rewarded. The roar of applause and excitement all around them heralded the appearance of the king and queen and their family on the balcony of Buckingham Palace, where they remained for some minutes acknowledging the crowds.

"They look just like the princesses in a fairy story," breathed Wenna, enchanted at the sight of the two little girls wearing their crowns. "How lucky they are!"

"Perhaps they are," Nick commented. "But they'll be living their lives in a goldfish bowl from now on. We're better off being anonymous."

"I'm not anonymous," she said indignantly. "And neither is Mom! She's far too beautiful to be anonymous."

"I'm not arguing with that," Nick grinned. "But I for one have had enough of all this standing about and adulation, so why don't we go off and find some tea rooms?"

"Yes please," Skye said feelingly. "It's been a heck of an experience to come all this way for a few minutes of actually seeing royalty. Olly will have had by far the best views on Theo's television set after all."

"You wouldn't have missed it though, would you, Mom?" Wenna said.

"Of course not. When will we ever get such a chance again?" she replied, as they fought their way through the sea of bodies still pressing forward as if to glimpse every last moment of history being enacted. It took an age to make their way through the crowds, and they thought they would never find a taxi, but by taking devious routes through unknown side streets, somehow they found one and fell inside it.

"Take us to the nearest Lyons cafe, please," Nick said.

"Righto, mate," the driver said cheerily. "First time up West, is it? You look done in. Big day though, ain't it?"

"A wonderful day," Skye told him, smiling.

It was as slow a crawl through the traffic as if they had been walking, but at least it was easier on the feet, and at last they drew up outside a Lyons. Once inside they were enveloped in the warm, crowded atmosphere, where all the talk was inevitably about the day's events. They ordered a welcome pot of tea and a selection of cakes.

"I was never so glad to sit down," Skye said. "As soon as we leave here, I want to get back to the hotel and take a hot bath. I feel as though I could sleep for a week. Thank goodness you persuaded me to stay for one more day before the long journey home, Nick. I simply couldn't face it tomorrow."

"We've got to do some more sightseeing, anyway," Wenna said determinedly. Skye groaned and closed her eyes for a brief instant.

There was a deafening mixture of voices and accents from every corner of the country all around them, as people outlined the events they had seen or missed that day. Then, through it all, one voice nearby seemed to ring out clearly in Skye's ears. A voice that was tantalisingly familiar, yet one she was unable to place immediately.

"Well, I tell yer, if I'd had to wear 'is bleedin' Majesty's crown on me 'ead for more than five minutes, I'd have keeled right over. Bleedin' 'ell, it must've weighed a ton at least!"

Skye turned her head sharply at the same time as Wenna did. It must have been ten years since either of them had heard the voice or the familiar phrase, and Wenna had been a small child, enchanted and awestruck by the daringly wicked words the flashy lady visitor had used.

"Fanny?" Skye said before she could stop herself. As she did so, the woman at the table near the window looked her way, and her heavily made-up face lit up with delight. She wound her way towards them at once, her arms outstretched, her fur stole sliding from her shoulders as she gaped from Skye to Wenna.

"Well, Gawd preserve us, if it ain't me old friend Skye. And this little beauty must be one of them lovely gels of yours, all grown up. Bleedin' 'ell, if this ain't a turn-up! You must come and meet my old feller," she chuckled.

"It's marvellous to see you, Fanny, but we were just going back to our hotel," Skye said, seeing Nick's frown, and remembering how he had disapproved of this old wartime acquaintance who had burst in on their lives with one of her 'gentleman friends' some years ago – and acquainted their small daughters with words they had never heard before.

"Pity, but Gawd Almighty, yer like a sight fer sore eyes. Well, if yer doing nothin' tonight, come and see our little establishment. I've come up in the world now, see," she said, dropping her voice. 'Betcha never thought I'd end up hitched, did yer, gel? Me and my Georgie run a small club – nothing seedy, mind. We get some class acts in, and we've got a lovely torch singer for tonight. Look, I can see Georgie's wantin' to move on now, but you be sure and come along tonight and have a meal wiv us after the show – all right?"

She shoved a card into Skye's hand, and before she could reply Fanny had turned away in a whiff of cheap scent to join the insignificant little man waiting impatiently for her by the door.

"Bleedin' 'ell," Wenna said beneath her breath, smothering a giggle.

Thankfully, Nick didn't hear her, but Skye did. She kicked her daughter beneath the table, but there was laughter in her eyes as she did so.

She looked at the business card, as pink and flashy as its owner, and proclaiming the name and address of the Flamingo Club, with the name of the proprieter George Rosenbloom beneath it.

"You might as well tear it up," Nick said. "It'll be some awful dive, and we're not going anywhere near it."

"You haven't asked me if I want to go there yet," Skye said as Wenna gave a howl.

"Why can't we go, Daddy? I've never been to a club before."

"You're not going now—"

"Why not? Must you be so stuffy, Nick? I'm sure it's respectable if Fanny's husband is anything to go by. He looked such an odd little man."

"He's a Jew," Nick said.

"What's wrong with that? They're people, aren't they?" Wenna said, disappointed and ready to argue. "Why must lawyers always try to stop people having fun?"

Skye realised that people were glancing their way as their voices rose. She said calmly that they would discuss it further at their hotel and not in a public place, which would be far more suitable for the dignity of Nicholas Pengelly, Solicitor at Law, she thought in annoyance.

He agreed, as she had known he would, and after a couple of hours of female persuasion he had also reluctantly given in to their request for a short visit to the Flamingo Club.

"But if it's in the least bit dubious, then we're coming straight back here," he warned.

Skye and Wenna smiled at once another, well pleased, and determined to make a night of it, whatever he said.

The Flamingo Club was a pleasant surprise. True to Fanny's word, it wasn't seedy at all. The decor was that of a discreet little nightclub, with a small area for dancing, and a raised platform where the various acts performed.

Wenna was instantly entranced by the glittering costumes of the dancers who performed acrobatic feats to music, and the comedian whose jokes bordered on schoolboy humour with veiled references to Herr Hitler and exaggerated goose-stepping. But what thrilled her most was the female torch singer, imported from America who sang in a deep, soulful voice to a piano accompaniment. The singer wore a long, creamy figure-hugging gown, and trailed a wispy chiffon scarf through her fingers as she wandered among the audience, exuding the kind of perfume that hadn't come out of Woolworth's. She was glamour personified, and Wenna was bowled over by her.

"Wasn't she simply marvellous?" she said, almost choked with emotion when the rendition came to an end.

"Marvellous," her father agreed. "But don't go getting any ideas, darling. You need real talent and self-confidence to be able to perform like that."

Wenna stared into the distance, the subtle and intimate lighting of the club made the room very romantic. No ideas of trying to emulate such a star had even entered her head. Not until now. Not until her father had unwittingly put them there. She swallowed.

"It must be lovely to entertain people and send them home feeling so happy, though."

"You stick to your piano playing and singing at the academy, Wenna. It's much safer to be well praised for your performances and to leave it at that, than to risk embarking on a precarious stage career," he said lightly, never realising how his words had taken root.

He might not, but Skye had. Her heart beat a little faster at the glow in her younger daughter's eyes. Celia had always been the confident one, while Wenna had always lagged a little behind, uncertain, unsure of herself, even with the undoubted talent she had inherited from Primmy Tremayne's superb piano playing. But Wenna had even more. She had a husky singing voice that was a faint echo of the American torch singer. With the right training and direction, it could be as intimate as the star performer's here tonight.

Skye shook herself, knowing she was letting her imagination run away with her on her daughter's behalf. And knowing too, that it wouldn't be the kind of future Nick would want for his daughter. But no matter how much she adored him, Nick would always have the lawyer's reserve on that score, while Skye was a free-spirited American, where the moon and stars were there for the taking.

The show was over, and she saw Fanny weaving her way towards them, with Georgie in tow.

"You came then, ducks," she shrilled out gleefully. "So what did you think of the acts? Wasn't Gloria del Mar the absolute bleedin' tops?"

"She was wonderful, Fanny," Skye agreed. "Wenna certainly thought so."

"Good, 'cos she's joining us for supper in the flat upstairs. You can meet her prop'ly then. She might even give us a tune or two if we talk nicely to 'er. We've got a piano up there, though Georgie's a bit rusty on it. Your Ma used to play, didn't she, Skye?"

"She was semi-professional," Skye said with a burst of pride. "Wenna takes after her. She can play and sing too."

"*Mom!*" Wenna said, agonised. It was one thing to have stars in your eyes. It was quite another to visualise accompanying the glamorous Miss Gloria del Mar.

Georgie suddenly spoke up, in a quiet, slightly lisping voice. It was clear that he rarely spoke at all while his wife held court, and they all looked at him in surprise.

"Perhaps the little lady would do us the honour of trying out the piano first of all. It needs someone who loves the instrument to get the best out of it, and I'm afraid such a description does not fit myself."

Wenna caught his shy smile and found herself smiling back. He was such an incongruous match for the awful, yet oddly endearing Fanny. The warmth of his welcome was like that of an indulgent grandfather, and she loved him at once.

"I could try, if you really want me to," she said.

Her heart was still skipping beats with monotonous regularity when they finally went up to the elegant flat above the club, and discovered that Fanny and Georgie lived quite the high life. Georgie obviously had other qualities besides a placid nature to complement his wife. There was someone to cook supper, and someone else to serve it.

Fanny had evidently fallen very much on her feet, and not for want of trying, Skye confided to Nick later, ignoring his jibe that it was more likely the time spent on her back that had finally produced the goods.

But by then, Wenna had realised the possibility of doors opening to her that she had never in her wildest dreams considered before.

Supper was a noisy, jolly affair, and Georgie proved to be a congenial, witty man with a dry sense of humour that was a complete foil to Fanny's brashness. That they adored one another was obvious to everyone. When they had eaten their fill and drunk copious amounts of wine and coffee, Gloria was persuaded to sing for them without too much urging. She declared that she was going to sing a song dedicated especially to them both.

"Are you going to play for me, honey?" she asked Wenna. "I hope you can follow the sheet music, but you probably know the song. Try it first. It was all the rage last year."

She opened the lid of the piano stool, clearly very much at home with the Rosenblooms, and handed the sheet music to Wenna with a smile. Music lessons at the academy involved mainly classical pieces, but Wenna was well acquainted with the more popular songs of the day, and to her relief she already knew this one.

Her fingers rippled over the keys for a few experimental bars, and then launched into the haunting, expressive melody of 'The Way You Look Tonight' while the others listened. Then she nodded to Gloria, who began to sing, lingering over the words with all the heartfelt emotion of the torch singer, and Wenna felt her throat close up. To offset the feeling, she found herself humming the tune very quietly as she played. So absorbed was she in the sheer aesthetic beauty of the words and the music that she didn't realise that Gloria had stopped singing.

She stopped playing at once, scarlet with embarassment.

"No, don't stop," Gloria said softly. "Why don't you sing it, honey? I'd love to hear you."

"Oh no, I couldn't possibly." she said, totally confused now.

"Go on, ducks," Fanny said encouragngly. "Gloria don't sit back and let someone else take centre stage unless she thinks there's a star in the makin'."

"I'm hardly that!"

They waited expectantly and she swallowed, placing her fingers on the piano keys she loved, letting the melody flow out again, and putting her own husky interpretation on the sensuous words.

". . . Love me . . . never, never change . . . keep that breathless charm . . ."

There was silence for a moment when she had finished. She felt the same acute embarrassment she had felt before, but there was exhilaration too, because she had put her heart and soul into it, feeling the emotions of the composer and lyricist, the way she always did whenever she performed anything. And then she heard the applause.

There were only five other people in the room, but the applause was loud and unstinting. Gloria put her arm round her shoulders and faced the others.

"I'm no clairvoyant, and I don't know what you folks have got in mind for this little gal, but she's clearly destined for Broadway. She's an absolute natural, and with that talent and those looks she could make it anywhere."

Nick cleared his throat, seeing his daughter's eyes glowing like sapphires. Her Swiss tutor's praise for her musical skills was as nothing compared with the future that Gloria del Mar was dangling in front of her, and it had to be curbed before Wenna got completely star struck. She was too young, too impressionable, still his little girl, even though he had been startled and deeply affected by the depth of emotion she had put into the song. In those moments she had no longer been his Wenna, but a sensual young woman yearning for her lover . . . and Nick needed to squash the unwelcome illusion at all costs.

"It's very kind of you to compliment her so much, but it's far too soon for Wenna to think about a career at all. When she finishes her tuition in Switzerland she'll be coming home to Cornwall, and that will be time enough to consider what direction she'll be taking."

"Oh, Daddy, don't be so pompous," Wenna said with a nervous giggle. "I'm not going to be a stuffy old lawyer like Olly, that's for sure."

Skye put a restraining hand on Nick's arm. Before the tension rose any further, Fanny said, "Your boy was just a babby when I visited you all them years back, Skye. I never had no dealings with infants as you know. Never knew which end of 'em was worst, if yer gets my meanin'. Going to be a lawyer, is he? Fancy that. He's made up his mind already then. And what about the other gel? Celia, weren't it?"

"She may be going to work in Berlin as a personal assistant for a company that buys a lot of our pottery. If I'd known I was going to see you again, Fanny, I'd have brought some of it for you as a gift," Skye said, thankful to turn the talk away from the magic of a potential stage career.

Not that she had the reservations that Nick had. In his eyes, such a life was consistent with debauchery at the very least, and filled with unsavoury characters, which, he had to admit, Gloria del Mar certainly was not. She was charming and delightful, but she was clearly wise enough to say nothing more about it as the Pengellys decided they really must leave for their hotel.

"Georgie will run you back, Skye. You'll never find a cab at this time of night."

"Oh, we couldn't put you out like that."

"It's no trouble," the congenial Georgie said, and before they left to slide into the vastness of his big Daimler, Fanny hugged Wenna.

"If you decide you want to try yer luck, darlin', you jest get in touch wiv us. We know the best agents who won't rip yer orf, and you'd be welcome to have a spot in the Flamingo. You could lodge wiv us in our spare room, so no harm would come to yer."

"Thank you," Wenna said, dazed, aware that Nick was edging

her out of the room before she committed herself. Not that she would, or could, right now. She was only seventeen years old, and she had until the end of the summer to finish her time at St Augustine's, but after that . . .

"Fanny's heart's in the right place," Georgie observed to no one in particular as he drove them away in the sleek motor car towards the smart London hotel where they were staying. "She'd be like a mother to your gel, as well as an eagle-eyed chaperon. She'd be well looked after if she came to us."

Skye leaned towards him before Nick could reply.

"I have no doubt of it, Georgie, and I thank you for the offer, but Wenna's always been a home-living girl and might well decide that she's been away from home for long enough."

Georgie glanced at the girl in question sitting in the corner of the back seat as she gazed out of the window at London's bright lights and the throngs of people who didn't seem to want this wonderful day to end, no matter how late the hour. He thought that the girl herself might have ideas of her own about that. Such talent was far too good to waste in a Cornish backwater.

It was obvious that the Pengellys would have to purchase one of the new-fangled television sets, even though the programmes were so very few as yet. It was the thing of the future, Theo boasted.

Olly was making the most of his painful ankle while still confined indoors, and secretly enjoyed being waited on by everyone. But his relentless pleading for a television set of their own, coupled with his enthusiasm and lordly comments that he had seen *far* more of the coronation day on the screen than the others had seen, finally won Nick over. Besides, Olly added slyly in a final burst of triumph, they surely didn't want his Uncle Theo to continue crowing over the fact that he could afford the luxury of something the Pengellys didn't own.

"Your son has all the makings of a lawyer," Nick observed to Skye as they drove into Truro to see about arranging delivery and installation. But she could see he wasn't displeased at the thought. Olly could argue with the best of them, and that was Nick's forte too.

She wanted peace and harmony in the house. There had been a small fracas when Wenna had declared to Olly that she was going to be a stage star, and Nick had flatly refused to listen to any such ideas until she had finished her education.

Wenna had since returned to Gstaad in a considerably more aggressive mood than usual, asserting her rights to anyone who would listen, including her sister.

Celia grinned. "And the awful Fanny would be willing to give you a home, would she? I can't imagine what kind of a place she lives in."

"It's a lovely flat, as a matter of fact, and you wouldn't know her now," Wenna said, defending her. "She's perfectly respectable, and Georgie's a lovely man."

"Well, you'd better not let the tutors hear you say you're going to be a star of stage and screen, or whatever, or you'll be thrown out of here as a bad influence on the younger girls!"

Wenna laughed at the thought, but her eyes were pleading, wanting Celia's approval. "You don't really think it's such a daft idea though, do you, sis?"

Celia suddenly saw how intense she was, and how important all this was to her. The idea that had been no more than a small seed of ambition now burned brightly in Wenna's soul.

Uncharacteristically, Celia gave her sister a hug.

"If you want it badly enough, don't let anyone try to stop you. Make sure it's truly what you want, that's all."

"Mom showed me some portraits of her mother when she played the piano in concerts. Old Uncle Albie had painted some that I hadn't even seen before," Wenna said. "She was so lovely, and I know I want to be just like her."

"Then I'm sure you will be," Celia said, touched. "Just don't push it too hard with Dad, that's all."

There was no point in doing anything about it yet, except to dream of what might be. She was too young to be allowed that freedom. Another year, and her parents might just think of letting her go to London alone. In any case, in a few months' time they would be losing one daughter when Celia went to work in Berlin. It was far too soon for them to think of losing another. She would have to be content with at least a spell of life in Cornwall once she left Gstaad. Until then, academic and cultural activities had to take precedence over everything else if she was to get the same coveted certificate of excellence that Celia had won in her own final term. All thoughts of a future career had to be put firmly to the back of her mind.

But it was far from the back of other peoples' minds. In London, there were three people who had become excited over the huge potential of the girl they believed they had discovered.

"I'd be more than willing to promote her," Georgie Rosenbloom said, never slow to back what he saw as a winner. "She'd need a good agent, and Gloria already has someone highly reliable in mind."

"She'd stay here wiv us, of course," Fanny said. "I'd make good my promise to Skye on that one. We don't want no greasy-haired gigolos hanging round and causin' bleedin' ructions. She's a good girl, and she'd need to be portrayed as such. She's a proper bleedin' angel with that voice of hers."

"You're right, honey," Gloria del Mar said thoughtfully. "And with the right kind of promotion and backing, she could be really big. I think we ought to write a careful letter to her parents and put our proposals to them. We can't do anything without their consent, since the girl is still a minor. Thinking ahead though, it won't do any of us any harm to let it be known eventually that we discovered her right here in the Flamingo Club. Didn't you say her mom used to be a journalist? That's to our advantage. She won't be averse to some cleverly worded publicity when the time comes. What we have to do is assure them that it's Wenna's future we're thinking of, and that there's no question of our trying to yank her out of that posh school before time."

They smiled at one another, well satisfied with what had so unexpectedly come their way. Georgie was more than happy at the thought of having a hand in handling this potential gold mine, and each of them was genuinely excited at the thought of steering this very likeable little lady to fame and fortune.

Seven

T heo swore vehemently as he scanned the official letter that had been delivered that morning. Coming hard on the heels of what that bastard Pengelly had been intimating recently, it smacked of intrigue going on behind his back. If there was one thing to get him riled up, it was that.

As always, when he was upset, his liver was affected, and he went about roaring and cursing at anyone who happened to come within earshot. It felt as if his entire guts were on fire and tied in knots on that fine June morning as his motor roared up to New World.

He scattered gravel in all directions as he hauled on the brake outside the house. He slammed the vehicle door behind him and hammered on the front door, bawling for admittance until Mrs Yardley answered him indignantly.

"Good morning to 'ee, Mr Theo, sir," she began, and then stepped hastily aside as he marched past her, hollering loudly for his cousin.

"If you'm wanting Mrs Pengelly, you'm out of luck, sir," she told him stiffly. "She's gone up to the pottery, and Mr Pengelly's away at Bodmin with the accountant. There's only young Master Oliver here and he's in his room with his books."

Her words as to Nick's whereabouts confirmed Theo's dark suspicions. He turned on his heel without another word, muttering obscenities beneath his breath. He shot away from the house in his motor, leaving the housekeeper sorely tempted to slam the front door behind him.

He arrived at White Rivers Pottery just as Skye was coming out, talking amiably with an important lady client, well pleased with her order for a dinner and a tea service that incorporated Seb's successful new design.

"I want to talk to you," Theo snapped, and Skye felt her face flame with colour.

"Certainly, Mr Tremayne. Please go into the office while I escort Lady Asher off the premises." She spoke pleasantly, but her eyes flashed dangerously at his crudeness. She walked on, her head held high, aware that Lady Asher glanced curiously at Theo's retreating back as her chauffeur opened her car door for her.

How *dare* he, Skye fumed, standing with her hands tightly clenched for several minutes until the car had moved smoothly away in the direction of St Austell. How *dare* he come here and disrupt her premises by such a display of rudeness? Lady Asher was as near to royalty as they would get in the county, and Skye was deeply honoured that she and her friends patronised the pottery. How *dare* Theo jeopardise that valuable clientele.

Inside the showroom, she ignored the huddled whispering of the two young women behind the counter, and went through to her office, where Theo was prowling, unable to keep still and barely able to contain his temper.

"Have you any knowledge of this, woman?" he bellowed, thrusting his letter under her nose. "And don't try to deny it, because I'm bloody sure your husband will have had a hand in it, and you'll be in cahoots with him."

"If you would kindly shut up for five minutes, Theo, we can discuss your outrageous appearance here in a civilised manner – if that's not asking the impossible!" she snapped.

Although she was shaking with anger, she sat down at her desk, forcing him to remain standing on the other side of it. Even sitting, with the desk between them she was still in control. In any case, she had the vocabulary to make mincemeat of him and he knew it. All he had ever had was bluster and blasphemies.

"*Well?*" he snarled, when she totally ignored the letter and declined to take it out of his hand.

"Well what? Or is all this dragon snorting supposed to be an unspoken apology for your rude behaviour?"

He crashed his hand down on her desk. She refused to be intimidated by him, and remained unblinking, her hands clenched tightly together. Only the whiteness of her knuckles revealed how she was controlling her temper.

"I'll see hell freeze over before I start apologising to a wench, and an outsider at that," he said explosively.

"Then we have nothing to say to one another," Skye said,

standing up so quickly that he stepped back a pace. As he did so, the door of the office opened, and Seb stepped inside.

"Is everything all right in here, Skye?"

Theo turned on his son at once. 'Don't come sniffing round my cousin's skirts and interfering wi' men's work, you milksop. Get back to your clay modelling where you belong."

Skye saw how Seb held himself in check with a huge effort. His father was a violent shade of red by now, and a fine candidate for a heart attack, Skye thought. The veins on his forehead stood out like purple ropes.

"You're a real bastard, aren't you?" Seb said at last, uncaring that it was his father he spoke to.

"Takes one to know one, boy," Theo roared, before he turned on his heel and went blundering out of the pottery. In the momentary silence in the office, they heard his car roar off with a screech of tyres.

"He didn't mean that, Sebby," Skye said quickly. "You know what he's like when he gets incensed."

"I know, I've had enough," the young man said bitterly. "I'm moving out, finding digs somewhere. I don't suppose . . ."

"If you're asking to move into New World, I don't think that would be a good idea, do you?" she said quietly.

"Probably not. After all, I'm not Irish. And I'm not female," he added, turning away.

When she was alone again, Skye sat down at her desk, drawing deep breaths, wondering just how this day had become so full of hate and resentment. The last thing she wanted to do was alienate Sebby from his father, and moving in with the Pengellys would certainly not help.

Trying not to dwell on that aspect, she re-read a letter that she too had received that morning. It would have been identical to Theo's. If only he didn't jump to hot-headed conclusions, usually the wrong ones, they could have discussed it sensibly.

With journalistic expertise, she ignored everything in the letter but the few sentences that mattered.

. . . and so this is our formal offer to purchase the part and parcel of the land and clayworks known as Killigrew Clay for the aforementioned sum. We would appreciate your early and considerate reply.

It was signed Zacharius Bourne and the address was Bourne and Yelland China-Clay Holdings Limited, Roche, Cornwall.

She shivered, wishing Nick had been there when the letter had arrived that morning, and just as quickly, glad that he was not. He had already suggested selling out, a suggestion that would have outraged old Morwen Tremayne and Theo's father Walter, who had loved the china clay with a passion only comparable with that for his wife, Cathy. Theo, Skye had long suspected, only loved it when it suited him, and when his covetous ownership was threatened.

But remembering the previous meeting between all three of them, she realised that Theo would naturally assume that Nick had been talking out of turn with Zacharius Bourne, and that this was the result. He would certainly think she had been allied with her husband. He had never trusted her or liked her comeuppance in the clay world, even though she was perfectly entitled to it. and now it seemed that Seb was against her too, with his snide reference to Karina.

Her thoughts shifted, wondering just how long Karina intended staying with them. She had cut her ties with Ireland, and was an undoubted family member, but she wasn't a substitute daughter. Skye had already sensed that Olly was tiring of her presence in his domain.

The uneasy question of what to do about Karina was taken out of her hands a few days later.

By then Nick had telephoned Theo and told him shortly that they need do nothing about the letters. He would send a formal reply on their behalf, if required, declining any interest in Bourne's offer. He had also assured him in no uncertain terms that he had had no prior knowledge of the matter, nor any personal interest in it.

But any ruffled feathers were forgotten when a frantic telephone call came from Lily one leisurely afternoon. Skye was sitting in the sunlit conservatory and reading the newspaper reports of the marriage in France of the ex-king and Mrs Simpson, now officially the Duke and Duchess of Windsor.

"It's Mrs Kingsley on the telephone, ma'am," Mrs Yardley said formally. "And she sounds in a right state," she added.

Skye went into the hall, and had to hold the instrument away from her ear as Lily's unusually shrill voice refused to make any sense for a few moments.

"You'll have to talk more slowly, Lily. I can't understand you—"

But it was impossible to quell Lily's flow, which continued to flood out in a long hysterical string of words.

"We were all sitting in mother's garden, and Karina was playing with the children, and mother was saying how she hoped the new Duchess would be happy now, despite all the fuss and upset she had caused, and then she just stopped talking in the middle of a sentence, and her head lolled to the side, and she was dead."

She stopped for breath with a huge shuddering gasp. Skye stared at the telephone for an instant, her mind unable to grasp the shock of such an unrelenting statement, and then her senses took control.

"Where are you now? Have you called the doctor?"

"I'm still here. At mother's. Karina's called David and the doctor, and has taken the boys home. I'm here with mother. Skye, I don't know what to do, and David's not here yet."

She was whimpering now, her earlier hysterical ramble reduced to short staccato sentences as shock took over. She had seen so much horror in France, stood up valiantly for women's rights and been a feminist long before her time, and now her nerves were simply shot to pieces by a second personal tragedy, coming so soon after her sister's death.

"I'll come right away," Skye said at once. "Hold on, darling. Just hold on."

She got into her car and drove to Truro like a wild thing, only pausing in her flight from the house to shout to Mrs Yardley to let Nick and Olly know what was happening when they returned from their ride along the sands.

By the time she arrived there were other cars outside Charlotte's impressive hillside house. It was full of a quietly dignified bustle as the doctor and the undertaker took charge.

Skye went into the terraced garden overlooking the sea, to find David holding his wife in his arms. She went to them and embraced them both, and the three of them stood silently locked together in mutual sorrow for some minutes.

"I need to get her home," David mouthed above Lily's head.

"She's had a terrible shock, and the doctor has given me a sedative for her."

"Not yet," Lily's voice came sharply. "And please don't talk about me as if I'm not here. I need to see that mother is taken carefully to the Chapel of Rest and made comfortable, and then I must tidy her house."

"You don't have to do any such thing!" Skye said, aghast.

"Yes I do. Mother hates an untidy house. She'll hate it if people come here and don't find everything in order."

"Lily darling, none of it will matter to your mother any more," Skye said gently.

"It matters to me," she said, as stubborn as ever. "Karina has taken the children home. My assistant can look after the showroom. It will be good for the boys to have a cheerful young person like Karina around them: I've asked her to stay with us for a while, since I'll be so busy here."

She almost faltered then, but her determination was strong, and she continued making plans as if needing to get the house ready for a party. She seemed driven, and after a while, David shrugged his shoulders and simply let her carry on. Everyone had their way of dealing with grief, and this seemed to be Lily's, Skye thought, horrified.

But more than a week later, when Charlotte had been laid to rest in the family vault beside her husband, Lily was still obstinately refusing to leave her old family home and resume normal living. David spoke desperately to Skye, knowing she was the one who always talked the most sense to his wife.

"She can't stay up there in that mausoleum for ever. In any case, it has to be sold. Charlotte made that clear in her will. The boys need her, Skye. They're fretting for their mother. And *I* need her."

"How does Karina feel about staying there?"

"She's a great girl, but I'm worried what people might be thinking. She's young and pretty, and she's living unchaperoned in my home with only myself and the boys. I don't need to tell you what gossips there are in a town like this, and a newspaper-man doesn't attract the best of neighbours."

Skye knew she would have to tread carefully. "Lily is fond of Karina, isn't she? She trusts her with the boys?"

"Immensely fond. She thinks of her as a daughter, which is

why she sees nothing wrong in her being there with me. There *is* nothing wrong, Skye. You believe that, don't you?"

"Of course. But I can also see that you're worried about your reputation, and Lily should see that too. I'll speak to her and try to get her to come home where she belongs."

He leaned forward and kissed her. "What the hell would any of us do without you?" he asked simply.

She left him then and drove to Charlotte's house, where Lily was still industriously cleaning, as if to dare any speck of dust to defile her mother's memory. Skye stilled her vigorous polishing by putting her hand on her cousin's arm.

"Lily, it's time to go home. It's time to care for your children and to be a loving wife to your husband."

Lily gasped, her face burning with colour.

"How can you say such a thing?" she said, her wild eyes brimming with tears. "I've just buried my mother."

"I buried mine, and my darling grandmother, *and* my husband. But life goes on, Lily darling. We all have to go on. You'll still grieve for her, but your mother doesn't need you now. Other people do. Frederick and Robert are pining, and so is David. He deserves more than to be shut out like this."

The last thing she had intended was to sound like a bloody saint, Skye thought irreverently. But everything she said was true. And as Lily became sullenly silent, there was still more to say. "Karina has been a gem in looking after the children for these past days, Lily. Do you think it would be a good idea to ask her to stay permanently? She's already like a big sister to them, and it would give you and David time to go out by yourselves sometimes if she was part of the household. It's only a suggestion but you might like to think about it."

"I can't think about anything like that just now," she said mutinously, but Skye knew the idea would take root. Lily had been badly shaken by her mother's death, but basically she was the strongest person Skye had ever known. She would survive this.

"You're a bit of a miracle worker, aren't you?" Nick said to his wife at bedtime a few weeks later, when the whole thing had been settled, and Karina had moved all her things out of New World and moved into the spare bedroom in the flat above the White Rivers showroom on Truro's waterfront.

"There's nothing magical about getting people to see what's right under their noses. It's obviously the right place for Karina, and we should have seen it all along."

"But it took Charlotte's death to bring it to fruition," he said thoughtfully. "As if it was all meant."

"Don't say that, Nick!" she said quickly. "I don't like to hear such things."

"And you a Cornishwoman?" he teased her. "Even if only a colonially attached one."

She threw a pillow at him, which he tossed right back. A few loose feathers flew, making her cough and splutter with laughter. Then she was captured in his arms and held close to his heart as they fell together across the bed.

"Do you know how long it is since I've made love to you?" he said, his voice urgent and aching with desire.

"Too long," Skye said, her breath catching in her throat. "Much, much too long."

"Then it's high time we put that to rights," he said softly, his fingers pushing aside the straps of her nightgown and bending forward to press his lips to her breasts. She strained towards him, wanting him with all the fierce desire of a wife, and all the uninhibited lust of a lover.

His hand slid beneath the hem of her nightgown and his fingers moved upwards tantalisingly slowly until they found their goal, making her gasp aloud with pleasure. She reached for him, glorying in the rampant desire she knew was there for her, caressing him and holding him, and needing him so much. So very much . . .

"If there's anything better than this on God's earth, I don't want to know about it," he murmured a long while later when the sweet preliminaries were over, and he was forging into her, each erotic thrust interspersed with kisses.

She could taste her own musky scent on his lips as his tongue roamed round her mouth, increasing her excitement as they reached the climax of their lovemaking. She clung to him as he gasped against her, holding her tightly to him as she felt the surging heat of him filling her.

He didn't move away from her quickly. They lay, their bodies still close, still part of each other, until it became obvious that they must break away. Only then did Skye feel the strange tears of release on her cheeks, the way they always were when she had been in the grip of an almost unbearably strong emotion.

Nick saw the tears and touched them with his fingertips. His voice was softly teasing again. "If I didn't know you so well, I would say you regretted what had just happened."

She put her fingers over his. "I have no regrets for anything, ever, my love," she whispered.

She felt no disrespect to Charlotte for having encouraged Lily to resume a normal life, and as time passed, she was relieved to hear from Karina that Lily was behaving more rationally and taking an interest in life again. She and David had even been to the theatre one evening, while Karina had looked after the children. It was a healthy beginning.

The Cornish community was always considerate in its deference to a family bereavement. Several months passed before a second letter arrived from Zacharius Bourne. It suggested that if the owners of Killigrew Clay weren't willing to sell outright it would be advantageous for them to merge, and Bourne would be happy to arrange a meeting between them and their solicitors to discuss the matter.

"Damn cheek," Skye said, ripping the letter to shreds. "Why on earth would we want to be part of a company with that odious little man?"

"Because there's strength in numbers," Nick pointed out.

"Yes, but we don't need his inferior clay for the pottery. Ours is by far the finest, production is good, and we have more than our needs for export. We don't need the Bourne clay, and he's not getting his hands on ours."

"I didn't know you were so possessive," Nick said.

"Yes, you did," she replied smartly. "And so is Theo. He'll have had a similar letter, I suppose. I wonder what his reaction to it is this time. He's calmed down a lot since Seb did what he threatened and moved out of the house. It gave him a considerable shock."

Theo didn't care about the Bourne offer one way or the other. He had seen mortality staring him in the face when his cousin Charlotte died. There were very few of the older members of the family left, and he was now the most senior one. The fact that his elder son could so coldly turn his back on him had been a further blow to his pride and his nerves.

Like many a bombastic man, when he felt the shadow of mortality hovering about his own shoulders, he crumbled. He didn't even bother to get in touch with Skye to let her know he had also received a second letter from Bourne. If she wanted to negotiate, it was up to her to contact him. With uncharacteristic melancholy, he told himself that perhaps it was time for him to think of retiring gracefully from the race and preserving his strength – but how long such a state of mind was destined to last was another matter. He had always been a man of chameleon-like moods, as contrary as the fluctuating clay fortunes, and his long-suffering family were only too well aware of it.

The only one to benefit from his unusually placid mood was Betsy, who fussed over him like a mother-hen, knowing that, like the calm before the storm, it couldn't last, but ready to enjoy it while it did.

As the academy year in Gstaad was nearing its end, Celia also received a letter, this one postmarked Berlin. She had already written back to Herr Vogl, saying she would be very interested in taking up the position and accommodation that he offered, and that she had her parents' full approval.

It was stretching it a bit, since Nick had not been nearly as agreeable as her mother, but fathers always worried about their ewe-lambs, as she had told anyone who would listen. Nick wasn't even her real father, just a bolted-on step-Dad, she sometimes added airily, enjoying the Celia-like drama of the words.

This new letter was not from Herr Vogl.

I will be in the Gstaad area on business shortly, and I would be delighted if we could meet and discuss the position Herr Vogl has offered you as my personal assistant.

A place and time were proposed for the meeting, and it was signed Stefan von Gruber. Celia replied at once, and long before the arranged date, she and Wenna had conjured up all kinds of images for the man.

"He's sure to be old and crabby with a name like that," Wenna decided. "I wonder if there's a Frau von Gruber, and any little von Grubers," she added, starting to giggle. "What a name to land your children with. He'll have a large red nose and an enormous pot belly at the very least."

"Hush, the tutors will hear you." Celia laughed.

"I don't care. I'm leaving this place soon and going *home*. I never realised I would long for it so much!"

"Oh, yes? What ever happened to the prospective star of stage and screen then? Has the great ambition disappeared in favour of Cornwall and selling Mother's pots?"

"Certainly not," Wenna said. "I'm just biding my time, as the saying goes, until I can leave home without causing any fuss. I'll have my name up in lights one day, you'll see."

"And pigs might fly," Celia said inelegantly.

Only to herself did she admit how nervous she was becoming as the time drew near for her to meet Herr von Gruber. This would be her first real job as part of a huge production company in the heart of Germany with a connection with her mother's pottery and with Killigrew Clay.

The charm of it didn't escape her. She wouldn't be losing touch entirely . . . and at the thought she straightened her shoulders, telling herself not to be as soft as Wenna in feeling the tug of home. The entire world was her home, and the thought of the insular little corner of it that Cornwall represented was no longer the be-all and end-all of existence for Celia. Plenty of Cornish diehards refused to accept that they were even part of England, clinging to their quaintness and mystical heritage, their omens and superstitions, as if they were talismen. Celia found herself smiling faintly as the thoughts came into her head, because she was Cornish too, and she had a good feeling about this appointment. The first step was to make a good impression on the oddly named Herr von Gruber.

She dressed carefully, wearing her best grey skirt and a silky white blouse, her waist tightly clinched by an emerald-green belt. It was meant to stamp her as a woman of fashion, and she hoped nervously that it wasn't too flashy.

Sophisticated was the word she wanted to apply, and she pinched her cheeks and added a touch of lip colour to her mouth, standing back from her mirror and trying to judge the effect through someone else's eyes. Maybe she should have had her hair cut, she moaned. The new marcel waves were all the rage, and more suitable to a working woman that her own long straight hair with the fringe almost touching her eyebrows. But neither she nor Wenna could bear to have their hair cut. Like Samson, she believed it kept her luck intact – and who was being superstitious now!

She put on her matching grey jacket with shaking fingers, and left the academy for the hotel lounge where she was to meet Herr von Gruber.

The hotel was quite crowded. The area was becoming prominent now, not only for winter sports, but for the year-round health-giving Swiss air, as clear as wine, and fragrant with the scent of flowers. Celia felt a brief nostalgia at having to leave this place that had been her home for several years, and tried to work out who Herr von Gruber might be.

She prayed it wouldn't be the monocled gentleman in the corner, and was relieved when an elderly lady joined him. Wenna had said he would probably be a sportsman in lederhosen and a hat with a feather tucked in the side, and she choked back a giggle at the thought, trying to compose her face.

"Miss Pengelly?" a strong male voice said in perfect English, with just the hint of an accent.

She whirled around and hoped that her eyes didn't widen too obviously at the man smiling down at her.

She had always believed in first impressions, and her first impression of Herr Stefan von Gruber was a world away from the image she and Wenna had pictured. He was not old or middle-aged, and he certainly wasn't fat. His hair was a Germanic silvery blond, and his eyes were as blue as Celia's own with laughter creases at the sides. His face was craggily good-looking, his nose aristocratically long, and his smile . . . his smile was wide and welcoming. He wore a light brown business suit that was impeccably tailored, covering a lean, athletic figure.

He held out his hand to Celia as she inclined her head, momentarily dumb. She placed her hand in his, and even though she was not the type to believe in love at first sight, or all the romantic and euphemistic trappings that went with it, she swore that she felt a definite, tingling shockwave run up her arm at the contact.

"Shall we find a table where we can talk privately, Miss

Pengelly?" the adorable Herr von Gruber said. She blinked, wondering how long she had been standing there like a ninny, with her hand still held in his, while a flood of sensations had surged through her head. It couldn't have been more than seconds, or he would have been looking at her very oddly, wondering if he was hiring a maniac to work for him. Instead of which, he was smiling at her very appreciatively indeed. Her heart glowed as she took her fingers out of his grasp.

She could still feel their warmth as they sat near a large bay window where they could see the brilliant green of the slopes and the dazzling display of wild flowers, and the white-tipped mountains far beyond.

It was a memory to cherish, Celia thought, without knowing why she thought it.

"You are somewhat unexpected, Miss Pengelly," Herr von Gruber said, when they had been served with a pot of tea and had both declined anything to eat.

"Am I?" she said, her heart plummeting.

Surely he wasn't going to say she was too young for the job, or that she looked too flighty? She should have had her hair bobbed, or twisted it into a knot as she sometimes did, she thought frantically. She should have thought of how she would appear to a sophisticated Berliner.

"Herr Vogl told me of the legendary beauty of your family, but I found it hard to believe, until now. He called it the Tremayne beauty, which I did not quite understand."

"It's kind of Herr Vogl to say so," Celia said, embarrassed. "The legend arose with my great-grandmother, Morwen Tremayne. She was reputed to be wildly beautiful, and although she had humble origins she married the son of the Killigrew Clay owner – the clay works whose name you will be familiar with, of course. All the women in the family since then have had the same colouring and distinctive looks, and somehow the tag of the Tremayne beauty has stuck."

She stopped abruptly, feeling her face flush as she realised she was talking too fast in her nervousness, and identifying herself with that beauty.

"I'm sorry. You must think me terribly conceited." she said quickly.

"Not at all. I think you are charming, and your pride in your ancestry is something we Germans respect and admire. It's delightful to hear you speak of it so warmly."

As he spoke, he put his hand briefly over hers as it rested on the small table, and again Celia felt that frisson of excitement at his touch. But she almost snatched her hand away from his, feeling gauche and confused at the force of her own emotions. Whatever she had once felt for Franz Vogl, was like a drop in the ocean compared with the empathy she felt towards von Gruber. It also frightened her to think that she was not in such control of her emotions as she had always believed.

"Herr von Gruber, won't you please tell me more about the position I am being offered – that is, if you still think I'm a suitable person. If you aren't already aware of it, I should tell you that I will be barely nineteen when the vacancy arises. You may think I am much too young, and I will understand if you have second thoughts."

She was virtually asking him to agree with her. She was in a blue funk, but she couldn't seem to stop herself. If fate decreed that she shouldn't take this job, she wouldn't. On the other hand, if it decreed otherwise . . .

"So you are nineteen – barely," he said solemnly. "And I am thirty-six, unmarried, with all my own teeth and hair, no dark secrets in my past, and desperately hoping that you will come to work for me. I would deem it an honour if you would say yes. Will you – please?"

She swallowed. He had told her far more personal details about himself than any job applicant needed to know. He had also told her nothing about the job requirements.

She looked into his eyes, and said yes.

A long while later, when business matters had finally been discussed and explained, Herr von Gruber bade her farewell until November. Celia returned to the academy, glad that Wenna was still at her classes and wouldn't seek her out, agog with curiosity, for at least another hour. She needed to be alone, to think about the future and what it might hold. She wasn't merely thinking of the prestige of having a highly paid position in a well-respected company.

She caught her breath, still seeing those so-blue eyes smiling down into hers; still seeing the curve of his mouth, with the small creases at the sides that reflected his charismatic personality.

Of *course* she didn't believe in love at first sight, she told herself as she lay on her bed gazing up at her uncompromising white ceiling. That was for idiots, or soft-hearted romantics like her sister. And her mother . . . her sweet, beautiful, romantic mother, whose wonderful story of how she and Nick Pengelly had looked into one another's eyes at someone else's wedding, and had just *known*, was indelibly imprinted on her daughters' minds.

Although she had known nothing of the magnetism passing between her mother and Nicholas Pengelly on that day, she could remember the occasion vividly. She and Wenna had been Vera's small bridesmaids. What Celia remembered most right now was Skye's beautiful shot-green silk outfit, and the way Aunt Charlotte had wailed that green was an unlucky colour.

It hadn't been unlucky for Skye, even though she had still been married to Celia's natural father, Philip Norwood. The colour and the sensual fabric of the outfit had enhanced her ethereal beauty. Skye had once confided in her daughter that despite her devotion to Philip, there had really been no turning back from the moment their eyes met, no matter how long it took for she and Nick to be together.

A long while after their father had died, when Skye and Nick had finally married, the children had mutually agreed to change their names to Pengelly. Celia remembered how her mother had worried that it was disloyal to Philip, but the children had insisted, and she had smiled ruefully, reflecting that no matter how many times the names changed, the old Tremayne spirit was still the same.

Unwittingly, her fingers touched the emerald-green belt at her waist. She shivered, wondering why she had chosen that colour, of all colours, to wear today.

She found herself whispering aloud, in a far deeper search for her inner feelings than usual.

"Oh, Mom, am I falling prey to what I've always thought was such romantic nonsense? Is this the legacy Granny Morwen left us; to follow our hearts, no matter where it leads us?"

Just like Morwen, and Primmy, and Skye.

Eight

Sebastian Tremayne could hardly contain his excitement as he reported to his father that night that his new pottery design had been approved by the German firm of Kauffmann's as well as Vogl's. Kauffmann's had been one of Killigrew Clay's major markets for decades, firstly buying china clay for their own pottery making and, more recently, importing finished goods of excellent quality and workmanship from White Rivers.

"What's that you say, boy?"

Theo's gaze was fixed on the flickering television screen that was now his passion, no matter what was showing on the very few programmes the new medium boasted, and finding it hard to concentrate on anything else.

"I thought old man Kauffmann had passed on years ago," he grunted in passing.

"So he has. It's his son who owns it now, and he's sent me a dummy of their new catalogue. My design is included in it as well as in Vogl's display material."

He thrust the pages underneath his father's nose. His determination to make Theo take an interest was twofold. Firstly, he wanted his father's approval of the way he was making a name for himself in the world of potters. And secondly, he wanted to stir Theo out of the alarming lethargy that seemed to have descended on him recently.

"Won't you take a look at the pictures, Theo?" Betsy coaxed him now. "Sebby's done so well, and is deservin' of a bit o' praise."

"Oh ah, turning a pot's clever enough, I'll grant you, though 'tis not what my father had in mind when he took on his shares in the clayworks. Walter Tremayne weren't afraid of gettin' his hands into the clay at its source, not when it was all prettied up for some fancy woman's table."

Seb's face darkened and he ignored his mother's warning look.

"That's true, Father, but a lump of raw clay's no good to anyone, is it? Until it's cleaned and refined and put to good use in medicine or paper-making, or turned into beautiful pieces of pottery or tableware, it's no more than it started out to be – a lump of raw clay."

He wasn't demeaning the basic material that had been their mainstay all these years, and his intention had never been to sneer, but he might have known his father would see it that way. Theo turned his eyes away from the television screen, and glared at his son.

"And mebbe that's what you think I be, too, just a lump of raw clay. If 'tweren't for all they who've gone before 'ee, there'd be none of it for 'ee now, and don't you forget it, you young whelp. I daresay you'll be hand in glove with the bloody Jerries next, with your fancy ideas—"

He was stopped by a bout of coughing, due not to any medical problem, but simply a lack of fresh air and exercise caused by the hours he sat hunched over the fire, no matter what time of the year, waiting impatiently for the next television programme until the day's viewing ended.

Despite his father's hawking and spitting, Seb's humiliation at such undeserved criticism made him lash out.

"My God, don't I know I did the right thing by moving out of here! You make me sick with your narrow-minded views. I envy Celia going to work in Berlin. At least the Germans know the meaning of civilised behaviour."

"Oh ah?" Theo shouted, snorting for breath. "Tell that to the poor buggers whose names are on the memorial crosses in St Austell and Truro. They weren't blown to bits and cut to ribbons through any bloody civilised behaviour."

Seb turned on his heel. His mother anxiously followed him to the kitchen.

"There's no reasoning with him any more," he raged. "He's a lout, Mother, and I don't know why you stay with him."

"He's my husband, that's why," Betsy said. "I promised to marry him for better or worse, and there's been worse times than this. He's got no taste for the wilder ways he once had, and he needs me now."

She had no intention of elaborating to her strapping son on

how many times in the past Theo Tremayne had come home reeking of cheap perfume, with the smell of another woman on his skin. It was enough, as she said, that he needed her now.

"Well, so much for showing him the dummy catalogue," Seb snapped. "I may as well throw it in the waste basket."

"No you won't," Betsy said more briskly. "You'll be proud of it, the way I am. But Sebby – you wouldn't go to work in Germany like Celia, would you? Your father would take it as a personal betrayal if you did. He does love you, you know."

She spoke awkwardly, because they were a family that didn't easily speak of love. Seb gave her a sudden hug.

"I promise you the only way I'd go there is wearing a uniform, and that would surely please him. But thank God that's not likely to happen again, is it?"

"Let's pray to God it never does," Betsy agreed, remembering to cross her fingers as she spoke.

Skye had begun to make regular visits to Killigrew Clay to discuss business matters with the site manager and pit captain. Since Theo had lost so much interest in the clayworks, she felt it was her duty to remind them that the family interest was still as strong as ever, no matter what some might still think of a woman clay boss.

That fine September afternoon, she walked the short distance across the firm moorland turf to the clayworks from the pottery, after a pleasurable time approving the German catalogues Seb had shown her so gleefully. She had no doubt both firms would be after similar stock once it was known that rivals were in full production of Seb's design.

Tom Vickery touched his hard hat as he saw her approach.

"Me and Mr Lovett were waiting for 'ee, ma'am. There's summat of importance we need to talk over."

"Oh dear, I hope that doesn't mean bad news," she said with a smile.

It was too fine a day to be hearing bad news. The girls were home from Switzerland, their school years over, and they were relaxing by taking a rowing boat on the river at Truro, having persuaded Justin and Olly to go with them.

"Depends," Vickery said in response to her comment.

Skye gave a sigh. Being closeted in the site manager's hut for even ten minutes was less than comfortable, with its rank smells of tobacco and sometimes steaming boots, as he dried the caking wet clay by his little fire. If this meeting went on for any length of time, she would as soon conduct it in the open air.

Once inside the hut, she tried to close her nose to the various unsavoury whiffs and shook Will Lovett's hand.

"I understand there's some problem that needs sorting out this afternoon," she said at once.

"It may take more'n an afternoon, ma'am," he warned. 'Tis this rumour that's going around, see?"

"What rumour? You should know as well I do, Will, that there's rarely any substance in rumours."

Although she knew only too well that there was frequently more than a touch of truth in them.

" 'Tis about we mergin' wi' Bourne's, missus," Tom Vickery broke in aggressively. "The clayers be up in arms about it, same as they've allus been when there's any such talk."

"And just where did you hear this?" Skye asked, amazed as ever at how quickly the moorland grapevine could transmit rumour and gossip. She knew she shouldn't be surprised. Families were so intertwined among the clayfolk that pillow talk could easily bring home the gossip from one pit to another, and it spread like wildfire.

"Don't matter where, Mrs Pengelly, ma'am," Lovett said. "The only thing that matters to we is whether or not 'tis true, and what 'twill mean to the clayers. One thing I can tell 'ee for certain sure, is that they don't like it."

"Theo Tremayne should be here explainin' things," Vickery growled. "The men 'ould listen to him—"

"And not to me?" Skye snapped.

He glared back at her, his eyes full of disrespect.

"I'll allow that they listened to your grandmother once, when times were threatening, but that was when another woman clay boss were in the runnin' for Killigrew Clay. This is different. Bourne's is a powerful name in Roche, and Zacharius Bourne's a hard man wi' money to burn. If 'tis likely you and Mr Theo are thinkin' of sellin' out or mergin', we've got a right to know of it – and what benefits we'd get out of it."

"You've got no such rights," Skye said, incensed. "Any

business dealings that my cousin and I choose to do are our business. We hold the purse strings here."

But his words made her go cold, intimating as they did that if Bourne offered substantially higher wages to the clayworkers, then a merger might be all too tempting if it came to a showdown between men and management.

"We do need to know where we stand, Mrs Pengelly, if only to prevent any talk of walkouts," Will Lovett said more quietly. "The autumn despatches are about due, and 'twould be a disaster if any were held up because of disputes that could be easily solved."

"Is that a threat, Will?"

"No. 'Tis common sense, ma'am," he said.

Skye took a deep breath. Despite the way her nostrils were closing up while being confined in this little hut, and her wish to get out of there before she threw up, she vastly preferred Will Lovett to the volatile Tom Vickery. He had the temperament to stir up trouble and strike action, while Will was more inclined to use diplomacy.

"You're absolutely right, Will," she said, appearing to back down. "Well, I can tell you that we have had offers to sell out or to merge with Bourne's –" she ignored Vickery's derisive snort at that point – "but my cousin and I have categorically refused both. There is no question of it, now or in the future, and you have my word on it."

"For what 'tis worth." Vickery muttered, and she rounded on him at once.

"Yes, Tom, and if my long and loyal family history in these clayworks mean anything, you will know that my word is worth everything to you – including your position here. I won't have men working for me who cannot trust me, or whom I can no longer trust. Do I make myself clear?"

"Aye, I reckon you do," he said sullenly.

"Then I suggest you and Mr Lovett relay all that I have said to the men, and get on with your work."

She left the hut, drawing in deep breaths of clean air, and began to stride back across the moors to reclaim her car at the pottery, more agitated than when she left.

Will Lovett called to her before she had gone more than a few yards.

"Thank you for that, ma'am," he said. "I'll smooth Tom over, never fear, and the clayers will be reassured."

"Good. It's all a storm in a teacup, Will, I promise you. It's a mystery how these rumours start, though."

" 'Tis no mystery. Young Jessie Vickery's courtin' one of Bourne's clayers, and she brought the news home to her pa."

So that was it. How much vindictiveness was in pretty little Jessie Vickery's mind at what she might see as scoring over the Killigrew dynasty – especially since Ethan Pengelly, very much a part of it, was no longer interested in her?

It hardly mattered, providing Skye had managed to squash any thought of uprising among their own clayworkers. It seemed likely, as the weeks passed without incident, and the autumn clay despatches got away on time to their various destinations, that she had done just that.

The weeks were passing all too quickly, she thought, as the time came for Celia to begin her new job in Berlin. They celebrated her birthday as a close-knit family event this time, just the five of them at home together as if this was an occasion that might never come again, not quite in the same way, anyway . . . the unwanted thought clouded Skye's mind. She was determinedly cheerful as she hugged her elder daughter as she prepared to leave.

"You be sure to write and tell us everything about your new life, honey. And you will take care, won't you?" Skye begged, hoping she didn't sound too much like clinging Betsy – but knowing exactly how Betsy felt now!

"Mom, I'll be just fine," Celia said, more than a little choked, but determined not to let it show. "And I'll be home for Christmas. You'll hardly have time to miss me."

She had to swallow hard as she said it. It was still a wrench to leave Cornwall and home, the way it had always been each time she left for Gstaad. But this time there was a new and exciting life awaiting her, and Stefan von Gruber was going to be a part of it.

As yet, she didn't know how great a part that was going to be. She knew she had to keep her feet on the ground, and remember that theirs was to be a working relationship. She also knew that in the past she had sometimes been too flirtatious for her own good, and she couldn't even be sure that the handsome German's attentions hadn't simply turned her head. After all, she had only met him once. The fact that he had filled her thoughts ever since, was no yardstick on which to base an everlasting love, Celia told herself severely, knowing herself too well.

As her immediate boss, von Gruber had arranged to meet her in Berlin and to drive her to the hostel where she was to live. It was far beyond his duties, and hardly usual for a managing director to take on the task for his new personal assistant.

He could have sent someone on his staff . . . or requested the *Hostel Frau* to meet her. Celia had been told she was a chaperone to the company employees, together with her husband, the hostel superintendent cum handyman.

But Celia didn't question the fact that Stefan had arranged to meet her himself. She only knew that her heart leapt the moment she saw him, and the pleasure in his eyes was far beyond that of a considerate employer.

"I'm so glad to see you again," he said, squeezing her hand. "The time has been long."

The simplicity and quaintness of the phrase charmed her. It wasn't over-gushing, but it said everything she would have said, had she dared.

As it was, for once, the sometimes arrogant, over-confident Celia Pengelly was briefly tongue-tied.

There was always a sense of strangeness when two people met again after being parted. A time of getting to know one another all over again, before they could fully relax and be themselves. But since they had had so little time to get to know one another before, there were no memories to share, save for that one afternoon in a hotel restaurant, with its view of the green slopes, the fragrant flower-filled valleys and the distant snow-capped mountains.

One memory of a stunning, evocative view, and a deep and certain knowledge that this was the man with whom she wanted to share the rest of her life. Celia's nerves prickled at the thought that hadn't even been fully formed in her mind, but which now seemed as inevitable as if it had been preordained.

She shivered slightly as she looked around the apartment in the hostel that was to be her home for the foreseeable future. The furniture was heavy and ornate in the German style, and more than comfortable.

"Is it to your liking?" he asked anxiously. "I saw you shiver.

Are you too cold? Perhaps the heating is not turned up high
enough—"

She shook her head. "I'm perfectly fine, and the apartment is
lovely," she said. "It was a goose stepping over my grave, that's
all."

She gave a forced laugh at his puzzled look. "I'm sorry. It's an
English expression. It means – well, I don't really know what it
means, except that sometimes you get a feeling of fate taking a
hand in your life, or of some memory of the past that intrudes
into the future. It's a Cornish legacy, if you like. We all have this
odd sense of *déjà vu* at times. It's silly, I suppose, to think
Cornish people should be any more perceptive than anyone else,
and now you'll be thinking I'm quite mad. I assure you I'm not
normally scatterbrained, Herr von Gruber, and I hope you will
be quite satisfied with my work."

He took her hands in his, laughing as she gabbled on, and
stopping her by raising one of her hands to his lips and kissing it
in the continental style.

"I'm quite sure I shall, Celia, providing you stop being so
nervous and talking so much, and you will please use my given
name except in the office building. I insist that you call me Stefan
this evening when I take you to dinner."

Her eyes widened as he dropped her hands. "Oh, but is this
usual? I mean, you're my employer—"

"It's my way of welcoming you to Berlin. I have every
confidence that our association will be fruitful. So I shall leave
you now to settle in, and I'll see you at seven thirty."

When he had gone, she watched him from her window as he
got into his powerful car and drove away. Her heart was
thudding as she saw him go and she felt momentarily alone.

A fruitful association seemed an odd way of putting it, but it
was one more example of his beautifully correct continental
phrasing.

She turned away from the window, took a deep breath and
looked around her slowly. On her arrival she had met the
motherly *Hostel Frau*, who had told her to let her know at once
if she needed anything. She knew that the hostel was full of other
employees of the Vogl empire, so she need never feel isolated in a
new country.

The company offices where she was to work with Stefan were

literally around the corner on the next block, within easy walking distance.

She was here, in her new life. In *his* life.

The restaurant where he took her for dinner that evening was small and intimate and seductive with soft rosy-hued lighting. Not knowing the kind of place it would be, she had worn a softly draping afternoon gown of pale green, without heeding any significance. It was simply a favourite of Celia's that did double duty as a semi-cocktail dress, and she knew it flattered her colouring.

Stefan had called for her at the hostel and handed her a small corsage to pin to her shoulder. It was so very elegant and grown-up, she found herself thinking. It was hardly any time at all since she had been involved in school activities, albeit as part-time teacher. But now it seemed like aeons ago, and she was a different person now, with different ideals and prospects.

"Why do you smile?" Stefan asked, when they had been shown to an intimate little alcove and he was smiling into her eyes through the soft candlelight.

"I was just thinking how quickly life can change. Here I am, away from home and family – with you."

"Do you question the decision? I have been told that your Cornish intuition tells you when something is right." He spoke teasingly. "What is it telling you now, I wonder?"

"To enjoy the moment," Celia said, smiling back.

"Then you should always trust your intuition, for such moments never come again," Stefan told her.

It was said light-heartedly, but it was a remark that Celia knew she would remember. To enjoy the moment for it would never come again . . . it was at once poignant and prosaically true. He was a wonderful and sensitive man with the ability to put such things into words so uninhibitedly and without embarrassment.

He behaved, as she had expected, like a perfect gentleman, but they were so comfortable with one another, Celia felt as if she had always known him. By the end of that evening, she knew she was in already half in love with him.

She ignored the fact that there was a considerable age difference between them. As he had pointed out with admirable dignity on their first meeting, she was nineteen – barely – and he was thirty-six. To Celia Pengelly such statistics were unimportant in the great scheme of things.

Love was the only thing that mattered. Love, and the special rapport between two people who refused to let any outside interference come between them. Even though it went unsaid in the weeks that followed, Celia knew in her heart that their feelings were the same.

In business and in pleasure, they were soulmates, she thought, with a dreamy smile that would have done justice to her sister's romantic heart.

Christmas, when she had left Berlin to spend the promised two weeks at home for the holidays, cemented it all. Her family was ecstatic to see her back, wanting to know everything about the new job, the new boss, and how she was enjoying everything. In those first few hours, the excitement of being at home eclipsed the tug of longing to be with Stefan.

"Let me get my breath back!" She laughed. "Berlin is a wonderful city and the job is marvellous. Stefan has taken me round the warehouses and showrooms, Mom, and our goods are very prominent everywhere, including Sebby's new design. Vogl's are making a big splash with it for the new year trade, and Stefan says it will do very well indeed."

"Stefan seems to be saying quite a lot," her father said with a smile. "What about the other girls in the hostel? I hope you've made some new friends among them."

"Oh, yes," she said quickly. "There are two girls in particular – Gerda and Maria. We go walking in the nearby park when the weather's not too cold, and I've been to several concerts with them too."

She caught Wenna's glance, and gave a faint smile, guessing that once they were alone she would want to know far more about Stefan von Gruber than about Gerda and Maria!

"I've brought presents for everyone," she went on quickly. "I'll fetch them from my room as soon as I've unpacked properly and put them under the tree, Mom. The house looks wonderful, by the way. I guess you all went out on the moors gathering berries and stuff. I missed that!"

When she had gone upstairs, still chattering, with Wenna at her heels, Skye looked thoughtfully at Nick.

"She's different. In these few weeks, she's changed."

"It's only to be expected, darling. She's earning her own money now, and feeling her independence. None of them will stay your chicks for ever, you have to accept that."

Skye shook her head. "I know, but it's more than that. It's something in the way she spoke."

About Stefan von Gruber . . . it came to her instantly. It was the way she said his name, the way she lingered slightly over it, the way it seemed she had to say it more than once when it wasn't strictly necessary. Skye knew the signs. She knew her girl was in love, and she prayed that this Stefan person wasn't going to break her heart.

He came highly praised from Herr Vogl as a man of integrity and breeding, and with an impeccable background – which the Germans set such store by – but he was still a stranger, a foreigner. Skye found herself smiling ruefully at the thought, because wasn't she herself just that, in many a Cornishman's eyes? Even now.

"What's so funny?" Nick asked.

"Nothing, honey. Nothing at all," she assured him. "I'm just so happy to have all the family at home once more. It's a good feeling."

Wenna was always direct.

"So tell me, what's he really like? Is he as spiffing as you thought he'd be?"

Celia laughed. There were some things you didn't tell, even to a best friend or a loving sister. You didn't tell about feelings and longings, and the new range of emotions that you didn't know were in you until you experienced them.

"He's very nice and I like him a lot, which is just as well, as we have to work together every day."

Every single, beautiful day.

"So are you going to marry him?"

Celia laughed again. "Good Lord, what a question! I should think he'd want to marry someone of his own age, not a dizzy nineteen-year-old."

The instant she said it, she wished she hadn't put the thought into words. She didn't want to consider the possibility, and one of the new, emotions she was experiencing was a searing jealousy.

"Oh, well, there's always Franz," Wenna said easily. "How is he, by the way?"

Celia had almost forgotten Franz Vogl's existence by now, which frightened her in a way, making her wonder if she was really shallow, or had been, until Stefan.

"I've only seen him once since going to Berlin, when I was invited to the Vogl home for dinner one evening."

"And?" Wenna persisted.

"And nothing. He's nice enough, but I don't have any special feelings for him, and I'm sure he felt nothing special for me. And that's quite enough inquisition for now."

She picked up the armfuls of Christmas parcels in their Christmas wrappings, obliging Wenna to follow her downstairs. She put the gifts beneath the tree with all the others, but her mind was full of the small gift-wrapped box that she had promised Stefan she wouldn't open until Christmas morning. A small box could mean many things and her heart always beat faster every time she wondered what it might be.

It was a tradition that the family ate breakfast together on Christmas morning and then Nick ceremoniously handed around the gifts. But long before then Celia's shaky hands had opened the glossy silver wrapping round the jeweller's box, and she had caught her breath at the ornate silver and pearl earrings inside.

There was a small, handwritten note with them.

'For a special lady. I hope you are not superstitious about pearls. If they are meant to indicate tears, then they will be mine at missing you.'

Her throat stung. There could surely be no more meaningful words. He missed her. She knew by now that he didn't say things he didn't mean. He could be funny and amusing, but basically he was a deep-thinking, serious man, and he missed her.

They were to have a large family dinner that evening. Lily and David and the boys, along with Karina, would be arriving during the afternoon, and the Pengelly brothers, Ethan and Adam, would be there too. Celia wore the earrings with the elegant new dress her mother had bought her. They were noticed at once.

"Are those new?" Lily asked. "They're beautiful, Celia, and they must have cost a pretty penny."

"Oh no, not that much," she said in confusion. "I saw them in the jeweller's window, and I just had to have them."

"Your daughter's becoming extravagant," David said teasingly to Skye. "I hear the German shops are full of expensive items to tempt a young lady."

Celia laughed, and said airily that since she was earning it, she might as well spend it. But she didn't look at her mother as she spoke.

Because of their business connections the family were closely allied with the Germans, but she hadn't ever considered how any of them might feel if things got serious between herself and Stefan. She had never considered anything beyond the sweet sensation of being truly in love for the first time.

As if to bring her brutally down to earth, she overheard a remark David Kingsley's made to her father as they all relaxed after a gargantuan meal. The two men were taking a turn in the conservatory, and were well out of earshot of the games being played by the rest of the family and the excited screams of Lily's little boys. But Celia's ears were attuned to the sombre note in David's voice as she took coffee and brandies out to them while they finished their cigars.

"You know these plans for air-raid shelters are going through, Nick. These are strange times, and I've had it on good authority that all school children are to be issued with gas masks in the new year. What does that tell you?"

"Either it doesn't bode well for the future, or it's just scare-mongering," Nick said.

"Whatever the truth of it, do you think it's wise to let Celia continue with this job in Berlin? It's one thing to keep the business contacts afloat, of course, but it could be fatal to leave her there in the thick of it if anything happened—"

Celia put the tray of drinks down on the small table beside them, her eyes blazing.

"I'll thank you to let me speak for myself, David. As for anything *happening*, as you put it, you seem to be the scaremonger. People in Berlin are going about their business the same as ordinary people everywhere. Anyway, if the government is going to put up air-raid shelters as you say, I think it's an insult to the Germans, as if we think they're going to start bombing us at any minute!"

She knew she was being unduly passionate, but it had nothing to do with governments or power-wielding leaders. It had to do with the fact that if the unthinkable happened, as these two were intimating, then she and Stefan would be torn apart. There would be no future for them if their two countries were at war. As the word slipped into her mind, she drew in her breath. Nick put his arms around her.

"Darling, we have to face facts. Adolph Hitler is no fairy-tale prince, and who knows what will happen in the future? None of us can see that, but I know this job means a lot to you, and of course there's no question of our asking you to come home."

"Good. Because I wouldn't come," she said in a brittle voice. "I'm really happy there, Dad, and you two have managed to spoil that, and to spoil Christmas too."

She rushed away from them, her eyes stinging. She didn't want their image of the future clouding her lovely new life. She reached her bedroom and tried to compose herself, knowing she would have to go and rejoin the others before anyone came looking for her, but feeling as if everything she had believed was so safe and secure was slipping away from her.

"Celia, are you in there?" she heard her mother's voice a few minutes later. Before she could answer, Skye had opened the bedroom door. "There's a telephone call for you. The line's very crackly, but I think he said it's Herr von Gruber – are you all right, honey?"

"I am now," Celia said, her smile suddenly brilliant, leaving Skye in no more doubt of her feelings.

She ran down to the telephone and clutched it to her ear.

"Hello," she said huskily.

"I don't wish to intrude on your family festivities, Celia, but I wanted to wish you a merry Christmas," came Stefan's voice, as close as if he was standing beside her.

"Thank you. And thank you so much for the earrings. They're beautiful and I'm wearing them now," she said.

"When you return to Berlin we must have an evening at the theatre and perhaps you will wear them then."

"Of course I will, and I shall look forward to it very much. I hope you're having a happy Christmas too, Stefan."

"A quiet one with my parents. So goodbye, *liebling* – until 1938. It sounds so far away," he added ruefully, "even though it will be no more than a week, so enjoy your time with your family until then."

"I will. Goodbye."

She hung up slowly, missing the sound of his voice the moment it was gone. And turning to find her mother near enough to have caught her last breathless words.

"So he's the one, is he, honey?" Skye said softly.

She couldn't lie. If she'd tried, her luminous eyes would have given her away.

"He's the one, Mom."

Nine

Fanny Rosenbloom, née Webb, was nothing if not big-hearted. She didn't hesitate when her husband put the question to her.

"If yer frettin' about yer folks losin' their livelihood, then o' course we must bring 'em over here," she declared. "There's plenty of room in the flat fer yer ma and pa. You go and wire 'em to pack up the shop and leave Vienna before old Adolph gets up to any more anti-Jewish larks."

"You're a good girl, Fanny," Georgie said warmly. "They made pure gold when they made you."

"Go on wiv yer," she said, pink-faced. "I lost my own folks so long ago, it'll be nice fer me to share a ma and pa again. It ain't just bein' noble!"

But she was glad he couldn't see her troubled face as he went off to wire his parents to leave Austria as soon as possible and come to London. The new year of 1938 hadn't begun well for the likes of Georgie's people, and she knew he kept a sharp eye on every newspaper report about the situation.

By the middle of March, Adolph Hitler had marched into Austria amid cheers of adulation as he reunited it with Germany and increased the Nazi stronghold. Austria was his homeland, and now he was its undoubted hero.

Very soon afterwards Austrian Jews faced up to the fact that even their most dignified professions were being closed to them; shops had to bear the slogan that they were 'Jewish-owned' and theatres and music halls were forbidden to allow the great Jewish artistes to perform.

For Georgie Rosenbloom it was a time of great sadness as he begged his parents to come to London where they would be safe, no matter what the future held. Their long-established family grocery business would dwindle dramatically, as folk became afraid to patronise something that was clearly anti-establishment now. But his parents were old and proud, and even though he begged, they refused to be hounded out of their home.

"You can't force 'em, Georgie, love," Fanny said sadly. "We can send 'em money, though, even if the shop has to close. They should be takin' things easy now, anyway, and they won't go short while the Flamingo continues to do good business."

"And if any Jewish artistes are looking a venue, we'll never close our doors to them," he declared.

"That's right, my duck," Fanny said, though they both knew the Flamingo Club was small fry compared with the likes of the Windmill Theatre. Still, it had its loyal clientele, and Gloria del Mar was still their regular star performer.

"I was thinkin' about the little Pengelly sweetheart the other day," Fanny said thoughtfully, more to take his mind off his worries than anything else. "I wonder if Skye would agree to let her come up to the smoke for a spell, just to try her wings, so to speak?"

"Maybe," Georgie said, not yet able to be distracted so readily from his gloomy thoughts.

"We could take a trip down there when we close over the Easter weekend. You ain't never been to Cornwall, have yer, Georgie? What do yer say? Make a bit of a holiday of it, eh?"

She was more than thankful she had made the suggestion when the horrifying news leaked out in British newspapers in April that some of the most influential Jewish figures in Vienna had been sent to Dachau concentration camp.

Just for being Jewish, she raged and wept on the telephone to her friend Skye Pengelly, while making the arrangements for a brief visit. And for once, Skye couldn't find the words to comfort her.

"All I know is that the more I hear of Mr Hitler, the more uneasy I am about Celia living and working in Berlin," she said anxiously to Nick.

"She's a sensible young woman, darling. If there's any kind of conflict likely in the months ahead, she'll have to come home, no question about it. She's not of age yet, and she must obey our wishes."

It was easy for him to say Celia must obey their wishes, but as the weeks of the new year progressed, the euphoric letters Skye received from her daughter, told her that wild horses wouldn't drag her away from Stefan von Gruber's side.

However far the relationship between them had developed hadn't yet been confided to Skye in so many words . . . but sometimes mere words were the last things that were needed when a mother's instinct knew it all. Especially a mother who had been down the same passionate road as her daughter.

But there was no point in fretting over it, she decided, as she prepared for Fanny and Georgie's visit. And those two could be guaranteed to bring a breath of fresh air to the unease in the whole country after the government announcement that all Britons were now to be fitted with gas masks. Wenna had declared that she would rather die than be confined in such a hideous thing.

"You may very well die without it," her brother Olly retorted. He was fast changing his intention of becoming a lawyer, for the far more exciting one of newspaper reporting. He spent much of his spare time at the *Informer* offices and was well up with political and world events.

"Well, I can hardly sing behind a stupid gas mask, can I?" Wenna snapped. "And Mom says I can have my voice trained properly if I want to. I may have to go to Bristol to learn with a qualified teacher, but Dad knows some people there where I can probably stay."

Even though it sounded exciting, she wasn't too sure about it. Her father's ex-partner lived in Bristol with his wife, where they ran a small antiques shop. Wenna didn't know them or the city, and she would far rather have gone to London. The fact that Fanny and Georgie were coming to Cornwall for a short break was filling her with excitement, as she remembered the heady evening she had sung with Gloria del Mar and had a tiny taste of stardom.

The Rosenblooms descended on them with the force of a whirlwind. Their large Daimler motor car crunched to a halt in front of the house and it seemed to take forever for Georgie to transport all Fanny's bags and cases into the house.

Somehow they managed to bring with them an air of glamour and stability in a fast-changing world, with the certainty in some folks' minds that another war was just around the corner.

Fanny simply refused to discuss such things in Georgie's presence, determined not to add to his anxiety over his parents. Only to Skye, when they were alone, did she confess how much she grieved for him.

"He'd go over there like a shot and bring 'em back wiv 'im, but he knows they wouldn't come. They say the only way they'll be moved outa their place is feet first, and you can't argue wiv old folk, can yer?"

"It won't come to that, Fanny."

"Won't it? The way things are going, there's some in London predictin' it'll be months rather than years before we're at war wiv the Jerries again." She gave a wry grin. "Whaddya say to the two of us doin' our bit again, duck? Bit long in the tooth fer it now, I daresay!"

But Skye had three nearly grown children who weren't too long in the tooth for it.

"I don't even want to think about it, so let's talk about something else. I want you to meet more of my family while you're here, Fanny, including our niece from Ireland. And you must see the pottery, of course."

She quickly changed the conversation so as not to think of sending her children to war. The very idea of it chilled her. It wouldn't happen. Couldn't happen again in her lifetime, but into her consciousness came the echo of a voice she hadn't heard for a long time.

"What's so special about your lifetime, Skye Tremayne?" asked the ghost of Granny Morwen.

"Are you all right, duck?" she heard the more raucous and very alive voice of Fanny Rosenbloom say. "I didn't mean to upset yer wiv all this war talk. Anyway, there's summat else I wanta talk to yer about."

She tucked her hand in her friend's arm as they strolled in the garden in the sunny April afternoon, and Fanny outlined her proposal for Skye's younger daughter.

"Absolutely not," Nick said sharply when Skye broached the subject in their bedroom that night. "I won't hear of it. It's bad enough that Celia's gone to live in Germany, without sending Wenna off to London."

"You were ready enough to send her to Bristol."

"That's different. Bristol's not the capital. London would be an enemy's prime target if the worst came to the worst."

Skye felt icy cold all over. "You think it will, then. You do, don't you, Nick?"

"I'm no clairvoyant, but yes, if you want my honest opinion, all the signs are pointing that way."

"Then Celia must come home!"

"I thought we were discussing Wenna. And don't raise your voice. The Rosenblooms will hear you."

"They'll have to know our feelings, anyway. And Wenna has to have her say in it too."

"She certainly does not. She's too young to make any such decision for herself."

She glared at him. 'Oh Nick, how can you be so pompous? They're not children any more."

"They're not adults, either. And I suggest you sleep on the matter, the same as I intend to do."

With that he reached out to turn off his bedside lamp and turned away from her, leaving her staring into the darkness. She could her the wind whining softly through the trees outside, and to her over-sensitive mind that night, it seemed horribly ominous.

Wenna rarely dug her heels in, the way Celia did. This time, she was ecstatic with excitement.

"Oh Mom, it's such a wonderful chance for me to get the feel for performing without having to take any old voice training lessons. It's not as if I want to be an opera singer or anything stuffy. And Fanny and Georgie will take such good care of me, it'll be like having a second set of parents!"

"That's enough to damn it before it even starts," Nick said darkly. "I can't allow it. Wenna—"

"If you keep on being so beastly to me, I'll just go anyway. One day you'll come home and I'll be gone," she said, her eyes brimming with tears, her voice full of furious passion. "Can't you see how important this is to me? You didn't stop Celia going to Berlin, and I bet you're going to let Olly have his way about working for the *Informer* too. Why must I always be the one who's victimised?"

"Darling, nobody's victimising you," Skye said, seeing how

Nick was becoming incensed at this unexpected little firecracker. "And we know you wouldn't really go without our permission—"

"I would, and I will," Wenna said stubbornly. "I've never wanted to do anything more in my whole life, and unless you tie me to the bedpost and starve me, I shall go back with Fanny if she'll take me."

"Good God, I thought it was a budding songstress we had here, not a Sarah Bernhardt," Nick snapped. "There's no need to be quite so melodramatic, Wenna."

"Then let me go, and don't try to ruin my life."

In the heavy silence that followed her statement, Nick shrugged.

"We'll think about it. I won't say any more than that."

Wenna swept out of the room, leaving her parents wilting after her sudden onslaught. Nick rounded on his wife.

"You see what comes of inviting your worldly friends down here? They've put all kinds of forward ideas into her head, and now she's fired up with the thought of becoming an overnight singing sensation."

Skye was enraged by his words. "*My* worldly friends, as you call them, are respectable business people, and since Wenna has my mother's musical talent and the voice of an angel, I won't stand in her way."

"You approve of all this then, do you? It's not enough that one daughter is living in a place of potential danger, you want to send the other one away as well."

"For pity's sake, Nick, you're scaremongering again, and exaggerating things out of all proportion." She put a hand on his arm, feeling the tension in it. "Anyway, once she's standing alone in the spotlight and singing in front of a crowd of strangers, she may hate it so much that it will be out of her system for good and all. But at least let her find that out for herself."

She didn't believe it for one minute, but she wasn't going to let Nick see that. She could still remember the way her mother's face had glowed with an inner euphoria when she came home from one of her piano concerts, still in her own aesthetic world until her senses returned to normality, filling Skye with a kind of possessive jealousy that her brother Sinclair never even noticed, and her father Cresswell completely understood.

While Primmy Tremayne was lost in the sensuality of her

music, she was transported to a place no one else could ever reach. Skye knew in her soul that it would be like that for Wenna. The pleasure and the success had been as potent as a drug for Primmy, the way that painting had been for Albert, and it would be so for Wenna. They had to let her go.

"You mean it?" Wenna said later to Skye, her voice choked. "I thought Dad was completely against the idea."

As Skye held her close, she could feel her fragile young body was as tense as a fledgling bird ready and eager to fly.

"Providing you promise to keep in touch, and if there's the slightest sign of trouble, you're to come home."

"What kind of trouble?"

But Skye couldn't name it. Putting it into words made the foolishness of it seem far too real.

How could there be another war? Hadn't they all learned lessons from the last one? Thomas Cook was offering summer holidays on the French Riviera for £8 17s 6d. Would any travel business be so reckless as to send British people flocking to the continent if there was real danger there?

But she shivered all the same. The Spanish civil war had erupted mercilessly, and there was always conflict somewhere in the world. What made *them* so special, so God-protected? Was she deliberately flouting fate by refusing to let herself be intimidated into keeping her daughters in the womb-like safety of Cornwall?

So in early May she let her daughter leave New World in the care and custody of Fanny and George Rosenbloom, and her luggage contained several special evening dresses for her performances in the Flamingo Club, as well as her now obligatory gas mask in its cardboard carrying box.

Theo telephoned Skye a few days later, by which time she had done her private weeping at parting from both her daughters. By then, all the family knew of what Wenna had called her big chance and most had wished her luck. Skye knew that Theo could be guaranteed to take the opposite view.

"You've done a foolish thing in letting the girl go off like that," he informed her, making her bristle and defensive at once.

"Oh? And what about Justin leaving home? He'll be living in

London while he does his medical training. Is it any more foolish for me to let Wenna go, than for Justin to be there?"

"He won't be flaunting himself in flimsies for all to see," he sneered. "You never know what kind o' queer folk frequent nightclubs these days."

"I know the kind of folk my friends are," she said frigidly, thinking that if they were face to face right now, she would cheerfully wring his neck. "No harm will come to Wenna while she's in their care. And I don't see what business it is of yours, anyway."

"Only passing an opinion, that's all, cuz," he grunted. "Betsy wants to know what news of t'other one, and what's this I hear of young Oliver wanting to work wi' Kingsley at the newspaper? What happened to his fancy lawyering prospects?"

The inference that the one job was so much less prestigious than the other made Skye fume as much as his bloody nosiness into her business.

"Journalism is an honourable profession, and I'll be very happy if Olly goes into it, since it was once my profession too. As for Celia, she's doing nicely, thank you. Next month she and her boss are going to a trade fair and business conference in Cologne. Displays of White Rivers pottery will be included on the stands."

"You should be pleased," she added, drawing breath, "since the items and brochures on display will include Sebby's new design, as well as the new pottery figurines that he's been working on."

"Is that so?" he said, with apparent disinterest.

"What's wrong with you, Theo? Don't you care that Sebby's making a success of his work?" Skye asked angrily.

"Oh ah. 'Tis fine for now until the Jerries decide that making bombs and aeroplanes is more commercial than fancy pots, and close all the factories down. Then where will you be – and Killigrew Clay as well? It happened once before, and anybody with any sense can see it happening again."

"Don't talk rot, Theo."

"And don't go thinking 'twill never happen. I read the newspapers too, and if I were you, I'd pull my girl out of there quicker'n blinking. But that's not what I want to talk to you about. 'Tis about the offer to merge wi' Bourne's. I've been talking to people, and they're all of the opinion that we should do it now. Once the foreign markets close down on us, they won't want to know. They're willing to pay a handsome sum for coming in with us and I say let's take their money while the offer's still there."

"You've got no right talking to outsiders about our business," she snapped, furious that words might have been bandied about at local hostelries and the like. "And why are you so certain the foreign markets will close down? We haven't done so well for years."

"It won't last," he said prophetically, suddenly calmer than she was. "Your own man believes it, and so do I."

Skye felt a chill like a presentiment run through her veins. Theo sneering and at his bombastic worst was something she could cope with. Theo being serious and far-seeing was out of character, and only underlined the way the world was heading in so many minds now. She clutched at the telephone, and her hands were clammy.

"I won't sell out and I won't merge with Bourne's," she said stubbornly, as if her own determination was a talisman that would keep them all safe.

"Then you're a fool," Theo said, and slammed down the telephone on her.

Skye replaced her own instrument slowly. It always unnerved her when Theo became sensible, and she almost preferred his hot-headed self. When he put things squarely to her, it made her doubt her own intuition, and that was something Skye Pengelly rarely did.

At the thought, it came to her that in her own way she was being as arrogant as Theo. Believing she was always right, and the rest of the world was wrong. She had to admit that Fanny had certainly looked anguished when she told her about her husband's fears for his Jewish family.

She turned with a sense of relief as her son came into the house like a tornado. For the moment at least, she could put aside all the large-scale doubts and worries, and see what it was that had got Olly so excited now. But the moment she got the whiff of him, she knew.

His fingers were stained, and the familiar and pungent scent of printer's ink wafted towards her, taking her back and firing her blood. As David Kingsley had once said, 'once a newshound, always a newshound', and she remembered chiding his nonsense with a laugh. How long ago it all seemed now.

"I've decided," Olly declared.

"Have you?" Skye said, but knowing what was coming.

"I've been at the *Informer* offices all day," he said, with rising excitement. "David's got this little machine that sends through the latest news from various agencies, and it's even faster than telephoning. It's amazing, Mom! I've got to work there. I couldn't do the kind of boring stuff that Nick does all day when I could be part of everything important in the world at the click of a button on a machine. What do you think? Would he be very disappointed in me?"

Skye hid a smile. "So you think sorting out people's personal problems is boring, do you, Olly?"

"I didn't mean that – I thought you'd understand—"

At his flustered look, she hugged him tight. He was fifteen years old now, a young man who had blossomed in the last few months. No longer a child, but still her baby, and she knew well enough not to let on so! She let him go after a quick peck on his cheek.

"Honey, of course I understand, and I would personally be delighted if you went into the reporting business. I'm sure Nick won't be offended that you don't want to be a lawyer. In fact, I'd say he already had a pretty good idea of the way things are going," she added.

"Then if there's another war, I can go to the Front and do what you did in the last one, can't I?" he said eagerly.

Skye's magnanimity vanished at once, and she had a hard job not to slap him.

"Don't say such things! You have no idea what it was like, and I hope you never do."

"But you'll let me start as a junior with David right away, won't you?" he pleaded. "He says I'll learn more about life through that kind of work than anything a dull old school can teach me now."

"Oh, he does, does he? And since when did David Kingsley have a say in my children's education?"

Olly looked uneasy. "I'm sure he didn't mean it that way, Mom. But I know what I want to do now, and Celia and Wenna got their own way, so why can't I?"

"We'll see what your father has to say about it, but I'm not promising anything," she replied, knowing darned well that he was going to get his way too.

And then there were none.

If Nick was disappointed that Olly wasn't going to follow in his footsteps after all, he hid it well. And since Olly was so intent on starting his new career right away, his plea to be allowed to start as a junior in Kingsley's office instead of going to college, was finally agreed to. To Olly's surprise, it was his cousin Justin who was the most sceptical.

"I can't think why you want to be a reporter. There's no glory in that. Who ever heard of a famous newspaperman?"

"Who cares about glory? Is your idea of being a doctor because of the glory?" Olly demanded. "I thought doctors were supposed to have a sense of vocation, like priests."

"I do have a sense of vocation. I want to help people by making them well again."

"So do I, by giving them the truth."

They were glaring at one another, arguing on what was supposed to be a pleasurable walk along the sands on a blue and golden Sunday afternoon. Olly suddenly grinned, wanting to break the tension between them. Wanting to be friends. He spoke recklessly.

"Tell you what. If war comes, like all these gloom merchants say it will, we'll run away and enlist. Then while you're patching up some poor devil at the Front, I'll write down his dying words of praise for his surgeon hero, and report it back to the *Informer*. How does that sound? Then we'll both get the glory."

They both laughed at that, but there was a sense of desperation in Justin's laughter.

"I hope to God it doesn't come to that," he muttered.

He sounded so serious it seemed to Oliver at that moment that the warm air was chilled for an instant, as if a small cloud had shadowed the sun. It hadn't, but the feeling in his gut was just as shivery.

"Come on, I'll race you to the water's edge," he shouted, with the strangest urge to be a small child again when nothing mattered but being pampered and loved.

* * *

Being pampered and loved was the last thing Karina Tremayne had expected when she came to Cornwall in search of a family. Nor had she intended to stay longer than a week or so. The family she had met since her arrival was charming and welcoming, and she adored looking after Lily and David Kingsley's small boys and being accepted into their home.

But it wasn't her home, and as a mellow spring had merged into a blistering summer, and the moorland turf grew browner and more burnt by the sun, she found herself thinking nostalgically of the green hills and meadows of Ireland.

" 'Tis the rain that does it, me darlin'," the old men who sprawled about on wooden benches outside the ale houses would chuckle. "Tis not called the Emerald Isle fer nuthin', and no matter how often you leave it, you'll always come back."

Well, she hadn't been back, but neither had she expected the longing for it to be quite as acute as it was now. Not only because she missed it so, but because she thought of it as a refuge from her trouble. Her only refuge, if she was to escape the shame and disgrace of it all.

She would tell Ethan that very night. Not the whole of it, of course. She would merely tell him she could no longer stay in Cornwall, without giving him a reason, even though it would break her heart to do so. But she wasn't going to burden him with her trouble. It was hers and hers alone.

As she brushed through her glossy hair that evening before he came to meet her for a stroll along the Truro riverbank, she knew that only a fool could miss the way her eyes were huge and dark in the pinched pallor of her face.

"Mother of God, forgive me," her lips murmured imperceptibly. " 'Tis lie upon lie, but it has to be done."

If there was anything ironic in the words she chose, she refused to notice it. It was lying in Ethan Pengelly's arms that had given her the trouble, which in any other circumstances would be the most wonderful thing on earth.

She passed a hand lightly over her stomach, feeling the imperceptible roundness of it, and her mouth trembled. How could she ever confess to this so-respectable family that passion had got the better of her and Ethan, and that this was the penalty for giving in to sin?

Even so, she wondered briefly how anyone could ever compare

the love and the oneness two people had shared so spectacularly, with words like giving in? It had been a mutual passion that had taken them to the stars but now it had to end, before she ruined a good man as well as herself.

If ever the sins of the mothers were to be borne by the daughters, she found herself thinking, remembering her own shock at discovering that her mother had been Bradley Tremayne's lover for all those years.

Once Karina had decided that bearing her disgrace alone was her penance, she knew she had to deal with it in her own way. It wasn't so easy to be strong when she saw Ethan's tall, powerful form striding along to meet her on that summer evening. She felt her heart turn over with love at the sight of him. He took her hand in his as he murmured her name, and his eyes looked adoringly at her.

"God, but I've missed you," he said. "Do you realise it's three whole days since I've seen you?"

They had reached their favourite secluded spot in a grassy hollow and sank down together. His body was half covering hers, his arms round her, caressing her through her thin summer dress. His mouth was warm and eager on hers before she found the strength to pull away from him.

"Ethan, I've got something to tell you," she said weakly.

"God, that sounds worrying. What have I done?" he teased.

She tried to smile. He would never know what he had done – what they had both done. It wasn't fair to burden him with this. If she stayed, she would be disgraced and ostracised, and so would he. If she left, she could merge into obscurity with a cheap wedding ring on her finger and claim to be a poor widow. It was the only way.

"Well, come on," he said, when she fell silent. "It can't be anything too awful. You're far too sweet-natured and beautiful to have committed a crime, so what is it?"

She held him close to her, unable to look into his eyes and see the misery she knew would be there in a few minutes. She didn't intend to tell anyone except him her decision, only Lily was going to know before she was safely on the boat for home. No one was going to stop her.

"My love, I'm going back to Ireland very soon. I have to go, and I shan't be coming back."

141

She murmured the words against his shoulder, and it was all she could say before her throat closed up. She felt him go rigid and then his fingers gripped her arms so hard she almost cried out.

"What are you saying?" he asked roughly. "What's brought this on? Are you ill?"

She shook her head. "No, not ill," she whispered.

"Then *tell* me, Karina. I have a right to know. I thought we meant everything to one another."

"So we do. Oh, so we do . . ."

He stared into her eyes as if he would see into her soul.

"Then why are you leaving me?" he said at last. "Is there someone else? Someone you knew before you came here?"

"There is no one else – not in the way you mean." The minute she had said it, she knew it was a mistake. She bit her lip hard, tasting blood, her eyes were lowered, she was unable to meet his gaze, her whole body trembling.

"My God," Ethan whispered. Without another word, his hand went down to her belly.

She gave a shuddering sob as he folded her to him.

"Is this the reason? Are you having a child – our child?"

She had been prepared to lie, but he held her captive, insisting that she looked into his eyes, and it was impossible for her to continue the lie.

"Yes," she mumbled. "But 'tis my trouble, not yours. 'Tis my decision to go, and I'll not force you into anything—"

"*Trouble*? You call the creation of a child between us a *trouble*? Don't you think we share this? And how dare you call it a trouble, or think that I would ever let you leave me."

She looked at him through tear-drowned eyes.

"No, my love, I can't let you do this. Think what people would say. Your family – Skye and Nick – I couldn't face them. I won't stay here to be shamed, and to shame you."

He didn't speak for a few moments. He just stroked her cheek, holding her close and feeling her erratic heartbeat.

"It's no shame for a married couple to have a child—"

"I'll not force you into marriage," she said fiercely. "My mother did no such thing, and neither will I."

She knew she was reminding him that she was illegitimate. Unwittingly she had opened the door to everything he wanted to say since she had given him the momentous news.

142

"Nobody's forcing me, darling girl. But I've no intention of letting my child – our child – be born out of wedlock. But you're right. You can't stay here, and neither can I. Your father went to Ireland and made a new life for himself, and you want to be back there where you belong. So we'll both go, and before we do, we'll be married quietly. The respectable Pengellys will have arrived to make a new start."

"We can't! What would you do? Your life is here. Your family is here. You're a skilled man, Ethan—"

He shushed her with a kiss. "Don't Irish folk need pots? As you say, I'm a skilled man, and I'll soon find work. As for my family here – what would any of them mean to me without you? *You're* my family now – you, and our child."

Before she knew what he was going to do, he had bent his head, and kissed her softly rounded belly. As she held his head close to her, she could have sworn she felt the baby give a slight movement, but she couldn't have done – not yet.

She took it as a sign though, a sign that this was the right thing to do. That their love and their decision was approved by the Holy One above, and for a lapsed Catholic, it was a feeling that was at once awesome and unutterably sweet.

Ten

They made their plans. They wanted no fuss. A number of letters needed to be written which would be delivered after the simple marriage service had been arranged, and they were safely on their way to Ireland. All anyone would be told was that they had married and decided to make a new life for themselves there. The only people who were to know of their departure in advance were Lily, and Ethan's older brother, Adam.

When Ethan went to see him, he was shocked at the uncared for state of the house that Vera had once kept so spick and span.

"What the hell have you been doing to yourself?" he exclaimed, seeing how unkempt his brother was, and seemingly not even noticing.

"Who cares about me?" he shrugged.

"Well, I do and so does Nick," Ethan said, but he was filled with guilt at the thought of how little he had seen of his brother since Vera's death.

Apart from being prised out of his hermit-like existence to spend Christmas at New World, Adam had insisted on being left alone, and they had all honoured his wish. But the sight of him and his surroundings was alarming.

"I'm going to open some windows. It's foul in here," Ethan went on. "And then I've got something to tell you in strictest confidence. I want you to do something for me."

"If you'm trying to get me married off again, you can forget it," Adam said roughly.

"I don't want to get you married off, you old fool. It's me that's getting married."

He hadn't meant to blurt it out like that, but at least it had the effect of making Adam's eyes show a flicker of interest. But before his brother could make some all-too emotive comment

145

like hoping Ethan hadn't got some young wench into trouble, he rushed on.

"Now listen, Adam. Me and Karina Tremayne have been seeing one another for some time and we want to get wed, but she's homesick for Ireland, so we're going there to live. You know how much of an uproar that will create in the family, so we aim to do it quietly and without any fuss."

At his brother's gaping look, he smiled faintly.

"I know it's a bit of a shock, but before you say anything else, there's no shotgun to my head. This is our choice, and naturally we'll need money behind us. So that's where you come in."

"Well, I ain't got no money to speak of, but you can have all I can spare," he said at once.

"That's not what I mean, Adam, but I thank you from my heart," Ethan said, touched at the ready response. "I won't be needing our old family house when Karina and me go to Ireland. I want you to get Nick to arrange the sale of it, and then see that the money's transferred to an Irish bank. Karina's getting in touch with her old lawyer, and he'll contact Nick to make further arrangements about the money."

"You've really thought all this out, haven't you?" Adam said with grudging admiration.

"I'm not your kid brother any longer, Adam. I'm twenty-six, in case you haven't noticed, and Karina's twenty-four, so we don't need anyone's permission."

"So since you're a man, why don't you ask Nick about all this yourself?"

"I told you. We don't want any fuss or arguments. We've made up our minds, and we just want to be together as soon as possible. You understand that, don't you?"

For the first time in a long time, Adam Pengelly's face softened. Oh yes, he remembered only too well when he and Vera only had eyes and hands for each other, and couldn't wait to be alone together, desperate for each other's touch.

"Aye, I understand. So when is all this to happen?"

"We're leaving next week. We're getting married in Newquay, and taking the afternoon ferry for Cork."

"You'll want someone to stand up for you," Adam said. "At least let me do that."

Ethan squeezed his arm, aware of how thin it had got, but

thankful that there was a spark more animation in his brother now than when he had arrived.

"I'd be honoured, bruth. And there's one more thing you can do for me."

"Name it. If I can, I'll do it."

"You can do it better than anyone else in the county. Your skill was once legendary, long before I was knee-high to throwing a pot, and Seb will be missing a good work partner when I leave. I want you to go back to your old job and get back in the world again. I mean it, Adam."

His brother didn't speak for a few moments, staring at the chair where Vera used to sit, and where his strong young brother was sitting so tensely now, reminding him that life went on, and that if he wanted to be, he was still part of it.

"And you think Skye will want me back, do you?" he said slowly, as if still needing confirmation. "You think Seb will want me as a work partner?"

"Why wouldn't they want the best?"

Adam suddenly laughed. "My God, if that's the kind of flattery you give Karina, no wonder she's fallen for you."

Ethan grinned. "Then you'll do it? All of it?"

Imperceptibly, Adam straightened his shoulders, and Ethan knew what a momentous decision he was making. To come out of the shadows and face the world again couldn't be easy.

"All of it, bruth. You have my word on it."

They were married at twelve noon on a bright June morning, and as Ethan slipped the ring onto Karina's finger and said the words that would bind them together for life, he saw the conflicting emotions on his brother's face, and knew he was remembering another day, another time.

But Adam had already changed, smartened his appearance, cut his wild hair. He was preparing, this very afternoon when the newly-weds had sailed for Ireland, to carry out the rest of his promises: to deliver letters, and to talk to the people whose approval Ethan still needed.

At the last moment, once Karina had told Lily of her plans and vowed that nothing would change them, Lily had arranged for someone to look after her children and insisted on coming to Newquay to see her and Ethan married. And when they had left

amid tears of mixed emotions, Lily and Adam drove back to the
moors above St Austell together.

"Now to face the music, eh?" she said quietly.

She glanced at him, knowing of his heartbreak when her sister
Vera had died, and wondering just how this day had affected
him. "Is there anything I can do for you, Adam?"

He shook his head. "I have to see Skye and Nick first of all,
and then I'll be calling on Seb Tremayne. I'm considering going
back to work at the pottery. What do you think?"

"I think it's the best damn news I've heard all day – well, apart
from the fact that the newly-weds looked so happy, of course.
Good for you, Adam. It's time."

"I know." And already, ever since his brother had made
the suggestion, his fingers were itching to hold the familiar,
sensuous wet clay in his hands and transform it to whatever
shape he desired. Her words were true. It was more than
time.

"I can't believe it!" Skye said, after she and Nick had read the
letters Adam delivered. "How could they go off and do this
without telling us?"

"It was the way they both wanted it," Adam told her. "It was
their choice. The letter to Nick explains everything about selling
the house. You'll see to it, won't you, Nick?"

"Of course I will, and there shouldn't be any problem about
selling it quickly, nor arranging for the proceeds to be paid into
an Irish bank," he answered.

Apart from feeling a mild resentment that his younger brother
hadn't confided in him first, he was more than thankful to see
Adam behaving like his old self, rather than the recluse he had
become.

Skye wasn't so ready to be mollified, having a woman's
natural reaction to being done out of a family wedding. It would
have been so lovely to have everyone there and given Karina a
beautiful send off. She wondered how Wenna was going to take
the news. Wenna had been crazy about Ethan ever since her
childhood, although the feeling had surely waned of late. Skye
turned her thoughts away from it, as something else came
uppermost in her mind.

"And what about the pottery – the orders we've got – I

suppose Ethan realises he's left us in the lurch without a master potter to work with Seb?"

"Seb will still have a master potter to work with – if you'll have me," Adam said.

The reaction from Theo was predictable, saying he'd expected trouble from the moment he laid eyes on the Irish wench. At which point Adam froze him with a look, reminding him that that first time was at Vera's burying.

"Well, good luck to them, I say," Betsy said. "It's the most romantic thing I've heard in a long time."

"Romantic," Theo snorted. "If that ain't just like a woman to give no thought to what the pair of 'em are going to do. What's the plan — to raise horses like old Freddie and Bradley did? A fat lot they'd know about that!"

"Leave it, Theo," Betsy said sharply. "You've got about as much romance in your soul as a toad. What does it matter what they do? It's nothing to do with us."

Theo turned his attenion to Adam, as if noticing for the first time that he had come out of his shell.

"So what's to do with you, then? I thought you'd taken root in that place of yours."

"I was beginning to think so too. That's what I've come to see Seb about."

He wasn't going to explain to this oaf that his need to work was becoming more urgent by the minute. He hadn't realised how much he'd missed it. A man's wife and a man's work – they couldn't compare – but in the matter of need they were one and the same to Adam Pengelly right now.

"Seb's still up at White Rivers," Betsy told him. "He's taken to staying on later now that he's making these little pottery figures. Here, I'll show you."

Adam followed Betsy into the parlour where a row of pottery dolphins looked back at him: there were single figures; sets of connected dolphin families; others were perched on the rims of ashtrays. Adam's skilled eyes recognised that all were superbly made. They made his pulses race.

"These are excellent," he said.

" 'Tis Sebby's new ideas," Betsy said with pride. "He's come a long way since you taught him how to fashion the clay."

"He certainly has. I think the pupil could show the teacher a thing or two," he murmured. "Anyway, I'd best be off. I have several more errands to do before dark."

And one of them was to hightail it up to White Rivers before Seb Tremayne left the premises, and see what other interesting ideas the boy had developed.

As he drove away from the house and started back up the long road towards the moors, he felt a rush of adrenalin such as he hadn't felt in a very long time. It wasn't the same feeling that a man felt for a woman, but it was a good and honest feeling all the same.

Skye worded the letter to her daughter very carefully. She had had several ecstatic letters from Wenna in the weeks since she had gone to London with Fanny, and she always made a regular weekend telephone call to her parents. But this was something Skye didn't want to tell her over the telephone. This was something that Wenna needed to read and digest alone. She had the added thought that if she needed to weep, Fanny's broad and comforting shoulder would surely be at the ready.

Fanny saw the way Wenna's smile faded a little as she stared at her mother's handwriting.

"Bad news, duck?" she asked.

"No. Unexpected, though," Wenna said, surprised that the stab of jealousy she would have expected didn't come.

So much had been happening in the last weeks that her childhood passion for Ethan Pengelly had been the last thing on her mind. Besides, she had known that he and Karina only had eyes for each other, and had mutely accepted it.

She went on hurriedly as she saw Fanny's expectant look. "My stepfather's brother and my Irish cousin have got married and left Cornwall to set up home in Ireland."

"Good Gawd, you folks do believe in keepin' it in the fam'ly, don't yer?" Fanny said with a chuckle. "I never heard of such going's-on."

"It's not going's-on," Wenna said. "Mom says everyone was surprised, but maybe we should have seen it coming, since they always got along well."

"*Very* well, I'd say," Fanny commented, but wisely said no

more. Whatever the circumstances behind the hasty nuptials of the couple, it was clear that this little sweetheart didn't suspect anything other than a whirlwind romance. She was far from dumb, but in some respects she was one of the world's innocents, and as such, Fanny felt as fiercely protective of her as if she had been her own. And for someone who had no maternal instincts whatsoever, it was a feeling that surprised her.

It was those eyes, she thought, those bleedin' beautiful blue eyes that could melt a man's heart and which were going to bring hoardes of customers to the Flamingo Club as soon as she was launched on the scene.

As yet, Wenna hadn't been tried out properly. She had to be eased in gently to a very different way of life. Fanny and Georgie had taken pains to introduce her first to the sights and sounds of London, and to various acquaintances.

As a preliminary test, and in order to steady the girl's nerve, it was suggested that she sang a couple of songs on several of their quieter evenings early in the week. It had been an undoubted success, especially when she had accompanied herself on the piano and revealed her second talent. Fanny soon realised that this was more than a good idea, it was a brilliant one. However nervous Wenna felt when she stood alone and faced the dimly lit audience, her nerves seemed to fall away when she had the prop of her beloved piano keys beneath those sensitive fingers. She caressed them and stroked them, putting all the feeling in the world into the music. The combination of the rippling notes and her soft, sensual voice was enough to send a shivery feeling through the most hardened club goer.

Oh yes, she was going to be an asset all right, Fanny thought lovingly. The customers already adored her. Gloria del Mar was still the glamorous Saturday night star performer at the Flamingo, but it was obvious that Wenna wasn't simply a decorative female who could sing in tune. It was clear to the talent-spotting Rosenblooms that this girl had depth as well as beauty.

Fanny blessed the day that Skye Tremayne, as she had been then, had come into her life during the Great War, and led her to this singing discovery. It was weird how a chance meeting in a war could lead you into directions you never anticipated, Fanny mused. Wars weren't all bad . . .

Her thoughts were brought up with a jolt, remembering the

hazardous lives of Georgie's family in Vienna. If this was a hint of things to come, then her thoughts were downright wicked. There was nothing good about a war. *Nothing*. Georgie's own recent letter from his father had been full of pain and humiliation at the news that Adolph Hitler had now forbidden German children to speak or play with Jewish children. It was the work of an evil man, to recruit children into such hatred, Georgie had declared savagely. Fanny shivered, and made herself listen to what Wenna was saying.

"Are you all right, Fanny?" Wenna asked her. "You look a little green about the gills, as they say."

"I'm fine, lovey, just wondering what else yer ma has ter say. Anything more to report?" she asked, forcing her own worries aside for now.

"Mom says Uncle Theo is still urging her to agree to merging the clayworks with another company. Mom will hold out though. Oh, and Nick's other brother is going back to work at the pottery. He's a master potter," she added proudly.

Fanny gave a small smile. No matter how long Wenna remained with them in London, she would never reject her Cornishness. They all had it. Few of them moved away for ever, at least not the ones she had met, which weren't that many, she conceded. Just the Tremaynes and their close-knit family, by whatever name they used.

Which brought her to something else she'd been meaning to say for a while, and she spoke carefully.

"Wenna, have you ever thought of changing' yer name? Havin' a stage name, I mean, summat glamorous like Gloria's. Wenna Pengelly's a bit of a mouthful, ain't it? It'd take up a lot of space on a billboard, fer instance."

Wenna heard nothing but that one word. Billboard.

"I can't imagine I'd ever have my name on a billboard, Fanny. Like famous people do, I mean!" she added, momentarily dazzled by the very idea.

"Why not?" Fanny saw the sudden gleam in Wenna's eyes, and pushed home the advantage, while giving her time to mull over the suggestion. "Why ever bleedin' not, gel?"

Wenna laughed again. The first time she and Celia ever met Fanny, they had been enchanted by the racy and daring way the woman spoke, and had shocked their stepfather by repeating the forbidden word. But Nick wasn't around now, and Wenna wasn't a gullible child any more. She grinned.

"Well, I'll think about it. Why ever bleedin' not!"

She wrote to Celia that night. Celia might think it was a disloyal thing to do to change her name. But since all three Norwood children had changed their names to Pengelly when their mother had married Nick, she couldn't see the difference. But as ever, Wenna needed her sister's approval and advice – and any suggestions for the glamorous new name she might choose.

If she did it, then the entire world was at her disposal, she slowly realised. She could be whatever and whoever she chose. And it would only be a stage name. It wouldn't change her real self. She couldn't deny a shiver of excitement at the very words – stage name – they evoked a world of glamour Wenna had never known existed until now. As yet, she had only got the merest glimpse of it. Fanny was a far stricter chaperon than anyone might have suspected. She was a dear friend, but Wenna already knew there were far greater prospects than being involved in this delightful little club of Fanny and Georgie's. The stage, and the movies, where the handsomest of Greek gods worshipped at their golden goddesses' feet.

And at that wild and heady thought, she came totally down to earth and told herself not to be so dippy.

"You have something on your mind, *liebling*," Stefan von Gruber said to his dinner companion.

Their final day at the three-day June trade fair and business conference was over, and tomorrow they would return to Berlin from the beautiful city of Cologne, and report their success to Herr Vogl.

White Rivers pottery was only a part of the goods that the Vogl empire supplied, but to Celia's pleasure it had created a lot of interest in its pure white simplicity.

She smiled apologetically. "I'm sorry, Stefan. I didn't mean to be rude. I'm still feeling surprised at the letter from my sister, and wondering how to answer it."

"Ah yes. The budding singing star," he said with a smile.

"Do you believe that?" she asked. "That she'll ever be a star, I mean – and famous?"

"Don't you? Is it so impossible to imagine?"

"Oh, I'm not denying that she has a beautiful voice, and she plays the piano superbly. Nor am I in the least jealous of her," Celia said hastily, in case he should think otherwise. "It's just that – well, to me, I suppose she's just Wenna."

"That's because you know her so well. To her, you're just Celia, while to me, you will never be 'just Celia'."

She felt her heartbeats quicken as his voice deepened. These three days and nights away from Berlin had been for official purposes. The hotel rooms that had been allocated to them were on the same floor for the convenience of business contacts. Nothing improper was intended, or had happened.

But Celia would be a fool if she didn't know that as the days passed, the sexual tension between herself and Stefan was reaching fever-pitch. Their successful business dealings had been as potent as an aphrodisiac to them both, and this was the last evening, when they could relax and be themselves.

He reached across the table and took her hand in his. His eyes were dark with desire, and she caught her breath.

"Celia, you know what I want more than anything, don't you, *liebling*?"

"Yes," she said softly, because she had never been less than honest with her own feelings and whatever he wanted, she wanted too. And all these months he had behaved with such impeccable manners.

"But as I told you once before, you're nineteen, and I'm thirty-six—"

"And what in hell's name does that have to do with anything?" she said in a cracked, almost inaudible voice, not noticing the words she used until she saw him smile.

"My lovely, adorable Celia, you are totally delightful, and it is just as you say. What in hell's name does that have to do with anything?"

Celia awoke with a feeling of tremendous warmth and well-being, stretching her limbs as slowly and elegantly as a sleek Persian cat. For a few seconds she couldn't think where she was, until she felt the soft breeze of someone else's breath on her skin. Her eyes flickered open slowly, as if to preserve the moment, as if to hold on to this most intimate of moments before she looked into the face of her lover . . . no longer merely her boss, but her *lover*.

She heard his voice, the words whispered close to her mouth, his lips moving over hers so sensuously. "No other morning will ever compare with today, my love, when we awoke in one another's arms."

She felt his arms tighten round her, and her naked body was being moulded to his, the way it had been through the wonderful, erotic hours of the night. She had adored him then and she adored him now, for not moving away from her, or making her feel that this had been wrong, or a mistake, or cheap, or an expected part of a business weekend. She couldn't have borne it if she had looked into his eyes and seen any of that. Instead, she saw only love, and the yearning to be where they had been only a few hours earlier, before sleep overcame them.

She yearned too, to be so much a part of him again that they were truly one. She *ached* for him to love her again.

"Do I shock you for wanting you so much, my sweet girl?" he murmured next, as she seemed so silent.

"Of course not," she whispered back. "The wanting is not only confined to you, Stefan."

Even so, her face was fiery as she said the words, as the teachings of the Swiss school surged into her mind. *Nice* girls didn't go with men until they were married, and even then, they didn't admit to wanton desires. *Nice* girls certainly didn't have clandestine relationships in hotel bedrooms.

He bent his head and kissed the burning cheeks.

"Then I thank God that you are not one of those prissy young ladies, when I feel the need to explore every inch of your loveliness all over again."

She gave up thinking of anything then, and let the sweet sensations of his lovemaking take control of her. Touching, and tasting, and caressing, and discovering the unknown pleasures in reciprocating, until their mutual need for fulfilment could no longer be denied.

When he finally gripped her tight and gasped against her, murmuring words of endearment in German that she couldn't even begin to understand, she knew that none of it mattered. All that mattered was that he was here with her, and that it was where she wanted him to stay for ever.

He remained, spent, against her body, for some moments, until she simply had to shift his weight slightly, if only to breathe. Even then, they simply rolled sideways, still a part of one another, until nature decreed otherwise.

"You see what you do to me, *liebling*," he teased, as she felt him dwindle. "You have taken everything."

"And you have taken everything from me," she whispered. "You do know that, don't you?"

His fingers caressed her hot cheeks, gently moving the dark hair back from her forehead.

"Do you think I don't know that I was the first? Or that I would have wanted it any other way? A man who finds purity in his wife is truly blessed."

"His wife?"

He looked into her eyes. "You must know that I want to marry you, Celia. I have always wanted it, but it was too soon, and you were too—"

She put her trembling fingers over his mouth. "If you say that I was too young, I shall hit you," she said. But reality was fast catching up with her now. "All the same there are others who will say I am too young for marriage, especially since I would need their permission."

Her own words made her feel even younger and more gauche and vulnerable, and she gave a small laugh.

"Anyway, you haven't asked me properly yet!"

Stefan laughed too, folding her in his arms and refusing to let any sign of a cloud dampen this moment.

"Then I'm asking you now, my beautiful Celia. No matter how long it takes, will you marry me?"

She caught her breath. "I will," she said solemnly, "no matter how long it takes." Then she came down to earth and wrinkled her nose ruefully. "As a matter of fact, Stefan, I know exactly how long it will take. My parents will refuse to let me marry anyone until I come of age."

And that was not until November of 1939, almost a year and a half away. Celia's eyes were full of consternation as she realised the fact. What worldly man like Stefan von Gruber would be willing to wait so long for a girl to become officially a woman? Even though, to them, that deed had already been accomplished.

Stefan kissed her fingertips with the utmost tenderness.

"Then we must be patient, *liebling*, and do nothing to betray your parents' trust."

She looked away. Did that mean no more lovemaking? she thought tremulously. Now that she had experienced desire and fulfilment, how could she bear to forget the joy of it for so long? But she couldn't ask him, or broach the subject so blatantly, even now when they had been everything to one another. There were some things a young lady didn't do, and even the outspoken Celia Pengelly didn't go that far.

A second letter from Wenna awaiting her when she got back to the hostel in Berlin told her that Stefan had been absolutely right. However strong their passion, she couldn't bear to bring disgrace on her family, nor on Stefan's. She knew little about his background, she realised, except that his parents were elderly and lived somewhere deep in the German countryside. He never discussed them.

She read Wenna's second letter, which was more frantic in tone than the first. It was little more than a note, really, and bursting with indignation.

What do think, sis? Fanny had a bit too much to drink the other night, and got very talkative. She reckons that Karina and Ethan are expecting a baby, and that's why they got married so quickly and ran away to Ireland. I didn't know what to think, but if it's true, I'm glad I don't have to have anything more to do with either of them. I think it's absolutely beastly and disgusting.

I'm thinking about changing my name to Penny Wood for stage purposes. What do you think? Does it sound all right? I thought it was quite clever – a mixture of Pengelly and Norwood to keep the parents happy. Do you get it?

Celia stared at the letter for a long time, ignoring the final effusiveness of Wenna's choice of name, and thinking only of the first part. Beastly and disgusting were not words she would associate with her recent ecstatic time with Stefan. But if the outcome should be the same as Fanny Rosenbloom was surmising about the other two . . . Celia shivered.

As if to add fuel to Stefan's determination to keep passion at bay between them, there was an urgent message for him a week after their return to Berlin. Celia took the message and relayed it to him anxiously.

"You're asked to telephone this number immediately, Herr von Gruber," she said formally, for the benefit of anyone else who might be within earshot.

She handed him the slip of paper on which she had written the number. He immediately picked up the telephone, and spoke rapidly once he was connected. Celia's German was excellent, and she had no difficulty in understanding the one-sided conversation. When it ended, Stefan's face was drawn, and he began automatically pushing things into his briefcase.

"My father has had a severe stroke and is in hospital," he informed Celia, glancing at his watch. "There is just time for me to catch the noon plane. Please contact Gunter Schmit and advise him to take over my duties until further notice. I'll leave you to deal with anything else pertaining to the trade fair. And also inform Herr Vogl that I will be in touch with him personally as soon as possible."

Celia wondered if he realised just how remote he sounded. Her hands were rigid by her sides, thinking him a stranger again, even while she understood his reactions. Of course she did. His father could be dying, and he needed to be by his side, but all the same, she felt as if she had just been given a slap in the face, as if she meant no more to him than any other employee to be given instructions while he was away. He had shared nothing with her, other than the stark facts of what he had just been told about his next movements. His words were cold and curt, as only a German could form them. The thought was in her head before she could stop it.

Without realising that she did so, she stepped back a pace, not quite knowing how to react if he was to clumsily apologise for his abruptness. He did not. He merely glanced about him to check on the habitually tidy state of his desk for his deputy manager to take over.

"I'll attend to everything," she murmured, "and I hope your father makes a full recovery."

"Thank you." He looked at her properly then. "Celia, I'm sorry. I'll call you as soon as there is any news, but my mind is so scattered I can think of nothing else at this moment."

"I understand, Stefan," she said generously, but if this precision of thought was that of a scattered mind, then what on earth must he think of everyday scatterbrains like hers!

"I'll call you," he said again, as if he could think of nothing more to say. As he passed her he squeezed her arm, and she felt her eyes sting at his lack of tenderness, when she knew he was capable of all the love in the world.

"What an idiot I am," she told herself angrily a few minutes later, as she watched from the window of the high office building as he hurried to his car and drove quickly away. "How can anyone be expected to behave in a normal fashion after hearing bad news? I didn't really expect a passionate goodbye here in the office, did I?"

She chided herself severely, and got down to the business that needed urgent attention. The first thing was to contact Gunter Schmit and ask him to report to the office to take over Stefan's duties as soon as possible. She disliked the oily little man intensely, and hoped she wouldn't need to work with him for very long. Then she telephoned Herr Vogl.

His voice was cordial when he answered.

"How pleasant to hear from you, Celia, although I'm sorry for von Gruber's sad news. But it's fortuitous that you telephoned, my dear, since I have been meaning to contact you. Perhaps you would like to come to dinner on Saturday evening? I have seen your report of the trade fair in Cologne, and congratulate you and von Gruber on your successful dealings there. But now I have a proposition for you that I hope you'll find interesting."

"Then I thank you for the dinner invitation, Herr Vogl. I shall look forward to seeing you on Saturday evening."

She put down the telephone slowly. A dinner invitation from the company head wasn't so much an invitation as a royal command. Her brain whirled, wondering just what kind of proposition he had in mind for her. An increase in salary, or a bonus after their successful trade fair results? As long as it wasn't extra duties within the company. She certainly didn't want that. She was happy here with Stefan.

She turned with a forced smile as Gunter Schmit's weasel-like face appeared at her office door, already puffed up with importance at the thought of taking over Stefan's managerial role for a while. She shivered, as if the mid-summer day had already turned a shade colder.

Eleven

"I've had very good reports of you, Celia, and you'll have discovered by now that I like to move my people around. It keeps them on their toes, as you English people say," Herr Vogl said easily, when dinner at the mansion was over, and the long-awaited proposition was finally about to be aired.

Until then, Celia had been in an agony of suspense, knowing better than to ask for information, and being obliged to listen to Frau Vogl's twittering praise of how Franz was now one of Herr Hitler's brownshirts. What little she knew of the fanatical rallies of this group smacked of a ghastly organisation intent on conquering and squashing lesser mortals, if not the world. But she smiled and tried to look interested, while being utterly thankful that her feelings for the arrogant Franz Vogl had long ago disappeared.

She turned her attention away from Frau Vogl to listen to her husband, and then she felt her face blanch.

"Our Cologne people were so impressed with you, Celia, that they have requested you be transferred to our office there for a time. I've now spoken at length with von Gruber on the telephone, and as his father is seriously ill, we have agreed that he must take indefinite leave until the situation is resolved one way or another. If the worst comes, he will need to remain there, of course. For the time being, Schmit will be in control of his department here, and it's reasonable for him to want to appoint his own assistant. So the way seems clear for you to accept the Cologne post, providing you approve the idea, naturally."

He kept smiling, but Celia knew that her approval was no more than a formality. She was being banished to Cologne to work with people she hardly knew. Stefan was out of her reach, somewhere in the German countryside caring for a desperately sick father, with all the signs suggesting he would stay there until he died. She had found out by now that Stefan was no pauper, so he would certainly be needed to administer his father's estate when the inevitable happened, as Herr Vogl said.

But to Celia, still reeling at the swiftness of how things were changing, it all seemed so cut and dried, as slick and efficient as she knew these people to be. And for the first time since coming to work in Germany, she felt as if she was in an alien country among people whose culture she didn't know or understand.

She swallowed. "Do I have a choice?" she dared to say.

Vogl's smile never wavered. "Well, of course you do, my dear. You can always go back to England and work for your mother, or take up some other employment. No one is holding you here against your will."

God, he was colder than an iceberg, Celia thought furiously. "But if I stay, I must go to Cologne and work there? Is there no other position for me in Berlin?"

She spoke calmly enough, but inwardly she was like a boiling cauldron, seething, not only at the indignity and unfairness of it all, but at the way she was practically grovelling to this pompous prig. It wasn't Celia Pengelly's style, and she resented it bitterly.

"We like to think of our management people as a team, Celia," Vogl said. "You and von Gruber worked well together. If and when he returns to the company, then naturally we shall think again."

"Is there a real doubt about his return then?" Celia said, all else forgotten for the moment, as her whole world seemed to fall apart.

Vogl looked at her thoughtfully. "How much do you know of him personally, Celia?"

Her face burned, wondering just what he meant by that remark, but thankfully, Frau Vogl intervened.

"Now you've embarrassed Celia, *liebe*. Please explain yourself properly."

He held up his hand in apology. Celia guessed he rarely did so verbally. She remembered his family's stiffness at her eighteenth birthday party, and began to wonder why the dickens she had come here in the first place.

"The von Grubers are a very old and wealthy family, and Stefan von Gruber will inherit vast areas of productive vineries on his father's death," he said. "He will not choose to leave it once he becomes the controller of the Von Gruber Estates."

"Why has he felt the need to leave it until now?" Celia heard herself saying numbly, tring to comprehend all he was telling her. "Why hasn't he always been the controller?"

She stumbled over the word, her mind spinning. She didn't know him at all, she realised. She didn't know any of them. None of them revealed more than they chose to outsiders. The insidious rise to power of Herr Adolph Hitler had proven such a trait only too well.

"His father insisted that Stefan made his own way in the world, and not to let it be known that he was due to inherit a fortune, for obvious reasons," Vogl went on. "Until now the estate has been managed by a caretaker controller. I'm sure that will change when the younger man is in charge."

"You knew nothing of this, Celia?" Frau Vogl asked.

"I did not. I was his personal assistant in the office, but we did not speak of private personal matters."

The distinction was bitterly ironic, when for one magical night they had been everything in the world to one another.

The memory of his whispered words when he had asked her to be his wife were like chaff to her now. Why would the wealthy and so cool-headed Stefan von Gruber, head of the Von Gruber Estates, ever want to marry a hot-blooded Cornish girl?

Especially one who might take advantage of the fact that he was due to inherit a fortune. The inference of fortune hunter did not escape her, and her face burned anew.

"May I have time to consider this offer, please?"

"Of course. There's no hurry. In fact, since Herr Schmit and his team will want to make their own arrangements in the office, I suggest that you take some time off. Go home for a month and decide what you want to do."

She kept her eyes lowered, wondering if she was really necessary to this company at all if he could so glibly offer her a month's holiday. She would damn well take it too, she thought furiously. There was no way she could work comfortably with Gunter Schmit and his team. He would have his own personal assistant, and there would be nothing for Celia to do. She had no intention of being passed over like a lost memo in the pending tray.

"Thank you, sir. I will take the month at home, and let you know my decision in due course," she said with dignity.

She cleared up her work at the office, and by the time she was ready to leave Berlin, she still had not heard from Stefan. She was bruised and shocked inside, and like a wounded animal she felt the need to run and hide, to be home where she belonged. She telephoned her mother in advance.

"How lovely that you're being given such a long holiday!" her mother said delightedly. "Tell us exactly when and where you'll be arriving, and we'll meet you."

Celia was choked at the warmth and pleasure in her mother's voice. Her pride hadn't let her reveal the whole situation, and she knew immediately she needed a little more time before she actually faced them all.

"Mom, would you mind if I stayed in London for a few days first? I haven't seen this place where Wenna's living, or what she's up to, and it will break the journey."

In the small pause before Skye answered, Celia knew her mother had heard far more than the impulsive words her daughter spoke. Her mother could always tell.

"I think that's a lovely idea, darling," Skye said. "Wenna will be thrilled to see you. I suppose you know she's going to go by the name of Penny Wood now?"

"So I heard. What do you think about it?" she said, making a huge effort to drag her thoughts round to the mundane question of Wenna's proposed stage name.

What the hell did it matter in the great scheme of things? What did anything matter but the fact that Celia was about to leave Germany, and that she would probably never see her lover again? She smothered a sob in her throat.

"She's sensible enough to know what she's doing," Skye said, "and so are you, my love. Come home when you're ready. Make it soon."

Skye replaced the telephone receiver slowly, more troubled than she wanted to admit. There had been desperation in Celia's voice and a resignation that wasn't healthy in someone so young – someone who had been on the brink of falling in love and having a wonderful life, if her mother had read all the signs correctly.

She didn't know what had gone wrong, but she was very sure that something had.

"It's surely unusual for her to be given an entire month's holiday, Nick," she said to her husband. "I'm tempted to contact Herr Vogl on some business pretext to find out if everything is all right. What do you think?"

"I think you should leave well alone," he said firmly. "Celia has been independent for some while now. Let her sort this out for herself – whatever it is. She certainly won't thank you for going behind her back and interfering."

"I know you're right," Skye said in frustration, "but it's never easy for a mother to know when a thing is interfering or just honest to goodness caring."

Nick put his arms around her. "Well, one thing's for sure, darling. She knows you care. You've always shown that you care for all of them. But you know it's important to let them go their own way. You didn't even raise your eyebrows at this damn nonsense of Wenna's about changing her name."

"Oh, Nick, you know the reason for that! If she's going to be a singer, she has to have a name that people will remember and can say easily. You must admit that Wenna Pengelly is a mouthful. I thought you'd be pleased that she combined both our names in the way she has."

His smile widened. "Of course I'm pleased. But the lawyer in me has to be objective and see every angle."

"Well then, you should see that this makes sense," she cut in neatly, guiltily glad to be diverted from worrying abut Celia for the moment. "Penny Wood is going to be a star. I can feel it in my bones."

"Just as long as she remembers she's still Wenna around here, and always will be to us," Nick couldn't resist adding.

Once Celia had made up her mind she couldn't wait to get away. Her decision to visit Wenna in London had been taken on the spur of the moment, but now it seemed totally the right thing to do, if only to get a little breathing-space before she faced the family at home. She never considered whether or not there would be room for her. She just knew that the warm-hearted Fanny would welcome her with open arms, the way she had welcomed Wenna.

She packed feverishly, and recklessly booked a flight to England rather than travelling by overland and ferry. The air travel was bumpy and scary and made her feel nauseous and, by the time she had gone the last miles of the journey in a hideously expensive taxi to the Flamingo Club, she was tired and tense and ready to burst into tears.

"My God, *Celia*!" Wenna exclaimed, as she opened the door to the flat. "What on earth are you doing here?"

"It's good to see you too," Celia retorted sarcastically. "So are you going to let me in or do I have to stand on the doorstep all day like a refugee?" she added, her voice cracking now, despite herself.

Still in shock at the sight of her sister unusually dishevilled, Wenna opened the door wider, noting for the first time the suitcase and collection of assorted bags. Celia never travelled light, she registered vaguely. Someone pushed past her and held out her arms to the visitor.

"Celia, by all that's bleedin' holy! Come on in and 'ave a cuppa tea and tell us what the bleedin' 'ell yer doing here and lookin' so done in, for Gawd's sake!"

Celia was suddenly enveloped in Fanny's welcoming arms, and held against her ample chest. Hearing the familiarly wicked expletives, Celia let her defences drop and burst into wild, angry and despairing sobs.

"Of course yer can stay," Fanny said, a long while later when the tears had been dried and several cups of strong sweet tea had been consumed. "Wenna – or Penny, I should say now – don't have anything much ter do in the daytimes, so she can show yer round." She cocked her head on one side thoughtfully. "You know, you two beautiful gels are the real spit of one another. I don't s'pose you ever thought of doin' a double act?"

It was enough to bring a watery smile to Celia's face. "I don't think you'd say that if you ever heard me sing! Thanks for the offer, but no thanks. Anyway, I'm not looking for a job, Fanny. Well, maybe I am. I don't know yet."

She hadn't meant to say any of it, but her words were so jerky and she was so clearly unhappy that Fanny wisely didn't say anything more. It was all going to come out later, Fanny was sure. Nobody could hold in such passionate feelings without letting them erupt like a volcano at some stage or other. Poor little bleeder, she thought, with her usual rough sympathy. I'll bet there's a man involved. There usually was, in Fanny's knowledgable opinion.

"So what's happened?" Wenna said later, once Celia had unpacked her things in the tiny boxroom after insisting that she didn't want to muscle in on Wenna's space by sharing her room – a decision that relieved both of them mightily.

"I've been given a month's holiday to consider a change of job in the company, and I wanted some time to myself before I went home," Celia said, having rehearsed the words well.

"*And?*" Wenna persisted. "What does your boss say to that? The lovely Stefan, I mean. How will he manage without you?"

She smiled encouragingly, not meaning anything by her words, but virtually tearing open Celia's heart. Aghast, Wenna saw her sister dissolve as she threw herself face down on the bed and sobbed her heart out.

"Celia – darling – please tell me what's wrong," Wenna begged, white-faced now. "I can't bear to see you like this. You were always so much stronger than me."

"Not any more," came the strangled sound from the bed.

"Yes you are," Wenna said, wrapping her arms round her. "Whatever's happened, you'll survive it, like you always do."

Celia sat up jerkily. "Perhaps I don't want to survive it," she said tragically.

"Now you're just being a drama-queen," Wenna said, surprisingly brisk. "I've heard better lines at the theatre. I'll take you there one night to see a good play."

Celia stared at her once-timid sister, who was now far stronger than she, and was aware of how their roles had changed in so short a space of time. Wenna's growing confidence had probably been inevitable in her new life, while Celia's nerves were still raw and painful from what she saw as rejection and betrayal.

"You're a good girl, Wenna," she said huskily. "Or do I have to get used to calling you Penny now?"

"Of course not! It's only for my image, as they say." She added, with a giggle: "My agent thinks it will help my career."

"Your agent?" Celia echoed.

"Darling, you don't know the half of it," Wenna teased her airily in her best luvvie voice, thankful to see that Celia had shown a spark of interest in her fortunes, however incredulous, and was less agitated than when she arrived.

Celia stayed in London for a week, and during that time they contacted Justin and spent an afternoon on the Thames with him, which reminded them nostalgically of the times they had spent rowing on the Truro river at home. Wenna had instructed Justin not to ask too any questions about just why Celia was here, and to his credit he managed to refrain.

Celia was moderately surprised at how enjoyable life was in the city. The weather was glorious and the parks were full of summer beauty. Whatever anxieties there were about European affairs, it was confined to governments and apparently had no effect on ordinary people going about their business. Since Fanny and Georgie refused to admit to their own growing fears about his family, and resolutely hid the newspapers after they had scoured both the English and German ones, the two girls were in blissful ignorance of just how dire the situation was in Vienna for Georgie's parents.

The biggest surprise of all for Celia was the way her little sister was being acclaimed in the Flamingo Club. On Friday and Saturday evenings the glamorous Gloria del Mar was still the star attraction and drew the weekend clientele, but for three evenings during the week, they were treated to the sweet and husky voice of Miss Penny Wood, accompanying herself on the piano, as the new posters outside the club proclaimed.

Celia was impressed. Not only by the status Wenna had deservedly attained, but by the performances she gave. It had never been like this in Gstaad, she reflected. As always she hastily blotted out the memories, since they also evoked a special afternoon in a hotel restaurant with a wonderful view of soft green slopes and flower-filled valleys and distant snow-capped mountains, when she had first set eyes on the love of her life.

Her resolve was never to think of him now, unless it was absolutely unavoidable. Unfortunately, those times were only too frequent when Wenna sang the emotional songs of love that went down so well with her listeners.

Wenna was so independent now, and far stronger than herself, Celia thought enviously, despite the fact that her sister and the Rosenblooms fondly believed she had recovered herself since being here. None of them knew the whole story, anyway, only the pieces she was prepared to tell. She was strong on the outside, but inside there was still a very different Celia. A compassionate word, a sentimental song, the sight of two lovers in the park, their arms entwined, could reduce her to a quivering jelly.

She felt she had stayed long enough and it was time to go home. There were hugs and kisses when she left, and sincere pleas from Fanny and Georgie for her to return any time she felt like a change from the wilds of Cornwall. They were bleedin' marvels, Celia thought with a rush of affection, finding Fanny's favourite word the best one to cover her unexpected emotion as the train from Paddington steamed and snorted out of the station and slowly began its long journey south-west.

As she was lulled by the rattle of the wheels on the track, she thought that at least there was one thing she could be thankful for. The slow drag on her insides the previous evening had heralded her regular monthly period. There was to be no issue out of her brief liaison with Stefan von Gruber, to use her stepfather's legal jargon. She was grateful for that, although by now the aching low-down pain in her stomach had given way to a peculiarly hollow feeling, as if there was nothing left to remember except that one blissful night spent in her lover's arms.

Back on home territory at last and in the sanctuary of New World, she was greeted by more hugs and kisses that left her feeling totally exhausted, like a dishcloth that had been thoroughly wrung out and left to dry.

"It's been a heck of a long journey, Mom and Dad," she said, by way of explanation for her request not to talk that night, but to go straight to bed.

They let her go, and she spent the best part of the night alternately weeping for what might have been, and telling herself severely not to be a bleedin' fool, but to face up to the fact that Stefan von Gruber had probably never really loved her. If he had, he would have contacted her before now. He must know she would be worried. He was cold and ruthless, like the rest of his race, and against all her principles she found herself turning against every damn one of them.

She had such a restless night that it was nearly dawn before she fell into a deep, impenetrable sleep. No one disturbed her until she crawled downstairs at noon. Nick was away in Bodmin, and

Skye didn't raise an eyebrow to question her refusal to eat anything other than toast and butter.

"So are you ready to tell me what's wrong, honey?" her mother asked her quietly that afternoon when they were sitting together in the sunlit conservatory.

Celia gave a shuddering breath. She knew the question had to be asked, just as she knew she had to answer it.

"A lot of things. Everything. So much of everything that I don't know where to start," she said jerkily.

"The beginning is always a good place," Skye said. She cringed at the inane remark, but she didn't know what else to say, becoming increasingly alarmed to see her self-sufficient daughter so disorientated.

"The beginning," Celia murmured, as if looking far into the past, "occurred when I arranged to meet a man in a hotel restaurant in Gstaad."

"You mean Stefan von Gruber?" Skye asked when she paused.

Celia hesitated, then the words came out in a torrent. "I loved him, Mom. I thought he loved me, but I've had no contact with him at all since his father became seriously ill and he left Berlin to be with his parents. I've had a lot of time to think since Herr Vogl gave me this long holiday. It seems probable that Stefan won't return to the company at all. His father's almost certain to die, and Stefan will then be a very rich and important man controlling a huge vinery and country estate, so why should he bother about me at all? And I can't help wondering if he suggested this post in Cologne for me just to be rid of me."

"For pity's sake, Celia, slow down," Skye said, as her daughter's voice quickened and rose higher. "Why on earth should you think any of these things? If the poor man's distraught about his father it's not likely that he's going to be on the telephone to you every five minutes, is it?"

"I don't need to hear his voice every five minutes," Celia said, angry at this censure. "Just once would be enough. Just to know that he still cares."

Skye hardly knew what to say to her. Celia looked frozen, despite the heat of the summer day, and her face was pinched and white. Dear God, surely she wasn't . . .

"Were you lovers, darling? Don't think you'll shock me by admitting it," she added softly.

Celia didn't answer for a moment.

"Just once," she said. "And since I can see what you're thinking, no, nothing came of it. Thank God."

Thank God indeed, thought Skye, recalling her own feeings long ago when she too had had such misgivings. Celia couldn't be placated right now, however much Skye yearned to hold her in her arms as if she was a child and tell her that she understood so very well the mixture of relief that there was no child inside her, and the grief that there was not. They were feelings that only another woman who had experienced the same deep love would understand.

She spoke more casually, deliberately ending the subject. "I'm going up to the moors this afternoon. I want to visit the pottery. As it's so hot and humid here today, why don't you come with me? The fresh air will do us both good."

"What's this? Therapy for the poor rejected lover?" Celia said, with a feeble spark of her old spirit.

"Something like that. So will you come?"

"All right," she said grudgingly. "I know you won't let me wallow for ever, however much I want to."

As far as their family was concerned, the moors had always done more for restoring the spirits than anywhere else. Skye prayed that it would do the same for Celia. Not that she expected her to get over this trauma quickly. Miracles rarely happened, and how could she recover quickly, when her heart was so patently broken?

But even hearts didn't stay broken for ever. They healed eventually, though Skye was wise enough not to tell Celia so now, knowing that she simply wouldn't believe her.

"We'll walk," she decided.

"Are you mad?" Celia asked. "What's wrong with the car?"

"What's wrong with your feet? My grandmother used to walk from the top of the moors where she lived in a cottage with her family, right down to Truro Fair along with the rest of the young folk who used to work at Killigrew Clay. It was the highlight of their year. And they had to walk back again unless they got a lift on a cart or a hay wagon for part of the way."

Celia allowed herself a small smile. "You always did set a lot of store on those old tales of your grandmother, didn't you, Mom?"

"Why wouldn't I? Morwen Tremayne was a remarkable woman. They made them tough in those days," she added.

"She must have been strong willed as well as beautiful to have married the boss's son," Celia said without thinking.

Skye saw her lips tremble as the contrast with her own position struck her. She tucked her hand in her daughter's arm as they left the roadside and began the stroll up the sun-scorched moors, the bracken crackling beneath their feet.

"She thought, like most of us, that when we meet our destiny that was the end of it. She adored Ben Killigrew. But after he died she realised she could love again, and when she married Ran Wainwright, she was twice blessed by love."

"I know what you're trying to say, Mom."

"Then let me say it," Skye went on relentlessly. "I loved your father just as much as Morwen loved Ben, and I was devastated when he died. And I love Nick just as much, but without feeling disloyal to your father in any way. We all have the capacity to love more than once, darling, and if Stefan never comes into your life again, believe me, it won't be the end of loving for you."

For a moment she felt the guilt and shame of knowing that her love for Philip Norwood had already died before he did. But it was all so long ago, and a little white lie was far preferable to seeing the haunted look in her daughter's eyes.

Celia didn't say anything for a while as they went steadily up towards the moors, where the sunlight glinted as always on the majestic sky tips of china-clay waste.

"I'm sure you're right," she said slowly at last. "But that doesn't mean I've entirely given up on Stefan, Mom. I thought I had, but listening to you has clarified my feelings and I know I didn't imagine the love we had. I'm glad we had this little talk. Whatever happens, I shan't give up hope – even thought I'm still very angry with him, especially if he thought I was some kind of fortune hunter," she added for good measure.

She released Skye's hand from her arm and strode on ahead. Skye wondered if she had done any good at all, or if she had simply made matters worse in making Celia doggedly believe that someday there would be a future for her and Stefan von Gruber, and in doing so closing her mind to any other kind of love.

Her daughter would be here for three weeks, and in that time Skye was determined to revive her spirits totally.

But for all that Celia was trying to keep cheerful and positive for her mother's sake, she was just as determined that if she hadn't heard from Stefan in those three weeks, she wouldn't go back to Germany at all. It was the yardstick by which she would decide her future.

Gunter Schmit was now in charge of what used to be Stefan's large Berlin office. His blonde personal assistant, whom he had hoped would become far more amenable to his advances now that he was a somebody in the company, had been instructed to clear out everything that was extraneous to the new team, after scrutinising it all thoroughly. She wasn't a very conscientious employee, and the correspondence in the pending tray had piled up in the couple of weeks since Gunter took over. She glanced through it, more taken up with her broken fingernail which needed urgent attention, and tossed what were obviously mostly advertising missives from other companies into the waste-paper bin. She missed several letters that should have called for more scrutiny. One of them was a personal letter addressed to Fraulein Celia Pengelly.

The loss of it wouldn't change the course of world history. It just proved Celia Pengelly's despairing thought that she meant no more to the company than a lost memo in a pending tray, and no more to Stefan von Gruber than a brief and delightful encounter.

Twelve

S eb Tremayne was openly glad to see Celia. He caught both her hands in his, ignoring the fact that her gloves were immediately covered in china-clay dust. Neither of them were too bothered about it.

"God, it's good to see you, Celia. It's been mighty dull here lately with none of you girls around."

She gave a slightly hysterical laugh.

"The day there are no girls around you I'll see pigs fly," she said, without thinking how, as children, she and Wenna as had always thought him a prize pig.

He wasn't now. He was tall and handsome, and his blue Tremayne eyes were admiring her slender figure and glossy dark hair, and noting how the exertion from the hill climb had made her cheeks glow and her eyes shine.

He laughed back. "There's none like you, though, cuz. I can't abide simpering females."

"You mean I've got an acid tongue, right?" she quipped.

"Something like that," he grinned, not sparing her. "So what are you doing here, anyway? I thought you were in Germany working with the enemy."

"Sebby, please," Skye put in sharply, her pleasure at the way Celia had become more animated dimmed at once by Seb's thoughtless remark.

"It's all right, Mom," the girl said now. "I'm home for a holiday, Seb, that's all. I needed a breathing-space and that's all you need to know."

"All right. If you're in Truro one evening, you can come and see a film with me if you like. No doubt you'll be doing the family rounds, and my mother's always glad to see a female relative. What do you say?"

"I'll think about it," Celia said airily, not ready to do the social

175

rounds just yet. She thought that if she had any sense at all she would certainly not sit around like a love-sick calf, waiting for a man to call.

She managed to keep the smile fixed on her face as she greeted Adam Pengelly, looking far more like his old self now that he was working with his beloved pots again.

The women stayed at White Rivers for a short while, watching the potters' skilled hands shaping their wares and sliding them onto the shelves to dry. Celia didn't miss the way Seb's hands caressed the slippery wet clay, coaxing it into whatever elegant shape he wanted, as tenderly as if he caressed a woman. She was shocked as the thought slid into her mind, and willed it away. She had no intention of thinking of Seb Tremayne in that way, now or ever. There was no room for anyone else in her heart but Stefan . . . certainly not her cousin, Sebastian Tremayne!

"I knew the walk would do you good," Skye remarked when they began the trek over the moors towards Killigrew Clay. "It always has that effect on people. My grandmother—"

"Your grandmother has a lot to answer for," Celia said with a brief smile. "Sometimes I swear she's practically at your shoulder dictating to you."

"I wish she was," Skye said. "Even after all these years, I miss her. She was one of reasons I came to Cornwall in the first place. Well, Granny Morwen and my mother, of course. I desperately wanted to discover all the places I'd dreamed about since I was a little girl. All the stories were so romantic, and Cornwall seemed such a magical, mystical place."

She stopped, seeing her daughter's sceptical face.

"You can scoff, Celia, but if it wasn't for Cornwall, you might recall that you wouldn't be here at all. If I'd stayed in America and married a homebody instead of wanting to find my roots, you might have been the product of some hard-headed American businessman, or even a humble New Jersey fisherman!"

"And you think it was worth it – finding your roots and discovering who you really are?"

"Of course! A million times yes! I'm no philosopher, but I believe that we're all who we are on account of those who have gone before us, honey."

Celia said nothing for a few moments, staring straight ahead to where the clay-spoil heaps soared so magnificently skywards. She was as steeped in her Cornish background as anyone. The sky tips, such a symbol of that background, were part of her heritage, her legacy. But only part of it.

"Maybe that's what I should do too," she said slowly.

"What are you talking about now?" Skye said. "Have I missed something?"

Celia looked at her. "You went back to your roots, Mom. So where are mine?"

"Right here, of course."

Celia shook her head. "It depends on how far back you take this ancestor thing, doesn't it? This is where your Granny Morwen was born, *and* your mother and so many of the Tremayne family. But then your mom went to America after she married my grandfather and that's where you and your brother were born. *Voilà!* My roots are in New Jersey."

"My Lord, I always thought the Tremayne side of the family was complicated enough, but you've just complicated it still more," Skye said with a laugh.

"No, I haven't. I've clarified it in my mind, anyway."

Skye suddenly realised just what she was getting at and looked at her in consternation.

"Oh honey, this isn't for you! You're just getting over a traumatic experience. It would be the biggest mistake to go halfway across the world in search of something that doesn't exist any more. My family home was sold years ago after my parents and my brother died. There's no one belonging to our family in New Jersey now."

"Then come with me and show me where you were born and the places you used to know; where my grandparents are buried; the magazine office where you used to work—"

"Stop it, Celia," Skye said firmly. "This has been my home for twenty-five years now, and here I stay. Surely you're not serious about this. You'd be a stranger in America. Tell me it's no more than a whim, for pity's sake."

"All right. I'm not serious. I'm just crazy, so let's forget I ever mentioned it."

Crazy was the word for it, thought Skye, but at least her daughter was behaving more positively than when she had arrived home. She easily forgot the conversation, but Celia didn't.

If Seb Tremayne had been glad to see her, Lily was positively overjoyed when she turned up at the pottery showroom in Truro.

"I can't tell you how much I've missed seeing you girls, and Karina too," she told her. "I'm surrounded by men here, well, David, and now Olly's started coming back with him in the evenings sometimes, and it's all men-talk or newspaper-talk until I could scream. And then there are the boys . . ."

"You're not tired of these little poppets, are you?" Celia said, laughing as Robert and Frederick climbed all over her.

"No, but they do tire me out. I should have had them when I was much younger," Lily groaned. She shooed them off Celia's lap and sent them out to play. "Tell me what brings you home, how long you're here, and when you're going back."

Celia answered Lily's usual quick-fire questions in the same quick-fire manner, without stopping to think.

"I'm home on an extended holiday because of changes in my office, to consider my future within the company. I'm not even sure that I'll be going back at all."

"Good Lord," Lily said. "I thought everything was wonderful, or is that something I shouldn't even ask about?"

"I don't know. Has my mother been talking?"

"Not specifically. But you looked so glowing when you were home at Christmas, darling, and I'm not slow at putting two and two together. So what's gone wrong?"

"Nothing and everything. But I don't really want to talk about it. Let me ask you something instead. Would you think I was completely crazy if I went to America for a time?"

"Crazy! I should say so. Just give me the chance to be so crazy," Lily said. "But you're serious, aren't you?"

"Why do people keep asking me that? Yes, I'm serious, though I denied it to my mother. But the more I think about it, I think it's what I have to do. Mom came to Cornwall to find her roots, and I feel the urge to do the same thing."

"Are you sure it's not just an excuse to run away from something?" Lily said, direct as ever.

"Could be," Celia said, just as honestly. "But since I don't know what I'm running away from, maybe I'll find the answer there."

"Well, in my opinion, if you've got a problem, you just take it with you wherever you go. It'll still be here when you get back, darling."

"But maybe I'll have been able to deal with it then," Celia told her. "Anyway, it's just a hypothetical question. I haven't definitely made up my mind to go."

"Haven't you?" Lily paused while they both digested the rhetorical question. "Well, if you're thinking of staying here for any length of time while you make up your mind, I could really do with someone to help me in the shop. It's getting hectic now with so many summer visitors coming to Cornwall. I think we've been 'discovered' too."

"Come here and work in the shop with you? I might just do that," Celia said.

Nick was against it, as she had half expected.

"For heaven's sake, Celia, you have a wonderful chance to work your way up in the German company, so why on earth would you want to work in a shop?"

"Mom wasn't so damn snobbish about it when the town turned against her when the clayworks and pottery employed some young German boys years ago," she snapped. "I heard all about that, *and* the way the town's ladies came to her rescue."

"You don't know the half of it," he snapped back. "The whole area was practically divided on account of the loutish way those youths behaved."

"And who won? The *women* did, because we're stronger and have more sense in seeing people as people. They didn't give in to madheads like Uncle Theo who would have crucified the German boys just because of past prejudices."

Nick gave a tight smile. "Your education isn't entirely complete, my dear. Your young Germans almost caused a riot when one of the clayworker's daughters became pregnant. It wasn't only the women who got them out of the country before murder could be done. Ask your mother."

Celia turned away from him and sought her mother out at once, bursting with rage at his lawyer's pomposity. She loved him dearly, but sometimes, just sometimes she wanted to hit him.

* * *

She found Skye in the midst of a fiery argument with her brother, and wondered hysterically if every family was like this, or only theirs.

Olly rounded on Celia at once, his eyes bright with fury, clearly intending to enlist her support.

"You don't think it's a stupid idea for me to want to move in with Lily and David, do you? They've got the room, and it makes perfect sense since David and I work together."

"My Lord, just listen to the little worm," Celia said before she could stop herself, in no mood to consider his needs. "Work with David indeed! I thought you were a junior tea boy, not a star reporter!"

The minute the words left her lips she saw the stricken look on Olly's face, and the shock on her mother's.

"Celia, that was unforgiveable. You will apologise to your brother at once."

"Don't bother," Olly yelled. "Everyone knows she's the favourite, anyway. Everything has to revolve around her, and I wish she'd never come back, making everyone creep around her as if she's half dead. I wish she'd go back to her fancy German employers where she belongs. And I *am* going to move in with David and Lily, if they'll have me. At least they see me as a person and not just as a tea boy!"

He stormed out of the room, and the next minute they saw him pedalling furiously away from the house on his bicycle.

For a moment the two women were too stunned to say anything. Then Celia held out her hands helplessly, hardly able to speak, her head throbbing with shame at the way she had humiliated her brother.

"Mom, I'm sorry. I didn't mean it. I don't know what's happening to me."

For once, Skye didn't take her in her arms and console her. This time, Celia had gone too far.

"What's happening to you is that you've become so self-pitying that you never consider anyone else's feelings, Celia. What's happening to you is that you think the world has to stop turning because you've had one little setback—"

"One little setback?" she said, choked.

"That's what I said. For pity's sake, pull yourself together and look at the world round you and see what's happening to other

people. As a start, you might care to read the letter I received
from Fanny this morning, and then tell me how important your
little setback really is."

She thrust the envelope into Celia's hands and left her to it.
Celia knew she had sought her mother out for a reason, but right
now the memory had vanished in the shock of hearing her
mother censure her so. It was so very rare. Simply to give her
trembling hands something to do, she pulled Fanny's letter out of
the envelope.

The words dazzled in front of her. Fanny was not an articulate
letter writer, but as Celia read on, the one long ungrammatical
paragraph made the horror all the more poignant.

We got a letter from Vienna a few days ago. It came from an
old friend of Georgie's folks. You knew they was shopkeepers
of course. Well it seems like the Jew-bashing bastards burned
their shop down one night and Georgie's parents was still in
bed and couldn't get out. It couldn't be proved who done it of
course and anyway who would care about an old Jewish
couple? The friend who wrote to tell us said it happened a
couple of weeks ago and there was nothing left of them to bury
properly. So some friends just had a secret service for them
and that was that. They begged Georgie not to go there as
everything's so bad now. But he's real cut up about it and he
cries all the time when he thinks I can't see. He don't like folk
to know any of it and Wenna thinks we've shut the club for a
week for painting. We'll have to open again soon though. You
can't sit back and let the buggers win can you gel?

Celia wept over the letter, knowing just why her mother had
wanted her to read it. It put everything into perspective. Poor,
poor Georgie . . . she wanted to run to the telephone and speak
to him, but she knew it wouldn't be wanted. He was so proud,
such a good man . . . and those terrible people had done this to
his family, just for being who they were.

She found Skye in the garden and gave back the letter.

"I'm so sorry. I didn't understand," she said in a small voice.
"Sometimes I think that for all my education, I don't know
anything at all. Fanny – even Fanny makes me feel humble – and
I know that sounds as snobbish as hell, Mom."

"Come here, honey," Skye said. "If you've realised that much, then I wouldn't say your education was wasted. Now what did you want to see me about? I know there was something."

She shook her head. "It doesn't matter now. I'm going into town to make my peace with Olly. That's more important than raking over old history." She hesitated. "You will let him move in with Lily and David, won't you? It would be good for him."

Even though the idea of working in the shop with Lily and suggesting that she herself should take the Kingsleys' spare room had been hovering in her mind, she knew that this was Olly's time, not hers.

A short while later, and with her mother's blessing, she got out her own bicycle and pedalled towards Truro. She caught up with Olly long before she reached the town. She caught sight of his own machine, thrown down on the grass above the cliffs, and saw his hunched shape, sitting with his hands clasped around his knees, a lone, miserable figure, and her heart went out to him.

"Olly, I'm so sorry," she said at once. "I didn't mean any of those things. Life has just been so bitchy lately, and I was just taking it out on you."

"Is that one of the fancy words they taught you at Gstaad?" he said, not yet prepared to compromise an inch, and staring resolutely out to sea, where a distant ocean-going liner was making its way steadily westwards on the calm, mirrored water.

Celia gave a small smile. "It's the way I feel right now, Olly. Why do you think I'm here?"

"How should I know?" he said bitterly. "Nobody ever tells me anything. At least David treats me like an adult and not like a baby."

"You want that room with David and Lily, don't you? And I think you should have it. You don't object to my putting in a good word for you, I hope. It's what older sisters do, and I know I can persuade Mom to let you do it."

So what if it was a little white lie as yet? Celia was damn sure she could swing it for her brother. The smile he gave her was worth any sacrifice she had to make. It was such a small sacrifice, anyway, she thought shamefacedly, still caught up with the dreadful thing that had happened to Georgie Rosenbloom's parents.

"You mean it?" he said eagerly. "But I thought you might be wanting to move there yourself."

"Not me," Celia said, her gaze also following the stately progress of the ocean-going liner. "I've got other ideas, and if you promise to keep it our secret for the time being, I might just tell you what they are."

She realised that never before in her life had she deigned to share a secret with her young brother. But seeing the look on his face she knew it was exactly the right thing to do to restore his hurt pride. It made her feel slightly better than she had for weeks. Life wasn't all bitchy.

A few days later, when she had made her peace with all concerned, it wasn't hard to wheedle out of Lily what had really happened all those years ago when a small group of German youths had been employed at Killigrew Clay and White Rivers, amid very mixed and vociferous reactions.

"Your mother was an angel then," Lily told her. "Though me and Vera didn't do so badly either. We became shopkeepers at White Rivers when nobody else would give us the time of day, and Vera withheld her favours from Adam, if you know what I mean. For a couple of newly-weds I don't think it went down very well with Adam," she added with a grin. "Anyway, Skye wrote a special newsletter that David published, saying how we should all let the past remain in the past and welcome good workers wherever they came from. Or words to that effect. I don't remember all of it now, except that it was addressed to the women of the area, and it turned the tide. The foreigners had to leave, of course. The situation was too volatile for anything else. But instead of Theo running 'em out of the country, your mum and dad smuggled them from their lodging house onto a ship in the dead of night and sent them back to Germany without any fuss. The poor little devils were terrified by then anyway, and all the fight had gone out of them."

Celia was open-mouthed at hearing all of this.

"We were all too young to know what was happening, and I had no idea it was such a traumatic time," she exclaimed. "You were all regular heroes, weren't you?"

"Oh, we had our moments, darling. Now what did you want to tell me? You know Olly's moving in and he's like a dog with two tails about it. I'd rather hoped it might be you, and that you'd decided to come and work for me. Are you?"

"I'm afraid not, Lily, but I'm not going back to Germany either. I've made up my mind and nobody's going to stop me."

"When did anybody ever try?" Lily said dryly.

Not everybody was so agreeable to her plan. Her stepfather thought it a mad idea to go to America in search of a dream, while Skye thought that Celia was simply putting as much distance as she could between herself and Stefan.

"I know why you're doing this," she told her daughter bluntly. "But you can't run away from your feelings for ever. At some stage you have to come back and face up to them."

"You didn't go back, did you? You came to Cornwall and you stayed. Why is it so impossible for me to do the same thing in reverse?"

Skye spoke softly. "I think you know the answer to that, honey. The time will come when you'll realise where your heart lies, and I don't believe it's in New Jersey."

Celia looked at her pleadingly. "I want your blessing, Mom. I feel too restless to stay here, and I can't go back to Germany, so where else is there for me to go? Anyway, the crossing only takes a little more than three days now. If I absolutely hate it, I can be back here in no time at all!"

Skye hugged her tightly, knowing that in the end she would give her blessing. Celia's complex feelings were tearing her apart, and the only place to sort them out clearly was as far as possible from everything familiar. Didn't she know that for herself?

"Then hadn't you better inform Herr Vogl that you won't be returning to Berlin? I'll write a separate letter to him explaining that you want to see something of the world and have decided to go travelling. I'll sort out some addresses and contacts for when you get to New Jersey."

"You're a darling, Mom," Celia whispered.

The plans were made, and nothing was going to change her mind. Celia stayed at home for the rest of her month's official holiday, but in early August she was a passenger on the *Queen Mary*, bound for New York. She left Cornwall with very mixed feelings, not least because of the letter that had finally arrived at New World a few days earlier, re-directed from the Vogl offices in

Berlin. She had shown it to no one, but the words Stefan wrote were imprinted in her heart.

I was devastated when you never replied to my earlier letter, Celia, and saddened that we had to part so abruptly. But if you wish to have no further contact with me, then I must accept your decision. Our paths are unlikely to cross again, since I have severed all connection with the Vogl company following the death of my father. My duty is here now.

I have been told that you declined to take the post in Cologne and have left the company. I can only assume that you preferred to be back in England with your own kind. My deepest regret is that I was clearly mistaken in the feelings I believed were genuine between us.

On my side, they were most sincere, but as I do not wish to put you under any obligation or sense of remorse, I will merely say that if ever you need me, I am here.

She couldn't read any more of it. It said so much, and yet it was so very stilted, and more like a formal office letter. Its tone was so unlike the lover who had held her and adored her, and even though she treasured his final words, she knew she would never contact him again.

Even his address, von Gruber Estates, heavily embossed in gilded letters at the top of the letter, set him apart from her. She should always have known it.

Where was this earlier letter she was supposed to have received, she raged? There had been no other letter, nor telephone call, nor message of any kind. Until now, she thought, he had forgotten her existence. This was his way of breaking all ties now that he was a rich landowner.

She clung to her anger. It was far safer than letting her emotions tear her apart. She told herself that he wasn't for her and never had been, and that she had to forget him, and travel to whatever fate awaited her on the other side of the Atlantic.

One thing was for sure. She wouldn't follow her mother's lead on her own long-ago voyage to Cornwall when she had met and fallen in love with Philip Norwood. This girl was keeping herself very much to herself for the few days of the voyage, and falling in love was not included in her itinerary.

"Well, that didn't last long, did it?" Seb asked his father when he heard the news. "I thought she was going to stay in Cornwall and get more involved in the business."

"She was always too high and mighty to think about throwing a few pots, boy," Theo said sneeringly.

"I didn't mean that. You never did have much time for Celia, did you?"

Theo scowled. "She was too sharp-tongued by far. And I've got no time for any of 'em while they remain so stubborn about mergin' with Bourne and Yelland. But I've got a trick or two up my sleeve that's soon going to change all that."

"Oh? And what's that?"

He laughed. "Oh, no, my lad. You'm too hand in glove with cousin Skye for me to give anything away. You'll all find out soon enough anyway."

He wasn't telling anyone about the deal he'd struck privately with Zacharius Bourne. The deal that was going to give him more say-so in what happened at the clayworks than he'd had since old Morwen Tremayne decreed that Skye should be a partner. He didn't know why he hadn't thought of it before.

The two partners at Bourne and Yelland, and himself, would be three-quarters of a thriving merger in which the fourth partner was not only a woman, but could always be outvoted. Once the two clayworks merged, Skye would be in the minority for decision making. The three men would hold the greater percentage of shares, which was the way it should be, Theo thought arrogantly.

Selected workers were already spreading the news at both clayworks that the merger was imminent. They said there was strength in numbers, and that all the clayworkers would benefit by it, especially from the fat bonuses the new combined company was prepared to pay as soon as things were settled.

That would be the clincher, Theo thought gleefully. Money talked, the way it always had. For the clayfolk, never the world's most affluent of workers, the golden handshake each of them would receive, would be irresistible. He and Zacharius Bourne had agreed to dip into their own pockets to see it through, which proved Theo's dogged intention to get his way over the American upstart.

He readily conceded that Bourne was a better negotiator than himself. The man had the gift of the gab without resorting to wild rages when things didn't go his way. This very day he was putting their case across to the two company lawyers far more eloquently than Theo could, which was why it had been decided that he would keep out of it for the time being. The fact that one of the lawyers concerned was Skye's own husband was a small fly in the proverbial, but Theo didn't anticipate any major problems now that he and Zach had sorted things out to their mutual satisfaction.

Nicholas Pengelly drove home to New World that evening at a greater speed than usual. There was no way he could object to the arguments that had been put to him today, and nor could he ignore the well-prepared documents that the Bourne and Yelland lawyer had produced. Private negotiations had clearly been going on for some time, and even though he was soured by the fact that Theo Tremayne had had a pretty hefty hand in it, he had to reluctantly agree that the conditions were fair and sensible.

As the fourth partner in the proposed merger, Skye wouldn't have any real choice about it, even though the entire workforces of the two companies would need to be drawn together to give a vote on it, the way they always did. To be seen to be fair and to give everyone their say, was the slogan, though in effect, it rarely worked that way. And there was little doubt what the outcome would be. The figures Bourne had produced for the bonuses, and the proposed rise in pay for the men, would see to that. Nick couldn't blame them. Nothing was stable in the world these days, and money in the men's pockets and food in their children's bellies counted for more than outdated principles.

He didn't relish the task of convincing his wife of it. She would see this merger as a betrayal of all her family stood for, despite the fact that Nick had been telling her for months that it made sense.

He waited until they had finished dinner before he told her he had something of importance to discuss with her.

"I think I know what it is," she said, looking at him unblinkingly in a way that he wished she wouldn't. That wide, blue-eyed gaze could always unnerve him, and it did his self-esteem no good at all to have to ask himself if he was a man or a mouse when it came to discussing things with his wife.

Right now she was looking at him as a businesswoman who knew very well he was about to destroy everything she had fought to preserve since the days when Morwen Tremayne had fought these same battles. *That* was what unnerved him, Nick thought savagely. This damn family thought they owned the world, and could do what they liked in it. The arrogant Theo Tremayne was proving that only too well. But in doing so, he diminished Skye.

"You can't know," he said briskly. "Unless you're able to read my mind, which wouldn't surprise me, with your so-called sixth sense," he added.

"I don't need a sixth sense to know why you're bringing your briefcase to the drawing room, and plying me with more wine than usual to soften me up."

"What a suggestion," Nick said, laughing.

Her voice sharpened. 'I don't need a sixth sense to know why Seb's been acting strangely for days now. He's been dropping hints as large as bricks as to why Theo's been spending so much time over at Roche lately."

Nick sighed. "This is like listening to your grandmother all over again."

"Thank you. I take that as a compliment, though I suspect it wasn't intended that way. But it doesn't get to the point of this discussion. So what is the proposal?"

"To merge," he said bluntly, "and to do it soon. Skye, you've seen the recent world figures for china clay. Prices are dropping alarmingly, and if it drops too far, then we'll have to lay men off, and if that happens we won't be able to fulfil our orders, and the pottery will suffer as well. We can no longer exist as a small company—"

"*Small?* Killigrew Clay was one of the largest—"

"It was once, but now it's one of the few independent companies left," he reminded her. "Others have merged and become stronger. Bourne and Yelland are offering excellent terms, and Theo's gone a long way to ensuring that the men get good bonuses. And before you say he shouldn't have done any of it without your knowledge, when have you been ready to listen? You've simply closed your ears to any of it, but you can't go on burying your head in the sand, darling."

Skye bit her lip as his impassioned voice went on.

"Listen to me, darling. Bourne's strength is that they're allied to several paper mills which give them guaranteed orders, which will stand us in good stead if the European markets close."

"And you think they will, don't you?" she said slowly. "You're convinced that the war is coming."

"As convinced as anyone can be without a crystal ball. Perhaps you'd have more faith in what everyone seems to take as inevitable if you consulted your old crone on the moors."

"That's the last thing I'll do!"

"Really? I got the impression you took more notice of her than your own husband."

Skye recognised his growing anger. She turned away from his accusing face, her emotions very near the surface.

"Nick, please don't let's fight over this. My mind is in a turmoil lately, what with everything."

"What everything?"

She moved away from him and went to stand by the window, staring out at the soft blue evening light. The crescent moon was just rising, and the sky was alive with stars almost close enough to be touched. It was a beautiful summer evening, calm and fragrant, with no hint of any conflict anywhere in the world. Not their world, or the wider world. So peaceful, so for ever. Skye shivered at the thought, knowing that nothing was for ever.

Nick came to stand behind her, and his arms folded around her, holding her, keeping her safe . . .

"I've kept my feelings to myself, Nick," she said slowly. "But everything is changing, and suddenly I feel so alone."

"You're not alone. I'm here. I'll always be here."

She leaned back against him, feeling his strength. Loving his strength. Loving him so much.

"But now we're just two, where we used to be five. Oh, I know they've been away to school, but they were children then, and now they're not. They're making their own way in the world and and they don't need us any more, and it all seems so weird and final. Whatever you think of Fanny, I was happy for Wenna to go to London because I knew she'd be safe with her. I always guessed that Olly had printer's ink in his veins, Nick, and Celia had such a future ahead of her in Berlin. But now . . ."

She paused for a moment as his hold on her tightened, knowing that it had to be said or she would burst.

"It's crazy I know, but it's as if I've only just realised that all our children have left home, and how much I shall miss them," she said, her voice catching. "The fact that Celia's assured future ended so disastrously makes me realise that I can no longer kiss them and make it better. We're not young any more, Nick, and we no longer have control over what our children do. Doesn't that frighten you?"

He twisted her around in his arms.

"Good God, woman, will you stop! If you're trying to say that we're in our dotage, then you'd better think again!" he said, making her give a half-smile.

"I don't mean that at all."

"Good. Then don't even think it. But I'll tell you exactly what I think. Our children are level-headed and intelligent. If Celia has to go halfway around the world to find what she's looking for, then so be it. Didn't you?"

As he echoed his daughter's own question, Skye felt his mouth on hers, warm and familiar, reminding her that life, and loving, didn't end because there were a few grey hairs in her still luxuriant black hair, and more than a sprinkle in Nick's. Love went on, passion could still be a flame. The kiss that began so tenderly was fast changing into something very different and demanding. His hands were pressing her into him, moulding their bodies together as he murmured against the softness of her lips.

"Since we seem to have wandered totally off the track, I think perhaps we had better finish this discussion about the clayworks in the morning."

"What clayworks?" she murmured back.

Thirteen

Before Nick left the next morning, Skye spoke quietly.

"If you really think the merger with Bourne and Yelland is the right thing to do, Nick, then I won't oppose it."

She was grateful that he didn't make a big show of his reaction, but simply accepted her decision. There would be time enough for crowing when Theo got to hear of it.

"Right. I'll inform Theo first of all, and then we'll set up a meeting between the combined owners and clayworkers. I don't see any real problems, but there are always some old diehards, and we don't want a strike on our hands because they don't approve of the idea."

"They don't approve? Whose business is it, anyway?" she was stung into saying.

"Yours, my love, but if you don't have willing workers, you don't have a business at all, do you?"

She was weary of arguing. "I know it. Just don't let Theo come crowing, that's all, or I shall throw something at him." Her mouth trembled as she said it. Although she just wanted it settled now, the enormity of it all was only just dawning on her. She still couldn't quite dismiss the thought that she was betraying everything those earlier Tremaynes and Killigrews had fought so hard to keep and, in particular, her grandmother's trust.

"Will you be all right?" she heard Nick say.

She forced a smile to her lips. "Of course I will. I'm not going to fall apart. I'm made of sterner stuff, remember?"

But it wasn't the way she felt inside. When he had gone, she wandered aimlessly about the empty house. Eventually she found herself in the round turreted room where many years ago the young Walter Tremayne and his sweetheart had hidden away, wanting so much to be together that they were prepared to defy everyone and risk a family scandal. If they hadn't been so passionate about one another, finally forcing both sets of parents to agree to their marriage, there would have been no Theo.

But it wasn't only love that conquered all things, Skye thought contrarily. Her mother, Primmy Tremayne, had had such an early aversion to her American cousin Cresswell that never could anyone have foreseen such a lifelong passion between them. Hate and love were sometimes so closely allied, that you had to experience one before you found the other.

She shivered. How anyone ever in this world found their soulmate was a mystery that only a romantic fool would try to comprehend. Or were they all fools, anyway? Maybe there was no such thing as a soulmate, and it was no more than a chemical reaction that drew two people together. What did love have to do with it?

"I must be going off my head," she muttered to herself, feeling beads of sweat on her forehead.

It was hot and airless in the little room, and although it had been a secure lovers' hiding place all those years ago, it was making Skye feel claustrophobic now. There was a small window, and she tugged at the unused fastenings until it opened and let the cool morning air filter in and throw welcome beams of sunlight across the room. Dust motes danced in the rays, and she followed their movements in a kind of charmed daze for a moment, her gaze finally setting on the boxes of old photographs and documents stored here.

The documents were mostly all musty accounts and letters that should have been thrown away years ago. There was nothing emotive in them, as there had been in old Morwen Tremayne's diaries that she had left to her granddaughter. After reading only one of them, Skye had been true to her vow that they were private and not for anyone else's eyes.

Once, she had thought of writing a book about the fiery and passionate Morwen Tremayne, based on the diaries, but in the end she couldn't do it. A person's life was her own, and a diary encapsulated all the thoughts and dreams that went into it. They were the only totally private things a person had, and should remain so. So all the diaries had been burned, reducing a lifetime's dreams to ashes. At the time it had seemed a right and noble thing to do.

"And that was crazy and over-emotional, if you like," Skye

went on muttering savagely, as if needing the reassurance of her own voice. "There was always something in Granny Morwen's words to comfort and reassure me."

She lifted the lid on one of the boxes. The photographs were old and brown and crackling with age, the mostly sepia tints doing little to enhance the vivacious faces of the family. Some of the faces and names Skye had virtually forgotten, all the Tremaynes and Killigrews and the girls they had married, and their friends and confidantes.

She stared at a picture of two young girls, laughing together, their arms wrapped around one another in friendship. They wore the long-ago garb of the bal maidens who had worked in the Cornish clayworks of a century ago: long white cotton dresses and aprons; bonnets framing their pretty faces; black lace-up boots caked with clay. It was as if the photographer had just captured these two in a rare moment of glorious happiness away from their work. Two such pretty faces, with bold, laughing eyes and rosy cheeks from a life spent in the open air, high on the moors, working in all winds and weathers.

Skye turned the photograph over, even though she was certain of the identity of these two, anticipating the names she would see scrawled there in the faded handwriting.

"Morwen and Celia the day before Truro Fair," she read. "On the look-out for young men as usual."

She wondered who had added the last sentence, since it was written in a different hand. One of Morwen's brothers, perhaps. It might even have been her beloved brother Matt, who had gone to America to seek his fortune, and whose own son had returned to Cornwall years later and whisked Primmy Tremayne off to America and married her. And in time they had had a daughter named Skye.

God, was there ever such a tangled family as theirs! But Morwen's life had been more fulfilled than anyone might have imagined from her humble beginnings. Skye knew it, because Granny Morwen had charmed her so in the telling. She had certainly fared better than the tragic Celia in the photograph, after whom Skye's own daughter was named. Morwen's friend had drowned herself in a clay pool, unable to face the disgrace of being raped and then committing the mortal sin of allowing a witchwoman to induce an abortion and burying the child in an unmarked moorland grave. Morwen had been a party to it all.

At the sudden sound of a disembodied female voice, Skye jumped visibly, her heart thudding wildly, as if those other two women were about to materialise in front of her eyes.

"Skye, what are you doing up there? Where are you?"

She swallowed as her ragged senses returned to normal, and croaked out a reply.

"I'm in the turret room, Lily."

She hastily dabbed at her face, until then unaware of the tears that had streaked down her cheeks. A few moments later Lily appeared in the litle room and gaped at her.

"What the dickens are you doing in here? You look as if you've seen a ghost," Lily said, as solid as ever, and not remotely like anything supernatural.

Skye's attempt to sound matter of fact failed dismally.

"Don't take any notice of me. I always get emotional when I see these old things."

"Good Lord, are those old family photographs?" Lily exclaimed. "There must be dozens of them here."

"Granny Morwen was a bit of a collector," Skye said with great understatement. "If you want to see them we'll take them down to the conservatory and have some tea. I'm stifled up here and the dust is tickling my throat."

She half-hoped Lily would decline. The photos were hers, she thought fiercely, and then she knew how foolish and selfish that was. They belonged to all of them. Lily was as much a part of this family as herself. Besides, Lily was married to a newspaperman and was just as keen as David at sensing a story. She proved that a couple of hours later, by which time she had scrutinised every one of the photos, put them in order, and tried to sort out who was who and where they all fitted into the intricate pattern of the family. Lily sat back and stared at Skye.

"These are amazing. They're a marvellous record of a past era. You should do a series of articles on the Tremayne family and the Killigrew Clay involvement with it for the newspaper, Skye, and let David use the photos to illustrate them. I know he'd be keen to collaborate with you."

"Oh, I don't think so," Skye said at once.

"Why ever not? The pottery hardly keeps you busy these days, does it? You've become a backseat owner. It doesn't suit you to sit around and do nothing. Now that the girls have gone, it would do you good to work, Skye. I haven't said anything, but I've been worried about you lately."

"Have you?" she said in surprise. "I can't think why. There's nothing wrong with me."

"Nothing that a good dose of working on some project or other wouldn't improve," Lily said astutely "Believe me, darling, I know what I'm talking about. Look what it's done for Adam to get him out of that gloomy little house where he just sat about mourning Vera! God knows I miss her too, but endless grieving won't bring her back."

"Are you talking about you and Vera, or me and Celia?"

And Wenna, and Olly, Skye thought.

"I'm talking about wanting to see you the way you used to be, when nobody could hold a candle to the quick-witted Skye Pengelly. Your writing always proved that. You had such style, Skye. Don't waste it by turning into a cabbage. I think I'd better leave now, before you throw something at me."

"I won't. I'll save that for Theo," Skye said with a grin. "As a matter of fact, it might be exactly the time to commemorate the end of an era by recording it all, as you so rightly said. I'd better explain."

Theo telephoned her that evening and was surprisingly docile, though Skye had no idea how much pressure Nick had put on him to curb his tongue. She had fully expected him to crow over her, but instead he said she had obviously inherited a lot of good sense after all, and left it at that. She remarked to Nick that it was almost as if all the fight had gone out of him, now he had got his way, which proved that there must be a first time for everything.

"Don't you believe it. He'll be saving it for the rally on the moors when the combined owners and workforce get together to thrash things out. He might be in agreement to merge with another company, but he'll leave them in no doubt who has the loudest voice when it comes to cursing and lording it over the rest of them."

Skye's eyes sparkled. "Is that so? Well, we all know his bigoted views of women in business, but he'll have to account to two other equals as well from now on, and Bourne and Yelland aren't going to sit back and let him dictate the terms, any more than I am."

"That's my girl," Nick said, chuckling at her vehemence. "You've got some of your old fizz back, anyway, and I'm not sure that it's entirely due to last night, flattering though the thought is. So what's been happening today?"

She laughed. Her eyes glowed with the memory of just how erotically pleasurable last night had been, when she had lain in his arms and nothing had been more important to either of them than loving and being loved.

"I haven't entirely forgotten last night either," she said provocatively, "but I can't say that today has been entirely wasted either. Lily came to visit, and we had quite an interesting time."

She outlined her vague plans for using the old family photographs with a series of articles for the *Informer* to trace back the history of Killigrew Clay, and in particular the Tremayne family involvement with it. After all, there had been only one Killigrew son, and five Tremayne children, who had all helped to shape the dynasty it had become.

"I think it's a marvellous idea," Nick said. "I'm sure Olly would be keen to be a part of it too."

"Don't think that hadn't escaped me," Skye said with a laugh. "Though of course I still have to interest David in the idea. It's his newspaper."

"And since when did David Kingsley ever turn down any suggestion that came from you?" he said, so coolly that she looked at him sharply. He laughed. "Good God, Skye, do you think I haven't known that the man's been in love with you for years?"

Shocked, Skye spoke quickly. "Please don't say that. He and Lily have such a lovely, comfortable life together."

"I'm not saying they don't. I'm sure he loves his wife and his boys, but he's always been more than a little in love with you. There's a difference."

"Well, I don't want to know about it," she said, almost crossly. "Anyway, 'being in love' is never as deep an emotion as loving someone and making a commitment to them."

"That's all right then, isn't it?" Nick said.

But she wished he'd never said it, or had known it, although Skye knew that David had never quite lost his feelings towards her, even though years ago he had turned easily enough to someone else when she had rebuffed him.

Maybe that was what 'being in love' really meant. In love with the feelings, but not with the person. Whatever it meant, she was going to stop being so analytical. It made no difference to her need to be a creative wordsmith again. She hadn't quite realised how great this was until Lily had made the suggestion. She should have done, of course. Writing had always been her salvation, through good times and bad just as it had been Morwen's, in a different way.

Even though she hadn't been well-educated, Morwen had recorded her thoughts in her diaries. Skye had often wondered if her own instinctive need to write had come from her grandmother. It was a lovely thought, and one that she cherished.

"Anyway, I'm not in love with David Kingsley and never could be," she told Nick firmly. "So don't let it worry you."

"I wasn't, but it's good to know," he said, smiling. "And I think your proposal for the newspaper is an excellent one, darling, and well timed in the circumstances. It will be good to remind the community of just how powerful Killigrew Clay once was, and how your family helped to shape it."

"That's what Lily and I thought too," she said, hugging him, and marvelling, as always, at how lucky she was to have him.

The rally was arranged for the end of the month. If it went through smoothly it would be in good time for the autumn despatches, when the proposed new company would have a new name which was still to be decided. That would cause another headache since neither company would be willing to relinquish their own.

Skye was very much against them being called Killigrew, Bourne and Yelland Holdings. In any case there would be arguments as to which name came first. Other companies had amalgamated several names, but she thought it was just too much of a mouthful; something neat and memorable would be preferable. It was one of the things she intended to bring up at the initial meeting of the four proposed owners and their lawyers in the Bodmin solicitor's chambers. Statements, orders and accounts had already been properly scrutinised on either side, and each party was satisfied that the merger would be advantageous to all.

But she was nervous as she and Nick drove to Bodmin on that bright August morning. She knew Zacharius Bourne slightly. He was portly and middle-aged and as aggressive as Theo, but always ready with an oily charm when it was needed. They were two of a kind, thought Skye.

Gideon Yelland was slightly younger and more submissive than his older partner, and Theo clearly thought him a nonentity when it came to swaying votes. Maybe there was an underlying steel about the man, but somehow Skye doubted it. He clearly looked the weaker partner.

"Well now, little lady," Bourne said expansively, once the four of them and their lawyers were seated. "I hope you and I are going to get along very well."

"I hope so too, Mr Bourne," she said pleasantly, "and I'm sure we will get off to a good start if you will refrain from addressing me in such a ridiculous fashion."

"Skye—" Nick said warningly, while Theo guffawed, and the other lawyer, a Mr Pascall, merely sniffed disapprovingly. He was small and wizened and clearly took his lead from Nick when it came to summing up a situation.

"Told you to watch your tongue when dealing with my cuz, didn't I, Zach? She's no pushover." jeered Theo.

"Thank you, Theo," she said coldly, "but I can answer for myself, and I suggest that we get down to business instead of indulging in useless chit-chat."

It was dawning on her that maybe she held the upper hand, after all, or at least as good a hand as any of them. The other three all wanted this merger desperately. As a woman she was in a minority of one, but women had their own methods, and if things became sticky for any reason, there were still ways of persuading the clayworkers to see her side of things. The power of the press combined with the power that wives and mothers held was something men would be foolish to ignore. It had worked once before when, by subtle means, the womenfolk of the whole area had proved their worth to their men.

She felt an unexpected sense of exhilaration. She would not let these men forget that she was as much a partner in this merger as any of them. She was a woman in a man's world, just as her grandmother had been, but Morwen Tremayne had always stood up for what she thought was right, no matter how much the rest of them tried to manipulate her. Skye had every intention of doing the same.

Nick cleared his throat.

"Will you all please open the folders that Mr Pascall and I have prepared for you, and we'll go through the various stages one at a time," he said.

Each of them complied and studied the facts and figures. On the face of it, Killigrew Clay had everything to gain and nothing to lose. Bourne and Yelland Holdings were a much smaller company in terms of actual pit size and production, but their undoubted advantage was in being allied to paper mills, which would stand them in good stead if overseas markets for raw clay faltered.

Everyone knew that the initial decision to merge had been made in all but signature. It only remained for the clayworkers' approval to go ahead immediately. But there was something still nagging in Skye's brain.

"There's one thing I'm not clear about. The clayworkers don't take kindly to change, so what exactly are we offering them as an incentive? This seems no more than a very modest pay rise," Skye said.

She saw Theo and Zach Bourne glance at one another, and braced herself. There had to be something more, and these two had probably been in collusion for some time. She glanced at Gideon Yelland who was keeping his gaze fixed on the proposal forms and guessed that she knew something that she did not.

"Well, Theo?" she said sharply. "Will you please explain? I refuse to sign anything until I have all the facts."

And if her husband knew them, why the hell hadn't he already informed her?

" 'Tis nothing that had to concern you, cuz, since me and Zach are putting our hands in our own pockets to subsidise matters. Though, because of our goodwill, we have an extra rider to add to the proposal—"

"What's this?" Nick said sharply. "Why haven't I been informed of this? Pascall, did you know of it?"

The other man scowled, his face reddening. "Only recently, sir, and I have still been debating the ethics of it. Naturally I was going to produce the rider I have prepared before we get down to the signatures."

"Really? It seems to me as if it had been conveniently for-gotten," Skye said, her blood boiling, disgusted by the under-hand methods her cousin was prepared to use. "And if that had happened, I presume the four signatures would have bound us to the merger, no matter what these two have cooked up between them."

"Now see here, little lady—" Bourne began aggressively, and was immediately silenced as Skye got to her feet, the chair legs scraping the floor behind her.

"No. *You* see here, Mr Bourne. Either you treat me with the respect I'm due, or I'm out of here this minute, and the merger will fail. My signature is of equal importance to my cousin's, and you can do nothing without it. We're not partners yet!"

"Of course. And I apologise, ma'am," Bourne said, changing his glower to an ingratiating smirk as Yelland put a restraining hand on his arm. "I meant no offence, I'm sure."

"Please sit down, Skye," Nick snapped. "This meeting was coming to an end, but it's clear that we have far more serious matters to discuss now."

"And Mr Tremayne," he addressed Theo formally, "you will please explain yourself. What exactly have you and Mr Bourne been arranging between you? Surely you know that you should have consulted me before any private arrangements were made?"

Theo immediately lost control and crashed his fists on the table. The veins on his forehead stood out like purple ropes as his face went a furious colour.

"You bloody snot-nosed lawyers think you rule the roost," he bellowed. "We'm perfectly capable of sorting out our own affairs, and I'll be buggered if I'll go cap in hand like a piss-assed schoolboy to ask your permission as to how I spend my money."

"Theo, for pity's sake, calm down," Skye snapped, disgusted with him as always, and mortified that it was her side of the table that was showing such a lack of control.

He glared at her, his eyes murderous. "Oh, ah, my fine wench, you can play the lah-de-dah colonial as much as you like, but it don't alter the fact that you came here and wormed your way into my grandmother's life, and thought you could take over what's been in my family for generations."

"It's my family too," she yelled back, furiously near to tears but determined not to show it. "What in hell's wrong with you, Theo? I never asked for any of this!"

But it was damn well hers now, and she'd fight tooth and nail to preserve her right to it.

"The deal's off," she announced tensely, standing again, and with her hands flat on the table surface as if to support every shaking nerve in her body.

"Skye, *no*," Nick said wearily. "I'm not going to let you back out of a sensible transaction on account of this buffoon's madness."

"Who the hell do you think you are to talk to me like that?" Theo rounded on him at once.

"I'm your lawyer and I suggest we all sit down again and get on with the business of the day."

"Damn right," Zach Bourne growled, seeing all their previous work dwindling away. Skye saw the flickering indecision on his face, and his jaw tightened as he went on. "Mrs Pengelly has a right to her opinions, and we must honour them. In view of all the dissension here today, I suggest that Tremayne and myself tear up the proposed rider to the incentives we've offered. For God's sake, let the bonuses stand but with no conditions attached."

The lawyer Pascall spoke cautiously. "Then before we go any further, do I have the meeting's permission to discuss the incentives, and the formal dismissal of the rider?"

"That would certainly seem like a good idea," Nick snapped, clearly wondering why the devil he had ever got involved with this volatile family in the first place.

Pascall continued. "Mr Tremayne and Mr Bourne decided to double the amount of the bonuses first suggested. They were prepared to pay these extra amounts themselves, which would undoubtedly have created goodwill among all concerned, and I trust they will honour that decision."

"I've said so, haven't I?" Bourne snapped.

"As to this rider," Pascall went on, clearly outraged at the implied slur on his reputation to be so involved in the first place, "it was to the effect that in consideration of these monetary offers, Mr Tremayne and Mr Bourne would each have a thirty per cent share in the new company, with Mrs Pengelly and Mr Yelland having twenty per cent each."

"They must have been out of their minds to suggest it," Nick said angrily. 'Show me the document, please."

Pascall handed it to him silently, while Skye was speechless. The rats, she raged, the double-dealers. It gave them more control than herself and the less dominant Yelland, who from the look of him, had been perfectly content to go along with it.

"This is not a legal document," Nick said. "It does not have the consent of all four parties, and I would strongly advise my wife to disassociate herself from it."

"You need have no fears on that score," Skye retorted. "What on earth were you thinking of, Theo? I always knew you were capable of some slimy dealings, but I didn't think you'd go so far as to cheat your own cousin."

"There's no cheating involved," he said, starting to bluster. "Twas merely a business arrangement that seemed perfectly fair, considering me and Zach Bourne were prepared to pay handsomely for the privilege."

"Bribing the clayworkers, more like," she snapped. "Well, this is what I think of it."

She picked up the document from the table, tore it in two pieces and threw it contemptuously towards her cousin.

"I think there's little more to be said here," Pascall began uneasily. "I suggest we leave things until another day."

Skye glared at him. "Certainly not. I think we all know a thing or two more about one another now. We came here to confirm our willingness to a merger, or do the other three parties wish to go back on it now?"

She heard Theo snigger at her vehemence, but his voice held the merest touch of grudging admiration as he spoke.

"Well, since 'tis clear that none of us will put one over on my cousin, and nor would we wish to," he added hastily, "I suggest we settle this deal once and for all, with equal shares between all four parties."

"Agreed," said Zach Bourne, with such alacrity that Skye guessed immediately who had made the initial suggestions as to what she could only see as a pay off.

"Then if that is the wish of you all," Nick said, taking charge as the senior lawyer, "it only remains for the new company to be given a suitable name. We can't present a *fait accompli* to the workforce without having it established. Have any of you given thought to it?"

Gideon Yelland made his voice heard properly for the first time. "It makes no difference, as long as the Killigrew folk don't shut us out. We ain't been established as long as they, but we've a good name in these parts."

"I agree, Mr Yelland," Skye said sweetly. "And neither do we want to lose the name of Killigrew Clay entirely. So what do you suggest?"

The man's face darkened with embarrassment, as she had suspected it would. He was the type to put forward a case, and then fizzle out because his thoughts never got past the first post. Pascall intervened quickly for his client in the small silence that followed.

"May I suggest that we get the initial agreements signed between all parties, and return here in a week's time? That will still give us a few days before the rally, and we'll have had time to choose a name that will satisfy everyone."

Nick nodded, more than ready to end the meeting.

"I agree. The agreement can be signed now, so the official deeds and documents can be drawn up before the new date, when the name of the new company can be inserted. After the rally, the final signatures and official seal will be put on the documents and the two companies will be officially one."

Just like a marriage, Skye thought. But with four partners instead of two.

"Thank God that's over," she said feelingly, when they were finally on their way home. "I couldn't have stood much more of Bourne's arrogance, or Yelland's fawning. As for Theo, well, he really overstepped the mark this time with his scheming."

"I think you made your point clear, and well done for seeing through him. At least you won't have to meet with the rest of them very often once the merger is finalised."

She glanced at him, seeing his set profile.

"You don't blame me for speaking up, do you? It was obvious there was something going on between him and Bourne, and I'm amazed that you hadn't already suspected it."

If he had, things might never have got this far.

"Are you blaming me for not doing my job properly?"

"Of course not! Nick, I didn't mean that—"

"It bloody well sounded like it, and I make no apologies for my language. Your family seems well used to it, anyway."

Skye gasped. "That was unforgiveable, and how dare you compare me with my loutish cousin! Oh, I wish – I wish . . ."

"What? That you'd continued hiding your head in the sand and thinking that Killigrew Clay could go on for ever? Face up to reality, Skye. It's doing little more than limp along at present, and you really had no option unless you wanted to close down like so many other Cornish pits."

"I never wanted that," she muttered. "I just wanted to preserve it as long as possible."

"And that's exactly what you did. Your grandmother would have been proud of you, but now it's time to let go."

She stared ahead as they drove over the moors and past the great silent sky tips that had never looked so calm and glintingly beautiful. No matter what happened, they wouldn't change. They would always be there, reminders of a more colourful age when the entire moorland was alive with the sight and sound of clayfolk, and the outmoded methods of extracting the clay from the earth. Skye remembered the tales of how the clay blocks had to be scraped by those white-bonneted women and left to dry for months in open air linhays before they were taken to St Austell port in huge, horse-drawn clay waggons, long before Ben Killigrew's little rail tracks had been built.

Oh yes, things had moved on since then. Nobody could cling to the past for ever. She had to be less possessive of her Cornish legacy, even though she knew she could never loosen all the ties that bound her to the past. Why should she? She was still part of it. But right now she would be better employed in thinking of a new name for the clayworks, and to start looking forward, not back.

Fourteen

"You realise it can't be solely your decision, don't you?"
Nick asked a few days later, by which time Skye had
become totally frustrated trying to coin different titles for the
new company, with a pile of screwed-up papers the only result.

"I know it, but I need to have something to offer, and I dread
to think what the others might come up with."

How arrogant that sounded, as if she was the only one with
any aesthetic ideas. Theirs would probably be far more practical
and perhaps that was the answer; something plain and simple,
like The China Clay Company. If only it didn't sound so damn
boring. No, that definitely wasn't it.

"I've tried twisting the names around, combining the letters
and so on, and nothing seems to work. KBY Holdings was one of
them, but it seems too cold and impersonal. The best thing I've
come up with is Bokilly Holdings. I'm sure Theo will object
because our name doesn't come first, but Killboy as an alternative is hardly going to attract customers, is it?"

Nick agreed. "Actually, Bokilly Holdings has a certain ring to
it. You know how to handle Theo, and if you're tactful enough
he'll end up believing he thought of it first, the way he did with
White Rivers."

"Well, I could try," she said. "I was thinking of going to Truro
this afternoon, anyway. I want to take the box of photographs to
show David and outline a few of my article ideas. I'll call in at
Theo's on the way back."

In fact, the more she thought about it, the more Bokilly
Holdings had a definite Cornish flavour and fluency about it,
as if it had been established for ever. All she had to do was
convince Theo of it so they could present a united front at the
next meeting before the final documents were signed and sealed.

But first, she was meeting David at the *Informer* offices and outlining her plans for the articles. She felt a real lift to her spirits as she drove her car towards Truro, and blessed Lily for urging her to do this. She had needed something positive to do after Celia left for America. Though by the sound of her enthusiastic phone calls and letters, Celia was no longer pining, Skye thought thankfully. Either that, or she was a pretty good actress.

At that moment, in the early morning sunshine, Celia was halfway up a ladder in the apple orchards of New Jersey, laughing down at the boy who was holding it steady.

"If you make this ladder wobble once more, I swear I'll kill you, Jarvis Stone," she giggled, feeling more light-hearted than she had in months.

"I couldn't rightly hear you, ma'am," the boy said, laughing back. "Was that kill or kiss?"

Celia clung on to the branch of the tree where the gleaming red apples exuded such a heavenly scent, and spoke to him in mock severity.

"You know very well what it was, and I'll have your mom and poppa on my tail if I don't do what I'm being paid for, so just hold this ladder still and let me get on with my work."

"Only if you promise to sit by me at supper this evening," he persisted. "You talk real pretty, and I can't always hear you with the rest of 'em jabbering."

"All right, I promise." Celia grinned.

She wouldn't have said she talked real pretty, but her accent was very different from these delightful American folk who had taken her in so readily. She hadn't thought she had an accent at all until it had been pointed out to her. She sometimes cashed in on it now to their delicious amusement.

She hadn't known what to do or what to expect when she had taken the bus from New York to the small New Jersey town of Mainstown. She had visited the magazine offices where Skye used to work many years ago, and been given a warm welcome. But apart from one or two older members, the staff there had changed, and once the information about her mother and family had been exhausted, Celia felt it was time to move on.

She had followed the detailed directions to the house called the Appletrees where her mother was born, and which was appropriately enough now a thriving fruit farm.

The farm was advertising a room for rent in exchange for fruit-picking duties, and in taking it on she had discovered the large, warm-hearted Stone family, whose sixteen-year-old son Jarvis had already declared himself madly in love with her, and had to be kept firmly in his place.

"Shoo, Jarvis, or I won't get this basket filled before supper."

She watched him go, dragging the twisted foot that set him apart from his younger brothers and sisters, but did nothing to stop his puppy-like exuberance. He was a sweetie, thought Celia, then concentrated on filling her basket ready for market in the morning. She had never been happier, except for one time that she refused to think about.

Even the growing anxiety over events in England and Europe couldn't dim her spirits these days. The Stone family's easy-going philosophy was to ignore things they couldn't see and couldn't help, and it was a philosophy that was spilling over onto Celia. Whatever upheavals were beginning to erupt on the other side of the Atlantic, they were all far away, and couldn't touch them here. This was Utopia, and sometimes she thought blissfully that she would stay here for ever.

Skye sat opposite David Kingsley in his office and waited while he studied the family photographs she had brought, together with the outline of her article.

She had worked hard on it, realising more and more how much she needed this project – and David's approval. So it came as a huge shock when he said, "In principle I like the idea very much, and I don't doubt your ability to do it justice."

"But?" she said, her heart jumping as he paused. "I know that tone of voice, David, and I know when I'm about to be fobbed off!"

"Not at all. Now don't go all sniffy on me, Skye. If you're completely set on working up a series of articles then I'll be more than happy to go ahead and publish them. You have a lifetime of memories here, but I'm wondering if this is the right outlet for it after all. It deserves so much more."

She forestalled him. "I know what you're about to suggest, David. I once thought about writing a work of fiction based on my grandmother and the diaries she left me. But I couldn't do it, and what's more I don't want to do it, so don't even think about trying to persuade me."

"I wasn't thinking about fiction. Hell's bells, Skye, you people are all the same, aren't you? Tremayne or Pengelly, you all go off half-cocked at a second's notice without listening to what anybody else has to say."

"I'm sorry," she said with a rueful laugh. "You're quite right, of course. So I'm listening."

"I wasn't about to suggest that you wrote a novel." He paused again. "Incidentally, do you still have those diaries?"

"I do not," she said crisply. "I burned them all."

"Pity. Well, as I was saying, you know as well as I do that a series of articles in a newspaper will only end up as firelighters. They're not kept, Skye, the way a bound book is. Now that more folk are coming to Cornwall they'll be looking for souvenirs to take home. The proof of that is already happening in the pottery shop, so why not offer them a small booklet about an industry that is at the very heart of Cornwall, written by a member of an old-established china-clay family? What do you say?"

"A booklet?" she said sceptically. "Who do you think would buy such a thing? And where would it be sold?"

"Tourists would buy it, Skye. And where better to sell it than in the White Rivers shop right here, alongside your pottery? Lily could make a big feature of it."

"Do you really think so?"

"Darling, I know so," David said. "As for the publishing and printing side, my contacts can see to that. All you have to do is produce the copy and the photographs. And of course you can have access to our archive material any time you feel like going into the office dungeons for a few hours. I really think you could be on to a real winner, Skye."

"I don't want to make a career out of this, David," she said faintly, as his voice rose with enthusiasm.

"You don't have to. One booklet isn't going to make your fortune, either. But I'll guarantee that years from now, tourists will still be buying it. Cash in on what upcountry folk see as the quaintness of the place and its industries. If you don't, somebody else will. Think about it, Skye. Who knows the history of the Killigrews and Tremaynes better than you do – and who will handle it more sensitively?"

"All right, you've made your point, and I promise I'll think about it," she said quickly, not ready to be bamboozled into making an instant decision.

"Good. Then how about taking a certain young man out for some afternoon tea, since I know he's itching to know what brings you here," he said with a smile.

"How is he doing?" Skye asked, glad to get her thoughts round something else for the moment.

David laughed broadly.

"You've got a budding reporter in the making in young Oliver," he said, "and I'm no idle flatterer when it comes to business. He's very keen, although I'm sure he thinks the jobs I'm giving him are a bit tame for his restless nature."

"What's that supposed to mean?"

"Oh, just that I think he'd prefer to be out in the middle of a war zone where's there's real action and plenty of blood and gore. It beats reporting the cosy doings at local village fêtes and domestic squabbles."

"Don't even think about it," Skye said with a shudder. "He's far too young for any of that nonsense, thank goodness."

But he wouldn't always be fifteen.

She caught up with Olly in the print room, and offered to buy him some tea and fruit buns in a local tea room. She hadn't seen him for a week or two since he'd been at Lily's, and already he seemed different. He had grown taller and as he leaned over the press he already seemed a young man, Skye thought with a shock. She was losing them all, even Olly.

But at her offer of tea and fruit buns he washed his hands quickly, and rolled down his sleeves, always ready to be taken out and treated. He hadn't changed that much then.

"So how do you like being a working man?" she asked him lightly, once he had wolfed down two buns in record time.

"It's spiffing, Mother, although it can be pretty dull at times," he said, echoing David's words. "But maybe that will all change if I'm allowed to go with him to the clayworkers' rally. I'm looking forward to that."

"For pity's sake, how do you know about it already?"

"Uncle Theo called in to the office and said we should be there in case of fireworks." He looked at her uneasily. "He wasn't speaking out of turn, was he? It would need to be reported in the newspaper, anyway."

Skye sighed. Of course it would need to be reported. The merger and change of name of an important industry was newsworthy. She knew that. It was just that so far the news hadn't become public property. Until it did, she could believe that everything was going on as usual.

"In fact, I was wondering if you would give me an exclusive interview, Mother," Olly went on, pushing his luck. "Then I might even persuade David to give me a byline."

She looked at his young, hopeful face and had to laugh, even though the laughter was tinged with a hint of anxiety. Oh yes, the ambition was already there, staring her in the face, and how far it might take him, only time would tell. Time, and the growing threat of Adolph Hitler's European domination.

"What's so funny about that?" Olly said, full of resentment. "I have to start somewhere, don't I?"

She pressed his arm. "Of course you do, honey, and of course I'll give you your interview when the time comes. You'll be the only one to get an exclusive, and you can do something for me in return. When you've got nothing else to do, you can sort out a pile of old newspapers in the archives ready for me to come in and study. There's no hurry, the merger is the most important thing at present."

She explained why she was interested in archive material, and saw how his interest was caught by her proposed project. How odd, she thought, as she finally left him and drove to Killigrew House where Theo and Betsy lived, that Olly should be the one to follow so closely in her footsteps. There was no reason why he shouldn't have done so, but she simply hadn't expected it, and their shared interest warmed her heart.

She put these thoughts to the back of her mind, as she learned from a whispering Betsy that Theo was in agony with the gout this afternoon, and in a filthy mood.

"He's best left alone, Skye," Betsy advised. "I just thank God that the vicar ain't likely to call, what with his foul language and all."

"I've probably heard it all before," Skye said. "Anyway, I have to see him and it won't wait, so I'll risk it."

He was in the drawing room, glaring mutinously at the blank television screen, and didn't even turn around to see who had come into the room.

"Why can't the fat-arsed buggers think of folk who have to be indoors all day and give 'em summat to watch?" he bellowed. "I ain't paid out good money for sitting and watching a snotty square box that don't do nothing."

Skye was about to open her mouth and say something witty that she hoped would make him grimace at least, when he suddenly hurled the nearest vase at the screen, shattering it into a thousand pieces.

"Well, now you've really done it, haven't you?" she said calmly. He swung round in his chair and glared at her as his wife came rushing in.

"What on earth's happened?" Betsy gasped.

"He's let his ridiculous temper get the better of him," Skye answered while he was still gathering breath. "He's acted like the spoilt brat he always was, and this is the result."

Betsy's mouth fell open even more. Few folk ever dared to speak about Theo like that. They might think it, but not even Sebby was so openly scathing unless he was seriously provoked. Theo looked as if he was about to burst every blood vessel in his body. Then they realised that instead of shaking with a seizure, he was roaring with laughter.

"By God, girl, you drive me off my head sometimes, but I probably should have married you. What a hell of a life we'd have had then, sparking off one another—"

"I doubt that very much. I'd almost certainly have killed you by now," Skye snapped, mortified that Betsy should have heard his words. Not that she seemed to care.

"Well, thank God we can get rid of the ugly thing now, and I never want to see another," Betsy said stiffly.

For one ludicrous moment Skye thought she was referring to Theo, then realised with a sense of rising hysteria that she meant the television set.

Theo ignored his wife and stumped across the room, his heavily bandaged foot huge and cumbersome.

"Whatever you've come to see me about, girl, let's get it over," he growled, "while somebody gets this mess cleared up."

"Somebody certainly will," Betsy retorted feelingly. "And

then somebody will get the house reorganised to a normal place where folk can sit around and talk to one another, instead of gawping at that one-eyed monstrosity."

Skye hid a smile, admiring the way the old insipid Betsy had come out of her shell and tackled Theo in the only way that worked.

"Since I'm here on business, shall we go to your study?" she asked him, as matter-of-factly as if nothing had happened.

"Theo, I'm really sorry you're in such pain," she said, once they were settled. From his tortured face there was no doubting that it was genuinely excruciating.

"I'll live," he muttered. "A few more noggins of whisky and I'll be in never-never land. So what do you want?"

"To discuss the new name for the company."

"Bloody hell, I can't bother about all that now."

"It's important, Theo. Haven't you given it any thought at all?"

He scowled. "No, I ain't. But we don't want nothing poncey like White Rivers, mind."

"Well, that certainly hasn't done us any harm! But that's not the issue here. I've been trying hard to merge the two company names, since I think we should try to keep as much of them as possible so we don't lose our identity. But whatever I come up with it doesn't seem to work. I mean, what would you say to the Killboy Company?" she asked innocently.

As she expected, he let out a derisive roar of fury.

"I think we'd be the laughing stock of the county wi' such a poncey name, that's what I think, woman!"

"That's what I think too."

His eyes narrowed. "Oh ah. And what little game are you playing now?"

"I'm not playing any game at all. But it hasn't been easy trying to twist the names around. You try it, and see if you have any better ideas."

"It's a waste of my bloody time."

"No, it isn't. We have to have something to present, Theo. I'm damn sure Bourne and Yelland are thinking up something to suit them, and if they have their way it will seem as if Killigrew Clay never existed."

As his bloodshot eyes gleamed she knew she had got his attention at last.

"All right. So what else have you thought up?"

"Nothing really," she said slowly. "Unless – no, that probably wouldn't work."

"What? *What*? Dammit woman, speak up!"

"Well, Killboy is obviously awful. Boykill is just as bad. We might leave a few letters out, but I don't know where. Bykill? I don't think so. Bokill?"

"Bollocks, more like! Try sticking an extra bit at the beginning or the end of it, if you must," Theo said.

"Such as *Bokilly*, I suppose?" She paused, as if considering, then spoke animatedly. "Actually, Theo, I quite like the sound of that, but it needs something more. Bokilly Clay or Bokilly Holdings maybe. Tell me what you think."

He didn't say anything for a couple of minutes, and she knew he was mulling over the name in his mind.

He finally growled at her in his usual fashion. "It's the best so far. I'll go along with that. And what I think is that you've just conned the conman. Now get out of here and leave me to my bed and the bloody whisky bottle."

She went home feeling elated. This had been a good day. The suggestion about the booklet could be put aside for now, but it would eventually give her many hours of pleasure after the undoubted trauma of signing half her life away was done. Melodramatic maybe, but she knew she would never have the same affinity for Bokilly Holdings as for Killigrew Clay. But times were changing, and she had to change with them.

She had brought back the box of photographs with her, along with her article outline, and she put them away until the time was more convenient for her to think about them. The stability of the business was the most important thing now, and when it came to the new name, Theo's gout had probably proved more of a help to her than a hindrance, she thought with a smile.

Though, regaling Nick that evening with the nonsensical result of her cousin's temper, it made her realise just how unpredictable he could be.

"I should probably have got his agreement to the proposed name in writing," she said, remembering it too late. "But he more or less believes he had the final say on it, so let's keep our fingers crossed."

213

"Then the sooner we get the next meeting over and everything agreed between all parties, the better. The rally has been fixed for the tenth of September."

"We should let David Kingsley know it then, since he'll want to cover it for the *Informer*. And I had better warn you that Olly wants me to give him an exclusive interview—"

"That child?" Nick said sceptically. "I suggest you'd better write it yourself unless you want it to sound like a schoolboy essay."

She reacted at once. "Give him some credit, Nick. He needs to do this and I'm not going to alter one word of it – once I've checked that he doesn't distort anything I say. Not that I think he will for one minute," she added hastily. "And he's not a child any longer, either."

"If you say so."

But by the following week when the new partners were due to meet again in Bodmin, Theo was confined to bed with a serious flare-up in his foot and leg that the doctor pronounced as phlebitis. Betsy informed Skye on the telephone with an unsympathetic note of I-told-you-so in her voice.

"He's not allowed to put his foot to the ground, and if he don't rest it he's in danger of losing his foot to the surgeon's knife. So that's put the wind up him, I can tell you, but he's driving me demented with his constant whining and demands for attention. I'm to tell you that Seb will be bringing you a signed note confirming your chosen name for the new company. He says 'tis secret until 'tis all agreed."

"So it is," Skye said, sure that by now Theo was quite convinced he'd thought of it himself. "Please tell him I'm sorry he's ill, but I'll let you know what's decided the minute I get back from Bodmin."

She couldn't help a sneaking feeling of relief. Everything always proceeded more smoothly when Theo wasn't around. She was sorry for him, though. Phlebitis could be very painful, as she knew from tending the soldiers in the field hospitals who had suffered from it in the Great War. Even worse, she had witnessed the physical and mental effects of gangrene and amputations . . . she shuddered, wishing such memories hadn't entered her mind.

She tried not to think of them as she and Nick drove to

Bodmin, as this was to be a momentous day. She wondered what name the Bourne and Yelland partners would produce and how many arguments there would be on the choice of a new company name.

In the end it was all a damp squib.

"My clients have thought of several names, but none that meet with any enthusiasm," Mr Pascall said tetchily. "So we await your suggestions in the matter."

"Then perhaps you will consider Bokilly Holdings," Nick said. "It is an amalgamation of the original names and has a substantial authority about it."

The look of relief on the other three faces told Skye that there had probably been considerable harassment between them all during this past week, and that they were simply thankful that someone else had taken the initiative. It was quickly apparent that the end result suited them all.

"Thank heavens for that," Skye said later, when they were on their way back to Truro to get Theo's signature on the documents. "Though it all feels a bit like an anti-climax, Nick. I was expecting fireworks and we didn't get any."

"That's because your cousin wasn't there. Even if it was his idea – or he thinks it was – he'd still have made some kind of fuss."

It was sad too, she thought. Such a huge decision to make, and it all been settled in a matter of minutes. And yes, crazy though it was, damn it, she had missed Theo's fireworks!

Incapacity certainly hadn't softened his temper. He was as irascible as Betsy had said, sitting up in bed with a huge wooden cradle over his leg beneath the bedclothes to keep any pressure off his painful limb.

"So how did it go?" he growled. "Did the buggers put up much of a fight?"

Skye saw him wince for a moment as he eased himself up higher in the bed, and thought how old he looked. Pain did that, of course, and he was no longer a young man. He was sixty-one years old, and looked every day of it right now.

"They agreed to Bokilly Holdings without any arguments, Theo," she told him. "In fact, they hadn't even been able to think up a title of their own."

"Typical," he sneered. "I always knew we were dealing with dullards when it came to using a bit of brain power."

Skye mentally counted to ten. He really was insufferable, and rarely gave anyone else any credit but himself. Zacharius Bourne was an intelligent and astute businessman, regardless of any underhand dealings. She didn't know Gideon Yelland that well, but he had certainly not struck her as a slouch. She was about to defend them, but Nick forestalled her with a sharp glance. She read it correctly. Once they got into any kind of arguments here, Theo was just as likely to refuse to sign the title document until he'd given it more thought.

The news had come through only that week that both the Vogl and Kauffmann firms had slimmed down their orders for raw china clay, so they couldn't afford to let anything go wrong now. If they must look for more home orders than exports, they needed this merger more than ever before. As yet the German orders were only slightly less than the previous ones, but with the uncertain European situation it could be the start of a more general slide.

"The other partners have signed the title document, Theo," Nick said crisply. "It only needs your signature."

He held out the document and the pen, and Skye saw her cousin give a sly smile.

"Gives me the final say, don't it, cuz?" he said. "If I choose to change my mind on this."

"I hardly think you'd be so foolish," she said. "After all, you've wanted this merger all along, and you made the final choice on the name, so I can't think why you would go back on your own triumph."

She was giving in, but she just wanted to get out of here, with its cloying sick-room smells and the overwhelming sense of betrayal that could still unexpectedlly stab her.

He signed quickly, and thrust the document back at Nick.

"Now leave me be to get some rest," he snarled. "I need to be fit for the rally, and I ain't planning to be wheeled there in a bloody bath chair."

They left him and declined Betsy's offer of tea. It was done, and it gave Skye no sense of satisfaction at all.

"I feel terrible," she said, once they reached the car. "Right until this moment, it never seemed quite real, but now it is and there's no turning back. You know damn well the clayworkers won't oppose anything with the bonuses Theo and Bourne are dangling in front of them. The rally will be no more than a farce and I don't want to be there."

"You have to be there, Skye. You have to show them that this was the only way Killigrew Clay could progress. It's part of something bigger and better now."

"Is it?" she said bitterly. "Oh, I know you're right from a business point of view. But I can't separate my head from my heart, and my heart still tells me it's wrong, and that something very precious has gone for good."

"That's why you're going to write about it," he said calmly. "So that what it was will never be forgotten."

He started up the car while she stared unseeingly ahead. He was so right, and she had the means and the skill to do something that no one else could do. So that something precious would never be forgotten.

"I'm so glad I've got you," she said thickly.

"Well, thank you, ma'am," he said, in a pseudo-Amercan voice to echo her own. "I'm glad I've got you too."

Her prophecy about the rally was proved correct. Where in times past, hundreds of clayworkers had gathered in belligerent fighting mood, or marched to the meeting-house in St Austell to argue their rights, this time it was a reasonably orderly mob who stood shuffling their feet in the hot sunshine of a September morning.

Each of the partners was to give the clayworkers their spiel, assuring them that they had their best interests at heart, and that this merger would benefit everyone. Zacharius Bourne was eloquent enough, but his partner declined at the last minute owing to a throat infection that rendered his voice hoarse and useless.

"More like a convenient way o' not riling the workers," Theo jeered. "None of 'em has much faith in the likes of that shirt-lifter."

Skye felt her face flame. Whatever Theo thought about Gideon Yelland, and she had begun to have similar suspicions, it was best kept to himself.

"It's a good thing you and I are seen to be so normal then, isn't it?" she hissed at him under cover of a rousing cheer as the bonuses were outlined. "If normal is the right word for a pig of a man," she added beneath her breath.

But she had to admit that he gave his speech his roaring best, interspersed with blasphemies that were undoubtedly his style, and one that the men knew and accepted. Then it was her turn, and she had barely begun when it was clear there was going to be some organised heckling.

Nick shouted back at them to give her a chance, but she stopped him with a glare and stood firm on the small platform that had been erected for the speakers.

"I thought you were all intelligent men with the gumption to know that what's being done is in your best interests, but if you aren't prepared to listen to me, then I suggest you all go back to work while you've still got a job to go to," she snapped.

"Who d'you think you are, missus, all done up in your fancy clobber and telling we what to do?" a few voices jeered.

"She ain't Morwen Tremayne, that's for certain sure," yelled another. From the look of his grizzled face he must have been near eighty years old, Skye thought, and still devoted to the clay and the old ways. It gave her a lead.

"No, I'm not Morwen Tremayne, nor ever could be," she said in a clear voice. "Some of you knew her, and those who didn't, knew what she stood for. I'm her granddaughter, and from the moment I met her, what I wanted most in the world was to be like her. I've done everything in my power to uphold her views and ideals and to preserve Killigrew Clay in the way my family controlled it."

"You should have thought o' that before selling out." A lone voice continued to yell amid more subdued mutterings.

"*Sir*," Skye said passionately, "I assure you it's the saddest thing in the world for my cousin and myself to accept that we can no long continue alone, and that Killigrew Clay has to be merged with another company. But many of you here know the integrity of Bourne and Yelland and that none of this has been considered lightly. Together we can grow stronger."

"So what's this new company to be called?" the grizzled one shouted. "You'm taking our clayworks, and the rumours say you'm taking our name too, and I ain't working for no Bourne and Yelland fancies."

"Leave it, Theo," she said, as he began to add his roars to the sudden outburst. "We all agreed that this was my time."

She was shaking inside. The new title, that had sounded so grand and perfect, was already stamped and registered, but these people had to be pleased. They had been a law unto themselves many times in the past, and could be now, if they chose to go on strike. And with the autumn despatches imminent, however much the orders were depleted, it was a risk she couldn't afford to take.

She held up her hand for silence, and spoke with as much dignity as she could.

"In any merger, just as in any marriage, both sides have their opinions, and the new title has been thought out carefully and agreed by all of us. We will no longer be Killigrew Clay –" she had to pause for opposing shouts and cheers – "but neither will we be Bourne and Yelland Holdings. Instead we have merged the names of the companies together and come up with a sensible solution. The new company will be known as Bokilly Holdings."

There was silence for a moment and then some slow hand-clapping from the back of the crowd was taken up by the rest. Like bloody sheep, Theo muttered. But knowing that David Kingsley and Olly were here, writing their reports for the *Informer*, Skye wasted no time on Theo's sneering asides.

It had been left to her to do this, and she had given up wondering if it had been a good idea. She just wanted to get the rally over and get back home. When the noise finally died down, she continued.

"As for working conditions, nothing will change. You all know your duties under your pit captains, and the central distribution of the china clay will be an administrative matter. When we have your ayes on it, you will separate into your old company groups and, as an act of goodwill, the bonuses will be paid out personally and immediately to each of you by Mr Bourne and Mr Yelland and by Mr Tremayne and myself."

"That's the blackmail, be it, missus?" a final heckler bawled out. "Once we've got our bonuses to sweeten the pill, there's no going back on it."

She gave him a wide smile, recognising him at once.

"That's about right, Ned Forest. I've learned a few of Morwen

Tremayne's tricks in my time, and I still don't know which of us is getting the better of the other. Do you?"

There was a ripple of laughter at this and the heckler was silenced. But once they had given their ayes on it, the lines were organised and they began to separate into two factions and shuffled forward to receive their bonuses, overseen by the two lawyers.

"By God, with all this money jingling in their pockets there'll be some business for the local kiddleywinks tonight," Theo muttered, handing out the packets into the grasping hands, and still begrudging the fact that he was willingly parting with his money.

"My Lord, I haven't heard that word in years," Skye said to him, as one and another clayworker touched his forehead to her by way of acknowledging their pay packets.

"They'm all called inns and hostelries now," Theo scowled. "But they still serve the same gut-rotting ale and clog the lungs wi' foul-smelling smoke."

But the thought of it filled his senses with an unexpected sense of nostalgia, and he knew he bloody well intended being in one of them tonight, whatever poncey name they gave the places now. He'd done his duty to Betsy for a good few years now, and he was feeling more like his randy old self since his medication had done its stuff.

Oh, yes, a few roisterous jars at a kiddleywink and a trip down memory lane – if that was all he could manage – at Miss Kitty's bawdy house, was definitely on the agenda for tonight. Even if it killed him.

Fifteen

The Pengelly girls read their mother's latest letters with varying emotions. Far away in New Jersey, sitting in the shade of an apple tree in the fruit farm where she was now firmly ensconced, Celia gazed into the distance and let the pages fall from her hands on to the grass.

"Bad news?" a voice beside her said, and as Jarvis's shadow passed between her and the sun, Celia smiled quickly.

"No, at least I don't think so. Not for me, anyway, and my mother seems quite positive about it."

"So are you going to tell me about it, or do I have to guess?" he asked encouragingly.

She laughed, gathering up the pages and stuffing them back into the envelope.

"It's just a merger between two china-clay companies in Cornwall that you wouldn't even have heard about, if I hadn't told you about my family connections. It's like the end of an era, of course, and I know I should feel sad, but somehow I don't. Life has to move on, doesn't it?"

"And there, fellow students, class of '38, speaks the voice of the nation," he said solemnly.

"Oh, very noble! Are you aiming to be the head of your college debating society or what?" she teased.

"Not really. I'd rather have a certain person agree to wear my college pin," he said, so coolly Celia thought she had misheard him for a minute.

And then she knew she hadn't.

"Jarvis, for pity's sake, you'll have your mom and poppa on my back for cradle-snatching," she said, scrambling to her feet. She gathered up her letter and the newspaper reports of the rally and the newly formed Bokilly Holdings. She was amazed at how astute her little brother had been in his exclusive interview with

221

their mother. But as the American boy's face flushed darkly, she realised she had humiliated him, and put her hand on his arm.

"I'm sorry. You know I didn't mean that. It's just that – well, you know how fond of you I am, of *all* of you," she emphasised. "But you're only just starting your college education—"

"And I'm lame," he said bluntly.

She stared at him, genuinely startled. "Do you think that would ever be an issue for someone who loved you, Jarvis?"

"Probably," he said. He turned away from her, his shoulders stiff, his frustration and anger making his limp more pronounced as he walked away.

She ached for him. He was more vulnerable than anyone might suppose, despite his brash manner. It was obvious that he had taken a real shine to her. Maybe it was time she moved on, too . . . except that she didn't want to. She loved it here. Anyway, Jarvis would be starting the new semester at college soon, so he wouldn't be a problem.

There were hints of a long-term position here for Celia. As well as helping with the various fruit harvests, she would be a child-minder-cum-book-keeper, and try to straighten out the chaotic accounts Poppa Stone returned to the IRS.

They had such a warm and relaxed way of life. Working with the younger ones, and as good as being a general dogsbody to the admittedly slapdash Momma Stone, would hardly be stretching her mind as the prestigious post in Berlin had done. But since all that was no longer part of her life, she was definitely tempted.

Besides, she thought, breathing in the sweet-scented grass of the orchard, what did she have to go back to Cornwall for? She would miss her mother, she still did, but she was too old for any of that homesick nonsense now. Her stepfather would definitely disapprove of any long-term arrangement here, of course, and would point out the wasted years at a Swiss finishing school.

Too bad, Celia thought defiantly. It was her life – and you had to be tough to survive these days. And anyway, what about Wenna's wasted academy years, which had led her to singing in a London nightclub!

Wenna burst into tears the minute she read her mother's letter. Fanny looked at her in dismay.

"Gawd Almighty, what's wrong, duck? Your Ma's not been taken ill, has she?"

"No," Wenna said, as soon as she could speak. "I'm being silly, that's all. I mean, I knew it was coming, but now it's settled, and it just seems so sad and final, that's all."

Fanny smiled faintly. She'd heard enough about the proposed merger of the clay companies to guess immediately what Wenna was getting at. Privately she thought it just made good business sense. She put her arms around the girl.

"You're just too soft-hearted fer yer own good, my duck. It's this clay-company stuff, I s'pose?"

Wenna nodded, her face full of misery. "Mom sounds so brave, and there's a bit in the letter where she tries to make me laugh about Uncle Theo smashing up his television set."

"Oh, my good Gawd!" Fanny said, staring. "You folk never do things by halves, do yer?"

"But I know she's really sad about it all," Wenna went on passionately. "Killigrew Clay was – well, I wouldn't go so far as to say it was in her soul like it was in my great-grandmother's – but it was so much a part of her life."

"Now you just listen to me," Fanny said briskly. "So these two companies have become one, and I'll refrain from makin' any funny-cum-naughty remarks about that, 'cos I can see yer ain't in the mood. But bleedin' 'ell, darlin', nobody's *died*, have they?"

As she paused for breath, Wenna felt her face flame with embarrassment.

"Oh, Fanny, I wasn't thinking. Poor Georgie—"

"I wasn't thinking about that neither, so stop yer frettin'. All I meant was, when it comes down to it, the most important thing in this world is having yer 'ealth and strength, and yer mother's got that in plenty. I bet by now she's thinkin' of other things, and she won't let any of this get her down for long. So don't you, neither. The last thing she'll want is a sob letter from you or a tearful phone call, so you just keep your pecker up, d'yer hear?"

She got a watery smile in return. "I know you're right, Fanny. But I've got to say something, just so she doesn't think that I don't care."

Fanny hugged her, her eyes suddenly moist. If she'd ever wanted a kid, she thought, she'd have wanted one exactly like this one.

223

"She knows you care, lovey."

Wenna wriggled free and continued perusing the letter with only the occasional sniff now. "She also says she might be doing some writing again. Proper writing this time – a sort of historical booklet."

"Fancy that now," Fanny said, never having had any inclination to do anything that sounded so dull, but readily admitting that Skye had quite a brainbox on her shoulders. Writing about anything, and especially about boring historical stuff, was well outside Fanny's limitations, but somebody had to do it, she supposed cheerfully.

"Anyway, Mom says the new company will do well, so I'm sure she means it. She's a great survivor," Wenna added proudly. "All our family were, wouldn't you say so, Fanny?"

"Course they were," Fanny said, not knowing the half of it, but thankful that Wenna was recovering fast.

For a minute she'd been afraid she would want to rush back to Cornwall and vegetate, when already there were big plans afoot to launch her in a Saturday spot in the new year, when Gloria del Mar would be starting rehearsals for a coveted role in a Broadway musical. Now might just be the right time to push ahead with the plans for Wenna, to cheer her up. It would cheer Georgie up too, she thought hopefully, knowing how his dark depressions over his parents came and went.

Lately they had got more frequent, and decidedly darker, she thought anxiously. He kept predicting that things could only get worse, that they had only seen the tip of the iceberg yet. She always hated it when he talked like that, as if he carried the weight of the world on his thin shoulders.

In November, Georgie Rosenbloom had another letter from an old friend that he couldn't bear to show even to his wife. The agony of what was happening in Germany was starting to affect him deeply, but the most recent news of what was virtually a massacre burned into his very soul.

According to Jackie Cohen, there had been an organised reign of terror carried out throughout the country; Jewish-owned shops had been looted, and innocent Jewish citizens beaten senseless. Thousands of people had died in one night. The reality of it was only just dawning on many of his countryfolk who were fleeing Germany in panic.

"I won't leave," the letter went on. "This is my home. Here I was born and here I will die, old friend, just as your mother and father did. All I will say is, pray for me, and for our brothers and sisters. I will write again when I can."

Georgie brooded over the letter continually, until the day Fanny discovered him silently weeping and she demanded to know what was wrong. Everything else faded out of existence as she held him in her arms. Whatever she had been in the past she was completely devoted to her Georgie, whose dry wit had sadly deserted him in recent times. It broke her heart to see him suffer like this.

Once she had got the gist of it, she was outraged.

"We must bring Jackie here to safety, and any others who want to come with him," she said at once.

He shook his head. "He won't do it. You've read the letter. He's a proud man and an old one. Why should he leave? The old ones are stubborn, but it's the children I'm sorry for. They're the innocent ones caught up in this evil. There's nothing we can do for them."

He was steeped in pessimism, and there was nothing she could say to comfort him. He spent long hours at the synagogue and she let him go, knowing it gave him strength, but privately thinking it did no good at all. Fanny admitted that her religious faith began and ended with what people could do for one another, not in some mumbo-jumbo candle-lighting rigmarole, or whatever it was they did.

The newspapers were soon full of the latest outrage, and the government was starting to take action, she reported to him. Many parts of the empire were offering to take in refugees, including Britain, the way it always had.

"I daresay," Georgie said, with a rare bitterness. "But your pompous Mr Chamberlain also says there's a limit to how many refugees Britain can accept."

"I s'pose there is. But he ain't my Mr Chamberlain," Fanny said vigorously. "I never voted for 'im."

"You never voted for anyone," Georgie reminded her.

She looked at him anxiously. If ever he needed a boost, it was now, and she knew just the way to give him one. She smothered the smile she felt coming on, knowing how she would have put a double meaning on her words on another day – another age, it seemed now.

"Wenna's going home to Cornwall for Christmas. I think we should go too. You know the invitation is always open to us, and it will take us out of ourselves."

"It won't change anything."

"It won't change anything by staying here, neither. Bleedin' 'ell, Georgie, think of something else for a while, can't yer? Think of *me*."

He looked at her in surprise, as if only just realising she was there at all, but the tortured look left his eyes for a second to be replaced by something else.

"There's nothing wrong, is there? If I thought I was losing you too—"

"No, there's nothing wrong," she scowled, almost wishing that there was for a minute, so he'd have something else to worry about. That was a wicked thing to think, because at least they both had their health and that counted for a hell of a lot in this world. "So shall I sort it out with Skye that we all go down there for Christmas?" she persisted. "She'll be glad of the extra company now Celia's gone to America."

"I doubt that she'll care if we're there or not, but do what you like," he said listlessly. "It's all the same to me where we are, since I won't be celebrating anything."

"Well, yer not going to put a bleedin' damper on things, neither," she snapped. "So yer can get that into yer head right away, my son."

"Yes, Mamma," he said, with the first ghost of a smile she'd seen on his face in weeks. But the smile was more haunted than Fanny realised.

Skye read the front-page features in the London newspapers as well as the *Informer* with growing horror. The headlines were huge and black, underlining the seriousness of the whole situation. With practised ease, she skimmed every article, picking out the essential facts. The tension grew with every day that passed and following Hitler's march into Czechoslovakia, it seemed obvious that his fanatical goal was to conquer Europe, if not the world. To do what he was doing to an entire race of people, was to fill every decent person with shame and outrage.

The small matter of their own European markets shrinking for both china clay and White Rivers pottery, seemed petty in the extreme now, compared with the suffering that was being endured elsewhere. It looked as though nothing was going to stop it.

"I've heard from Wenna," she told Nick one evening, "and she says Fanny and Georgie want to come here with her for Christmas. They'll be closing the Flamingo Club for a couple of weeks apparently, and Wenna says she'll have some exciting news to tell us about that. You don't have any objection to them all coming here, do you?"

Her eyes dared him to do so, and he shrugged, saying he could always keep himself occupied if Fanny's coarseness and Georgie's laboured humour all got too much for him. But then he relented, seeing the indignation on her face.

"Of course I don't mind. The poor devil's had enough to put up with lately, anyway. This house is big enough for an army, and it may be the last Christmas of its kind that we'll see for a while, so let's enjoy it while we can."

Skye wouldn't comment, knowing exactly what he meant, and refusing to put it into words.

"I'll call Fanny this evening, and tell her we'd love to see them," she said.

But before she could do so, Fanny called her. It wasn't a long call, she just stated the facts in a strange, calm voice that didn't sound like Fanny's voice at all, then she said that she had to go away and see to things.

Wenna came on the line, and the mood was totally different.

"Oh Mom, it was terrible," Wenna wept hysterically. "One minute everything was fine, and then – and then – oh, I don't know how to say it—"

"Just slow down, honey. Take a deep breath and tell me exactly what happened," Skye said.

Wenna gave a huge gulp. "We were having dinner, and Georgie wasn't eating a thing. He just sat staring at his plate, and Fanny was scolding him, you know the way she does. Then suddenly Georgie got up from the table and said there was something he had to do, and we were to get on with our dinner and not to wait for him."

"And?" Skye prompted.

"So we did. Got on with our dinner, I mean, which just seems so awful now, but we didn't know, did we? How *could* we have known?"

"Then what happened?" Skye asked sharply.

"Well, we didn't have to open the club as it was Sunday, and when he didn't come back Fanny got the hump as she calls it, and said we should go to bed. So we did, and in the middle of the night there was a loud hammering on the door that woke us both up. I heard Fanny go downstairs to answer it, yelling to Georgie that for two pins she'd make him stand outside all night if he'd forgotten his key. A few minutes later I heard her screaming."

Wenna found herself reciting the story parrot-fashion, as if to hold the horror of it all at bay.

"I ran down to see what was happening, and two policemen were holding her up. One of them told me to fetch her some brandy. Then they told me that Georgie had walked calmly along Westminster Bridge, climbed onto the parapet and jumped. If a passer-by hadn't seen it and reported it, they might not have found him for days. His wallet was still in his pocket, which was how they identified him."

"Dear God," Skye said, horrified, visualising it all too well. "That poor sweet man! His state of mind must have been in turmoil for him to do such a thing."

"I know. And now Fanny's blaming herself for not seeing it coming. But how could she? Georgie kept everything so much to himself these last months. And I – I just don't know what to say to her any more."

Skye heard the bewilderment and grief in her young voice, and knew at once what she had to do.

"I'll be with you in a day or two, darling, just as soon as I can arrange it, and I won't leave until you're both ready to come back to Cornwall with me."

Cornwall. Where she had once believed in her naivety that everything could be solved, and all ills could be healed.

As she thought it, Skye realised how foolish and infantile that had been. Nothing could heal the pain that Fanny was going through now, except time. And pathetic though the platitude sounded to her, Skye knew it was true.

*   *   *

"You're going to London?" Nick asked.

"I have to. Fanny needs me, and so does Wenna. Once the funeral's over I'll bring them both back here as soon as possible. They were coming for Christmas, anyway."

"A bright Christmas it's going to be, isn't it?"

"What would you have me do then – leave them to spend a miserable time alone in that flat above the empty club? I thought you had more compassion than that," she said angrily. "Fanny must be in a terrible state, and this has obviously hit Wenna hard. She was so very fond of Georgie."

"I'm sorry, darling," he said, contrite at once. "You're right, and they must come down here as soon as possible."

"What I also have to do is write to Celia," she said uneasily, her thoughts leaping ahead. "We all know what demons drove Georgie to this, and I wonder if it will affect any remaining feelings she has for Stefan von Gruber."

"Why on earth should it? You can't stamp all Germans in the same mould as that madman, Hitler. You of all people know that. Herr Vogl would never have been a party to such evil doings, and nor would any other sane person going about his daily business."

"I know. But I can't help being thankful that nothing more came of the romance between Celia and Stefan. What would have become of them if they had married and their countries were heading for war – as you keep reminding me they are?"

She shivered as the enormity of it filled her mind, blocking out for a moment the horror of what had happened to Georgie Rosenbloom. But their fates were all linked together, and in those moments she found it hard to separate the one from the other.

"I'm sure Celia's glad she's well out of it," Nick reassured her. "Now, I'll find out when there's a suitable train for you, and I suggest you get some sleep, darling."

But she insisted on going into her study and writing to Celia first. She couldn't put it off. How could she ever sleep, when once her head touched the pillow she knew it would be filled with images she didn't want, but couldn't avoid. Images of Georgie jumping off Westminster Bridge and sinking into the sinister dark water of the Thames and giving no resistance while he was sucked under and drowned.

Her forehead was beaded with sweat as other, unwanted,

images crowded into her mind. Were her family and everyone they touched cursed with this same awful self-destructive urge? She remembered how Granny Morwen's friend Celia had drowned herself in a milky clay pool all those years ago. How Theo's father Walter had walked into the sea when everything became too much for him. Now Georgie Rosenbloom. Was there a terrible pattern to all this that none of them could avoid . . .

"Drink this, Skye," ordered Nick. A glass of spirit was thrust into her hand. "You can't take on everyone else's burdens, my love."

"It seems to me that's just what Georgie did," she said, as she swallowed the bitter spirit with a grimace. "And I know it can't be done."

"Then write your letter and come to bed. And maybe later you can write a personal obituary for the *Informer*. People here won't have known Georgie, but they'll know of our connection with him, and it may help them to understand things happening in Germany more personally. It will help you, too."

She didn't speak for a long moment and then she shook her head. "I love you for your understanding, Nick, but I don't think that's a sensible idea. I'm afraid it might just remind people of the time we brought the German youths here to work, and stir things up all over again. We're all involved in this now, whether we like it or not. In our own small backwater way, we're already at war, aren't we?"

The thought of it loomed ahead of her like a spectre. Already, times were changing at a breakneck speed and there was no way it could be stopped, not by ineffectual governments or by personal tragedies. Only a fool could deny it.

Two days later she reached London at the end of a long and wearisome journey, and took a taxi to the Flamingo Club. Wenna fell into her arms and began to cry helplessly.

"I'm so glad to see you, Mom. Fanny's being so odd and working feverishly, and the place is full of strangers."

"What kind of strangers?"

"Policemen and doctors and reporters and accountants and clients from the club, of course, and the new manager."

"What new manager?" Skye said, starting to feel like an echo as her daughter faltered.

Wenna sniffed back the tears and linked her arm in her mother's as they went up to the flat with her suitcase.

"The one Fanny called among all the other people she's been calling. It seems tasteless to me, but she keeps saying it's what Georgie would have wanted, that he hadn't built up this club from nothing to see it all fall apart, so she sent for Martin Russell, an agent-manager, who comes here often, and asked him to take over the running of the club in the new year. We shan't re-open until then."

"And you don't think it's right for Fanny to have contacted this Martin Russell so soon?" Skye said, ignoring the rest of it.

"I think it's awful. Why couldn't she have waited? Georgie's not even buried yet and I've even heard her laughing with this other man."

Skye sensed her outrage. Youth had such fixed ideas. She had known Fanny a very long while and knew that laughter could also hide tears and heartbreak.

"Honey, everyone faces grief in their own way, and no single way is the right one. Remember how Adam turned inwards and became almost a recluse after Vera died, and how Lily furiously cleaned her mother's house until no speck of dust would have dared to enter it? If this is Fanny's way, then it's the only way for her, and we have no right to question it. Now then, dry your tears and stop letting your resentment show, while I go and find her."

She left Wenna sitting on the bed and sought out the sitting room where the noise was coming from. Fanny was surrounded by a small group of people, but the moment she saw Skye she turned to her and held out her hands.

"I knew you'd come," she said simply. "Come and have a drink, fer Gawd's sake. You look fair perished."

Only someone who knew her well would have seen the anguish in her eyes and recognised the tremor in her voice. Fanny was suffering all right, thought Skye, but she'd never show it. She was a real trouper and if the show didn't have to go on until the new year, it would bleedin' well go on then, she thought in Fanny's style.

"This is Martin Russell who's takin' over the management of the club," she said next. "I ain't a businesswoman, Skye, so I need somebody I can trust, and me and Martin go back a long way. He'll be handling Wenna's future, too – I should say Penny Wood's, o' course. Me mind plays tricks these days."

Skye wasn't surprised. As the moments passed and the chatter resumed with no mention of Georgie at all, she began to feel as if she was in a kind of charade. Fanny was acting out the part of hostess so well, talking too loudly, making sure everyone had a drink, and putting people at ease. It was more like a social occasion than a pre-wake, and it alarmed Skye. Despite what she had said to Wenna, it wasn't natural. It wasn't right.

It was only when they had all gone and it was just the two of them sitting together on the sofa, that Fanny's shoulders drooped and she looked old for the first time since Skye had known her. Gone was the brashness and the brittle tarty look, and in its place was a broken woman who had just lost her husband and didn't know how to handle it except by surrounding herself with people.

"I know Wenna thinks I'm wicked and that I don't care," she said, pouring herself another drink with shaking hands. "But she don't understand, Skye. It's because I care too much about Georgie that I can't just sit back and weep. I daren't even let myself think too much. I just have to go on. *You* understand, don't yer?"

"You know I do. We went through too much together during the war not to know how grief affects different people."

"And I can't cry in front of 'er, can I? She's too young to know how it feels. And I can't cry in front of anybody else, neither. I ain't cried at all yet, Skye. It's like I was waitin' fer somebody's shoulder. It used to be Georgie's, but now there's nobody."

"Yes there is, Fanny," Skye said softly. "There's me."

She held out her arms, and as she did so, Fanny gave an agonising cry like that of an animal in pain.

It went straight to Skye's heart as Fanny leant heavily against her and cried her heart out. It went on and on, while she poured out all the details of her personal and passionate life with Georgie that Skye didn't need to hear but couldn't avoid.

At one point during the hours of sorrowing, she saw Wenna's frightened face over Fanny's heaving shoulders, as she stood hesitatingly at the door, and she shook her head as she motioned her daughter out of the room. This was Fanny's time, and one that she desperately needed.

*　　*　　*

The following day Fanny was nearly as brash as ever. Only her shadowed eyes showed evidence of a night's releasing weeping. Wenna made no more criticisms of her behaviour, and simply put her arms around her.

"I'm sorry. I didn't understand," she whispered. "I'm glad Mom's here."

"So am I, duck," said Fanny crisply. "So when are yer goin' to show her the poster?"

"Oh. I thought after – you know—"

"After we've seen Georgie on 'is way to the sweet bye-and-bye? Nah. He wouldn't want yer to miss out on yer bit of excitement. Go on now."

"What's all this?" Skye asked, when Wenna had gone hurrying to her room.

Fanny smiled faintly. "There's no point in making the poor little bugger suffer on account o' Georgie's passing, is there? She's been dying to let yer know what's happening in the new year, and we was goin' to spill the beans at Christmas, but now seems as good a time as any."

"You're still coming to Cornwall, aren't you, Fanny?" Skye said urgently. "I'm not going back until you agree."

"O' course I am. Me and Georgie are looking forward to it." She stopped abruptly. "Bugger it. I'll have to get out of the habit of speakin' fer two, won't I?"

Wenna came back into the room, relieving Skye of finding a reply that didn't sound trite. She turned to her daughter quickly as she unrolled the poster and held it up.

"My Lord!" Skye exclaimed.

Wenna grinned. "I thought you'd be surprised. There's going to be a bigger one outside the club, and these smaller ones are going to be distributed around the area. This one's a souvenir for you. Are you impressed?"

Skye scanned the words surrounding the photograph of her daughter – a sensuous, yet still tasteful photograph, showing the glowing sapphire eyes to best advantage, the mouth half-smiling, and the dark hair curling provocatively around her heart-shaped face.

"Celebrate the New Year of 1939," she read, "with the opening Saturday evening debut of the beautiful Cornish songbird, MISS PENNY WOOD."

"My Lord," Skye said again, as if they were the only words she knew.

Fanny chuckled. "Are yer praying, or just thanking the Almighty fer giving yer such a luscious daughter?"

"Both," Skye said at once.

"Oh Mom," Wenna said, embarrassed. "It was all down to the photographer's skill, though Georgie was as flattering as usual and said it didn't even do me justice."

She clapped her hand over her mouth at once, her eyes full of dismay, and Fanny wagged a finger at her.

"Now look here, my gel. If yer goin' ter stop using Georgie's name, it'll be as if he never existed at all, and I won't have that. My Georgie was a good judge of yooman nature and he loved yer like 'is own."

"I know," Wenna said, her voice catching.

Already Skye could see that they had moved on from the depths of shock and sorrow that should have drawn them together, but had instead driven them temporarily apart.

She asked about the plans for the new-year opening, and learned that Martin Russell would play a big part in promoting, as well as managing, the club in future, which clearly went some way to mollifying Wenna to his existence.

"So when is Mother coming home?" Oliver said resentfully to his father, on hearing the news that Skye had gone rushing up to London.

"Soon. As soon as the funeral's over, and Fanny feels ready to travel."

Nick looked at his son through narrowed eyes. He was only fifteen, but there was already a hardness about him that reeked of David Kingsley's influence. David was constantly reiterating that a newsman had to be hard-headed and unemotional, no matter how harrowing the story, and God knew it was the same for a lawyer, but sometimes Nick thought his son was taking the advice too far.

"They'll still be suffering from shock after Georgie Rosenbloom's death," he went on. "We must make this Christmas as comfortable for Fanny as possible in the circumstances."

"I still think I could ask her to give me some comments on how she sees the German situation," Olly said.

"That's exactly what you are not going to do," Nick snapped. "Do you have no sensitivity at all? If you can't be tactful then I suggest you stay away."

"That's just what I'll do then," he shouted. "Lily said I can have Christmas dinner with them if I wanted to, and I jolly well will. It's not going to be much fun here, is it? Adam's going there for the day too, so you can all stew in your own juice for all I care."

"Oliver, come back here," Nick raged, incensed, but his son banged out of the house and went pedalling furiously away on his bicycle in the direction of Truro.

So much for a family holiday, Nick fumed. Not that it would have been any easier with Olly around. They constantly rubbed one another up the wrong way lately. It was probably better like this, though he wasn't at all sure that was how Skye would see it. She was a great one for family get-togethers and it looked as if this one was going to consist of just themselves, Wenna and Fanny Rosenbloom.

Theo's family were also spending the holiday in their own home, with Justin coming down from London. There had been a time, thought Nick, when this old house had been bursting with people at the least opportunity, but all that was changing. He regretted the fact his elder daughter seemed to have no inclination to come home at all.

Sixteen

F anny Rosenbloom, née Webb, was nothing if not resilient. However much crying she did in private she did none of it in public. She had been born illegitimate, living hand to mouth with her feckless mother in London's East End, and learning how to survive. Once she was alone in the world she had clawed herself up from nothing, through good times as well as bad, and meeting Georgie had been the best thing of all. They had made a good and respectable life for themselves, and she wasn't letting go of it now. She owed it to him to follow his dream, and to make the Flamingo Club a success.

But if Georgie had been a dreamer, Fanny was also a realist. Throughout the funeral service, eyeing the men, in their bespoke tailored black suits, who had come to honour and remember him, she noted that they were of a class who wouldn't have given her their nose-droppings in her early years. It was all due to Georgie's modestly warm and generous personality, of course, and together with Martin Russell's management and her new star in the making, she vowed that it would continue. There was work to be done.

By the time she and the protective Pengelly women were on the train bound for Cornwall, Fanny's eyes had lost much of their haunted look, and she was already thinking positively about the future. Yesterday was gone, but a brighter tomorrow was just around the corner, she thought cheerfully. You had to bleedin' well believe it or go under.

"I want ter say something, Skye," she announced, after they had all dozed for a while as the train clattered westwards. "I don't want gloomy faces on my account, and Georgie wouldn't have wanted it neither. If yer planning parties and suchlike, yer must go ahead wiv 'em."

"We weren't, actually," Skye began.

"Why ever not? It's Christmas, ain't it? Bleedin' 'ell, ain't yer planning a knees-up or nothin', gel? I might as well have stayed at home and looked at me four walls!"

Wenna started to laugh. "Oh, Fanny, you're priceless!"

"Oh yeah? And what's that s'posed ter mean?"

"Just that I love you," Wenna said quickly, in case she thought she was being patronising.

"We all do," Skye said. "And if it's a party you want, then a party you shall have. Just as long as you're sure."

"I'm sure."

Skye raised her eyebrows slightly as she glanced at her daughter. How anybody could think of a party at such a time was beyond her, but if Fanny wanted it and needed it, they would have it. It wasn't right to spoil everyone else's Christmas, anyway, even though she had been prepared to do it. But there were others to think about, she thought guiltily. There was her husband and her children.

"Olly said *what*?" she asked Nick, some time after they had arrived at New World late that night, and Wenna and Fanny had gone to bed.

"Don't worry. I put him off the idea damn quickly."

"I should think so, indeed. How could he think of interviewing Fanny at this time? How dare he think about dissecting her feelings? And I suppose you both argued about it as usual," Skye said, touchy after the endless train journey and not needing to hear any of this.

"When did we not?" Nick retorted. "But I made him see sense. Anyway, he's now planning to spend Christmas Day with Lily and David—"

"He certainly is not! He'll be here where he belongs, and they'll all be invited too, and so will Adam. People need to be together at Christmas. It's bad enough that Celia will be so far away without the family splitting up unnecessarily."

She felt angry and ridiculously tearful at that moment and dashed the feeling away. But with the recently revealed instructions about what everyone should do in case of war, and now news of the government spending an exorbitant amount of money on air-raid shelters, it made the prospect seem desperately real. She felt an urgency to gather her family around her like a mother hen with her chicks.

Nick's arms held her close and she leaned against him. They had been apart for more than two weeks, and she desperately needed him in a way that Fanny could never physically have Georgie again.

The thought sent a wave of erotic sensation through her and, while it shocked her, it was an unchangeable fact that she and Nick were warm and alive, with normal feelings and emotions. Whatever happened to the world around them, they mustn't lose that feeling.

"Can we sleep on it, honey?" she said huskily. "Let's talk about it tomorrow."

"Of course we can," he said at once. "I was forgetting how exhausted you must be, darling."

"I'm not," she whispered against him. "I just want to go to bed and to feel you holding me."

She raised her face to his, with all the love she felt for him mirrored in her eyes. His answering kiss was very sweet on her lips.

Lily was uncertain, and openly shocked.

"Are you sure this is what Fanny wants?" she asked Skye, while making a duty visit and guiltily relieved to find that Fanny and Wenna had gone out. "As far as I'm concerned, I'll be delighted to let your people do all the Christmas cooking, but is it right?"

"If you mean, does she want to forget Georgie, then of course she doesn't, and she won't. But this is her way, Lily. She wants what she calls a good old knees-up. I don't know that we'll go that far, but she needs people around her, and I want to humour her before she and Wenna go back to London."

"Well, if you say so. I hope David will agree once I explain, and anyway, our boys love it here."

"They'll make all the difference," Skye assured her. "Children make Christmas, and although Fanny never had any, she always says she enjoys other people's, because she can always hand them back."

"I know the feeling," Lily said with a grin.

"Oh, and one more thing, please prime David and Olly – well, I think you know what I'm trying to say."

"Don't worry. I've already warned them to walk on eggshells when they come in contact with her."

"Well, you didn't need to go that far. She's marvellous as always, and full of the big splash that Miss Penny Wood is going to make in the new year," Skye said, and remembered to show her Wenna's advertising poster.

"This is wonderful," Lily said. "You must let David see it. Wenna really is going places, as they say. And how about your plans?"

Skye looked at her blankly. What plans did she have, apart from wondering if Bokilly Holdings was really going to be the success they hoped, or if the shock of the drastically reduced china-clay orders from Kauffmann's was going to make Bourne and Yelland wish they had never suggested the merger at all.

"Your writing, Skye!" Lily reminded her. "The booklet you were planning."

"Good Lord, I haven't given that a second thought. There's plenty of time for all that, and right now I don't have the heart for it." She felt something akin to anger at even being reminded of it.

"Well, don't let other people's worries eat into you the way you always do. They have to sort out their own lives."

"There's no danger of that," Skye said dryly, hearing the raucous laughter that heralded Fanny's homecoming. Tinged with hysteria it may be, but it was laughter all the same.

Celia telephoned on Christmas Day, and Skye told her to wait a minute until she closed the door to the drawing room, as she couldn't hear a thing for the noise.

"What's happening there, Mom?" Celia yelled. "It sounds like a herd of elephants rampaging through the house."

"No. It's just Fanny organising them all in a game of charades," Skye replied.

"Good God. It didn't take her long to get back on form, did it? Anyway, I can't talk for long, or it will cost Poppa Stone a fortune – and he won't let me pay for the call. I just wanted to wish you all a happy Christmas, and to thank you for the gifts you sent – and I wish I was there too."

"I wish it too, honey. So when are you coming home?"

"Well, not just yet. I'm going to be doing some extra work for Poppa Stone. It is all right, isn't it, Mom?"

"Just don't stay away for ever. We miss you."

"I miss you too. Listen, I'll have to go now, but say hello to everyone for me, won't you?" she said, before she choked up altogether.

She hung up the receiver on the wall hook, blinking the tears from her eyes. What an idiot she was to get so emotional when she had just made up her mind to stay here for a few more months at least. But it wouldn't be for ever, she vowed. This place was heaven, but it wasn't home.

She could visualise them all there now, with Fanny holding court and being the life and soul of the party. And for one scintillating and completely unexpected moment, Celia identified with Fanny totally. She understood that need to throw yourself into a brash and noisy party atmosphere, as if it could blot out the pain inside. But it wouldn't make Fanny forget, even for a moment, her love for that funny little Georgie Rosenbloom.

Just as if it could make *her* forget, even for a moment, the love that she had felt, and would always feel, for Stefan von Gruber.

"Are you coming back to the party?" Jarvis Stone's voice interrupted her thoughts. "Did you manage to call your folks?"

"I did, and yes, I'm coming back," she said brightly, and then squealed as Jarvis caught her under a sprig of mistletoe and just missed her mouth with his enthusiastic kiss as she managed to twist her head away.

"Nearly caught you that time!" He laughed.

"Go find your sweetheart, Jarvis," she said, laughing back, and more than thankful that he had at last found a sweet little farm girl to court. Then she was being chased by the younger Stone siblings who all screeched and hollered as they fought to kiss their adored Celia under the mistletoe, and for a few blissful minutes, it was almost like being home.

Skye was thankful that the holiday passed smoothly after all. Once it was over she was relieved to have no more of Fanny's enforced exuberance, though she was sad to see Wenna leave for London. But the feeling was reversed when Lily arrived a few days later to show her a belated Christmas card and letter from Ireland. Skye's eyes widened as she read it.

"I'm sure Wenna doesn't have any serious feelings about Ethan now," Skye said. "But the news that he and Karina have a child might have revived them again."

"And so soon after the marriage," Lily said meaningly. "No wonder it was all so hastily arranged. But they seem to be doing well enough with their pigs and sheep."

Skye pulled a face. "It's not something I ever imagined them doing. I can still remember the awful farmyard smells whenever I visited Aunt Em in Padstow. Poor Em," she added wistfully. "I never thought the 'flu would see her and Will off so quickly. They always seemed so strong."

"That doesn't mean a thing, apparently. I'm sure Karina will be writing to you as well, but I thought you'd like to know that there's now a Ryan Pengelly in the family."

"I'll telephone and congratulate them," Skye said, trying not to mind that Lily had got the news first. But since Karina had been part of her household for quite a while, she supposed it was understandable.

Ethan might have been embarrassed to speak to Nick, she conceded, since it was obvious that the child had been conceived before their marriage. She readily forgave them for any lapse of protocol.

"So how are you, now that you've got the house to yourself again?" Lily went on.

"How am I?" She considered the question. "Lonely. Quiet. Missing Wenna. Missing Celia. Missing Fanny too."

"Well, that sums it all up neatly. And what about Olly? Don't you miss him?"

"Well, yes. Does that mean you're tired of him?"

"Of course not. I love having him around. It's just that you didn't include him in your list of missing persons," Lily said shrewdly.

Skye gave a sigh. "I'm afraid he and Nick clash more often than they agree these days. I know it's an awful admission to make about my own son. I love him dearly, but the house is much calmer when he's not around."

"Calm? Lonely? Skye, I'm worried about you!"

"Why on earth should you be? I'm perfectly fine."

Lily shook her head. "I don't think you are, darling. You look peaky, and I think you're losing weight. It doesn't suit you, and perhaps you should see the doctor."

Skye began to laugh. "I promise you there's nothing wrong with me, Lily, and I'm not going to turn into a hypochondriac like cousin Theo. Betsy tells me he calls the doctor out on any pretext now, the old buffoon!"

"You're not going to divert my attention by telling me any tales about Theo," Lily said sternly. "Promise me you'll think about yourself for a change instead of thinking about everybody else, and about business worries. It will all survive without you, Skye."

"Oh, well, that really fills me with confidence! Are you suggesting I'm about to hang up my boots at any minute?" she said. The accompanying small shiver reminded her that she shouldn't tempt fate.

"Of course not. You're indestructable, darling, and in any case, what would we all do without you?"

Lily blew her a kiss as she took her leave. Skye was still smiling in the doorway as she drove her car away at her usual gear-crunching speed. But once she had gone, all was silent again, and Skye turned slowly back indoors, and felt the smile slipping away from her mouth.

There was nothing wrong with her, she thought, at least nothing that a new interest wouldn't put right. The pottery was in good hands now, with Adam and Seb doing such good work, and the showroom was under the control of an efficient manager and an assistant.

She certainly wasn't needed at the clayworks, nor was she obliged to be present at any meeting other than the quarterly meetings of the four new partners of Bokilly Holdings. Orders, shipping, accounts and audits were all taken care of by others, and the lawyers kept their eagle eyes over it all.

Once, the clay bosses had been deep into every facet of the industry, knowing where every penny was spent, and dealing with every problem, large or small. Now, providing her signature was obtained on each document that needed it, she was no more than a figurehead.

Perhaps that was the reason Theo Tremayne had turned in on himself, she thought suddenly. He was no longer the chief of the Indians, either, and studying and querying his own health was one way to keep attention on him. It was the way old folk behaved, and it wasn't going to happen to her, Skye thought in panic.

She knew she should make a start on the booklet she was

promising to do, but somehow she couldn't even gather up the stamina or the interest in it, and that was alarming too. The combination of remembering Theo's antics, which didn't seem so funny any more, and Lily's anxiety about her, was beginning to remind her sharply that she too was middle-aged. And she didn't like what she saw.

"Tell me something, honestly. Do you think I'm getting old?" she asked Nick that evening.

"Not by my reckoning," he said with a laugh, and then he saw that she was serious. "Of course you're not getting old, no more than the rest of us. What's brought this on, anyway?"

"Oh, just something Lily said. I'm being silly to take any notice of it. I've probably got too much time on my hands lately. Which reminds me of the reason she came here. Ethan and Karina have had a son."

"And they haven't let us know themselves?" Nick said, anger flaring in his eyes. "Well, that's rich, I must say, considering that Ethan's my brother and that we took the girl in. It happened mighty quickly, didn't it?"

"Don't let's judge them for that, honey. I'm sure Ethan felt too embarrassed to tell you himself. Anyway, I telephoned them this afternoon, and Karina's not too well." She hesitated. "Actually I wondered if I might go over there for a few weeks to help out. What do you think?"

"Why should you? She's not your responsibility."

"But she doesn't have anyone else, and Ethan's busy with the farm. You could always come too. He is your brother, and I'd love to see the baby."

Nick was clearly more put out than she was that Ethan hadn't let them know about the child, but finally he nodded.

"I couldn't spare the time to stay away for long, but I'll take you and stay a few days, and then fetch you back when you're ready. Just don't stay away too long, Skye."

"Don't be crazy. It won't be for ever," she said.

She was guiltily relieved that he would only stay for a few days. London had been harrowing after Georgie died, and although Fanny had been in fine form over Christmas, Skye had still felt obliged to keep an eye on her, and on Wenna too, who had loved Georgie like a substitute father. There had been all the trauma over the recent business merger, and even a satisfactory conclusion could take its toll on the nerves. She hadn't even realised, until this new opportunity arose, that she needed time to herself; time to get away from everything. She would find peace and tranquillity in Ireland, and the sweet remembered joy of caring for a new baby.

She smiled ruefully as these thoughts assaulted her. Oh yes, she may not be getting old in Nick's eyes, and thank heaven for that, but she definitely felt the need to slow down and take stock of her life.

"My mother's going to Ireland for a few weeks," Wenna said to Fanny, after their weekly telephone call.

"What the 'ell would she want to go there for? They have pigs and sheep and chickens running in and out of their houses, don't they?"

"Oh, Fanny, I'm sure they don't!" Wenna said, laughing. "Although my relatives do have a small farm."

"There you are then," Fanny said. "What relatives are these, anyway?"

"Karina's a sort of Irish cousin, and her husband happens to be Nick's younger brother," she said, almost surprised to note that there were no painful palpitations in her heart as she said the words.

"Blimey, gel, you do like ter keep it in the fam'ly, don't yer?" Fanny said, not for the first time. "Yer ma's parents were cousins as well, weren't they?"

Wenna nodded. "It makes you believe in fate though, doesn't it? I mean, my grandfather was born and brought up in America, and my grandmother was as Cornish as the clay. But they found one another out of all the people in the world. Don't you think that's beautiful?"

Fanny suddenly gave her one of her bear hugs. "I think you're a sentimental sweetheart, that's what I think. No wonder yer can put so much feelin' into yer songs."

"Well, you have to live the words, don't you?"

And she certainly did that, Fanny thought happily. She put her heart and soul into every song she sang, and the Flamingo audiences were well aware of it. On this very Saturday night little Wenna Pengelly, alias Miss Penny Wood, was going to be their shining light.

Her delight faltered just for a moment, thinking how much Georgie would have loved all this. Georgie had loved *her*, his little Cornish cup-cake, loved her like a daughter.

"Fanny, are you all right?" Wenna asked her now.

"Course I am, duck. And this afternoon you and me are goin' round the sales to buy yer a new frock for tonight."

"But I've got my blue, and I don't need anything else."

Fanny shook her head. "White and virginal is what yer need to set off them lovely blue eyes and dark hair, my duck. Trust me and never mind the coffers."

In the audience at the Flamingo Club that night there was a theatre critic sent along, under protest, by his editor. More used to covering plays and revues for the weekly theatre guide, it wasn't Austin Marsh's idea of an interesting night out to visit a small club well away from the West End. But his editor had been sent details of a new female singer called Penny Wood by an agent friend, and had decided that their paper may as well cover it. Austin had been given the assignment, and taken along a bored woman colleague in the interests of remaining incognito.

"It's better than some, I suppose," she commented. "Nice enough decor, anyway, and the clients look well-heeled."

Austin glanced around at the black-suited gentlemen and their ladies. He really hadn't known what to expect of the Flamingo Club, some low dive, perhaps, but this certainly wasn't it. It had class, he thought in surprise. At least he could report on that, even if the singer wasn't up to much. He'd seen enough amateur nights to last a lifetime, and he didn't hold out much hope for some little country girl from the wilds of Cornwall.

An hour later he had completely reversed his opinion.

"Put your eyes back in their sockets, Austin," his companion said in her usual cynical drawl, drawing heavily on her cigarette before exhaling blue smoke and blurring his vision for a moment.

He ignored her. He was too intent on watching and listening to the lovely girl on the stage, who had already enchanted the audience with her singing and piano playing. Her performance was magical, but it was more than that. He had never believed how a beautifully straight posture that curved so deliciously into a slender waist could be so erotic. Now, after an interval, someone else was playing the piano, and the vision in the sensuously silky white gown was weaving her way slowly around the audience as she sang a plaintive love song in that soft, husky voice that surely touched the heartstrings of everyone who heard it.

For a hard-bitten theatre critic who had seen and heard it all, Austin Marsh was completely bowled over by this angel whose eyes were more lustrously blue than any eyes he had ever seen before. He reminded himself severely that he was here to make a report for his column and not to fall in love.

Wenna had almost reached their table. He could breathe in her subtle perfume. He could see the delicate sheen on her faintly flushed skin and the perfect contours of her face. Her seductive shape was caressed by the white silk dress and he felt an urge to replace that white silk with his hands and touch that lovely warm young body.

"Come back, Austin. She's not for you," he heard his colleague say, and he glanced into her so sophisticated eyes that were a world away from those of the girl nearing them.

What would Maggie Stubbs know who was and wasn't for him, he thought resentfully. Her mission in life was to get her claws into him, as well as every other man on the paper, but he had never fallen for it. She was too brash, in a worldly, unfeminine way that wasn't to his taste. Until now, he had never met a woman who was.

Until now . . .

The golden-voiced girl had reached their table. Several people had reached out to shake her hand as she slowly circled the room, and she had made each of them feel important, as if she sang especially for them.

Austin stretched out his hand to clasp those slim, ringless fingers in his for a moment, and smiled into her eyes. He was positive he saw them widen imperceptibly, and the flush in her cheeks deepened, but it may just have been a trick of the lighting – and then she had moved on.

He applauded with the rest of the clientele as the performance came to an end, and finished his drink quickly.

"I'm going to ask for an interview," he said briefly.

Maggie gave him a knowing look. "My God, I do believe you're smitten. She's no different from a hundred other girls singing for a crust."

"Yes, she is. She's very different."

The woman pulled her fake fur stole around her shoulders and gave a disinterested shrug.

"Well, you can hang around here if you like. Personally I'm bored by the whole thing. I'll leave you to it and see you at the office tomorrow."

"I'll call a cab for you."

"Don't bother. Just be sure and tell me tomorrow if you made a conquest."

She went out laughing, and Austin immediately forgot her as he wove his way between the tables to where the blowsy woman who owned the club was watching his progress.

If this handsome bloke thought he was going to make a play for her Wenna, Fanny thought keenly, he was out of luck.

"Mrs Rosenbloom?" he asked her, and thrust his business card under her nose. "Is it possible for me to have a few words with Miss Penny Wood? I was very impressed by her, and I intend to give her a good review, but I'd like some personal background information for my readers."

And for yourself, I'll bet, thought Fanny. But now that she had seen the credentials on his card, she knew better than to refuse him. This could lead to something big for Wenna.

"Wait here, and I'll see if she's prepared to talk to you," she said, as cool as you like.

She left him and went to the little dressing room where Wenna was sitting motionless on a stool, gazing at her reflection in the mirror. She turned at once, her face more flushed than ever.

"Was I all right, Fanny? Do you think they liked me? I couldn't really tell, though there seemed to be plenty of applause. I was a bag of nerves from start to finish."

"Sweetheart, you was the tops and you know it. And we ain't the only ones. There's a theatre critic bloke who wants to talk to yer. Martin says he's all right, so do yer want me to send him in? He don't look the type to start any funny business, but in any case I'll be right outside the door."

Wenna laughed, her nerves starting to unwind at last at Fanny's threatening words.

"Oh, let's get it over with, then I can change out of this dress and have something to eat. I'm starving."

248

"That's just reaction," Fanny told her. "Here's the bloke's card then, and remember, I'll be right outside."

Wenna glanced into the mirror again as she heard the tap on the door and called to the stranger to come in. It was only an instant before she turned round to face him, but it felt like an eternity. It was one of those weird moments in life that you wanted to hold on to for ever, knowing it could never come again.

She shook off the feeling and rose quickly to shake the man's hand. She felt the same tingle in her fingers that she had felt before. Somewhere in the back of her consciousness she remembered Celia telling her about a similar sensation the first time she had touched Stefan von Gruber's hand. With a small sense of something like fright, she almost snatched her hand away from Austin Marsh's as she asked him to sit down.

"I thought you were marvellous," he said simply.

"Oh – well, thank you."

He had taken her by surprise. She had expected the kind of interview that David Kingsley was so good at, and that her brother Olly was emulating, firing crisp questions at her that were as unnerving as they were efficient. But this man – this Austin Marsh with the almost autocratic features and crisp dark hair – seemed content to simply look at her for long moments, which was just as unnerving in a different way.

"What did you want to ask me?" she said huskily. "My brother works on a newspaper in Truro, so I know the form."

She felt her cheeks burn. It sounded so pathetic, as if she was trying to prove that she was a sophisticated Londoner like himself, which she certainly wasn't. In fact she felt all fingers and thumbs. He gave a small smile.

"I hope your brother has such delightful assignments as mine has been tonight," Austin went on. "Is Truro your home?"

"Nearby. Do you know the area?"

He shook his head. "I've never been to Cornwall, but I've heard that the scenery is stunning and that Cornishwomen are beautiful. Now I know that much is true."

Wenna blushed at the blatant compliment. She wasn't used to such outspokenness from strangers, and asked him again what he wanted to know.

He took out a small notebook. "I can write a review of what

I've seen and heard here tonight, and I assure you it will be a good one," he said, more briskly. "But our readers like to know a few personal details too. For instance, do you mind telling me your age, Miss Wood?"

She smiled at the name, still not used to it. Even though she had been working on and off at the club for some time it seemed suddenly unreal that Wenna Pengelly was being interviewed for a London theatre guide.

"I'll tell you mine if you tell me yours," she said mischievously, without stopping to think.

Austin paused in surprise, and then laughed.

"I'm twenty-five, a bachelor of this parish, and I live in an apartment overlooking the Thames."

"My goodness, that sounds very grand," Wenna said.

"Not really. My parents bought it for me as a university-leaving gift. So now that you know more about me than I know about you, are you going to come clean, or are you about to show me a picture of a female Dorian Gray in the attic?"

For a moment she looked blank, and then remembered the story by Oscar Wilde, and she laughed.

"I'm nearly nineteen," she told him.

"What a wonderful age to have the world at your feet," he said, scribbling in his notebook.

"I don't know that I want the world at my feet," she heard herself say. "I just want what every other woman wants."

"Oh yes?" he said, interested at once. "And what's that? Marriage? Children?"

He merely asked the question to get a useful quote to add to his review. She didn't answer immediately, and when she did, her voice was husky again.

"Of course marriage and children, when the right man comes along."

"But how will you know? I'm sorry, this is becoming far too personal, but as a mere man such comments intrigue me. Women always seem to have an instinct about these things."

"Especially Cornishwomen," she said softly.

Right at that moment, right on cue, as if to disperse the suddenly charged atmosphere between them, her stomach rumbled. She gasped and pressed her hand to the offending object.

"I apologise for that, Mr Marsh. I never eat before I perform, and this is the result."

"Then would you let me take you out to supper? I promise that nothing you say will be taken down and used in my review, cross my heart. But only if you'll call me Austin and allow me to call you Penny."

"I'd much rather you called me Wenna, since it's my real name. But you must promise not to reveal it in your paper."

"Your secret is safe with me, ma'am," he said solemnly.

"Then perhaps you'd wait in the club while I change," she said pointedly, when he made no attempt to move.

"I'm sorry. It's difficult for me to take my eyes off you, and I find myself wanting to look at you for ever."

But he left her then, and she had changed out of the white gown with shaking hands by the time Fanny came into the little room.

"Is everything all right, duck? He was a mighty long time in here, and Martin's talking to 'im now just to make sure he's who he says he is. He's on the up and up all right."

"He was absolutely delightful," Wenna said dreamily. "And he's taking me out to supper."

Fanny's face changed. "Is he now? I ain't sure I approve of that. I'm sure yer ma wouldn't approve of yer going out wiv a man yer've only just met, neither. Maybe I should come wiv yer as a chaperon."

"Well, you said yourself that he's on the up and up, so I'm sure you can stop worrying. And I don't want him to think I'm a baby, do I? I'm sure he's perfectly respectable, and I can take care of myself, truly."

She knew she was talking too fast to justify the fact that wild horses wouldn't have permitted her to let Fanny come along. She turned away to continue with her toiletry, afraid that her eyes would reveal what her heart was already telling her, with every bit of Cornish intuition bursting forth in her veins.

That he was the one. He was the one.

Seventeen

S kye felt her stomach heave as the boat lurched, dipped and then threatened to fall into eternity on the choppy Irish Sea. It was icy cold at the end of January, which had been the earliest time that Nick could get away. He had flatly refused to let her make the journey by herself. She was more than thankful for his company now, as the apparently endless voyage continued. Yet it was such a short distance compared with the great adventure she had made all those years ago, travelling from New York to Cornwall, and finding love on the way.

She could think of Philip with fond affection now. She remembered both their passionate love and the difficult last years when he had suffered so badly from the effects of the Great War, as if it had happened to someone else. She was oddly detached from it all, and if she stopped to think about that too deeply, the feeling alarmed her.

These days she seemed detached from everything. Her children had all gone; Nick was kept ever more busy with his legal work; the clayworks and pottery got along very well without her; she wasn't needed by anyone. She was useless. Not even Nick guessed how desperately she clung to the hope that Karina really needed her to help with the baby. It had begun to feel like a lifeline to her.

"What's wrong, darling?" Nick asked quietly, when she had said nothing for a long while, but gazed unseeingly out at the pewter-grey water.

"Nothing, really."

"Please credit me with more sense than that, Skye. There's clearly something wrong," he said, eyeing her pinched face as she sat huddled up in a thick coat and scarf, her hat pulled well down over her ears to keep out the wind, her hands clenched tightly together in her leather gloves.

She forced a smile to her cold lips, trying to reassure him without revealing the awful hollow feeling in her stomach. "I guess I've lost the knack of being a good sailor after all these years, honey. The Atlantic was never as rough as this."

He looked relieved. "And that's all? You're just feeling seasick and nothing more?"

"Well, if you call that *all*, then yes," she said with a touch more spirit. "I'll be fine once we get onto dry land."

"I hope so. Ethan's meeting us, so let's hope it's not too far to the farmhouse and that it's good and warm."

She was glad she'd planned to stay for a month. Years ago, making the pilgrimage from her home in New Jersey to meet her Cornish family, she had so longed to be in Cornwall, and now she couldn't wait to get away from it. She couldn't even begin to understand why. She didn't even want Nick around any longer than the several days he planned to be here. She didn't want anything any more.

She was intelligent enough to know it was her mid-life crisis, and dumb enough to have thought it would never affect her the way it did other women. She had imagined she would sail through it all, keeping busy, keeping her interests alive, living vicariously through her children's careers.

Her thoughts went off at a tangent, and she allowed them to do so to take her mind off the heaving sea. Olly was becoming hard, which wasn't such a bad thing in a newspaper reporter, but he was still barely sixteen and she mourned the passing of his childhood. Celia had always been self-sufficient, needing no one, and would overcome all the knocks life threw at her. And Wenna . . . Skye's face softened, remembering her daughter's phone call a few nights ago.

"His name's Austin, Mom, and I'm sending you a copy of my review from the paper where he works. Isn't it funny that he's in journalism too? His father's a member of parliament and his mother's so nice. I met them both at the weekend."

"So soon? I thought you hardly knew this man, Wenna."

She had laughed happily. "Oh, well, you know how it is with some people. You feel as if you've always known them, don't you? That's how it is with Austin and me."

Skye had felt a lump in her throat, hearing in her daughter's voice all the things she wasn't yet prepared to say: all the tremulous, first-love words that were too private to reveal to anyone but the beloved – if it had gone that far.

"Wenna, be careful. I think you know what I mean."

"I do, and you really needn't worry, Mom. Austin is an honourable man, and I know you'll love him."

"I'm going to meet him then? And incidentally, what does Fanny say to all this?"

"Fanny thinks he's lovely now that she's invited him round for tea and given him a proper once-over, as she grandly calls it."

Skye had felt utterly cheated at that moment. Fanny was doing all the things she should be doing. Fanny had met the man that Wenna had obviously fallen head over heels for, and Skye had been left out in the cold. Ridiculous as it seemed, she hadn't been able to shake off that feeling. She prayed uneasily that she wasn't thinking of this baby of Karina's as a substitute for her own lost chicks.

"Not long now," she heard Nick say, and felt a surge of relief as the land became more evident. All she wanted was to get off this boat and on to dry land before the bile in her throat came up and humiliated her.

A short while later, as the flat grey coastline merged into recognisable shapes and contours, they saw Ethan on the quay. At last they left the boat behind, and were being clasped in his arms.

"It's so good to see you both," he said, "but come to the car quickly, for you must be frozen. Karina's got a hot meal waiting for you at the farm."

Skye realised he was nervous, rightly so, she supposed. His news had been a shock to everyone, but the child was here, and had been born in wedlock, and she was sure she would love him as much as they did. Ethan had grown in stature, she realised. He was a husband and father now, and he looked every inch of it.

"How is Karina?" she asked, once they were in the welcome warmth of the car and driving away from the quay.

"She still doesn't have much energy, and the doctor says she's anaemic. She's desperately looking forward to having you here, Skye. She regards you as a second mother, you know."

"Does she? I thought that was reserved for Lily."

"Not at all. It was always you she wanted to please."

The sincerity of his words helped to settle some of the akwardness of the reunion, and the queasiness she still felt in her stomach – though she hoped that the hot meal was going to be a plain one.

She concentrated on watching the changing countryside as the two men talked, and fell in love with the greenness of it, with the smoky blue hills in the distance, in just the way her Uncles Freddie and Bradley must have done all those years ago when they first came here. There was a family tradition here too, she thought, and the charm of it warmed her heart.

Once they reached the valley and glimpsed the white-painted farmhouse with the curl of smoke drifting straight up into the sky, she knew exactly what had drawn them here.

She was shocked to see how thin Karina had grown. When she hugged her, Skye could almost feel her bones through her woollen dress. She needed pampering, and she was going to get it. When Ethan brought the baby down from his crib upstairs and put him in Skye's arms, she looked into his blue eyes and fell in love all over again.

"He's beautiful," she said, "and I hope you'll let me care for him while you get your strength back, Karina. That's what I'm here for, remember."

She breathed in his baby smell and felt her heart lift.

"Just as long as you don't overdo it," Karina said. "You don't look so well yourself."

"I'll be fine once I settle down after that boat trip."

But she wasn't. It took a few days before she felt anything like her old self, and caring for Ryan took more energy than she had expected. It was too cold to take him out in his baby carriage for more than short walks, but she was more than content to hold him by the fire and croon to him, the way she had always done for her own children.

By the time she had been there a couple of weeks, and Nick had long since returned to Cornwall, she had become used to the easy pace of life, even though she knew it couldn't last for ever. It was an idyll, no more, a month out of time, out of her life, to pause and take stock of herself. She still hadn't come to any conclusions as the days sauntered on towards the end of February.

"It suits you," Karina said with a smile, when she came

downstairs one afternoon from her regular afternoon nap, to find Skye dozing by the fire with Ryan sleeping in her arms. Karina was so much better now, and the doctor's pills were restoring her colour and her health.

"What suits me?" Skye asked lazily, still half asleep.

"You with a baby in your arms. Did you never think of having any more children, Skye?"

"Don't you think three was quite enough?" she said with a laugh. "Anyway, it's a little late now!"

But even as she said it, she knew immediately what had been wrong with her all these weeks.

The queasiness, the irritability, the disorientation, the tearfulness at the least provocation, she had put it all down to the midlife changes in her body. Now she was just as certain that the absence of her monthly periods meant something quite different.

"Skye, are you all right? You look quite pale. I haven't said something to upset you, have I?" Karina said.

"No. Just a goose walking over my grave, that's all," she replied quickly, because no one was going to hear about the spectacular thing that was happening to her until Nick heard it first. Until she was reassured by his love and his care that he was delighted by this late-stage child.

At the thought she gave a shiver. Because it was a late-stage child, of course, and anything could go wrong. She was no longer a young woman. She was forty-seven years old, and Nick was fifty-two. They had three adult children. How would they view the prospect of a brother or sister? She didn't know how they would react to this news.

"If you're ready to take over this little honey-bee," she said to Karina, in as normal a voice as possible, "would you mind if I go and lie down in my room for a while? I have quite a headache."

"Of course. Can I get you anything?"

"No. I'll be fine after a little while."

As she reached the door, she heard Karina speak softly.

"You miss them all, don't you, Skye? A month is a long time to be away, and you'll be glad to see Nick again."

"I expect that's what it is," she murmured.

She realised she was nervous of seeing him again. What if he hated the thought of another child? What if he rejected the very idea? But why should he? It would be her fourth, but Nick's first-born. Her thoughts raced on. What if her own children despised her for putting them in an embarrassing position? She lay down on her bed as the imaginary headache became a real one and she pressed her hand to her belly as if to protect the child against all comers.

If it actually was a child. Her imagination began to make nightmare images, wondering if it there was a hideous cancerous growth inside her instead. She turned her head into the pillow with a sob, wondering if she was going mad.

She had forced herself to think more soberly before she went downstairs again. Nick was due to arrive in a few days' time, and she decided to judge the effect of the infant Ryan Pengelly on him, and to see her own doctor to confirm just what was wrong with her before she said anything at all.

He had dire news. Wenna's latest letter was full of indignation and jitters because thousands of air-raid shelters were going up in London in the event of bombing.

"They look just like horrid steel tunnels," Wenna had written, "and Fanny's saying she wouldn't be seen dead in one of them if her life depended on it."

"Which makes sense to Fanny, if not to the rest of us," Skye commented as she read the words aloud to their hosts.

"So what else do you have to tell me?" she asked Nick, knowing there was more to come.

"Both our main German outlets have cut their orders by half," he said brutally, "and Herr Vogl has sent a personal letter of apology in his usual pompous manner, saying it's doubtful they will be able to continue to do business with us if all the portents are to be believed."

"In other words, if war comes."

"No, my love. *When* war comes," he said. "Why else would all this frantic government activity be going on, if it wasn't inevitable? We have to face it, and make plans."

"What plans?" she said, the ever-threatening tears beginning to surface. "What do you expect us to do? Go and hide away in some South Sea island out of harm's way until the conflict is all over?"

"You could stay here. Move to Ireland and be near us. That would be perfect," Karina said eagerly.

Skye gave her a half-smile. She was so young. She didn't know what it was to go through a war. But Skye did and Nick did. They had both lost people in the last one, and the prospect of a new horror was too awful to contemplate. But one thing was certain. They didn't run away from it.

"Honey, I wasn't being serious," she told her. "We belong in Cornwall, and that's where we'll stay, whatever happens."

"At least Celia's safely away from it all," Karina went on unthinkingly. "You'll be glad of that."

Skye didn't answer. Glad of it? With so much uncertainty on a world scale, and so much uncertainty in her own heart?

What she wanted more than anything was to have all her family around her, to know that every one of them was safe. Like a mother hen, she thought again, she needed her brood.

"Oh, by the way, Herr Vogl included a letter for Celia," Nick said. "I sent it on to her before I came here."

Skye looked at him listlessly. If Herr Vogl was thinking of offering Celia her old job back, he was a bigger fool than she took him for! But it wouldn't be that, of course. In the circumstances, she thought with a shudder, the sooner all foreign workers got out of Germany, the better.

Celia recognised her stepfather's handwriting on the bulky envelope, and put the letter aside to read later, as the younger Stone siblings clamoured for her attention. It wasn't until after supper that she remembered it. There was just a short note from Nick, enclosing another letter that had arrived for her recently. The second envelope bore a German stamp, and her heart leapt as she recognised Stefan's handwriting. She tore the envelope open.

'My darling Celia,' she read, noting at once the carefully correct words that were always so stilted, no matter how deep the sentiments.

It's been so very long since we were together, and I must apologise contritely for my tardiness in not contacting you before. I tried to do so after I left Berlin, and I assumed that you did not care to continue our association. Since then I have learned that you went home to Cornwall, but I cannot leave things as they were without knowing if your feelings are the same as mine.

My life has been turned upside down since those halcyon days, and God knows when we will be together again. You will be as aware as I am of the precarious situation between our two countries, and how dangerous everything seems these days. Some of our Jewish workers have simply disappeared and no one can trace them. I fear the worst, and although it would be my dearest wish to come to you, or to beg you to come to me, who knows what disaster that would produce in the future?

On a different level, I have to tell you that my circumstances have undergone a radical change since both my parents have died. I have many people dependent on me for their livelihood now and I cannot abandon the estate unless I sell it. I suspect that this will be my course eventually, as I've no heart for the family business. But until this present situation is resolved, I feel the best thing to do is to sit tight, as you English say, and await developments.

Or come here, Celia found herself imploring him silently. Come to America where we are both safe.

The most important thing I wanted to tell you, my Celia, is that I loved you then and I love you now, and nothing will change that. Whatever happens in the future, I ask you to believe in us, and to believe that one day we will be together for always. Please write to me if you can, for who knows how long such a correspondence will be available to us?

These last words struck a black chord in her heart. It seemed more ominous that anything else she had heard lately. Being so far away from home had removed the sense of urgency that she realised everyone in Europe must be feeling now. Reading Stefan's words made it seem even more real. Both sides were going to suffer. It wouldn't only be governments that were at war, ordinary people would be affected too. Just as employing some German youths soon after the last war had resulted in violence and murder in the clay industry, there would be no place for lovers whose countries were on opposing sides.

She swallowed a huge sob as the enormity of it sank into her brain. Her earlier thought about being safe here seemed hollow now, as she remembered that America had been drawn into the last conflict. If that happened again, there would be no safe place for lovers like Celia Pengelly and Stefan von Gruber.

The portly Poppa Stone found her in the family room, staring into the distance, her face as white as chalk. He put his head on one side, as if trying to read her mind.

"Is this some kind of Cornish trance, honey?" he said with a chuckle. "If so, I don't want to disturb it, but Momma Stone and me were wondering if you'd care for a game of cards now the young 'uns have gone to bed?"

"Do you mind if I don't?" she said in a choked voice. "I have a lot of thinking to do tonight."

"My Lord, you don't want to do too much of that, girl. It rots your brain," he said. His voice grew anxious as he realised how serious she looked. "What's wrong, honey?"

She took a deep breath. "I think it's time I went home," she said slowly, her eyes wide and dark.

She had expected him to argue with her, but, as perceptive as any Cornishman, he nodded and hugged her.

"If you think it's time, it's time," he said.

But first of all she wrote to Stefan, to tell him she understood everything he was careful not to put into words, that her feelings for him had never changed, and never would. She told him what she had been doing all this time, and that now she was going home to Cornwall. She told him she loved him with all her heart.

What she didn't tell him was that part of her reason for going home was because she would feel a little closer to him without an ocean separating them. They would then only be divided by the evil intent of a madman who wanted to conquer the world.

"Celia's coming home," Skye said joyfully to Nick, when they had been back at New World for two weeks.

She had still said nothing about her suspected condition. Every time she was about to do so, something held her back, and now she attributed her reticence to this new development. Celia was coming home, and that was a good omen. Once her daughter was here, that would be the time.

She still felt unwell for hours on end. When Nick told her angrily that she should see a doctor, she simply told him it was perfectly normal for a woman of her age going through these changes, and that he wasn't to fuss.

"Are you sure it's no more than that?" Lily had already asked her. "You're not – good God, Skye, you're surely not—"

"Don't be ridiculous," she had snapped. "A woman of my age? People would be staring at me as if I had two heads or something. Imagine my having to tell Olly!"

But Lily's incredulity and her own embarrassment seemed to sum up what she felt. It also filled her with guilt, as if she was rejecting the child she was sure she was expecting. Once Celia came home, she was just as sure she would have her support and that everything would be all right. She clung to that fact like a talisman.

It was the middle of March before they finally welcomed their daughter home. Sebby had insisted on going to Falmouth to meet her from the ship and bring her home to New World. Once they had all fallen on one another's shoulders with hugs and kisses and tears, and he had discreetly left them to it, Celia addressed her mother in a shocked voice.

"What the heck have you been doing to yourself while I've been away, Mom? You look terrible!"

"Well, that's a nice way to greet your mother, I must say," Nick commented.

"Well, can't you see it? Have you seen a doctor, Mom?"

"Not yet," Skye said weakly. "I intend to, though."

She really meant it. It had to be done soon, if only to see if she needed iron for her blood, the way Karina had done. She felt so weak these days. In fact, right now, she felt as though the room was starting to spin, and she fought to hold her senses together. It would be a terrible homecoming for Celia if she passed out here and now.

She was vaguely aware of drifting in and out of consciousness for what seemed an age, but when she came around properly, there was a terrible dragging ache in her belly.

She realised she was in her own bed. The doctor was looking down at her accusingly, and Nick and Celia looked strained and anxious.

"Why haven't you come to see me before, Mrs Pengelly? We could have prevented this. Your age is no barrier to producing a healthy child, providing sensible precautions were taken, but that would include not subjecting yourself to excursions on the Irish Sea and taking on another woman's burden."

"It is a child then?" she asked huskily.

It seemed an age before he slowly shook his head. She saw Celia and Nick clutch one another's hands as she heard the doctor speak more gently, in the tone he always used whenever he had to give bad news.

"My dear, I'm afraid you've suffered a miscarriage."

"Skye," Nick pushed past him to take her cold hand in his. "Why didn't you tell me? I had a right to know."

She turned her face away. It wasn't easy to speak of personal, womanly things, even to the one you loved the most. It was the stupid indoctrination of the age they lived in, but now she realised too late that by her stupidity, she had denied him something precious. She should have allowed him to share in these early weeks of anticipation. He could hate her for not doing so, just as she hated herself now, and wept inside for the child that was never to be.

But he didn't hate her, and although it took her months rather than weeks to get over the trauma, he was always there when she needed him, and if he wasn't, then Celia was. Her beloved Celia, who had come home when she needed her most.

"My grandmother's best friend was called Celia," Skye told her one morning when they were sitting outside on a warm June day. "And you needn't think I've gone crazy to mention it without reason," she added. "We named you after that other Celia. Did I ever tell you that?"

"Only about a hundred times," Celia said uneasily. "What made you think of that now, anyway?"

"I was thinking how Granny Morwen picked herself up so many times when things went wrong, and here am I, wallowing in my own troubles, when all around me the world is facing disaster. What right do I have to feel so sorry for myself?"

"Every right. You're a person, aren't you?"

She looked at her daughter. "And so are you, my love. And I never asked you properly why you happened to come home exactly when I needed you. Was that Cornish, or what?"

Celia hesitated, and then spoke truthfully. "I'm afraid it was what, Mom. I had a letter from Stefan at last, and I thought coming home to Cornwall would bring me that much nearer to him. That's crazy if you like, isn't it?"

"No darling, it's not crazy," Skye said. "It's exactly what I would have done for someone I loved. Why don't we go for a walk on the moors and you can tell me all about it?"

"Are you sure? You haven't wanted to go anywhere lately, let alone take a strenuous walk."

"It's high time I did. Good Lord, people must be sick of coming to visit me when I'm not even ill. How selfish can you get, for pity's sake? I need to get back in the world again!"

"That's my Mom," Celia said thankfully.

"My mother's better," Wenna told Fanny, putting down the telephone. "Celia says she's going out of the house at last and seeing people. Thank God. I still feel horribly guilty that I haven't been home to see her."

"Now you know yer Dad said you wasn't to make her feel bad about taking yer away from yer work. And she takes such pleasure in seeing all them good reviews yer keep getting now, my duck."

"I know, and not just from Austin, either," Wenna said, cheering up at once. "He's the best though, isn't he, Fanny?"

"If yer say so," Fanny said dryly.

"I do. And you'll never guess what else Celia said."

"Well, that's for sure, unless yer tells me."

"They're going to offer to take in some London children at New World for families who want to evacuate them to the country. That's just like Mom, and of course, Celia's been looking after children in New Jersey until recently, so I daresay she'll have a hand in it too. It makes the threat of war seem even more certain, though."

"Well, I'll tell yer one thing, gel. I ain't going to be evacuated on account of old Hitler, no matter how many bombs he drops on London," Fanny said determinedly.

"Neither am I," Wenna declared. "And neither is Austin. Whatever happens, we'll stick together like the three musketeers, won't we?"

"If yer say so. Though in your case, I reckon it'll be more like the two bleedin' musketeers stickin' together, if yer get my meaning. Yer won't want a third party around when you do yer canoodlin'.

"Oh, Fanny, you'll make me blush," Wenna said, laughing.

"Good. That means yer still taking care of yerself then."

"Of course I am. And Austin's taking good care of me too, so stop fishing for details, because you're not getting any!"

All the same, she was more than thankful that Austin didn't pressure her to go further than she wanted to go. He was more worldly than she was, and he had a passionate nature. So did she, Wenna had discovered, but there was an unspoken rule between them that dictated how far they would go with their lovemaking.

Kissing and touching – fondling even, Wenna thought with a thrill at the erotic-sounding word – was permitted on both sides. But doing the actual thing was going to wait. She was young yet, but one day they would be married. They were so deeply in love that nothing else would do.

This summer was turning out to be so wonderful for her career. People were coming to the club time and time again on Saturday nights when she had the star spot, and Fanny was delighted with the good business her little Cornish songbird was bringing in. It was almost as good as being discovered for the movies, Wenna told Austin, although she had never wanted to be an actress.

"Singing's a kind of acting, sweetheart," he pointed out.

"Yes, but I don't have to say anything. I know I'm giving a performance, but I can forget my shyness once I throw myself into the words and the melodies, and just live the emotions."

He laughed, pressing her to him as they strolled arm in arm along the riverbank on that warm, still evening. It was high summer now, and London had never looked so beautiful, the elegant bridges bathed in the reddening sunlight, the ethereal colours of the sky reflected in the water.

"Sometimes I think your shyness is something of a myth, Wenna," he teased. "At least as far as I'm concerned."

"Only as far as you're concerned," she retorted, her cheeks warm, knowing how hard it was for him to resist their mutual desires at times, but loving him all the more for his patience and understanding.

"I know it," he said, more soberly. "And I consider myself the luckiest man on earth to have found you. Do you realise that if my paper hadn't persuaded me to go along to the Flamingo Club that evening, we might never have met?"

"Oh, but we would," Wenna said with supreme confidence.

"You're sure of that, are you?" he said with a grin.

"Of course! I'm Cornish, and we know these things. You and I were destined to meet, and no power on earth was going to stop that!"

"Not even—"

"Don't say it," Wenna broke in quickly. "I don't want anything to spoil this lovely evening, Austin."

Especially not thoughts of a German dictator and his machinations. The colour of the sky deepened still more as the sun began to slide below the horizon, and the river, so serene and beautiful just moments ago, turned an ominous blood-red.

Eighteen

"The bastards have done it then," Theo Tremayne bawled, bursting into New World while Skye and Celia were enjoying an afternoon cup of tea in the garden.

His presence was hardly a surprise, since they had heard the screech of his car as it roared to a halt, and had been relishing the few moments' peace before he found them.

"Would you like some tea, Theo?" Skye asked mildly.

"I don't want your tea, cuz. I want to know what we're going to do now that the bloody Germans have pulled out of every contract they had with us."

Celia got to her feet. "I think I'll leave you two to sort out your business problems, Mom," she said. "In any case I have a meeting in Truro this afternoon with the ladies' evacuee committee."

"What's that?" Theo said, diverted for a moment as he watched her trim figure go back into the house. "You're not going through with this daft idea of bringing London brats down here, are you? Outsiders don't belong here."

She had long been thought of as an outsider, too.

"I don't remember you objecting when we brought the German boys over here years ago," Skye pointed out. "In fact, it may even have been mostly your idea, Theo."

"It was a bloody bad one, whoever thought of it." He scowled, not admitting anything. "And now look what's happened. You are acquainted with the situation, I suppose, in between your flower-arranging and poxy female occupations."

Skye held on to her temper with an effort at his patronising sneer, and snapped back a reply. "Naturally I know what's happening. And if you mean do we have to think of where else to sell the clay, then no, we don't. Our partners have got it all under control, and we should be thankful they have their other outlets."

His eyes narrowed in his florid face. "You're in a mighty forgiving mood, considering you never wanted us to merge with 'em in the first place."

"Times change," she said evenly. "In fact, I've been giving the whole business serious thought lately."

"Oh ah," he said, alert at once. "And what wonderful conclusions have you come up with?"

His tone implied that it could be nothing of major importance, especially coming from a woman. He was in one of his most belligerent and macho moods, but she had never been afraid of standing up to him, and she wasn't afraid now.

"Perhaps it's time we sold out completely after all," she said coolly. "And before you throw a fit, hear me out, Theo."

But she could see that he was too dumbstruck by her words to say anything at all for a moment. She certainly hadn't meant to blurt it out. It had been no more than a seed of an idea at first, but one that had steadily grown in her mind, as insidiously as the mist descending over the moors.

He sat down on the chair vacated by Celia and folded his arms as best he could over his bulging belly.

"Go on," he snapped. "I'd never taken you for a turncoat, so your reasoning had better be good."

"I'm tired," she said flatly. "Very tired. The miscarriage took more out of me than I realised, and although Celia and Nick think I'm perfectly well again, I know I'm not. I'm telling you this in confidence, Theo, and I'm appealing to your better nature, if that's not an impossibility."

"Go on." He grunted again, for once not making any snide comment at her frankness, but not missing her pallor.

She spoke slowly, needing to explain her thoughts to herself as well as him.

"I've come to realise that I don't have the same interest in the clay that I once did, Theo. My heart is no longer in it, and I don't think yours is, either. Our day is past, and it's time we realised it before it's too late."

"Too late for what?"

"Too late for all of us to make any profit out of a business that's dwindling rapidly. Bourne and Yelland are in a much better position than we are. They have the goodwill of the paper mills and medical supplies trade, but without the regular German firms buying our clay, we're doing no more than giving lip service to the partnership. That embarrasses me, and I've no wish to feel like a poor relation."

"And how do you think our grandmother would see this backing down of all she stood for?" he couldn't resist sneering. "So much for your fine principles, cuz."

Skye bit her dry lips. "I have a feeling that Granny Morwen would applaud my common sense. There's a time for holding on and a time for letting go. I think we've reached that time."

"And do you think our offspring will think the same about losing their inheritance?" he demanded.

"It's not for them to say whether or not we decide to sell. Naturally, they'd all be compensated. But I suggest we put the matter to them all to see what they think."

He leapt to his feet, his ungainly bulk blotting out the sunlight from her gaze, his eyes spitting fire, his brief sense of compassion gone.

"I'll tell 'ee exactly what they'll think without askin' their bloody opinion. Yes, they'll get compensated all right, but your girls couldn't give a tinker's cuss about the clay, and your son's got so toffee-nosed with the newspaper trade he won't care, neither. Justin's already turned his back on it all to become a doctor, so that leaves only one, don't it?"

"It's Sebby I'm most concerned about," Skye said carefully. "I do understand, Theo—"

"No, you bloody don't! You came here from America and stepped right into your grandmother's affections. For all the rest of us knew, you wormed your way right into her will an' all. You knew nothing about what my father had worked for all his life, and his father and brothers before him. You knew *nothing* except for some romantic idea of where your parents came from – and it's mighty kind of you to be so concerned about Sebastian," he added, seething with sarcasm now. "But if you're that bothered, why don't we go and ask him what he thinks about selling out, and by-pass all the rest?"

"*Now?*" she said, appalled at his vindictiveness, and his smouldering resentment of her that she thought had been dead and buried long ago.

"Yes, *now*," he snapped. "While we're both in the mood."

* * *

Seb Tremayne looked up from his work to see the small deputa-
tion making their way through to the workroom from the White
Rivers showroom. When he saw the expressions on their faces he
grinned wryly at his working partner.

"Stand by for fireworks, Adam. When these two get together
with that look, something's definitely up."

Seb stopped working his wheel and slid the pot expertly on to
the base board before wiping his hands on a rag as Skye and his
father came into the room.

"To what do we owe this pleasure?" he asked. "Checking up
on us, are you, Father?"

Theo scowled. The boy had far too sharp a tongue on him, he
mused, and just as quickly conceded that it was far too much like
his own for comfort.

"We've come to talk to 'ee on an important and personal
matter, boy," he stated.

"Then I'll leave you folks to it," Adam said.

"No, you stay, Adam. Whatever business there is to discuss,
we'll do it in the open air," Seb said at once, taking command.

This was his domain, his and Adam's – and Skye's, of course,
he thought, though she didn't look too well. He wondered at
once if they should discuss whatever it was indoors after all. But
it was too late now, and she was already following his father
outside again.

"Shall we walk over the moors, or would you prefer to sit in
the car to talk, Skye?" he said. "You do look weary."

"I'm well enough," she said. "Let's walk."

She had had enough of sitting beside Theo in the confines of
his car. He had never smelled too sweet and it seemed now that
he never bothered to keep himself particularly clean. How Betsy
must hate it, although maybe she preferred his natural bodily
stink to his reeking of the floosies he used to visit. Skye gave a
shudder, thankful that her husband was a decent man.

They strode across the moors in the heady summer freshness,
until they reached the outcrop of smooth rocks where they could
sit down and take a breather. In the distance was the Larnie
Stone, the tall, holed standing stone, from where you could see
the distant sea, and where Morwen Tremayne had once glimpsed
her lover, Ben Killigrew, after taking a witchwoman's potion.

Skye pushed the thoughts out of her head, even though they

were never more vivid than here, where it had all begun. The sweet liaison had become a powerful dynastic concern, which she and Theo were about to dissolve. A sob caught in her throat and she wondered after all, if she was doing the right thing.

"Are you sure you're feeling quite well, Skye?" Sebby asked her again.

"She's all right, boy," Theo said crudely. "Just listen to me, and give us your thoughts without interrupting."

He listened silently as his father explained what he and Skye were contemplating.

"Is this really what you want to do?" he said, turning to Skye. "I can hardly believe you want to turn your back on the clay-works."

He ignored his father. It was Skye he was most concerned with, the lovely woman who was looking more careworn than he had ever seen her before. She was still beautiful in middle age, but so fragile and so vulnerable. It was not the way he liked to see Skye Pengelly. Impulsively, he caught at her cold hands.

"Skye? Have you really had a hand in this, or have you been pushed into it by my father?"

He heard Theo give a raucous laugh.

"Well, if that ain't a proper show of confidence in your father, I don't think!" he said angrily. "The woman can speak for herself, and always has done."

"Then why don't you let me?" Skye said, her quiet voice echoed across the rustling bracken. She looked at Seb. When they were children her daughters had always called him a prize pig, and so he had been in those days, but not any more. Now, she had the greatest fondness for him.

"Sebby, it was my idea," she said gently. "I feel it's time I stood aside, and naturally, you'll have your opinion on it, but it's not only the clayworks I'm thinking of selling."

Both men gasped as she said the words that seemed to fall from her lips of their own accord. But once said, she knew it was the way forward.

"I also know how important the pottery is to you and to Adam. You may hate the idea of working for someone else—"

"Neither us would agree to it," he said sharply. "I'm sure I speak for Adam as well as myself. If you're going to sell out, then you must give us first refusal."

His reply took her aback. It was what she had tentatively intended to offer, but Seb's response was immediate and decisive. She had expected remonstrations, perhaps anger, but not quite such swiftness of thought that turned a negative situation into a positive one. She should have expected it. Sebby was a man after old Morwen Tremayne's heart, her eyes stung as the sweet thought slid into her mind with consummate ease.

"Now wait a minute, boy. Never mind the bloody pottery. 'Tis the clayworks that's the main concern here. Shares should come to you and the rest of 'em by right, and there are things to discuss –" Theo began hotly.

"There's nothing to discuss as far as I'm concerned, Father. The pottery is Skye's property, and once I've discussed it with Adam, I'm sure we'll be able to make an offer for it with my share of the money from the sale of the clayworks. I don't imagine you'll get any opposition from my brother and cousins, providing you see us all right on that, since we'll be losing our true inheritance. Is that your plan, Father?"

Skye could hardly contain her smile at his so-innocent words. He could sum up a situation in a moment, and oh, Theo, she thought, you may have scored over a thousand people in your lifetime, but you'll never put one over on your own son!

"Of course," Theo said coldly. "You're agreeable then?"

He held out his hand and Seb grasped it firmly. Then it was Skye's turn and, as she felt Seb's fingers close around hers, she could have sworn she heard a faintly cackling laugh creep over the moors, as if in triumph that the Killigrews and Tremaynes were to be finally severed from all that had been theirs for nearly a century.

But when she looked around quickly, there was nothing there, except a small breeze blowing through her heart.

Nothing could be done swiftly. There had to be further meetings between all the partners and their lawyers to ensure the best deal on all sides. Skye knew that Nick was openly relieved that she had finally decided to relinquish her interests in business matters. Though he was surprised she had decided to sell the pottery as well.

"I surprised myself, but it just seemed the right time," she said "and I won't be losing all my interest. The pottery will still be a family concern with Seb and Adam taking charge, and Lily minding the shop in Truro. I won't be letting go entirely."

"You'd have had to, if Seb hadn't offered to buy," he pointed out. Then he saw the look on her face.

"My God, you had no doubt of it, did you, woman? Did you prime him on it beforehand?"

She shook her head. "Truly I didn't, Nick. But I knew in my heart what would happen. He's the right one to carry on. Him and Adam. I rather like the idea of their partnership, don't you? It cements our two families."

"I thought the two of us had already done that pretty effectively," he said meaningly.

Skye laughed, but the laugh was shaky as she turned away from him. The memory of of what might have been still lingered in her mind with a great sadness. As the weeks and months passed, the time for their baby to be born would soon be here. It was as though she had to go through the normal gestation period as a time of mourning until she was completely whole again. It wasn't even something she felt able to discuss with Nick, whom she loved more than life. It was her pain and her sorrowing, and hers alone.

She felt an undoubted sense of relief now that the idea of selling out had been approved by all concerned. It had only needed the resolve to carry out what her heart had been telling her for months. To free herself of business responsibilities she had never sought, and be herself. A wife and mother and, above all, a woman.

True to what she and Theo had surmised, neither Oliver nor Justin had raised any objection to the plans. And her girls had openly applauded the decision.

"It's time you took things easy, Mom," Wenna had phoned from London. "You've worked far too hard all these years, and you're not young any more."

"Oh, really! And what was that all about?" Skye had asked, hearing the explosive noise in the background.

After a few minutes Wenna's voice came back on the line, full of suppressed laughter.

"It was Fanny telling me off for implying that you're past it. She's a scream, isn't she, Mom?"

"Is that what you think, then? That I'm past it?"

"Good Lord no! But you won't be worrying your head about how much money the businesses are making or losing from now on, will you? You can be a proper lady of leisure at last."

"That's not quite what I had in mind," Skye said mildly.

"Well, I'm glad you won't be rushing around so much, because Austin and I plan to come down for a visit at the end of August."

Skye was diverted at once. "That's marvellous news, darling! So I'm going to meet this wonder man at last, am I?"

"And we'll have some special news to tell you then. But I'm not going to spoil the surprise by telling you now. I'll give you a tiny hint, though. Austin will want to have a word with you and Daddy."

She would say no more. Skye was fizzing with excitement when she hung up the phone, guessing at once what the tiny word was going to be. Austin Marsh wanted to marry her daughter. And when he did, Skye would become a mother-in-law, and in time, a grandmother. The thought of it was at once thrilling and alarming.

Time moved on, and with it, so did she. Not for the first time when she had something on her mind, whether good or bad, she felt an oppressive need to get out of the house. Like all the Tremayne women before her, she needed the clean invigorating air of the moors to be able to think clearly.

It was funny, but she had naturally expected Celia to be the one to bring this news home. Celia was more forceful, more sure of herself, and had fallen in love first. For all her early flirtatious ways, Celia had become a one-man-woman, Skye thought with deep affection, and until Stefan was free to come to her, there would be no one else. While Wenna, shy, quiet Wenna, had fallen just as hard.

It occurred to Skye as she drove to the moors and parked her car before striding out aross the short stubbly turf, with the whole of St Austell bay shimmering far befow in the sunlight, that she had never met either of the men her daughters were so determined to marry. But that didn't matter, as long as they were happy and fulfilled. Happiness was all that counted in this world.

Nick's peevishness, for example over who had been told first about Ethan and Karina's baby had faded away the moment they saw how blissful they all were in their idyllic Irish farm.

She and Nick might have been just as blissful with their own baby being born any day now . . . the mortality that was everyone's destiny would have been continued in a new son or daughter.

In a weird way, the loss of that child had been one of the things that had prompted her desire to sell her partnership in the clayworks and the pottery. She needed time to do what had been no more than a vague idea suggested to her some time ago by David Kingsley. She wanted to perpetuate what had always belonged to the Killigrews and the Tremaynes, and now the Pengellys. She *would* write that booklet, so that all the children that followed, would know – and that those who remained, wouldn't forget . . .

"What noble thoughts be goin' round and round in that pretty head o' yourn, my fine lady?" she heard a wheezing voice cackle close by.

She didn't need to turn around to know who was hobbling up behind her. Perhaps she had come this way especially for the sake of coming face to face with old Helza, for whatever reason fate decreed, thought Skye. How old was she now, she wondered, as the old witchwoman literally rocked on her spindly legs as if they would barely hold her up.

"I'm looking for answers," she said simply, the words escaping her lips without any forethought. She felt as light-headed as she always did when faced with this self-styled all-seeing, all-knowing old creature. She began to wish she had stayed safely at home.

"Before 'ee can find answers, there must be questions, my pretty," the wizened old woman croaked, her head cocked to one side like an enquiring bird.

"But how can I find the answers when I don't know the questions?" Skye said, knowing she was being ridiculously enigmatic.

Helza's eyes screwed up to slits in the brightness of the sun, accentuating the corrugated lines of her ancient face to gargoyle proportions.

"Mebbe the answer is inside yourself, lady. You're strong enough to find it wi'out anybody's help."

With that she turned and hobbled away. She seemed to disappear into nothingness, but common sense told Skye it was simply a dip in the hillside that hid her from view.

She stood motionless for a while, letting the warm, caressing breezes of the moors wrap softly around her. She had already found the answer. Life didn't end, even if her own baby's had ended before it had begun. In the great overall plan of things, life went on, and she had already decided what she was going to do with hers.

August, that had once seemed an eternity away, was into its middling days now. The sun was hot, reviving the spirit, and the countryside she loved was serenely beautiful. Her sky tips, no longer strictly hers, but which would always be so in her heart, were sparkling like diamonds as she turned towards them to reach her car. In essence, they would never change, and nor would she.

Thoughts of wars, of conflicts that were none of her making, nor of anyone who belonged to her, were as far removed from her mind as that distant life-giving sun. The solidity from deep inside the earth in the form of the pure white china clay that was her heritage, always gave her a feeling of peace, as it had done for all the women in her family.

She was much calmer by the time she reached New World once more, where she found Celia in a state verging on hysteria. There had been a telephone call from Stefan.

"He's in Gstaad for a week or so, and he asks if I can meet him there." Her voice shook with excitement, and Skye felt her heart stop at the yearning in her daughter's face.

"I wouldn't even try to stop you, honey, if you're sure it's what you want to do."

"I have to go to him. It's unwise for him to come here, for if the worst comes to the worst, there's a great danger that he'd be interned, and he forbids me to go to Germany. But in Gstaad we shall be on neutral ground. You understand, don't you, Mom? I couldn't bear to miss this chance of being with him again for a short while."

Skye hugged her, feeling the tension in her taut young body. "Of course I understand. In your place I would do exactly the same. Daddy will make all the arrangements—"

Celia shook her head. "Too late. I've called David and he's organised everything through his connections. I fly out tomorrow afternoon on a private aeroplane."

She gave a gulp. Her eyes were huge and vibrantly blue as she looked at her mother. "I'm so excited – and so scared. What if we take one look at each other, and everything's changed?"

"Do you believe that's how it will be?" Skye murmured.

"No. But I just can't believe it's really true that we're going to be together again," Celia said tremulously.

"Not for too long," Skye said, hating to take the sparkle from her eyes, but obliged to remind her that this was no more than a temporary reunion. "Stefan will have to go back to Germany, honey, and you'll be needed here once the evacuee children descend on us. I'll be depending on you."

"I know. But I'd rather spend a week with Stefan than a lifetime with anybody else. And if a week is all we have . . ."

They hugged one another, and into Skye's mind came the fleeting thought that it wasn't only a clayworks and a pottery that had been the family legacy. All the women had felt this passionately about their lovers, and that passion had given them strength, in the way that women everywhere had found the strength to send their men away when necessary. It was a sweet and sobering thought.

But such introspection had to take second place to Celia's frantic haste to prepare for her journey. Every moment she and Stefan were apart was obviously a moment wasted, for who knew whether or not this lovers' meeting would be the first of many, or one that must last for ever?

Celia was realistic enough to know how lucky she and Stefan were to have this second chance. If she hadn't come home when she had, she might still have been halfway across the world in New Jersey. Stefan wouldn't have been able to contact her from Gstaad in time for her to get there before he returned to Germany. She shivered, thinking how fragile and dependent on coincidence life could be.

These thoughts were far behind her when at last she took the taxi cab to the hotel in Gstaad where they had first met. The town was pristine and fragrant now, the meadows and foothills of the mountains clothed in wild summer flowers, turning the whole area into a fairyland of colour. The man who rose from the window table to greet her was dear and familiar, and the love of her life. She whispered his name and was enfolded in his arms.

"God, how I've missed you," Stefan breathed against her mouth. "How I've wanted you and ached for this moment."

"And so have I. Oh, so have I, Stefan."

They could hardly bear to break apart, and had it not been for the amused stares of other hotel guests they might have stood there all day, locked in one another's arms. But they both had other needs, and although for the sake of her reputation as well as the hotel's, he had booked them into separate rooms, Celia knew they would not be apart that night, nor for any of the nights to come.

Later, when they had had dinner and drunk a bottle of the hotel's best wine, they retired to their adjoining rooms, and she undressed nervously. It had been a long time since they had been together and when she heard his tap on her door, she opened it with shaking hands. Her drew her into his arms and looked down searchingly into her darkening eyes.

"Are you afraid, *liebling*?" he said softly.

She shook her head. "Only of not pleasing you. Of not being everything you expect of me."

"You are all that and more, and always will be, my Celia. And if I don't possess you this minute, I think I shall go mad. Does it not shock you that I'm so impatient to feel your body next to mine?"

She felt her heart soar to meet him. "No, it doesn't shock me! It only makes me love you more, if that's possible, because I feel the same way."

She could say no more as he swept her up in his arms and took her to the bed, kissing her mouth every step of the way.

Then he removed the silky nightgown from her shoulders and let it fall to the ground, pausing a moment to gaze down at her as if to imprint her luscious shape on his mind for eternity, before disrobing and sliding into the bed beside her.

They had all night . . . but they had been too long apart and their need was too great. Hands and mouths sought and found their goals, and the sensations were at once new and erotically familiar, and then she felt him enter her and she cried out with the sheer remembered pleasure of it.

A long while later, when their passion was spent, they still lay in one another's arms, dreaming impossible dreams of a future together, and finally coming back to reality.

"*Liebling*, if this was all we had, I would die happy tomorrow," he whispered against her mouth, and her eyes stung, because it echoed her own thoughts so much.

"This won't be all we have, Stefan," she whispered back. "However long it takes, we'll be together again, I know it."

"Is this your famous Cornish intuition speaking?"

"No. I know because I love you," she said. She was glad to her soul that it was her Cornish passion that allowed her to say these words in such an uninhibited way.

"Then I must tell you the special reason I wanted us to meet here, *liebling*. In time I intend to move here to Gstaad, possibly to go into the luxury hotel business. I will not desert the people who depend on me, and I ask you again to accept that decision. But when the time is right I will ask you to marry me and to start our life together here. I do not ask it now, while the future is so uncertain—"

"But I will give you my answer now," Celia broke in, knowing that his words became more formal the more nervous he became, and loving him for not taking her for granted. "Whenever you ask me to marry you, I will marry you, Stefan, whether it's today, tomorrow, or a hundred years from now."

"I trust it will not be so long to wait," he said. "But if you're sure—"

"I was never more sure of anything in my whole life."

"Then I will ask you formally. Will you do me the honour of marrying me, Celia?"

Her answer was on her lips before the question was properly ended. By the time she returned home to Cornwall, on the third finger of her left hand was a pearl and garnet ring that had belonged to Stefan's mother. They knew that contact between them might well become sparse or non-existent in the days to come, but to Celia, the ring was a talisman and a sweet reminder that love never died.

It was ironic that Wenna's arrival back in Cornwall coincided with the day that Skye's baby would have been born.

She woke with a heavy feeling in her heart and spent a few self-pitying moments weeping into her pillow. Nick found her there, and held her close while she finally spilled out all her emotions.

"Did you think I didn't know – or didn't care?" he said gently. "We both knew this day must come, and tomorrow it will be over. Isn't that the way you've always coped with things, my darling? Even the worst, most heartbreaking things?"

Her snappy reply died on her lips as she looked into his tortured eyes, and knew that her pain was also his. All this time Nick had had to face this day too, and she had never considered his feelings.

"We have to go on, don't we?" she whispered.

"It's the only way," he said evenly. "But we go on together, and we're luckier than most. We'll have all our family around us soon. Wenna and Austin will be here by tonight, and Celia will be back from Gstaad tomorrow. Olly's keen to meet this beau of Wenna's, and is insisting that we have a family party at the weekend, just our own crowd for once, and not all the rest of the horde. But you only have to say no if you don't feel up to it."

She drew a deep breath. "Of course I'm up to it. When did you ever hear a Tremayne woman refuse a party?"

"Or even a Pengelly one," he said.

So on the last day of August, Wenna and Austin Marsh boarded the train for Cornwall, having decided it was far too long a drive for his old boneshaker of a car. By the time they arrived at New World it was late in the evening, and once the ecstatic reunion was over and Austin had been welcomed and silently approved, Wenna spoke soberly.

"It was a ghastly journey, Mom. We hadn't realised how many children were being sent out of London to the country today, so the trains were full of the poor little things, all with labels round their necks and carrying their bags and gas masks. A lot of them were crying. It was horrible, I can tell you."

She looked around the familiar surroundings with huge affection, wanting Austin to see it all exactly as she saw it. A refuge, a haven – or more properly, a heaven on earth.

"I can understand why you and Celia want to bring some of them here," she went on. "I really envy them their first sight of the moors and the sea."

"But you're just as determined to go back to London, I presume," Skye pointed out.

Her daughter smiled at the young man sitting beside her. "I belong there now just as much as Austin does. I never thought I'd say it, but it's true. We have a good life there."

She was so grown up, Skye thought, with a catch in her throat. She had not only changed, she had blossomed. Skye doubted that it was just her career that had done that for her. She was so clearly in love with the handsome young man who patently adored her.

"I'm so glad you came home today," she said, without thinking.

"What's special about today?" Wenna asked in surprise.

Skye caught Nick's glance and smiled into his eyes.

"Nothing at all, except that your father and I are old-stick-in-the-muds and like having our children around us."

"Well, you've got one more now," Wenna teased. "That is, if you'll have Austin as a sort of extra son."

"Wenna, not yet—" Austin said, getting a word in at last in this exuberant family gathering, but she brushed him aside with a squeeze of her hand.

"Oh, they all know why we're here, don't you?"

"You're here to make this day a special one," Nick said, in the small pause that followed, and the glance between him and his wife was one of perfect understanding.

They were all glad Wenna and Austin had got here in advance of Celia, so that their own news wasn't overshadowed by Celia's. Celia wore her betrothal ring on her finger, even though her future was so uncertain. Olly was full of dire and excited predictions about what would happen in the next few days.

"Olly's an out-and-out newspaperman," Wenna confided to Austin as they strolled on the sands below New World and looked out towards the horizon and the stately progress of the ships way out on the Atlantic Ocean. "A real one, I mean, and is always bragging he has advanced news of world affairs."

"He probably has," Austin said. "But anyone would have to be wearing blinkers not to know that we're on the brink of war, my love."

She hugged his arm, suddenly afraid. Down here, far from the capital, she had expected the urgency of the crisis to be left behind, but she hadn't been able to forget the sight of those evacuee children. It seemed as if everything was closing in on her.

"What will it mean to us, Austin? How will life change for us, personally, I mean?"

"Oh, I'll probably enlist and be a war correspondent, and you'll sing to the troops at camp concerts and have every soldier swooning over you," he said jokingly.

"You don't mean it – about enlisting?" she said.

"Every red-blooded man will want to do the same," he retorted, and then he saw the panic in her eyes. "Hey, sweetheart, I'm not planning to get shot, I promise you!"

"Nobody ever does," she muttered. "But it happens."

"Well, don't let's spoil our few days here worrying about what might happen. We've got a party tonight, and I've heard rumours that the Pengelly parties are famous around here."

Wenna pulled a face. "So they are. Mom intended this one to be just for us, but word got around, and now you'll meet the rest of the clan. The house will be bursting at the seams as usual. You may as well know what you're in for in one fell swoop," she said with a grin.

"It'll be bursting with evacuee children pretty soon, won't it? Your sister was telling me she's involved with the billeting committee in Truro and they'll be allocated with however many your parents are prepared to take in."

"I know. And although I think Mom's crazy, she's looking forward to it. She thinks we don't know how she grieved over losing that baby, and she misses having children around, but she couldn't keep us children for ever."

"Thank God," Austin said, cementing the words with a very satisfactory kiss.

In the end the party was a noisy and frenetic affair, with Theo and Betsy and Seb arriving with Justin, down from his university term, an unexpected visit that tempered Theo's normally sarcastic manner.

Lily and David Kingsley came with the twins, and Lily reminded Celia that it was a foretaste of how the house would be disrupted when the evacuees arrived, and to everyone's surprise Adam brought along a lady friend. The festivities went on until the early hours of the morning, and Skye gloried in the fact that they were all united in friendship and love. There were no enemies here.

At that moment, she caught sight of Celia's face as she took a breather outside on the terrace. Skye's heart turned over, thinking how very alone she looked in the midst of this family gathering, and the reason for it was crystal clear. Soon, very soon now, Celia's beloved Stefan would be classed as one of the enemy. It was an impossible position for lovers to be in. She went outside in the cool of the evening air, and tucked her arm through her daughter's.

In the comparative quiet of the lovely starlit night, with the laughter and noise muffled inside the house, Celia spoke softly without needing to turn her head to acknowledge her mother's presence. "Do you see that star, Mom? That very bright star that's brighter than all the rest? That's our star, Stefan's and mine. As long as that star still shines, we know that some day we'll be together, no matter what happens. We pledged to look at that star every night that we're apart. Don't you think that was a beautiful thing to do?"

To Skye, it seemed as if she was compelled to repeat the words like a mantra. It was only when she had finished that she turned to look at her mother with brimming eyes. They hugged one another close. Skye looked back through the years, knowing exactly what war could do and how it could tear people apart; while Celia looked ahead, full of uncertainty and dread, and ultimately hope.

"Let's go inside, darling," Skye said huskily. "There's a party going on, and we'll be missed."

They still held on tightly to one another, and as they went back into the house, it seemed to Skye as if the rest of their close-knit family was drawn towards them by an invisible thread. She could hear Olly's eager chatter with Austin Marsh, as to the part he too would play as a war correspondent, if he got the chance; Wenna's eyes were full of guilty dreams as she imagined herself on a makeshift stage surrounded by adoring homesick soldiers.

Celia turned to Skye with a smile that reminded her so startlingly of her own mother that she drew in her breath.

"As long as we always have one another, we'll be all right, won't we, Mom?" she said softly.

"Amen to that," Nick said, coming closer and circling them both in his arms.

Skye looked up at him, her beloved Nick, older and wiser, and knowing better than any of them that no day was ever going to be the same again, and that they had to hold on to the lovely memories of this one for as long as possible.

This precious day, whose stars were already beginning to fade with the coming dawn of a perfect September morning.